The SFWA
GRAND MASTERS

VOLUME THREE

LESTER DEL REY

FREDERIK POHL

DAMON KNIGHT

A. E. VAN VOGT

JACK VANCE

EDITED BY

FREDERIK POHL

A TOM DOHERTY ASSOCIATES BOOK

NEW YORK

THE SFWA GRAND MASTERS: VOLUME THREE

A Tor Book
Published by Tom Doherty Associates, LLC
175 Fifth Avenue
New York, NY 10010

www.tor.com

Library of Congress Cataloging-in-Publication Data

The SFWA grand masters / edited by Frederik Pohl.—1st ed.
     p. cm.
    "A Tom Doherty Associates book."
    Contents: Lester Del Rey—Frederik Pohl—Damon Knight—
A. E. van Vogt—Jack Vance
    ISBN 0-312-86877-4 (alk. paper)
    1. Science fiction, American. I. Pohl, Frederik. II. Science
Fiction Writers of America. III. Title: Grand masters.
  PS648.S3S44   2001
  813'.0876208—dc21   99-21933
                                                 CIP

First Edition: June 2001

Printed in the United States of America

0 9 8 7 6 5 4 3 2 1

CONTENTS

INTRODUCTION

This is the third—and at least for the moment the last—in the series of anthologies devoted to the works of the "Grand Masters of Science Fiction and Fantasy." These are the handful of writers who have been chosen for the award by their professional organization, the Science Fiction and Fantasy Writers of America. Collectively these Grand Masters have produced a lifetime body of work that is not only commendable in itself, but has done a great deal to shape the stories that came after.

However, they aren't the only ones involved. We must not forget that other class of being, the editors, for science fiction is nearly unique among literatures in that the talents and personalities of its editors have had as much to do with its present form as the writers themselves. So it is worthwhile to look at some of these seminal figures, starting with the very first of them all.

In the beginning was Hugo Gernsback, the man for whom the "Hugos" are named. In April, 1926, he brought out the first issue of the world's first magazine dedicated entirely to science fiction, *Amazing Stories*.

Gernsback can't be said to have imprinted much of his own personal stamp on science fiction. It isn't that he wouldn't have liked to. He simply didn't have the chance, for in those early days there was no existing body of active science fiction writers from whose output he could pick and choose for his newborn *Amazing Stories*. Gernsback's options were sharply limited. He was constantly scrambling to fill the magazine each month, frequently by including reprints of ancient stories by H. G. Wells, Edgar Allan Poe, and others. For the rest, if a story was readable and could by any stretch be considered SF, Gernsback published it.

Later on the situation eased for him as new writers discovered the magazine and began to produce stories specifically designed for it. But by then Gernsback had troubles of his own, exacerbated by the 1929 stock market crash and the beginnings of the Great

Depression. He lost control of *Amazing Stories*. He started publishing other science fiction magazines almost at once; but there was no more pioneering for Hugo Gernsback. Single-handed, he had created this new genre of science fiction, but he no longer had anything new to add. As far as the development of the SF field was concerned, Gernsback's work was done.

Then, in 1930, along came a new magazine, fulsomely entitled *Astounding Stories of Super Science*, with a new editor, Harry Bates. A writer himself (and sometimes a very good one; his story "Alas All Thinking" is an early masterpiece in the field), Bates had no intention of putting out a carbon copy of *Amazing*. Bates's background was in the action-adventure pulps, and it was the slam-bang action potential of science fiction that attracted him.

It was Harry Bates, more than any other editor, who sealed that early connection between SF and the buckeye pulp magazines. *Amazing* had published a goodish number of interplanetary shoot-'em-ups, but it had also found room for every other kind of story as well. Bates was less eclectic. He had no time for reflective thought or poetic writing. He wanted something violent to happen on just about every page. He got what he wanted, and thus set the pattern for *Planet Stories* and *Thrilling Wonder* and all the other SF pulps that would follow.

The Depression was still going strong, however. Bates's tenure came to an end when his publishing company was swallowed up by the pulp giant, Street & Smith, in 1933. In acquiring a new publisher, *Astounding* also acquired a new editor, F. Orlin Tremaine.

Let the record show that I have a personal fondness for Tremaine. As a struggling teenage writer, I didn't hope for much personal attention from editors. By and large I didn't get it, either, but Tremaine was the exception. He not only let me come into his office and talk, he went so far as to take me out to lunch a couple of times. In retrospect I think I know why. Tremaine had become a science fiction editor without ever having had any experience in the field. He had no idea what a science fiction reader was like, and when a representative sample of that species of mankind came to his office— namely me—he was glad enough to have the chance to try to figure out what made us tick.

Apart from inexperience, Tremaine was in a fortunate position. As part of the vast Street & Smith empire, *Astounding* was well financed. It paid its writers a lordly full penny a word for everything it bought, and it paid them immediately on acceptance. Its only competitors were what was left of *Amazing* and Gernsback's other attempt, *Wonder Stories*. Both of them were bimonthlies, while *Astounding* came out every month without fail; both of them paid only half as much per word as *Astounding*, and they paid on publication—sometimes, indeed, only on lawsuit. So *Astounding* made the running for the whole field and, while Tremaine never actually contributed much that was original to the development of science fiction, he knew enough to know who did. When he was promoted past the editorship of a single magazine, he hand-picked his replacement. The man chosen was a regular contributor, and his name was John W. Campbell, Jr.

Simply put, John Campbell was the best editor science fiction ever had.

He was not a man without flaw. While he was revolutionizing *Astounding* he occasionally threw the baby out with the bath. For example, he continued only grudgingly to publish such old masters as Edward E. Smith, Ph.D., and made it clear how little he valued them by paying for their stories at a lower rate than those of his own discoveries. And he had a worrisome habit of falling for weird and improbable new "scientific" discoveries, mostly of the nature he called "psionic."

No matter. As an editor he was splendid. Single-handed he brought into the field nearly half of the Grand Masters we celebrate in these volumes, from Asimov to van Vogt. He fed his writers story ideas—had plenty of those to feed them, too, because he had been a good writer himself and now he preferred to let others write the ideas that kept on coming to him. Most important of all, he brought a revelatory new doctrine into science fiction. Don't write me stories about marvelous inventions or aliens invading the Earth, he begged his writers. The kind of stories I want, he said, are the kind of stories that could appear as contemporary literature—in a magazine published in the Twenty-fifth Century.

That, of course, is a description of most of the best science fiction stories that have appeared ever since.

Campbell was not the last editor to bring something new to science fiction. By the 1950s there were two, H. L. Gold, whose *Galaxy* emphasized hard-edged satire, and Anthony Boucher, who stressed literary style over adventure in *The Magazine of Science Fic-*

tion and Fantasy. Each one of them brought about a paradigm shift. Put them all together—Gernsback and Bates, Tremaine and Campbell, Boucher and Gold—and you have all the ingredients that science fiction writers have explored ever since.

Oh, they couldn't have done it without the writers, our Grand Masters included. But what the editors did was provide a place where the writers could experiment, and learn, and grow. Without them the field would be a lot poorer today.

Let me end on a personal note.

It has been my custom to write a short introduction to the works of each of the Grand Masters. For this volume, that made a problem, since one of the writers who had received the Grand Master award in this batch was me.

So I turned to an independent critic to write this particular introduction. Her name is Elizabeth Anne Hull, Ph.D. She is a former president of the Science Fiction Research Association, a professor who teaches science fiction at William Rainey Harper College, and an author in her own right. She therefore has all the skills required to bring an objective viewpoint to this task. Besides, she's my wife.

—Frederik Pohl

The SFWA
GRAND MASTERS

VOLUME THREE

LESTER DEL REY

1915–1993

One of the very few things we know for sure about the early life of Lester del Rey is that "Lester del Rey" was not the name he was born to. His birth name may have been Ramon Felipe San Juan Mario Silvio Enrico Smith Heathcourt-Brace Sierra y Alvarez-del Rey y de los Verdes, as he frequently maintained. Or it may have been Leonard Knapp, a name said to have been that of a cousin which (Lester said) he had been forced to use for legal purposes at one time, since his own birth records had been destroyed. But, from the early 1940s on, it was as Lester del Rey that he lived, voted, married, died—and wrote.

When Lester first appeared in recorded society he was living in Washington, D.C., and struggling to make a living. He worked for a time in an aircraft plant, and for a longer spell as a fry cook in a White Castle hamburger restaurant. He had been a reader of science fiction from early on, and in 1938 he began writing stories. His first sale was "The Faithful," to John Campbell's *Astounding*, followed quickly by the tenderly moving story which some critics still think his best, "Helen O'Loy," about a female robot and her love for her human owner.

I first met Lester in 1940; I was editing two science fiction magazines, *Astonishing Stories* and *Super Science Stories*, and Lester dropped in at the office to offer me a couple of stories John Campbell had rejected. (I rejected them, too. So, apparently, did everyone else, because they were never published anywhere and somewhere along the line Lester lost the manuscripts.) He was in a prolific period, appearing regularly in Campbell's *Astounding* and, when it came along, in its fantasy companion magazine, *Unknown;* with Asimov, de Camp, Van Vogt, Heinlein, and others, he was one of the major figures in Campbell's "golden age." In 1942 Lester published the novella "Nerves," about a cataclysmic explosion in a nuclear power plant—forty-odd years before Chernobyl—and after World War II he began writing his award-winning science fiction juveniles.

In the early 1950s Lester del Rey and his wife, Evelyn, came out to our home near Red Bank, New Jersey, to spend the weekend. They stayed fifteen years. Not all of it was in our house; before long, Lester and Evvie bought a place of their own down the street. Distance did not imply separation. We were in and out of each others' houses, went to cons together, frequently engaged in all-night canasta marathons, got involved together in local politics; the del Reys were Aunt Evvie and Uncle Lester to my children as they grew, and Lester and I collaborated on two not very remarkable novels, *Preferred Risk* and *The Sky Is Falling*. (Collaborating together was a bad idea, though. Lester had his own idiosyncratic work habits—he liked to work out an entire story in his mind before he put the first word on paper—and I had my own quite opposite ones, preferring to make it up as I went along. The collaborations were painful, and so by mutual consent we decided we would rather remain friends than to write any more books together.) And Lester and I shared a not very secret vice. Once or twice a week one or both of us would take the late train into New York City to sit in on Long John Nebel's all-night radio talk show, in the company of assorted scientists, politicians, celebrities, and a long list of flying saucer weirdos. I don't know how many times Lester and I did the Long John show—hundreds, at least—and I certainly don't know why. Perhaps it was just that both of us liked to talk.

Then, tragically, Evelyn was killed in a car smash in Virginia, on their way to a Florida holiday. Lester did not have the heart to stay in their house after that; he moved back to New York City, and we saw him only occasionally for a year or two.

While I was editor of the magazines *Galaxy* and *If*, my publisher had suggested that it would be a good idea to add a fantasy magazine to the string, to be called *Worlds of Fantasy*. Since Lester knew more about fantasy than I, I asked him to edit it. He did, and thus made the acquaintance of my assistant editor, a young woman named Judy-Lynn Benjamin. A few years later, Judy-Lynn and Lester married.

By then Judy-Lynn had become the science fiction editor for Ballantine Books. She was vastly successful (the imprint, Del Rey Books, is named for her) and when she, too, wanted to add more fantasy titles to the line, she, too, turned to Lester to edit them. He was just as successful as she. His specialty was taking manuscripts by unknown authors and turning them into million-copy bestsellers.

Some editors are relaxed and undemanding in their relations with their writers. Lester was too energetic for that. He went over those hundred-thousand-word manuscripts line by line and word by word, and insisted that their writers work as hard as he did on them. Not all of his writers enjoyed that process, and some moved on to less taxing editors. Still, the results spoke for themselves; Lester's publisher told me once that at that point in time Lester del Rey was clearly the most financially profitable editor in the publishing business. But all of that left him no time to do any writing of his own.

Then Judy-Lynn, too, died without warning. She was a young woman still, but she suffered a massive stroke, hung on in a coma for a while, and then was gone.

The fun of editing for Del Rey Books had gone out of it for Lester. He finished up all the works in progress and announced his retirement. It was his plan, he said, to devote the next few years to writing the immense, multivolume fantasy novel that he had wanted to do for a long time.

By then I had moved to the midwest, but we stayed in touch. When in New York I made a point of asking him how the great novel was progressing. He assured me that it was going very well— but only in his mind; he had not yet begun the business of putting any of it on paper.

He never did. His health declined, and in 1993 he suffered a couple of major heart attacks and died.

Recommended Reading
by Lester del Rey

THE FAITHFUL

Today, in a green and lovely world, here in the mightiest of human cities, the last of the human race is dying. And we of Man's creation are left to mourn his passing, and to worship the memory of Man, who controlled all that he knew save only himself.

I am old, as my people go, yet my blood is still young and my life may go on for untold ages yet, if what this last of Men has told me is true. And that also is Man's work, even as we and the Ape-People are his work in the last analysis. We of the Dog-People are old, and have lived a long time with Man. And yet, but for Roger Stren, we might still be baying at the moon and scratching the fleas from our hides, or lying at the ruins of Man's empire in dull wonder at his passing.

There are earlier records of dogs who mouthed clumsily a few Man words, but Hungor was the pet of Roger Stren, and in the labored efforts at speech, he saw an ideal and a life work. The operation on Hungor's throat and mouth, which made Man-speech more nearly possible, was comparatively simple. The search for other "talking" dogs was harder.

But he found five besides Hungor, and with this small start he began. Selection and breeding, surgery and training, gland implantation and X-ray mutation were his methods, and he made steady progress. At first money was a problem, but his pets soon drew attention and commanded high prices.

When he died, the original six had become thousands, and he had watched over the raising of twenty generations of dogs. A generation of my kind then took only three years. He had seen his small backyard pen develop into a huge institution, with a hundred followers and students, and had found the world eager for his success. Above all, he had seen tail-wagging give place to limited speech in that short time.

The movement he had started continued. At the end of two thousand years, we had a place beside Man in his work that would have been inconceivable to Roger Stren himself. We had our schools, our houses, our work with Man, and a society of our own. Even our independence, when we wanted it. And our life-span was not fourteen, but fifty years or more.

Man, too, had traveled a long way. The stars were almost within his grasp. The barren moon had been his for centuries. Mars and Venus lay beckoning, and he had reached them twice, but not to return. That lay close at hand. Almost, Man had conquered the universe.

But he had not conquered himself. There had been many setbacks to his progress because he had to go out and kill others of his kind. And now, the memory of his past called again, and he went out in battle against himself. Cities crumbled to dust, the plains to the south became barren deserts again, Chicago lay covered in a green mist. That death killed slowly, so that Man fled from the city and died, leaving it an empty place. The mist hung there, clinging days, months, years—after Man had ceased to be.

I, too, went out to war, driving a plane built for my people, over the cities of the Rising Star Empire. The tiny atomic bombs fell from my ship on houses, on farms, on all that was Man's, who had made my race what it was. For my Men had told me I must fight.

Somehow, I was not killed. And after the last Great Drive, when half of Man was already dead, I gathered my people about me, and we followed to the North, where some of my Men had turned to find a sanctuary from the war. Of Man's work, three cities still stood— wrapped in the green mist, and useless. And Man huddled around little fires and hid himself in the forest, hunting his food in small clans. Yet hardly a year of the war had passed.

For a time, the Men and my people lived in peace, planning to rebuild what had been, once the war finally ceased. Then came the Plague. The anti-toxin which had been developed was ineffective as the Plague increased in its virulency. It spread over land and sea, gripped Man who had invented it, and killed him. It was like a strong dose of strychnine, leaving Man to die in violent cramps and retchings.

For a brief time, Man united against it, but there was no control. Remorselessly it spread, even into the little settlement they had founded in the north. And I watched in sorrow as my Men around me were seized with its agony. Then we of the Dog-People were left alone in a shattered world from whence Man had vanished. For weeks we labored at the little radio we could operate, but there was no answer; and we knew that Man was dead.

There was little we could do. We had to forage our food as of old, and cultivate our crops in such small way as our somewhat modified forepaws permitted. And the barren north country was not suited to us.

I gathered my scattered tribes about me, and we began the long trek south. We moved from season to season, stopping to plant our food in the spring, hunting in the fall. As our sleds grew old and broke down, we could not replace them, and our travel became even slower. Sometimes we came upon our kind in smaller packs. Most of them had gone back to savagery, and these we had to mold to us by force. But little by little, growing in size, we drew south. We sought Men; for fifty thousand years we of the Dog-People had lived with and for Man, and we knew no other life.

In the wilds of what had once been Washington State we came upon another group who had not fallen back to the law of tooth and fang. They had horses to work for them, even crude harnesses and machines which they could operate. There we stayed for some ten years, setting up a government and building ourselves a crude city. Where Man had his hands, we had to invent what could be used with our poor feet and our teeth. But we had found a sort of security, and had even acquired some of Man's books by which we could teach our young.

Then into our valley came a clan of our people, moving west, who told us they had heard that one of our tribes sought refuge and provender in a mighty city of great houses lying by a lake in the east. I could only guess that it was Chicago. Of the green mist they had not heard—only that life was possible there.

Around our fires that night we decided that if the city were habitable, there would be homes and machines designed for us. And it might be there were Men, and the chance to bring up our young in the heritage which was their birthright. For weeks we labored in preparing ourselves for the long march to Chicago. We loaded our supplies in our crude carts, hitched our animals to them, and began the eastward trip.

It was nearing winter when we camped outside the city, still mighty and imposing. In the sixty years of the desertion, nothing had perished that we could see; the fountains to the west were still playing, run by automatic engines.

We advanced upon the others in the dark, quietly. They were living in a great square, littered with filth, and we noted that they had not even fire left from civilization. It was a savage fight, while it lasted, with no quarter given nor asked. But they had sunk too far, in the lazy shelter of Man's city, and the clan was not as large as we had heard. By the time the sun rose there was not one of them but had been killed or imprisoned until we could train them in our ways. The ancient city was ours, the green mist gone after all those years.

Around us were abundant provisions, the food factories which I knew how to run, the machines that Man had made to fit our needs, the houses in which we could dwell, power drawn from the bursting core of the atom, which needed only the flick of a switch to start. Even without hands, we could live here in peace and security for ages. Perhaps here my dreams of adapting our feet to handle Man's tools and doing his work were possible, even if no Men were found.

We cleared the muck from the city and moved into Greater South Chicago, where our people had had their section of the city. I, and a few of the elders who had been taught by their fathers in the ways of Man, set up the old regime, and started the great water and light machines. We had returned to a life of certainty.

And four weeks later, one of my lieutenants brought Paul Kenyon before me. Man! Real and alive, after all this time! He smiled, and I motioned my eager people away.

"I saw your lights," he explained. "I thought at first some men had come back, but that is not to be; but civilization still has its followers, evidently, so I asked one of you to take me to the leaders. Greetings from all that is left of Man!"

"Greetings," I gasped. It was like seeing the return of the gods. My breath was choked; a great peace and fulfillment surged over me. "Greetings, and the blessings of your God. I had no hope of seeing Man again."

He shook his head. "I am the last. For fifty years I have been searching for Men—but there are none. Well, you have done well. I should like to live among you, work with you—when I can. I survived the Plague somehow, but it comes on me yet, more often now, and I can't move nor care for myself then. That is why I have come to you.

"Funny." He paused. "I seem to recognize you. Hungor Beowulf XIV? I am Paul Kenyon. Perhaps you remember me? No? Well, it was a long time, and you were young. Perhaps my smell has changed with the disease. But that white streak under the eye still shows, and I remember you."

I needed no more to complete my satisfaction at his home-coming.

Now one had come among us with hands, and he was of great help. But most of all, he was of the old Men, and gave point to our working. But often, as he had said, the old sickness came over him, and he lay in violent convulsions, from which he was weak for days. We learned to care for him, and help him when he needed it, even as we learned to fit our society to his presence. And at last, he came to me with a suggestion.

"Hungor," he said, "if you had one wish, what would it be?"

"The return of Man. The old order, where we could work to-gether. You know as well as I how much we need Man."

He grinned crookedly. "Now, it seems, Man needs you more. But if that were denied, what next?"

"Hands," I said. "I dream of them at night and plan for them by day, but I will never see them."

"Maybe you will, Hungor. Haven't you ever wondered why you go on living, twice normal age, in the prime of your life? Have you never wondered how I have withstood the Plague which still runs in my blood, and how I still seem only in my thirties, though nearly seventy years have passed since a Man has been born?"

"Sometimes," I answered. "I have no time for wonder, now, and when I do—Man is the only answer I know."

"A good answer," he said. "Yes, Hungor, Man is the answer. That is why I remember you. Three years before the war, when you were just reaching maturity, you came into my laboratory. Do you remem-ber now?"

"The experiment," I said. "That is why you remembered me?"

"Yes, the experiment. I altered your glands somewhat, implanted certain tissues into your body, as I had done to myself. I was seeking the secret of immortality. Though there was no reaction at the time, it worked, and I don't know how much longer we may live—or you may; it helped me resist the Plague, but did not overcome it."

So that was the answer. He stood staring at me a long time. "Yes, unknowingly, I saved you to carry on Man's future for him. But we were talking of hands.

"As you know, there is a great continent to the east of the Americas, called Africa. But did you know Man was working there on the great apes, as he was working here on your people? We never made as much progress with them as with you. We started too late. Yet they spoke a simple language and served for common work. And we changed their hands so the thumb and fingers opposed, as do mine. There, Hungor, are your hands."

Now Paul Kenyon and I laid plans carefully. Out in the hangars of the city there were aircraft designed for my people's use; heretofore, I had seen no need of using them. The planes were in good condition, we found on examination, and my early training came back to me as I took the first ship up. They carried fuel to circle the globe ten times, and out in the lake the big fuel tanks could be drawn on when needed.

Together, though he did most of the mechanical work between spells of sickness, we stripped the planes of all their war equipment. Of the six hundred planes, only two were useless, and the rest would serve to carry some two thousand passengers in addition to the pilots. If the apes had reverted to complete savagery, we were equipped with tanks of anesthetic gas by which we could overcome them and strap them in the planes for the return. In the houses around us, we built accommodations for them strong enough to hold them by force, but designed for their comfort if they were peaceable.

At first, I had planned to lead the expedition. But Paul Kenyon pointed out that they would be less likely to respond to us than to him. "After all," he said, "Men educated them and cared for them, and they probably remember us dimly. But your people they know only as the wild dogs who are their enemies. I can go out and contact their leaders, guarded, of course, by your people. But otherwise, it might mean battle."

Each day I took up a few of our younger ones in the planes and taught them to handle the controls. As they were taught, they began the instruction of others. It was a task which took months to finish, but my people knew the need of hands as well as I; any faint hope was well worth trying.

It was late spring when the expedition set out. I could follow their progress by means of television, but could work the controls only with difficulty. Kenyon, of course, was working the controls at the other end, when he was able.

They met with a storm over the Atlantic Ocean, and three of the ships went down. But under the direction of my lieutenant and Kenyon, the rest weathered the storm. They landed near the ruins of Capetown, but found no trace of the Ape-People. Then began weeks of scouting over the jungles and plains. They saw apes, but on capturing a few they found them only the primitive creatures which nature had developed.

It was by accident they finally met with success. Camp had been made for the night, and fires had been lit to guard against the savage beasts which roamed the land. Kenyon was in one of his rare moments of good health. The telecaster had been set up in a tent near the outskirts of the camp, and he was broadcasting a complete account of the day. Then, abruptly, over the head of the Man was raised a rough and shaggy face.

He must have seen the shadow, for he started to turn sharply, then caught himself and moved slowly around. Facing him was one of the apes, He stood there silently, watching the ape, not knowing whether it was savage or well disposed. It, too, hesitated; then it advanced.

"Man—Man," it mouthed. "You came back. Where were you? I am Tolemy, and I saw you, and I came."

"Tolemy," said Kenyon, smiling. "It is good to see you, Tolemy. Sit down; let us talk. I am glad to see you. Ah, Tolemy, you look old; were your father and mother raised by Man?"

"I am eighty years, I think. It is hard to know. I was raised by Man long ago. And now I am old; my people say I grow too old to lead. They do not want me to come to you, but I know Man. He was good to me. And he had coffee and cigarettes."

"I have coffee and cigarettes, Tolemy." Kenyon smiled. "Wait, I will get them. And your people, is not life hard among them in the jungle? Would you like to go back with me?"

"Yes, hard among us. I want to go back with you. Are you many?"

"No, Tolemy." He set the coffee and cigarettes before the ape, who drank eagerly and lit the smoke gingerly from a fire. "No, but I have friends with me. You must bring your people here, and let us get to be friends. Are there many of you?"

"Yes. Ten times we make ten tens—a thousand of us, almost. We are all that was left in the city of Man after the great fight. A Man freed us, and I led my people away, and we lived here in the jungle. They wanted to be in small tribes, but I made them one, and we are safe. Food is hard to find."

"We have much food in a big city, Tolemy, and friends who will help you, if you work for them. You remember the Dog-People, don't you? And you would work with them as with Man if they treated you as Man treated you, and fed you, and taught your people?"

"Dogs? I remember the Man-Dogs. They were good. But here the dogs are bad. I smelled dog here; it was not like the dog we smell each day, and my nose was not sure. I will work with Man-Dogs, but my people will be slow to learn them."

Later telecasts showed rapid progress. I saw the apes come in by twos and threes and meet Paul Kenyon, who gave them food, and introduced my people to them. This was slow, but as some began to lose their fear of us, others were easier to train. Only a few broke away and would not come.

Cigarettes that Man was fond of—but which my people never used—were a help, since they learned to smoke with great readiness.

It was months before they returned. When they came, there were over nine hundred of the Ape-People with them, and Paul and Tolemy had begun their education. Our first job was a careful medical examination of Tolemy, but it showed him in good health, and with much of the vigor of a younger ape. Man had been lengthening the ages of his kind, as it had ours, and he was evidently a complete success.

Now they have been among us three years, and during that time we have taught them to use their hands at our instructions. Overhead, the great monorail cars are running, and the factories have started to work again. They are quick to learn, with a curiosity that makes them eager for new knowledge. And they are thriving and multiplying here. We need no longer bewail the lack of hands; perhaps in time to come, with their help, we can change our forepaws further, and learn to walk on two legs, as did Man.

Today, I have come back from the bed of Paul Kenyon. We are often together now—perhaps I should include the faithful Tolemy—when he can talk, and among us there has grown a great friendship.

I laid certain plans before him today for adapting the apes mentally and physically until they are Men. Nature did it with an apelike brute once; why can we not do it with the Ape-People now? The Earth would be peopled again, science would rediscover the stars, and Man would have a foster child in his own likeness.

And—we of the Dog-People have followed Man for fifty thousand years. That is too long to change. Of all Earth's creatures, the Dog-People alone have followed Man thus. My people cannot lead now. No dog was ever complete without the companionship of Man. The Ape-People will be Man.

It is a pleasant dream, surely not an impossible one.

Kenyon smiled as I spoke to him, and cautioned me in the jesting way he uses when most serious, not to make them too much like Man, lest another Plague destroy them. Well, we can guard against that. I think he, too, had a dream of Man reborn, for there was a hint of tears in his eyes, and he seemed pleased with me.

There is but little to please him now, alone among us, wracked by pain, waiting the slow death he knows must come. The old trouble has grown worse, and the Plague has settled harder on him.

All we can do is give him sedatives to ease the pain now, though Tolemy and I have isolated the Plague we found in his blood. It seems a form of cholera, and with that information, we have done some work. The old Plague serum offers a clue, too. Some of our serums have seemed to ease the spells a little, but they have not stopped them.

It is a faint chance. I have not told him of our work, for only a stroke of luck will give us success before he dies.

Man is dying. Here in our laboratory, Tolemy keeps repeating something; a prayer, I think it is. Well, maybe the God whom he has learned from Man will be merciful, and grant us success.

Paul Kenyon is all that is left of the old world which Tolemy and I loved. He lies in the ward, moaning in agony, and dying. Sometimes he looks from his windows and sees the birds flying south; he gazes at them as if he would never see them again. Well, will he? Something he muttered once comes back to me:

"For no man knoweth—"

THE PIPES OF PAN

Beyond the woods on either side were well-kept fields and fertile farm land, but here the undergrowth ran down to the dirt road and hid the small plot of tilled ground, already overrun with weeds. Behind that, concealed by thicker scrub timber, lay a rude log house. Only the trees around, which had sheltered it from the heavy winds, had kept it from crumbling long before.

Pan recognized the lazy retreat to nature that had replaced his strong worship of old. He moved carefully through the tangled growth that made way for him, his cloven hoofs clicking sharply on the stones. It was a thin and saddened god that approached the house and gazed in through a hole that served as a window.

Inside, Fred Emmet lay on a rude pallet on the floor, a bag of his possessions beside him. Across from him was a stone fireplace, and between the two, nothing. A weak hand moved listlessly, brushing aside the vermin that knew his sickness; perhaps they sensed that the man was dying, and their time was short. He gave up the struggle against them and reached for a broken crock that contained water, but the effort was too great.

"Pan!" The man's voice reached out, and the god stepped away from the window and through the warped doorway. He moved to the pallet and leaned over his follower. The man looked up.

"Pan!" Emmet's face was startled, but there was a reverent note in his labored voice, though another might have mistaken the god for a devil. The tangled locks of Pan's head were separated by two goat horns and the thin sharp face ended in a ragged beard that seemed the worse for the weather. Then the neck led down to a bronzed torso that might have graced Hercules, only to end in the hips and legs of a goat, covered with shaggy hair. Horror and comedy mingled grotesquely, except for the eyes, which were deep and old, filled now with pity.

Pan nodded. "You've been calling me, Frank Emmet, and it's a poor god that wouldn't answer the appeal of his last worshiper. All the others of your kind have deserted me for newer gods, and only you are left now."

It was true enough. Over the years, Pan had seen his followers fall off and dwindle until his great body grew lean and his lordly capering among the hills became a slow march toward extinction. Now even this man was dying. He lifted the tired head and held the crock of water to Emmet's mouth.

"Thanks!" The man mulled it over slowly. "So when I'm gone there's no others. If I'd a-known, Pan, I might have raised up kids to honor your name, but I thought there were others. Am I—?"

"Dying," the god answered. The blunt truth was easier than half-believed lies.

"Then take me outside, where the sun can shine on me."

Pan nodded and lifted him easily, bearing him out as gently as a mother might her child, but a spasm of pain shot over the man's face as Pan laid him down. The time was almost up, the god knew. From a pocket in his tattered loincloth he drew out a small syrinx, or pipe of seven reeds, and blew softly across it. A bird heard the low murmuring melody and improvised a harmony, while a cricket marked time in slow chirps.

Emmet's face relaxed slowly and one of his hands came out to lie on the hairy thigh. "Thanks, Pan. You've always been a good god to me, and I'm hoping you'll have good l—" The voice trailed away and disappeared into the melody of the syrinx. Pan rose slowly, drawing a last lingering note from it, dropped the arm over the still chest and closed the eyes. Nearby was a rusty spade, and the earth was soft and moist.

Pan's great shoulders drooped as he wiped the last of the earth from his hands. Experimentally, he chirped at the cricket, but there was no response, and he knew that the law governing all gods still applied. When the last of their worshipers was gone, they either died or were forced to eke out their living in the world of men by some human activity. Now there would be hunger to satisfy and, in satisfying it, other needs of a life among men would present themselves.

Apollo was gone, long since, choosing in his pride to die, and the other gods had followed slowly, some choosing work, some death. But they had at least the advantage of human forms, while he knew himself for a monster his own mother had fled from. But then, the modern clothes were more concealing than the ancient ones.

Inside the house he found Emmet's other clothes, more or less presentable, and a hunting knife and soap. Men were partial to their own appearance, and horns were a stigma among them. Reluctantly, he brought the knife up against the base of one, cutting through it. Pain lanced through him at first, but enough of his godhood remained to make the stumps heal over almost instantly. Then the other one followed, and the long locks of hair. He combed it out and hacked it into such form as he could.

As the beard came away he muttered ungodly phrases at the knife that took off skin with the hair. But even to his own eyes the smooth-shaven face was less forbidding. The lips, as revealed, were firm and straight, and the chin was good, though a mark of different color showed where the beard had been.

He fingered his tail thoughtfully, touching it with the blade of the knife, then let it go; clothes could hide it, and Pan had no love for the barren spine that men regarded as a mark of superiority. The tail must stay. Shoes were another problem, but he solved it by carving wooden feet to fit them, and making holes for his hoofs. By lacing the shoes on firmly, he found half an hour's practice enough to teach him to walk. The underclothes, which scratched against the hair on his thighs and itched savagely, were another factor he had no love for, but time might improve that.

Hobbling about in the rough walk his strange legs necessitated, he came on a few pieces of silver in another broken crock and pocketed them. From the scraps of conversation he had heard, work was hard enough for unskilled men to find, and he might need this small sum before he found occupation. Already hunger was creeping over him, or he guessed it was hunger. At least the vacuum in his stomach was as abhorrent to him as to nature. Heretofore, he had supped lightly on milk and honey as the mood suited him, but this was a man-sized craving.

Well, if work he must, work he would. The others had come to it, such as still lived. Ishtar, or Aphrodite, was working somewhere in the East as a nursemaid, though her old taste for men still cost her jobs as fast as she gained them. Pan's father, Hermes, had been working as a Western Union messenger the last he'd seen of him. Even Zeus, proudest of all, was doing an electrician's work somewhere, leaving only Ares still thriving in full godhood. What his own talents might be, time alone would tell, but the rippling muscles of his body must be put to some good use.

Satisfied that there was no more he could do, he trotted out and plowed his way through the underbrush that failed to make way for him as it should have done. He jingled the money in one pocket thoughtfully as he hit the road, then drew out the syrinx and began a reedy tune of defiance on it. Work there must be, and he'd find it.

It was less than half an hour later, but the god's feet were already aching in the tight boxes he had made for them, and his legs threatened to buckle under the effort it took to ape man's walk. He moved past the ugly square house and toward the barn where the farmer was unhitching his team.

"Handout or work?" The man's voice was anything but enthusiastic.

"I'm looking for work."

"Uh-huh. Well, you do look strong enough. Living near the city the way I do, I get a lot of fellows in here, figuring they can always work in the country. But their arms wouldn't make toothpicks for a jaybird. Know anything about farming?"

"Something." It was more in Demeter's line, but he knew something about everything that grew. "I'm not asking more than a room and board and a little on the side."

The farmer's eyes were appraising. "You do look as if you'd seen fresh air, at that. And you're homely enough to be honest. Grab a-holt here, and we'll talk it over. I don't rightly need a man now, but—Hey! Whoa, there!"

Pan cursed silently. His godhood was still clinging to him, and the horses sensed the urge to wildness that was so intimately a part of him. As his hands fell on the tugs, they reared and bucked, lunging against their collars. He caught at the lines to steady them, but they flattened back their ears and whinnied wildly. That was enough; Pan moved back and let the farmer quiet them.

"Afraid I can't use you." The farmer's words were slow and decisive. "I use a right smart amount of horseflesh here, and some people just don't have the knack with them; animals are funny that way—finicky, you might say. Easy there, Nelly! Tried any other places?"

"All the other farms along the road. They're not hiring hands."

"Hm-mm. Wouldn't be, of course. Bunch of city men. Think they can come out and live in the country and do a little farming on the side. If I had the money, I'd sell out and move somewhere where people knew what the earth was made for. You won't find any work around here." He slapped a horse on the withers and watched as it stretched out and rolled in the short grass. "Stay for lunch?"

"No." He wasn't hungry enough to need food yet, and the delay might cost him a job elsewhere. "Any sheep-herding done around here?" As the god of the shepherds, it should come natural to him, and it was work that would be more pleasant than any in the tight closeness of the city.

"Not around here. Out West they have, but the Mexicans do all that. If you're a sheep man, though, that's why the horses didn't take to you; they hate the smell of sheep."

Again the limitations of a human life imposed themselves; instead of transporting himself to the sheep-herding country in a night, he'd have to walk there slowly, or ride. "How much would it cost to go out West?"

"Blamed if I know. Seventy dollars, maybe more."

So that was out. It would have to be the city, after all, where the fetid stench of close-packed humans tainted the air, and their meaningless yammering beat incessantly in one's ears. "I guess I'll have to go on into town," he said ruefully.

"Might be best. Nowadays, the country ain't what it used to be. Every fool that fails in town thinks he can fall back on the country, and every boy we have that amounts to anything goes to the city. Machinery's cutting down the number of men we need, and prices are shot haywire, even when a mortgage doesn't eat up all we make. You traveling on Shank's mare?"

Pan nodded, and the other studied him again. "Uh-huh. Well, down the road a piece you'll see a brick house set way back behind some oaks. Go in there and tell Hank Sherman I said you was a friend of mine. He's going into the city, and you might as well ride along. Better hurry, though."

Pan made his thanks hastily and left. If memory served him right, the friendliness of the farmer was the last he'd see. In the cities, even in the old days, men were too busy with their own importance and superiority to bother with others. But beggars made ill choosers.

•   •   •

The god clumped down the hot sidewalk, avoiding the press of the one-o'clock rush, and surveyed the signs thoughtfully. Food should come first, he guessed, but the prices were discouraging. One read:

BUSINESS MAN'S LUNCH
Blue plate special, $2.00

He cut away from the large street into an older part of the city, and found that the prices dropped steadily. Finally a sign that suited his pocketbook came into view, and he turned in, picking the only vacant booth. Now he was thankful for the time he'd believed wasted in studying men's ways.

The menu meant little to him. He studied it carefully, and decided that the safest course was to order one of their combinations. Fish—no, that was food for Poseidon. But the lamb plate looked better, and the price fell within his means. "Lamb," he ordered.

The waitress shifted her eyes from the man behind the counter and wrote it down in the manner of all waitresses who expect no tip from the customer. "Coffeetearmilk?" she asked. "Rollerwhiterye?"

"Eh? Oh, milk and roll." Pan had a word for her type in several languages, and was tempted to use one. As a god—but he wasn't a god now, and men no longer respected their gods, anyway. The cashier eyed his clothes thoughtfully until he moved in irritation, jingling the few coins in his pocket. Then she went back to her tickets, flipping gum from one tooth to another in an abstracted manner.

The food, when it came, was to him a soggy-looking mess, but that was true of all human food, and he supposed it was good enough for the price. At least the plate was better filled than those he had seen through the windows of the more expensive places, and Pan's appetite was immense. He stuffed half a roll in his mouth and chewed on it quickly.

Not bad; in fact, he might grow to like this business of eating. His stomach quieted down and made itself at home, while another half-bun followed the first. As he started to pick up the cut of meat and swallow it, he caught the eyes of another diner and rumbled unhappily. Should he know the sissies nipped off shavings with their knives and minced the food down? But he put the meat back on the plate and fell to as they did. It was best to ape them.

"Mind if I sit here, old-timer?" Pan looked up at a clean-cut young man. "The other booths are filled, you know."

Where the man sat was no business of Pan's. The seat opposite him was vacant, and he motioned to it. "I didn't buy it, and your face isn't misshapen. Sit down."

The other grinned good-naturedly and inspected the menu. "Lamb any good?"

"Seems all right." He was no judge of food, naturally, but it wasn't burned, and he had seen no dirt on it. He cleaned the last of the gravy from his plate with a bun and transferred it to his mouth. "At least, it partly fills a—a man."

"Okay, lamb it is." This time the waitress showed more interest, and even brought water, a thing she'd neglected before. "Make it lamb, sugar. And a beer. How about you, stranger?"

"Eh?" Unless he was mistaken, that was an invitation, and a welcome one. It was long years since he'd had a chance to sample even the anemic brew of the modern world, but that had been none of his choosing.

"Have a beer?"

"Why not?" As an afterthought, he added an ungodlike thanks. The man was likable, he decided, though friendliness among city men was not what he had expected. "You wouldn't know about work in this city, would you—ah—?"

"Bob Bailey."

"Men call me Pan—or Faunus, sometimes."

"Tried the want ads yet, Pan—or the employment agencies?" Bailey pulled a folded newspaper from his pocket and handed it over. "There might be a job in the back there. What kind of work?"

"Whatever I can do." Pan began at the bottom and skimmed up the list from xylophone players to bartenders. "But nothing they have here. I'm supposed to be good at herding and playing the syrinx, but that's about all."

"Syrinx?" Bailey inspected the instrument Pan held out, and amusement danced in his eyes. "Oh, that. Afraid it wouldn't do, Mr. Faunus. You don't happen to play the clarinet?"

"Never tried it."

"Then you don't. I'm, looking for someone who does, right now, for my band. Bob Bailey's Barnstormers. Ever hear of it? Well, you're not the only one. Since we lost the best darned clarinetist in the business, we've slipped plenty. Playing the third-rate spots now with the substitute we had to hire. He used to be on the Lady Lee Lullaby hour, and never got over it."

"Why not get a good one then?" The talk made little sense to the god, but the solution seemed obvious.

"Where? We get plenty of applicants—there's an ad running in there now. But they'd either put the crowd to sleep or rattle the strings off the doghouse. Not a good clear tone in the bunch. All the good guys are signed up or starting their own outfits."

They finished the beers and Pan counted out the amount marked on his ticket, estimating the length of time his remaining money would last; two days, maybe, by going half-hungry. He grunted. "Where are these employment agencies you mentioned?"

"One just down the street. It's a U.S. employment center, so they won't try to rob you. Good luck, Faunus."

"And to you. My thanks for the beer." Then they separated, and Pan headed down the street toward the mecca of the jobless. The ads had all called for training of some sort, but there must be other work in this town that needed no previous experience. Perhaps meeting two friendly men in one day was a good omen. He hoped so.

The girl at the desk, when he finally found the right division, looked as bored as had the waitress. Looking over the collection of people waiting, Pan felt she had more reason. There were the coarsened red faces of professional sots, the lackluster stares of men whose intelligence ranked slightly below the apes, and the dreary faces of people who struggle futilely for a life that brings nothing but death to break its monotony.

But there were others there who looked efficient and purposeful, and these were the ones Pan feared. They had at least some training, some experience, and their appearance was better than his. Surely the preference would go to them, and even as a minority there were still many of that type there.

He studied the applicants and strained his ears to familiarize himself with the questions asked, holding down his impatience as best he could. But the machine ground slowly on, and his turn finally came, just as the hot, fetid air was becoming unbearable. "Your name," said the girl, studying him impersonally.

"Pan—Pan Faunus."

Many strange names had passed over the desk to her, and her expression remained the same. "Middle name?"

"Uh . . . Sylvanus." The Romans had done him a good turn in

doubling up on their names for him, though he preferred the Greek. "Address?"

For a moment that stumped him. Then he gave the address of the restaurant, figuring that he might be able to arrange with the cashier to accept any mail that came there; he'd heard another man talking of that scheme while he waited, and it was as good as any. "Age?"

"Seven thou—*ulp!* Forty-five." Since a pack of lies was needed of him, they might as well be good ones. "Born June 5, 1912."

There were more questions, and at some of his answers the girl looked up sharply, but his wits had always been good and he passed the test with some fair success. Then came what he had been dreading.

"Experience and type of work?"

"General work in the country," he decided. "No trade, and I can't give references, since my former foll—employer is dead."

"Social Security number?"

"Eh?" He had been hearing that asked of the applicants, but it still meant nothing to him. "I don't have one."

"But—" She frowned, then shrugged. "You should have, even for farm work. Well, all right, I guess you'll have to make out an application."

Finally it was done and he was sent into a cubbyhole where a man asked more questions and made marks on a piece of paper. Some of Pan's answers were true; Hermes was his father, at least. Even that questioning came to an end leaving him sweating and cursing the underclothes that itched again in the hot room. The man leaned back and surveyed him.

"We haven't much of a job for you, Mr. Faunus. As a matter of fact, you'd probably do much better in the country where you came from. But"—he searched through his records—"this call just came in for an office boy and for some reason they want someone of your age. It pays only the minimum, but they didn't mention experience. Want to try it?"

Pan nodded emphatically and blessed the luck that had turned up the job at precisely the right moment; he'd seen enough people turned away to know how small his chances were. He wasted no time in taking the little address slip and tracking the job to its lair.

•   •   •

Late afternoon found him less enthusiastic about the work. The air in the office was thick and stuffy and there was an incessant jarring of comptometers, thudding from the typewriters, and the general buzz that men think necessary to business. He leaned over on the table, taking some of the ache from his tired feet and cursing the endless piles of envelopes that needed sealing and stamping.

This was work for a fool or one of the machines that men were so proud of. Pick up an envelope, draw one finger under the flap to lift it, roll the flap over the wet roller, and close it with the other hand as it came off. Lift, roll, seal, lift, roll, seal. No wonder men shut themselves in tight houses, away from the good, clean winds and light of the sun; they were ashamed of what served for life among them, and with good reason.

But if it had to be done he was willing to try. At first the exultation of getting the work had served to keep his mind off it. Lying and deceit were not his specialty, and only a driving urge to adapt himself had made him use them to the extent that had been necessary. Now the men had put him on work that shriveled the mind and did the muscles no good.

The former office boy came up to inspect his work and Pan understood, looking at him, why the manager no longer wanted boys. The kid didn't know as yet that his job was being taken over but thought he was in line for promotion, and was cocky enough for two. He seized the envelope rudely and ran it over the roller with a flourish.

"Awful dumb help they're sending out these days," he told the air. "Now I told you these had to go out tonight and I find you loafing. Keep moving. You don't catch me laying down on the job. Ain't you never had a job before?"

Pan looked at him, a sidelong glance that choked off the kid's words, and fell to on the envelopes again. The air was getting the best of him. His head felt numb and thick and his whole body was logy and dull. With what was supposed to be a chummy air the boy sat his overgrown body on the desk and opened up his reservoir of personal anecdotes.

"Boy, you shoulda been with me last night. Good-looking babes! Man! And boy, did they ever go for me! One little babe saw me work on the football team last year, and that didn't do me no harm. Best high school team in the state we had. You like football, guy?"

Pan's lips twitched. "No!" He redid an envelope that hadn't been properly moistened and reviewed the reasons for not committing mayhem on the boy. They were good reasons but their value was depreciating with the passage of time in the stinking office—and with each new visit from the boy. The direct bluntness he longed to use came out a little in his voice and the kid bounced off the table, scowling.

"Okay, don't let it get you. Hey, whatcha think stamps are? Don't tear them that way. Some of you hicks are ignorant enough to eat them."

The god caught himself on the table again, throbbing pains running through his head. There was a conference around the manager's desk and cigar smoke was being added to the thickness of the room. He groped out behind him for a stool and eased himself down on it. Something sharp cut into him and brought him up with a wild bellow!

The boy giggled. "Dawgone, I didn't think you'd fall for it. Oldest gag there is, and you still sat right down on that tack. Boy, you shoulda seen yourself!"

Pan wasn't seeing himself but he was seeing red. Homeric Greek is probably the most expressive of all languages and his command of it included a good deal Homer had forgotten to mention. With a sharp leap, his head came down and his body jerked forward. He missed the horns now, but his hard skull in the boy's midsection served well enough.

Sudden confusion ran through the office and the manager rose quickly from his chair and headed toward the scene. Pan's senses were returning and he knew it was time to leave. The back door opened on an alley and he didn't wait to ask for directions.

The outer air removed the last traces of his temper and sobered him down, but there was no regret in his mind. What was done was done and there was no room in his philosophy for regrets. Of course, word of it would get back to the employment agency and he'd have no more jobs from them, but he wanted no more of such jobs. Maybe Apollo had the right idea in dying.

He made a slow meal in the restaurant; Bailey was not there. He'd liked that young man. With a rush of extravagance he bought a beer for himself and hung around, half-waiting in hopes of Bailey's appearance and half-planning for tomorrow; but nothing came of his plans.

Finally he got up and moved out into a little park across from the restaurant, just as darkness began to replace the twilight. Sleeping accommodations were the least of his worries. He found a large bush which concealed his body and lay down on the ground under it. Sleep came quickly.

When he awoke he found himself better for the sleep, though the same wasn't true for his clothes. He located his shoes and clamped his hoofs into them again, muttering dark thoughts about cobblers in general. If this kept up he'd get bog spavins yet.

He made his way across to the restaurant again, where the waitress who was on at that hour regarded him with less approval than the other had. Out of the great pity of her heart, her actions said, she'd condescend to serve him, but she'd be the last to object to his disappearance. The sweet bun he got must have been well chosen for dryness.

"Hello there, old-timer." Bob Bailey's easy voice broke in on his gloom and the young man sat down opposite him. Bailey's eyes studied the god's clothes and the man nodded faintly to himself, but made no comment. "Have any luck yesterday?"

"Some, if you'd call it that." Pan related his fortunes shortly. Bailey grinned faintly.

"The trouble with you," Bailey said around a mouthful of eggs, "is that you're a man; employers don't want that. They want self-repairing machines with self-starters and a high reverence for so-called business ideals. Takes a man several years to get inculcated with the proper liking for all kinds of knuckling under. You're supposed to lie down and take it, no matter how little you like it."

"Even from empty fools who hold themselves better than the gods?"

"That or worse; I know something about it myself. Stood all I could of a two-bit white-collar job before I organized the Barnstormers."

Pan considered the prospect and wondered how long it would take him to starve. "Slavery isn't what I'm looking for. Find your musician?"

"Not a chance. When they've got rhythm they don't bother learning music, and most of them don't have it. Smoke?"

Pan took the cigarette doubtfully and mimicked the other's actions. He'd seen men sucking smoke for centuries now but the urge to try it had never come to him. He coughed over the first puff, letting out a bleat that startled the couple in the next booth, then set about mastering it. Once the harsh sting of the tobacco was gone there was something oddly soothing about it, and his vigorous good health threw off any toxic effect it might have had.

Bob finished his breakfast and picked up the checks. "On me, Faunus," he said. "The shows should open in a few minutes. Want to take one in?"

Pan shook his head vigorously. The close-packed throng of humans in a dark theater was not his idea of a soothing atmosphere. "I'm going over to the park again. Maybe in the outdoor air I can get an idea."

"Okay, we'll make it a twosome, if it's all right with you. Time to kill is about the only thing I have now." As he paid the checks, Pan noticed, the man's pocketbook was anything but overflowing, and he guessed that one of Bailey's difficulties was inability to pay for a first-class musician.

They found a bench in the shade and sat down together, each thinking of his own troubles and mulling over the other's. It was the best way in the world to feel miserable. Above them in a tree a bird settled down to a high, bubbling little song and a squirrel came over to them with the faint hope of peanuts clearly in its mind.

Pan clucked at it, making clicking sounds that brought its beady little eyes up at him quickly. It was a fat, well-fed squirrel that had domesticated man nicely for its purposes, and there was no fear about it. When even the animals had learned to live with man and like it, surely a god could do as well.

He tapped his thigh slowly and felt the syrinx under his hand. The squirrel regarded him carefully as he drew it out, saw there was no bag of peanuts there, and started to withdraw. The first low notes blown from the reeds called it back, and it sat down on its tail, paws to its mouth in a rapt attitude that aped a critic listening to Bach.

Pan took courage and the old bluff laughter fell from his lips. He lifted the syrinx again and began a quick, wild air on the spur of the moment, letting the music roam through the notes as it would. There was no set tempo, but his feet tapped lightly on the graveled path, and the bird fell into time with him.

Bailey looked up in surprise, his fingers twitching at the irregular rhythm. There was a wildness to it, a primitiveness that barely escaped savagery, and groped out toward man's first awareness of the fierce, wild joy of living. Now the notes formed a regular cadence that could be followed, and Bailey whistled an impromptu harmony. The squirrel swayed lightly from side to side, twitching its tail.

"Crazy, isn't he?" Bob asked, as Pan paused. "I've never seen music hit an animal that way before. Where'd you learn the piece?"

"Learn it?" Pan shook his head. "Music isn't learned—it's something that comes from inside."

"You mean you made that up as you went along? *Wow!* But you can play a regular tune, can't you?"

"I never tried."

"Uh. Well, here's one." He pursed his lips and began whistling one of the standard popular things his orchestra played at, but never hit. Pan listened to it carefully, only half-sure he liked it, then put the syrinx to his lips, beat his foot for time, and repeated it. But there were minor variations that somehow lifted it and set the rhythm bouncing along, reaching out to the squirrel and making its tail twitch frenziedly.

Bailey slapped him on the back, beaming. "Old-timer," he chuckled, "you've got the least to make it with in that whistle, but when you hit it, you *send*. Man, I'd like to have the boys hear the way you take off on the bit and go supersonic!"

Pan's face was blank, though the voice had seemed approving. "Can't you speak English?"

"Sure. I'm telling you you're hot. Give the crowds an earful of that and you couldn't miss top billing. Come on."

Pan followed him uncertainly. "Where?"

"Over to the boys. If you can learn to wrap your lips around a clarinet the way you do that thing, our worries are over. And I'm betting now that you can."

It was their last night's engagement at the Grotto a month later, and Pan stood up, roaring out the doggerel words in a rich basso that caught and lifted the song. Strictly speaking, his voice was a shade too true for popular styling, but the boisterous paganism in it was like a beat note from a tuba, something that refused to let feet be still. Then it ended and the usual clamor followed. His singing was a recent experiment but it went over.

Bob shook hands with himself and grinned. "Great, Pan! You've got it tonight!" Then he stepped to the microphone. "And now, for our last number, folks, I'd like to present a new tune for the first time ever played. It's called *The Gods Got Rhythm*, and we think you'll like it. Words and music by Tin Pan Faunus. Okay, Tin Pan, take it!"

Pan cuddled the clarinet in his mouth and watched the crowd stampede out onto the floor. Bob winked at him and he opened up, watching the dancers. This was like the rest, a wild ecstasy that refused to let them stay still. Primitive, vital, every nerve alive to the music. Even the nymphs of old had danced less savagely to his piping.

One of the boys held a note where he could see it, and he glanced at it as he played. "Boys, we're set. Peterson just gave Bob the signal, and that means three months at the Crystal Palace. Good-by blues!"

Pan opened up, letting the other instruments idle in the background, and went in for a private jam session of his own. Out on the floor were his worshipers, every step an act of homage to him. Homage that paid dividends, and was as real in its way as the sacrifices of old; but that was a minor detail. Right now, he was hot.

He lifted the instrument higher, drawing out the last wild ecstasy from it. Under his clothes, his tail twitched sharply, but the dancers couldn't see that, and wouldn't have cared if they could. Tin Pan Faunus was playing, and that was enough.

THE COPPERSMITH

In the slanting rays of the morning sun, the figure trudging along the path seemed out of place so near the foothills of the Adirondacks. His scant three feet of stocky height was covered by a tattered jerkin of brown leather that fell to his knees, and above was a russet cap with turned-back brim and high, pointed crown. Below, the dusty sandals were tipped up at the toes and tied back to the ankles, and on each a little copper bell tinkled lightly as he walked.

Ellowan Coppersmith moved slowly under the weight of the bag he bore on his shoulders, combing out his beard with a stubby brown hand and a humming in time with the jingling bells. It was early still and a whole day lay before him in which to work. After the long sleep, back in the hills where his people lay dormant, work would be good again.

The path came to an end where it joined a well-kept highway, and the elf eased the bag from his shoulder while he studied the signpost. There was little meaning for him in the cryptic marker that bore the cabalistic 30, but the arrow below indicated that Wells lay half a mile beyond. That must be the village he had spied from the path; a very nice little village, Ellowan judged, and not unprosperous. Work should be found in plenty there.

But first, the berries he had picked in the fields would refresh him after the long walk. His kindly brown eyes lighted with pleasure as he pulled them from his bag and sat back against the signpost. Surely even these few so late in the season were an omen of good fortune to come. The elf munched them slowly, savoring their wild sweetness gratefully.

When they were finished, he reached into his bag again and brought forth a handful of thin sticks, which he tossed on the ground and studied carefully. "Sixscore years in sleep," he muttered. "Eh, well, though the runes forecast the future but poorly, they seldom lie of the past. Sixscore years it must be."

He tossed the runes back into the bag and turned toward a growing noise that had been creeping up on him from behind. The source of the sound seemed to be a long, low vehicle that came sweeping up the road and flashed by him so rapidly that there was only time to catch a glimpse of the men inside.

"These men!" Ellowan picked up his bag and headed toward the village, shaking his head doubtfully. "Now they have engines inside their carriages, and strange engines at that, from the odor. Even the air of the highway must be polluted with the foul smell of machines. Next it's flying they'll be. Methinks 'twere best to go through the fields to the village."

He pulled out his clay pipe and sucked on it, but the flavor had dried out while he had lain sleeping, and the tobacco in his pouch had molded away. Well, there'd be tobacco in the village, and coppers to buy it with. He was humming again as he neared the town and studied its group of houses, among which the people were just beginning to stir. It would be best to go from house to house rather than disturb them by crying his services from the street. With an expectant smile on his weathered old face, Ellowan rapped lightly and waited for a response.

"Whatta you want?" The woman brushed back her stringy hair with one hand while holding the door firmly with the other, and her eyes were hard as she caught sight of the elf's bag. "We don't want no magazines. You're just wastin' your time!"

From the kitchen came the nauseating odor of scorching eggs, and the door was slammed shut before Ellowan could state his wants. Eh, well, a town without a shrew was a town without a house. A bad start and a good ending, perchance. But no one answered his second knock, and he drew no further response than faces pressed to the window at the third.

A young woman came to the next door, eyeing him curiously, but answering his smile. "Good morning," she said doubtfully, and the elf's hopes rose.

"A good morning to you, mistress. And have you pots to mend, pans or odds that you wish repaired?" It was good to speak the words again. "I'm a wonderful tinker, none better, mistress. Like new they'll be, and the better for the knack that I have and that which I bring in my bag."

"I'm sorry, but I haven't anything; I've just been married a few weeks." She smiled again, hesitantly. "If you're hungry, though . . . well, we don't usually feed men who come to the door, but I guess it'd be all right this time."

"No, mistress, but thank'ee. It's only honest labor I want." Ellowan heaved the bag up again and moved down the steps. The girl turned to go in, glancing back at him with a feeling of guilt that there was no work for the strange little fellow. On impulse, she called after him.

"Wait!" At her cry, he faced her again. "I just thought; Mother might have something for you. She lives down the street—the fifth house on the right. Her name's Mrs. Franklin."

Ellowan's face creased in a twinkling smile. "My thanks again, mistress, and good fortune attend you."

Eh, so, his luck had changed again. Once his skill was known, there'd be no lack of work for him. "A few coppers here and a farthing there, from many a kettle to mend; with solder and flux and skill to combine, there's many a copper to spend."

He was still humming as he rounded the house and found Mrs. Franklin hanging out dish towels on the back porch to dry. She was a somewhat stout woman, with the expression of fatigue that grows habitual in some cases, but her smile was as kindly as her daughter's when she spied the elf.

"Are you the little man my daughter said mended things?" she asked. "Susan phoned me that you'd be here—she took quite a fancy to you. Well, come up here on the porch and I'll bring out what I want fixed. I hope your rates aren't too high?"

"It's very reasonable you'll find them, mistress." He sank down on a three-legged stool he pulled from his bag and brought out a little table, while she went inside for the articles that needed repairs. There were knickknacks, a skillet, various pans, a copper wash boiler, and odds and ends of all sorts; enough to keep him busy till midday.

She set them down beside him. "Well, that's the lot of them. I've been meaning to throw most of them away, since nobody around here can fix them, but it seems a shame to see things wasted for some little hole. You just call me when you're through."

Ellowan nodded briskly and dug down into his seemingly bottomless bag. Out came his wonderful fluxes that could clean the thickest tarnish away in a twinkling, the polish that even the hardest grease and oldest soot couldn't defy, the bars of solder that became one with the metal, so that the sharpest eye would fail to note the difference; and out came the clever little tools that worked and smoothed the repair into unity with the original. Last of all, he drew forth a tiny anvil and a little charcoal brazier whose coals began to burn as he set it down. There was no fan or bellows, yet the coals in the center glowed fiercely at white heat.

The little elf reached out for the copper boiler, so badly dented that the seam had sprung open all the way down. A few light taps on his anvil straightened it back into smoothness. He spread on his polish, blew on it vigorously, and watched the dirt and dullness disappear, then applied his flux, and drew some of the solder onto it with a hot iron, chuckling as the seams became waterproof again. Surely now, even the long sleep had cost him none of his skill. As he laid it down, there was no sign to show that the boiler had not come freshly from some shop, or new out of the maker's hands.

The skillet was bright and shiny, except for a brown circle on the bottom, and gleamed with a silvery luster. Some magic craftsman must have made it, the elf thought, and it should receive special pains to make sure that the spell holding it so bright was not broken. He rubbed a few drops of polish over it carefully, inspected the loose handle, and applied his purple flux, swabbing off the small excess. Tenderly he ran the hot iron over the solder and began working the metal against the handle.

But something was very wrong. Instead of drawing firmly to the skillet, the solder ran down the side in little drops. Such as remained was loose and refused to stick. With a puzzled frown, Ellowan smelled his materials and tried again; there was nothing wrong with the solder or flux, but they still refused to work. He muttered softly and reached out for a pan with a pin hole in it.

Mrs. Franklin found him sitting there later, his tools neatly before him, the pots and pans stacked at his side, and the brazier glowing brightly. "All finished?" she asked cheerfully. "I brought you some coffee and a cinnamon bun I just baked; I thought you might like them." She set them down before the elf and glanced at the pile of utensils again. Only the boiler was fixed. "What—" she began sharply, but softened her question somewhat as she saw the bewildered frustration on his face. "I thought you said you could fix them?"

Ellowan nodded glumly. "That I did, mistress, and that I tried to do. But my solder and flux refused all but the honest copper, yonder, and there's never a thing I can make of them. Either these must be wondrous metals indeed, or my art has been bewitched."

"There's nothing very wonderful about aluminum and enamelware—nor stainless steel, either, except the prices they charge." She picked up the wash boiler and inspected his work. "Well, you did do this nicely, and you're not the only one who can't solder aluminum, I guess, so cheer up. And eat your roll before it's cold!"

"Thank'ee, mistress." The savory aroma of the bun had been tantalizing his stomach, but he had been waiting to make certain that he was welcome to it. "It's sorry I am to have troubled you, but it's a long time ago that I tinkered for my living, and this is new to me."

Mrs. Franklin nodded sympathetically; the poor little man must have been living with a son, or maybe working in a side show—he was short enough, and his costume was certainly theatrical. Well, hard times were hard times. "You didn't trouble me much, I guess. Besides, I needed the boiler tomorrow for wash day, so that's a big help, anyway. What do I owe you for it?"

"Tu'pence ha'penny," Ellowan said, taking out for the bun. Her look was uncertain, and he changed it quickly. "Five pence American, that is, mistress."

"Five cents! But it's worth ten times that!"

"It's but an honest price for the labor, mistress." Ellowan was putting the tools and materials back in his bag. "That's all I can take for the small bit I could do."

"Well—" She shrugged. "All right, if that's all you'll take, here it is." The coin she handed him seemed strange, but that was to be expected. He pocketed it with a quick smile and another "thank'ee," and went in search of a store he had noticed before.

The shop was confusing in the wide variety of articles it carried, but Ellowan spied tobacco and cigars on display and walked in. Now that he had eaten the bun, the tobacco was a more pressing need than food.

"Two pennies of tobacco, if it please you," he told the clerk, holding out the little leather pouch he carried.

"You crazy?" The clerk was a boy, much more interested in his oiled hair than in the customers who might come in. "Cheapest thing I can give you is Duke's Mixture, and it'll cost you five cents, cash."

Regretfully Ellowan watched the nickel vanish over the counter; tobacco was indeed a luxury at the price. He picked up the small cloth bag, and the pasteboard folder the boy thrust at him. "What might this be?" he asked, holding up the folder.

"Matches." The boy grinned in fine superiority. "Where you been all your life? Okay, you do this . . . see? Course, if you don't want 'em—"

"Thank'ee." The elf pocketed the book of matches quickly and hurried toward the street, vastly pleased with his purchase. Such a great marvel as the matches alone surely was worth the price. He filled his clay pipe and struck one of them curiously, chuckling in delight as it flamed up. When he dropped the flame regretfully, he noticed that the tobacco, too, was imbued with magic, else surely it could never have been cured to such a mild and satisfying flavor. It scarcely bit his tongue.

But there was no time to be loitering around admiring his new treasures. Without work there could be no food, and supper was still to be taken care of. Those aluminum and enamelware pans were still in his mind, reminding him that coppers might be hard to get. But then, Mrs. Franklin had mentioned stainless steel, and only a mighty wizard could prevent iron from rusting; perhaps her husband was a worker in enchantments, and the rest of the village might be served in honest copper and hammered pewter. He shook his shoulders in forced optimism and marched down the street toward the other houses, noting the prices marked in a store window as he passed. Eh, the woman was right; he'd have to charge more for his services to eat at those rates.

The road was filled with the strange carriages driven by engines, and Ellowan stayed cautiously off the paving. But the stench from their exhausts and the dust they stirred up were still thick in his nostrils. The elf switched the bag from his left shoulder to his right and plodded on grimly, but there was no longer a tune on his lips, and the little bells refused to tinkle as he walked.

The sun had set, and it was already growing darker, bringing the long slow day to a close. His last call would be at the house ahead, already showing lights burning, and it was still some distance off. Ellowan pulled his belt tighter and marched toward it, muttering in slow time to his steps.

"Al-u-mi-num and en-an-el-ware and stain-less STEEL!" A row of green pans, red pots and ivory bowls ran before his eyes, and everywhere there was a glint of silvery skillets and dull white kettles. Even the handles used were no longer honest wood, but smelled faintly resinous.

Not one proper kettle in the whole village had he found. The housewives came out and looked at him, answered his smile, and brought forth their work from him in an oddly hesitant manner as if they were unused to giving out such jobs at the door. It spoke more of pity than of any desire to have their wares mended.

"No, mistress, only copper. These new metals refuse my solder, and them I cannot mend." Over and again he'd repeated the words until they were as wooden as his knocks had grown; and always, there was no copper. It was almost a kindness when they refused to answer his knock.

He had been glad to quit the village and turn out on the road to the country, even though the houses were father apart. Surely among the farming people, the older methods would still be in use. But the results were no different. They greeted him kindly and brought out their wares to him with less hesitancy than in the village—but the utensils were enamelware and aluminum and stainless steel!

Ellowan groped for his pipe and sank down on the ground to rest, noting that eight miles still lay between him and Northville. He measured out the tobacco carefully, and hesitated before using one of the new matches. Then, as he lit it, he watched the flame dully and tossed it listlessly aside. Even the tobacco tasted flat now, and the emptiness of this stomach refused to be fooled by the smoke, though it helped to take his mind away from his troubles. Eh, well, there was always that one last house to be seen, where fortune might smile on him long enough to furnish a supper. He shouldered the bag with a grunt and moved on.

A large German shepherd came bounding out at the elf as he turned in the gate to the farmhouse. The dog's bark was gruff and threatening, but Ellowan clucked softly and the animal quieted, walking beside him toward the house, its tail wagging slowly. The farmer watched the performance and grinned.

"Prinz seems to like you," he called out. "'Tain't everyone he takes to like that. What can I do for you, lad?" Then, as Ellowan drew nearer, he looked more sharply. "Sorry—my mistake. For a minute there, I thought you were a boy."

"I'm a tinker, sir. A coppersmith, that is." The elf stroked the dog's head and looked up at the farmer wistfully. "Have you copper pots or pans, or odds of any kind, to be mended? I do very good work on copper, sir, and I'll be glad to work for only my supper."

The farmer opened the door and motioned him in. "Come on inside, and we'll see. I don't reckon we have, but the wife knows better." He raised his voice. "Hey, Louisa, where are you? In the kitchen?"

"In here, Henry." The voice came from the kitchen, and Ellowan followed the man back, the dog nuzzling his hand companionably. The woman was washing the last few dishes and putting the supper away as they entered, and the sight of food awoke the hunger that the elf had temporarily suppressed.

"This fellow says he's good at fixin' copper dishes, Louisa," Henry told his wife. "You got anything like that for him?" He bent over her ear and spoke in an undertone, but Ellowan caught the words.

"If you got anything copper, he looks like he needs it, Lou. Nice little midget, seems to be, and Prinz took quite a shine to him."

Louisa shook her head slowly. "I had a couple of old copper kettles, only I threw them away when we got the aluminum cooking set. But if you're hungry, there's plenty of food still left. Won't you sit down while I fix it for you?"

Ellowan looked eagerly at the remains of the supper, and his mouth watered hotly, but he managed a smile, and his voice was determined. "Thank'ee kindly, mistress, but I can't. It's one of the rules I must live by not to beg or take what I cannot earn. But I'll be thanking you both for the thought, and wishing you a very good night."

They followed him to the door, and the dog trotted behind him until its master's whistle called it back. Then the elf was alone on the road again, hunting a place to sleep. There was a haystack back off the road that would make a good bed, and he headed for that. Well, hay was hardly nourishing, but chewing on it was better than nothing.

Ellowan was up with the sun again, brushing the dirt off his jerkin. As an experiment, he shook the runes out on the ground and studied them for a few minutes. "Eh, well," he muttered, tossing them back in the bag, "they speak well, but it's little faith I'd have in them for what is to come. It's too easy to shake them the way I'd want them to be. But perchance there'll be a berry or so in the woods yonder."

There were no berries, and the acorns were still green. Ellowan struck the highway again, drawing faint pleasure from the fact that few cars were on the road at that hour. He wondered again why their fumes, though unpleasant, bothered him a little as they did. His brothers, up in the grotto hidden in the Adirondacks, found even the smoke from the factories a deadening poison.

The smell of a good wood fire, or the fumes from alcohol in the glass-blower's lamp were pleasant to them. But with the coming of coal, a slow lethargy had crept over them, driving them back one by one into the hills to sleep. It had been bad enough when coal was burned in the hearths, but that Scotchman, Watts, had found that power could be drawn from steam, and the factories began spewing forth the murky fumes of acrid coal smoke. And the Little Folk had fled hopelessly from the poison, until Ellowan Coppersmith alone was left. In time, even he had joined his brothers up in the hills.

Now he had awakened again, without rhyme or reason, when the stench of the liquid called gasoline was added to that of coal. All along the highway were pumps that supplied it to the endless cars, and the taint of it in the air was omnipresent.

"Eh, well," he thought. "My brothers were ever filled with foolish pranks instead of honest work, while I found my pleasure in labor. Methinks the pranks weakened them against the poison, and the work gives strength; it was only after I hexed the factory owner that the sleep crept into my head, and sixscore years must surely pay the price of one such trick. Yet, when I first awakened, it's thinking I was that there was some good purpose that drew me forth."

The sight of an orchard near the road caught his attention, and the elf searched carefully along the strip of grass outside the fence in the hope that an apple might have been blown outside. But only inside was there fruit, and to cross the fence would be stealing. He left the orchard reluctantly and started to turn in at the road leading to the farmhouse. Then he paused.

After all, the farms were equipped exactly as the city now, and such faint luck as he'd had yesterday had been in the village. There was little sense in wasting his effort among the scattered houses of the country, in the unlikely chance that he might find copper. In the city, at least, there was little time wasted, and it was only by covering as man places as he could that he might hope to find work. Ellowan shrugged, and turned back on the highway; he'd save his time and energy until he reached Northville.

It was nearly an hour later when he came on the boy, sitting beside the road and fussing over some machine. Ellowan stopped as he saw the scattered parts and the worried frown on the lad's face. Little troubles seemed great to twelve-year-olds.

"Eh, now, lad," he asked, "is it trouble you're having there? And what might be that contrivance of bars and wheels?"

"It's a bicycle; ever'body knows that." From the sound of the boy's voice, tragedy had reared a large and ugly head. "And I've only had it since last Christmas. Now it's broke and I can't fix it."

He held up a piece that had come from the hub of the rear wheel. "See? That's the part that swells up when I brake it. It's all broken, and a new coaster brake costs five dollars."

Ellowan took the pieces and smelled them; his eyes had not been deceived. It was brass. "So?" he asked. "Now that's a shame, indeed. And a very pretty machine it was. But perchance I can fix it."

The boy looked up hopefully as he watched the elf draw out the brazier and tools. Then his face fell. "Naw, mister. I ain't got the money. All I got's a quarter, and I can't get it, 'cause it's in my bank, and mom won't let me open it."

The elf's reviving hopes of breakfast faded away, but he smiled casually. "Eh, so? Well, lad, there are other things than money. Let's see what we'll be making of this."

His eyes picked out the relation of the various parts, and his admiration for the creator of the machine rose. That hub was meant to drive the machine, to roll free, or to brake as the user desired. The broken piece was a split cylinder of brass that was arranged to expand against the inside of the hub when braking. How it could have been damaged was a mystery, but the ability of boys to destroy was no novelty to Ellowan.

Under his hands, the rough edges were smoothed down in a twinkling, and he ran his strongest solder into the break, filling and drawing it together, then scraping and abrading the metal smooth again. The boy's eyes widened.

"Say, mister, you're good! Them fellers in the city can't do it like that, and they've got all kinds of tools, too." He took the repaired piece and began threading the parts back on the spindle. "Gosh, you're little. D'you come out of a circus?"

Ellowan shook his head, smiling faintly. The questions of children had always been candid, and honest replies could be given them. "That I did not, lad, and I'm not a midget, if that's what you'd be thinking. Now didn't your grandmother tell you the old tales of the elves?"

"An elf!" The boy stopped twisting the nuts back on. "Go on! There ain't such things—I don't guess." His voice grew doubtful, though, as he studied the little brown figure. "Say, you do look like the pi'tures I seen, at that, and it sure looked like magic the way you fixed my brake. Can you really do magic?"

"It's never much use I had for magic, lad. I had no time for learning it, when business was better. The honest tricks of my trade were enough for me, with a certain skill that was ever mine. And I wouldn't be mentioning this to your parents, if I were you."

"Don't worry, I won't; they'd say I was nuts." The boy climbed on the saddle, and tested the brake with obvious satisfaction. "You goin' to town? Hop on and put your bag in the basket here. I'm goin' down within a mile of there—if you can ride on the rack."

"It would be a heavy load for you, lad, I'm thinking." Ellowan was none too sure of the security of such a vehicle, but the ride would be most welcome.

"Naw. Hop on. I've carried my brother, and he's heavier'n you. Anyway, that's a Mussimer two-speed brake. Dad got it special for Christmas." He reached over for Ellowan's bag, and was surprised by its lightness. Those who help an elf usually found things easier than they expected. "Anyway, I owe you sumpin' for fixin' it."

Ellowan climbed on the luggage rack at the rear and clutched the boy tightly at first. The rack was hard, but the paving smoothed out the ride, and it was far easier than walking. He relaxed and watched the road go by in a quarter of the time he could have traveled it on foot. If fortune smiled on him, breakfast might be earned sooner than he had hoped.

"Well, here's where I stop," the boy finally told him. "The town's down there about a mile. Thanks for fixin' my bike."

Ellowan dismounted cautiously, and lifted out his bag. "Thank'ee for helping me so far, lad. And I'm thinking the brake will be giving you little trouble hereafter." He watched the boy ride off on a side road, and started toward the town, the serious business of breakfast uppermost in his mind.

Breakfast was still in his mind when midday had passed, but there was no sign that it was nearer his stomach. He came out of an alley and stopped for a few draws on his pipe and a chance to rest his shoulders. He'd have to stop smoking soon; on an empty stomach, too much tobacco is nauseating. Over the smell of the smoke, another odor struck his nose, and he turned around slowly.

It was the clean odor of hot metal in a charcoal fire, and came from a sprawling old building a few yards away. The sign above was faded, but he made out the words: MICHAEL DONAHUE— HORSESHOEING AND AUTO REPAIRS. The sight of a blacksmith shop aroused memories of pleasanter days, and Ellowan drew nearer.

The man inside was in his fifties, but his body spoke of strength and clean living, and the face under the mop of red hair was open and friendly. At the moment, he was sitting on a stool, finishing a sandwich. The odor of the food reached out and stirred the elf's stomach again, and he scuffed his sandals against the ground uneasily. The man looked up.

"Saints preserve us!" Donahue's generous mouth opened to its widest. "Sure, and it's one o' the Little Folk, the loike as me feyther tolt me. Now fwhat—Och, now, but it's hungry ye'd be from the look that ye have, and me eatin' before ye! Here now, me hearty, it's yerself as shud have this bread."

"Thank'ee." Ellowan shook his head with an effort, but it came harder this time. "I'm an honest worker, sir, and it's one of the rules that I can't be taking what I cannot earn. But there's never a piece of copper to be found in all the city for me to mend." He laid his hands on a blackened bench to ease the ache in his legs.

"Now that's a shame." The brogue dropped from Donahue's speech, now that the surprise of seeing the elf was leaving him. "It's a good worker you are, too, if what my father told me was true. He came over from the old country when I was a bit of a baby, and his father told him before that. Wonderful workers, he said you were."

"I am that." It was a simple statement as Ellowan made it; boasting requires a certain energy, even had he felt like it. "Anything of brass or copper I can fix, and it'll be like new when I finish."

"Can you that?" Donahue looked at him with interest. "Eh, maybe you can. I've a notion to try you out. You wait here." He disappeared through the door that divided his smithy from the auto servicing department and came back with a large piece of blackened metal in his hand. The elf smelled it questioningly and found it was brass.

Donahue tapped it lightly. "That's a radiator, m'boy. Water runs through these tubes here and these little fins cool it off. Old Pete Yaegger brought it in and wanted it fixed, but it's too far ruined for my hands. And he can't afford a new one. You fix that now, and I'll be giving you a nice bit of money for the work."

"Fix it I can." Ellowan's hands were trembling as he inspected the corroded metal core, and began drawing out his tools. "I'll be finished within the hour."

Donahue looked doubtfully at the elf, but nodded slowly. "Now maybe you will. But first, you'll eat, and we'll not be arguing about that. A hungry man never did good work, and I'm of the opinion the same applies to yourself. There's still a sandwich and a bit of pie left, if you don't mind washing it down with water."

The elf needed no water to wash down the food. When Donahue looked at him next, the crumbs had been licked from the paper, and Ellowan's deft hands were working his clever little tools through the fins of the radiator, and his face was crinkling up into its usual merry smile. The metal seemed to run and flow through his hands with a will of its own, and he was whistling lightly as he worked.

Ellowan waited intently as Donahue inspected the finished work. Where the blackened metal had been bent and twisted, and filled with holes, it was now shining and new. The smith could find no sign to indicate that it was not all one single piece, now, for the seams were joined invisibly.

"Now that's craftsmanship," Donahue admitted. "I'm thinking we'll do a deal of business from now on, the two of us, and there's money in it, too. Ellowan, m'boy, with work like that we can buy up old radiators, remake them, and at a nice little profit for ourselves we can sell them again. You'll be searching no further for labor."

The elf's eyes twinkled at the prospect of long lines of radiators needing to be fixed, and a steady supply of work without the need of searching for it. For the first time, he realized that industrialization might have its advantages for the worker.

Donahue dug into a box and came out with a little metal figure of a greyhound, molded on a threaded cap. "Now, while I get something else for you, you might be fixing this," he said. " 'Tis a godsend that you've come to me ... Eh, now that I think of it, what brings you here, when I thought it'd be in the old country you worked?"

"That was my home," the elf agreed, twisting the radiator cap in his hands and straightening out the broken threads. "But the people became too poor in the country, and the cities were filled with coal smoke. And then there was word of a new land across the sea, so we left, such of us as remained, and it was here we stayed until the smoke came again, and sent us sleeping into the hills. Eh, it's glad I am now to be awake again."

Donahue nodded. "And it's not sorry I am. I'm a good blacksmith, but there's never enough of that for a man to live now, and mostly I work on the autos. And there, m'boy, you'll be a wonderful help to be sure. The parts I like least are the ignition system and generator, and there's copper in them where your skill will be greater than mine. And the radiators, of course."

Ellowan's hands fumbled on the metal, and he set it down suddenly. "Those radiators, now—they come from a car?"

"That they do." Donahue's back was turned as he drew a horseshoe out of the forge and began hammering it on the anvil. He could not see the twinkle fade from the elf's eyes and the slowness with which the small fingers picked up the radiator cap.

Ellowan was thinking of his people, asleep in the hills, doomed to lie there until the air should be cleared of the poisonous fumes. And here he was, working on parts of the machines that helped to make those fumes. Yet, since there was little enough else to do, he had no choice but to keep on; cars or no cars, food was still the prime necessity.

Donahue bent the end of a shoe over to a calk and hammered it into shape, even with the other one. "You'll be wanting a place to sleep?" he asked casually. "Well, now, I've a room at the house that used to be my boy's, and it'll just suit you. The boy's at college and won't be needing it."

"Thank'ee kindly." Ellowan finished the cap and put it aside distastefully.

"The boy'll be a great engineer some day," the smith went on with a glow of pride. "And not have to follow his father in the trade. And it's a good thing, I'm thinking. Because some day, when they've used up all their coal and oil, there'll be no money in the business at all, even with the help of these newfangled things. My father was a smith, and I'm by way of being smith and mechanic—but not the boy."

"They'll use up all the coal and oil—entirely?"

"They will that, now. Nobody knows when, but the day's acoming. And then they'll be using electricity or maybe alcohol for fuel. It's a changing world, lad, and we old ones can't change to keep with it."

Ellowan picked up the radiator cap and polished it again. Eh, so. One day they'd use up all the sources of evil, and the air would be pure again. The more cars that ran, the sooner that day would come, and the more he repaired, the more would run.

"Eh, now," he said gayly. "I'll be glad for more of those radiators to mend. But until then, perchance I could work a bit of yonder scrap brass into more such ornaments as this one."

Somehow, he was sure, when his people came forth again, there'd be work for all.

FOR I AM A JEALOUS PEOPLE!

I

. . . the keepers of the house shall tremble, and the strong men shall bow themselves . . . and the doors shall be shut in the streets, when the sound of the grinding is low . . . they shall be afraid of that which is high, and fears shall be in the way, and the almond tree shall flourish . . . because man goeth to his long home, and the mourners go about the streets . . .

ECCLESIASTES, XII, 3–5.

There was the continuous shrieking thunder of an alien rocket overhead as the Reverend Amos Strong stepped back into the pulpit. He straightened his square, thin shoulders slightly, and the gaunt hollows in his cheeks deepened. For a moment he hesitated, while his dark eyes turned upwards under bushy grizzled brows. Then he moved forward, placing the torn envelope and telegram on the lectern with his notes. The blue-veined hand and knobby wrist that projected from the shiny black serge of his sleeve hardly trembled.

His eyes turned toward the pew where his wife was not. Ruth would not be there this time. She had read the message before sending it on to him. Now she could not be expected. It seemed strange to him. She hadn't missed service since Richard was born nearly thirty years ago.

The sound hissed its way into silence over the horizon, and Amos stepped forward, gripping the rickety lectern with both hands. He straightened and forced into his voice the resonance and calm it needed.

"I have just received word that my son was killed in the battle of the moon," he told the puzzled congregation. He lifted his voice, and the resonance in it deepened. "I had asked, if it were possible, that this cup might pass from me. Nevertheless, not as I will, Lord, but as Thou wilt."

He turned from their shocked faces, closing his ears to the sympathetic cry of others who had suffered. The church had been built when Wesley was twice its present size, but the troubles that had hit the people had driven them into the worn old building until it was nearly filled. He pulled his notes to him, forcing his mind from his own loss to the work that had filled his life.

"The text today is drawn from Genesis," he told them. "Chapter seventeen, seventh verse; and chapter twenty-six, fourth verse. The promise which God made to Abraham and to Isaac." He read from the Bible before him, turning the pages unerringly at the first try.

" 'And I will establish my covenant between me and thee and thy seed after thee in their generations for an everlasting covenant, to be a God unto thee, and to thy seed after thee.

" 'And I will make thy seed to multiply as the stars of heaven, and will give unto thy seed all these countries, and in thy seed shall all the nations of the earth be blessed.' "

He had memorized most of his sermon, no longer counting on inspiration to guide him as it had once done. He began smoothly, hearing his own words in snatches as he drew the obvious and comforting answer to their uncertainty. God had promised man the earth as an everlasting covenant. Why then should men be afraid or lose faith because alien monsters had swarmed down out of the emptiness between the stars to try man's faith? As in the days of bondage in Egypt or captivity in Babylon, there would always be trials and times when the fainthearted should waver, but the eventual outcome was clearly promised.

He had delivered a sermon from the same text in his former parish of Clyde when the government had first begun building its base on the moon, drawing heavily in that case from the reference to the stars of heaven to quiet the doubts of those who felt that man had no business in space. It was then that Richard had announced his commission in the lunar colony, using Amos' own words to defend his refusal to enter the ministry. It had been the last he saw of the boy.

He had used the text one other time, over forty years before, but the reason was lost, together with the passion that had won him fame as a boy evangelist. He could remember the sermon only because of the shock on the bearded face of his father when he had misquoted a phrase. It was one of his few clear memories of the period before his voice changed and his evangelism came to an abrupt end.

He had tried to recapture his inspiration after ordination, bitterly resenting the countless intrusions of marriage and fatherhood on his spiritual forces. But at last he had recognized that God no longer intended him to be a modern Peter the Hermit, and resigned himself to the work he could do. Now he was back in the parish where he had first begun; and if he could no longer fire the souls of his flock, he could at least help somewhat with his memorized rationalizations for the horror of the alien invasion.

Another ship thundered overhead, nearly drowning his words. Six months before, the great ships had exploded out of space and had dropped carefully to the moon, to attack the forces there. In another month, they had begun forays against Earth itself. And now, while the world haggled and struggled to unite against them, they were setting up bases all over and conquering the world mile by mile.

Amos saw the faces below him turn up, furious and uncertain. He raised his voice over the thunder, and finished hastily, moving quickly through the end of the service.

He hesitated as the congregation stirred. The ritual was over and his words were said, but there had been no real service. Slowly, as if by themselves, his lips opened, and he heard his voice quoting the Twenty-seventh Psalm. " 'The Lord is my light and my salvation; whom shall I fear?' "

His voice was soft, but he could feel the reaction of the congregation as the surprisingly timely words registered. " 'Though an host should encamp against me, my heart shall not fear: though war should rise against me, in this will I be confident.' " The air seemed to quiver, as it had done long ago when God had seemed to hold direct communion with him, and there was no sound from the pews when he finished. " 'Wait on the Lord: be of good courage, and he shall strengthen thine heart: wait, I say, on the Lord.' "

The warmth of that mystic glow lingered as he stepped quietly from the pulpit. Then there was the sound of motorcycles outside, and a pounding on the door. The feeling vanished.

Someone stood up and sudden light began pouring in from outdoors. There was a breath of the hot, droughty physical world with its warning of another dust storm, and a scattering of grasshoppers on the steps to remind the people of the earlier damage to their crops. Amos could see the bitterness flood back over them in tangible waves, even before they noticed the short, plump figure of Dr. Alan Miller.

"Amos! Did you hear?" He was wheezing as if he had been running. "Just came over the radio while you were in here gabbling."

He was cut off by the sound of more motorcycles. They swept down the single main street of Wesley, heading west. The riders were all in military uniform, carrying weapons and going at top speed. Dust erupted behind them, and Doc began coughing and swearing. In the last few years, he had grown more and more outspoken about his atheism; when Amos had first known him, during his first pastorate, the man had at least shown some respect for the religion of others.

"All right," Amos said sharply. "You're in the house of God, Doc. What came over the radio?"

Doc caught himself and choked back his coughing fit. "Sorry. But damn it, man, the aliens have landed in Clyde, only fifty miles away. They've set up a base there! That's what all those rockets going over meant."

There was a sick gasp from the people who had heard, and a buzz as the news was passed back to others.

Amos hardly noticed the commotion. It had been Clyde where he had served before coming here again. He was trying to picture the alien ships dropping down, scouring the town ahead of them with gas and bullets. The grocer on the corner with his nine children, the lame deacon who had served there, the two Aimes sisters with their horde of dogs and cats and their constant crusade against younger sinners. He tried to picture the green-skinned, humanoid aliens moving through the town, invading the church, desecrating the altar! And there was Anne Seyton, who had been Richard's sweetheart, though of another faith . . .

"What about the garrison nearby?" a heavy farmer yelled over the crowd. "I had a boy there, and he told me they could handle any ships when they were landing! Shell their tubes when they were coming down—"

Doc shook his head. "Half an hour before the landing, there was a cyclone up there. It took the roof off the main building and wrecked the whole training garrison."

"Jim!" The big man screamed out the name, and began dragging his frail wife behind him, out toward his car. "If they got Jim—"

Others started to rush after him, but another procession of motorcycles stopped them. This time they were traveling slower, and a group of tanks was rolling behind them. The rear tank drew abreast, slowed, and stopped, while a dirty-faced man in an untidy major's uniform stuck his head out.

"You folks get under cover! Ain't you heard the news? Go home and stick to your radios, before a snake plane starts potshooting the bunch of you for fun. The snakes'll be heading straight over here if they're after Topeka, like it looks!" He jerked back down and began swearing at someone inside. The tank jerked to a start and began heading away toward Clyde.

There had been enough news of the sport of the alien planes in the papers. The people melted from the church. Amos tried to stop them for at least a short prayer and to give them time to collect their thoughts, but gave up after the first wave shoved him aside. A minute later, he was standing alone with Doc Miller.

"Better get home, Amos," Doc suggested. "My car's half a block down. Suppose I give you a lift?"

Amos nodded wearily. His bones felt dry and brittle, and there was a dust in his mouth thicker than that in the air. He felt old and, for the first time, almost useless. He followed the doctor quietly, welcoming the chance to ride the six short blocks to the little house the parish furnished him.

A car of ancient age and worse repair rattled toward them as they reached Doc's auto. It stopped, and a man in dirty overalls leaned out, his face working jerkily. "Are you prepared, brothers? Are you saved? Armageddon has come, as the Book foretold. Get right with God, brothers! The end of the world as foretold is at hand, amen!"

"Where does the Bible foretell alien races around other suns?" Doc shot at him.

The man blinked, frowned, and yelled something about sinners burning forever in hell before he started his rickety car again. Amos sighed. Now, with the rise of their troubles, fanatics would spring up to cry doom and false gospel more than ever, to the harm of all honest religion. He had never decided whether they were somehow useful to God or whether they were inspired by the forces of Satan.

" 'In my Father's house are many mansions,' " he quoted to Doc, as they started up the street. "It's quite possibly an allegorical reference to other worlds in the heavens."

Doc grimaced, and shrugged. Then he sighed and dropped one hand from the wheel onto Amos' knee. "I heard about Dick, Amos. I'm sorry. The first baby I ever delivered—and the handsomest!" He sighed again, staring toward Clyde as Amos found no words to answer. "I don't get it. Why can't we drop atom bombs on them? What happened to the moon base's missiles?"

Amos got out at the unpainted house where he lived, taking Doc's hand silently and nodding his thanks.

He would have to organize his thoughts this afternoon. When night fell and the people could move about without the danger of being shot at by chance alien planes, the church bell would summon them, and they would need spiritual guidance. If he could help them to stop trying to understand God, and to accept Him . . .

There had been that moment in the church when God had seemed to enfold him and the congregation in warmth—the old feeling of true fulfillment. Maybe, now in the hour of its greatest need, some measure of inspiration had returned.

He found Ruth setting the table. Her small, quiet body moved as efficiently as ever, though her face was puffy and her eyes were red. "I'm sorry I couldn't make it, Amos. But right after the telegram, Anne Seyton came. She'd heard—before we did. And—"

The television set was on, showing headlines from the *Kansas City Star*, and he saw there was no need to tell her the news. He put a hand on one of hers. "God has only taken what he gave, Ruth. We were blessed with Richard for thirty years."

"I'm all right." She pulled away and turned toward the kitchen, her back frozen in a line of taut misery. "Didn't you hear what I said? Anne's here. Dick's wife! They were married before he left, secretly—right after you talked with him about the difference in religion. You'd better see her, Amos. She knows about her people in Clyde."

He watched his wife go. The slam of the outside door underlined the word. He'd never forbidden the marriage; he had only warned the boy, so much like Ruth. He hesitated, and finally turned toward the tiny, second bedroom. There was a muffled answer to his knock, and the lock clicked rustily.

"Anne?" he said. The room was darkened, but he could see her blond head and the thin, almost unfeminine lines of her figure. He put out a hand and felt her thin fingers in his palm. As she turned toward the weak light, he saw no sign of tears, but her hand shook with her dry shudders. "Anne, Ruth has just told me that God has given us a daughter—"

"God!" She spat the word out harshly, while the hand jerked back. "God, Reverend Strong? Whose God? The one who sends meteorites against Dick's base, plagues of insects, and drought against our farms? The God who uses tornadoes to make it easy for the snakes to land? That God, Reverend Strong? Dick gave you a daughter, and he's dead! Dead!"

Amos backed out of the room. He had learned to stand the faint mockery with which Doc pronounced the name of the Lord, but this was something that set his skin into goosepimples and caught at his throat. Anne had been of a different faith, but she had always seemed religious before.

It was probably only hysteria. He turned toward the kitchen door to call Ruth and send her in to the girl.

Overhead, the staccato bleating of a ram-jet cut through the air in a sound he had never heard. But the radio description fitted it perfectly. It could be no Earth ship!

Then there was another and another, until they blended together into a steady drone.

And over it came the sudden firing of a heavy gun, while a series of rapid thuds came from the garden behind the house.

Amos stumbled toward the back door. "Ruth!" he cried.

There was another burst of shots. Ruth was crumpling before he could get to the doorway.

II

My God, my God, why hast thou forsaken me? . . . I am poured out like water, and all my bones are out of joint: my heart is like wax; it is melted in the midst of my bowels. My strength is dried up like a potsherd; and my tongue cleaveth to my jaws; and thou has brought me into the dust of death.

PSALMS, XXII, 1, 14, 15.

There were no more shots as he ran to gather her into his arms. The last of the alien delta planes had gone over, heading for Topeka or whatever city they were attacking.

Ruth was still alive. One of the ugly slugs had caught her in the abdomen, ripping away part of the side, and it was bleeding horribly. But he felt her heart still beating, and she moaned faintly. Then as he put her on the couch, she opened her eyes briefly, saw him, and tried to smile. Her lips moved, and he dropped his head to hear.

"I'm sorry, Amos. Foolish. Nuisance. Sorry."

Her eyes closed, but she smiled again after he bent to kiss her lips. "Glad now. Waited so long."

Anne stood in the doorway, staring unbelievingly. But as Amos stood up, she unfroze and darted to the medicine cabinet, to come back and begin snipping away the ruined dress and trying to staunch the flow of blood.

Amos reached blindly for the phone. He mumbled something to the operator, and a minute later to Doc Miller. He'd been afraid that the doctor would still be out. He had a feeling that Doc had promised to come, but could remember no words.

The flow of blood outside the wound had been stopped, but Ruth was white, even to her lips. Anne forced him back to a chair, her fingers gentle on his arm.

"I'm sorry, Father Strong. I—I—"

He stood up and went over to stand beside Ruth, letting his eyes turn toward the half-set table. There was a smell of something burning in the air, and he went out to the old wood-burning stove to pull the pans off and drop them into the sink. Anne followed, but he hardly saw her, until he heard her begin to cry softly. There were tears this time.

"The ways of God are not the ways of man, Anne," he said, and the words released a flood of his own emotions. He dropped tiredly to a chair, his hands falling limply onto his lap. He dropped his head against the table, feeling the weakness and uncertainty of age. "We love the carnal form and our hearts are broken when it is gone. Only God can know all of any of us or count the tangled threads of all our lives. It isn't good to hate God!"

She dropped beside him. "I don't, Father Strong. I never did." He couldn't be sure of the honesty of it, but he made no effort to question her, and she sighed. "Mother Ruth isn't dead yet!"

He was saved from any answer by the door being slammed open

as Doc Miller came rushing in. The plump little man took one quick look at Ruth, and was beside her, reaching for plasma and his equipment. He handed the plasma bottle to Anne, and began working carefully.

"There's a chance," he said finally. "If she were younger or stronger, I'd say there was an excellent chance. But now, since you believe in it, you'd better do some fancy praying."

"I've been praying," Amos told him, realizing that it was true. The prayers had begun inside his head at the first shot, and they had never ceased.

They moved her gently, couch and all, into the bedroom where the blinds could be drawn, and where the other sounds of the house couldn't reach her. Doc gave Anne a shot of something and sent her into the other room. He turned to Amos, but didn't insist when the minister shook his head.

"I'll stay here, Amos," he said. "With her. Until we know, or I get another call. The switchboard girl knows where I am."

He went into the bedroom and closed the door. Amos stood in the center of the living room, his head bowed, for long minutes.

The sound of the television brought him back. Topeka was off the air, but another station was showing scenes of destruction.

Hospitals and schools seemed to be their chief targets. The gas had accounted for a number of deaths, though those could have been prevented if instructions had been followed. But now the incendiaries were causing the greatest damage.

And the aliens had gotten at least as rough treatment as they had meted out. Of the forty that had been counted, twenty-nine were certainly down.

"I wonder if they're saying prayers to God for their dead?" Doc asked. "Or doesn't your God extend his mercy to races other than man?"

Amos shook his head slowly. It was a new question to him. But there could be only one answer. "God rules the entire universe, Doc. But these evil beings surely offer him no worship!"

"Are you sure? They're pretty human!"

Amos looked back to the screen, where one of the alien corpses could be seen briefly. They did look almost human, though squat and heavily muscled. Their skin was green, and they wore no clothes. There was no nose, aside from two orifices under their curiously flat ears that quivered as if in breathing. But they were human enough to pass for deformed men, if they were worked on by good make-up men.

They were creatures of God, just as he was! And as such, could he deny them? Then his mind recoiled, remembering the atrocities they had committed, the tortures that had been reported, and the utter savagery so out of keeping with their inconceivably advanced ships. They were things of evil who had denied their birthright as part of God's domain. For evil, there could be only hatred. And from evil, how could there be worship of anything but the powers of darkness?

The thought of worship triggered his mind into an awareness of his need to prepare a sermon for the evening. It would have to be something simple; both he and his congregation were in no mood for rationalizations. Tonight he would have to serve God through their emotions. The thought frightened him. He tried to cling for strength to the brief moment of glory he had felt in the morning, but even that seemed far away.

There was the wail of a siren outside, rising to an ear-shattering crescendo, and the muffled sound of a loud-speaker driven beyond its normal operating level.

He stood up at last and moved out onto the porch with Doc as the tank came by. It was limping on treads that seemed to be about to fall apart, and the amplifier and speakers were mounted crudely on top. It pushed down the street, repeating its message over and over.

"Get out of town! Everybody clear out! This is an order to evacuate! The snakes are coming! Human forces have been forced to retreat to regroup. The snakes are heading this way, heading toward Topeka. They are looting and killing as they go. Get out of town! Everybody clear out!"

It paused, and another voice blared out, sounding like that of the major who had stopped before. "Get the hell out, all of you! Get out while you've still got your skins outside of you. We been licked. Shut up, Blake! We've had the holy living pants beat off us, and we're going back to momma. Get out, scram, vamoose! The snakes are coming! Beat it!"

It staggered down the street, rumbling its message, and now other stragglers began following it—men in cars, piled up like cattle; men in carts of any kind, drawn by horses. Then another amplifier sounded from one of the wagons.

"Stay under cover until night! Then get out! The snakes won't be here at once. Keep cool. Evacuate in order, and under cover of darkness. We're holing up ourselves when we get to a safe place. This is your last warning. Stay under cover now, and evacuate as soon as it's dark."

There was a bleating from the sky, and alien planes began dipping down. Doc pulled Amos back into the house, but not before he saw men being cut to ribbons by shots that seemed to fume and burst into fire as they hit. Some of the men on the retreat made cover. When the planes were gone, they came out and began regrouping, leaving the dead and hauling the wounded with them.

"Those men need me!" Amos protested.

"So does Ruth," Doc told him. "Besides, we're too old, Amos. We'd only get in the way. They have their own doctors and chaplains, probably. They're risking their lives to save us, damn it— they've piled all their worst cases there and left them to warn us and to decoy the planes away from the rest who are probably sneaking back through the woods and fields. They'd hate your guts for wasting what they're trying to do. I've been listening to one of the local stations, and it's pretty bad."

He turned on his heel and went back to the bedroom. The television program tardily began issuing evacuation orders to all citizens along the road from Clyde to Topeka, together with instructions. For some reason, the aliens seemed not to spot small objects in movement at night, and all orders were to wait until then.

Doc came out again, and Amos looked up at him, feeling his head bursting, but with one clear idea fixed in it. "Ruth can't be moved, can she, Doc?"

"No, Amos." Doc sighed. "But it won't matter. You'd better go in to her now. She seems to be coming to. I'll wake the girl and get her ready."

Amos went into the bedroom as quietly as he could, but there was no need for silence. Ruth was already conscious, as if some awareness of her approaching death had forced her to use the last few minutes of her life. She put out a frail hand timidly to him. Her voice was weak, but clear.

"Amos, I know. And I don't mind now, except for you. But there's something I had to ask you. Amos, do you—?"

He dropped beside her when her voice faltered, wanting to bury his head against her, but not daring to lose the few remaining moments of her sight. He fought the words out of the depths of his mind, and then realized it would take more than words. He bent over and kissed her again, as he had first kissed her so many years ago.

"I've always loved you, Ruth," he said. "I still do love you."

She sighed and relaxed. "Then I won't be jealous of God any more, Amos. I had to know."

Her hand reached up weakly, to find his hair and to run through it. She smiled, the worn lines of her face softening. Her voice was soft and almost young. "And forsaking all others, cleave only unto thee—"

The last syllable whispered out, and the hand dropped.

Amos dropped his head at last, and a single sob choked out of him. He folded her hands tenderly, with the worn, cheap wedding ring uppermost, and arose slowly with his head bowed.

"'Then shall the dust return to the earth as it was; and the spirit shall return unto God who gave it.' Father, I thank thee for this moment with her. Bless her, O Lord; and keep her for me."

He nodded to Doc and Anne. The girl looked sick and sat staring at him with eyes that mixed shock and pity.

"You'll need some money, Anne," he told her as Doc went into the bedroom. "I don't have much, but there's a little—"

She drew back, choking, and shook her head. "I've got enough, Reverend Strong. I'll make out. Doctor Miller has told me to take his car. But what about you?"

"There's still work to be done," he said. "I haven't even written my sermon. And the people who are giving up their homes will need comfort. In such hours as these, we all need God to sustain us."

She stumbled to her feet and into the bedroom after Miller. Amos opened his old desk and reached for pencil and paper.

III

The wicked have drawn out the sword, and have bent their bow, to cast down the poor and needy, and to slay such as be of upright conversation.

I have seen the wicked in great power, and spreading himself like a green bay tree.

PSALMS, XXXVII, 14, 35.

Darkness was just beginning to fall when they helped Anne out into the doctor's car, making sure that the tank was full. She was quiet, and had recovered herself, but avoided Amos whenever possible. She turned at last to Doc Miller.

"What are you going to do? I should have asked before, but—"

"Don't worry about me, girl," he told her, his voice as hearty as when he was telling an old man he still had forty years to live. "I've got other ways. The switchboard girl is going to be one of the last to leave, and I'm driving her in her car. You go ahead, the way we mapped it out. And pick up anyone else you find on the way. It's safe; it's still too early for men to start turning to looting, rape, or robbery. They'll think of that a little later."

She held out a hand to him, and climbed in. At the last minute, she pressed Amos' hand briefly. Then she stepped on the accelerator and the car took off down the street at its top speed.

"She hates me," Amos said. "She loves men too much and God too little to understand."

"And maybe you love your God too much to understand that you love men, Amos. Don't worry, she'll figure it out. The next time you see her, she'll feel different. I'll see you later."

Doc swung off toward the telephone office, carrying his bag. Amos watched him, puzzled as always at anyone who could so fervently deny God and yet could live up to every commandment of the Lord except worship. They had been friends for a long time, while the parish stopped fretting about it and took it for granted, yet the riddle was no nearer solution.

There was the sound of a great rocket landing, and the smaller stutterings of the peculiar alien ram-jets. The ship passed directly overhead, yet there was no shooting this time.

Amos faced the bedroom window for a moment, and then turned toward the church. He opened it, throwing the door wide. There was no sign of the sexton, but he had rung the bell in the tower often enough before. He took off his work coat and grabbed the rope.

It was hard work, and his hands were soft. Once it had been a pleasure, but now his blood seemed too thin to suck up the needed oxygen. The shirt stuck wetly to his back, and he felt giddy when he finished.

Almost at once, the telephone in his little office began jangling nervously. He staggered to it, panting as he lifted it to hear the voice of Nellie, shrill with fright. "Reverend what's up? Why's the bell ringing?"

"For prayer meeting, of course," he told her. "What else?"

"Tonight? Well, I'll be—" She hung up.

He lighted a few candles and put them on the altar, where their glow could be seen from the dark street, but where no light would shine upwards for alien eyes. Then he sat down to wait, wondering what was keeping the organist.

There were hushed calls from the street and nervous cries. A car started, to be followed by another. Then a group took off at once. He went to the door, partly for the slightly cooled air. All along the street, men were moving out their possession and loading up, while others took off. They waved to him, but hurried on by. He heard telephones begin to ring, but if Nellie was passing on some urgent word, she had forgotten him.

He turned back to the altar, kneeling before it. There was no articulate prayer in his mind. He simply clasped his gnarled fingers together and rested on his knee, looking up at the outward symbol of his life. Outside, the sounds went on blending together. It did not matter whether anyone chose to use the church tonight. It was open, as the house of God must always be in times of stress. He had long since stopped trying to force religion on those not ready for it.

And slowly, the strains of the day began to weave themselves into the pattern of his life. He had learned to accept; from the death of his baby daughter on, he had found no way to end the pain that seemed so much a part of life. But he could bury it behind the world of his devotion, and meet whatever his lot was to be without anger at the will of the Lord. Now, again, he accepted things as they were ordered.

There was a step behind him. He turned, not bothering to rise, and saw the dressmaker, Angela Anduccini, hesitating at the door. She had never entered, though she had lived in Wesley since she was eighteen. She crossed herself doubtfully, and waited.

He stood up. "Come in, Angela. This is the house of God, and all His daughters are welcome."

There was a dark, tight fear in her eyes as she glanced back to the street. "I thought—maybe the organ—"

He opened it for her and found the switch. He started to explain the controls, but the smile on her lips warned him that it was unnecessary. Her calloused fingers ran over the stops, and she began playing, softly as if to herself. He went back to one of the pews, listening. For two years he had blamed the organ, but now he knew that there was no fault with the instrument, but only with its player before. The music was sometimes strange for his church, but he liked it.

A couple who had moved into the old Surrey farm beyond the town came in, holding hands, as if holding each other up. And a minute later, Buzz Williams stumbled in and tried to tiptoe down the aisle to where Amos sat. Since his parents had died, he'd been the town problem. Now he was half-drunk, though without his usual boisterousness.

"I ain't got no car and I been drinking," he whispered. "Can I stay here till maybe somebody comes or something?"

Amos sighed, motioning Buzz to a seat where the boy's eyes had centered. Somewhere, there must be a car for the four waifs who had remembered God when everything else had failed them. If one of the young couple could drive, and he could locate some kind of a vehicle, it was his duty to see that they were sent to safety.

Abruptly, the haven of the church and the music came to an end, leaving him back in the real world—a curiously unreal world now.

He was heading down the steps, trying to remember whether the Jameson boy had taken his flivver, when a panel truck pulled up in front of the church. Doc Miller got out, wheezing as he squeezed through the door.

He took in the situation at a glance. "Only four strays, Amos? I thought we might have to pack them in." He headed for Buzz. "I've got a car outside, Buzz. Gather up the rest of this flock and get going!"

"I been drinking," Buzz said, his face reddening hotly.

"Okay, you've been drinking. At least you know it, and there's no traffic problem. Head for Salina and hold it under forty and you'll be all right." Doc swept little Angela Anduccini from the organ and herded her out, while Buzz collected the couple. "Get going, all of you!"

They got, with Buzz enthroned behind the wheel and Angela beside him. The town was dead. Amos closed the organ and began shutting the doors to the church.

"I've got a farm tractor up the street for us, Amos," Doc said at last. "I almost ran out of tricks. There were more fools than you'd think who thought they could hide out right here. At that, I probably missed some. Well, the tractor's nothing elegant, but it can take those back roads. We'd better get going."

Amos shook his head. He had never thought it out, but the decision had been in his mind from the beginning. Ruth still lay waiting a decent burial. He could no more leave her now than when she was alive. "You'll have to go alone, Doc."

"I figured." The doctor sighed, wiping the sweat from his forehead. " . . . I'd remember to my dying day that believers have more courage than an atheist! No sale, Amos. It isn't sensible, but that's how I feel. We'd better put out the candles, I guess."

Amos snuffed them reluctantly, wondering how he could persuade the other to leave. His ears had already caught the faint sounds of shooting; the aliens were on their way.

The uncertain thumping of a laboring motor sounded from the street, to wheeze to silence. There was a shout, a pause, and the motor caught again. It might have run for ten seconds before it backfired, and was still.

Doc opened one of the doors. In the middle of the street, a man was pushing an ancient car while his wife steered. But it refused to start again. He grabbed for tools, threw up the hood, and began a frantic search for the trouble.

"If you can drive a tractor, there's one half a block down," Doc called out.

The man looked up, snapped one quick glance behind him, and pulled the woman hastily out of the car. In almost no time, the heavy roar of the tractor sounded. The man revved it up to full throttle and tore off down the road, leaving Doc and Amos stranded. The sounds of the aliens were clearer now, and there was some light coming from beyond the bend of the street.

There was no place to hide. They found a window where the paint on the imitation stained glass was loose, and peeled it back enough for a peephole. The advance scouts of the aliens were already within view. They were dashing from house to house. Behind them, they left something that sent up clouds of glowing smoke that seemed to have no fire connected to their brilliance. At least, no buildings were burning.

Just as the main group of aliens came into view, the door of one house burst open. A scrawny man leaped out, with his fat wife and fatter daughter behind him. They raced up the street, tearing at their clothes and scratching frantically at their reddened skin.

Shots sounded. All three jerked, but went racing on. More shots sounded. At first, Amos thought it was incredibly bad shooting. Then he realized that it was even more unbelievably good marksmanship. The aliens were shooting at the hands first, then moving up the arms methodically, wasting no chance for torture.

For the first time in years, Amos felt fear and anger curdle solidly in his stomach. He stood up, feeling his shoulders square back and his head come up as he moved toward the door. His lips were moving in words that he only half understood. "'Arise, O Lord; O God, lift up thine hand; forget not the humble. Wherefore doth the wicked condemn God? He hath said in his heart, Thou wilt not require it. Thou hast seen it, for thou beholdest mischief and spite, to requite it with thy hand: the poor committeth himself unto thee; thou art the helper of the fatherless. Break thou the arm of the wicked and the evil ones; seek out their wickedness till thou find none. . . .'"

"Stop it, Amos!" Doc's voice rasped harshly in his ear. "Don't be a fool! And you're misquoting that last verse!"

It cut through the fog of his anger. He knew that Doc had deliberately reminded him of his father, but the trick worked, and the memory of his father's anger at misquotations replaced his cold fury. "We can't let that go on!"

Then he saw it was over. They had used up their targets. But there was the sight of another wretch, unrecognizable in half of his skin . . .

Doc's voice was as sick as he felt. "We can't do anything, Amos. I can't understand a race smart enough to build star ships and still going in for this. But it's good for our side, in the long run. While our armies are organizing, they're wasting time on this. And it makes resistance tougher, too."

The aliens didn't confine their sport to humans. They worked just as busily on a huge old tomcat they found. And all the corpses were being loaded onto a big wagon pulled by twenty of the creatures.

The aliens obviously had some knowledge of human behavior. At first they had passed up all stores, and had concentrated on living quarters. The scouts had passed on by the church without a second glance. But they moved into a butcher shop at once, to come out again, carrying meat which was piled on the wagon with the corpses.

Now a group was assembling before the church, pointing up toward the steeple where the bell was. Two of them shoved up a mortar of some sort. It was pointed quickly and a load was dropped in. There was a muffled explosion, and the bell rang sharply, its pieces rattling down the roof and into the yard below.

Another shoved the mortar into a new position, aiming it straight for the door of the church. Doc yanked Amos down between two pews. "They don't like churches, damn it! A fine spot we picked. Watch out for splinters!"

The door smashed in and a heavy object struck the altar, ruining it and ricocheting onto the organ. Amos groaned at the sound it made.

There was no further activity when they slipped back to their peepholes. The aliens were on the march again, moving along slowly. In spite of the delta planes, they seemed to have no motorized ground vehicles, and the wagon moved on under the power of the twenty green-skinned things, coming directly in front of the church.

Amos stared at it in the flickering light from the big torches burning in the hands of some of the aliens. Most of the corpses were strangers to him. A few he knew. And then his eyes picked out the twisted, distorted upper part of Ruth's body, her face empty in death's relaxation.

He stood up wearily, and this time Doc made no effort to stop him. He walked down a line of pews and around the wreck of one of the doors. Outside the church, the air was still hot and dry, but he drew a long breath into his lungs. The front of the church was in the shadows, and no aliens seemed to be watching him.

He moved down the stone steps. His legs were firm now. His heart was pounding heavily, but the clot of feelings that rested leadenly in his stomach had no fear left in it. Nor was there any anger left, nor any purpose.

He saw the aliens stop and stare at him, while a jabbering began among them.

He moved forward with the measured tread that had led him to his wedding the first time. He came to the wagon, and put his hand out, lifting one of Ruth's dead-limp arms back across her body.

"This is my wife," he told the staring aliens quietly. "I am taking her home with me."

He reached up and began trying to move the other bodies away from her. Without surprise, he saw Doc's arms moving up to help him, while a steady stream of whispered profanity came from the man's lips.

He hadn't expected to succeed. He had expected nothing.

Abruptly, a dozen of the aliens leaped for the two men. Amos let them overpower him without resistance. For a second, Doc struggled, and then he too relaxed while the aliens bound them and tossed them onto the wagon.

IV

He hath bent his bow like an enemy: he stood with his right hand as an adversary, and slew all that were pleasant to the eye in the tabernacle of the daughter of Zion: he poured out his fury like fire.

The Lord was as an enemy: he hath swallowed up Israel, he hath swallowed up all her palaces: he hath destroyed his strong holds, and hath increased in the daughter of Judah mourning and lamentation.

The Lord hath cast off his altar, he hath abhorred his sanctuary, he hath given up into the hand of the enemy the walls of her palaces; they have made a noise in the house of the Lord, as in the day of a solemn feast.

LAMENTATIONS, II, 4, 5, 7.

Amos' first reaction was one of dismay at the ruin of his only good suit. He struggled briefly on the substance under him, trying to find a better spot. A minister's suit might be old, but he could never profane the altar with such stains as these. Then some sense of the ridiculousness of his worry reached his mind, and he relaxed as best he could.

He had done what he had to do, and it was too late to regret it. He could only accept the consequences of it now, as he had learned to accept everything else God had seen fit to send him. He had never been a man of courage, but the strength of God had sustained him through as much as most men had to bear. It would sustain him further.

Doc was facing him, having flopped around to lie facing toward him. Now the doctor's lips twisted into a crooked grin. "I guess we're in for it now. But it won't last forever, and maybe we're old enough to die fast. At least, once we're dead, we won't know it, so there's no sense being afraid of dying."

If it was meant to provoke him into argument, it failed. Amos considered it a completely hopeless philosophy, but it was better than none, probably. His own faith in the hereafter left something to be desired; he was sure of immorality and the existence of heaven and hell, but he had never been able to picture either to his own satisfaction.

The wagon had been swung around and was now being pulled up the street, back toward Clyde. Amos tried to take his mind off the physical discomforts of the ride by watching the houses, counting them to his own. They drew near it finally, but it was Doc who spotted the important fact. He groaned. "My car!"

Amos strained his eyes, staring into the shadows through the glare of the torches. Doc's car stood at the side of the house, with the door open! Someone must have told Anne that he hadn't left, and she'd swung back around the alien horde to save him!

He began a prayer that they might pass on without the car being noticed, and it seemed at first that they would. Then there was a sudden cry from the house, and he saw her face briefly at a front window. She must have seen Doc and himself lying on the wagon!

He opened his mouth to risk a warning, but it was too late. The door swung back, and she was standing on the front steps, lifting Richard's rifle to her shoulder. Amos' heart seemed to hesitate with the tension of his body. The aliens still hadn't noticed. If she'd only wait . . .

The rifle cracked. Either by luck or some skill he hadn't suspected, one of the aliens dropped. She was running forward now, throwing another cartridge into the barrel. The gun barked again, and an alien fell to the ground, bleating horribly.

There was no attempt at torture this time, at least. The leading alien jerked out a tubelike affair from a scabbard at his side and a single sharp explosion sounded. Anne jerked backward as the heavy slug hit her forehead, the rifle spinning from her dead hands.

The wounded alien was trying frantically to crawl away. Two of his fellows began working on him mercilessly, with as little feeling as if he had been a human. His body followed that of Anne toward the front of the wagon, just beyond Amos' limited view.

She hadn't seemed hysterical this time, Amos thought wearily. It had been her tendency to near hysteria that had led to his advising Richard to wait, not the difference in faith. Now he was sorry he'd had no chance to understand her better.

Doc sighed, and there was a peculiar pride under the thickness of his voice. "Man," he said, "has one virtue which is impossible to any omnipotent force like your God. He can be brave. He can be brave beyond sanity, for another man or for an idea. Amos, I pity your God if man ever makes war on Him!"

Amos flinched, but the blasphemy aroused only a shadow of his normal reaction. His mind seemed numbed. He lay back, watching black clouds scudding across the sky almost too rapidly. It looked unnatural, and he remembered how often the accounts had mentioned a tremendous storm that had wrecked or hampered the efforts of human troops. Maybe a counteract had begun, and this was part of the alien defense. If they had some method of weather control, it was probable. The moonlight was already blotted out by the clouds.

Half a mile further on, there was a shout from the aliens, and a big tractor chugged into view, badly driven by one of the aliens, who had obviously only partly mastered the human machine. With a great deal of trial and error, it was backed into position and coupled to the wagon. Then it began churning along at nearly thirty miles an hour, while the big wagon bucked and bounced behind. From then on, the ride was physical hell. Even Doc groaned at some of the bumps, though his bones had three times more padding than Amos'.

Mercifully, they slowed when they reached Clyde. Amos wiped the blood off his bitten lip and managed to wriggle to a position where most of the bruises were on his upper side. There was a flood of brilliant lights beyond the town where the alien rockets stood, and he could see a group of nonhuman machines busy unloading the great ships. But the drivers of the machines looked totally unlike the other aliens.

One of the alien trucks swung past them, and he had a clear view of the creature steering it. It bore no resemblance to humanity. There was a conelike trunk, covered with a fine white down, ending in four thick stalks to serve as legs. From its broadest point, four sinuous limbs spread out to the truck controls. There was no head, but only eight small tentacles waving above it.

He saw a few others, always in control of machines, and no machines being handled by the green-skinned people as they passed through the ghost city that had been Clyde. Apparently there were two races allied against humanity, which explained why such barbarians could come in space ships. The green ones must be simply the fighters, while the downy cones were the technicians. From their behavior, though, the pilots of the planes must be recruited from the fighters.

Clyde had grown since he had been there, unlike most of the towns about. There was a new supermarket just down the street from Amos' former church, and the tractor jolted to a stop in front of it. Aliens swarmed out and began carrying the loot from the wagon into its big food lockers, while two others lifted Doc and Amos.

But they weren't destined for the comparatively merciful death of freezing in the lockers. The aliens threw them into a little cell that had once apparently been a cashier's cage, barred from floor to ceiling. It made a fairly efficient jail, and the lock that clicked shut as the door closed behind them was too heavy to be broken.

There was already one occupant—a medium-built young man whom Amos finally recognized as Smithton, the Clyde dentist. His shoulders were shaking with sporadic sobs as he sat huddled in one corner. He looked at the two arrivals without seeing them. "But I surrendered," he whispered. "I'm a prisoner of war. They can't do it. I surrendered—"

A fatter-than-usual alien, wearing the only clothes Amos had seen on any of them, came waddling up to the cage, staring in at them, and the dentist wailed off into silence. The alien drew up his robe about his chest and scratched his rump against a counter without taking his eyes off them. "Humans," he said in a grating voice, but without an accent, "are peculiar. No standardization."

"I'll be damned!" Doc swore. "English!"

The alien studied them with what might have been surprise, lifting his ears. "Is the gift of tongues so unusual, then? Many of the priests of the Lord God Almighty speak all the human languages. It's a common miracle, not like levitation."

"Fine. Then maybe you'll tell us what we're being held for?" Doc suggested.

The priest shrugged. "Food, of course. The *grethi* eat any kind of meat—even our people—but we have to examine the laws to find whether you're permitted. If you are, we'll need freshly killed specimens to sample, so we're waiting with you."

"You mean you're attacking us for *food?*"

The priest grunted harshly. "No! We're on a holy mission to exterminate you. The Lord commanded us to go down to Earth where abominations existed and to leave no living creature under your sun."

He turned and waddled out of the store, taking the single remaining torch with him, leaving only the dim light of the moon and reflections from further away.

Amos dropped onto a stool inside the cage. "They had to lock us in a new building instead of one I know," he said. "If it had been the church, we might have had a chance."

"How?" Doc asked sharply.

Amos tried to describe the passage through the big, unfinished basement under the church, reached through a trap door. Years before, a group of teen-agers had built a sixty-foot tunnel into it and had used it for a private club until the passage had been discovered and bricked over from outside. The earth would be soft around the bricks, however. Beyond, the outer end of the tunnel opened in a wooded section, which led to a drainage ditch that in turn connected with the Republican River. From the church, they could have moved to the stream and slipped down that without being seen, unlike most of the other sections of the town.

Doc's fingers were trembling on the lock when Amos finished. "If we could get the two hundred feet to the church—They don't know much about us, Amos, if they lock us in where the lock screws are on our side. Well, we'll have to chance it."

Amos' own fingers shook as he felt the screwheads. He could see what looked like a back door to the store. If they could come out into the alley that had once been there, they could follow it nearly to the church—and then the trees around that building would cut off most of the light. It would be a poor chance. But was it chance? It seemed more like the hand of God to him.

"More like the carelessness of the aliens to me," Doc objected. "It would probably be a lot less complicated in most other places, the way they light the town. Knock the bottom out of the money drawer and break off two slats. I've got a quarter that fits these screws."

Smithton fumbled with the drawer, praying now—a childhood prayer for going to sleep. But he succeeded in getting two slats Doc could place the quarter between.

It was rough going, with more slipping than turning of the screws, but the lock had been meant to keep outsiders out, not cashiers in. Three of the screws came loose, and the lock rotated on the fourth until they could force the cage open.

Doc stopped and pulled Smithton to him. "Follow me, and do

what I do. No talking, no making a separate break, or I'll break your neck. All right!"

The back door was locked, but on the inside. They opened it to a backyard filled with garbage. The alley wasn't as dark as it should have been, since open lots beyond let some light come through. They hugged what shadows they could until they reached the church hedge. There they groped along, lining themselves up with the side office door. There was no sign of aliens.

Amos broke ahead of the others, being more familiar with the church. It wasn't until he had reached the door that he realized it could have been locked; it had been kept that way part of the time. He grabbed the handle and forced it back—to find it open!

For a second, he stopped to thank the Lord for their luck. Then the others were with him, crowding into the little kitchen where social suppers were prepared. He'd always hated those functions, but now he blessed them for a hiding place that gave them time to find their way.

There were sounds in the church, and odors, but none that seemed familiar to Amos. Something made the back hairs of his neck prickle. He took off his shoes and tied them around his neck, and the other followed suit.

The trap door lay down a small hall, across in front of the altar, and in the private office on the other side.

They were safer together than separated, particularly since Smithton was with them. Amos leaned back against the kitchen wall to catch his breath. His heart seemed to have a ring of needled pain around it, and his throat was so dry that he had to fight desperately against gagging. There was water here, but he couldn't risk rummaging across the room to the sink.

He was praying for strength, less for himself than the others. Long since, he had resigned himself to die. If God willed his death, he was ready; all he had were dead and probably mutilated, and he had succeeded only in dragging those who tried to help him into mortal danger. He was old, and his body was already treading its way to death. He could live for probably twenty more years, but aside from his work, there was nothing to live for—and even in that, he had been only a mediocre failure. But he was still responsible for Doc Miller, and even for Smithton now.

He squeezed his eyes together and squinted around the doorway. There was some light in the hall that led toward the altar, but he could see no one, and there were drapes that gave a shadow from which they could spy the rest of their way. He moved to it softly, and felt the others come up behind him.

He bent forward, parting the drapes a trifle. They were perhaps twenty feet in front of the altar, on the right side. He spotted the wreckage that had once stood as an altar. Then he frowned as he saw evidence of earth piled up into a mound of odd shape.

He drew the cloth back further, surprised at the curiosity in him, as he had been surprised repeatedly by the changes taking place in himself.

There were two elaborately robed priests kneeling in the center of the chapel. But his eyes barely noticed them before it was attracted to what stood in front of the new altar.

A box of wood rested on an earthenware platform. On it were four marks which his eyes recognized as unfamiliar, but which his mind twisted into a sequence from the alphabets he had learned, unpronounceable yet compelling. And above the box was a veil, behind which Something shone brightly without light.

In his mind, a surge of power pulsed, making patterns that might almost have been words through his thoughts—words like the words Moses once had heard—words that Amos, heartsick, knew. . . .

"I AM THAT I AM, who brought those out of bondage from Egypt and who wrote upon the wall before Belshazzar, MENE, MENE, TEKEL, UPHARSIN, as it shall be writ large upon the Earth, from this day forth. For I have said unto the seed of Mikhtchah, thou art my chosen people and I shall exalt thee above all the races under the heavens!"

V

And it was given unto him to make war with the saints, and to overcome them: and power was given him over all kindreds, and tongues, and nations.

He that leadeth into captivity shall go into captivity: he that killeth with the sword must be killed with the sword.

REVELATIONS, XIII, 7, 10.

The seed of Mikhtchah. The seed of the invaders. . . .

There was no time and all time, then. Amos felt his heart stop, but the blood pounded through his arteries with a vigor it had lacked for decades. He felt Ruth's hand in his, stirring with returning life, and knew she had never existed. Beside him, he saw Doc Miller's hair turn snow-white and knew that it was so, though there was no way he could see Doc from his position.

He felt the wrath of the Presence rest upon him, weighing his every thought from his birth to his certain death, where he ceased completely and went on forever, and yet he knew that the Light behind the veil was unaware of him, but was receptive only to the two Mikhtchah priests who knelt, praying.

All of that was with but a portion of his mind so small that he could not locate it, though his total mind encompassed all time and space, and that which was neither; yet each part of his perceptions occupied all of his mind that had been or ever could be, save only the present, which somehow was a concept not yet solved by the One before him.

He saw a strange man on a low mountain, receiving tablets of stone that weighed only a pennyweight, engraved with a script that all could read. And he knew the man, but refused to believe it, since the garments were not those of his mental image, and the clean-cut face fitted better with the strange headpiece than with the language the man spoke.

He saw every prayer of his life tabulated. But nowhere was there the mantle of divine warmth which he had felt as a boy and had almost felt again the morning before. And there was a stirring of unease at his thought, mixed with wrath; yet while the thought was in his mind, nothing could touch him.

Each of those things was untrue, because he could find no understanding of that which was true.

It ended as abruptly as it had begun, either a microsecond or a million subjective years after. It left him numbered, but newly alive. And it left him dead as no man had ever been hopelessly dead before.

He knew only that before him was the Lord God Almighty, He who had made a covenant with Abraham, with Isaac, and with Jacob, and with their seed. And he knew that the covenant was ended. Mankind had been rejected, while God now was on the side of the enemies of Abraham's seed, the enemies of all the nations of earth.

Even that was too much for a human mind no longer in touch with the Presence, and only a shadow of it remained.

Beside him, Amos heard Doc Miller begin breathing again,

brushing the white hair back from his forehead wonderingly as he muttered a single word, "God!"

One of the Mikhtchah priests looked up, his eyes turning about; there had been a glazed look on his face, but it was changing.

Then Smithton screamed! His open mouth poured out a steady, unwavering screaming, while his lungs panted in and out. His eyes opened, staring horribly. Like a wooden doll on strings, the man stood up and walked forward. He avoided the draperies and headed for the Light behind the veil. Abruptly, the Light was gone, but Smithton walked toward it as steadily as before. He stopped before the falling veil, and the scream cut off sharply.

Doc had jerked silently to his feet, tugging Amos up behind him. The minister lifted himself, but he knew there was no place to go. It was up to the will of God now . . . Or . . .

Smithton turned on one heel precisely. His face was rigid and without expression, yet completely mad. He walked mechanically forward toward the two priests. They sprawled aside at the last second, holding two obviously human-made automatics, but making no effort to use them. Smithton walked on toward the open door at the front of the church.

He reached the steps, with the two priests staring after him. His feet lifted from the first step to the second and then he was on the sidewalk.

The two priests fired!

Smithton jerked, halted, and suddenly cried out in a voice of normal, rational agony. His legs kicked frantically under him and he ducked out of the sight of the doorway, his faltering steps sounding further and further away. He was dead—the Mikhtchah marksmanship had been as good as it seemed always to be—but still moving, though slower and slower, as if some extra charge of life were draining out like a battery running down.

The priests exchanged quick glances and then darted after him, crying out as they dashed around the door into the night. Abruptly, a single head and hand appeared again, to snap a shot at the draperies from which Smithton had come. Amos forced himself to stand still, while his imagination supplied the jolt of lead in his stomach. The bullet hit the draperies, and something else.

The priest hesitated, and was gone again.

Amos broke into a run across the chapel and into the hall at the other side of the altar. He heard the faint sound of Doc's feet behind him.

The trap door was still there, unintentionally concealed under carpeting. He forced it up and dropped through it into the four-foot depth of the uncompleted basement, making room for Doc. They crouched together as he lowered the trap and began feeling his way through the blackness toward the other end of the basement. It had been five years since he had been down there, and then only once for a quick inspection of the work of the boys who had dug the tunnel.

He thought he had missed it at first, and began groping for the small entrance. It might have caved in, for that matter. Then, two feet away, his hand found the hole and he drew Doc after him.

It was cramped, and bits of dirt had fallen in places and had to be dug out of the way. Part of the distance was covered on their stomachs. They found the bricked-up wall ahead of them and began digging around it with their bare hands. It took another ten minutes, while distant sounds of wild yelling from the Mikhtchah reached them faintly. They broke through at last with bleeding hands, not bothering to check for aliens near. They reached a safer distance in the woods, caught their breath, and went on.

The biggest danger lay in the drainage trench, which was low in several places. But luck was with them, and those spots lay in the shadow.

Then the little Republican River lay in front of them, and there was a flatbottom boat nearby.

Moments later, they were floating down the stream, resting their aching lungs, while the boat needed only a trifling guidance. It was still night, with only the light from the moon, and there was little danger of pursuit by the alien planes. Amos could just see Doc's face as the man fumbled for a cigarette.

He lighted it and exhaled deeply. "All right, Amos—you were right, and God exists. But damn it, I don't feel any better for knowing that. I can't see how God helps me—nor even how He's doing the Mikhtchah much good. What do they get out of it, beyond a few miracles with the weather? They're just doing God's dirty work."

"They get the Earth, I suppose—if they want it," Amos said doubtfully. He wasn't sure they did. Nor could he see how the other aliens tied into the scheme; if he had known the answers, they were gone now. "Doc, you're still an atheist, though you now know God is."

The plump man chuckled bitterly. "I'm afraid you're right. But at least I'm myself. You can't be, Amos. You've spent your whole life on the gamble that God is right and that you must serve him—when the only way you could serve was to help mankind. What do you do now? God is automatically right—but everything you've ever believed makes Him completely wrong, and you can only serve Him by betraying your people. What kind of ethics will work for you now?"

Amos shook his head wearily, hiding his face in his hands. The same problem had been fighting its way through his own thoughts. His first reaction had been to acknowledge his allegiance to God without question; sixty years of conditioned thought lay behind that. Yet now he could not accept such a decision. As a man, he could not bow to what he believed completely evil, and the Mikhtchah were evil by every definition he knew.

Could he tell people the facts, and take away what faith they had in any purpose in life? Could he go over to the enemy, who didn't even want him, except for their feeding experiments? Or could he encourage people to fight with the old words that God was with them—when he knew the words were false, and their resistance might doom them to eternal hellfire for opposing God?

It hit him then that he could remember nothing clearly about the case of a hereafter—either for or against it. What happened to a people when God deserted them? Were they only deserted in their physical form, and still free to win their spiritual salvation? Or were they completely lost? Did they cease to have souls that could survive? Or were those souls automatically consigned to hell, however noble they might be?

No question had been answered for him. He knew that God existed, but he had known that before. He knew nothing now beyond that. He did not even know when God had placed the Mikhtchah before humanity. It seemed unlikely that it was as recent as his own youth. Yet otherwise, how could he account for the strange spiritual glow he had felt as an evangelist?

"There's only one rational answer," he said at last. "It doesn't make any difference what I decide! I'm only one man."

"So was Columbus when he swore the world was round. And he

didn't have the look on his face you've had since we saw God, Amos! I know now what the Bible means when it says Moses' face shone after he came down from the mountain, until he had to cover it with a veil. If I'm right, God help mankind if you decide wrong!"

Doc tossed the cigarette over the side and lighted another, and Amos was shocked to see that the man's hands were shaking. The doctor shrugged, and his tone fell back to normal. "I wish we knew more. You've always thought almost exclusively in terms of the Old Testament and a few snatches of Revelations—like a lot of men who become evangelists. I've never really thought about God—I couldn't accept Him, so I dismissed Him. Maybe that's why we got the view of Him we did. I wish I knew where Jesus fits in, for instance. There's too much missing. Too many imponderables and hiatuses. We have only two facts, and we can't understand either. There is a manifestation of God which has touched both Mikhtchah and mankind; and He has stated now that he plans to wipe out mankind. We'll have to stick to that."

Amos made one more attempt to deny the problem that was facing him. "Suppose God is only testing man again, as He did so often before?"

"Testing?" Doc rolled the word on his tongue, and seemed to spit it out. The strange white hair seemed to make him older, and the absence of mockery in his voice left him almost a stranger. "Amos, the Hebrews worked like the devil to get Canaan; after forty years of wandering around a few square miles God suddenly told them this was the land—and then they had to take it by the same methods men have always used to conquer a country. The miracles didn't really decide anything. They got out of Babylon because the old prophets were slaving night and day to hold them together as one people, and because they managed to sweat it out until they finally got a break. In our own time, they've done the same things to get Israel, and with no miracles! It seems to me God took it away, but they had to get it back by themselves. I don't think much of that kind of a test in this case."

Amos could feel all his values slipping and spinning. He realized that he was holding himself together only because of Doc; otherwise, his mind would have reached for madness, like any intelligence forced to solve the insoluble. He could no longer comprehend himself, let alone God. And the feeling crept into his thoughts that God couldn't wholly understand Himself, either.

"Can a creation defy anything great enough to create it, Doc? And should it, if it can?"

"Most kids have to," Doc said. He shook his head. "It's your problem. All I can do is point a few things out. And maybe it won't matter, at that. We're still a long ways inside Mikhtchah territory, and it's getting along toward daylight."

The boat drifted on, while Amos tried to straighten out his thoughts and grew more deeply tangled in a web of confusion. What could any man who worshipped devoutly do if he found his God was opposed to all else he had ever believed to be good?

A version of Kant's categorical imperative crept into his mind; somebody had once quoted it to him—probably Doc. "So act as to treat humanity, whether in thine own person or in that of any other, in every case as an end withal, never as a means only." Was God now treating man as an end, or simply as a means to some purpose, in which man had failed? And had man ever seriously treated God as an end, rather than as a means to spiritual immortality and a quietus to the fear of death?

"We're being followed!" Doc whispered suddenly. He pointed back, and Amos could see a faint light shining around a curve in the stream. "Look—there's a building over there. When the boat touches shallow water, run for it!"

He bent to the oars, and a moment later they touched bottom and were over the side, sending the boat back into the current. The building was a hundred feet back from the bank, and they scrambled madly toward it. Even in the faint moonlight, they could see that the building was a wreck, long since abandoned. Doc went in through one of the broken windows, dragging Amos behind him.

Through a chink in the walls, they could see another boat heading down the stream, lighted by a torch and carrying two Mikhtchah. One rowed, while the other sat in the prow with a gun, staring ahead. They rowed on past.

"We'll have to hole up here," Doc decided. "It'll be light in half an hour. Maybe they won't think of searching a ruin like this."

They found rickety steps, and stretched out on the bare floor of a huge upstairs closet. Amos groaned as he tried to find a position in which he could get some rest. Then, surprisingly, he was asleep.

He woke once with traces of daylight coming into the closet, to hear sounds of heavy gunfire not far away. He was just drifting back to sleep when hail began cracking furiously down on the roof. When it passed, the gunfire was stilled.

Doc woke him when it was turning dark. There was nothing to eat, and Amos' stomach was sick with hunger. His body ached in every joint, and walking was pure torture. Doc glanced up at the stars, seemed to decide on a course, and struck out. He was wheezing and groaning in a way that indicated he shared Amos' feelings.

But he found enough energy to begin the discussion again. "I keep wondering what Smithton saw, Amos? It wasn't what we saw. And what about the legends of war in heaven? Wasn't there a big battle there once, in which Lucifer almost won? Maybe Lucifer simply stands for some other race God cast off?"

"Lucifer was Satan, the spirit of evil. He tried to take over God's domain."

"Mmm. I've read somewhere that we have only the account of the victor, which is apt to be pretty biased history. How do we know the real issues? Or the true outcome? At least he thought he had a chance, and he apparently knew what he was fighting."

The effort of walking made speech difficult. Amos shrugged, and let the conversation die. But his own mind ground on.

If God was all-powerful and all-knowing, why had He let them spy upon Him? Or was He all-powerful over a race He had dismissed? Could it make any difference to God what man might try to do, now that He had condemned him? Was the Presence they had seen the whole of God—or only one manifestation of Him?

His legs moved on woodenly, numbed to fatigue and slow from hunger, while his head churned with his basic problem. Where was his duty now? With God or against Him?

They found food in a deserted house, and began preparing it by the hooded light of a lantern, while they listened to the news from a small battery radio that had been left behind. It was a hopeless account of alien landings and human retreats, yet given without the tone of despair they should have expected. They were halfway through the meal before they discovered the reason.

"Flash!" the radio announced. "Word has just come through from the Denver area. A second atomic missile, piloted by a suicide crew, has fallen successfully! The alien base has been wiped out, and every ship is ruined. It is now clear that the trouble with earlier bombing attempts lay in the detonating mechanism. This is being investigated, while more volunteers are being trained to replace this undependable

part of the bomb. Both missiles carrying suicide bombers have succeeded. Captive aliens of both races are being questioned in Denver
now, but the same religious fanaticism found in Portland seems to
make communication difficult."

It went back to reporting alien landings, while Doc and Amos
stared at each other. It was too much to absorb at once.

Amos groped in his mind, trying to dig out something that might
tie in the success of human bombers, where automatic machinery
was miraculously stalled, with the reaction of God to his thoughts
of the glow he had felt in his early days. Something about man . . .

"They can be beaten!" Doc said in a harsh whisper.

Amos sighed as they began to get up to continue the impossible
trek. "Maybe. We know God was at Clyde. Can we be sure He was
at the other places to stop the bombs by His miracles?"

They slogged on through the night, cutting across country in the
dim light, where every footstep was twice as hard. Amos turned it
over, trying to use the new information for whatever decision he
must reach. If men could overcome those opposed to them, even for
a time . . .

It brought him no closer to an answer.

The beginnings of dawn found them in a woods. Doc managed
to heave Amos up a tree, where he could survey the surrounding
terrain. There was a house beyond the edge of the woods, but it
would take dangerous minutes to reach it. They debated, and then
headed on.

They were just emerging from the woods when the sound of an
alien plane began its stuttering shriek. Doc turned and headed back
to where Amos was behind him. Then he stopped. "Too late! He's
seen something. Gotta have a target!"

His arms swept out, shoving Amos violently back under the
nearest tree. He swung and began racing across the clearing, his fat
legs pumping furiously as he covered the ground in straining leaps.
Amos tried to lift himself from where he had fallen, but it was too
late.

There was the drumming of gunfire and the earth erupted around
Doc. He lurched and dropped, to twitch and lie still.

The plane swept over, while Amos disentangled himself from a
root. It was gone as he broke free. Doc had given it a target, and
the pilot was satisfied, apparently.

He was still alive as Amos dropped beside him. Two of the shots had hit, but he managed to grin as he lifted himself on one elbow. It was only a matter of minutes, however, and there was no help possible. Amos found one of Doc's cigarettes and lighted it with fumbling hands.

"Thanks," Doc wheezed after taking a heavy drag on it. He started to cough, but suppressed it, his face twisting in agony. His words came in an irregular rhythm, but he held his voice level. "I guess I'm going to hell, Amos, since I never did repent—if there is a hell! And I hope there is! I hope it's filled with the soul of every poor damned human being who died in less than perfect grace. Because I'm going to find some way—"

He straightened suddenly, coughing and fighting for breath. Then he found one final source of strength and met Amos' eyes, a trace of his old cynical smile on his face.

"—some way to open a recruiting station!" he finished. He dropped back, letting all the fight go out of his body. A few seconds later, he was dead.

VI

. . . Thou shalt have no other peoples before me . . . Thou shalt make unto them no covenant against me . . . Thou shalt not foreswear thyself to them, nor serve them . . . for I am a jealous people . . .

EXULTATIONS, XII, 2–4.

Amos lay through the day in the house to which he had dragged Doc's body. He did not even look for food. For the first time in his life since his mother had died when he was five, he had no shield against his grief. There was no hard core of acceptance that it was God's will to hide his loss at Doc's death. And with the realization of that, all the other losses hit at him as if they had been no older than the death of Doc.

He sat with his grief and his newly sharpened hatred, staring toward Clyde. Once, during the day, he slept. He awakened to a sense of a tremendous sound and shaking of the earth, but all was quiet when he finally became conscious. It was nearly night, and time to leave.

For a moment, he hesitated. It would be easier to huddle here, beside his dead, and let whatever would happen come to him. But within him was a sense of duty that drove him on. In the back of his mind, something stirred, telling him he still had work to do.

He found part of a stale loaf of bread and some hard cheese and started out, munching on them. It was still too light to move safely, but he was going through woods again, and he heard no alien planes. When it grew darker, he turned to the side roads that led in the direction of Wesley.

In his mind was the knowledge that he had to return there. His church lay there; if the human fighters had pushed the aliens back, his people might be there. If not, it was from there that he would have to follow them.

His thoughts were too deep for conscious expression, and too numbed with exhaustion. His legs moved on steadily. One of his shoes had begun to wear through, and his feet were covered with blisters, but he went grimly on. It was his duty to lead his people, now that the aliens were here, as he had led them in easier times. His thinking had progressed no further.

He holed up in a barn that morning, avoiding the house because of the mutilated things that lay on the doorstep where the aliens had apparently left them. And this time he slept with the soundness of complete fatigue, but he awoke to find one fist clenched and extended toward Clyde. He had been dreaming that he was Job, and that God had left him sitting unanswered on his boils until he died, while mutilated corpses moaned around him, asking for leadership he would not give.

It was nearly dawn before he realized that he should have found himself some kind of a car. He had seen none, but there might have been one abandoned somewhere. Doc could probably have found one. It was too late to bother, then. He had come to the outskirts of a tiny town, and started to head beyond it, before realizing that all the towns must have been well searched by now. He turned down the small street, looking for a store where he could find food.

There was a small grocery with a door partly ajar. Amos pushed it open, to the clanging of a bell. Almost immediately, a dog began barking, and a human voice came sharply from the back.

"Down, Shep! Just a minute, I'm a-coming." A door to the rear opened, and a bent old man emerged, carrying a kerosene lamp. "Darned electric's off again! Good thing I stayed. Told them I had to mind my store, but they wanted me to get with them. Had to hide out in the old well. Darned nonsense about—"

He stopped, his eyes blinking behind thick lenses, and his mouth dropped open. He swallowed, and his voice was startled and shrill. "*Mister, who are you?*"

"A man who just escaped from the aliens," Amos told him. He hadn't realized the shocking appearance he must present by now. "One in need of food and a chance to rest until night. But I'm afraid I have no money on me."

The old man tore his eyes away slowly, seeming to shiver. Then he nodded, and pointed to the back. "Never turned nobody away hungry yet," he said, but the words seemed automatic.

An old dog backed slowly under a couch as Amos entered. The man put the lamp down and headed into a tiny kitchen to begin preparing food. Amos reached for the lamp and blew it out. "There really are aliens—worse than you heard," he said.

The old man bristled, met his eyes, and then nodded slowly. "If *you* say so. Only it don't seem logical God would let things like that run around in a decent state like Kansas."

He shoved a plate of eggs onto the table, and Amos pulled it to him, swallowing a mouthful eagerly. He reached for a second, and stopped. Something was violently wrong, suddenly. His stomach heaved, the room began to spin, and his forehead was cold and wet with sweat. He gripped the edge of the table, trying to keep from falling. Then he felt himself being dragged to a cot. He tried to protest, but his body was shaking with ague, and the words that spilled out were senseless. He felt the cot under him, and waves of sick blackness spilled over him.

It was the smell of cooking food that awakened him finally, and he sat up with a feeling that too much time had passed. The old man came from the kitchen, studying him. "You sure were sick, Mister. Guess you ain't used to going without decent food and rest. Feeling okay?"

Amos nodded. He felt a little unsteady, but it was passing. He pulled on the clothes that had been somewhat cleaned for him, and found his way to the table. "What day is it?"

"Saturday, evening," the other answered. "At least the way I figure. Here, eat that and get some coffee in you." He watched until Amos began on the food, and then dropped to a stool to begin cleaning an old rifle and loading it. "You said a lot of things. They true?"

For a second, Amos hesitated. Then he nodded, unable to lie to his benefactor. "I'm afraid so."

"Yeah, I figured so, somehow, looking at you." The old man sighed. "Well, I hope you make wherever you're going."

"What about you?" Amos asked.

The old man sighed, running his hands along the rifle. "I ain't leaving my store for any bunch of aliens. And if the Lord I been doing my duty by all my life decides to put Himself on the wrong side, well, maybe He'll win. But it'll be over my dead body!"

Nothing Amos could say would change his mind. He sat on the front step of the store, the rifle on his lap and the dog at his side, as Amos headed down the street in the starlight.

The minister felt surprisingly better after the first half mile. Rest and food, combined with crude treatment of his sores and blisters, had helped. But the voice inside him was driving him harder now, and the picture of the old man seemed to lend it added strength. He struck out at the fastest pace he could hope to maintain, leaving the town behind and heading down the road that the old man had said led to Wesley.

It was just after midnight that he saw the lights of a group of cars or trucks moving along another road. He had no idea whether they were driven by men or aliens, but he kept steadily on. There were sounds of traffic another time on a road that crossed the small one he followed. But he knew now he was approaching Wesley, and speeded up his pace.

When the first light came, he made no effort to seek shelter. He stared at the land around him, stripped by grasshoppers that could have been killed off if men had worked as hard at ending the insects as they had at their bickerings and wars. He saw the dry, arid land, drifting into dust, and turning a fertile country into a nightmare. Men could put a stop to that.

It had been no act of God that had caused this ruin, but man's own follies. And without help from God, man might set it right in time.

God had deserted men. But mankind hadn't halted. On his own, man had made a path to the moon and had unlocked the atom. He'd found a means, out of his raw courage, to use those bombs against the aliens when miracles were used against him. He had done everything but conquer himself—and he could do that, if he were given time.

Amos saw a truck stop at the crossroads ahead and halted, but the driver was human. He saw the open door and quickened his step toward it. "I'm bound for Wesley!"

"Sure." The driver helped him into the seat. "I'm going back for more supplies myself. You sure look as if you need treatment at the aid station there. I thought we'd rounded up all you strays. Most of them came in right after we sent out the word on Clyde."

"You've taken it?" Amos asked.

The other nodded wearily. "We took it. Got 'em with a bomb, like sitting ducks, then we've been mopping up since. Not many aliens left."

They were nearing the outskirts of Wesley, and Amos pointed to his own house. "If you'll let me off there—"

"Look, I got orders to bring all strays to the aid station," the driver began firmly. Then he swung and faced Amos. For a second, he hesitated. Finally he nodded quietly. "Sure. Glad to help you."

Amos found the water still running. He bathed slowly. Somewhere, he felt his decision had been made, though he was still unsure of what it was. He climbed from the tub at last, and began dressing. There was no suit that was proper, but he found clean clothes. His face in the mirror looked back at him, haggard and bearded, as he reached for the razor.

Then he stopped as he encountered the reflection of his eyes. A shock ran over him, and he backed away a step. They were eyes foreign to everything in him. He had seen a shadow of what lay in them only once, in the eyes of a great evangelist; and this was a hundred times stronger. He tore his glance away to find himself shivering, and avoided them all through the shaving. Oddly, though, there was a strange satisfaction in what he had seen. He was beginning to understand why the old man had believed him, and why the truck driver had obeyed him.

Most of Wesley had returned, and there were soldiers on the streets. As he approached the church, he saw the first-aid station, hectic with business. And a camera crew was near it, taking shots for television of those who had managed to escape from alien territory after the bombing.

A few people called to him, but he went on until he reached the church steps. The door was still in ruins and the bell was gone. Amos stood quietly waiting, his mind focusing slowly as he stared at the people who were just beginning to recognize him and to spread hasty words from mouth to mouth. Then he saw little Angela An-duccini, and motioned for her to come to him. She hesitated briefly, before following him inside and to the organ.

The little Hammond still functioned. Amos climbed to the pul-pit, hearing the old familiar creak of the boards. He put his hands on the lectern, seeing the heavy knuckles and blue veins of age as he opened the Bible and made ready for his Sunday-morning con-gregation. He straightened his shoulders and turned to face the pews, waiting as they came in.

There were only a few at first. Then more and more came, some from old habit, some from curiosity, and many only because they had heard that he had been captured in person, probably. The camera crew came to the back and set up their machines, flooding him with bright lights and adjusting their telelens. He smiled on them, nod-ding.

He knew his decision now. It had been made in pieces and tatters. It had come from Kant, who had spent his life looking for a basic ethical principle, and had boiled it down in his statement that men must be treated as ends, not as means. It had been distilled from Doc's final challenge, and the old man sitting in his doorway.

There could be no words with which to give his message to those who waited. No orator had ever possessed such a command of lan-guage. But men with rude speech and limited use of what they had had fired the world before. Moses had come down from a mountain with a face that shone, and had overcome the objections of a stiff-necked people. Peter the Hermit had preached a thankless crusade to all of Europe, without radio or television. It was more than words or voice.

He looked down at them when the church was filled and the organ hushed.

"My text for today," he announced, and the murmurs below him hushed as his voice reached out to the pews. "Ye shall know the truth and the truth shall make men free!"

He stopped for a moment, studying them, feeling the decision in his mind, and knowing he could make no other. The need of him lay here, among those he had always tried to serve while believing he was serving God through them. He was facing them as an end, not as a means, and he found it good.

Nor could he lie to them now, and deceive them with false hopes. They would need all the facts if they were to make an end to their bickerings and to unite themselves in the final struggle for the fullness of their potential glory.

"I have come back from captivity among the aliens," he began. "I have seen the hordes who have no desire but to erase the memory of man from the dust of the earth that bore him. I have stood at the altar of their God. I have heard the voice of God proclaim that He is also our God, and that He has cast us out. I have believed Him, as I believe Him now."

He felt the strange, intangible something that was greater than words or oratory flow out of him, as it had never flowed in his envied younger days. He watched the shock and the doubt arise and disappear slowly as he went on, giving them the story and the honest doubts he still had. He could never know many things, or even whether the God worshipped on the altar was wholly the same God who had been in the hearts of men for a hundred generations. No man could understand enough. They were entitled to all his doubts, as well as to all that he knew.

He paused at last, in the utter stillness of the chapel. He straightened and smiled down at them, drawing the smile out of some reserve that had lain dormant since he had first tasted inspiration as a boy. He saw a few smiles answer him, and then more—uncertain, doubtful smiles that grew more sure as they spread.

"God has ended the ancient covenants and declared Himself an enemy of all mankind," Amos said, and the chapel seemed to roll with his voice. "I say this to you: He has found a worthy opponent."

FREDERIK POHL

b. 1919

Frederik Pohl was a boy genius who's grown into one of the Grand Masters. And he continues to produce high quality, readable fiction for fans who eagerly await each new book or story. But not to neglect those early years, I have to tell you of the various ways he contributed to shaping the field as we know it today.

For example, he had a turn as one of the most powerful literary agents in the field of SF in the early 1950s, representing nearly everyone who is still remembered, including many of the other Grand Masters like his lifelong friend and fellow Futurian Isaac Asimov, and Hal Clement (Harry Stubbs), our most recent Grand Master. He won awards for his magazine editing also in the 1950s and 1960s, and served several major publishers as a book editor into the 1970's. Kingsley Amis, in his seminal analysis of SF, *The New Maps of Hell*, had already described Fred as "the most consistently able writer" science fiction had produced, even though at that time Fred hadn't yet written either of his Nebula-winning novels, *Man Plus* and *Gateway*. He still lectures all over the world and teaches at colleges and universities from time to time.

The list of SF awards he has won includes the Edward E. Smith and Donald A. Wolheim Awards, the French *Prix Apollo*, the Yugoslavian *Vizija*, two John W. Campbell Memorial Awards (for best novel of the year), and of course three Nebulas and six Hugos, with the distinction among Hugo winners of being the only one to earn them as both editor and writer. From academia he's also won the Science Fiction Research Association's Thomas Clareson Award for service to their organization and the Popular Culture Association annual award. In the mundane world he's received the American

Book Award and the United Nations Society of Writers Award. He's an elected fellow of the British Interplanetary Society and the American Association for the Advancement of Science. Golly! Our home is so full of plaques and scrolls and sculpted awards that we don't have shelf or wall space to display most of them. He served his fellow writers as a member of the Authors' Guild council and as president of the Science Fiction Writers of America and of World SF, the international association for professionals in SF.

What a life it's been! Although it is more a chronicle of the development of science fiction than an autobiography, if you want to know what his earlier years were like, I highly recommend his memoir, *The Way the Future Was*.

The Fred I've known for the last twenty-five years has always been a rather private fellow. In company he's quite cordial and urbane, but his preference is for solitude, and he told me early on in our relationship, "Watching a writer work is a pretty boring business. The exciting part is going on in my head where no one else can see it. I spend a lot of time just staring into space." Being a space-starer a lot of the time myself, I knew then I had met my soulmate.

Although I've read nearly everything Fred's ever written, it's not easy to tell you what he writes about. Malcolm Edwards, a British editor, once tried to explain why it was so hard to "market" Fred. (Editors and publishers talk about writers as if they were merely commodities, but since Fred's been on that side of the business, I've never seen him resent it.) Malcolm declared: "With most other SF writers, you can get a feel for what they've done before and aim toward the target reader who likes that sort of thing with a here's-more-of-the-same pitch. But the reason I like Fred's work and keep buying it is that it's practically *never* the same, even when it's a sequel or part of a series. I treasure the unknown and unfamiliar. The only thing I can count on with a Fred Pohl story is that he'll surprise me. And I hope to reach the market that also values that creativity."

Years ago Ellen Pedersen, interviewing me for a fanzine in Denmark, asked me to identify Fred's principal themes or concerns. Given that each story or novel seems to be not just different in plot and characters but also concerned with some other social issue from the last one—usually something in contemporary society that is bothering Fred at that moment—I was taken aback for a moment. Then before I knew the words were coming out of my mouth I said, "I think Fred really wants everyone to play nice. He's trying to get us all to be more civilized toward each other and be kinder."

Fred makes it a practice to write every day, wherever we are, at home or stuck in some hotel somewhere while it pours outside, whether it's a holiday or not, with a miserable cold or flu, recovering from surgery in the hospital, no matter the circumstances. Fred once described his friend Isaac Asimov as "a perfect writing machine," adding that Isaac had never seen a blank piece of paper he didn't want to cover with words. Now *that's* projecting!

We do a lot of traveling for research, although unlike most researchers we seldom have any fixed idea of what we're looking for, other than something we haven't seen before. (That's not altogether true: we both love England, especially London, and willingly spend time there at least once a year, or as often as possible, and I doubt that we could ever use it up.) When we went to China Fred began *Black Star Rising;* on a more recent trip to Turkey Fred found the setting and main character for "The Boy Who Would Live Forever." If we're stranded somewhere in an airport or train station due to equipment failure or because of a work stoppage, Fred uses the time to write by hand, on a lined yellow pad with a fine-line black felt-tip pen. Fred claims, "For a writer there's no such thing as good experience and bad experience. It's all just experience. It's all grist for my mill."

Another interest we share which has shown up repeatedly in Fred's writing is politics. In a world where most "nice" people affect not to be interested in politics or at least don't want to discuss the subject with anyone but their closest friends, Fred is willing to go out on a limb to express controversial ideas. Years ago he wrote a nonfiction book, a how-to-get-elected primer called *Practical Politics.* It's now a collector's item, if it can be found at all, since libraries rarely purchased paperbacks in those days and they weren't printed on acid-free paper. One of his novels that *can* usually be found in public libraries with any sizable collection of SF is his much under-rated book, *The Years of the City,* a future history of his beloved New York City. Among his more intriguing ideas in this story is the selective service Congress, whereby representatives are chosen from among all citizens by lot rather than by ballot, eliminating the need for fund-raising for campaign financing, with its concomitant evils of favors owed to large donors. By this method, lots of rogues and dim minds get chosen, of course, but then there are many of those in Congress as it is, aren't there? And the big advantage is that *most* people are honest and will rise to the call, trying their best to enact just laws, if for no other reason than that they themselves will have to live with the consequences of their legislation when they return to civilian life at the end of their relatively short tour of duty.

Fred likes to think about the future and about the changes that might occur, at least some of which will be pleasant for us, although surely not all. His own favorite of all his stories is here in this collection, "Day Million"—a projection a million days into the future. This is another one written before we met, but he reports that he wrote it in a single sitting, without effort, without his customary method of painstaking rewriting of rewriting. He is so fond of it, in fact, that he says he'd be pleased to have it used as an epitaph, engraved on his tombstone. Doesn't that make you want to start reading it right now?

—Elizabeth Anne Hull

Recommended Reading
by Frederik Pohl

The Space Merchants (with C. M. Kornbluth)
Gateway
Man Plus
The World at the End of Time
The Voices of Heaven

LET THE ANTS TRY

Gordy survived the Three-Hour War, even though Detroit didn't; he was on his way to Washington, with his blueprints and models in his bag, when the bombs struck.

He had left his wife behind in the city, and not even a trace of her body was ever found. The children, of course, weren't as lucky as that. Their summer camp was less than twenty miles away, and unfortunately in the direction of the prevailing wind. But they were not in any pain until the last few days of the month they had left to live. Gordy managed to fight his way back through the snarled, frantic airline controls to them. Even though he knew they would certainly die of radiation sickness, and they suspected it, there was still a whole blessed week of companionship before the pain got too bad.

That was about all the companionship Gordy had for that whole year.

He came back to Detroit, as soon as the radioactivity had died down; he had nowhere else to go. He found a house on the outskirts of the city, and tried to locate someone to buy it from. But the Emergency Administration laughed at him. "Move in, if you're crazy enough to stay."

When Gordy thought about it all, it occurred to him that he was in a sort of state of shock. His fine, trained mind almost stopped functioning. He ate and slept, and when it grew cold he shivered and built fires, and that was all. The War Department wrote him two or three times, and finally a government man came around to ask what had happened to the things that Gordy had promised to bring to Washington. But he looked queerly at the pink, hairless mice that fed unmolested in the filthy kitchen, and he stood a careful distance away from Gordy's hairy face and torn clothes.

He said, "The Secretary sent me here, Mr. Gordy. He takes a personal interest in your discovery."

Gordy shook his head. "The Secretary is dead," he said. "They were all killed when Washington went."

"There's a new Secretary," the man explained. He puffed on his cigarette and tossed it into the patch Gordy was scrabbling into a truck garden. "Arnold Cavanagh. He knows a great deal about you, and he told me, 'If Salva Gordy has a weapon, we must have it. Our strength has been shattered. Tell Gordy we need his help.' "

Gordy crossed his hands like a lean Buddha.

"I haven't got a weapon," he said.

"You have something that can be used as a weapon. You wrote to Washington, before the war came, and said—"

"The war is over," said Salva Gordy. The government man sighed, and tried again, but in the end he went away. He never came back. The thing, Gordy thought, was undoubtedly written off as a crackpot idea after the man made his report; it was exactly that kind of a discovery, anyhow.

It was May when John de Terry appeared. Gordy was spading his garden. "Give me something to eat," said the voice behind Gordy's back.

Salva Gordy turned around and saw the small, dirty man who spoke. He rubbed his mouth with the back of his hand. "You'll have to work for it," he said.

"All right." The newcomer set down his pack. "My name is John de Terry. I used to live here in Detroit."

Salva Gordy said, "So did I."

Gordy fed the man, and accepted a cigarette from him after they had eaten. The first puffs made him light-headed—it had been that long since he'd smoked—and through the smoke he looked at John de Terry amiably enough. Company would be all right, he thought. The pink mice had been company, of a sort; but it turned out that the mutation that made them hairless had also given them an appetite for meat. And after the morning when he had awakened to find tiny toothmarks in his leg, he'd had to destroy them. And there had been no other animal since, nothing but the ants.

"Are you going to stay?" Gordy asked.

De Terry said, "If I can. What's your name?" When Gordy told him, some of the animal look went out of his eyes, and wonder took its place. "*Doctor* Salva Gordy?" he asked. "Mathematics and physics in Pasadena?"

"Yes, I used to teach at Pasadena."

"And I studied there." John de Terry rubbed absently at his ruined clothes. "That was a long time ago. You didn't know me; I majored in biology. But I knew you."

Gordy stood up and carefully put out the stub of his cigarette. "It was too long ago," he said. "I hardly remember. Shall we work in the garden now?"

Together they sweated in the spring sunlight that afternoon, and Gordy discovered that what had been hard work for one man went quickly enough for two. They worked clear to the edge of the plot before the sun reached the horizon. John de Terry stopped and leaned on his spade, panting.

He gestured to the rank growth beyond Gordy's patch. "We can make a bigger garden," he said. "Clear out that truck, and plant more food. We might even—" He stopped. Gordy was shaking his head.

"You can't clear it out," said Gordy. "It's rank stuff, a sort of crabgrass with a particularly tough root. I can't even cut it. It's all around here, and it's spreading."

De Terry grimaced. "Mutation?"

"I think so. And look." Gordy beckoned to the other man and led him to the very edge of the cleared area. He bent down, picked up something red and wriggling between his thumb and forefinger.

De Terry took it from his hand. "Another mutation?" He brought the thing close to his eyes. "It's almost like an ant," he said. "Except—well, the thorax is all wrong. And it's soft-bodied." He fell silent, examining the thing.

He said something under his breath, and threw the insect from him. "You wouldn't have a microscope, I suppose? No—and yet, that thing is hard to believe. It's an ant, but it doesn't seem to have a tracheal breathing system at all. It's something different."

"Everything's different," Gordy said. He pointed to a couple of abandoned rows. "I had carrots there. At least, I thought they were carrots; when I tried to eat them they made me sick." He sighed heavily. "Humanity has had its chance, John," he said. "The atomic bomb wasn't enough; we had to turn everything into a weapon. Even I, I made a weapon out of something that had nothing to do with war. And our weapons have blown up in our faces."

De Terry grinned. "Maybe the ants will do better. It's their turn now."

"I wish it were." Gordy stirred earth over the boiling entrance to an anthole and watched the insects in their consternation. "They're too small, I'm afraid."

"Why, no. These ants are different Dr. Gordy. Insects have always been small because their breathing system is so poor. But these are mutated. I think—I think they actually have lungs. They could grow, Dr. Gordy. And if ants were the size of men . . . they'd rule the world."

"Lunged ants!" Gordy's eyes gleamed. "Perhaps they will rule the world, John. Perhaps when the human race finally blows itself up once and for all . . ."

De Terry shook his head, and looked down again at his tattered, filthy clothes. "The next blow-up is the last blow-up," he said. "The ants come too late, by millions and millions of years."

He picked up his spade. "I'm hungry again, Dr. Gordy," he said.

They went back to the house and, without conversation, they ate. Gordy was preoccupied, and de Terry was too new in the household to force him to talk.

It was sundown when they had finished, and Gordy moved slowly to light a lamp. Then he stopped.

"It's your first night, John," he said. "Come down cellar. We'll start the generator and have real electric lights in your honor."

De Terry followed the older man down a flight of stairs, groping in the dark. By candlelight they worked over a gasoline generator; it was stiff from disuse, but once it started it ran cleanly. "I salvaged it from my own," Gordy explained. "The generator—and that."

He swept an arm toward a corner of the basement. "I told you I invented a weapon," he added. "That's it."

De Terry looked. It was as much like a cage as anything, he thought—the height of a man and almost cubical. "What does it do?" he asked.

For the first time in months, Salva Gordy smiled. "I can't tell you in English," he said. "And I doubt that you speak mathematics. The closest I can come is to say that it displaces temporal co-ordinates. Is that gibberish?"

"It is," said de Terry. "What does it do?"

"Well, the War Department had a name for it—a name they borrowed from H. G. Wells. They called it a Time Machine." He met de Terry's shocked, bewildered stare calmly. "A time machine," he repeated. "You see, John, we can give the ants a chance after all, if you like."

Fourteen hours later they stepped into the cage, its batteries charged again and its strange motor whining . . .

And, forty million years earlier, they stepped out onto quaking, humid soil.

Gordy felt himself trembling, and with an effort managed to stop. "No dinosaurs or saber-toothed tigers in sight," he reported.

"Not for a long time yet," de Terry agreed. Then, "My Lord!"

He looked around him with his mouth open wide. There was no wind, and the air was warm and wet. Large trees were clustered quite thickly around them—or what looked like trees; de Terry decided they were rather some sort of soft-stemmed ferns of fungi. Overhead was deep cloud.

Gordy shivered. "Give me the ants," he ordered.

Silently de Terry handed them over. Gordy poked a hole in the soft earth with his finger and carefully tilted the flask, dropped one of the ant queens he had unearthed in the back yard. From her belly hung a slimy mass of eggs. A few yards away—it should have been farther, he thought, but he was afraid to get too far from de Terry and the machine—he made another hole and repeated the process.

There were eight queens. When the eighth was buried he flung the bottle away and came back to de Terry.

"That's it," he said.

De Terry exhaled. His solemn face cracked in a sudden embarrassed smile. "I—I guess I feel like God," he said. "Good Lord, Dr. Gordy! Talk about your great moments in history—this is all of them! I've been thinking about it, and the only event I can remember that measures up is the Flood. Not even that. We've created a race!"

"If they survive, we have." Gordy wiped a drop of condensed

moisture off the side of his time machine and puffed. "I wonder how they'll get along with mankind," he said.

They were silent for a moment, considering. From somewhere in the fern jungle came a raucous animal cry. Both men looked up in quick apprehension, but moments passed and the animal did not appear.

Finally de Terry said, "Maybe we'd better go back."

"All right." Stiffly they climbed into the closet-sized interior of the time machine.

Gordy stood with his hand on the control wheel, thinking about the ants. Assuming that they survived—assuming that in 40,000,000 years they grew larger and developed brains—what would happen? Would men be able to live in peace with them? Would it—might it not make men brothers, joined against an alien race?

Might this thing prevent human war, and—his thoughts took an insane leap—could it have prevented the war that destroyed Gordy's family!

Beside him, de Terry stirred restlessly. Gordy jumped, and turned the wheel, and was in the dark mathematical vortex which might have been a fourth dimension.

They stopped the machine in the middle of a city, but the city was not Detroit. It was not a human city at all.

The machine was at rest in a narrow street, half blocking it. Around them towered conical metal structures, some of them a hundred feet high. There were vehicles moving in the street, one coming toward them and stopping.

"Dr. Gordy!" de Terry whispered. "Do you see them?"

Salva Gordy swallowed. "I see them," he said.

He stepped out of the time machine and stood waiting to greet the race to which he had given life.

For these were the children of ants in the three-wheeled vehicle. Behind a transparent windshield he could see them clearly.

De Terry was standing close behind him now, and Gordy could feel the younger man's body shaking. "They're ugly things," Gordy said mildly.

"Ugly! They're filthy!"

The antlike creatures were as big as a man, but hard-looking and as obnoxious as black beetles. Their eyes, Gordy saw with surprise, had mutated more than their bodies. For, instead of faceted insect eyes, they possessed iris, cornea and pupil—not round, or vertical like a cat's eyes, or horizontal like a horse's eyes, but irregular and blotchy. But they seemed like vertebrate's eyes, and they were strange and unnatural in the parchment blackness of an ant's bulged head.

Gordy stepped forward, and simultaneously the ants came out of their vehicle. For a moment they faced each other, the humans and the ants, silently.

"What do I do now?" Gordy asked de Terry over his shoulder.

De Terry laughed—or gasped. Gordy wasn't sure. "Talk to them," he said. "What else is there to do?"

Gordy swallowed. He resolutely did not attempt to speak in English to these creatures, knowing as surely as he knew his name that English—and probably any other language involving sound—would be incomprehensible to them. But he found himself smiling pacifically to them, and that was of course as bad . . . the things had no expressions of their own, that he could see, and certainly they would have no precedent to help interpret a human smile.

Gordy raised his hand in the semantically sound gesture of peace, and waited to see what the insects would do.

They did nothing.

Gordy bit his lip and, feeling idiotic, bowed stiffly to the ants.

The ants did nothing. De Terry said from behind, "Try talking to them, Dr. Gordy."

"That's silly," Gordy said. "They can't hear." But it was no sillier than anything else. Irritably, but making the words very clear, he said, "We . . . are . . . friends."

The ants did nothing. They just stood there, with the unwinking pupiled eyes fixed on Gordy. They didn't shift from foot to foot as a human might, or scratch themselves, or even show the small movement of human breathing. They just stood there.

"Oh, for heaven's sake," said de Terry. "Here, let me try."

He stepped in front of Gordy and faced the ant-things. He pointed to himself. "I am human," he said. "Mammalian." He pointed to the ants. "You are insects. That"—he pointed to the time machine—"took us to the past, where we made it possible for you to exist." He waited for reaction, but there wasn't any. De Terry clicked his tongue and began again. He pointed to the tapering metal structures. "This is your city," he said.

Gordy, listening to him, felt the hopelessness of the effort. Something disturbed the thin hairs at the back of his skull, and he reached absently to smooth them down. His hand encountered something hard and inanimate—not cold, but, like spongy wood, without temperature at all. He turned around. Behind them were half a dozen larger ants. Drones, he thought—or did ants have drones? "John," he said softly . . . and the inefficient, fragile-looking pincer that had touched him clamped his shoulder. There was no strength to it, he thought at once. Until he moved, instinctively, to get away, and then a thousand sharp serrations slipped through the cloth of his coat and into the skin. It was like catching oneself on a cluster of tiny fishhooks. He shouted, "John! Watch out!"

De Terry, bending low for the purpose of pointing at the caterpillar treads of the ant vehicle, straightened up, startled. He turned to run, and was caught in a step. Gordy heard him yell, but Gordy had troubles of his own and could spare no further attention for de Terry.

When two of the ants had him, Gordy stopped struggling. He felt warm blood roll down his arm, and the pain was like being flayed. From where he hung between the ants, he could see the first two, still standing before their vehicle, still motionless.

There was a sour reek in his nostrils, and he traced it to the ants that held him, and wondered if he smelled as bad to them. The two smaller ants abruptly stirred and moved forward rapidly on eight thin legs to the time machine. Gordy's captors turned and followed them, and for the first time since the scuffle he saw de Terry. The younger man was hanging limp from the lifted forelegs of a single ant, with two more standing guard beside. There was pulsing blood from a wound on de Terry's neck. Unconscious, Gordy thought mechanically, and turned his head to watch the ants at the machine.

It was a disappointing sight. They merely stood there, and no one moved. Then Gordy heard de Terry grunt and swear weakly. "How are you, John?" he called.

De Terry grimaced. "Not very good. What happened?"

Gordy shook his head, and sought for words to answer. But the two ants turned in unison from the time machine and glided toward de Terry, and Gordy's words died in his throat. Delicately one of them extended a foreleg to touch de Terry's chest.

Gordy saw it coming. "John!" he shrieked—and then it was all over, and de Terry's scream was harsh in his ear and he turned his head away. Dimly from the corner of his eye he could see the sawlike claws moving up and down, but there was no life left in de Terry to protest.

Salva Gordy sat against a wall and looked at the ants who were looking at him. If it hadn't been for that which was done to de Terry, he thought, there would really be nothing to complain about.

It was true that the ants had given him none of the comforts that humanity lavishes on even its criminals . . . but they had fed him, and allowed him to sleep—when it suited their convenience, of course—and there were small signs that they were interested in his comfort, in their fashion. When the pulpy mush they first offered him came up thirty minutes later, his multi-legged hosts brought him a variety of foods, of which he was able to swallow some fairly palatable fruits. He was housed in a warm room, And, if it had neither chairs or windows, Gordy thought, that was only because ants had no use for these themselves. And he couldn't ask for them.

That was the big drawback, he thought. That . . . and the memory of John de Terry.

He squirmed on the hard floor until his shoulderblades found a new spot to prop themselves against, and stared again at the committee of ants who had come to see him.

They were working an angular thing that looked like a camera—at least, it had a glittering something that might be a lens. Gordy stared into it sullenly. The sour reek was in his nostrils again. . . .

Gordy admitted to himself that things hadn't worked out just as he had planned. Deep under the surface of his mind—just now beginning to come out where he could see it—there had been a furtive hope. He had hoped that the rise of ants, with the help he had given them, would aid and speed the rise of mankind. For hatred, Gordy knew, started in the recoil from things that were different. A man's first enemy is his family—for he sees them first—but he sides with them against the families across the way. And still his neighbors are allies against the Ghettos and Harlems of his town—and his town to him is the heart of the nation—and his nation commands life and death in war.

For Gordy, there had been a buried hope that a separate race would make a whipping-boy for the passions of humanity. And that, if there were struggle, it would not be between man and man, but between the humans . . . and the ants.

There had been this buried hope, but the hope was denied. For the ants simply had not allowed man to rise.

The ants put up their camera-like machine, and Gordy looked up in expectation. Half a dozen of them left, and two stayed on. One was the smallish creature with a bangle on the foreleg which seemed to be his personal jailer; the other a stranger to Gordy, as far as he could tell.

The two ants stood motionless for a period of time that Gordy found tedious. He changed his position, and lay on the floor, and thought of sleeping. But sleep would not come. There was no evading the knowledge that he had wiped out his own race—annihilated them by preventing them from birth, forty million years before his own time. He was like no other murderer since Cain, Gordy thought, and wondered that he felt no blood on his hands.

There was a signal that he could not perceive, and his guardian ant came forward to him, nudged him outward from the wall. He moved as he was directed—out the low exit-hole (he had to navigate it on hands and knees) and down a corridor to the bright day outside.

The light set Gordy blinking. Half blind, he followed the bangled ant across a square to a conical shed. More ants were waiting there, circled around a litter of metal parts. Gordy recognized them at once. It was his time machine, stripped piece by piece.

After a moment the ant nudged him again, impatiently, and Gordy understood what they wanted. They had taken the machine apart for study, and they wanted it put together again.

Pleased with the prospect of something to do with his fingers and his brain, Gordy grinned and reached for the curious ant-made tools. . . .

He ate four times, and slept once, never moving from the neighborhood of the cone-shaped shed. And then he was finished.

Gordy stepped back. "It's all yours," he said proudly. "It'll take you anywhere. A present from humanity to you."

The ants were very silent. Gordy looked at them and saw drone-ants in the group, all still as statues.

"Hey!" he said in startlement, unthinking. And then the needle-jawed ant claw took him from behind.

Gordy had a moment of nausea—and then terror and hatred swept it away.

Heedless of the needles that laced his skin, he struggled and kicked against the creatures that held him. One arm came free, leaving gobbets of flesh behind, and his heavy shod foot plunged into a pulpy eye. The ant made a whistling, gasping sound and stood erect on four hairy legs.

Gordy felt himself jerked a dozen feet into the air, then flung free in the wild, silent agony of the ant. He crashed into the ground, cowering away from the staggering monster. Sobbing, he pushed himself to his feet; the machine was behind him; he turned and blundered into it a step ahead of the other ants, and spun the wheel.

A hollow insect leg, detached from the ant that had been closest to him, was flopping about on the floor of the machine; it had been that close.

Gordy stopped the machine where it had started, on the same quivering, primordial bog, and lay crouched over the controls for a long time before he moved.

He had made a mistake, he and de Terry; there weren't any doubts left at all. And there was . . . there *might* be a way to right it.

He looked out at the Coal Measure forest. The fern trees were not the fern trees he had seen before; the machine had been moved in space. But the time, he knew, was identically the same; trust the machine for that. He thought: I gave the world to the ants, right here. I can take it back. I can find the ants I buried and crush them underfoot . . . or intercept myself before I bury them. . . .

He got out of the machine, suddenly panicky. Urgency squinted his eyes as he peered around him.

Death had been very close in the ant city; the reaction still left Gordy limp. And was he safe there? He remembered the violent animal scream he had heard before, and shuddered at the thought of furnishing a casual meal to some dinosaur . . . while the ant queens lived safely to produce their horrid young.

A gleam of metal through the fern trees made his heart leap. Burnished metal here could mean but one thing—the machine!

Around a clump of fern trees, their bases covered with thick club mosses, he ran, and saw the machine ahead. He raced toward it—then came to a sudden stop, slipping on the damp ground. For there were *two* machines in sight.

The farther machine was his own, and through the screening

mosses he could see two figures standing in it, his own and de Terry's.

But the nearer was a larger machine, and a strange design.

And from it came a hastening mob—not a mob of men, but of black insect shapes racing toward him.

Of course, thought Gordy, as he turned hopelessly to run—of course, the ants had infinite time to work in. Time enough to build a machine after the pattern of his own—and time to realize what they had to do to him, to insure their own race safety.

Gordy stumbled, and the first of the black things was upon him.

As his panicky lungs filled with air for the last time, Gordy knew what animal had screamed in the depths of the Coal Measure forest.

THE TUNNEL UNDER THE WORLD

On the morning of June 15th, Guy Burckhardt woke up screaming out of a dream.

It was more real than any dream he had ever had in his life. He could still hear and feel the sharp, ripping-metal explosion, the violent heave that had tossed him furiously out of bed, the searing wave of heat.

He sat up convulsively and stared, not believing what he saw, at the quiet room and the bright sunlight coming in the window.

He croaked, "Mary?"

His wife was not in the bed next to him. The covers were tumbled and awry, as though she had just left it, and the memory of the dream was so strong that instinctively he found himself searching the floor to see if the dream explosion had thrown her down.

But she wasn't there. Of course she wasn't, he told himself, looking at the familiar vanity and slipper chair, the uncracked window, the unbuckled wall. It had only been a dream.

"Guy?" His wife was calling him querulously from the foot of the stairs. "Guy, dear, are you all right?"

He called weakly, "Sure."

There was a pause. Then Mary said doubtfully, "Breakfast is ready. Are you sure you're all right? I thought I heard you yelling."

Burckhardt said more confidently, "I had a bad dream, honey. Be right down."

In the shower, punching the lukewarm-and-cologne he favored, he told himself that it had been a beaut of a dream. Still bad dreams weren't unusual, especially bad dreams about explosions. In the past thirty years of H-bomb jitters, who had not dreamed of explosions?

Even Mary had dreamed of them, it turned out, for he started to tell her about the dream, but she cut him off. "You *did?*" Her voice was astonished. "Why, dear, I dreamed the same thing! Well, almost the same thing. I didn't actually *hear* anything. I dreamed that something woke me up, and then there was a sort of quick bang, and then something hit me on the head. And that was all. Was yours like that?"

Burckhardt coughed. "Well, no," he said. Mary was not one of the strong-as-a-man, brave-as-a-tiger women. It was not necessary, he thought, to tell her all the little details of the dream that made it seem so real. No need to mention the splintered ribs, and the salt bubble in his throat, and the agonized knowledge that this was death. He said, "Maybe there really was some kind of explosion downtown. Maybe we heard it and it started us dreaming."

Mary reached over and patted his hand absently. "Maybe," she agreed. "It's almost half-past eight, dear. Shouldn't you hurry? You don't want to be late to the office."

He gulped his food, kissed her and rushed out—not so much to be on time as to see if his guess had been right.

But downtown Tylerton looked as it always had. Coming in on the bus, Burckhardt watched critically out the window, seeking evidence of an explosion. There wasn't any. If anything, Tylerton looked better than it ever had before. It was a beautiful crisp day, the sky was cloudless, the buildings were clean and inviting. They had, he observed, steam-blasted the Power & Light Building, the town's only skyscraper—that was the penalty of having Contro Chemical's main plant on the outskirts of town; the fumes from the cascade stills left their mark on stone buildings.

None of the usual crowd were on the bus, so there wasn't anyone Burckhardt could ask about the explosion. And by the time he got out at the corner of Fifth and Lehigh and the bus rolled away with a muted diesel moan, he had pretty well convinced himself that it was all imagination.

He stopped at the cigar stand in the lobby of his office building, but Ralph wasn't behind the counter. The man who sold him his pack of cigarettes was a stranger.

"Where's Mr. Stebbins?" Burckhardt asked.

The man said politely, "Sick, sir. He'll be in tomorrow. A pack of Marlins today?"

"Chesterfields," Burckhardt corrected.

"Certainly, sir," the man said. But what he took from the rack and slid across the counter was an unfamiliar green-and-yellow pack.

"Do try these, sir," he suggested. "They contain an anti-cough factor. Ever notice how ordinary cigarettes make you choke every once in a while?"

Burckhardt said suspiciously, "I never heard of this brand."

"Of course not. They're something new." Burckhardt hesitated, and the man said persuasively, "Look, try them out at my risk. If you don't like them, bring back the empty pack and I'll refund your money. Fair enough?"

Burckhardt shrugged. "How can I lose? But give me a pack of Chesterfields, too, will you?"

He opened the pack and lit one while he waited for the elevator. They weren't bad, he decided, though he was suspicious of cigarettes that had the tobacco chemically treated in any way. But he didn't think much of Ralph's stand-in; it would raise hell with the trade at the cigar stand if the man tried to give every customer the same high-pressure sales talk.

The elevator door opened with a low-pitched sound of music. Burckhardt and two or three others got in and he nodded to them as the door closed. The thread of music switched off and the speaker in the ceiling of the cab began its usual commercials.

No, not the *usual* commercials, Burckhardt realized. He had been exposed to the captive-audience commercials so long that they hardly registered on the outer ear any more, but what was coming from the recorded program in the basement of the building caught his attention. It wasn't merely that the brands were mostly unfamiliar; it was a difference in pattern.

There were jingles with an insistent, bouncy rhythm, about soft drinks he had never tasted. There was a rapid patter dialogue between what sounded like two ten-year-old boys about a candy bar, followed by an authoritative bass rumble: "Go right out and get a DELICIOUS Choco-Bite and eat your TANGY Choco-bite *all up*. That's *Choco-Bite!*" There was a sobbing female whine: "I *wish* I had a Feckle Freezer! I'd do *anything* for a Feckle Freezer!" Burckhardt reached his floor and left the elevator in the middle of the last one. It left him a little uneasy. The commercials were not for familiar brands; there was no feeling of use and custom to them.

But the office was happily normal—except that Mr. Barth wasn't in. Miss Mitkin, yawning at the reception desk, didn't know exactly why. "His home phoned, that's all. He'll be in tomorrow."

"Maybe he went to the plant. It's right near his house."

She looked indifferent. "Yeah."

A thought struck Burckhardt. "But today is June 15th! It's quarterly tax return day—he has to sign the return!"

Miss Mitkin shrugged to indicate that that was Burckhardt's problem, not hers. She returned to her nails.

Thoroughly exasperated, Burckhardt went to his desk. It wasn't that he couldn't sign the tax returns as well as Barth, he thought resentfully. It simply wasn't his job, that was all; it was a responsibility that Barth, as office manager for Contro Chemicals' downtown office, should have taken.

He thought briefly of calling Barth at his home or trying to reach him at the factory, but he gave up the idea quickly enough. He didn't really care much for the people at the factory and the less contact he had with them, the better. He had been to the factory once, with Barth; it had been a confusing and, in a way, a frightening experience. Barring a handful of executives and engineers, there wasn't a soul in the factory—that is, Burckhardt corrected himself, remembering what Barth had told him, not a *living* soul—just the machines.

According to Barth, each machine was controlled by a sort of computer which reproduced, in its electronic snarl, the actual memory and mind of a human being. It was an unpleasant thought. Barth, laughing, had assured him that there was no Frankenstein business of robbing graveyards and implanting brains in machines. It was only a matter, he said, of transferring a man's habit patterns from brain cells to vacuum-tube cells. It didn't hurt the man and it didn't make the machine into a monster.

But they made Burckhardt uncomfortable all the same.

He put Barth and the factory and all his other little irritations out of his mind and tackled the tax returns. It took him until noon to verify the figures—which Barth could have done out of his memory and his private ledger in ten minutes, Burckhardt resentfully reminded himself.

He sealed them in an envelope and walked out to Miss Mitkin. "Since Mr. Barth isn't here, we'd better go to lunch in shifts," he said. "You can go first."

"Thanks." Miss Mitkin languidly took her bag out of the desk drawer and began to apply makeup.

Burckhardt offered her the envelope. "Drop this in the mail for me, will you? Uh—wait a minute. I wonder if I ought to phone Mr. Barth to make sure. Did his wife say whether he was able to take phone calls?"

"Didn't say." Miss Mitkin blotted her lips carefully with a Kleenex. "Wasn't his wife, anyway. It was his daughter who called and left the message."

"The kid?" Burckhardt frowned. "I thought she was away at school."

"She called, that's all I know."

Burckhardt went back to his own office and stared distastefully at the unopened mail on his desk. He didn't like nightmares; they spoiled his whole day. He should have stayed in bed, like Barth.

A funny thing happened on his way home. There was a disturbance at the corner where he usually caught his bus—someone was screaming something about a new kind of deep-freeze—so he walked an extra block. He saw the bus coming and started to trot. But behind him, someone was calling his name. He looked over his shoulder; a small harried-looking man was hurrying toward him.

Burckhardt hesitated, and then recognized him. It was a casual acquaintance named Swanson. Burckhardt sourly observed that he had already missed the bus.

He said, "Hello."

Swanson's face was desperately eager. "Burckhardt?" he asked inquiringly, with an old intensity. And then he just stood there silently, watching Burckhardt's face, with a burning eagerness that dwindled to a faint hope and died to a regret. He was searching for something, waiting for something, Burckhardt thought. But whatever it was he wanted, Burckhardt didn't know how to supply it.

Burckhardt coughed and said again, "Hello, Swanson."

Swanson didn't even acknowledge the greeting. He merely sighed a very deep sigh.

"Nothing doing," he mumbled, apparently to himself. He nodded abstractedly to Burckhardt and turned away.

Burckhardt watched the slumped shoulders disappear in the crowd. It was an *odd* sort of day, he thought, and one he didn't much like. Things weren't going right.

Riding home on the next bus, he brooded about it. It wasn't anything terrible or disastrous; it was something out of his experience entirely. You live your life, like any man, and you form a network of impressions and reactions. You *expect* things. When you open your medicine chest, your razor is expected to be on the second shelf; when you lock your front door, you expect to have to give it a slight extra tug to make it latch.

It isn't the things that are right and perfect in your life that make it familiar. It is the things that are just a little bit wrong—the sticking latch, the light switch at the head of the stairs that needs an extra push because the spring is old and weak, the rug that unfailingly skids underfoot.

It wasn't just that things were wrong with the pattern of Burckhardt's life; it was that the *wrong* things were wrong. For instance, Barth hadn't come into the office, yet Barth *always* came in.

Burckhardt brooded about it through dinner. He brooded about it, despite his wife's attempt to interest him in a game of bridge with the neighbors, all through the evening. The neighbors were people he liked—Anne and Farley Dennerman. He had known them all their lives. But they were odd and brooding, too, this night and he barely listened to Dennerman's complaints about not being able to get good phone service or his wife's comments on the disgusting variety of television commercials they had these days.

Burckhardt was well on the way to setting an all-time record for continuous abstraction when, around midnight, with a suddenness that surprised him—he was strangely *aware* of it happening—he turned over in his bed and, quickly and completely, fell asleep.

On the morning of June 15th, Burckhardt woke up screaming.

It was more real than any dream he had ever had in his life. He could still hear the explosion, feel the blast that crushed him against a wall. It did not seem right that he should be sitting bolt upright in bed in an undisturbed room.

His wife came pattering up the stairs. "Darling!" she cried. "What's the matter?"

He mumbled, "Nothing. Bad dream."

She relaxed, hand on heart. In an angry tone, she started to say: "You gave me such a shock—"

But a noise from outside interrupted her. There was a wail of sirens and a clang of bells; it was loud and shocking.

The Burckhardts stared at each other for a heartbeat, then hurried fearfully to the window.

There was no rumbling fire engines in the street, only a small panel truck, cruising slowly along. Flaring loudspeaker horns crowned its top. From them issued the screaming sound of sirens, growing in intensity, mixed with the rumble of heavy-duty engines and the sound of bells. It was a perfect record of fire engines arriving at a four-alarm blaze.

Burckhardt said in amazement, "Mary, that's against the law! Do you know what they're doing? They're playing records of a fire. What are they up to?"

"Maybe it's a practical joke," his wife offered.

"Joke? Waking up the whole neighborhood at six o'clock in the morning?" He shook his head. "The police will be here in ten minutes," he predicted. "Wait and see."

But the police weren't—not in ten minutes, or at all. Whoever the pranksters in the car were, they apparently had a police permit for their games.

The car took a position in the middle of the block and stood silent for a few minutes. Then there was a crackle from the speaker, and a giant voice chanted:

> "Feckle Freezers!
> Feckle Freezers!
> Gotta have a
> Feckle Freezer!
> Feckle, Feckle, Feckle,
> Feckle, Feckle, Feckle—"

It went on and on. Every house on the block had faces staring out of windows by then. The voice was not merely loud; it was nearly deafening.

Burckhardt shouted to his wife, over the uproar, "What the hell is a Feckle Freezer?"

"Some kind of a freezer, I guess, dear," she shrieked back unhelpfully.

Abruptly the noise stopped and the truck stood silent. It was still misty morning; the sun's rays came horizontally across the rooftops. It was impossible to believe that, a moment ago, the silent block had been bellowing the name of a freezer.

"A crazy advertising trick," Burckhardt said bitterly. He yawned and turned away from the window. "Might as well get dressed. I guess that's the end of—"

The bellow caught him from behind; it was almost like a hard slap on the ears. A harsh, sneering voice, louder than the archangel's trumpet, howled:

"Have you got a freezer? *It stinks!* If it isn't a Feckle Freezer, *it stinks!* If it's a last year's Feckle Freezer, *it stinks!* Only this year's Feckle Freezer is any good at all! You know who owns an Ajax Freezer? Fairies own Ajax Freezers! You know who owns a Triplecold Freezer? Commies own Triplecold Freezers! Every freezer but a brand-new Feckle Freezer *stinks!*"

The voice screamed inarticulately with rage. "I'm warning you! Get out and buy a Feckle Freezer right away! Hurry up! Hurry for Feckle! Hurry for Feckle! Hurry, hurry, hurry, Feckle, Feckle, Feckle, Feckle, Feckle, Feckle, Feckle . . ."

It stopped eventually. Burckhardt licked his lips. He started to say to his wife, "Maybe we ought to call the police about—" when the speakers erupted again. It caught him off guard; it was intended to catch him off guard. It screamed:

"Feckle, Feckle, Feckle, Feckle, Feckle, Feckle, Feckle, Feckle. Cheap freezers ruin your food. You'll get sick and throw up. You'll get sick and die. Buy a Feckle, Feckle, Feckle, Feckle! Ever take a piece of meat out of the freezer you've got and see how rotten and moldy it is? Buy a Feckle, Feckle, Feckle, Feckle, Feckle. Do you want to eat rotten, stinking food? Or do you want to wise up and buy a Feckle, Feckle, Feckle—"

That did it. With fingers that kept stabbing the wrong holes, Burckhardt finally managed to dial the local police station. He got a busy signal—it was apparent that he was not the only one with the same idea—and while he was shakily dialing again, the noise outside stopped.

He looked out the window. The truck was gone.

•   •   •

Burckhardt loosened his tie and ordered another Frosty-Flip from the waiter. If only they wouldn't keep the Crystal Cafe so *hot!* The new paint job—searing reds and blinding yellows—was bad enough, but someone seemed to have the delusion that this was January instead of June; the place was a good ten degrees warmer than outside.

He swallowed the Frosty-Flip in two gulps. It had a kind of peculiar flavor, he thought, but not bad. It certainly cooled you off, just as the waiter had promised. He reminded himself to pick up a carton of them on the way home; Mary might like them. She was always interested in something new.

He stood up awkwardly as the girl came across the restaurant toward him. She was the most beautiful thing he had ever seen in Tylerton. Chin-height, honey-blond hair and a figure that—well, it was all hers. There was no doubt in the world that the dress that clung to her was the only thing she wore. He felt as if he were blushing as she greeted him.

"Mr. Burckhardt." The voice was like distant tomtoms. "It's wonderful of you to let me see you, after this morning."

He cleared his throat. "Not at all. Won't you sit down, Miss—"

"April Horn," she murmured, sitting down—beside him, not where he had pointed on the other side of the table. "Call me April, won't you?"

She was wearing some kind of perfume, Burckhardt noted with what little of his mind was functioning at all. It didn't seem fair that she should be using perfume as well as everything else. He came to with a start and realized that the waiter was leaving with an order for *filets mignon* for two.

"Hey!" he objected.

"Please, Mr. Burckhardt." Her shoulder was against his, her face was turned to him, her breath was warm, her expression was tender and solicitous. "This is all on the Feckle Corporation. Please let them—it's the *least* they can do."

He felt her hand burrowing into his pocket.

"I put the price of the meal into your pocket," she whispered conspiratorially. "Please do that for me, won't you? I mean I'd appreciate it if you'd pay the waiter—I'm old-fashioned about things like that."

She smiled meltingly, then became mock-businesslike. "But you must take the money," she insisted. "Why, you're letting Feckle off lightly if you do! You could sue them for every nickel they've got, disturbing your sleep like that."

With a dizzy feeling, as though he had just seen someone make a rabbit disappear into a top hat, he said, "Why, it really wasn't so bad, uh, April. A little noisy, maybe, but—"

"Oh, Mr. Burckhardt!" The blue eyes were wide and admiring. "I *knew* you'd understand. It's just that—well, it's such a *wonderful* freezer that some of the outside men get carried away, so to speak. As soon as the main office found out about what happened, they sent representatives around to every house on the block to apologize. Your wife told us where we could phone you—and I'm so very pleased that you were willing to let me have lunch with you, so that I could apologize, too. Because truly, Mr. Burckhardt, it is a *fine* freezer.

"I shouldn't tell you this, but"—the blue eyes were shyly lowered—"I'd do almost anything for Feckle Freezers. It's more than a job to me." She looked up. She was enchanting. "I bet you think I'm silly, don't you?"

Burckhardt coughed. "Well, I—"

"Oh, you don't want to be unkind!" She shook her head. "No, don't pretend. You think it's silly. But really, Mr. Burckhardt, you wouldn't think so if you knew more about the Feckle. Let me show you this little booklet—"

Burckhardt got back from lunch a full hour late. It wasn't only the girl who delayed him. There had been a curious interview with a little man named Swanson, whom he barely knew, who had stopped him with desperate urgency on the street—and then left him cold.

But it didn't matter much. Mr. Barth, for the first time since Burckhardt had worked there, was out for the day—leaving Burckhardt stuck with the quarterly tax returns.

What did matter, though, was that somehow he had signed a purchase order for a twelve-cubic-foot Feckle Freezer, upright model, self-defrosting, list price $625, with a ten per cent "courtesy" discount—"Because of that *horrid* affair this morning, Mr. Burckhardt," she had said.

And he wasn't sure how he could explain it to his wife.

THE TUNNEL UNDER THE WORLD   123

•   •   •

He needn't have worried. As he walked in the front door, his wife
said almost immediately, "I wonder if we can't afford a new freezer,
dear. There was a man here to apologize about that noise and—well,
we got to talking and—"

She had signed a purchase order, too.

It had been the damnedest day, Burckhardt thought later, on his
way up to bed. But the day wasn't done with him yet. At the head
of the stairs, the weakened spring in the electric light switch refused
to click at all. He snapped it back and forth angrily and, of course,
succeeded in jarring the tumbler out of its pins. The wires shorted
and every light in the house went out.

"Damn!" said Guy Burckhardt.

"Fuse?" His wife shrugged sleepily. "Let it go till the morning,
dear."

Burckhardt shook his head. "You go back to bed. I'll be right
along."

It wasn't so much that he cared about fixing the fuse, but he
was too restless for sleep. He disconnected the bad switch with a
screwdriver, tumbled down into the black kitchen, found the flashlight and climbed gingerly down the cellar stairs. He located a spare
fuse, pushed an empty trunk over to the fuse box to stand on and
twisted out the old fuse.

When the new one was in, he heard the starting click and steady
drone of the refrigerator in the kitchen overhead.

He headed back to the steps, and stopped.

Where the old trunk had been, the cellar floor gleamed oddly
bright. He inspected it in the flashlight beam. It was metal!

"Son of a gun," said Guy Burckhardt. He shook his head unbelievingly. He peered closer, and rubbed the edges of the metallic
patch with his thumb and acquired an annoying cut—the edges were
sharp.

The stained cement floor of the cellar was a thin shell. He found
a hammer and cracked it off in a dozen spots—everywhere was metal.

The whole cellar was a copper box. Even the cement-brick walls
were false fronts over a metal sheath!

Baffled, he attacked one of the foundation beams. That, at least,
was real wood. The glass in the cellar windows was real glass.

He sucked his bleeding thumb and tried the base of the cellar stairs. Real wood. He chipped at the bricks under the oil burner. Real bricks. The retaining walls, the floor—they were faked.

It was as though someone had shored up the house with a frame of metal and then laboriously concealed the evidence.

The biggest surprise was the upside-down boat hull that blocked the rear half of the cellar, relic of a brief home-workshop period that Burckhardt had gone through a couple of years before. From above, it looked perfectly normal. Inside, though, where there should have been thwarts and seats and lockers, there was a mere tangle of braces, rough and unfinished.

"But I *built* that!" Burckhardt exclaimed, forgetting his thumb. He leaned against the hull dizzily, trying to think this thing through. For reasons beyond his comprehension, someone had taken his boat and his cellar away, maybe his whole house, and replaced them with a clever mock-up of the real thing.

"That's crazy," he said to the empty cellar. He stared around in the light of the flash. He whispered, "What in the name of Heaven would anybody do that for?"

Reason refused an answer; there wasn't any reasonable answer. For long minutes, Burckhardt contemplated the uncertain picture of his own sanity.

He peered under the boat again, hoping to reassure himself that it was a mistake, just his imagination. But the sloppy, unfinished bracing was unchanged. He crawled under for a better look, feeling the rough wood incredulously. Utterly impossible!

He switched off the flashlight and started to wriggle out. But he didn't make it. In the moment between the command to his legs to move and the crawling out, he felt a sudden draining weariness flooding through him.

Consciousness went—not easily, but as though it were being taken away, and Guy Burckhardt was asleep.

On the morning of June 16th, Guy Burckhardt woke up in a cramped position huddled under the hull of the boat in his basement—and raced upstairs to find it was June 15th.

The first thing he had done was to make a frantic, hasty inspection of the boat hull, the faked cellar floor, the imitation stone. They were all as he had remembered them, all completely unbelievable.

The kitchen was its placid, unexciting self. The electric clock was purring soberly around the dial. Almost six o'clock, it said. His wife would be waking at any moment.

Burckhardt flung open the front door and stared out into the quiet street. The morning paper was tossed carelessly against the steps, and as he retrieved it, he noticed that this was the 15th day of June.

But that was impossible. *Yesterday* was the 15th of June. It was not a date one would forget, it was quarterly tax-return day.

He went back into the hall and picked up the telephone; he dialed for Weather Information, and got a well-modulated chant: "—and cooler, some showers. Barometric pressure thirty point zero four, rising . . . United States Weather Bureau forecast for June 15th. Warm and sunny, with high around—"

He hung the phone up. June 15th.

"Holy heaven!" Burckhardt said prayerfully. Things were very odd indeed. He heard the ring of his wife's alarm and bounded up the stairs.

Mary Burckhardt was sitting upright in bed with the terrified, uncomprehending stare of someone just waking out of a nightmare.

"Oh!" she gasped, as her husband came in the room. "Darling, I just had the most *terrible* dream! It was like an explosion and—"

"Again?" Burckhardt asked, not very sympathetically. "Mary, something's funny! I *knew* there was something wrong all day yesterday and—"

He went on to tell her about the copper box that was the cellar, and the odd mock-up someone had made of his boat. Mary looked astonished, then alarmed, then placatory and uneasy.

She said, "Dear, are you *sure*? Because I was cleaning that old trunk out just last week and I didn't notice anything."

"Positive!" said Guy Burckhardt. "I dragged it over to the wall to step on it to put a new fuse in after we blew the lights out and—"

"After we what?" Mary was looking more than merely alarmed.

"After we blew the lights out. You know, when the switch at the head of the stairs stuck. I went down to the cellar and—"

Mary sat up in bed. "Guy, the switch didn't stick. I turned out the lights myself last night."

Burckhardt glared at his wife. "Now I *know* you didn't! Come here and take a look!"

He stalked out to the landing and dramatically pointed to the bad switch, the one that he had unscrewed and left hanging the night before . . .

Only it wasn't. It was as it had always been. Unbelieving, Burckhardt pressed it and the lights sprang up in both halls.

Mary, looking pale and worried, left him to go down to the kitchen and start breakfast. Burckhardt stood staring at the switch for a long time. His mental processes were gone beyond the point of disbelief and shock; they simply were not functioning.

He shaved and dressed and ate his breakfast in a state of numb introspection. Mary didn't disturb him; she was apprehensive and soothing. She kissed him good-by as he hurried out to the bus without another word.

Miss Mitkin, at the reception desk, greeted him with a yawn. "Morning," she said drowsily. "Mr. Barth won't be in today."

Burckhardt started to say something, but checked himself. She would not know that Barth hadn't been in yesterday, either, because she was tearing a June 14th pad off her calendar to make way for the "new" June 15th sheet.

He staggered to his own desk and stared unseeingly at the morning's mail. It had not even been opened yet, but he knew that the Factory Distributors envelope contained an order for twenty thousand feet of the new acoustic tile, and the one from Finebeck & Sons was a complaint.

After a long while, he forced himself to open them. They were.

By lunchtime, driven by a desperate sense of urgency, Burckhardt made Miss Mitkin take her lunch hour first—the June-fifteenth-that-was-yesterday, *he* had gone first. She went, looking vaguely worried about his strained insistence, but it made no difference to Burckhardt's mood.

The phone rang and Burckhardt picked it up abstractedly. "Contro Chemicals Downtown, Burckhardt speaking."

The voice said, "This is Swanson," and stopped.

Burckhardt waited expectantly, but that was all. He said, "Hello?"

Again the pause. Then Swanson asked in sad resignation, "Still nothing, eh?"

"Nothing what? Swanson, is there something you want? You came up to me yesterday and went through this routine. You—"

The voice crackled: "Burckhardt! Oh, my good heavens, *you* remember! Stay right there—I'll be down in half an hour!"

"What's this all about?"

"Never mind," the little man said exultantly. "Tell you about it when I see you. Don't say any more over the phone—somebody may be listening. Just wait there. Say, hold on a minute. Will you be alone in the office?"

"Well, no. Miss Mitkin will probably—"

"Hell. Look, Burckhardt, where do you eat lunch? Is it good and noisy?"

"Why, I suppose so. The Crystal Cafe. It's just about a block—"

"I know where it is. Meet you in half an hour!" And the receiver clicked.

The Crystal Cafe was no longer painted red, but the temperature was still up. And they had added piped-in music interspersed with commercials. The advertisements were for Frosty-Flip, Marlin Cigarettes—"They're sanitized," the announcer purred—and something called Choco-Bite candy bars that Burckhardt couldn't remember ever having heard of before. But he heard more about them quickly enough.

While he was waiting for Swanson to show up, a girl in the cellophane skirt of a nightclub cigarette vendor came through the restaurant with a tray of tiny scarlet-wrapped candies.

"Choco-Bites are *tangy*," she was murmuring as she came close to his table. "Choco-Bites are *tangier* than tangy!"

Burckhardt, intent on watching for the strange little man who had phoned him, paid little attention. But as she scattered a handful of the confections over the table next to his, smiling at the occupants, he caught a glimpse of her and turned to stare.

"Why, Miss Horn!" he said.

The girl dropped her tray of candies.

Burckhardt rose, concerned over the girl. "Is something wrong?" But she fled.

The manager of the restaurant was staring suspiciously at Burckhardt, who sank back in his seat and tried to look inconspicuous. He hadn't insulted the girl! Maybe she was just a very strictly reared young lady, he thought—in spite of the long bare legs under the cellophane skirt—and when he addressed her, she thought he was a masher.

Ridiculous idea. Burckhardt scowled uneasily and picked up his menu.

"Burckhardt!" It was a shrill whisper.

Burckhardt looked up over the top of his menu, startled. In the seat across from him, the little man named Swanson was sitting, tensely poised.

"Burckhardt!" the little man whispered again. "Let's get out of here! They're on to you now. If you want to stay alive, come on!"

There was no arguing with the man. Burckhardt gave the hovering manager a sick, apologetic smile and followed Swanson out. The little man seemed to know where he was going. In the street, he clutched Burckhardt by the elbow and hurried him off down the block.

"Did you see her?" he demanded. "That Horn woman, in the phone booth? She'll have them here in five minutes, believe me, so hurry it up!"

Although the street was full of people and cars, nobody was paying any attention to Burckhardt and Swanson. The air had a nip in it—more like October than June, Burckhardt thought, in spite of the weather bureau. And he felt like a fool, following this mad little man down the street, running away from some "them" toward— toward what? The little man might be crazy, but he was afraid. And the fear was infectious.

"In here!" panted the little man.

It was another restaurant—more of a bar, really, and a sort of second-rate place that Burckhardt had never patronized.

"Right straight through," Swanson whispered; and Burckhardt, like a biddable boy, sidestepped through the mass of tables to the far end of the restaurant.

It was L-shaped, with a front on two streets at right angles to each other. They came out on the side street, Swanson staring coldly back at the question-looking cashier, and crossed to the opposite sidewalk.

They were under the marquee of a movie theater. Swanson's expression began to relax.

"Lost them!" he crowed softly. "We're almost there."

He stepped up to the window and bought two tickets. Burckhardt trailed him into the theater. It was a weekday matinee and the place was almost empty. From the screen came sounds of gunfire and horse's hoofs. A solitary usher, leaning against a bright brass rail, looked briefly at them and went back to staring boredly at the picture as Swanson led Burckhardt down a flight of carpeted marble steps.

They were in the lounge and it was empty. There was a door for men and one for ladies; and there was a third door, marked "MANAGER" in gold letters. Swanson listened at the door, and gently opened it and peered inside.

"Okay," he said, gesturing.

Burckhardt followed him through an empty office, to another door—a closet, probably, because it was unmarked.

But it was no closet. Swanson opened it warily, looked inside, then motioned Burckhardt to follow.

It was a tunnel, metal-walled, brightly lit. Empty, it stretched vacantly away in both directions from them.

Burckhardt looked wondering around. One thing he knew and knew full well:

No such tunnel belonged under Tylerton.

There was a room off the tunnel with chairs and a desk and what looked like television screens. Swanson slumped in a chair, panting.

"We're all right for a while here," he wheezed. "They don't come here much any more. If they do, we'll hear them and we can hide."

"Who?" demanded Burckhardt.

The little man said, "Martians!" His voice cracked on the word and the life seemed to go out of him. In morose tones, he went on: "Well, I think they're Martians. Although you could be right, you know; I've had plenty of time to think it over these last few weeks, after they got you, and it's possible they're Russians after all. Still—"

"Start from the beginning. Who got me when?"

Swanson sighed. "So we have to go through the whole thing again. All right. It was about two months ago that you banged on my door, late at night. You were all beat up—scared silly. You begged me to help you—"

"*I* did?"

"Naturally you don't remember any of this. Listen and you'll understand. You were talking a blue streak about being captured and threatened, and your wife being dead and coming back to life, and all kinds of mixed-up nonsense. I thought you were crazy. But—well, I've always had a lot of respect for you. And you begged me to hide you and I have this darkroom, you know. It locks from the inside only. I put the lock on myself. So we went in there—just to humor you—and along about midnight, which was only fifteen or twenty minutes after, we passed out."

"Passed out?"

Swanson nodded. "Both of us. It was like being hit with a sandbag. Look, didn't that happen to you again last night?"

"I guess it did." Burckhardt shook his head uncertainly.

"Sure. And then all of a sudden we were awake again, and you said you were going to show me something funny, and we went out and bought a paper. And the date on it was June 15th."

"June 15th? But that's today! I mean—"

"You got it, friend. It's *always* today!"

It took time to penetrate.

Burckhardt said wonderingly, "You've hidden out in that darkroom for how many weeks?"

"How can I tell? Four of five, maybe, I lost count. And every day the same—always the 15th of June, always my landlady, Mrs. Keefer, is sweeping the front steps, always the same headline in the papers at the corner. It gets monotonous, friend."

It was Burckhardt's idea and Swanson despised it, but he went along. He was the type who always went along.

"It's dangerous," he grumbled worriedly. "Suppose somebody comes by? They'll spot us and—"

"What have we got to lose?"

Swanson shrugged. "It's dangerous," he said again. But he went along.

Burckhardt's idea was very simple. He was sure of only one thing—the tunnel went somewhere. Martians or Russians, fantastic plot or crazy hallucination, whatever was wrong with Tylerton had an explanation, and the place to look for it was at the end of the tunnel.

They jogged along. It was more than a mile before they began to see an end. They were in luck—at least no one came through the tunnel to spot them. But Swanson had said that it was only at certain hours that the tunnel seemed to be in use.

Always the fifteenth of June. Why? Burckhardt asked himself. Never mind the how. *Why?*

And falling asleep, completely involuntarily—everyone at the same time, it seemed. And not remembering, never remembering anything—Swanson had said how eagerly he saw Burckhardt again, the morning after Burckhardt had incautiously waited five minutes too many before retreating into the darkroom. When Swanson had come to, Burckhardt was gone. Swanson had seen him in the street that afternoon, but Burckhardt had remembered nothing.

And Swanson had lived his mouse's existence for weeks, hiding in the woodwork at night, stealing out by day to search for Burckhardt in pitiful hope, scurrying around the fringe of life, trying to keep from the deadly eyes of *them.*

Them. One of "them" was the girl named April Horn. It was by seeing her walk carelessly into a telephone booth and never come out that Swanson had found the tunnel. Another was the man at the cigar stand in Burckhardt's office building. There were more, at least a dozen that Swanson knew of or suspected.

They were easy enough to spot, once you knew where to look, for they alone in Tylerton changed their roles from day to day. Burckhardt was on that 8:51 bus, every morning of every day-that-was-June-15th, never different by a hair or a moment. But April Horn was sometimes gaudy in the cellophane skirt, giving away candy or cigarettes; sometimes plainly dressed; sometimes not seen by Swanson at all.

Russians? Martians? Whatever they were, what could they be hoping to gain from this mad masquerade?

Burckhardt didn't know the answer, but perhaps it lay beyond the door at the end of the tunnel. They listened carefully and heard distant sounds that could not quite be made out, but nothing that seemed dangerous. They slipped through.

And, through a wide chamber and up a flight of steps, they found they were in what Burckhardt recognized as the Contro Chemicals plant.

Nobody was in sight. By itself, that was not so very odd; the automatized factory had never had very many persons in it. But

Burckhardt remembered, from his single visit, the endless, ceaseless busyness of the plant, the valves that opened and closed, the vats that emptied themselves and filled themselves and stirred and cooked and chemically tasted the bubbling liquids they held inside themselves. The plant was never populated, but it was never still.

Only now it *was* still. Except for the distant sounds, there was no breath of life in it. The captive electronic minds were sending out no commands; the coils and relays were at rest.

Burckhardt said, "Come on." Swanson reluctantly followed him through the tangled aisles of stainless steel columns and tanks.

They walked as though they were in the presence of the dead. In a way, they were, for what were the automatons that once had run the factory, if not corpses? The machines were controlled by computers that were really not computers at all, but the electronic analogues of living brains. And if they were turned off, were they not dead? For each had once been a human mind.

Take a master petroleum chemist, infinitely skilled in the separation of crude oil into its fractions. Strap him down, probe into his brain with searching electronic needles. The machine scans the patterns of the mind, translates what it sees into charts and sine waves. Impress these same waves on a robot computer and you have your chemist. Or a thousand copies of your chemist, if you wish, with all of his knowledge and skill, and no human limitations at all.

Put a dozen copies of him into a plant and they will run it all, twenty-four hours a day, seven days of every week, never tiring, never overlooking anything, never forgetting.

Swanson stepped up closer to Burckhardt. "I'm scared," he said.

They were across the room now and the sounds were louder. They were not machine sounds, but voices; Burckhardt moved cautiously up to a door and dared to peer around it.

It was a smaller room, lined with television screens, each one—a dozen or more, at least—with a man or woman sitting before it, staring into the screen and dictating notes into a recorder. The viewers dialed from scene to scene; no two screens ever showed the same picture.

The pictures seemed to have little in common. One was a store, where a girl dressed like April Horn was demonstrating home freezers. One was a series of shots of kitchens. Burckhardt caught a glimpse of what looked like the cigar stand in his office building.

It was baffling and Burckhardt would have loved to stand there and puzzle it out, but it was too busy a place. There was the chance that someone would look their way or walk out and find them.

They found another room. This one was empty. It was an office, large and sumptuous. It had a desk, littered with papers. Burckhardt stared at them, briefly at first—then as the words on one of them caught his attention, with incredulous fascination.

He snatched up the topmost sheet, scanned it, and another, while Swanson was frenziedly searching through the drawers.

Burckhardt swore unbelievingly and dropped the papers to the desk.

Swanson, hardly noticing, yelped with delight: "Look!" He dragged a gun from the desk. "And it's loaded, too!"

Burckhardt stared at him blankly, trying to assimilate what he had read. Then, as he realized what Swanson had said, Burckhardt's eyes sparked. "Good man!" he cried. "We'll take it. We're getting out of here with that gun, Swanson. And we're not going to the police! Not the cops in Tylerton, but the F.B.I., maybe. Take a look at this!"

The sheaf he handed Swanson was headed: "Test Area Progress Report. Subject: Marlin Cigarettes Campaign." It was mostly tabulated figures that made little sense to Burckhardt and Swanson, but at the end was a summary that said:

Although Test 47-K3 pulled nearly double the number of new users of any of the other tests conducted, it probably cannot be used in the field because of local sound-truck control ordinances.

The tests in the 47-K12 group were second best and our recommendation is that retests be conducted in this appeal, testing each of the three best campaigns with and without the addition of sampling techniques.

An alternative suggestion might be to proceed directly with the top appeal in the K12 series, if the client is unwilling to go to the expense of additional tests.

All of these forecast expectations have an 80% probability of being within one-half of one per cent of results forecast, and more than 99% probability of coming within 5%.

Swanson looked up from the paper into Burckhardt's eyes. "I don't get it," he complained.

Burckhardt said, "I don't blame you. It's crazy, but it fits the facts, Swanson, *it fits the facts*. They aren't Russians and they aren't Martians. These people are advertising men! Somehow—heaven knows how they did it—they've taken Tylerton over. They've got us, all of us, you and me and twenty or thirty thousand other people, right under their thumbs.

"Maybe they hypnotize us and maybe it's something else; but however they do it, what happens is that they let us live a day at a time. They pour advertising into us the whole damned day long. And at the end of the day, they see what happened—and then they wash the day out of our minds and start again the next day with different advertising."

Swanson's jaw was hanging. He managed to close it and swallow. "Nuts!" he said flatly.

Burckhardt shook his head. "Sure, it sounds crazy, but this whole thing is crazy. How else would you explain it? You can't deny that most of Tylerton lives the same day over and over again. You've *seen* it! And that's the crazy part and we have to admit that that's true— unless *we* are the crazy ones. And once you admit that somebody, somehow, knows how to accomplish that, the rest of it makes all kinds of sense.

"Think of it, Swanson! They test every last detail before they spend a nickel on advertising! Do you have any idea what that means? Lord knows how much money is involved, but I know for a fact that some companies spend twenty or thirty million dollars a year on advertising. Multiply it, say, by a hundred companies. Say that every one of them learns how to cut its advertising cost by only ten per cent. And that's peanuts, believe me!

"If they know in advance what's going to work, they can cut their costs in half—maybe to less than half, I don't know. But that's saving two or three hundred million dollars a year—and if they pay only ten or twenty per cent of that for the use of Tylerton, it's still dirt cheap for them and a fortune for whoever took over Tylerton."

Swanson licked his lips. "You mean," he offered hesitantly, "that we're a—well, a kind of captive audience?"

Burckhardt frowned. "Not exactly." He thought for a minute. "You know how a doctor tests something like penicillin? He sets up a series of little colonies of germs on gelatin disks and he tries the stuff on one after another, changing it a little each time. Well, that's us—we're the germs, Swanson. Only it's even more efficient than that. They don't have to test more than one colony, because they can use it over and over again."

It was too hard for Swanson to take in. He only said, "What do we do about it?"

"We go to the police. They can't use human beings for guinea pigs!"

"How do we get to the police?"

Burckhardt hesitated. "I think—" he began slowly. "Sure. This is the office of somebody important. We've got a gun. We'll stay right here until he comes along. And he'll get us out of here."

Simple and direct. Swanson subsided and found a place to sit, against the wall, out of sight of the door. Burckhardt took up a position behind the door itself—

And waited.

The wait was not as long as it might have been. Half an hour, perhaps. Then Burckhardt heard approaching voices and had time for a swift whisper to Swanson before he flattened himself against the wall.

It was a man's voice, and a girl's. The man was saying, "—reason why you couldn't report on the phone? You're ruining your whole day's test! What the devil's the matter with you, Janet?"

"I'm sorry, Mr. Dorchin," she said in a sweet, clear tone. "I thought it was important."

The man grumbled, "Important! One lousy unit out of twenty-one thousand."

"But it's the Burckhardt one, Mr. Dorchin. Again. And the way he got out of sight, he must have had some help."

"All right, all right. It doesn't matter, Janet; the Choco-Bite program is ahead of schedule anyhow. As long as you're this far, come on in the office and make out your worksheet. And don't worry about the Burckhardt business. He's probably just wandering around. We'll pick him up tonight and—"

They were inside the door. Burckhardt kicked it shut and pointed the gun.

"That's what you think," he said triumphantly.

It was worth the terrified hours, the bewildered sense of insanity, the confusion and fear. It was the most satisfying sensation Burckhardt had ever had in his life. The expression on the man's face was one he had read about but never actually seen: Dorchin's mouth fell open and his eyes went wide, and though he managed to make a sound that might have been a question, it was not in words.

The girl was almost as surprised. And Burckhardt, looking at her, knew why her voice had been so familiar. The girl was the one who had introduced herself to him as April Horn.

Dorchin recovered himself quickly. "Is this the one?" he asked sharply.

The girl said, "Yes."

Dorchin nodded. "I take it back. You were right. Uh, you— Burckhardt. What do you want?"

Swanson piped up, "Watch him! He might have another gun."

"Search him then," Burckhardt said. "I'll tell you what we want, Dorchin. We want you to come along with us to the FBI and explain to them how you can get away with kidnaping twenty thousand people."

"Kidnapping?" Dorchin snorted. "That's ridiculous, man! Put that gun away; you can't get away with this!"

Burckhardt hefted the gun grimly. "I think I can."

Dorchin looked furious and sick—but oddly, not afraid. "Damn it—" he started to bellow, then closed his mouth and swallowed. "Listen," he said persuasively, "you're making a big mistake. I haven't kidnapped anybody, believe me!"

"I don't believe you," said Burckhardt bluntly. "Why should I?"

"But it's true! Take my word for it!"

Burckhardt shook his head. "The FBI can take your word if they like. We'll find out. Now how do we get out of here?"

Dorchin opened his mouth to argue.

Burckhardt blazed, "Don't get in my way! I'm willing to kill you if I have to. Don't you understand that? I've gone through two days of hell and every second of it I blame on you. Kill you? It would be a pleasure and I don't have a thing in the world to lose! Get us out of here!"

Dorchin's face went suddenly opaque. He seemed about to move; but the blond girl he had called Janet slipped between him and the gun.

"Please!" she begged Burckhardt. "You don't understand. You mustn't shoot!"

"Get out of my way!"

"But, Mr. Burckhardt—"

She never finished. Dorchin, his face unreadable, headed for the door. Burckhardt had been pushed one degree too far. He swung the gun, bellowing. The girl called out sharply. He pulled the trigger. Closing on him with pity and pleading in her eyes, she came again between the gun and the man.

Burckhardt aimed low instinctively, to cripple, not to kill. But his aim was not good.

The pistol bullet caught her in the pit of the stomach.

Dorchin was out and away, the door slamming behind him, his footsteps racing into the distance.

Burckhardt hurled the gun across the room and jumped to the girl.

Swanson was moaning. "That finishes us, Burckhardt. Oh, why did you do it? We could have got away. We could have gone to the police. We were practically out of here! We—"

Burckhardt wasn't listening. He was kneeling beside the girl. She lay flat on her back, arms helterskelter. There was no blood, hardly any sign of the wound; but the position in which she lay was one that no living human being could have held.

Yet she wasn't dead.

She wasn't dead—and Burckhardt, frozen beside her, thought: *She isn't alive, either.*

There was no pulse, but there was a rhythmic ticking of the outstretched fingers of one hand.

There was no sound of breathing, but there was a hissing, sizzling noise.

The eyes were open and they were looking at Burckhardt. There was neither fear nor pain in them, only a pity deeper than the Pit.

She said, through lips that writhed erratically, "Don't—worry, Mr. Burckhardt. I'm—all right."

Burckhardt rocked back on his haunches, staring. Where there should have been blood, there was a clean break of a substance that was not flesh; and a curl of thin golden-copper wire.

Burckhardt moistened his lips.

"You're a robot," he said.

The girl tried to nod. The twitching lips said, "I am. And so are you."

•   •   •

Swanson, after a single inarticulate sound, walked over to the desk and sat staring at the wall. Burckhardt rocked back and forth beside the shattered puppet on the floor. He had no words.

The girl managed to say, "I'm—sorry all this happened." The lovely lips twisted into a rictus sneer, frightening on that smooth young face, until she got them under control. "Sorry," she said again. "The—nerve center was right about where the bullet hit. Makes it difficult to—control this body."

Burckhardt nodded automatically, accepting the apology. Robots. It was obvious, now that he knew it. In hindsight, it was inevitable. He thought of his mystic notions of hypnosis or Martians or something stranger still—idiotic, for the simple fact of created robots fitted the facts better and more economically.

All the evidence had been before him. The automatized factory, with its transplanted minds—why not transplant a mind into a humanoid robot, give it its original owner's features and form?

Could it know that it was a robot?

"All of us," Burckhardt said, hardly aware that he spoke out loud. "My wife and my secretary and you and the neighbors. All of us the same."

"No." The voice was stronger. "Not exactly the same, all of us. I chose it, you see. I"—this time the convulsed lips were not a random contortion of the nerves—"I was an ugly woman, Mr. Burckhardt, and nearly sixty years old. Life had passed me. And when Mr. Dorchin offered me the chance to live again as a beautiful girl, I jumped at the opportunity. Believe me, I *jumped*, in spite of its disadvantages. My flesh body is still alive—it is sleeping, while I am here. I could go back to it. But I never do."

"And the rest of us?"

"Different, Mr. Burckhardt. I work here. I'm carrying out Mr. Dorchin's orders, mapping the results of the advertising tests, watching you and the others live as he makes you live. I do it by choice, but you have no choice. Because, you see, you are dead."

"Dead?" cried Burckhardt; it was almost a scream.

The blue eyes looked at him unwinkingly and he knew that it was no lie. He swallowed, marveling at the intricate mechanisms that let him swallow, and sweat, and eat.

He said: "Oh. The explosion in my dream."

"It was no dream. You are right—the explosion. That was real and this plant was the cause of it. The storage tanks let go and what the blast didn't get, the fumes killed a little later. But almost everyone died in the blast, twenty-one thousand persons. You died with them and that was Dorchin's chance."

"The damned ghoul!" said Burckhardt.

The twisted shoulders shrugged with an odd grace. "Why? You were gone. And you and all the others were what Dorchin wanted—a whole town, a perfect slice of America. It's as easy to transfer a pattern from a dead brain as a living one. Easier—the dead can't say no. Oh, it took work and money—the town was a wreck—but it was possible to rebuild it entirely, especially because it wasn't necessary to have all the details exact.

"There were the homes where even the brain had been utterly destroyed, and those are empty inside, and the cellars that needn't be too perfect, and the streets that hardly matter. And anyway, it only has to last for one day. The same day—June 15th—over and over again; and if someone finds something a little wrong, somehow, the discovery won't have time to snowball, wreck the validity of the tests, because all errors are canceled out at midnight."

The face tried to smile. "That's the dream, Mr. Burckhardt, that day of June 15th, because you never really lived it. It's a present from Mr. Dorchin, a dream that he gives you and then takes back at the end of the day, when he has all his figures on how many of you respond to what variation of which appeal, and the maintenance crews go down the tunnel to go through the whole city, washing out the new dream with their little electronic drains, and then the dream starts all over again. On June 15th.

"Always June 15th, because June 14th is the last day any of you can remember alive. Sometimes the crews miss someone—as they missed you, because you were under your boat. But it doesn't matter. The ones who are missed give themselves away if they show it—and if they don't, it doesn't affect the test. But they don't drain us, the ones of us who work for Dorchin. We sleep when the power is turned off, just as you do. When we wake up, though, we remember." The face contorted wildly. "If I could only forget!"

Burckhardt said unbelievingly, "All this to sell merchandise! It must have cost millions!"

The robot called April Horn said, "It did. But it has made millions for Dorchin, too. And that's not the end of it. Once he finds the master words that make people act do you suppose he will stop with that? Do you suppose—"

The door opened, interrupting her. Burckhardt whirled. Belatedly remembering Dorchin's flight, he raised the gun.

"Don't shoot," ordered the voice calmly. It was not Dorchin; it was another robot, this one not disguised with the clever plastics and cosmetics, but shining plain. It said metallically, "Forget it, Burckhardt. You're not accomplishing anything. Give me that gun before you do any more damage. Give it to me *now*."

Burckhardt bellowed angrily. The gleam on this robot torso was steel; Burckhardt was not at all sure that his bullets would pierce it, or do much harm if they did. He would have put it to the test—

But from behind him came a whimpering, scurrying whirlwind: its name was Swanson, hysterical with fear. He catapulted into Burckhardt and sent him sprawling, the gun flying free.

"Please!" begged Swanson incoherently, prostrate before the steel robot. "He would have shot you—please don't hurt me! Let me work for you, like that girl. I'll do anything, anything you tell me—"

The robot voice said, "We don't need your help." It took two precise steps and stood over the gun—and spurned it, left it lying on the floor.

The wrecked blond robot said, without emotion, "I doubt that I can hold out much longer, Mr. Dorchin."

"Disconnect if you have to," replied the steel robot.

Burckhardt blinked. "But you're not Dorchin!"

The steel robot turned deep eyes on him. "I am," it said. "Not in the flesh—but this is the body I am using at the moment. I doubt that you can damage this one with the gun. The other robot body was more vulnerable. Now will you stop this nonsense? I don't want to have to damage you; you're too expensive for that. Will you just sit down and let the maintenance crews adjust you?"

Swanson groveled. "You—you won't punish us?"

The steel robot had no expression, but its voice was almost surprised. "Punish you?" it repeated on a rising note. "How?"

Swanson quivered as though the word had been a whip; but Burckhardt flared: "Adjust *him*, if he'll let you—but not me! You're going to have to do me a lot of damage, Dorchin. I don't care what I cost or how much trouble it's going to be to put me back together again. But I'm going out of that door! If you want to stop me, you'll have to kill me. You won't stop me any other way!"

The steel robot took a half-step toward him, and Burckhardt involuntarily checked his stride. He stood poised and shaking, ready for death, ready for attack, ready for anything that might happen.

Ready for anything except what did happen. For Dorchin's steel body merely stepped aside, between Burckhardt and the gun, but leaving the door free.

"Go ahead," invited the steel robot. "Nobody's stopping you."

Outside the door, Burckhardt brought up sharp. It was insane of Dorchin to let him go! Robot or flesh, victim or beneficiary, there was nothing to stop him from going to the FBI or whatever law he could find away from Dorchin's sympathetic empire, and telling his story. Surely the corporations who paid Dorchin for test results had no notion of the ghoul's technique he used; Dorchin would have to keep it from them, for the breath of publicity would put a stop to it. Walking out meant death, perhaps, but at that moment in his pseudo-life, death was no terror for Burckhardt.

There was no one in the corridor. He found a window and stared out of it. There was Tylerton—an ersatz city, but looking so real and familiar that Burckhardt almost imagined the whole episode a dream. It was no dream, though. He was certain of that in his heart and equally certain that nothing in Tylerton could help him now.

It had to be the other direction.

It took him a quarter of an hour to find a way, but he found it— skulking through the corridors, dodging the suspicion of footsteps, knowing for certain that his hiding was in vain, for Dorchin was undoubtedly aware of every move he made. But no one stopped him, and he found another door.

It was a simple enough door from the inside. But when he opened it and stepped out, it was like nothing he had ever seen.

First there was light—brilliant, incredible, blinding light. Burck-hardt blinked upward, unbelieving and afraid.

He was standing on a ledge of smooth, finished metal. Not a dozen yards from his feet, the ledge dropped sharply away; he hardly dared approach the brink, but even from where he stood he could see no bottom to the chasm before him. And the gulf extended out of sight into the glare on either side of him.

No wonder Dorchin could so easily give him his freedom! From the factory there was nowhere to go. But how incredible this fantastic gulf, how impossible the hundred white and blinding suns that hung above!

A voice by his side said inquiringly, "Burckhardt?" And thunder rolled the name, mutteringly soft, back and forth in the abyss before him.

Burckhardt wet his lips. "Y-yes?" he croaked.

"This is Dorchin. Not a robot this time, but Dorchin in the flesh, talking to you on a hand mike. Now you have seen, Burckhardt. Now will you be reasonable and let the maintenance crews take over?"

Burckhardt stood paralyzed. One of the moving mountains in the blinding glare came toward him.

It towered hundreds of feet over his head; he stared up at its top, squinting helplessly into the light.

It looked like—

Impossible!

The voice in the loudspeaker at the door said, "Burckhardt?" But he was unable to answer.

A heavy rumbling sigh. "I see," said the voice. "You finally understand. There's no place to go. You know it now. I could have told you, but you might not have believed me, so it was better for you to see it yourself. And after all, Burckhardt, why would I reconstruct a city just the way it was before? I'm a businessman; I count costs. If a thing has to be full-scale, I build it that way. But there wasn't any need to in this case."

From the mountain before him, Burckhardt helplessly saw a lesser cliff descend carefully toward him. It was long and dark, and at the end of it was whiteness, five-fingered whiteness . . .

"Poor little Burckhardt," crooned the loudspeaker, while the echoes rumbled through the enormous chasm that was only a workshop. "It must have been quite a shock for you to find out you were living in a town built on a table top."

It was the morning of June 15th, and Guy Burckhardt woke up screaming out of a dream.

It had been a monstrous and incomprehensible dream, of explosions and shadowy figures that were not men and terror beyond words.

He shuddered and opened his eyes.

Outside his bedroom window, a hugely amplified voice was howling.

Burckhardt stumbled over to the window and stared outside. There was an out-of-season chill to the air, more like October than June; but the scene was normal enough—except for a sound-truck that squatted at curbside halfway down the block. Its speaker horns blared:

"Are you a coward? Are you a fool? Are you going to let crooked politicians steal the country from you? NO! Are you going to put up with four more years of graft and crime? NO! Are you going to vote straight Federal Party all up and down the ballot? YES! *You just bet you are!*"

Sometimes he screams, sometimes he wheedles, threatens, begs, cajoles . . . but his voice goes on and on through one June 15th after another.

DAY MILLION

On this day I want to tell you about, which will be about a thousand years from now, there was a boy, a girl and a love story.

Now although I haven't said much so far, none of it is true. The boy was not what you and I would normally think of as a boy, because he was a hundred and eighty-seven years old. Nor was the girl a girl, for other reasons; and the love story did not entail that sublimation of the urge to rape and concurrent postponement of the instinct to submit which we at present understand in such matters. You won't care much for this story if you don't grasp these facts at once. If, however, you will make the effort you'll likely enough find it jam-packed, chockful and tiptop-crammed with laughter, tears and poignant sentiment which may, or may not, be worthwhile. The reason the girl was not a girl was that she was a boy.

How angrily you recoil from the page! You say who the hell wants to read about a pair of queers? Calm yourself. Here are no hot-breathing secrets of perversion for the coterie trade. In fact, if you were to see this girl, you would not guess that she was in any sense a boy. Breasts, two; vagina, one. Hips, Callipygean; face, hairless; supra-orbital lobes, non-existent. You would term her female at once, although it is true that you might wonder just what species she was a female of, being confused by the tail, the silky pelt or the gill slits behind each ear.

Now you recoil again. Cripes, man, take my word for it. This is a sweet kid, and if you, as a normal male, spent as much as an hour in a room with her, you would bend heaven and earth to get her in the sack. Dora (we will call her that; her "name" was omicron-Dibase seven-group-totteroot S Doradus 5314, the last part of which is a color-specification corresponding to a shade of green)—Dora, I say, was feminine, charming and cute. I admit she doesn't sound that way. She was, as you might put it, a dancer. Her art involved qualities of intellection and expertise of a very high order, requiring both tremendous natural capacities and endless practice; it was performed in null-gravity and I can best describe it by saying that it was something like the performance of a contortionist and something like classical ballet, maybe resembling Danilova's dying swan. It was also pretty damned sexy. In a symbolic way, to be sure; but face it, most of the things we call "sexy" are symbolic, you know, except perhaps an exhibitionist's open fly. On Day Million when Dora danced, the people who saw her panted; and you would too.

About this business of her being a boy. It didn't matter to her audiences that genetically she was male. It wouldn't matter to you, if you were among them, because you wouldn't know it—not unless you took a biopsy cutting of her flesh and put it under an electron-microscope to find the XY chromosome—and it didn't matter to them because they didn't care. Through techniques which are not only complex but haven't yet been discovered, these people were able to determine a great deal about the aptitudes and easements of babies quite a long time before they were born—at about the second horizon of cell-division, to be exact, when the segmenting egg is becoming a free blastocyst—and then they naturally helped those aptitudes along. Wouldn't we? If we find a child with an aptitude for music we give him a scholarship to Juilliard. If they found a child whose aptitudes were for being a woman, they made him one. As sex had long been dissociated from reproduction this was relatively easy to do and caused no trouble and no, or at least very little, comment.

How much is "very little"? Oh, about as much as would be caused by our own tampering with Divine Will by filling a tooth. Less than would be caused by wearing a hearing aid. Does it still sound awful? Then look closely at the next busty babe you meet and reflect that she may be a Dora, for adults who are genetically male but somatically female are far from unknown even in our own time. An accident of environment in the womb overwhelms the blueprints of heredity. The difference is that with us it happens only by accident and we don't know about it except rarely, after close study; whereas the people of Day Million did it often, on purpose, because they wanted to.

Well, that's enough to tell you about Dora. It would only confuse you to add that she was seven feet tall and smelled of peanut butter. Let us begin our story.

On Day Million Dora swam out of her house, entered a transportation tube, was sucked briskly to the surface in its flow of water and ejected in its plume of spray to an elastic platform in front of her—ah—call it her rehearsal hall. "Oh, shit!" she cried in pretty confusion, reaching out to catch her balance and finding herself tumbled against a total stranger, whom we will call Don.

They met cute. Don was on his way to have his legs renewed. Love was the farthest thing from his mind; but when, absentmindedly taking a short cut across the landing platform for submarinites and finding himself drenched, he discovered his arms full of the loveliest girl he had ever seen, he knew at once they were meant for each other. "Will you marry me?" he asked. She said softly, "Wednesday," and the promise was like a caress.

Don was tall, muscular, bronze and exciting. His name was no more Don than Dora's was Dora, but the personal part of it was Adonis in tribute to his vibrant maleness, and so we will call him Don for short. His personality color-code, in Angstrom units, was 5290, or only a few degrees bluer than Dora's 5314, a measure of what they had intuitively discovered at first sight, that they possessed many affinities of taste and interest.

I despair of telling you exactly what it was that Don did for a living—I don't mean for the sake of making money, I mean for the sake of giving purpose and meaning to his life, to keep him from going off his nut with boredom—except to say that it involved a lot of traveling. He traveled in interstellar spaceships. In order to make a spaceship go really fast about thirty-one male and seven genetically female human beings had to do certain things, and Don was one of the thirty-one. Actually he contemplated options. This involved a lot of exposure to radiation flux—not so much from his own station in the propulsive system as in the spillover from the next stage, where a genetic female preferred selections and the subnuclear particles making the selections she preferred demolished themselves in a shower of quanta. Well, you don't give a rat's ass for that, but it meant that Don had to be clad at all times in a skin of light, resilient, extremely strong copper-colored metal. I have already mentioned this, but you probably thought I meant he was sunburned.

More than that, he was a cybernetic man. Most of his ruder parts had been long since replaced with mechanisms of vastly more permanence and use. A cadmium centrifuge, not a heart, pumped his blood. His lungs moved only when he wanted to speak out loud, for a cascade of osmotic filters rebreathed oxygen out of his own wastes. In a way, he probably would have looked peculiar to a man from the twentieth century, with his glowing eyes and seven-fingered hands; but to himself, and of course to Dora, he looked mighty manly and grand. In the course of his voyages Don had circled Proxima Centauri, Procyon and the puzzling worlds of Mira Ceti; he had carried agricultural templates to the planets of Canopus and brought back warm, witty pets from the pale companion of Aldebaran. Blue-hot or red-cool, he had seen a thousand stars and their ten thousand planets. He had, in fact, been traveling the starlanes with only brief leaves on Earth for pushing two centuries. But you don't care about that, either. It is people that make stories, not the circumstances they find themselves in, and you want to hear about these two people. Well, they made it. The great thing they had for each other grew and flowered and burst into fruition on Wednesday, just as Dora had promised. They met at the encoding room, with a couple of well-wishing friends apiece to cheer them on, and while their identities were being taped and stored they smiled and whispered to each other and bore the jokes of their friends with blushing repartee. Then they exchanged their mathematical analogues and went away. Dora to her dwelling beneath the surface of the sea and Don to his ship.

It was an idyll, really. They lived happily ever after—or anyway, until they decided not to bother anymore and died.

Of course, they never set eyes on each other again.

Oh, I can see you now, you eaters of charcoal-broiled steak, scratching an incipient bunion with one hand and holding this story with the other, while the stereo plays d'Indy or Monk. You don't believe a word of it, do you? Not for one minute. People wouldn't live like that, you say with an irritated and not amused grunt as you get up to put fresh ice in a stale drink.

And yet there's Dora, hurrying back through the flushing commuter pipes toward her underwater home (she prefers it there; has had herself somatically altered to breathe the stuff). If I tell you with what sweet fulfillment she fits the recorded analogue of Don into the symbol-manipulator, hooks herself in and turns herself on . . . if I try to tell you any of that you will simply stare. Or glare; and grumble, what the hell kind of lovemaking is this? And yet I assure you, friend, I really do assure you that Dora's ecstasies are as creamy and passionate as any of James Bond's lady spies, and one hell of a lot more so than anything you are going to find in "real life." Go ahead, glare and grumble. Dora doesn't care. If she thinks of you at all, her thirty-times-great-great-grandfather, she thinks you're a pretty primordial sort of brute. You are. Why, Dora is farther removed from you than you are from the Australopithecines of five thousand centuries ago. You could not swim a second in the strong currents of her life. You don't think progress goes in a straight line, do you? Do you recognize that it is an ascending, accelerating, maybe even exponential curve? It takes Hell's own time to get started, but when it goes it goes like a bomb. And you, you Scotch-drinking steak-eater in your Relax-acizer chair, you've just barely lighted the primacord of the fuse. What is it now, the six or seven hundred thousandth day after Christ? Dora lives in Day Million. A thousand years from now. Her body fats are polyunsaturated, like Crisco. Her wastes are hemo-dialyzed out of her bloodstream while she sleeps—that means she doesn't have to go to the bathroom. On whim, to pass a slow half-hour, she can command more energy than the entire nation of Portugal can spend today, and use it to launch a weekend satellite or remold a crater on the Moon. She loves Don very much. She keeps his every gesture, mannerism, nuance, touch of hand, thrill of intercourse, passion of kiss stored in symbolic-mathematical form. And when she wants him, all she has to do is turn the machine on and she has him.

And Don, of course, has Dora. Adrift on a sponson city a few hundred yards over her head or orbiting Arcturus, fifty light-years away, Don has only to command his own symbol-manipulator to rescue Dora from the the ferrite files and bring her to life for him, and there she is; and rapturously, tirelessly they ball all night. Not in the flesh, of course; but then his flesh has been extensively altered and it wouldn't really be much fun. He doesn't need the flesh for pleasure. Genital organs feel nothing. Neither do hands, nor breasts, nor lips; they are only receptors, accepting and transmitting impulses. It is the brain that feels, it is the interpretation of those impulses that makes agony or orgasm; and Don's symbol-manipulator gives him the analogue of cuddling, the analogue of kissing, the analogue of wildest, most ardent hours with the eternal, exquisite and incorruptible analogue of Dora. Or Diane. Or sweet Rose, or laughing Alicia; for to be sure, they have each of them exchanged analogues before, and will again.

Balls, you say, it looks crazy to me. And you—with your aftershave lotion and your little red car, pushing papers across a desk all day and chasing tail all night—tell me, just how the hell do you think you would look to Tiglath-Pileser, say, or Attila the Hun?

THE GOLD AT THE STARBOW'S END

CONSTITUTION ONE

Log of Lt-Col Sheffield N. Jackman, USAF, commanding U.S. Starship *Constitution*, Day 40.

All's well, friends. Thanks to Mission Control for the batch of personal messages. We enjoyed the concert you beamed us, in fact we recorded most of it so we can play it over again when communication gets hairy.

We are now approaching the six-week point in our expedition to Alpha Centauri, Planet Aleph, and now that we've passed the farthest previous manned distance from Earth we're really beginning to feel as if we're on our way. Our latest navigation check confirms Mission Control's plot, and we estimate we should be crossing the orbit of Pluto at approximately 1631 hours, ship time, of Day 40, which is today. Letski has been keeping track of the time dilation effect, which is beginning to be significant now that we are traveling about some 6 percent of the speed of light, and says this would make it approximately a quarter of two in the morning your time, Mission Control. We voted to consider that the "coastal waters" mark. From then on we will have left the solar system behind and thus will be the first human beings to enter upon the deeps of interstellar space. We plan to have a ceremony. Letski and Ann Becklund have made up an American flag for jettisoning at that point, which we will do through the Number Three survey port, along with the prepared stainless steel plaque containing the President's commissioning speech. We are also throwing in some private articles for each of us. I am contributing my Air Academy class ring.

Little change since previous reports. We are settling down nicely to our routine. We finished up all our post-launch checks weeks ago, and as Dr. Knefhausen predicted we began to find time hanging heavy on our hands. There won't be much to keep us busy between now and when we arrive at the planet Alpha-Aleph that is really essential to the operating of the spaceship. So we went along with Kneffie's proposed recreational schedule, using the worksheets prepared by the Nasa Division of Flight Training and Personnel Management. At first (I think the boys back in Indianapolis are big enough to know this!) it met with what you might call a cool reception. The general consensus was that this business of learning number theory and the calculus of statement, which is what they handed us for openers, was for the birds. We figured we weren't quite desperate enough for that yet, so we fooled around with other things. Ann and Will Becklund played a lot of chess. Dot Letski began writing a verse adaptation of *War and Peace*. The rest of us hacked around with the equipment, and making astronomical observations and gabbing. But all that began to get tiresome pretty fast, just as Kneffie said it would at the briefings. We talked about his idea that the best way to pass time in a spaceship was learning to get interested in mathematical problems—no mass to transport, no competitive element to get tempers up and all that. It began to make sense. So now Letski is in his tenth day of trying to find a formula for primes, and my own dear Flo is trying to prove Goldbach's Conjecture by means of the theory of congruences. (This is the girl who two months ago couldn't add up a laundry list!) It certainly passes the time.

Medically, we are all fit. I will append the detailed data on our blood pressures, pulses, etc., as well as the tape from the rocket and navigating systems readouts. I'll report again as scheduled. Take care of Earth for us—we're looking forward to seeing it again, in a few years!

WASHINGTON ONE

There was a lull in the urban guerrilla war in Washington that week. The chopper was able to float right in to the South Lawn of the White House—no sniper fire, no heat-seeking missiles, not even rock-throwing. Dr. Dieter von Knefhausen stared suspiciously at the knot of weary-looking pickets in their permitted fifty yards of space along the perimeter. They didn't look militant, probably Gay Lib or, who knew what, maybe nature-food or single-tax; at any rate no rocks came from them, only a little disorganized booing as the helicopter landed. Knefhausen bowed to Herr Omnes sardonically, hopped nimbly out of the chopper and got out of the way as it took off again, which it did at once. He didn't trouble to run to the White House. He strolled. He did not fear these simple people, even if the helicopter pilot did. Also he was not really eager to keep his appointment with the President.

The ADC who frisked him did not smile. The orderly who conducted him to the West Terrace did not salute. No one relieved him of the dispatch case with his slides and papers, although it was heavy. You could tell right away when you were in the doghouse, he thought, ducking his head from the rotor blast as the pilot circled the White House to gain altitude before venturing back across the spread-out city.

It had been a lot different in the old days, he thought with some nostalgia. He could remember every minute of those old days. It was right here, this portico, where he had stood before the world's press and photographers to tell them about the Alpha-Aleph Project. He had seen his picture next to the President's on all the front-pages, watched himself on the TV newscasts, talking about the New Earth that would give America an entire colonizable planet four light-years away. He remembered the launch at the Cape, with a million and a half invited guests from all over the world: foreign statesmen and scientists eating their hearts out with envy, American leaders jovial with pride. The orderlies saluted then, all right. His lecture fees had gone clear out of sight. There was even talk of making him the Vice Presidential candidate in the next election—and it could have happened, too, if the election had been right then, and if there hadn't been the problem of his being born in another country.

Now it was all different. He was taken up in the service elevator. It wasn't so much that Knefhausen minded for his own sake, he told himself, but how did the word get out that there was trouble? Was it only the newspaper stories? Was there a leak?

The Marine orderly knocked once on the big door of the Cabinet room, and it was opened from inside.

Knefhausen entered.

No "Come in, Dieter, boy, pull up a pew." No Vice President jumping up to grab his arm and slap his back. His greeting was thirty silent faces turned toward him, some reserved, some frankly hostile. The full Cabinet was there, along with half a dozen department heads and the President's personal action staff, and the most hostile face around the big oval table was the President's own.

Knefhausen bowed. An atavistic hankering for lyceum-cadet jokes made him think of clicking his heels and adjusting a monocle, but he didn't have a monocle and didn't yield to impulses like that. He merely took his place standing at the foot of the table and, when the President nodded, said, "Good morning, gentlemen, and ladies. I assume you want to see me about the stupid lies the Russians are spreading about the Alpha-Aleph program."

Roobarooba, they muttered to each other. The President said in his sharp tenor, "So you think they are just lies?"

"Lies or mistakes, Mr. President, what's the difference? We are right and they are wrong, that's all."

Roobaroobarooba. The Secretary of State looked inquiringly at the President, got a nod and said: "Dr. Knefhausen, you know I've been on your team a long time and I don't want to disagree with any statement you care to make, but are you so sure about that?

They's some mighty persuasive figures comin' out of the Russians."

"They are false, Mr. Secretary."

"Ah, well, Dr. Knefhausen. I might be inclined to take your word for it, but they's others might not. Not cranks or malcontents, Dr. Knefhausen, but good, decent people. Do you have any evidence for such as them?"

"With your permission, Mr. President?" The President nodded again, and Knefhausen unlocked his dispatch case and drew out a slim sheaf of slides. He handed them to a major of Marines, who looked to the President for approval and then did what Knefhausen told him. The room lights went down and, after some fiddling with the focus, the first slide was projected over Knefhausen's head. It showed a huge array of Y-shaped metal posts, stretching away into the distance of a bleak, powdery-looking landscape.

"This picture is our radio telescope on Farside, the Moon," he said. "It is never visible from the Earth, because that portion of the Moon's surface is permanently turned away from us, for which reason we selected it for the site of the telescope. There is no electrical interference of any kind. The instrument is made up of thirty-three million separate dipole elements, aligned with an accuracy of one part in several million. Its actual size is an approximate circle eighteen miles across, but by virtue of the careful positioning its performance is effectively equal to a telescope with a diameter of some twenty-six miles. Next slide, please."

Click. The picture of the huge RT display swept away and was replaced by another similar—but visibly smaller and shabbier—construction.

"This is the Russian instrument, gentlemen. And ladies. It is approximately one quarter the size of ours in diameter. It has less than one-tenth as many elements, and our reports—they are classified, but I am informed this gathering is cleared to receive this material? Yes—our reports indicate the alignment is very crude. Even terrible, you could say.

"The difference between the two instruments in information-gathering capacity is roughly a hundred to one, in our favor. Lights, please.

"What this means," he went on smoothly, smiling at each of the persons around the table in turn as he spoke, "is that if the Russians say 'no' and we say 'yes,' bet on 'yes.' Our radio telescope can be trusted. Theirs cannot."

The meeting shifted uneasily in its chairs. They were as anxious to believe Knefhausen as he was to convince them, but they were not sure.

Representative Belden, the Chairman of the House Ways and Means Committee, spoke for all of them. "Nobody doubts the quality of your equipment. Especially," he added, "since we still have bruises from the job of paying for it. But the Russians made a flat statement. They said that Alpha Centauri can't have a planet larger than one thousand miles in diameter, or nearer than half a billion miles to the star. I have a copy of the Tass release here. It admits that their equipment is inferior to our own, but they have a statement signed by twenty-two academicians that says their equipment could not miss on any object larger or nearer than what I have said, or on any body of any kind which would be large enough to afford a landing place for our astronauts. Are you familiar with this statement?"

"Yes, of course, I have read it—"

"Then you know that they state positively that the planet you call 'Alpha-Aleph' does not exist."

"Yes, that is what they state."

"Moreover, statements from authorities at the Paris Observatory and the UNESCO Astrophysical Center at Trieste, and from England's Astronomer Royal, all say that they have checked and confirmed their figures."

Knefhausen nodded cheerfully. "That is correct, Representative Belden. They confirm that if the observations are as stated, then the conclusions drawn by the Soviet installation at Novy Brezhnevgrad on Farside naturally follow. I don't question the arithmetic. I only say that the observations are made with inadequate equipment, and thus the Soviet astronomers have come to a false conclusion. But I do not want to burden your patience with an unsupported statement," he added hastily as the Congressman opened his mouth to speak again, "so I will tell you all there is to tell. What the Russians say is theory. What I have to counter is not merely better theory, but also objective fact. I know Alpha-Aleph is there because I have seen it! Lights again, Major! And the next slide, if you please."

The screen lit up and showed glaring bare white with a sprinkling of black spots, like dust. A large one appeared in the exact center of the screen, with a dozen lesser ones sprinkled around it. Knefhausen picked up a flash pointer and aimed its little arrowhead of light at the central dot.

"This is a photographic negative," he said, "which is to say that it is black where the actual scene is white and vice versa. Those objects are astronomical. It was taken from our Briareus Twelve satellite near the orbit of Jupiter, on its way out of Neptune fourteen months ago. The central object is the star Alpha Centauri. It was photographed with a special instrument which filters out most of the light from the star itself, electronic in nature and something like the coronascope which is used for photographing prominences on our own Sun. We hoped that by this means we might be able actually to photograph the planet Alpha-Aleph. We were successful, as you can see." The flash pointer laid its little arrow next to the nearest small dot to the central star. "That, gentlemen, and ladies, is Alpha-Aleph. It is precisely where we predicted it from radio telescope data."

There was another buzz from the table. In the dark it was louder than before. The Secretary of State cried sharply, "Mr. President! Can't we release this photograph?"

"We will release it immediately after this meeting," said the President.

Roobarooba. Then the committee chairman: "Mr. President, I'm sure if you say that's the planet we want, then it's the planet. But others outside this country may wonder, for indeed all those dots look about alike to me. I wonder if Knefhausen could satisfy a layman's curiosity. *How* do we know that's Alpha-Aleph?"

"Slide Number Four, please—and keep Number Three in the carriage." The same scene, subtly different. "Note that in this picture, gentlemen, that one object, there, is in a different position. It has moved. You know that the stars show no discernible motion, of course. It has moved because this photograph was taken eight months later, as Briareus Twelve was returning from the Neptune flyby, and the planet Alpha-Aleph had revolved in its orbit. This is not theory, it is evidence; and I add that the original tapes from which the photoprint was made are stored in Goldstone, so there is no question that arises of foolishness." *Roobarooba,* but in a higher and excited key. Gratified, Knefhausen nailed down his point. "So, Major, if you will now return to Slide Three, yes—And if you will flip back and forth, between Three and Four, as fast as you can—Thank you." The little black dot called Alpha-Aleph bounced back and forth like a tennis ball, while all the other star points remained motionless. "This is what is called the blink comparator process, you see. I point out that if what you are looking at is not a planet, it is, excuse me, Mr. President, the damnedest funniest star you ever saw. Also it is exactly at the distance and exactly with the orbital period we specified based on the RT data. Now, are there any more questions?"

"No, sir!" "That's great, Kneffie!" "Clear as a cow's ass to the stud bull." "I think that wraps it up." "That'll show the Commies." The President's voice overrode them all.

"I think we can have the lights on now, Major Merton," he said. "Dr. Knefhausen, thank you. I'd appreciate it if you would remain nearby for a few minutes, so you can join Murray and myself in the study to check over the text of our announcement before we release these pictures." He nodded sober dismissal to his chief science advisor and then, reminded by the happy faces of his cabinet, remembered to smile with pleasure.

CONSTITUTION TWO

Sheffield Jackman's log. Starship *Constitution*. Day 95.

According to Letski we are now traveling at just about 15% of the speed of light, almost 30,000 miles per second. The fusion thrust is operating smoothly and well. Fuel, power, and life-support curves are sticking tight to optimum. No sweat of any kind with the ship, or, actually, with anything else.

Relativistic effects have begun to show up as predicted. Jim Barstow's spectral studies show the stars in front of us are showing a shift to the blue end, and the Sun and the other stars behind us are shifting to the red. Without the spectroscope you can't see much, though. Beta Circini looks a little funny, maybe. As for the Sun, it's still very bright—Jim logged it as minus-six magnitude a few hours ago—and as I've never seen it in quite that way before, I can't tell whether the color looks bright or not. It certainly isn't the golden yellow I associate with type GO, but neither is Alpha Centauri ahead of us, and I don't really see a difference between them. I think the reason is simply that they are so bright that the color impressions are secondary to the brightness impressions, although the spectroscope, as I say, does show the differences. We've all taken turns at looking back. Naturally enough, I guess. We can still make out the Earth and even the Moon in the telescope, but it's chancy. Ski almost got an eyeful of the Sun at full light-gathering amplitude yesterday because the visual separation is only about twelve seconds of arc now. In a few more days they'll be too close to separate.

Let's see, what else?

We've been having a fine time with the recreational-math program. Ann has taken to binary arithmetic like a duck to water. She's involved in what I take to be some sort of statistical experimentation (we don't pry too much into what the others are doing until they're ready to talk about it), and, of all things, she demanded we produce coins to flip. Well, naturally none of us had taken any money with us! Except that it turns out two of us did. Ski had a Russian silver ruble that his mother's uncle had given him for luck, and I found an old Philadelphia transit token in my pocket. Ann rejected my transit token as too light to be reliable, but she now spends happy hours flipping the ruble, heads or tails, and writing down the results as a series of six-place binary numbers, heads for 1 and tails for 0. After about a week my curiosity got too much so I began hinting to find out what she was doing. When I ask she says things like, "By means of the easy and the simple we grasp the laws of the whole world." When I say that's nice but what does she hope to grasp by flipping the coin? she says, "When the laws of the whole world are grasped, therein lies perfection." So, as I say, we don't press each other and I leave it there. But it passes the time.

Kneffie would be proud of himself if he could see how our recreation keeps us busy. None of us has managed to prove Fermat's Last Theorem yet or anything like that, but of course that's the whole point. If we could *solve* the problems, we'd have used them up, and then what would we do for recreation? It does exactly what it was intended to. It keeps us mentally alert on this long and intrinsically rather dull boat-ride.

Personal relationships? Jes' fine, fellows, jes' fine. A lot better than any of us really hoped, back there at the personal-hygiene briefings in Mission Control. The girls take the stripey pills every day until three days before their periods, then they take the green pills for four days, then they lay off pills for four days, then back to the stripes. There was a little embarrassed joking about it at first, but now it's strictly routine, like brushing the teeth. We men take our red pills every day (Ski christened them "stop lights") until our girls tell us they're about to lay off (you know what I mean, each of our individual girls tells her husband), then we take the Blue Devil (that's what we call the antidote) and have a hell of a time until the girls start on the stripes again. None of us thought any of this would work, you know. But it works fine. I don't even think sex until Flo kisses my ear and tells me she's getting ready to, excuse the expression, get in heat, and then like wow. Same with everybody. The aft chamber with the nice wide bunks we call Honeymoon Hotel. It belongs to whoever needs it, and never once have both bunks been used. The rest of the time we just sleep wherever is convenient, and nobody gets uptight about it.

Excuse my getting personal, but you told me you wanted to know everything, and there's not much else to tell. All systems remain optimum. We check them over now and again, but nothing has given any trouble, or even looked as though it might be thinking about giving trouble later on. And there's absolutely nothing worth looking at outside but stars. We've all seen them about as much as we need to by now. The plasma jet thrums right along at our point-seven-five Gee. We don't even hear it anymore.

We've even got used to the recycling system. None of us really thought we'd get with the suction toilet, not to mention what happens to the contents, but it was only a little annoying the first few days. Now it's fine. The treated product goes into the algae tanks, feces and urine together. The sludge from the algae goes into the hydroponic beds, but by then, of course, it's just greeny-brown vegetable matter like my father used to get out of his mulch bed. That's all handled semi-automatically anyway, of course, so our first real contact with the system comes in the kitchen. The food we eat comes in the form of nice red tomatoes and nourishing rice pilaf and stuff like that. (We do miss animal protein a little; the frozen stores have to last a long time, so each hamburger is a special feast, and we only have them once a week or so.) The water we drink comes actually out of the air, condensed by the dehumidifiers into the reserve supply, where we get it to drink. It's nicely aerated and chilled and tastes fine. Of course, the way it gets into the air in the first place is by being sweated out of our pores or transpired from the plants (which are irrigated direct from the treated product of the reclamation tanks), and we all know, when we stop to think of it, that every molecule of it has passed through all our kidneys forty times by now. But not directly. That's the point. What we drink is clear sweet dew. And if it once was something else, can't you say the same of Lake Erie?

Well. I think I've gone on long enough. You've probably got the idea by now: We're happy in the service, and we all thank you for giving us this pleasure cruise!

WASHINGTON TWO

Waiting for his appointment with the President, Dr. Knefhausen reread the communique from the spaceship, chuckling happily to himself. "Happy in the service." "Like wow." "Kneffie would be proud of himself"—indeed Kneffie was. And proud of them, those little wonders, there! So brave. So strong.

He took as much pride in them as if they had been his own sons and daughters, all eight of them. Everybody knew the Alpha-Aleph project was Knefhausen's baby, but he tried to conceal from the world that, in his own mind, he spread his fatherhood to include the crew. They were the pick of the available world, and it was he who had put them where they were. He lifted his head, listening to the distant chanting from the perimeter fence where today's disgusting exhibition of mob violence was doing its best to harass the people who were making the world go. What great lumps they were out there, with their long hair and their dirty morals. The heavens belonged only to angels, and it was Dieter von Knefhausen who had picked the angels. It was he who had established the selection procedures (and if he had done some things that were better left unmentioned to make sure the procedures worked, what of it?). It was he who had conceived and adapted the highly important recreation schedule, and above all he who had conceived the entire project and persuaded the President to make it come true. The hardware was nothing, only money. The basic scientific concepts were known; most of the components were on the shelves; it took only will to put them together. The will would not have existed if it had not been for Knefhausen, who announced the discovery of Alpha-Aleph from his radio-observatory on Farside (and gave it that name, although as everyone realized he could have called it by any name he chose, even his own) and carried on the fight for the project by every means available until the President bought it.

It had been a hard, bitter struggle. He reminded himself with courage that the worst was still ahead. No matter. Whatever it cost, it was done, and it was worthwhile. These reports from *Constitution* proved it. It was going exactly as planned, and—

"Excuse me, Dr. Knefhausen."

He looked up, catapulted back from almost half a light-year away.

"I said the President will see you now, Dr. Knefhausen," repeated the usher.

"Ah," said Knefhausen. "Oh, yes, to be sure. I was deep in thought."

"Yes, sir. This way, sir."

They passed a window and there was a quick glimpse of the turmoil at the gates, picket signs used like battle-axes, a thin blue cloud of tear gas, the sounds of shouting. "King Mob is busy today," said Knefhausen absently.

"There's no danger, sir. Through here, please."

The President was in his private study, but to Knefhausen's surprise he was not alone. There was Murray Amos, his personal secretary, which one could understand; but there were three other men in the room. Knefhausen recognized them as the Secretary of State, the Speaker of the House and, of all people, the Vice President. How strange, thought Knefhausen, for what was to have been a confidential briefing for the President alone! But he rallied quickly.

"Excuse me, Mr. President," he said cheerfully. "I must have understood wrong. I thought you were ready for our little talk."

"I am ready, Knefhausen," said the President. The cares of his years in the White House rested heavily on him today, Knefhausen thought critically. He looked very old and very tired. "You will tell these gentlemen what you would have told me."

"Ah, yes, I see," said Knefhausen, trying to conceal the fact that he did not see at all. Surely the President did not mean what his words said; therefore it was necessary to try to see what was his thought. "Yes to be sure. Here is something, Mr. President. A new report from the *Constitution*! It was received by burst transmission from the Lunar Orbiter at Goldstone just an hour ago, and has just come from the decoding room. Let me read it to you. Our brave astronauts are getting along splendidly, just as we planned. They say—"

"Don't read us that just now," said the President harshly. "We'll hear it, but first there is something else. I want you to tell this group the full story of the Alpha-Aleph project."

"The full story, Mr. President?" Knefhausen hung on gamely. "I see. You wish me to begin with the very beginning, when first we realized at the observatory that we had located a planet—"

"No, Knefhausen. Not the cover story. The truth."

"Mr. President!" cried Knefhausen in sudden agony. "I must in-form you that I protest this premature disclosure of vital—"

"The truth, Knefhausen!" shouted the President. It was the first time Knefhausen had ever heard him raise his voice. "It won't go out of this room, but you must tell them everything. Tell them why it is that the Russians were right and we lied! Tell them why we sent the astronauts on a suicide mission, ordered to land on a planet that we knew all along did not exist!"

CONSTITUTION THREE

Shef Jackman's journal, Day 130.

It's been a long time, hasn't it? I'm sorry for being such a lousy correspondent. I was in the middle of a thirteen-game chess series with Eve Barstow—she was playing the Bobby Fischer games, and I was playing in the style of Reshevsky—and Eve said something that made me think of old Kneffie, and that, of course, reminded me I owed you a transmission. So here it is.

In my own defense, though, it isn't only that we've been busy with other things. It takes a lot of power for these chatty little letters. Some of us aren't so sure they're worthwhile. The farther we get the more power we need to accumulate for a transmission. Right now it's not so bad yet, but, well, I might as well tell you the truth, right? Kneffie made us promise that. Always tell the truth, he said, because you're part of the experiment, and we need to know what you're doing, all of it. Well, the truth in this case is that we were a little short of disposable power for a while because Jim Barstow needed quite a lot for research purposes. You will probably wonder what the research is, but we have a rule that we don't criticize, or even talk about, what anyone else is doing until they're ready, and he isn't ready yet. I take the responsibility for the whole thing, not just the power drain but the damage to the ship. I said he could go ahead with it.

We're going pretty fast now, and to the naked eye the stars fore and aft have blue-shifted and red-shifted nearly out of sight. It's funny, but we haven't been able to observe Alpha-Aleph yet, even with the disk obscuring the star. Now, with the shift to the blue, we probably won't see it at all until we slow down. We can still see the Sun, but I guess what we're seeing is ultraviolet when it's home. Of course the relativistic frequency shifts mean we need extra compensating power in our transmissions, which is another reason why, all in all, I don't think I'll be writing home every Sunday, between breakfast and the baseball game, the way I ought to!

But the mission's going along fine. The "personal relationships" keep on being just great. We've done a little experimental research there too that wasn't on the program, but it's all OK. No problems. Worked out great. I think maybe I'll leave out some of the details, but we found some groovy ways to do things. Oh, hell, I'll give you one hint: Dot Letski says I should tell you to get the boys at Mission Control to crack open two of the stripey pills and one of the Blue Devils, mix them with a quarter-teaspoon of black pepper and about 2 cc of the conditioner fluid from the recycling system. Serve over orange sherbet, and oh boy. After the first time we had it Flo made a crack about its being "seminal," which I thought was a private joke, but it broke everybody up. Dot figured it out for herself weeks ago. We wondered how she got so far so fast with *War and Peace* until she let us into the secret. Then we found out what it could do for you, both emotionally and intellectually: the creative over the arousing, as they say.

Ann and Jerry Letski used up their own recreational programs early (real early—they were supposed to last the whole voyage!), so they swapped microfiches, on the grounds that each was interested in an aspect of causality and they wanted to see what the other side had to offer. Now Ann is deep into people like Kant and Carnap, and Ski is sore as a boil because there's no *Achillea millefolium* in the hydroponics garden. Needs the stalks for his researches, he says. He is making do with flipping his ruble to generate hexagrams; in fact, we all borrow it now and then, but it's not the right way. Honestly, Mission Control, he's right. Some thought should have been given to our other needs, besides sex and number theory. We can't even use chop bones from the kitchen wastes, because there isn't any kitchen waste. I know you couldn't think of everything, but still— Anyway, we improvise as best we can, and mostly well enough.

Let's see, what else? Did I send you Jim Barstow's proof of Goldbach's Conjecture? Turned out to be very simple once he had devised his multiplex parity analysis idea. Mostly we don't fool with that sort of stuff anymore, though. We got tired of number theory after we'd worked out all the fun parts, and if there is any one thing that we all work on (apart from our private interests) it is probably the calculus of statement. We don't do it systematically, only as time permits from our other activities, but we're all pretty well convinced that a universal grammar is feasible enough, and it's easy enough to see what that leads to. Flo has done more than most of us. She asked me to put in that Boole, Venn and all those old people were on the wrong track, but she thinks there might be something to Leibniz's "calculus ratiocinator" idea. There's a J. W. Swanson suggestion that she likes for multiplexing languages. (Jim took off from it to work out his parity analysis.) The idea is that you devise a double-vocabulary language. One set of meanings is conveyed, say, by phonemes—that is, the shape of the words themselves. Another set is conveyed by pitch. It's like singing a message, half of it conveyed by the words, the other half by the tune. Like rock music. You get both sets of meanings at the same time. She's now working on third, fourth, and nth dimensions so as to convey many kinds of meanings at once, but it's not very fruitful so far (except for using sexual intercourse as one of the communications media). Most of the senses available are too limited to convey much. By the way, we checked out all the existing "artificial languages" as best we could—put Will Becklund under hypnotic regression to recapture the Esperanto he'd learned as a kid, for instance. But they were all blind alleys. Didn't even convey as much as standard English or French.

Medical readouts follow. We're all healthy. Eve Barstow gave us a medical check to make sure. Ann and Ski had little rough spots in a couple of molars so she filled them for the practice more than because they needed it. I don't mean practice in filling teeth; she wanted to try acupuncture instead of procaine. Worked fine.

We all have this writing-to-Daddy-and-Mommy-from-Camp-Tanglewood feeling and we'd like to send you some samples of our home handicrafts. The trouble is there's so much of it. Everybody has something he's personally pretty pleased with, like Barstow's proof of most of the classic math problems and my multimedia adaptation of *Sur le pont d'Avignon*. Its hard to decide what to send you with the limited power available, and we don't want to waste it with junk. So we took a vote and decided that the best thing was Ann's verse retelling of *War and Peace*. It runs pretty long. I hope the power holds it. I'll transmit as much of it as I can. . . .

WASHINGTON THREE

Spring was well advanced in Washington. Along the Potomac the cherry blossoms were beginning to bud, and Rock Creek Park was the pale green of new leaves. Even through the *whap, whap* of the helicopter rotor Knefhausen could hear an occasional rattle of small-arms fire from around Georgetown, and the Molotov cocktails and tear gas from the big Water Gate apartment development at the river's edge were steaming the sky with smoke and fumes. They never stopped, thought Knefhausen irritably. What was the good of trying to save people like this?

It was distracting. He found himself dividing his attention into three parts—the scarred, greening landscape below; the escort fire-ships that orbited around his own chopper; and the papers on his lap. All of them annoyed him. He couldn't keep his mind on any of them. What he liked least was the report from the *Constitution*. He had had to get expert help in translating what it was all about, and he didn't like the need, and even less liked the results. What had gone wrong? They were his kids, handpicked. There had been no hint, for instance, of hippiness in any of them, at least not past the age of twenty, and only for Ann Becklund and Florence Jackman even then. How had they got into this *I Ching* foolishness, and this stupid business with the *Achillea millefolium*, better known as the common yarrow? What "experiments"? Who started the disgustingly antiscientific acupuncture thing? How dared they depart from their programmed power budget for "research purposes," and what were the purposes? Above all, what was the "damage to the ship"?

He scribbled on a pad:

With immediate effect, cut out the nonsense. I have the impression you are all acting like irresponsible children. You are letting down the ideals of our program.

Knefhausen

After running the short distance from the chopper pad to the shelter of the guarded White House entrance, he gave the slip to a page from the Message Center for immediate encoding and transmission to the *Constitution* via Goldstone, Lunar Orbiter and Farside Base. All they needed was a reminder, he persuaded himself, then they would settle down. But he was still worried as he peered into a mirror, patted his hair down, smoothed his moustache with the tip of a finger and presented himself to the President's chief secretary.

This time they went down, not up. Knefhausen was going to the basement chamber that had been successively Franklin Roosevelt's swimming pool, the White House press lounge, a TV studio for taping jolly little two-shots of the President with congressmen and senators for the folks back home to see, and, now, the heavily armored bunker in which anyone trapped in the White House in the event of a successful attack from the city outside could hold out for several weeks, during which time the Fourth Armored would surely be able to retake the grounds from its bases in Maryland. It was not a comfortable room, but it was a safe one. Besides being armored against attack, it was as thoroughly soundproof, spyproof and leakproof as any chamber in the world, not excepting the Under-Kremlin or the Colorado NOROM base.

Knefhausen was admitted and seated, while the President and a couple of others were in whispered conversation at one end of the room, and the several dozen other people present craned their necks to stare at Knefhausen.

After a moment the President raised his head. "All right," he said. He drank from a crystal goblet of water, looking wizened and weary, and disappointed at the way a boyhood dream had turned out: the Presidency wasn't what it had seemed to be from Muncie, Indiana. "We all know why we're here. The government of the United States has given out information which was untrue. It did so knowingly and wittingly, and we've been caught at it. Now we want you to know the background, and so Dr. Knefhausen is going to explain the Alpha-Aleph project. Go ahead, Knefhausen."

Knefhausen stood up and walked unhurryingly to the little lectern set up for him, off to one side of the President. He opened his papers on the lectern, studied them thoughtfully for a moment with his lips pursed, and said:

"As the President has said, the Alpha-Aleph project is a camouflage. A few of you learned this some months ago, and then you referred to it with other words. 'Fraud.' 'Fake.' Words like that. But if I may say it in French, it is not any of those words, it is a legitimate *ruse de guerre*. Not the *guerre* against our political enemies, or even against the dumb kids in the streets with their Molotov cocktails and bricks. I do not mean those wars; I mean the war against ignorance.

For you see, there were certain sings—certain *things* we had to know for the sake of science and progress. Alpha-Aleph was designed to find them out for us.

"I will tell you the worst parts first," he said. "Number one, there is no such planet as Alpha-Aleph. The Russians were right. Number two, we knew this all along. Even the photographs we produced were fakes, and in the long run the rest of the world will find this out and they will know of our *ruse de guerre*. I can only hope that they will not find out too soon, for if we are lucky and keep the secret for a while, then I hope we will be able to produce good results to justify what we have done. Number three, when the *Constitution* reaches Alpha Centauri there will be no place for them to land, no way to leave their spacecraft, no sources of raw materials which they might be able to use to make fuel to return, no nothing but the star and empty space. This fact has certain consequences. The *Constitution* was designed with enough hydrogen fuel capacity for a one-way flight, plus maneuvering reserve. There will not be enough for them to come back, and the source they had hoped to tap, namely the planet Alpha-Aleph, does not exist, so they will not come back. Consequently they will die there. Those are the bad things to which I must admit."

There was a sighing murmur from the audience. The President was frowning absently to himself. Knefhausen waited patiently for the medicine to be swallowed, then went on.

"You ask, then, why have we done this thing? Condemning eight young people to their death? The answer is simple: knowledge. To put it with other words, we must have the basic scientific knowledge we need to protect the free world. You are all familiar, I si—I believe, with the known fact that basic scientific advances have been very few these past ten years and more. Much R&D. Much technology. Much applications. But in the years since Einstein, or better since Weizsäcker, very little basic.

"But without the new basic knowledge, the new technology must soon stop developing. It will run out of steam, you see.

"Now I must tell you a story. It is a true scientific story, not a joke; I know you do not want jokes from me at this time. There was a man named de Bono, a Maltese, who wished to investigate the process of creative thinking. There is not very much known about this process, but he had an idea how he could find something out. So he prepared for an experiment a room that was stripped of all furniture, with two doors, one across from the other. You go into one door, you go through the room, you walk out the other. He put at the door that was the entrance some material—two flat boards, some ropes. And he got as his subjects some young children. Now he said to the children, 'Now, this is a game we will play. You must go through this room and out the other door, that is all. If you do that, you win. But there is one rule. You must not touch the floor with your feet or your knees or with any part of your body or your clothing. We had here a boy,' he said, 'who was very athletic and walked across on his hands, but he was disqualified. You must not do that. Now go, and whoever does it fastest will win some chocolates.'

"So he took away all of the children but the first one and, one by one, they tried. There were ten or fifteen of them, and each of them did the same thing. Some it took longer to figure out, some figured it out right away, but it always was the same trick: They sat down on the floor, they took the boards and the ropes, and they tied one board to each foot and they walked across the room like on skis. The fastest one thought of the trick right away and was across in a few seconds. The slowest took many minutes. But it was the same trick for all of them, and that was the first part of the experiment.

"Now this Maltese man, de Bono, performed the second part of the experiment. It was exactly like the first, with one difference. He did not give them two boards. He only gave them one board.

"And in the second part every child worked out the same trick, too, but it was of course a different trick. They tied the rope to the end of the single board and then they stood on it, and jumped up, tugging the rope to pull the board forward, hopping and tugging, moving a little bit at a time, and every one of them succeeded. But in the first experiment the average time to cross was maybe forty-five seconds. And in the second experiment the average time was maybe twenty seconds. With one board they did their job faster than with two.

"Perhaps now some of you see the point. Why did not any of the children in the first group think of this faster method of going across the room? It is simple. They looked at what they were given to use for materials and, they are like all of us, they wanted to use everything. But they did not need everything. They could do better with less, in a different way."

Knefhausen paused and looked around the room, savoring the

moment. He had them now, he knew. It was just as it had been with the President himself, three years before. They were beginning to see the necessity of what had been done, and the pale, upturned faces were no longer as hostile, only perplexed and a little afraid.

He went on:

"So that is what Project Alpha-Aleph is about, gentlemen and ladies. We have selected eight of the most intelligent human beings we could find—healthy, young, very adventurous. Very creative. We played on them a nasty trick, to be sure. But we gave them an opportunity no one has ever had. The opportunity to *think*. To think for *ten years*. To think about basic questions. Out there they do not have the extra board to distract them. If they want to know something they cannot run to the library and look it up, and find that somebody has said that what they were thinking could not work. They must think it out for themselves.

"So in order to make this possible we have practiced a deception on them, and it will cost them their lives. All right, that is tragic, yes. But if we take their lives we give them in exchange immortality.

"How do we do this? Trickery again, gentlemen and ladies. I do not say to them, 'Here, you must discover new basic approaches to science and tell them to us.' I camouflage the purpose, so that they will not be distracted even by that. We have told them that this is recreational, to help them pass the time. This too is a *ruse de guerre*. The 'recreation' is not to help them make the trip; it is the whole purpose of the trip.

"So we start them out with the basic tools of science. With numbers: that is, with magnitudes and quantification, with all that scientific observations are about. With grammar. This is not what you learned when you were thirteen years old, it is a technical term; it means with the calculus of statement and the basic rules of communication: that is so they can learn to think clearly by communicating fully and without fuzzy ambiguity. We give them very little else, only the opportunity to mix these two basic ingredients and come up with new forms of knowledge.

"What will come of these things? That is a fair question. Unfortunately there is no answer. Not yet. If we knew the answer in advance, we would not have to perform the experiment. So we do not know what will be the end result of this, but already they have accomplished very much. Old questions that have puzzled the wisest of scientists for hundreds of years they have solved already. I will give you one example. You will say, 'Yes, but what does it *mean?*' I will answer, 'I do not know'; I only know that it is so hard a question that no one else has ever been able to answer it. It is a proof of a thing which is called Goldbach's Conjecture. Only a conjecture; you could call it a guess. A guess by an eminent mathematician some many years ago, that every even number can be written as the sum of two prime numbers. This is one of those simple problems in mathematics that everyone can understand and no one can solve. You can say, 'Certainly, sixteen is the sum of eleven and five, both of which are prime numbers, and thirty is the sum of twenty-three and seven, which also are both prime, and I can give you such numbers for any even number you care to name.' Yes, you can; but can you prove that for *every* even number it will *always* be possible to do this? No. You cannot. No one has been able to, but our friends on the *Constitution* have done it, and this was in the first few months. They have yet almost ten years. I cannot say what they will do in that time, but it is foolish to imagine that it will be anything less than very much indeed. A new relativity, a new universal gravitation—I don't know, I am only saying words. But much."

He paused again. No one was making a sound. Even the President was no longer staring straight ahead without expression, but was looking at him.

"It is not yet too late to spoil the experiment, and so it is necessary for us to keep the secret a bit longer. But there you have it, gentlemen and ladies. That is the truth about Alpha-Aleph." He dreaded what would come next, postponed it for a second by consulting his papers, shrugged, faced them and said: "Now, are there any questions?"

Oh, yes there were questions. Herr Omnes was stunned a little, took a moment to overcome the spell of the simple and beautiful truths he had heard, but then first one piped up, then another, then two or three shouting at once. There were questions, to be sure. Questions beyond answering. Questions Knefhausen did not have time to hear, much less answer, before the next question was on him. Questions to which he did not know the answers. Questions, worst of all, to which the answers were like pepper in the eyes, enraging, blinding the people to sense. But he had to face them, and he tried to answer them. Even when they shouted so that, outside the thick double doors, the Marine guards looked at each other uneasily and wondered what made the dull rumble that penetrated the very good sound-proofing of the room. "What I want to know, who put you up to this?" "Mr. Chairman, nobody; it is as I have said." "But see now, Knefhausen, do you mean to tell us you're murderin' these good people for the sake of some Goldbach's theory?" "No, Senator, not for Goldbach's Conjecture, but for what great advances in science will mean in the struggle to keep the free world free." "You're confessing you've dragged the United States into a palpable fraud?" "A legitimate ruse of war, Mr. Secretary, because there was no other way." "The photographs, Knefhausen?" "Faked, General, as I have told you. I accept full responsibility." And on and on, the words "murder" and "fraud" and even "treason" coming faster and faster.

Until at last the President stood up and raised his hand. Order was a long time coming, but at last they quieted down.

"Whether we like it or not, we're in it," he said simply. "There is nothing else to say. You have come to me, many of you, with rumors and asked for the truth. Now you have the truth, and it is classified Top Secret and must not be divulged. You all know what this means. I will only add that I personally propose to see that any breach of this security is investigated with all the resources of the government, and punished with the full penalty of the law. I declare this a matter of national emergency, and remind you that the penalty includes the death sentence when appropriate—and I say that in this case it is appropriate." He looked very much older than his years, and he moved his lips as though something tasted bad in his mouth. He allowed no further discussion, and dismissed the meeting.

Half an hour later, in his private office, it was just Knefhausen and the President.

"All right," said the President, "it's all hit the fan. The next thing is: The world will know it. I can postpone that a few weeks, maybe even months. I can't prevent it."

"I am grateful to you, Mr. President, for—"

"Shut up, Knefhausen. I don't want any speeches. There is one thing I want from you, and that is an explanation. What the hell is this about mixing up narcotics and free love and so on?"

"Ah," said Knefhausen, "you refer to the most recent communication from the *Constitution*. Yes. I have already dispatched, Mr.

President, a strongly worded order. Because of the communications lag it will not be received for some months, but I assure you the matter will be corrected."

The President said bitterly, "I don't want any assurances, either. Do you watch television? I don't mean *I Love Lucy* and the ball games; I mean news. Do you know what sort of shape this country is in? The bonus marches in 1932, the race riots in 1967—they were nothing. Time was when we could call out the National Guard to put down disorder. Last week I had to call out the Army to use against three companies of the Guard. One more scandal and we're finished, Knefhausen, and this is a big one."

"The purposes are beyond reproach—"

"Your purposes may be. Mine may be, or I try to tell myself it is for the good of science I did this, and not so I will be in the history books as the president who contributed a major breakthrough. But what are the purposes of your friends on the *Constitution*? I agreed to eight martyrs, Knefhausen. I didn't agree to forty billion dollars out of the nation's pockets to give your eight young friends ten years of gang-bangs and dope."

"Mr. President, I assure you this is only a temporary phase. I have instructed them to straighten out."

"And if they don't, what are you going to do about it?" The President, who never smoked, stripped a cigar, bit off the end and lit it. He said, "It's too late for me to say I shouldn't have let you talk me into this. So all I will say is you have to show results from this flim-flam before the lid blows off, or I won't be President anymore, and I doubt that you will be alive."

CONSTITUTION FOUR

This is Shef again and it's, oh, let me see, about Day 250. 300? No, I don't think so. Look, I'm sorry about the ship date, but I honestly don't think much in those terms anymore. I've been thinking about other things. Also I'm a little upset. When I tossed the ruble the hexagram was K'an, which is danger, over Li, the Sun. That's a bad mood to be communicating with you in. We aren't vengeful types, but the fact is that some of us were pretty sore when we found out what you'd done. I don't *think* you need to worry, but I wish I'd got a better hexagram.

Let me tell you the good parts first. Our velocity is pushing point four oh C now. The scenery is beginning to get interesting. For several weeks now the stars fore and aft have been drifting out of sight as the ones in front get up into the ultraviolet and the ones behind sink into the infrared. You'd think that as the spectrum shifts the other parts of the EMF bands would come into the visible range. I guess they do, but the stars peak in certain frequencies, and most of them seem to do it in the visible frequencies, so the effect is that they disappear. The first thing was that there was a sort of round black spot ahead of us where we couldn't see anything at all, not Alpha Centauri, not Beta Centauri, not even the bright Circini stars. Then we lost the Sun behind us, and a little later we saw the blackout spread to a growing circle of stars there. Then the circles began to widen.

Of course, we know that the stars are really there. We can detect them with phase-shift equipment, just as we can transmit and receive your message by shifting the frequencies. But we just can't see them anymore. The ones in direct line of flight, where we have a vector velocity of .34c or .37c (depending on whether they are in front of us or behind us) simply aren't radiating in the visible band anymore. The ones farther out to the side have been displaced visually because of the relativistic effects of our speed. But what it looks like is that we're running the hell out of Nothing, in the direction of Nothing, and it is frankly a little scary.

Even the stars off to one side are showing relativistic color shifts. It's almost like a rainbow, one of those full-circle rainbows that you see on the clouds beneath you from an airplane sometimes. Only this circle is all around us. Nearest the black hole in front the stars have frequency-shifted to a dull reddish color. They go through orange and yellow and a sort of leaf green to the band nearest the black hole in back, which are bright blue shading to purple. Jim Barstow has been practicing his farsight on them, and he can relate them to the actual sky map. But I can't. He sees something in the black hole in front of us that I can't see, either. He says he thinks it's a bright radio source, probably Centaurus A, and he claims it is radiating strongly in the whole visible band now. He means strongly for him, with his eyes. I'm not sure I can see it at all. There *may* be a sort of very faint, diffuse glow there, like the *gegenschein*, but I'm not sure. Neither is anyone else.

But the starbow itself is beautiful. It's worth the trip. Flo has been learning oil painting so she can make a picture of it to send you for your wall, although when she found out what you'd been up to she got so sore she was thinking of booby-trapping it with a fusion bomb or something. (But she's over that now, I think.)

So we're not so mad at you anymore, although there was a time when, if I'd been communicating with you at exactly that moment, I would have said some bad things.

. . . I just played this back, and it sounds pretty jumbled and confused. I'm sorry about that. It's hard for me to do this. I don't mean hard like intellectually difficult (the way chess problems and tensor analysis used to be), but hard like shoveling sand with a teaspoon. I'm just not used to constricting my thoughts in this straitjacket anymore. I tried to get one of the others to communicate this time instead of me, but there were no takers. I did get a lot of free advice. Dot says I shouldn't waste my time remembering how we used to talk. She wanted to write an eidetic account in simplified notation for you, which she estimated a crash program could translate for you in reasonable time, a decade or two, and would give you an absolutely full account of everything. I objected that that involved practical difficulties. Not in preparing the account, I don't mean. Shucks, we can all do that now. I don't forget anything, except irrelevant things like the standard-reckoning day that I don't want to remember in the first place, and neither does anyone else. But the length of transmission would be too much. We don't have the power to transmit the necessary number of groups, especially since the accident. Dot said we could Gödelize it. I said you were too dumb to de-Gödelize it. She said it would be good practice for you.

Well, she's right about that, and it's time you all learned how to communicate in a sensible way, so if the power holds out I'll include Dot's eidetic account at the end. In Gödelized form. Lots of luck. I won't honestly be surprised if you miss a digit or something and it all turns into *Rebecca of Sunnybrook Farm* or some missing books of apocrypha or, more likely of course, gibberish. Ski says it won't do you any good in any case, because Henle was right. I pass that on without comment.

Sex. You always want to hear about sex. It's great. Now that we don't have to fool with the pills anymore we've been having some marvelous times. Flo and Jim Barstow began making it as part of a multiplexed communications system that you have to see to believe. Sometimes when they're going to do it we all knock off and just sit around and watch them, cracking jokes and singing and helping with the auxiliary computations. When we had that little bit of minor surgery the other day (now we've got the bones seasoning), Ann and Ski decided to ball instead of using anesthesia, and they said it was better than acupuncture. It didn't block the sensation. They were aware of their little toes being lopped off, but they didn't perceive it as pain. So then Jim, when it was his turn, tried going through the amputation without anything at all in the expectation that he and Flo would go to bed together a little later, and that worked well too. He was all het up about it; claimed it showed a reverse causality that his theories predicted but that had not been demonstrated before. Said at last he was over the cause-preceding-the-effect hangup. It's like the Red Queen and the White Queen, and quite puzzling until you get the hang of it. (I'm not sure I've gotten the hang of it yet.) Suppose he hadn't balled Flo? Would his toe have hurt retroactively? I'm a little mixed up on this, Dot says because I simply don't understand phenomenology in general, and I think I'll have to take Ann's advice and work my way through Carnap, although the linguistics are so poor that it's hard to stay with it. Come to think of it, I don't have to. It's all in the Gödelized eidetic statement, after all. So I'll transmit the statement to you, and while I'm doing that it will be a sort of review for me and maybe I'll get my head right on causality.

Listen, let me give you a tip. The statement will also include Ski's trick of containing plasma for up to 500K milliseconds, so when you figure it out you'll know how to build those fusion power reactors you were talking about when we left. That's the carrot before your nose, so get busy on de-Gödelizing. The plasma dodge works fine, although of course we were sorry about what happened when we converted the drive. The explosion killed Will Becklund outright, and it looked hairy for all of us.

Well, anyway. I have to cut this short because the power's running a little low and I don't want to chance messing up the statement. It follows herewith:

$1973^{354} + 331^{852} + 17^{2008} + 5^{47} + 3^{9606} + 2^{88}$ take away 78.

Lots of luck, fellows!

WASHINGTON FOUR

Knefhausen lifted his head from the litter of papers on his desk. He rubbed his eyes, sighing. He had given up smoking the same time as the President, but, like the President, he was thinking of taking it up again. It could kill you, yes. But it was a tension-reducer, and he needed that. And what was wrong with something killing you? There were worse things than being killed, he thought dismally.

Looking at it any way you could, he thought objectively, the past two or three years had been hard on him. They had started so well and had gone so bad. Not as bad as those distant memories of childhood when everybody was so poor and Berlin was so cold and what warm clothes he had came from the *Winterhilfe*. By no means as hard as the end of the war. Nothing like as bad as those first years in South America and then in the Middle East, when even the lucky and famous ones, the Von Brauns and the Ehrickes, were having trouble getting what was due them and a young calf like Knefhausen had to peel potatoes and run elevators to live. But harder and worse than a man at the summit of his career had any reason to expect.

The Alpha-Aleph project, fundamentally, was sound! He ground his teeth, thinking about it. It would work—no, by God, it *was* working, and it would make the world a different place. Future generations would see.

But the future generations were not here yet, and in the present things were going badly.

Reminded, he picked up the phone and buzzed his secretary. "Have you got through to the President yet?" he demanded.

"I'm sorry, Dr. Knefhausen. I've tried every ten minutes, just as you said."

"Ah," he grunted. "No, wait. Let me see. What calls are there?"

Rustle of paper. "The news services, of course, asking about the rumors again. Jack Anderson's office. The man from CBS."

"No, no. I will not talk to press. Anyone else?"

"Senator Copley called, asking when you were going to answer the list of questions his committee sent you."

"I will give him an answer. I will give him the answer Götz von Berlichingen gave to the Bishop of Bamberg."

"I'm sorry, Dr. Knefhausen, I didn't quite catch—"

"No matter. Anything else?"

"Just a long-distance call, from a Mr. Hauptmann. I have his number."

"Hauptmann?" The name was puzzlingly familiar. After a moment Knefhausen placed it: to be sure, the photo technician who had cooperated in the faked pictures from Briareus Twelve. Well, he had his orders to stay out of sight and shut up. "No, that's not important. None of them are, and I do not wish to be disturbed with such nonsense. Continue as you were, Mrs. Ambrose. If the President is reached you are to put me on at once, but no other calls."

He hung up and returned to his desk.

He looked sadly and fondly at the papers. He had them all out: the reports from the *Constitution*, his own drafts of interpretation and comment, and more than a hundred footnoted items compiled by his staff, to help untangle the meanings and implications of those, ah, so cryptic sometimes reports from space:

"*Henle*. Apparently refers to Paul Henle (note appended); probably the citation intended is his statement, 'There are certain symbolisms in which certain things cannot be said.' Conjecture that English language is one of those symbolisms."

"*Orange sherbet sundae*. A classified experimental study was made of the material in Document Ref. No. CON-130, Para. 4. Chemical analysis and experimental testing have indicated that the recommended mixture of pharmaceuticals and other ingredients produce a hallucinogen-related substance of considerable strength and not wholly known qualities. 100 subjects ingested the product or a placebo in a double-blind controlled test. Subjects receiving the actual substance report reactions significantly different from the placebo. Effects reported include feelings of immense competence and deepened understanding. However, data is entirely subjective. Attempts were made to verify claims by standard I.Q., manipulative, and other tests, but the subjects did not cooperate well, and several have since absented themselves without leave from the testing establishment."

"*Gödelized language*. A system of encoding any message of any kind as a single very large number. The message is first written out in clear language and then encoded as bases and exponents. Each letter of the message is represented in order by the natural order of primes—that is, the first letter is represented by the base 2, the second by the base 3, the third by the base 5, then 7, 11, 13, 17, etc. The identity of the letter occupying that position in the message is given by the exponent: simply, the exponent 1 meaning that the letter in that position is an A, the exponent 2 meaning that it is a B, 3 a C, etc. The message as a whole is then rendered as the product of all the bases and exponents. *Example.* The word "cab" can thus be represented as $2^3 \times 3^1 \times 5^2$, or 600. (=8×3×25.) The name 'Abe' would be represented by the number 56,250, or $2^1 \times 3^2 \times 5^5$. (=2×9×3125.) A sentence like 'John lives,' would be represented by the product of the following terms: $2^{10} \times 3^{15} \times 5^8 \times 7^{14} \times 11^0 \times 13^{12} \times 17^9 \times 19^{22} \times 23^5 \times 29^{19} \times 31^{27}$ (in which the exponent '0' has been reserved for a space and the exponent '27' has been arbitrarily assigned to indicate a full stop). As can be seen, the Gödelized form for even a short message involves a very large number, although such numbers may be transmitted quite compactly in the form of a sum of bases and exponents. The example transmitted by the *Constitution* is estimated to equal the contents of a standard unabridged dictionary."

"*Farsight.* The subject James Madison Barstow is known to have suffered from some nearsightedness in his early school years, apparently brought on by excessive reading, which he attempted to cure through eye exercises similar to the 'Bates method' (note appended). His vision at time of testing for Alpha-Aleph project was optimal. Interviews with former associates indicate his continuing interest in increasing visual acuity. *Alternate explanation.* There is some indication that he was also interested in paranormal phenomena such as clairvoyance or prevision, and it is possible, though at present deemed unlikely, that his use of the term refers to 'looking ahead' in time."

And so on, and on.

Knefhausen gazed at the litter of papers lovingly and hopelessly, and passed his hand over his forehead. The kids! They were so marvelous . . . but so unruly . . . and so hard to understand. How unruly of them to have concealed their true accomplishments. The secret of hydrogen fusion! That alone would justify, more than justify, the entire project. But where was it? Locked in that number-jumber gibberish. Knefhausen was not without appreciation of the elegance of the method. He, too, was capable of taking seriously a device of such luminous simplicity. Once the number was written out you had only to start by dividing it by two as many times as possible, and the number of times would give you the first letter. Then divide by the next prime, three, and that number of times would give you the second letter. But the practical difficulties! You could not get even the first letter until you had the whole number, and IBM had refused even to bid on constructing a bank of computers to write that number out unless the development time was stretched to twenty-five years. *Twenty-five years.* And meanwhile in that number was hidden probably the secret of hydrogen fusion, possibly many greater secrets, most certainly the key to Knefhausen's own well-being over the next few weeks. . . .

His phone rang.

He grabbed it and shouted into it at once: "Yes, Mr. President!"

He had been too quick. It was only his secretary. Her voice was shaking but determined.

"It's not the President, Dr. Knefhausen, but Senator Copley is on the wire and he says it is urgent. He says—"

"No!" shouted Knefhausen and banged down the phone. He regretted it even as he was doing it. Copley was very high, chairman of the Armed Forces Committee; he was not a man Knefhausen wished to have as an enemy, and he had been very careful to make him a friend over years of patient fence-building. But he could not speak to him, or to anyone, while the President was not answering his calls. Copley's rank was high, but he was not in the direct hierarchical line over Knefhausen. When the top of that line refused to talk to him, Knefhausen was cut off from the world.

He attempted to calm himself by examining the situation objectively. The pressures on the President just now: They were enormous. There was the continuing trouble in the cities, all the cities. There were the political conventions coming up. There was the need to get elected for a third term, and the need to get the law amended to make that possible. And yes, Knefhausen admitted to himself, the worst pressure of all was the rumors that were floating around about the *Constitution*. He had warned the President. It was unfortunate the President had not listened. He had said that a secret known to two people is compromised and a secret known to more than two is not secret. But the President had insisted on the disclosure to that ever-widening circle of high officials—sworn, of course to secrecy, but what good was that?—and, of course, in spite of everything, there had been leaks. Fewer than one might have feared. More than one could stand.

He touched the reports from *Constitution* caressingly. Those beautiful kids, they could still make everything right, so wonderful. . . .

Because it was he who had made them wonderful, he confessed to himself. He had invented the idea. He had selected them. He had done things which he did not quite even yet reconcile himself to, to make sure that it was they and not some others who were on the crew. He had, above all, made assurance doubly sure by insuring their loyalty in every way possible. Training. Discipline. Ties of affection and friendship. More reliable ties: loading their food supplies, their entertainment tapes, their programmed activities with every sort of advertising inducement, M/R compulsion, psychological reinforcement he could invent or find, so that whatever else they did they did not fail to report faithfully back to Earth. Whatever else happened, there was that. The data might be hard to untangle, but it would be there. They could not help themselves; his commandments were stronger than God's; like Martin Luther, they must say *Ich kann night anders*, and come Pope or inquisition, they must stand by it. They would learn, and tell what they learned, and thus the investment would be repaid. . . .

The telephone!

He was talking before he had it even to his mouth. "Yes, yes! this is Dr. Knefhausen, yes!" he gabbled. Surely it must be the President now—

It was not.

"Knefhausen!" shouted the man on the other end. "Now, listen, I'll tell you what I told that bitch pig girl of yours, if I don't talk to you on the phone *right now* I'll have Fourth Armored in there to arrest you and bring you to me in twenty minutes. So listen!"

Knefhausen recognized both voice and style. He drew a deep voice and forced himself to be calm. "Very well, Senator Copley," he said, "what is it?"

"The game is blown, boy! That's what it is. That boy of yours in Huntsville, what's his name, the photo technician—"

"*Hauptmann?*"

"That's him! Would you like to know where he is, you dumb Kraut bastard?"

"Why, I suppose—I should think in Huntsville—"

"Wrong, boy! Your Kraut bastard friend claimed he didn't feel good and took some accrued sick time. Intelligence kept an eye on him up to a point, didn't stop him, wanted to see what he'd do. Well, they saw. They saw him leaving Orly Airport an hour ago in an Aeroflot plane. Put your big Kraut brain to work on that one, Knefhausen! He's defected. Now start figuring out what you're going to do about it, and it better be good."

Knefhausen said something, he did not know what, and hung up the phone, he did not remember when. He stared glassily into space for a time.

Then he flicked the switch for his secretary and said, not listening to her stammering apologies, "That long-distance call that came from Hauptmann before, Mrs. Ambrose. You didn't say where it was from."

"It was an overseas call, Dr. Knefhausen. From Paris. You didn't give me a chance to—"

"Yes, yes. I understand. Thank you. Never mind." He hung up and sat back. He felt almost relieved. If Hauptmann had gone to Russia it could only be to tell them that the picture was faked and not only was there no planet for the astronauts to land on but it was not a mistake, even, actually a total fraud. So now it was all out of his hands. History would judge him now. The die was cast. The Rubicon was crossed.

So many literary allusions, he thought deprecatingly. Actually it was not the judgment of history that was immediately important but the judgment of certain real people now alive and likely to respond badly. And they would judge him not so much by what might be or what should have been, as by what was. He shivered in the cold of that judgment and reached for the telephone to try once more to call the President. But he was quite sure the President would not answer, then or ever again.

CONSTITUTION FIVE

Old reliable peed-off Shef here. Look, we got your message. I don't want to discuss it. You've got a nerve. You're in a bad mood, aren't you?

If you can't say anything nice, don't say anything at all. We do the best we can, and that's not bad, and if we don't do exactly what you want us to, maybe it's because we know quite a lot more than you did when you fired us off at that blob of moonshine you call Alpha-Aleph. Well, thanks a lot for nothing.

On the other hand, thanks a little for what little you did do, which at least worked out to get us where we are, and I don't mean spatially. So I'm not going to yell at you. I just don't want to talk to you at all. I'll let the others talk for themselves.

Dot Letski speaking. This is important. Pass it on. I have three things to tell you that I do not want you to forget. *One: Most problems have grammatical solutions.* The problem of transporting people from the Earth to another planet does not get solved by putting pieces of steel together one at a time at random, and happening to find out you've built the *Constitution* by accident. It gets solved by constructing a model (= equation (= grammar)) which describes the necessary circumstances under which the transportation occurs. Once you have the grammatical model, you just put the metal around it and it goes like gangbusters.

When you have understood this you will be ready for: *Two: There is no such thing as causality.* What a waste of time it has been, trying to assign "causes" to "events"! You say things like, "Striking a match causes it to burn." True statement? No, false statement. You find yourself in a whole waffle about whether the "act" of "striking" is "necessary" and/or "sufficient" and you get lost in words. Pragmatically useful grammars are without tenses. In a decent grammar (which this English-language one, of course, is not, but I'll do the best I can) you can make a statement like "There exists a conjunction of forms of matter (specified) which combine with the release of energy at a certain temperature (specified) (which may be the temperature associated with heat of friction)." Where's the causality? "Cause" and "effect" are in the same timeless statement. So, *Three: There are no such thing as empirical laws.* When Ski came to understand that, he was able to contain the plasma in our jet indefinitely, not by pushing particles around in brute-force magnetic squeezes but by encouraging them to want to stay together. There are other ways of saying what he does (="creates an environment in which centripetal exceed centrifugal forces"), but the way I said it is better because it tells something about your characters. Bullies, all of you. Why can't you be nice to things if you want them to be nice to you? Be sure to pass this on to T'in Fa at Tiantsin, Professor Morris at All Soul's, and whoever holds the Carnap chair at UCLA.

Flo's turn. My mother would have loved my garden. I have drumsticks and daffodils growing side by side in the sludgy sand. They do so please us, and we them: I will probably transmit a full horticultural handbook at a future date, but meanwhile it is shameful to eat a radish. Carrots, on the other hand, enjoy it.

A statement of William Becklund, deceased. I emerged into the world between feces and urine, learned, grew, ate, worked, moved and died. Alternatively, I emerged from the hydrogen flare, shrank, disgorged, and reentered the womb one misses so. You may approach it from either end; it makes no difference at all which way you look at it.

Observational datum, Letski. At time *t*, a Dirac number incommensurable with GMT, the following phenomenon is observed:
    The radio source Centaurus A is identified as a positionally stable single collective object rather than two intersecting gas clouds and is observed to contract radially toward a center. Analysis and observation reveal it to be a Black Hole of which the fine detail is not detectable as yet. One infers all galaxies develop such central vortices, with implications of interest to astronomers and eschatologists. I, Seymour Letski, propose to take a closer look but the others prefer to continue programmed flight first. Harvard-Smithsonian notification service, please copy.

"Starbow," a preliminary study for a rendering into English of a poem by James Barstow:
    Gaggle of goslings but pick of our race
    We waddle through relativistic space.
    Dilated, discounted, despondent we scan:
    But vacant the Sign of the Horse and the Man.
    Vacant the Sign of the Man and the Horse,

And now we conjecture the goal of our course.
Tricked, trapped and cozened, we ruefully run
After the child of the bachelor sun.
The trick is revealed and the trap is confessed
And we are the butts of the dimwitted jest.
O Gander who made us, O Goose who laid us,
How lewdly and twistedly you betrayed us!
We owe you a debt. We won't forget.
With fortune and firmness we'll pay you yet.
Give us some luck and we'll timely send
Your pot of gold from the starbow's end.

Ann Becklund.

I think it was Stanley Weinbaum who said that from three facts a truly superior mind should be able to deduce the whole universe (Ski thinks it is possible with a finite number, but considerably larger than that). We are so very far from being truly superior minds by those standards, or even by our own. Yet we have a much larger number of facts to work with than three, or even three thousand, and so we have deduced a good deal.

This is not as valuable to you as you might have hoped, dear old bastardly Kneffie and all you bastardly others, because one of the things that we have deduced is that we can't tell you everything, because you wouldn't understand. We would help you along, some of you, if you were here, and in time you would be able to do what we do easily enough, but not at remote control.

But all is not lost, folks! Cheer up! You don't deduce like we deduce, but on the other hand you have so very much more to work from. Try. Get smart. You can do it if you want to. Set your person at rest, compose your mind before you speak, make your relations firm before you ask for something. Try not to be loathsome about it. Don't be like the fellow in the Changes. "He brings increase to no one. Indeed, someone even strikes him."

We've all grown our toes back now, even Will, although it was particularly difficult for him since he had been killed, and we've inscribed the bones and used them with very good effect in generating the hexagrams. I hope you see the point of what we did. We could have gone on with tossing coins or throwing the yarrow stalks, or at least with the closest Flo could breed to yarrow stalks. We didn't want to do that because it's not the optimum way.

The person who doesn't keep his heart constantly steady might say, "Well, what's the difference?" That's a poor sort of question to ask. It implies a deterministic answer. A better question to that is, "Does it make a difference?" and the answer to that is, "Yes, probably, because in order to do something right you must do it right." That is the law of identity, in any language.

Another question you might ask is, "Well, what source of knowledge are you actually tapping when you consult the hexagrams?" That's a better kind of question in that it doesn't *force* a wrong answer, but the answer is, again, indeterminate. You might view the *I Ching* as a sort of Rorschach bundle of squiggles that has no innate meaning but is useful because your own mind interprets it and puts sense into it. Feel free! You might think of it as a sort of memory bank of encoded lore. Why not? You might skip it entirely and come to knowledge in some other tao, any tao you like. ("The superior man understands the transitory in the light of the eternity of the end.") That's fine, too!

But whatever way you do it, you should *do* it that way. We needed inscribed bones to generate hexagrams, because that was the right way, and so it was no particular sacrifice to lop off a toe each for the purpose. It's working out nicely, except for one thing. The big hangup now is that the translations are so degraded, Chinese to German, German to English, and error seeping in at every step, but we're working on that now.

Perhaps I will tell you more at another time. Not now. Not very soon. Eve will tell you about that.

Eve Barstow, the Dummy, comes last and, I'm afraid, least.

When I was a little girl I used to play chess, badly, with very good players, and that's the story of my life. I'm a chronic over-achiever. I can't stand people who aren't smarter and better than I am, but the result is that I'm the runt of the litter every time. They are all very nice to me here, even Jim, but they know what the score is and so do I.

So I keep busy and applaud what I can't do. It isn't a bad life. I have everything I need, except pride.

Let me tell you what a typical day is like here between Sol and Centaurus. We wake up (if we have been sleeping, which some of us still do) and eat (if we are still eating, as all but Ski and, of course,

Will Becklund do). The food is delicious and Florence has induced it to grow cooked and seasoned where that is desirable, so it's no trouble to go over and pick yourself a nice poached egg or clutch of French fries. (I really prefer brioche in the mornings, but for sentimental reasons she can't manage them.) Sometimes we ball a little or sing old campfire songs. Ski comes down for that, but not for long, and then he goes back to looking at the universe. The starbow is magnificent and appalling. It is now a band about 40° across, completely surrounding us with colored light. One can always look in the other frequencies and see ghost stars before us and behind us, but in the birthright bands the view of the front and rear is now dead black and the only light is that beautiful banded ring of powdery stars.

Sometimes we write plays or have a little music. Shef had deduced four lost Bach piano concerti, very reminiscent of Corelli and Vivaldi, with everything going at once in the tuttis, and we've all adapted them for performance. I did mine on the Moog, but Ann and Shef synthesized whole orchestras. Shef's is particularly cute. You can tell that the flautist has early emphysema and two people in the violin section have been drinking, and he's got Toscanini conducting like a *risorgimento* metronome. Flo's oldest daughter made up words and now she sings a sort of nursery-rhyme adaptation of some Buxtehude chorales; oh, I didn't tell you about the kids. We have eleven of them now. Ann, Dot and I have one apiece, and Florence has eight. (But they're going to let me have quadruplets next week.) They let me take care of them pretty much for the first few weeks, while they're little, and they're *so* darling.

So mostly I spend my time taking care of the kids and working out tensor equations that Ski kindly gives me to do for him, and, I must confess it, feeling a little lonely. I *would* like to watch a TV quiz show over a cup of coffee with a friend! They let me do over the interior of our mobile home now and then. The other day I redid it in Pittsburgh suburban as a joke. Would you believe French windows in interstellar space? We never open them, of course, but they look real pretty with the chintz curtains and lace tiebacks. And we've added several new rooms for the children and their pets (Flo grew them the cutest little bunnies in the hydroponics plot).

Well, I've enjoyed this chance to gossip, so will sign off now. There is one thing I have to mention. The others have decided we don't want to get any more messages from you. They don't like the way you try to work on our subconsciouses and all (not that you succeed, of course, but you can see that it's still a little annoying), and so in future the dial will be set at six-six-oh, all right, but the switch will be in the "off" position. It wasn't my idea, but I was glad to go along. I *would* like some slightly less demanding company from time to time, although not, of course, yours.

WASHINGTON FIVE

Once upon a time the building that was known as DoD Temp Restraining Quarters 7—you might as well call it with the right word, "jail," Knefhausen thought—had been a luxury hotel in the Hilton chain. The maximum security cells were in the underground levels, in what had been meeting rooms. There were no doors or windows to the outside. If you did get out of your own cell you had a flight of stairs to get up before you were at ground level, and then the guards to break through to get to the open. And then, even if there happened not to be an active siege going on at the moment, you took your chances with the roaming addicts and activists outside.

Knefhausen did not concern himself with these matters. He did not think of escape, or at least didn't after the first few panicky moments, when he realized he was under arrest. He stopped demanding to see the President after the first few days. There was no point in appealing to the White House for help when it was the White House that had put him here. He was still sure that if only he could talk to the President privately for a few moments he could clear everything up. But as a realist he had faced the fact that the President would never talk to him privately again.

So he counted his blessings.

First, it was comfortable here. The bed was good, the rooms were warm. The food still came from the banquet kitchens of the hotel, and it was remarkably good for jailhouse fare.

Second, the kids were still in space and still doing some things, great things, even if they did not report what. His vindication was still a prospect.

Third, the jailers let him have newspapers and writing materials, although they would not bring him his books or give him a television set.

He missed the books, but nothing else. He didn't need TV to

tell him what was going on outside. He didn't even need the news-papers, ragged, thin and censored as they were. He could hear for himself. Every day there was the rattle of small-arms fire, mostly far-off and sporadic, but once or twice sustained and heavy and almost overhead, Brownings against AK-47s, it sounded like, and now and then the slap and smash of grenade launchers. Sometimes he heard sirens hooting through the streets, punctuated by clanging bells, and wondered that there was still a civilian fire department left to bother. (Or was it still civilian?) Sometimes he heard the grinding of heavy motors that had to be tanks. The newspapers did little to fill in the details, but Knefhausen was good at reading between the lines. The Administration was holed up somewhere—Key Biscayne or Camp David or Southern California, no one was saying where. The cities were all in red revolt. Herr Omnes had taken over.

For these disasters Knefhausen felt unjustly blamed. He com-posed endless letters to the President, pointing out that the serious troubles of the Administration had nothing to do with Alpha-Aleph; the cities had been in revolt for most of a generation, the dollar had become a laughingstock since the Indochinese wars. Some he de-stroyed, some he could get no one to take from him, a few he man-aged to dispatch—and got no answers.

Once or twice a week a man from the Justice Department came to ask him the same thousand pointless questions once again. They were trying to build up a dossier to prove it was all his fault, Knef-hausen suspected. Well, let them. He would defend himself when the time came. Or history would defend him. The record was clear. With respect to moral issues, perhaps, not so clear, he conceded. No matter. One could not speak of moral questions in an area so vital to the search for knowledge as this. The dispatches from the *Constitution* had already produced so much!—although, admittedly, some of the most significant parts were hard to understand. The Gödel message had not been unscrambled, and the hints of its contents remained only hints.

Sometimes he dozed and dreamed of projecting himself to the *Constitution*. It had been a year since the last message. He tried to imagine what they had been doing. They would be well past the midpoint now, decelerating. The starbow would be broadening and diffusing every day. The circles of blackness before and behind them would be shrinking. Soon they would see Alpha Centauri as no man had ever seen it. To be sure, they would then see that there was no planet called Aleph circling the primary, but they had guessed that somehow long since. Brave, wonderful kids! Even so they had gone on. This foolishness with drugs and sex, what of it? One opposed such goings-on in the common run of humanity, but it had always been so that those who excelled and stood out from the herd could make their own rules. As a child he had learned that the plump, proud air leader sniffed cocaine, that the great warriors took their sexual pleasure sometimes with each other. An intelligent man did not concern himself with such questions, which was one more indication that the man from the Justice Department, with his constant hinting and prying into Knefhausen's own background, was not really very intelligent.

The good thing about the man from the Justice Department was that one could sometimes deduce things from his questions, and rarely—oh, very rarely—he would sometimes answer a question himself. "Has there been a message from the *Constitution?*" "No, of course not, Dr. Knefhausen; now, tell me again, who suggested this fraudulent scheme to you in the first place?"

Those were the highlights of his days, but mostly the days just passed unmarked.

He did not even scratch them off on the wall of his cell, like the prisoner in the Chateau d'If. It would have been a pity to mar the hardwood paneling. Also, he had other clocks and calendars. There was the ticking of the arriving meals, the turning of the seasons as the man from the Justice Department paid his visits. Each of these was like a holiday—a holy day, not joyous but solemn. First there would be a visit from the captain of the guards, with two armed soldiers standing in the door. They would search his person and his cell on the chance that he had been able to smuggle in a—a what? A nuclear bomb, maybe. Or a pound of pepper to throw in the Justice man's eyes. They would find nothing, because there was nothing to find. And then they would go away, and for a long time there would be nothing. Not even a meal, even if a meal time happened to be due. Nothing at all, until an hour or three hours later the Justice man would come in with his own guard at the door, equally vigilant inside and out, and his engineer manning the tape recorders, and his questions.

And then there was the day when the man from the Justice Department came and he was not alone. With him was the President's secretary, Murray Amos.

•   •   •

How treacherous is the human heart! When it has given up hope, how little it takes to make it hope again!

"Murray!" cried Knefhausen, almost weeping. "It's so good to see you again! The President, is he well? What can I do for you? Have there been developments?"

Murray Amos paused in the doorway. He looked at Dieter von Knefhausen and said bitterly, "Oh, yes, there have been developments. Plenty of them. The Fourth Armored has just changed sides, so we are evacuating Washington. And the President wants you out of here at once."

"No, no! I mean—oh, yes, it is good that the President is concerned about my welfare, although it is bad about the Fourth Armored. But what I mean, Murray, is this: Has there been a message from the *Constitution?*"

Amos and the Justice Department man looked at each other. "Tell me, Dr. Knefhausen," said Amos silkily, "how did you manage to find that out?"

"Find it out? How could I find it out? No, I only asked because I hoped. There has been a message, yes? In spite of what they said? They have spoken again?"

"As a matter of fact, there has been," said Amos thoughtfully. The Justice Department man whispered piercingly in his ear, but Amos shook his head. "Don't worry, we'll be coming in a second. The convoy won't go without us. . . . Yes, Knefhausen, the message came through to Goldstone two hours ago. They have it at the decoding room now."

"Good, very good!" cried Knefhausen. "You will see, they will justify all. But what do they say? Have you good scientific men to interpret it? Can you understand the contents?"

"Not exactly," said Amos, "because there's one little problem the code room hadn't expected and wasn't prepared for. The message wasn't coded. It came in clear, but the language was Chinese."

CONSTITUTION SIX

Ref.: CONSIX T51/11055/*7
CLASSIFIED MOST SECRET

Subject: Transmission from U.S. Starship *Constitution*.

The following message was received and processed by the decrypt section according to standing directives. Because of its special nature, an investigation was carried out to determine its provenance. Radio-direction data received from Farside Base indicate its origin along a line of sight consistent with the present predicted location of the *Constitution*. Strength of signal was high but within appropriate limits, and degradation of frequency separation was consistent with relativistic shifts and scattering due to impact with particle and gas clouds.

Although available data do not prove beyond doubt that this transmission originated with the starship, no contraindications were found.

On examination, the text proved to be a phonetic transcription of what appears to be a dialect of Middle Kingdom Mandarin. Only a partial translation has been completed. (See note appended to text.) The translation presented unusual difficulties for two reasons: One, the difficulty of finding a translator of sufficient skill who could be granted appropriate security status; two, because (conjecturally) the language used may not correspond exactly to any dialect but may be an artifact of the *Constitution*'s personnel. (See PARA EIGHT, Lines 43–51 below, in this connection.)

This text is PROVISIONAL AND NOT AUTHENTICATED and is furnished only as a first attempt to translate the contents of the message into English. Efforts are being continued to translate the full message, and to produce a less corrupt text for the section herewith. Later versions and emendations will be forwarded when available.

TEXT FOLLOWS:

1 PARA ONE. The one who speaks for all [*Lt-Col*
2 *Sheffield N. Jackman?*] rests. With righteous
3 action comes surcease from care. I [*identity*
4 *not certain, but probably Mrs. Annette Marin*
5 *Becklund, less probably one of the other three*
6 *female personnel aboard, or one of their de-*
7 *scendants*] come in his place, moved by charity
8 and love.

9   PARA TWO. It is not enough to study or to do
10   deeds which make the people frown and bow
11   their heads. It is not enough to comprehend
12   the nature of the sky or the sea. Only through
13   the understanding of all can one approach wis-
14   dom, and only through wisdom can one act
15   rightly.
16   PARA THREE. These are the precepts as it is
17   given us to see them.
18   PARA FOUR. The one who imposes his will by
19   force lacks justice. Let him be thrust from a
20   cliff.
21   PARA FIVE. The one who causes another to
22   lust for a trifle of carved wood or a sweetmeat
23   lacks courtesy. Let him be restrained from the
24   carrying out of wrong practices.
25   PARA SIX. The one who ties a knot and says, "I
26   do not care who must untie it," lacks foresight.
27   Let him wash the ulcers of the poor and carry
28   nightsoil for all until he learns to see the day
29   to come as brother to the day that is.
30   PARA SEVEN. We who are in this here should
31   not impose our wills on you who are in that
32   here by force. Understanding comes late. We
33   regret the incident of next week, for it was
34   done in haste and in error. The one who
35   speaks for all acted without thinking. We who
36   are in this here were sorry for it afterward.
37   PARA EIGHT. You may wonder [*literally: ask*
38   *thoughtless questions of the hexagrams*] why
39   we are communicating in this language. The
40   reason is in part recreational, in part heuristic
41   [*literally: because on the staff hand one*
42   *becomes able to strike a blow more ably when*
43   *blows are struck repeatedly*], but the nature
44   of the process is such that you must go through
45   it before you can be told what it is. Our steps
46   have trodden this path. In order to reconstruct
47   the Chinese of the *I Ching* it was first neces-
48   sary to reconstruct the German of the trans-

49 lation from which the English was made. Error
50 lurks at every turn. [*Literally: false apparitions*
51 *shout at one each time the path winds.*] Many
52 flaws mark our carving. Observe it in silence
53 for hours and days until the flaws become part
54 of the work.
55 PARA NINE. It is said that you have eight days
56 before the heavier particles arrive. The dead
57 and broken will be few. It will be better if all
58 airborne nuclear reactors are grounded until
59 the incident is over.
60 PARA TEN. When you have completed rebuild-
61 ing send us a message, directed to the planet
62 Alpha-Aleph. Our home should be prepared
63 by then. We will send a ferry to help colonists
64 cross the stream when we are ready.

The above text comprises the first 852 groups of the transmission. The remainder of the text, comprising approximately 7500 groups, has not been satisfactorily translated. In the opinion of a consultant from the Oriental Languages Department at Johns Hopkins it may be a poem.

/s/ Durward S RICHTER

Durward S RICHTER
Maj Gen USMC
Chief Cryptographer
Commanding

Distribution: X X X BY HAND ONLY

WASHINGTON SIX

The President of the United States (Washington) opened the storm windows of his study and leaned out to yell at his Chief Science Adviser. "Harry, get the lead out! We're waiting for you!"

Harry looked up and waved, then continued doggedly plowing through the dripping jungle that was the North Lawn. Between the overgrown weeds and the rain and the mud it was slow going, but the President had little sympathy. He slammed down the window and said, "Damn that man, he just goes out of his way to aggravate me. How long am I supposed to wait for him so I can decide if we're gonna have to move the capital or not?"

The Vice President looked up from her knitting. "Jimbo, honey, why do you fuss yourself like that? Why don't we just move and get it over with?"

"Well, it looks so lousy." He threw himself into a chair despondently. "I was really looking forward to the Tenth Anniversary parade," he complained. "Ten years, that's really worth bragging about! I don't want to hold it the hell out in the sticks, I want it right down Constitution Avenue, just like the old days, with the people cheering and the reporters and the cameras all over and everything. Then let that son of a bitch in Omaha say I'm not the real President."

His wife said placidly, "Don't fuss yourself about him, honey. You know what I've been thinking, though? The parade might look a little skimpy on Constitution Avenue anyway. It would be real nice on a kind of littler street."

"Oh, what do you know? Anyway, where would we go? If Washington's under water, what makes you think Bethesda would be any better?"

His Secretary of State put down his solitaire cards and looked interested. "Doesn't have to be Bethesda," he said. "I got some real nice land up near Dulles we could use. It's high there."

"Why, sure. Lots of nice land over to Virginia," the Vice President confirmed. "Remember when we went out on that picnic after your Second Inaugural? That was at Fairfax Station. There was hills there all around. Just beautiful."

The President slammed his fist on the coffee table and yelled, "I'm not the President of Fairfax Station, I'm the President of the U.S. of A.! What's the capital of the U.S. of A.? Washington! My God, don't you see how those jokers in Houston and Omaha and Salt Lake and all would laugh if they heard I had to move out of my own capital?"

He broke off, because his Chief Science Advisor was coming in the door, shaking himself, dripping mud as he got out of his oilskin slicker. "Well?" demanded the President. "What did they say?"

Harry sat down. "It's terrible out there. Anybody got a dry cigarette?"

The President threw him a pack. Harry dried his fingers on his shirt front before he drew one out. "Well," he said, "I went to every boat captain I could find. They all said the same. Ships they talked to, places they'd been. All the same. Tides rising all up and down the coast."

He looked around for a match. The President's wife handed him a gold cigarette lighter with the Great Seal of the United States on it, which, after some effort, he managed to ignite. "It don't look good, Jimmy. Right now it's low tide and that's all right, but it's coming in. And tomorrow it'll come in a little higher. And there's going to be storms, not just rain like this, I mean, but you got to figure on a tropical depression coming up from the Bahamas now and then."

"We're not in the tropics," said the Secretary of State suspiciously.

"It doesn't mean that," said the Science Advisor, who had once given the weather reports over the local ABC television station, when there was such a thing as a television network. "It means storms. Hurricanes. But they're not the worst things; it's the tides. If the ice is melting then they're going to keep getting higher regardless."

The President drummed his fingers on the coffee table. Suddenly he shouted, "I don't *want* to move my capital!"

No one answered. His temper outbursts were famous. The Vice President became absorbed in her knitting, the Secretary of State picked up his cards and began to shuffle, the Science Advisor picked up his slicker and carefully hung it on the back of a door.

The President said, "You got to figure it this way. If we move out, then all those local yokels that claim to be the President of the United States are going to be just that much better off, and the eventual reunification of our country is going to be just that much more delayed." He moved his lips for a moment, then burst out, "I don't ask nothing for myself! I never have. I only want to play the part I have to play in what's good for all of us, and that means keeping up my position as the *real* President, according to the U.S. of A. Constitution as amended. And that means I got to stay right here in the real White House, no matter what."

His wife said hesitantly, "Honey, how about this? The other Presidents had like a Summer White House, and Camp David and like that. Nobody fussed about it. Why couldn't you do the same as they did? There's the nicest old farm house out near Fairfax Station that we could fix up to be real pretty."

The President looked at her with surprise. "Now, that's good thinking," he declared. "Only we can't move permanently, and we have to keep this place garrisoned so nobody else will take it away from us, and we have to come back here once in a while. How about that, Harry?"

His Science Advisor said thoughtfully, "We could rent some boats, I guess. Depends. I don't know how high the water might get."

"No 'guess'! No 'depends'! That's a national priority. We have to do it that way to keep that bastard in Omaha paying attention to the real President."

"Well, Jimbo, honey," said the Vice President after a moment, emboldened by his recent praise, "you have to admit they don't pay a lot of attention to us right now. When was the last time they paid their taxes?"

The President looked at her foxily over his glasses. "Talking about that," he said, "I might have a little surprise for them anyway. What you might call a secret weapon."

"I hope it does better than we did in the last war," said his wife, "because if you remember, when we started to put down the uprising in Frederick, Maryland, we got the pee kicked out of us."

The President stood up, indicating the Cabinet meeting was over.

"Never mind," he said sunnily. "You go on out again, Harry, and see of you can find any good maps in the Library of Congress where they got the fires put out. Find us a nice high place within, um, twenty miles if you can. Then we'll get the Army to condemn us a Summer White House like Mae says, and maybe I can sleep in a bed that isn't moldy for a change."

His wife looked worried, alerted by his tone. "What are you going to do, Jim?"

He chuckled. "I'm going to check out my secret weapon."

He shooed them out of his study and, when they were gone, went to the kitchen and got himself a bottle of Fresca from the six-pack in the open refrigerator. It was warm, of course. The Marine guard company was still trying to get the gas generator back in operation, but they were having little success. The President didn't mind. They were his personal Praetorians and, if they lacked a little as appliance repairmen, they had proved their worth when the chips were down. The President was always aware that during the Troubles he had been no more than any other Congressman—appointed to fill a vacancy, at that—and his rapid rise to Speaker of the House and Heir Apparent, finally to the Presidency itself, was due not only to his political skills and know-how, but also to the fact that he was the only remotely legitimate heir to the Presidency who also happened to have a brother-in-law commanding the Marine garrison in Washington.

The President was, in fact, quite satisfied with the way the world was going. If he envied Presidents of the past (missiles, fleets of nuclear bombers, billions of dollars to play with), he certainly saw nothing, when he looked at the world around him, to compare with his own stature in the real world he lived in.

He finished the soda, opened his study door a crack and peered out. No one was nearby. He slipped out and down the back stairs. In what had once been the public parts of the White House you could see the extent of the damage more clearly. After the riots and the trashings and the burnings and coups, the will to repair and fix up had gradually dwindled away. The President didn't mind. He didn't even notice the charred walls and the fallen plaster. He was listening to the sound of a distant gasoline pump chugging away, and smiling to himself as he approached the underground level where his secret weapon was locked up.

The secret weapon, whose name was Dieter von Knefhausen, was trying to complete the total defense of every act of his life that he called his memoirs.

He was less satisfied with the world than the President. He could have wished for many changes. Better health, for one thing; he was well aware that his essential hypertension, his bronchitis, and his gout were fighting the last stages of a total war to see which would have the honor of destroying their mutual battleground, which was himself. He did not much mind his lack of freedom, but he did mind the senseless destruction of so many of his papers.

The original typescript of his autobiography was long lost, but he had wheedled the President—the pretender, that is, who called himself the President—into sending someone to find what could be found of them. A few tattered and incomplete carbon copies had turned up. He had restored some of the gaps as best his memory and available data permitted, telling again the story of how he had planned Project Alpha-Aleph and meticulously itemizing the details of how he had lied, forged and falsified to bring it about.

He was as honest as he could be. He spared himself nothing. He admitted his complicity in the "accidental" death of Ann Barstow's first husband in a car smash, thus leaving her free to marry the man he had chosen to go with the crew to Alpha Centauri. He had confessed he had known that the secret would not last out the duration of the trip, thus betraying the trust of the President who made it possible. He put it all in, all he could remember, and boasted of his success.

For it was clear to him that his success was already proved. What could be surer evidence of it than what had happened ten years ago? The "incident of next week" was as dramatic and complete as anyone could wish. If its details were still indecipherable, largely because of the demolition of the existing technology structure it had brought about, its main features were obvious. The shower of heavy particles—baryon? perhaps even quarks?—had drenched the Earth. The source had been traced to a point in the heavens identical with that plotted for the *Constitution*.

Also there were the messages received, and, take them together, there was no doubt that the astronauts had developed knowledge so far in advance of anything on Earth that, from two light-years out, they could impose their will on the human race. They had done it. In one downpour of particles, the entire military-industrial complex of the planet was put out of action.

How? How? Ah, thought Knefhausen, with envy and pride, that was the question. One could not know. All that was known was that every nuclear device—bomb, powerplant, hospital radiation source or stockpile—had simultaneously soaked up the stream of particles and at that moment ceased to exist as a source of nuclear energy. It was not rapid and catastrophic, like a bomb. It was slow and long-lasting. The uranium and the plutonium simply melted in the long, continuous reaction that was still bubbling away in the seething lava lakes where the silos had stood and the nuclear power plants had generated electricity. Little radiation was released, but a good deal of heat.

Knefhausen had long since stopped regretting what could not be helped, but wistfully he still wished he had the opportunity to measure the total heat flux properly. Not less than 10^{16} watt-years, he was sure, just to judge by the effects on the Earth's atmosphere, the storms, the gradual raising of temperature all over, above all by the rumors about the upward trend of sea level that bespoke the melting of the polar ice caps. There was no longer even a good weather net, but the fragmentary information he was able to piece together suggested a world increase of four, maybe as many as six or seven degrees Celsian already, and the reactions still seething away in Czechoslovakia, the Congo, Colorado, and a hundred lesser infernos.

Rumors about the sea level?

Not rumors, no, he corrected himself, lifting his head and staring at the snake of hard rubber hose that began under the duckboards at the far end of the room and ended outside the barred window, where the gasoline pump outside did its best to keep the water level inside his cell low enough to keep the water below the boards. Judging by the inflow, the grounds of the White House must be nearly awash.

The door opened. The President of the United States (Washington) walked in, patting the shoulder of the thin, scared, hungry-looking kid who was guarding the door.

"How's it going, Knefhausen?" the President began sunnily. "You ready to listen to a little reason yet?"

"I'll do whatever you say, Mr. President, but as I have told you there are certain limits. Also I am not a young man, and my health—"

"Screw your health and your limits," shouted the President. "Don't start up with me, Knefhausen!"

"I am sorry, Mr. President," whispered Knefhausen.

"Don't be sorry! What I got to judge by is results. You know what it takes to keep that pump going just so you won't drown? Gas is rationed, Knefhausen! Takes a high national priority to get it! I don't know how long I'm gonna be able to justify this continuous drain on our resources if you don't cooperate."

Sadly, but stubbornly, Knefhausen said: "As far as I am able, Mr. President, I cooperate."

"Yeah. Sure." But the President was in an unusually good mood today, Knefhausen observed with the prisoner's paranoid attention to detail, and in a moment he said: "Listen, let's not get uptight about this. I'm making you an offer. Say the word and I'll fire that dumb son-of-a-bitch Harry Stokes and make you my Chief Science Advisor. How would that be? Right up at the top again. An apartment of your own. Electric lights! Servants—you can pick 'em out yourself, and there's some nice-looking little girls in the pool. The best food you ever dreamed of. A chance to perform a real service for the U.S. of A., helping to reunify this great country to become once again the great power it should and must be!"

"Mr. President," Knefhausen said, "naturally, I wish to help in any way I can. But we have been all over this before. I'll do anything you like, but I don't know how to make the bombs work again. You saw what happened, Mr. President. They're gone."

"I didn't say bombs, did I? Look, Kneffie, I'm a reasonable man. How about this. You promise to use your best scientific efforts *in any way you can*. You say you can't make bombs; all right. But there will be other things."

"What other things, Mr. President?"

"Don't push me, Knefhausen. Anything at all. Anything where you can perform a service for your country. You give me that promise and you're out of here today. Or would you rather I just turned off the pump?"

Knefhausen shook his head, not in negation but in despair. "You do not know what you are asking. What can a scientist do for you today? Ten years ago, yes. Even five years ago. We could have worked something out maybe; I could have done something. But now the preconditions do not exist. When all the nuclear plants went out— When the fertilizer plants couldn't fix nitrogen and the insecticide plants couldn't deliver—When the people began to die of hunger and the pestilences started—"

"I know all that, Knefhausen. Yes or no?"

The scientist hesitated, looking thoughtfully at his adversary. A gleam of the old shrewdness appeared in his eyes.

"Mr. President," he said slowly. "You know something. Something has happened."

"Right," crowed the President. "You're smart. Now tell me; what is it I know?"

Knefhausen shook his head. After seven decades of vigorous life, and another decade of slowly dying, it was hard to hope again. This terrible little man, this upstart, this lump—he was not without a certain animal cunning, and he seemed very sure. "Please, Mr. President. Tell me."

The President put a finger to his lips, and then an ear to the door. When he was convinced no one could be listening, he came closer to Knefhausen and said softly:

"You know that I have trade representatives all over, Knefhausen. Some in Houston, some in Salt Lake, some even in Montreal. They are not always there just for trade. Sometimes they find things out, and tell me. Would you like to know what my man in Anaheim has just told me?"

Knefhausen did not answer, but his watery old eyes were imploring.

"A message," whispered the President.

"From the *Constitution*?" cried Knefhausen. "But no, it is not possible! Farside is gone, Goldstone is destroyed, the orbiting satellites are running down—"

"It wasn't a radio message," said the President. "It came from Mount Palomar. Not the big telescope, because that got ripped off too, but what they call a Schmidt. Whatever that is. It still works. And they still have some old fogies who look through it now and then, for old times' sake. And they got a message, in laser light. Plain Morse code. From what they said was Alpha Centauri. From your little friends, Knefhausen."

He took a sheaf of paper from his pocket and held it up.

Knefhausen was racked by a fit of coughing, but he managed to croak: "Give it to me!"

The President held it away. "A deal, Knefhausen?"

"Yes, yes! Anything you say, but give me the message!"

"Why, certainly," smiled the President, and passed over the much-creased sheet of paper. It said:

PLEASE BE ADVISED. WE HAVE CREATED THE PLANET ALPHA-ALEPH. IT IS BEAUTIFUL AND GRAND. WE WILL SEND OUR FERRIES TO BRING SUITABLE PERSONS AND OTHERS TO STOCK IT AND TO COMPLETE CERTAIN OTHER BUSINESS. OUR SPECIAL REGARDS TO DR. DIETER VON KNEFHAUSEN, WHOM WE WANT TO TALK TO VERY MUCH. EXPECT US WITHIN THREE WEEKS OF THIS MESSAGE.

Knefhausen read it over twice, stared at the President and read it again. "I—I am very glad," he said inadequately.

The President snatched it back, folded it and put it in his pocket, as though the message itself was the key to power. "So you see," he said, "it's simple. You help me, I help you."

"Yes. Yes, of course," said Knefhausen, staring past him.

"They're your friends. They'll do what you say. All those things you told me that they can do—"

"Yes, the particles, the ability to reproduce, the ability, God save us, to build a planet—" Knefhausen might have gone on cataloging the skills of the spacemen indefinitely, but the President was impatient:

"So it's only a matter of days now, and they'll be here. You can imagine what they'll have! Guns, tools, everything—and all you have to do is get them to join me in restoring the United States of America to its proper place. I'll make it worth their while, Knefhausen! And yours, too. They—"

The President stopped, observing the scientist carefully. Then he cried "Knefhausen!" and leaped forward to catch him.

He was too late. The scientist had fallen limply to the duckboards. The guard, when ordered, ran for the White House doctor, who limped as rapidly to the scene as his bad legs and brain soaked with beer would let him, but he was too late too. Everything was too late for Knefhausen, whose old heart had failed him . . . as it proved a few days later (when the great golden ships from Alpha-Aleph landed and disgorged their bright, terrible crewmen to clean up the Earth), just in time.

DAMON KNIGHT

b. 1922

Damon Knight was born and raised in Oregon, and—after protracted stays in New York, Pennsylvania, Florida, and London—lives there now. Like many of the other Grand Masters, Knight caught the science fiction bug in his teens. Not yet twenty, he moved to New York City in 1941 to get closer to where the action was, and there became an instant member of the New York SF fan club, the Futurians. Knight's first thought of a career in science fiction was as an illustrator—his first professional sale was a cartoon, to *Amazing Stories*—but in the print-oriented company of Isaac Asimov, James Blish, Donald A. Wollheim, and the other Futurians he could not avoid turning to writing. His first published story was "Resilience," though it would not be accurate to describe it as his first "sale." The story appeared in Wollheim's short-lived magazine, *Stirring Science Stories*, which had the lowest budget of any newsstand science fiction magazine in history; it paid most of its contributors nothing at all. Judging by what happened to Knight's story, it would seem the printers weren't paid much better. "Resilience" was a tricky little story about a race of rubbery aliens visiting the Earth. As Knight wrote it, from the aliens' point of view, it was not until the aliens referred to human beings as "the Brittle People" that the reader discovered what they were like. Unfortunately, there was a problem at the press. Somehow, after the story had been proofread, someone seems to have dropped the type. When they restored it "the Brittle People" had become "the Little People," and the story no longer had any point at all.

"Resilience" was a one-off story; Knight wrote little fiction for the next few years, concentrating on beginning his career as a critic—in no-pay, small-circulation science fiction fan magazines to start, since there was no professional market for science-fiction criticism at the time. Then, in 1943, he commenced a new career.

I had just been inducted into the Army Air Forces; my position as an editor for the pulp chain of Popular Publications was thus about to become vacant. I took Damon into the office to meet the boss, Alden H. Norton, who hired him as my replacement on the spot.

Damon Knight was one of the most perceptive and adventurous editors the field of science fiction has ever had, but it took quite a while for that to become evident. The few years he spent at Popular Publications gave him a good grounding in the mechanics of editing and the magazine publishing process, but there, as an assistant to Norton, he had little freedom to pursue his own ideas. After World War II he became editor of the magazine *Worlds Beyond,* but the timing was poor and it survived for only three issues; later still he took over the magazine *If,* but again only for a few issues. It was not until 1966 that he began editing his *Orbit* series of anthologies of original science fiction stories; which gave first publication to a number of the field's best writers and set the standards for the whole genre for a period of years.

It was criticism, though, that interested Knight most in his early years. As the book publishing industry belatedly took note of science fiction and hardbound volumes began to appear in the late 1940s, Damon switched his critical medium from the fan magazines to the pros, notably to writing a regular review column for *The Magazine of Fantasy and Science Fiction;* many of those early critical essays were collected in Knight's book, *In Search of Wonder,* which won him a Hugo in 1956. He also participated, with James Blish and Judith Merril, in establishing the Milford Science-Fiction Writers Workshop, the first of its kind. Milford was not only a trade school for science fiction writers but, for a time, the principal milieu for discussion of science fiction as literature. (Knight later became a regular in-house instructor for the Clarion Workshop, Milford's successor.) Then, in the early 1950s he almost single-handed created the field's trade union, the Science Fiction Writers of America, churning out invitations to join to every single person who had a story in any science fiction publication. Naturally enough, he also served as SFWA's first president. In recognition of all these services to the cause of elevating the literary and critical standards of the field, the Science Fiction Research Association, the group that comprises the academic wing of science fiction, gave Knight its Pilgrim award in 1975. Other honors include the Charles Erskine Scott Wood award, and the honorary Doctorate of Humanities, conferred by Michigan State University in 1996.

Meanwhile, starting in the late 1940s, Knight had hit his stride as a writer. In collaboration with James Blish he published several workmanlike stories in Campbell's *Astounding*—by then well past its "Golden Age" but still for a time the leader in the field. When the two new challengers, *Galaxy* and *The Magazine of Fantasy and Science Fiction*, commenced publication Knight was a regular in their pages from their earliest issues. In 1949 he published the end-of-the-world story, "Not with a Bang," the first of his stories to attract wide attention, followed by perhaps his most famous story, "To Serve Man" (aliens visiting Earth carry a volume bearing that title; it turns out to be a cookbook), "The Country of the Kind," "Babel II," and dozens of others. All were marked by inventiveness, graceful prose, and terse, ironic compression, the very models of what a science fiction short story should be. That decade of the 1950s was a vintage season for short stories in the field. C. M. Kornbluth, Fritz Leiber, Robert Sheckley, and others were producing them in great volume and at the top of their form, but even in that remarkable field Knight's work stood out.

The novels came along, too, starting with *Hell's Pavement* in 1955 and followed by a dozen others over the years. They are all worth reading, but it is primarily Knight's brilliant shorter work, as well as his contributions in criticism and teaching, that made him an inevitable candidate for the Grand Master award.

Recommended Reading
by Damon Knight

THE HANDLER

When the big man came in, there was a movement in the room like bird dogs pointing. The piano player quit pounding, the two singing drunks shut up, all the beautiful people with cocktails in their hands stopped talking and laughing.

"Pete!" the nearest woman shrilled, and he walked straight into the room, arms around two girls, hugging them tight. "How's my sweetheart? Susy, you look good enough to eat, but I had it for lunch. George, you pirate"—he let go both girls, grabbed a bald blushing little man and thumped him on the arm—"you were great, sweetheart, I mean it, really great. Now HEAR THIS!" he shouted, over all the voices that were clamoring Pete this, Pete that.

Somebody put a martini in his hand and he stood holding it, bronzed and tall in his dinner jacket, teeth gleaming white as his shirt cuffs. "We had a show!" he told them.

A shriek of agreement went up, a babble of did we have a *show* my God Pete listen a *show*—

He held up his hand. "It was a good show!"

Another shriek and babble.

"The sponsor kinda liked it—he just signed for another one in the fall!"

A shriek, a roar, people clapping, jumping up and down. The big man tried to say something else, but gave up, grinning, while men and women crowded up to him. They were all trying to shake his hand, talk in his ear, put their arms around him.

"I love ya all!" he shouted. "Now what do you say, let's live a little!"

The murmuring started again as people sorted themselves out. There was a clinking form the bar. "Jesus, Pete," a skinny pop-eyed little guy was saying, crouching in adoration, "when you dropped that fishbowl I thought I'd pee myself, honest to God—"

The big man let out a bark of happy laughter. "Yeah, I can still see the look on your face. And the fish, flopping all over the stage. So what can I do, I get down there on my knees—" the big man did so, bending over and staring at imaginary fish on the floor. "And I say, 'Well, fellows, back to the drawing board!' "

Screams of laughter as the big man stood up. The party was arranging itself around him in arcs of concentric circles, with people in the back standing on sofas and the piano bench so they could see. Somebody yelled, "Sing the goldfish song, Pete!"

Shouts of approval, please-do-Pete, the goldfish song.

"Okay, okay." Grinning the big man sat on the arm of a chair and raised his glass. "And a vun, and a doo—vere's de moosic?" A scuffle at the piano bench. Somebody banged out a few chords. The big man made a comic face and sang, "Ohhh—how I wish . . . I was a little fish . . . and when I want some quail . . . I'd flap my little tail."

Laughter, the girls laughing louder than anybody and their red mouths farther open. One flushed blonde had her hand on the big man's knee, and another was sitting close behind him.

"But seriously—" the big man shouted. More laughter.

"No seriously," he said in a vibrant voice as the room quieted, "I want to tell you in all seriousness I couldn't have done it alone. And incidentally I see we have some foreigners, litvaks and other members of the press here tonight, so I want to introduce all the important people. First of all, George here, the three-fingered band leader—and there isn't a guy in the world could have done what he did this afternoon—George, I love ya." He hugged the blushing little bald man.

"Next my real sweetheart, Ruthie, where are ya? Honey, you were the greatest, really perfect—I mean it, baby—" He kissed a dark girl in a red dress who cried a little and hid her face on his broad shoulder. "And Frank—" he reached down and grabbed the skinny pop-eyed guy by the sleeve. "What can I tell you? A sweetheart?" The skinny guy was blinking, all choked up; the big man thumped him on the back. "Sol and Ernie and Mack, my writers, Shakespeare should have been so lucky—" One by one, they came up to shake the big man's hand as he called their names; the women kissed him and cried. "My stand-in," the big man was calling out, and "my caddy," and "Now," he said, as the room quieted a little, people flushed and sore-throated with enthusiasm, "I want you to meet my handler."

The room fell silent. The big man looked thoughtful and startled, as if he had had a sudden pain. Then he stopped moving. He sat without breathing or blinking his eyes. After a moment there was a jerky motion behind him. The girl who was sitting on the arm of the chair got up and moved away. The big man's dinner jacket split open in the back, and a little man climbed out. He had a perspiring brown face under a shock of black hair. He was a very small man, almost a dwarf, stoop-shouldered and round-backed in a sweaty brown singlet and shorts. He climbed out of the cavity in the big man's body, and closed the dinner jacket carefully. The big man sat motionless and his face was doughy.

The little man got down, wetting his lips nervously. Hello, Harry, a few people said. "Hello," Harry called, waving his hand. He was about forty, with a big nose and big soft brown eyes. His voice was cracked and uncertain. "Well, we sure put on a show, didn't we?"

Sure did, Harry, they said politely. He wiped his brow with the back of his hand. "Hot in there," he explained, with an apologetic grin. Yes I guess it must be, Harry, they said. People around the outskirts of the crowd were beginning to turn away, form conversational groups; the hum of talk rose higher. "Say, Tim, I wonder if I could have something to drink," the little man said. "I don't like to leave him—you know—" He gestured toward the silent big man.

"Sure, Harry, what'll it be?"

"Oh—you know—a glass of beer?"

Tim brought him a beer in a pilsener glass and he drank it thirstily, his brown eyes darting nervously from side to side. A lot of people were sitting down now; one or two were at the door leaving.

"Well," the little man said to a passing girl, "Ruthie, that was quite a moment there, when the fishbowl busted, wasn't it?"

"Huh? Excuse me, honey, I didn't hear you." She bent nearer.

"Oh—well, it don't matter. Nothing."

She patted him on the shoulder once, and took her hand away.

"Well excuse me, sweetie, I have to catch Robbins before he leaves." She went on toward the door.

The little man put his beer glass down and sat, twisting his knobby hands together. The bald man and the pop-eyed man were the only ones still sitting near him. An anxious smile flickered on his lips; he glanced at one face, then another. "Well," he began, "that's one show under our belts, huh, fellows, but I guess we got to start, you know, thinking about—"

"Listen, Harry," said the bald man seriously, leaning forward to touch him on the wrist, "why don't you get back inside?"

The little man looked at him for a moment with sad hound-dog eyes, then ducked his head, embarrassed. He stood up uncertainly, swallowed and said, "Well—" He climbed up on the chair behind the big man, opened the back of the dinner jacket and put his legs in one at a time. A few people were watching him, unsmiling. "Thought I'd take it easy a while," he said weakly, "but I guess—" He reached in and gripped something with both hands, then swung himself inside. His brown, uncertain face disappeared.

The big man blinked suddenly and stood up. "Well hey there," he called, "what's a matter with this party anyway? Let's see some life, some action—" Faces were lighting up around him. People began to move in closer. "What I mean, let me hear that beat!"

The big man began clapping his hands rhythmically. The piano took it up. Other people began to clap. "What I mean, are we alive here or just waiting for the wagon to pick us up? How's that again, can't hear you!" A roar of pleasure as he cupped his hand to his ear. "Well come on, let me hear it!" A louder roar. Pete, Pete; a gabble of voices. "I got nothing against Harry," said the bald man earnestly in the middle of the noise, "I mean for a square he's a nice guy." "Know what you mean," said the pop-eyed man, "I mean like he doesn't mean it." "Sure," said the bald man, "but Jesus that sweaty undershirt and all . . ." The pop-eyed man shrugged. "What are you gonna do?" Then they both burst out laughing as the big man made a comic face, tongue lolling, eyes crossed. Pete, Pete, Pete; the room was really jumping; it was a great party, and everything was all right, far into the night.

DIO

I

It is noon. Overhead the sky like a great silver bowl shimmers with heat; the yellow sand hurls it back; the distant ocean is dancing with white fire. Emerging from underground, Dio the Planner stands blinking a moment in the strong salt light; he feels the heat like a cap on his head, and his beard curls crisply, iridescent in the sun.

A few yards away are five men and women, their limbs glinting pink against the sand. The rest of the seascape is utterly bare; the sand seems to stretch empty and hot for miles. There is not even a gull in the air. Three of the figures are men; they are running and throwing a beach ball at one another, with far-off shouts. The two women are half reclining, watching the men. All five are superbly muscled, with great arched chests, ponderous as Percherons. Their skins are smooth; their eyes sparkle. Dio looks at his own forearm: is there a trace of darkness? is the skin coarsening?

He drops his single garment and walks toward the group. The sand's caress is briefly painful to his feet; then his skin adapts, and he no longer feels it. The five incuriously turn to watch him approach. They are all players, not students, and there are two he does not even know. He feels uncomfortable, and wishes he had not come. It isn't good for students and players to meet informally; each side is too much aware of the other's good-natured contempt. Dio tires to imagine himself a player, exerting himself to be polite to a student, and as always, he fails. The gulf is too wide. It takes both kinds to make a world, students to remember and make, players to consume and enjoy; but the classes should not mix.

Even without their clothing, these are players: the wide, innocent eyes that flash with enthusiasm, or flicker with easy boredom; the soft mouths that can be gay or sulky by turns. Now he deliberately looks at the blonde woman, Claire, and in her face he sees the same unmistakable signs. But, against all reason and usage, the soft curve of her lips is beauty; the poise of her dark-blonde head on the strong neck wrings his heart. It is illogical, almost unheard-of, perhaps abnormal; but he loves her.

Her gray eyes are glowing up at him like sea-agates; the quick pleasure of her smile warms and soothes him. "I'm so glad to *see* you." She takes his hand. "You know Katha of course, and Piet. And this is Tanno, and that's Mark. Sit here and talk to me, I can't move, it's so hot."

The ball throwers go cheerfully back to their game. The brunette, Katha, begins talking immediately about the choirs at Bethany: has Dio heard them? No? But he must; the voices are stupendous, the choir-master is brilliant; nothing like it has been heard for centuries.

The word "centuries" falls carelessly. How old is Katha—eight hundred, a thousand? Recently, in a three-hundred-year-old journal, Dio has been surprised to find a reference to Katha. Evidently he had known her briefly, forgotten her completely. There are so many people; it's impossible to remember. That's why the students keep journals; and why the players don't. He might even have met Claire before, and forgotten . . . "No," he says, smiling politely, "I've been busy with a project."

"Dio is an Architectural Planner," says Claire, mocking him with the exaggerated syllables; and yet there's a curious, inverted pride in her voice. "I told you, Kat, he's a student among students. He rebuilds this whole sector, every year."

"Oh," says Katha, wide-eyed, "I think that's absolutely fascinating." A moment later, without pausing, she has changed the subject to the new sky circus in Littlam—perfectly vulgar, but hilarious. The sky clowns! The tumblers! The delicious mock animals!

Claire's smooth face is close to his, haloed by the sun, gilded from below by the reflection of the hot sand. Her half-closed eyelids are delicate and soft, bruised by heat; her pupils are contracted, and the wide gray irises are intricately patterned. A fragment floats to the top of his mind, something he has read about the structure of the iris: ray-like dilating muscles interlaced with a circular contractile set, pigmented with a little melanin. For some reason, the thought is distasteful, and he pushes it aside. He feels a little lightheaded; he has been working too hard.

"Tired?" she asks gently.

He relaxes a little. The brunette, Katha, is still talking; she is one of those who talk and never care if anyone listens. He answers, "This is our busiest time. All the designs are coming back for a final check before they go into the master integrator. It's our last chance to find any mistakes."

"Dio, I'm sorry," she says. "I know I shouldn't have asked you." Her brows go up; she looks at him anxiously under her lashes. "You should rest, though."

"Yes," says Dio.

She lays her soft palm on the nape of his neck. "Rest, then. Rest."

"Ah," says Dio wearily, letting his head drop into the crook of his arm. Under the sand where he lies are seventeen inhabited levels, of which three are his immediate concern, over a sector that reaches from Alban to Detroy. He has been working almost without sleep for two weeks. Next season there is talk of beginning an eighteenth level; it will mean raising the surface again, and all the force-planes will have to be shifted. The details swim past, thousands of them; behind his closed eyes, he sees architectural tracings, blueprints, code sheets, specifications.

"Darling," says her caressing voice in his ear, "you know I'm happy you came, anyhow, even if you didn't want to. *Because* you didn't want to. Do you understand that?"

He peers at her with one half-open eye. "A feeling of power?" he suggests ironically.

"*No.* Reassurance is more like it. Did you know I was jealous of your work? . . . I am, very much. I told myself, if he'll leave it, now, today—"

He rolls over, smiling crookedly up at her. "And yet you don't know one day from the next."

Her answering smile is quick and shy. "I know, isn't it awful of me: but *you* do."

As they look at each other in silence, he is aware again of the gulf between them. *They need us*, he thinks, *to make their world over every year—keep it bright and fresh, cover up the past—but they dislike us because they know that whatever they forget, we keep and remember.*

His hand finds hers. A deep, unreasoning sadness wells up in him; he asks silently, *Why should I love you?*

He has not spoken, but he sees her face contract into a rueful, pained smile; and her fingers grip hard.

Above them, the shouts of the ball throwers have changed to noisy protests. Dio looks up. Piet, the cotton-headed man, laughing, is afloat over the heads of the other two. He comes down slowly and throws the ball; the game goes on. But a moment later Piet is in the air again: the others shout angrily, and Tanno leaps up to wrestle with him. The ball drops, bounds away: the two striving figures turn and roll in midair. At length the cotton-headed man forces the other down to the sand. They both leap up and run over, laughing.

"Someone's got to tame this wild man," says the loser, panting. "I can't do it, he's too slippery. How about you, Dio?"

"He's resting," Claire protests, but the others chorus, "Oh, yes!"

"Just a fall or two," says Piet, with a wide grin, rubbing his hands together. "There's lots of time before the tide comes in—unless you'd rather not?"

Dio gets reluctantly to his feet. Grinning, Piet floats up off the sand. Dio follows, feeling the taut surge of back and chest muscles, and the curious sensation of pressure on the spine. The two men circle, rising slowly. Piet whips his body over, head downward, arms slashing for Dio's legs. Dio overleaps him, and, turning, tries for a leg-and-arm; but Piet squirms away like an eel and catches him in a waist lock. Dio strains against the taut chest, all his muscles knotting; the two men hang unbalanced for a moment. Then, suddenly, something gives way in the force that buoys Dio up. They go over together, hard and awkwardly into the sand. There is a surprised babble of voices.

Dio picks himself up. Piet is kneeling nearby, white-faced, holding his forearm. "Bent?" asks Mark, bending to touch it gently.

"Came down with all my weight," says Piet. "Wasn't expecting—" He nods at Dio. "That's a new one."

"Well, let's hurry and fix it," says the other, "or you'll miss the spout." Piet lays the damaged forearm across his own thighs. "Ready?" Mark plants his bare foot on the arm, leans forward and presses sharply down. Piet winces, then smiles; the arm is straight.

"Sit down and let it knit," says the other. He turns to Dio. "What's this?"

Dio is just becoming aware of a sharp pain in one finger, and dark blood welling. "Just turned back the nail a little," says Mark. "Press it down, it'll close in a second."

Katha suggests a word game, and in a moment they are all sitting in a circle, shouting letters at each other. Dio does poorly; he cannot forget the dark blood falling from his fingertip. The silver sky seems oppressively distant; he is tired of the heat that pours down on his head, of the breathless air and the sand like hot metal under his body. He has a sense of helpless fear, as if something terrible had already happened; as if it were too late.

Someone says, "It's time," and they all stand up, whisking sand from their bodies. "Come on," says Claire over her shoulder. "Have you ever been up the spout? It's fun."

"No, I must get back, I'll call you later," says Dio. Her fingers lie softly on his chest as he kisses her briefly, then he steps away. "Goodbye," he calls to the others, "Goodbye," and turning, trudges away over the sand.

The rest, relieved to be free of him, are halfway to the rocks above the water's edge. A white feather of spray dances from a fissure as the sea rushes into the cavern below. The water slides back, leaving mirror-wet sand that dries in a breath. It gathers itself; far out a comber lifts its green head, and rushes onward. "Not this one, but the next," calls Tanno.

"Claire," says Katha, approaching her, "it was so peculiar about your friend. Did you notice? When he left, his finger was still bleeding."

The white plume leaps, higher, provoking a gust of nervous laughter. Piet dances up after it, waving his legs in a burlesque entrechat. "What?" says Claire. "You must be wrong. It couldn't have been."

"Now, come on, everybody. Hang close!"

"All the same," says Katha, "it was bleeding." No one hears her; she is used to that.

Far out, the comber lifts its head menacingly high; it comes onward, white-crowned, hard as bottle glass below, rising, faster, and as it roars with a shuddering of earth into the cavern, the Immortals are dashed high on the white torrent, screaming their joy.

Dio is in his empty rooms alone, pacing the resilient floor, smothered in silence. He pauses, sweeps a mirror into being on the bare wall; leans forward as if to peer at his own gray face, then wipes the mirror out again. All around him the universe presses down, enormous, inexorable.

The time stripe on the wall has turned almost black: the day is over. He has been here alone all afternoon. His door and phone circuits are set to reject callers, even Claire—his only instinct has been to hide.

A scrap of yellow cloth is tied around the hurt finger. Blood has saturated the cloth and dried, and now it is stuck tight. The blood has stopped, but the hurt nail has still not reattached itself. There is something wrong with him; how could there be anything wrong with him?

He has felt it coming for days, drawing closer, invisibly. Now it is here.

It has been eight hours . . . his finger has not healed itself.

He remembers that moment in the air, when the support dropped away under him. Could that happen again? He plants his feet firmly now, thinks, *Up*, and feels the familiar straining of his back and chest. But nothing happens. Incredulously, he tries again. Nothing!

His heart is thundering in his chest; he feels dizzy and cold. He sways, almost falls. It isn't possible that this should be happening to him. . . . Help; he must have help. Under his trembling fingers the phone index lights; he finds Claire's name, presses the selector. She may have gone out by now, but sector registry will find her. The screen pulses grayly. He waits. The darkness is a little farther away. Claire will help him, will think of something.

The screen lights, but it is only the neutral gray face of an autosec. "One moment please."

The screen flickers; at last, Claire's face!

"—is a recording, Dio. When you didn't call, and I couldn't reach you, I was very hurt. I know you're busy, but—Well, Piet has asked me to go over to Toria to play skeet polo, and I'm going. I may stay a few weeks for the flower festival, or go on to Rome. I'm sorry, Dio, we started out so nicely. Maybe the classes really don't mix. Goodbye."

The screen darkens. Dio is down on his knees before it. "Don't go," he says breathlessly. "Don't go." His last courage is broken; the hot, salt, shameful tears drop from his eyes.

The room is bright and bare, but in the corners the darkness is gathering, curling high, black as obsidian, waiting to rush.

II

The crowds on the lower level are a river of color, deep electric blue, scarlet, opaque yellow, all clean, crisp and bright. Flower scents puff from the folds of loose garments; the air is filled with good-natured voices and laughter. Back from five months' wandering in Africa, Pacifica and Europe, Claire is delightfully lost among the moving ways of Sector Twenty. Where the main concourse used to be, there is a maze of narrow adventure streets, full of gay banners and musky with perfume. The excursion cars are elegant little baskets of silver filigree, hung with airy grace. She gets into one and soars up the canyon of windows on a long, sweeping curve, past terraces and balconies, glimpse after intimate glimpse of people she need never see again: here a woman feeding a big blue macaw, there a couple of children staring at her from a garden, solemn-eyed, both with ragged yellow hair like dandelions. How long it has been since she last saw a child! . . . She tries to imagine what it must be like, to be a child now in this huge strange world full of grown people, but she can't. Her memories of her own childhood are so far away, quaint and small, like figures in the wrong side of an opera glass. Now here is a man with a bushy black beard, balancing a bottle on his nose for a group of laughing people . . . off it goes! Here are two couples obliviously kissing . . . Her heart beats a little faster; she feels the color coming into her cheeks. Piet was so tiresome, after a while; she wants to forget him now. She has already forgotten him; she hums in her sweet, clear contralto, "Dio, Dio, Dio . . ."

On the next level she dismounts and takes a robocab. She punches Dio's name; the little green-eyed driver "hunts" for a moment, flickering; then the cab swings around purposefully and gathers speed.

The building is unrecognizable; the whole street has been done over in baroque façades of vermilion and frost green. The shape of the lobby is familiar, though, and here is Dio's name on the directory.

She hesitates, looking up the uninformative blank shaft of the elevator well. Is he there, behind that silent bulk of marble? After a moment she turns with a shrug and takes the nearest of a row of fragile silver chairs. She presses "3"; the chair whisks her up, decants her.

She is in the vestibule of Dio's apartment. The walls are faced with cool blue-veined marble. On one side, the spacious oval of the shaft opening; on the other, the wide, arched doorway, closed. A mobile turns slowly under the lofty ceiling. She steps on the annunciator plate.

"Yes?" A pleasant male voice, but not a familiar one. The screen does not light.

She gives her name. "I want to see Dio—is he in?"

A curious pause. "Yes, he's *in* . . . Who sent you?"

"No one *sent* me." She has the frustrating sense that they are at cross purposes, talking about different things. "Who are you?"

"That doesn't matter. Well, you can come in, though I don't know when you'll get time today." The doors slide open.

Bewildered and more than half angry, Claire crosses the threshold. The first room is a cool gray cavern: overhead are fixed-circuit screens showing views of the sector streets. They make a bright frieze around the walls, but shed little light. The room is empty; she crosses it to the next.

The next room is a huge disorderly space full of machinery carelessly set down; Claire wrinkles her nose in distaste. Down at the far end, a few men are bending over one of the machines, their backs turned. She moves on.

The third room is a cool green space, terrazzo-floored, with a fountain playing in the middle. Her sandals click pleasantly on the hard surface. Fifteen or twenty people are sitting on the low curving benches around the walls, using the service machines, readers and so on: it's for all the world like the waiting room of a fashionable healer. Has Dio taken up mind-fixing?

Suddenly unsure of herself, she takes an isolated seat and looks around her. No, her first impression was wrong, these are not clients waiting to see a healer, because, in the first place, they are all students—every one.

She looks them over more carefully. Two are playing chess in an alcove; two more are strolling up and down separately; five or six are grouped around a little table on which some papers are spread; one of these is talking rapidly while the rest listen. The distance is too great; Claire cannot catch any words.

Farther down on the other side of the room, two men and a woman are sitting at a hooded screen, watching it intently, although at this distance it appears dark.

Water tinkles steadily in the fountain. After a long time the inner doors open and a man emerges; he leans over and speaks to another man sitting nearby. The second man gets up and goes through the inner doors; the first moves out of sight in the opposite direction. Neither reappears. Claire waits, but nothing more happens.

No one has taken her name, or put her on a list; no one seems to be paying her any attention. She rises and walks slowly down the room, past the group at the table. Two of the men are talking vehemently, interrupting each other. She listens as she passes, but it is all student gibberish: "the delta curve clearly shows . . . a stochastic assumption . . ." She moves on to the three who sit at the hooded screen.

The screen still seems dark to Claire, but faint glints of color move on its glossy surface, and there is a whisper of sound.

There are two vacant seats. She hesitates, then takes one of them and leans forward under the hood.

Now the screen is alight, and there is a murmur of talk in her ears. She is looking into a room dominated by a huge oblong slab of gray marble, three times the height of a man. Though solid, it appears to be descending with a steady and hypnotic motion, like a waterfall.

Under this falling curtain of stone sit two men. One of them is a stranger. The other—

She leans forward, peering. The other is in shadow; she cannot see his features. Still, there is something familiar about the outlines of his head and body. . . .

She is almost sure it is Dio, but when he speaks she hesitates again. It is a strange, low, hoarse voice, unlike anything she has ever heard before: the sound is so strange that she forgets to listen for the words.

Now the other man is speaking: ". . . these notions. It's just an ordinary procedure—one more injection."

"No," says the dark man with repressed fury, and abruptly stands up. The lights in that pictured room flicker as he moves, and the shadow swerves to follow him.

"Pardon me," says an unexpected voice at her ear. The man next to her is leaning over, looking inquisitive. "I don't think you're authorized to watch this session, are you?"

Claire makes an impatient gesture at him, turning back fascinated to the screen. In the pictured room, both men are standing now; the dark man is saying something hoarsely while the other moves as if to take his arm.

"Please," says the voice at her ear, "*are* you authorized to watch this session?"

The dark man's voice has risen to a hysterical shout—hoarse and thin, like no human voice in the world. In the screen, he whirls and makes as if to run back into the room.

"Catch him!" says the other, lunging after.

The dark man doubles back suddenly, past the other who reaches for him. Then two other men run past the screen; then the room is vacant; only the moving slab drops steadily, smoothly, into the floor.

The three beside Claire are standing. Across the room, heads turn. "What is it?" someone calls.

One of the men calls back, "He's having some kind of a fit!" In a lower voice, to the woman, he adds, "It's the discomfort, I suppose . . ."

Claire is watching, uncomprehendingly, when a sudden yell from the far side of the room makes her turn.

The doors have swung back, and in the opening a shouting man is wrestling helplessly with two others. They have his arms pinned and he cannot move any farther, but that horrible, hoarse voice goes on shouting, and shouting . . .

There are no more shadows: she can see his face.

"Dio!" she calls, getting to her feet.

Through his own din, he hears her and his head turns. His face gapes blindly at her, swollen and red, the eyes glaring. Then with a violent motion he turns away. One arm comes free, and jerks up to shield his head. He is hurrying away; the others follow. The doors close. The room is full of standing figures, and a murmur of voices.

Claire stands where she is, stunned, until a slender figure separates itself from the crowd. That other face seems to hang in the air, obscuring his—red and distorted, mouth agape.

The man takes her by the elbow, urges her toward the outer door. "What are you to Dio? Did you know him before?"

"Before what?" she asks faintly. They are crossing the room of machines, empty and echoing.

"Hm. I remember you now—I let you in, didn't I? Sorry you came?" His tone is light and negligent; she has the feeling that his attention is not really on what he is saying. A faint irritation at this is the first thing she feels through her numbness. She stirs as they walk, disengaging her arm from his grasp. She says, "What was wrong with him?"

"A very rare complaint," answers the other, without pausing. They are in the outer room now, in the gloom under the bright frieze, moving toward the doors. "Didn't you know?" he asks in the same careless tone.

"I've been away." She stops, turns to face him. "Can't you tell me? What *is* wrong with Dio?"

She sees now that he has a thin face, nose and lips keen, eyes bright and narrow. "Nothing you want to know about," he says curtly. He waves at the door control, and the doors slide noiselessly apart. "Goodbye."

She does not move, and after a moment the doors close again. "What's *wrong with him?*" she says.

He sighs, looking down at her modish robe with its delicate clasps of gold. "How can I tell you? Does the verb 'to die' mean anything to you?"

She is puzzled and apprehensive. "I don't know . . . isn't it something that happens to the lower animals?"

He gives her a quick mock bow. "Very good."

"But I don't know what it is. Is it—a kind of fit, like—" She nods toward the inner rooms.

He is staring at her with an expression half compassionate, half wildly exasperated. "Do you really want to know?" He turns abruptly and runs his finger down a suddenly glowing index stripe on the wall. "Let's see . . . don't know what there is in this damned reservoir. Hm. Animals, terminus." At his finger's touch, a cabinet opens and tips out a shallow oblong box into his palm. He offers it.

In her hands, the box lights up; she is looking into a cage in which a small animal crouches—a white rat. Its fur is dull and rough-looking; something is caked around its muzzle. It moves unsteadily, noses a cup of water, then turns away. Its legs seem to fail; it drops and lies motionless except for the slow rise and fall of its tiny chest.

Watching, Claire tries to control her nausea. Students' cabinets are full of nastinesses like this; they expect you not to show any distaste. "Something's the matter with it," is all she can find to say.

"Yes. It's dying. That means to cease living: to stop. Not to be any more. Understand?"

"No," she breathes. In the box, the small body has stopped moving. The mouth is stiffly open, the lip drawn back from the yellow teeth. The eye does not move, but glares up sightless.

"That's all," says her companion, taking the box back. "No more rat. Finished. After a while it begins to decompose and make a bad smell, and a while after that, there's nothing left but bones. And that has happened to every rat that was ever born."

"I don't *believe* you," she says. "It isn't like that; I never heard of such a thing."

"Didn't you ever have a pet?" he demands. "A parakeet, a cat, a tank of fish?"

"Yes," she says defensively, "I've had cats, and birds. What of it?"

"What happened to them?"

"Well—I don't know, I suppose I lost them. You know how you lose things."

"One day they're there, the next, not," says the thin man. "Correct?"

"Yes, that's right. But why?"

"We have such a tidy world," he says wearily. "Dead bodies would clutter it up; that's why the house circuits are programmed to remove them when nobody is in the room. Every one: it's part of the basic design. Of course, if you stayed in the room, and didn't turn your back, the machine would have to embarrass you by cleaning up the corpse in front of your eyes. But that never happens. Whenever you saw there was something wrong with any pet of yours, you turned around and went away, isn't that right?"

"Well, I really can't remember—"

"And when you came back, how odd, the beast was gone. It wasn't 'lost,' it was dead. They die. They all die."

She looks at him, shivering. "But that doesn't happen to *people*."

"No?" His lips are tight. After a moment he adds, "Why do you think he looked that way? You see he knows; he's known for five months."

She catches her breath suddenly. "That day at the beach!"

"Oh, were you there?" He nods several times, and opens the door again. "Very interesting for you. You can tell people you saw it happen." He pushes her gently out into the vestibule.

"But I want—" she says desperately.

"What? To love him again, as if he were normal? Or do you want to help him? Is that what you mean?" His thin face is drawn tight, arrow-shaped between the brows. "Do you think you could stand it? If so—" He stands aside, as if to let her enter again.

"Remember the rat," he says sharply.

She hesitates.

"It's up to you. Do you really want to help him? He could use some help, if it wouldn't make you sick. Or else—Where were you all this time?"

"Various places," she says stiffly. "Littlam, Paris, New Hol."

He nods. "Or you can go back and see them all again. Which?"

She does not move. Behind her eyes, now, the two images are intermingled: she sees Dio's gorged face staring through the stiff jaw of the rat.

The thin man nods briskly. He steps back, holding her gaze. There is a long suspended moment; then the doors close.

III

The years fall away like pages from an old notebook. Claire is in Stambul, Winthur, Kumoto, BahiBlanc . . . other places, too many to remember. There are the intercontinental games, held every century on the baroque wheel-shaped ground in Campan: Claire is one of the spectators who hover in clouds, following their favorites. There is a love affair, brief but intense; it lasts four or five years; the man's name is Nord, he has gone off now with another woman to Deya, and for nearly a month Claire has been inconsolable. But now comes the opera season in Milan, and in Tusca, afterwards, she meets some charming people who are going to spend a year in Papeete. . . .

Life is good. Each morning she awakes refreshed; her lungs fill with the clean air; the blood tingles in her fingertips.

On a spring morning, she is basking in a bubble of green glass, three-quarters submerged in an emerald-green ocean. The water sways and breaks, frothily, around the bright disk of sunlight at the top. Down below where she lies, the cool green depths are like mint to the fire-white bite of the sun. Tiny flat golden fishes swarm up to the bubble, turn, glinting like tarnished coins, and flow away again. The memory unit near the floor of the bubble is muttering out a muted tempest of Wagner: half listening, she hears the familiar music mixed with a gabble of foreign syllables. Her companion, with his massive bronze head almost touching the speakers, is listening attentively. Claire feels a little annoyed; she prods him with a bare foot: "Ross, turn that horrible thing off, won't you please?"

He looks up, his blunt face aggrieved. "It's *The Rhinegold*."

"Yes, I know, but I can't understand a word. It sounds as if they're clearing their throats. . . . Thank you."

He has waved a dismissing hand at the speakers, and the guttural chorus subsides. "Billions of people spoke that language once," he says portentously. Ross is an artist, which makes him almost a player, really, but he has the student's compulsive habit of bringing out these little kernels of information to lay in your lap.

"And I can't even stand four of them," she says lazily. "I only listen to opera for the music, anyhow, the stories are always so foolish; why is that, I wonder?"

She can almost see the learned reply rising to his lips; but he represses it politely—he knows she doesn't really want an answer—and busies himself with the visor. It lights under his fingers to show a green chasm, slowly flickering with the last dim ripples of the sunlight.

"Going down now?" she asks.

"Yes, I want to get those corals." Ross is a sculptor, not a very good one, fortunately, nor a very devoted one, or he would be impossible company. He has a studio on the bottom of the Mediterranean, in ten fathoms, and spends part of his time concocting gigantic menacing tangles of stylized undersea creatures. Finished with the visor, he touches the controls and the bubble drifts downward. The waters meet overhead with a white splash of spray; then the circle of light dims to yellow, to lime color, to deep green.

Beneath them now is the coral reef—acre upon acre of bare skeletal fingers. A few small fish move brilliantly among the pale branches. Ross touches the controls again; the bubble drifts to a stop. He stares down through the glass for a moment, then gets up to open the inner lock door. Breathing deeply, with a distant expression, he steps in and closes the transparent door behind him. Claire sees the water spurt around his ankles. It surges up quickly to fill the airlock; when it is chest high, Ross opens the outer door and plunges out in a cloud of air bubbles.

He is a yellow kicking shape in the green water; after a few moments he is half obscured by clouds of sediment. Claire watches, vaguely troubled; the largest corals are like bleached bone.

She fingers the memory unit for the Sea Pieces from *Peter Grimes*, without knowing why; it's cold, northern ocean music, not appropriate. The cold, far calling of the gulls makes her shiver with sadness, but she goes on listening.

Ross grows dimmer and more distant in the clouding water. At length he is only a flash, a flicker of movement down in the dusky green valley. After a long time she sees him coming back, with two or three pink corals in his hand.

Absorbed in the music, she has allowed the bubble to drift until the entrance is almost blocked by corals. Ross forces himself between them, levering himself against a tall outcropping of stone, but in a moment he seems to be in difficulty. Claire turns to the controls and backs the bubble off a few feet. The way is clear now, but Ross does not follow.

Through the glass she sees him bend over, dropping his specimens. He places both hands firmly and strains, all the great muscles of his limbs and back bulging. After a moment he straightens again, shaking his head. He is caught, she realizes; one foot is jammed into a crevice of the stone. He grins at her painfully and puts one hand to his throat. He has been out a long time.

Perhaps she can help, in the few seconds that are left. She darts into the airlock, closes and floods it. But just before the water rises over her head, she sees the man's body stiffen.

Now, with her eyes open under water, in that curious blurred light, she sees his gorged face break into lines of pain. Instantly, his face becomes another's—Dio's—vividly seen through the ghost of a dead rat's grin. The vision comes without warning, and passes.

Outside the bubble, Ross's stiff jaw wrenches open, then hangs slack. She sees the pale jelly come bulging slowly up out of his mouth; now he floats easily, eyes turned up, limbs relaxed.

Shaken, she empties the lock again, goes back inside and calls Antibe Control for a rescue cutter. She sits down and waits, careful not to look at the still body outside.

She is astonished and appalled at her own emotion. It has nothing to do with Ross, she knows: he is perfectly safe. When he breathed water, his body reacted automatically: his lungs exuded the protective jelly, consciousness ended, his heartbeat stopped. Antibe Control will be here in twenty minutes or less, but Ross could stay like that for years, if he had to. As soon as he gets out of the water, his lungs will begin to resorb the jelly; when they are clear, heartbeat and breathing will start again.

It's as if Ross were only acting out a part, every movement stylized and meaningful. In the moment of his pain, a barrier in her mind has gone down, and now a doorway stands open.

She makes an impatient gesture, she is not used to being tyrannized in this way. But her arm drops in defeat; the perverse attraction of that doorway is too strong. *Dio*, her mind silently calls. *Dio*.

The designer of Sector Twenty, in the time she has been away, has changed the plan of the streets "to bring the surface down." The roof of every level is a screen faithfully repeating the view from the surface, and with lighting and other ingenious tricks the weather up there is parodied down below. Just now it is a gray cold November day, a day of slanting gray rain: looking up, one sees it endlessly falling out of the leaden sky: and down here, although the air is as always pleasantly warm, the great bare slabs of the building fronts have turned bluish gray to match, and silvery insubstantial streamers are twisting endlessly down, to melt and disappear before they strike the pavement.

Claire does not like it; it does not feel like Dio's work. The crowds have a nervous air, curious, half-protesting; they look up and laugh, but uneasily, and the refreshment bays are full of people crammed together under bright yellow light. Claire pulls her metallic cloak closer around her throat; she is thinking with melancholy of the turn of the year, the earth growing cold and hard as iron, the trees brittle and black against the unfriendly sky. This is a time for blue skies underground, for flushed skins and honest laughter, not for this echoed grayness.

In her rooms, at least, there is cheerful warmth. She is tired and perspiring from the trip; she does not want to see anyone just yet. Some American gowns have been ordered; while she waits for them, she turns on the fire-bath in the bedroom alcove. The yellow spiky flames jet up with a black-capped *whoom*, then settle to a high murmuring curtain of yellow-white. Claire binds her head in an insulating scarf, and without bothering to undress, steps into the fire.

The flame blooms up around her body, cool and caressing; the fragile gown flares and is gone in a whisper of sparks. She turns, arms outspread against the flow. Depilated, refreshed, she steps out again. Her body tingles, invigorated by the flame. Delicately, she brushes away some clinging wisps of burnt skin; the new flesh is glossy pink, slowly paling to rose-and-ivory.

In the wall mirror, her eyes sparkle; her lips are liquidly red, as tender and dark as the red wax that spills from the edge of a candle.

She feels a somber recklessness; she is running with the tide. Responsive to her mood, the silvered ceiling begins to run with swift bloody streaks, swirling and leaping, striking flares of light from the bronze dado and the carved crystal lacework of the furniture. With a sudden exultant laugh, Claire tumbles into the great yellow bed: she rolls there, half smothered, the luxuriant silky fibers cool as cream to her skin; then the mood is gone, the ceiling dims to grayness; and she sits up with an impatient murmur.

What can be wrong with her? Sobered, already regretting the summery warmth of the Mediterranean, she walks to the table where Dio's card lies. It is his reply to the formal message she sent en route: it says simply:

THE PLANNER DIO WILL BE AT HOME.

There is a discreet chime from the delivery chute, and fabrics tumble in in billows of canary yellow, crimson, midnight blue. Claire chooses the blue, anything else would be out of key with the day; it is gauzy but long-sleeved. With it she wears no rings or necklaces, only a tiara of dark aquamarines twined in her hair.

She scarcely notices the new exterior of the building; the ascensor shaft is dark and padded now, with an endless chain of cushioned seats that slowly rise, occupied or not, like a disjointed flight of stairs. The vestibule above slowly comes into view, and she feels a curious shock of recognition.

It is the same: the same blue-veined marble, the same mobile idly turning, the same arched doorway.

Claire hesitates, alarmed and displeased. She tries to believe that she is mistaken: no scheme of decoration is ever left unchanged for as much as a year. But here it is, untouched, as if time had queerly stopped here in this room when she left it: as if she had returned, not only to the same choice, but to the same instant.

She crosses the floor reluctantly. The dark door screen looks back at her like a baited trap.

Suppose she had never gone away—what then? Whatever Dio's secret is, it has had ten years to grow, here behind this unchanged door. There it is, a darkness, waiting for her.

With a shudder of almost physical repulsion, she steps onto the annunciator plate.

The screen lights. After a moment a face comes into view. She sees without surprise that it is the thin man, the one who showed her the rat. . . .

He is watching her keenly. She cannot rid herself of the vision of the rat, and of the dark struggling figure in the doorway. She says, "Is Dio—" She stops, not knowing what she meant to say.

"At home?" the thin man finishes. "Yes, of course. Come in."

The doors slide open. About to step forward, she hesitates again, once more shocked to realize that the first room is also unchanged. The frieze of screens now displays a row of gray-lit streets; that is the only difference; it is as if she were looking into some far-distant world where time still had meaning, from this still, secret place where it has none.

The thin man appears in the doorway, black-robed. "My name is Benarra," he says, smiling. "Please come in; don't mind all this, you'll get used to it."

"Where is Dio?"

"Not far . . . But we make a rule," the thin man says, "that only students are admitted to see Dio. Would you mind?"

She looks at him with indignation. "Is this a joke? Dio sent me a note . . ." She hesitates; the note was noncommittal enough, to be sure.

"You can become a student quite easily," Benarra says. "At least, you can begin, and that would be enough for today." He stands waiting, with a pleasant expression; he seems perfectly serious.

She is balanced between bewilderment and surrender. "I don't— what do you want me to do?"

"Come and see." He crosses the room, opens a narrow door. After a moment she follows.

He leads her down an inclined passage, narrow and dark. "I'm living on the floor below now," he remarks over his shoulder, "to keep out of Dio's way." The passage ends in a bright central hall from which he leads her through a doorway into dimness.

"Here your education begins," he says. On both sides, islands of light glow up slowly: in the nearest, and brightest, stands a curious group of beings, not ape, not man: black skins with a bluish sheen, tiny eyes peering upward under shelving brows, hair a dusty black. The limbs are knob-jointed like twigs; the ribs show; the bellies are soft and big. The head of the tallest comes to Claire's waist. Behind them is a brilliant glimpse of tropical sunshine, a conical mass of what looks like dried vegetable matter, trees and horned animals in the background.

"Human beings," says Benarra.

She turns a disbelieving, almost offended gaze on him. "Oh, no!"

"Yes, certainly. Extinct several thousand years. Here, another kind."

In the next island the figures are also black-skinned, but taller— shoulder high. The woman's breasts are limp leathery bags that hang to her waist. Claire grimaces. "Is something wrong with her?"

"A different standard of beauty. They did that to themselves, deliberately. Woman creating herself. See what you think of the next."

She loses count. There are coppery-skinned ones, white ones, yellowish ones, some half naked, others elaborately trussed in metal and fabric. Moving among them, Claire feels herself suddenly grown titanic, like a mother animal among her brood: she has a flash of absurd, degrading tenderness. Yet, as she looks at these wrinkled gnomish faces, they seem to hold an ancient and stubborn wisdom that glares out at her, silently saying, *Upstart!*

"What happened to them all?"

"They died," says Benarra. "Every one."

Ignoring her troubled look, he leads her out of the hall. Behind them, the lights fall and dim.

The next room is small and cool, unobtrusively lit, unfurnished except for a desk and chair, and a visitor's seat to which Benarra waves her. The domed ceiling is pierced just above their heads with round transparencies, each glowing in a different pattern of simple blue and red shapes against a colorless ground.

"They are hard to take in, I know," says Benarra. "Possibly you think they're fakes."

"No." No one could have imagined those fierce, wizened faces; somewhere, sometime, they must have existed.

A new thought strikes her. "What about *our* ancestors—what were they like?"

Benarra's gaze is cool and thoughtful. "Claire, you'll find this hard to believe. Those were our ancestors."

She is incredulous again. "Those—absurdities in there?"

"Yes. All of them."

She is stubbornly silent a moment. "But you said, they *died*."

"They did; they died. Claire—did you think our race was always immortal?"

"Why—" She falls silent, confused and angry.

"No, impossible. Because if we were, where are all the old ones? No one in the world is older than, perhaps, two thousand years. That's not very long. . . . What are you thinking?"

She looks up, frowning with concentration. "You're saying it happened. But how?"

"It didn't happen. We did it, we created ourselves." Leaning back, he gestures at the glowing transparencies overhead. "Do you know what those are?"

"No. I've never seen any designs quite like them. They'd make lovely fabric patterns."

He smiles. "Yes, they are pretty, I suppose, but that's not what they're for. These are enlarged photographs of very small living things—too small to see. They used to get into people's bloodstreams and make them die. That's bubonic plague"—blue and purple dots alternating with larger pink disks—"that's tetanus"—blue rods and red dots—"that's leprosy"—dark spotted blue lozenges with a cross-hatching of red behind them. "That thing that looks something like a peacock's tail is a parasitic fungus called *streptothrix actinomyces*. That one"—a particularly dainty design of pale blue with darker accents—"is from a malignant oedema with gas gangrene."

The words are meaningless to her, but they call up vague images that are all the more horrible for having no definite outlines. She thinks again of the rat, and of a human face somehow assuming that stillness, that stiffness . . . frozen into a bright pattern, like the colored dots on the wall. . . .

She is resolved not to show her disgust and revulsion. "What happened to them?" she asks in a voice that does not quite tremble.

"Nothing. The planners left them alone, but changed us. Most of the records have been lost in two thousand years, and of course we have no real science of biology as they knew it. I'm no biologist, only a historian and collector." He rises. "But one thing we know they did was to make our bodies chemically immune to infection. Those things"—he nods to the transparencies above—"are simply irrelevant now, they can't harm us. They still exist—I've seen cultures taken from living animals. But they're only a curiosity. Various other things were done, to make the body's chemistry, to put it crudely, more stable. Things that would have killed our ancestors by toxic reactions—poisoned them—don't harm us. Then there are the protective mechanisms, and the paraphysical powers that *homo sapiens* had only in potential. Levitation, regeneration of lost organs. Finally, in general we might say that the body was very much more homeostatized than formerly, that is, there's a cycle of functions which always tends to return to the norm. The cumulative processes that used to impair function don't happen—the 'matrix' doesn't thicken, progressive dehydration never gets started, and so on. But you see all these are just delaying actions, things to prevent you and me from dying prematurely. The main thing"—he fingers an index stripe, and a linear design springs out on the wall—"was this. Have you ever read a chart, Claire?"

She shakes her head dumbly. The chart is merely an unaesthetic curve drawn on a reticulated background: it means nothing to her. "This is a schematic way of representing the growth of an organism," says Benarra. "You see here, this up-and-down scale is numbered in one-hundredths of mature weight—from zero here at the bottom, to one hundred per cent here at the top. Understand?"

"Yes," she says doubtfully. "But what good is that?"

"You'll see. Now this other scale, along the bottom, is numbered according to the age of the organism. Now: this sharply rising curve here represents all other highly developed species except man. You see, the organism is born, grows very rapidly until it reaches almost its full size, then the curve rounds itself off, becomes almost level. Here it declines. And here it stops: the animal dies."

He pauses to look at her. The word hangs in the air; she says nothing, but meets his gaze.

"Now this," says Benarra, "this long shallow curve represents man as he was. You notice it starts far to the left of the animal curve. The planners had this much to work with: man was already unique, in that he had this very long juvenile period before sexual maturity. Here: see what they did."

With a gesture, he superimposes another chart on the first.

"It looks almost the same," says Claire.

"Yes. Almost. What they did was quite a simple thing, in principle. They lengthened that juvenile period still further, they made the curve rise still more slowly . . . and never quite reach the top.

The curve now becomes asymptotic, that is, it approaches sexual maturity by smaller and smaller amounts, and never gets there, no matter how long it goes on."

Gravely, he returns her stare.

"Are you saying," she asks, "that we're *not* sexually mature? Not anybody?"

"Correct," he says. "Maturity in every complex organism is the first stage of death. We never mature, Claire, and that's why we don't die. We're the eternal adolescents of the universe. That's the price we paid."

"The price . . ." she echoes. "But I still don't see." She laughs. "Not *mature*—" Unconsciously she holds herself straighter, shoulders back, chin up.

Benarra leans casually against the desk, looking down at her. "Have you ever thought to wonder why there are so few children? In the old days, loving without any precautions, a grown woman would have a child a year. Now it happens perhaps once in a hundred billion meetings. It's an anomaly, a freak of nature, and even then the woman can't carry the child to term herself. Oh, we *look* mature; that's the joke—they gave us the shape of their own dreams of adult power." He fingers his glossy beard, thumps his chest. "It isn't real. We're all pretending to be grownup, but not one of us knows what it's really like."

A silence falls.

"Except Dio?" says Claire, looking down at her hands.

"He's on the way to find out. Yes."

"And you can't stop it . . . you don't know why."

Benarra shrugs. "He was under strain, physical and mental. Some link of the chain broke, we may never know which one. He's already gone a long way up that slope—I think he's near the crest now. There isn't a hope that we can pull him back again."

Her fists clench impotently. "Then what good is it all?"

Benarra's eyes are hooded; he is playing with a memocube on the desk. "We learn," he says. "We can do something now and then, to alleviate, to make things easier. We don't give up."

She hesitates. "How long?"

"Actually, we don't know. We can guess what the maximum is; we know that from analogy with other mammals. But with Dio, too many other things might happen." He glances up at the transparencies.

"Surely you don't mean—" The bright ugly shapes glow down at her, motionless, inscrutable.

"Yes. Yes. He had one of them already, the last time you saw him—a virus infection. We were able to control it; it was what our ancestors used to call 'the common cold'; they thought it was mild. But it nearly destroyed Dio—I mean, not the disease itself, but the moral effect. The symptoms were unpleasant. He wasn't prepared for it."

She is trembling. "Please."

"You have to know all this," says Benarra mercilessly, "or it's no use your seeing Dio at all. If you're going to be shocked, do it now. If you can't stand it, then go away now, not later." He pauses, and speaks more gently. "You can see him today, of course; I promised that. Don't try to make up your mind now, if it's hard. Talk to him, be with him this afternoon; see what it's like."

Claire does not understand herself. She has never been so foolish about a man before: love is all very well; love never lasts very long and you don't expect that it should, but while it lasts, it's pleasantness. Love is joy, not this wrenching pain.

Time flows like a strong, clean torrent, if only you let things go. She could give Dio up now and be unhappy, perhaps, a year or five years, or fifty, but then it would be over, and life would go on just the same.

She sees Dio's face, vivid in memory—not the stranger, the dark shouting man, but Dio himself, framed against the silver sky: sunlight curved on the strong brow, the eyes gleaming in shadow.

"We've got him full of antibiotics," says Benarra compassionately. "We don't think he'll get any of the bad ones. . . . But aging itself is the worst of them all. . . . What do you say?"

IV

Under the curtain of falling stone, Dio sits at his workbench. The room is the same as before; the only visible change is the statue which now looms overhead, in the corner above the stone curtain: it is the figure of a man reclining, weight on one elbow, calf crossed over thigh, head turned pensively down toward the shoulder. The figure is powerful, but there is a subtle feeling of decay about it: the bulging muscles seem about to sag; the face, even in shadow, has a deformed, damaged look. Forty feet long, sprawling immensely across the corner of the room, the statue has a raw, compulsive power: it is supremely ugly, but she can hardly look away.

A motion attracts her eye. Dio is standing beside the bench, waiting for her. She advances hesitantly: the statue's face is in shadow, but Dio's is not, and already she is afraid of what she may see there.

He takes her hand between his two palms; his touch is warm and dry, but something like an electric shock seems to pass between them, making her start.

"Claire—it's good to see you. Here, sit down, let me look." His voice is resonant, confident, even a trifle assertive; his eyes are alert and preternaturally bright. He talks, moves, holds himself with an air of suppressed excitement. She is relieved and yet paradoxically alarmed: there is nothing really different in his face; the skin glows clear and healthy, his lips are firm. And yet every line, every feature, seems to be hiding some unpleasant surprise; it is like looking at a mask which will suddenly be whipped aside.

In her excitement, she laughs, murmurs a few words without in the least knowing what she is saying. He sits facing her across the corner of the desk, commandingly intent; his eyes are hypnotic.

"I've just been sketching some plans for next year. I have some ideas . . . it won't be like anything people expect." He laughs, glancing down; the bench is covered with little gauzy boxes full of shadowy line and color. His tools lie in disorderly array, solidopens, squirts, calipers. "What do you think of this, by the way?" He points up, behind him, at the heroic statue.

"It's very unusual . . . yours?"

"A copy, from stereographs—the original was by Michelangelo, something called 'Evening.' But I did the copy myself."

She raises her eyebrows, not understanding.

"I mean I didn't do it by machine. I carved the stone myself—with mallet and chisel, in these hands, Claire." He holds them out, strong, calloused. It was those flat pads of thickened skin, she realizes, that felt so warm and strange against her hand.

He laughs again. "It was an experience. I found out about texture, for one thing. You know, when a machine melts or molds a statue, there's no texture, because to a machine granite is just like cheese. But when you carve, the stone fights back. Stone has character, Claire, it can be stubborn or evasive—it can throw chips in your face, or make your chisel slip aside. Stone fights." His hand clenches, and again he laughs that strange, exultant laugh.

In her apartment late that evening, Claire feels herself confused and overwhelmed by conflicting emotions. Her day with Dio has been like nothing she ever expected. Not once has he aroused her pity: he is like a man in whom a flame burns. Walking with her in the streets, he has made her see the Sector as he imagines it: an archaic vision of buildings made for permanence rather than for change; of masonry set by hand, woods hand-carved and hand-polished. It is a terrifying vision, and yet she does not know why. People endure; things should pass away. . . .

In the wide cool rooms an air whispers softly. The border lights burn low around the bed, inviting sleep. Claire moves aimlessly in the outer rooms, letting her robe fall, pondering a languorous stiffness in her limbs. Her mouth is bruised with kisses. Her flesh remembers the touch of his strange hands. She is full of a delicious weariness; she is at the floating, bodiless zenith of love, neither demanding nor regretting.

Yet she wanders restively through the rooms, once idly evoking a gust of color and music from the wall; it fades into an echoing silence. She pauses at the door of the playroom, and looks down into the deep darkness of the diving well. To fall is a luxury like bathing in water or flame. There is a sweetness of danger in it, although the danger is unreal. Smiling, she breathes deep, stands poised, and steps out into emptiness. The gray walls hurtle upward around her: with an effort of will she withholds the pulse of strength that would support her in midair. The floor rushes nearer, the effort mounts intolerably. At the last minute she releases it; the surge buoys her up in a brief paroxysmal joy. She comes to rest, inches away from the hard stone. With her eyes dreamily closed, she rises slowly again to the top. She stretches: now she will sleep.

V

First come the good days. Dio is a man transformed, a demon of energy. He overflows with ideas and projects; he works unremittingly, accomplishes prodigies. Sector Twenty is the talk of the continent, of the world. Dio builds for permanence, but, dissatisfied, he tears down what he has built and builds again. For a season all his streets are soaring, incredibly beautiful lace-works of stone; then all the ornament vanishes and his buildings shine with classical purity: the streets are full of white light that shines from the stone. Claire waits for the cycle to turn again, but Dio's work becomes ever more massive and crude; his stone darkens. Now the streets are narrow and full of shadows; the walls frown down with heavy magnificence. He builds no more ascensor shafts; to climb in Dio's buildings, you walk up ramps or even stairs, or ride in closed elevator cars. The people murmur, but he is still a novelty; they come from all over the planet to protest, to marvel, to complain; but they still come.

Dio's figure grows heavier, more commanding: his cheeks and chin, all his features thicken; his voice becomes hearty and resonant. When he enters a public room, all heads turn: he dominates any company; where his laugh booms out, the table is in a roar.

Women hang on him by droves; drunken and triumphant, he sometimes staggers off with one while Claire watches. But only she knows the defeat, the broken words and the tears, in the sleepless watches of the night.

There is a timeless interval when they seem to drift, without anxiety and without purpose, as if they had reached the crest of the wave. Then Dio begins to change again, swiftly and more swiftly. They are like passengers on two moving ways that have run side by side for a little distance, but now begin to diverge.

She clings to him with desperation, with a sense of vertigo. She is terrified by the massive, inexorable movement that is carrying her off: like him, she feels drawn to an unknown destination.

Suddenly the bad days are upon them. Dio is changing under her eyes. His skin grows slack and dull; his nose arches more strongly. He trains vigorously, under Benarra's instruction; when streaks of gray appear in his hair, he conceals them with pigments. But the lines are cutting themselves deeper around his mouth and at the corners of the eyes. All his bones grow knobby and thick. She cannot bear to look at his hands, they are thick-fingered, clumsy; they hold what they touch, and yet they seem to fumble.

Claire sometimes surprises herself by fits of passionate weeping. She is thin; she sleeps badly and her appetite is poor. She spends most of her time in the library, pursuing the alien thoughts that alone make it possible for her to stay in touch with Dio. One day, taking the air, she passes Katha on the street, and Katha does not recognize her.

She halts as if struck, standing by the balustrade of the little stone bridge. The building fronts are shut faces, weeping with the leaden light that falls from the ceiling. Below her, down the long straight perspective of the stair, Katha's little dark head bobs among the crowd and is lost.

The crowds are thinning; not half as many people are here this season as before. Those who come are silent and unhappy; they do not stay long. Only a few miles away, in Sector Nineteen, the air is full of streamers and pulsing with music: the light glitters, people are hurrying and laughing. Here, all colors are gray. Every surface is amorphously rounded, as if mumbled by the sea; here a baluster is missing, here a brick has fallen; here, from a ragged alcove in the wall, a deformed statue leans out to peer at her with its malevolent terra cotta face. She shudders, averting her eyes, and moves on.

A melancholy sound surges into the street, filling it brim-full. The silence throbs; then the sound comes again. It is the tolling of the great bell in Dio's latest folly, the building he calls a "cathedral." It is a vast enclosure, without beauty and without a function. No one uses it, not even Dio himself. It is an emptiness waiting to be filled. At one end, on a platform, a few candles burn. The tiled floor is always gleaming, as if freshly damp; shadows are piled high along the walls. Visitors hear their footsteps echo sharply as they enter; they turn uneasily and leave again. At intervals, for no good reason, the great bell tolls.

Suddenly Claire is thinking of the Bay of Napol, and the white gulls wheeling in the sky: the freshness, the tang of ozone, and the burning clear light.

As she turns away, on the landing below she sees two slender figures, hand in hand: a boy and a girl, both with shocks of yellow hair. They stand isolated; the slowly moving crowd surrounds them with a changing ring of faces. A memory stirs: Claire recalls the other afternoon, the street, so different then, and the two small yellow-haired children. Now they are almost grown; in a few more years they will look like anyone else.

A pang strikes at Claire's heart. She thinks, *If we could have a child* . . .

She looks upward in a kind of incredulous wonder that there

should be so much sorrow in the world. Where has it all come from? How could she have lived for so many decades without knowing of it?

The leaden light flickers slowly and ceaselessly along the blank stone ceiling overhead.

Dio is in his studio, tiny as an ant in the distance, where he swings beside the shoulder of the gigantic, half-carved figure. The echo of his hammer drifts down to Claire and Benarra at the doorway.

The figure is female, seated; that is all they can distinguish as yet. The blind head broods, turned downward; there is something malign in the shapeless hunch of the back and the thick, half-defined arms. A cloud of stone dust drifts free around the tiny shape of Dio; the bitter smell of it is in the air; the white dust coats everything.

"Dio," says Claire into the annunciator. The chatter of the distant hammer goes on. "Dio."

After a moment the hammer stops. The screen flicks on and Dio's white-masked face looks out at them. Only the dark eyes have life; they are hot and impatient. Hair, brows and beard are whitened; even the skin glitters white, as if the sculptor had turned to stone.

"Yes, what is it?"

"Dio—let's go away for a few weeks. I have such a longing to see Napol again. You know, it's been years."

"You go," says the face. In the distance, they see the small black figure hanging with its back turned to them, unmoving beside the gigantic shoulder. "I have too much to do."

"The rest would be good for you," Benarra puts in. "I advise it, Dio."

"I have too much to do," the face repeats curtly. The image blinks out; the chatter of the distant hammer begins again. The black figure blurs in a new cloud of dust.

Benarra shakes his head. "No use." They turn and walk out across the balcony, overlooking the dark reception hall. Benarra says, "I didn't want to tell you this just yet. The Planners are going to ask Dio to resign his post this year."

"I've been afraid of it," says Claire after a moment. "Have you told them how it will make him feel?"

"They say the Sector will become an Avoided Place. They're right; people already are beginning to have a feeling about it. In another few seasons they would stop coming at all."

Her hands are clasping each other restlessly. "Couldn't they give it to him, for a Project, or a museum, perhaps—?" She stops; Benarra is shaking his head.

"He's got this to go through," he says. "I've seen it coming."

"I know." Her voice is flat, defeated. "I'll help him . . . all I can."

"That's just what I don't want you to do," Benarra says.

She turns, startled; he is standing erect and somber against the balcony rail, with the gloomy gulf of the hall below. He says, "Claire, you're holding him back. He dyes his hair for you, but he has only to look at himself when he has been working in the studio, to realize what he actually looks like. He despises himself . . . he'll end hating you. You've got to go away now, and let him do what he has to."

For a moment she cannot speak; her throat aches. "What does he have to do?" she whispers.

"He has to grow old, very fast. He's put it off as long as he can." Benarra turns, looking out over the deserted hall. In a corner, the old cloth drapes trail on the floor. "Go to Napol, or to Timbuk. Don't call, don't write. You can't help him now. He has to do this all by himself."

In Djuba she acquires a little ring made of iron, very old, shaped like a serpent that bites its own tail. It is a curiosity, a student's thing; no one would wear it, and besides it is too small. But the cold touch of the little thing in her palm makes her shiver, to think how old it must be. Never before has she been so aware of the funnel-shaped maw of the past. It feels precarious, to be standing over such gulfs of time.

In Winthur she takes the waters, makes a few friends. There is a lodge on the crest of Mont Blanc, new since she was last here, from which one looks across the valley of the Doire. In the clear Alpine air, the tops of the mountains are like ships, afloat in a sea of cloud. The sunlight is pure and thin, with an aching sweetness; the cries of the skiers echo up remotely.

In Cair she meets a collector who has a curious library, full of scraps and oddments that are not to be found in the common supply. He has a baroque fancy for antiquities; some of his books are actually made of paper and bound in synthetic leather, exact copies of the originals.

" 'Again, the Alfurs of Poso, in Central Celebes,' " she reads aloud, " 'tell how the first men were supplied with their requirements direct from heaven, the Creator passing down his gifts to them by means of a rope. He first tied a stone to the rope and let it down from the sky. But the men would have none of it, and asked somewhat peevishly of what use to them was a stone. The Good God then let down a banana, which, of course, they gladly accepted and ate with relish. This was their undoing. "Because you have chosen the banana," said the deity, "you shall propagate and perish like the banana, and your offspring shall step into your place. . . ." ' " She closes the book slowly. "What was a banana, Alf?"

"A phallic symbol, my dear," he says, stroking his beard, with a pleasant smile.

In Prah, she is caught up briefly in a laughing horde of athletes, playing follow-my-leader: they have volplaned from Omsk to the Baltic, tobogganed down the Rose Club chute from Danz to Warsz, cycled from there to Bucur, ballooned, rocketed, leaped from precipices, run afoot all night. She accompanies them to the mountains; they stay the night in a hostel, singing, and in the morning they are away again, like a flock of swallows. Claire stands grave and still; the horde rushes past her, shining faces, arrows of color, laughs, shouts. "Claire, aren't you coming?" . . . "Claire, what's the matter?" . . . "Claire, come with us, we're swimming to Linz!" But she does not answer; the bright throng passes into silence.

Over the roof of the world, the long cloud-packs are moving swiftly, white against the deep blue. They come from the north; the sharp wind blows among the pines, breathing of icy fiords.

Claire steps back into the empty forum of the hostel. Her movements are slow; she is weary of escaping. For half a decade she has never been in the same spot more than a few weeks. Never once has she looked into a news unit, or tried to call anyone she knows in Sector Twenty. She has even deliberately failed to register her whereabouts: to be registered is to expect a call, and expecting one is halfway to making one.

But what is the use? Wherever she goes, she carries the same darkness with her.

The phone index glows at her touch. Slowly, with unaccustomed fingers, she selects the sector, the group, and the name: Dio.

The screen pulses; there is a long wait. Then the gray face of an autosec says politely, "The registrant has removed, and left no forwarding information."

Claire's throat is dry. "How long ago did his registry stop?"

"One moment please." The blank face falls silent. "He was last registered three years ago, in the index of November thirty."

"Try central registry," says Claire.

"No forwarding information has been registered."

"I know. Try central, anyway. Try everywhere."

"There will be a delay for checking." The blank face is silent a long time. Claire turns away, staring without interest at the living frieze of color which flows along the borders of the room. "Your attention please."

She turns. "Yes?"

"The registrant does not appear in any sector registry."

For a moment she is numb and speechless. Then, with a gesture, she abolishes the autosec, fingers the index again: the same sector, same group; the name: Benarra.

The screen lights: his remembered face looks out at her. "Claire! Where are you?"

"In Cheky. Ben, I tried to call Dio, and it said there was no registry. Is he—?"

"No. He's still alive, Claire; he's retreated. I want you to come here as soon as you can. Get a special; my club will take care of the overs, if you're short."

"No, I have a surplus. All right, I'll come."

"This was made the season after you left," says Benarra. The wall screen glows: it is a stereo view of the main plaza in Level Three, the Hub section: dark, unornamented buildings, like a cliff-dwellers' canyon. The streets are deserted; no face shows at the windows.

"Changing Day," says Benarra. "Dio had formally resigned, but he still had a day to go. Watch."

In the screen, one of the tall building fronts suddenly swells and crumbles at the top. Dingy smoke spurts. Like a stack of counters, the building leans down into the street, separating as it goes into individual bricks and stones. The roar comes dimly to them as the next building erupts, and then the next.

"He did it himself," says Benarra. "He laid all the explosive charges, didn't tell anybody. The council was horrified. The integrators weren't designed to handle all that rubble—it had to be amorphized and piped away in the end. They begged Dio to stop, and finally he did. He made a bargain with them, for Level One."

"The whole level?"

"Yes. They gave it to him; he pointed out that it would not be for long. All the game areas and so on up there were due to be changed, anyhow; Dio's successor merely canceled them out of the integrator."

She still does not understand. "Leaving nothing but the bare earth?"

"He wanted it bare. He got some seeds from collectors, and planted them. I've been up frequently. He actually grows cereal grain up there, and grinds it into bread."

In the screen, the canyon of the street has become a lake of dust. Benarra touches the controls; the screen blinks to another scene.

The sky is a deep luminous blue; the level land is bare. A single small building stands up blocky and stiff; behind it there are a few trees, and the evening light glimmers on fields scored in parallel rows. A dark figure is standing motionless beside the house; at first Claire does not recognize it as human. Then it moves, turns its head. She whispers, "Is that Dio?"

"Yes."

She cannot repress a moan of sorrow. The figure is too small for any details of face or body to be seen, but something in the proportions of it makes her think of one of Dio's grotesque statues, all stony bone, hunched, shrunken. The figure turns, moving stiffly, and walks to the hut. It enters and disappears.

She says to Benarra, "Why didn't you tell me?"

"You didn't leave any word; I couldn't reach you."

"I know, but you should have told me. I didn't know . . ."

"Claire, what do you feel for him now? Love?"

"I don't know. A great pity, I think. But maybe there is love mixed up in it too. I pity him because I once loved him. But I think that much pity is love, isn't it, Ben?"

"Not the kind of love you and I used to know anything about," says Benarra, with his eyes on the screen.

He was waiting for her when she emerged from the kiosk.

He had a face like nothing human. It was like a turtle's face, or a lizard's: horny and earth-colored, with bright eyes peering under the shelf of brow. His cheeks sank in; his nose jutted, and the bony shape of the teeth bulged behind the lips. His hair was white and fine, like thistledown in the sun.

They were like strangers together, or like visitors from different planets. He showed her his grain fields, his kitchen garden, his stand of young fruit trees. In the branches, birds were fluttering and chirping. Dio was dressed in a robe of coarse weave that hung awkwardly from his bony shoulders. He had made it himself, he told her; he had also made the pottery jug from which he poured her a clear tart wine, pressed from his own grapes. The interior of the hut was clean and bare. "Of course, I get food supplements from Ben, and a few things like needles, thread. Can't do everything, but on the whole, I haven't done too badly." His voice was abstracted; he seemed only half aware of her presence.

They sat side by side on the wooden bench outside the hut. The afternoon sunlight lay pleasantly on the flagstones; a little animation came to his withered face, and for the first time she was able to see the shape of Dio's features there.

"I don't say I'm not bitter. You remember what I was, and you see what I am now." His eyes stared broodingly; his lips worked. "I sometimes think, why did it have to be me? The rest of you are going on, like children at a party, and I'll be gone. But, Claire, I've discovered something. I don't quite know if I can tell you about it."

He paused, looking out across the fields. "There's an attraction in it, a beauty. That sounds impossible, but it's true. Beauty in the ugliness. It's symmetrical, it has its rhythm. The sun rises, the sun sets. Living up here, you feel that a little more. Perhaps that's why we went below."

He turned to look at her. "No, I can't make you understand. I don't want you to think, either, that I've surrendered to it. I feel it coming sometimes, Claire, in the middle of the night. Something coming up over the horizon. Something—" He gestured. "A feeling. Something very huge, and cold. Very cold. And I sit up in my bed, shouting, 'I'm not ready yet!' No, I don't want to go. Perhaps if I had grown up getting used to the idea, it would be easier now. It's a big change to make in your thinking. I tried—all this—and the sculpture, you remember—but I can't quite do it. And yet—now, this is the curious thing. I wouldn't go back, if I could. That sounds funny. Here I am, going to die, and I wouldn't go back. You see, I want to be myself; yes, I want to go on being myself. Those other men were not me, only someone on the way to be me."

They walked back together to the kiosk. At the doorway, she turned for a last glimpse. He was standing, bent and sturdy, white-haired in his rags, against a long sweep of violet sky. The late light glistened grayly on the fields; far behind, in the grove of trees the birds' voices were stilled. There was a single star in the east.

To leave him, she realized suddenly, would be intolerable. She stepped out, embraced him: his body was shockingly thin and fragile in her arms. "Dio, we mustn't be apart now. Let me come and stay in your hut; let's be together."

Gently he disengaged her arms and stepped away. His eyes gleamed in the twilight. "No, no," he said. "It wouldn't do, Claire. Dear, I love you for it, but you see . . . you see, you're a goddess. An immortal goddess—and I'm a man."

She saw his lips work, as if he were about to speak again, and she waited, but he only turned, without a word or gesture, and began walking away across the empty earth: a dark spindling figure, garments flapping gently in the breeze that spilled across the earth. The last light glowed dimly in his white hair. Now he was only a dot in the middle distance. Claire stepped back into the kiosk, and the door closed.

VI

For a long time she cannot persuade herself that he is gone. She has seen the body, stretched in a box like someone turned to painted wax: it is not Dio, Dio is somewhere else.

She catches herself thinking, *When Dio comes back* . . . as if he had only gone away, around to the other side of the world. But she knows there is a mound of earth over Sector Twenty, with a tall polished stone over the spot where Dio's body lies in the ground. She can repeat by rote the words carved there:

> Weak and narrow are the powers implanted in the limbs of man; many the woes that fall on them and blunt the edges of thought; short is the measure of the life in death through which they toil. Then are they borne away; like smoke they vanish into air; and what they dream they know is but the little that each hath stumbled upon in wandering about the world. Yet boast they all that they have learned the whole.

Vain fools! For what that is, no eye hath seen, no ear hath heard, nor can it be conceived by the mind of man.

—EMPEDOCLES (5TH CENT B.C.)

One day she closes up the apartment; let the Planner, Dio's successor, make of it whatever he likes. She leaves behind all her notes, her student's equipment, useless now. She goes to a public inn and that afternoon the new fashions are brought to her: robes in flame silk and in cold metallic mesh; new perfumes, new jewelry. There is new music in the memory units, and she dances to it tentatively, head cocked to listen, living into the rhythm. Already it is like a long-delayed spring; dark withered things are drifting away into the past, and the present is fresh and lovely.

She tries to call a few old friends. Katha is in Centram, Ebert in the South; Piet and Tanno are not registered at all. It doesn't matter; in the plaza of the inn, before the day is out, she makes a dozen new friends. The group, pleased with itself, grows by accretion; the resulting party wanders from the plaza to the Vermilion Club gardens, to one member's rooms and then another's, and finally back to Claire's own apartment.

Leaving the circle toward midnight, she roams the apartment alone, eased by comradeship, content to hear the singing blur and fade behind her. In the playroom, she stands idly looking down into the deep darkness of the diving well. How luxurious, she thinks, to fall and fall, and never reach the bottom . . .

But the bottom is always there, of course, or it would not be a diving well. A paradox: the well must be a shaft without an exit at the bottom; it's the sense of danger, the imagined smashing impact, that gives it its thrill. And yet there is no danger of injury: levitation and the survival instinct will always prevent it.

"We have such a tidy world. . . ."

Things pass away; people endure.

Then where is Piet, the cottony haired man, with his laughter and his wild jokes? Hiding, somewhere around the other side of the world, perhaps; forgetting to register. It often happens; no one thinks about it. But then, her own mind asks coldly, where is the woman named Marla, who used to hold you on her knee when you were small? Where is Hendry, your own father, whom you last saw . . . when? Five hundred, six hundred years ago, that time in Rio. Where do people go when they disappear . . . the people no one talks about?

The singing drifts up to her along the dark hallway. Claire is staring transfixed down into the shadows of the well. She thinks of Dio, looking out at the gathering darkness: "I feel it coming sometimes, up over the horizon. Something very huge, and cold."

The darkness shapes itself in her imagination into a gray face, beautiful and terrible. The smiling lips whisper, for her ears alone, *Some day.*

NOT WITH A BANG

Ten months after the last plane passed over, Rolf Smith knew beyond doubt that only one other human being had survived. Her name was Louise Oliver, and he was sittin' opposite her in a department-store café in Salt Lake City. They were eating canned Vienna sausages and drinking coffee.

Sunlight struck through a broken pane like a judgment. Inside and outside, there was no sound; only a stifling rumor of absence. The clatter of dishware in the kitchen, the heavy rumble of streetcars: never again. There was sunlight; and silence; and the watery, astonished eyes of Louise Oliver.

He leaned forward, trying to capture the attention of those fishlike eyes for a second. "Darling," he said, "I respect your views, naturally. But I've got to make you see that they're impractical."

She looked at him with faint surprise, then away again. Her head shook slightly. *No. No, Rolf, I will not live with you in sin.*

Smith thought of the women of France, of Russia, of Mexico, of the South Seas. He had spent three months in the ruined studios of a radio station in Rochester, listening to the voices until they stopped. There had been a large colony in Sweden, including an English cabinet minister. They reported that Europe was gone. Simply gone; there was not an acre that had not been swept clean by radioactive dust. They had two planes and enough fuel to take them anywhere on the Continent; but there was nowhere to go. Three of them had the plague; then eleven; then all.

There was a bomber pilot who had fallen near a government radio station in Palestine. He did not last long, because he had broken some bones in the crash; but he had seen the vacant waters where the Pacific Islands should have been. It was his guess that the Arctic ice fields had been bombed.

There were no reports from Washington, from New York, from London, Paris, Moscow, Chungking, Sydney. You could not tell who had been destroyed by disease, who by the dust, who by bombs.

Smith himself had been a laboratory assistant in a team that was trying to find an antibiotic for the plague. His superiors had found one that worked sometimes, but it was a little too late. When he left, Smith took along with him all there was of it—forty ampoules, enough to last him for years.

Louise had been a nurse in a genteel hospital near Denver. According to her, something rather odd had happened to the hospital as she was approaching it the morning of the attack. She was quite calm when she said this, but a vague look came into her eyes and her shattered expression seemed to slip a little more. Smith did not press her for an explanation.

Like himself, she had found a radio station which still functioned, and when Smith discovered that she had not contracted the plague, he agreed to meet her. She was, apparently, naturally immune. There must have been others, a few at least; but the bombs and the dust had not spared them.

It seemed very awkward to Louise that not one Protestant minister was left alive.

The trouble was, she really meant it. It had taken Smith a long time to believe it, but it was true. She would not sleep in the same hotel with him, either; she expected, and received, the utmost courtesy and decorum. Smith had learned his lesson. He walked on the outside of the rubble-heaped sidewalks; he opened doors for her, when there were still doors; he held her chair; he refrained from swearing. He courted her.

Louise was forty or thereabouts, at least five years older than Smith. He often wondered how old she thought she was. The shock of seeing whatever it was that had happened to the hospital, the patients she had cared for, had sent her mind scuttling back to her childhood. She tacitly admitted that everyone else in the world was dead, but she seemed to regard it as something one did not mention.

A hundred times in the last three weeks, Smith had felt an almost irresistible impulse to break her thin neck and go his own way. But there was no help for it; she was the only woman in the world, and he needed her. If she died, or left him, he died. Old bitch! he thought to himself furiously, and carefully kept the thought from showing on his face.

"Louise, honey," he told her gently, "I want to spare your feelings as much as I can. You know that."

"Yes, Rolf," she said, staring at him with the face of a hypnotized chicken.

Smith forced himself to go on. "We've got to face the facts, unpleasant as they may be. Honey, we're the only man and the only woman there are. We're like Adam and Eve in the Garden of Eden."

Louise's face took on a slightly disgusted expression. She was obviously thinking of fig leaves.

"Think of the generations unborn," Smith told her, with a tremor in his voice. Think about me for once. Maybe you're good for another ten years, maybe not. Shuddering, he thought of the second stage of the disease—the helpless rigidity, striking without warning. He'd had one such attack already, and Louise had helped him out of it. Without her, he would have stayed like that till he died, the hypodermic that would save him within inches of his rigid hand. He thought desperately, If I'm lucky, I'll get at least two kids out of you before you croak. Then I'll be safe.

He went on, "God didn't mean for the human race to end like this. He spared us, you and me, to—" he paused; how could he say it without offending her? "parents" wouldn't do—too suggestive—"to carry on the torch of life," he ended. There. That was sticky enough.

Louise was staring vaguely over his shoulder. Her eyelids blinked regularly, and her mouth made little rabbitlike motions in the same rhythm.

Smith looked down at his wasted thighs under the tabletop. I'm not strong enough to force her, he thought. Christ, if I were strong enough!

He felt the futile rage again, and stifled it. He had to keep his head, because this might be his last chance. Louise had been talking lately, in the cloudy language she used about everything, of going up in the mountains to pray for guidance. She had not said "alone," but it was easy enough to see that she pictured it that way. He had to argue her around before her resolve stiffened. He concentrated furiously and tried once more.

The pattern of words went by like a distant rumbling. Louise heard a phrase here and there; each of them fathered chains of thought, binding her reverie tighter. "Our duty to humanity . . ." Mama had often said—that was in the old house on Waterbury Street, of course, before Mama had taken sick—she had said, "Child, your duty is to be clean, polite, and God-fearing. Pretty doesn't matter. There's plenty of plain women that have got themselves good, Christian husbands."

Husbands . . . To have and to hold . . . Orange blossoms, and the bridesmaids; the organ music. Through the haze, she saw Rolf's lean, wolfish face. Of course, he was the only one she'd ever get; *she* knew that well enough. Gracious, when a girl was past twenty-five, she had to take what she could get.

But I sometimes wonder if he's really a *nice* man, she thought.

". . . in the eyes of God . . ." She remembered the stained-glass windows in the old First Episcopalian Church, and how she always thought God was looking down at her through that brilliant transparency. Perhaps He was still looking at her, though it seemed sometimes that He had forgotten. Well, of course she realized that marriage customs changed, and if you couldn't have a regular minister . . . But it was really a shame, an outrage almost, that if she were actually going to marry this man, she couldn't have all those nice things. . . . There wouldn't even be any wedding presents. Not even that. But of course Rolf would give her anything she wanted. She saw his face again, noticed the narrow black eyes staring at her with ferocious purpose, the thin mouth that jerked in a slow, regular tic, the hairy lobes of the ears below the tangle of black hair.

He oughtn't to let his hair grow so long, she thought. It isn't quite decent. Well, she could change all that. If she did marry him, she'd certainly make him change his ways. It was no more than her duty.

He was talking now about a farm he'd seen outside town—a

good big house and a barn. There was no stock, he said, but they could get some later. And they'd plant things, and have their own food to eat, not go to restaurants all the time.

She felt a touch on her hand, lying pale before her on the table. Rolf's brown, stubby fingers, black-haired above and below the knuckles, were touching hers. He had stopped talking for a moment, but now he was speaking again, still more urgently. She drew her hand away.

He was saying, ". . . and you'll have the finest wedding dress you ever saw, with a bouquet. Everything you want, Louise, everything . . ."

A wedding dress! And flowers, even if there couldn't be any minister! Well, why hadn't the fool said so before?

Rolf stopped halfway through a sentence, aware that Louise had said quite clearly, "Yes, Rolf, I will marry you if you wish."

Stunned, he wanted her to repeat it but dared not ask, "What did you say?" for fear of getting some fantastic answer, or none at all. He breathed deeply. He said, "Today, Louise?"

She said, "Well, *today* . . . I don't know quite . . . Of course, if you think you can make all the arrangements in time, but it does seem . . ."

Triumph surged through Smith's body. He had the advantage now, and he'd ride it. "Say you will, dear," he urged her. "Say yes, and make me the happiest man . . ."

Even then, his tongue balked at the rest of it; but it didn't matter. She nodded submissively. "Whatever you think best, Rolf."

He rose, and she allowed him to kiss her pale, sapless cheek. "We'll leave right away," he said. "If you'll excuse me for just a minute, dear?"

He waited for her "Of course" and then left, making footprints in the furred carpet of dust down toward the end of the room. Just a few more hours he'd have to speak to her like that, and then, in her eyes, she'd be committed to him forever. Afterward, he could do with her as he liked—beat her when he pleased, submit her to any proof of his scorn and revulsion, use her. Then it would not be too bad, being the last man on earth—not bad at all. She might even have a daughter. . . .

He found the washroom door and entered. He took a step inside, and froze, balanced by a trick of motion, upright but helpless. Panic struck at his throat as he tried to turn his head and failed; tried to scream, and failed. Behind him, he was aware of a tiny click as the door, cushioned by the hydraulic check, shut forever. It was not locked; but its other side bore the warning MEN.

I SEE YOU

You are five, hiding in a place only you know. You are covered with bark dust, scratched by twigs, sweaty and hot. A wind sighs in the aspen leaves. A faint steady hiss comes from the viewer you hold in your hands; then a voice: "Lorie, I see you—under the barn, eating an apple!" A silence. "Lorie, come on out, I see you." Another voice. "That's right, she's in there." After a moment, sulkily: "Oh, okay."

You squirm around, raising the viewer to aim it down the hill. As you turn the knob with your thumb, the bright image races toward you, trees hurling themselves into red darkness and vanishing, then the houses in the compound, and now you see Bruce standing beside the corral, looking into his viewer, slowly turning. His back is to you; you know you are safe, and you sit up. A jay passes with a whir of wings, settles on a branch. With your own eyes now you can see Bruce, only a dot of blue beyond the gray shake walls of the houses. In the viewer, he is turning toward you, and you duck again. Another voice: "Children, come in and get washed for dinner now." "Aw, Aunt Ellie!" "Mom, we're playing hide and seek. Can't we just stay fifteen minutes more?" "Please, Aunt Ellie!" "No, come on in now— you'll have plenty of time after dinner." And Bruce: "Aw, okay. All out's in free." And once more they have not found you; your secret place is yours alone.

Call him Smith. He was the president of a company that bore his name and which held more than a hundred patents in the scientific instrument field. He was sixty, a widower. His only daughter and her husband had been killed in a plane crash in 1978. He had a partner who handled the business operations now; Smith spent most of his time in his own lab. In the spring of 1990 he was working on an image-intensification device that was puzzling because it was too good. He had it on his bench now, aimed at a deep shadow box across the room; at the back of the box was a card ruled with black, green, red and blue lines. The only source of illumination was a single ten-watt bulb hung behind the shadow box; the light reflected from the card did not even register on his meter, and yet the image in the screen of his device was sharp and bright. When he varied the inputs to the components in a certain way, the bright image vanished and was replaced by shadows, like the ghost of another image. He had monitored every television channel, had shielded the device against radio frequencies, and the ghosts remained. Increasing the illumination did not make them clearer. They were vaguely rectilinear shapes without any coherent pattern. Occasionally a moving blur traveled slowly across them.

Smith made a disgusted sound. He opened the clamps that held the device and picked it up, reaching for the power switch with his other hand. He never touched it. As he moved the device, the ghost images had shifted; they were dancing now with the faint movements of his hand. Smith stared at them without breathing for a moment. Holding the cord, he turned slowly. The ghost images whirled, vanished, reappeared. He turned the other way; they whirled back.

Smith set the device down on the bench with care. His hands were shaking. He had had the thing clamped down on the bench all the time until now. "Christ almighty, how dumb can one man get?" he asked the empty room.

You are six, almost seven, and you are being allowed to use the big viewer for the first time. You are perched on a cushion in the leather chair at the console; your brother, who has been showing you the controls with a bored and superior air, has just left the room, saying, "All right, if you know so much, do it yourself."

In fact, the controls on this machine are unfamiliar; the little viewers you have used all your life have only one knob, for nearer or farther—to move up/down, or left/right, you just point the viewer where you want to see. This machine has dials and little windows with numbers in them, and switches and pushbuttons, most of which you don't understand, but you know they are for special purposes and don't matter. The main control is a metal rod, right in front of you, with a gray plastic knob on the top. The knob is dull from years of handling; it feels warm and a little greasy in your hand. The console has a funny electric smell, but the big screen, taller than you are, is silent and dark. You can feel your heart beating against your breastbone. You grip the knob harder, push it forward just a little. The screen lights, and you are drifting across the next room as if on huge silent wheels, chairs and end tables turning into reddish silhouettes that shrink, twist and disappear as you pass through them, and for a moment you feel dizzy because when you notice the red numbers jumping in the console to your left, it is as if the whole house were passing massively and vertiginously through itself; then you are floating out the window with the same slow and steady motion, on across the sunlit pasture where two saddle horses stand with their heads up, sniffing the wind; then a stubbled field, dropping away; and now, below you, the co-op road shines like a silver-gray stream. You press the knob down to get closer, and drop with a giddy swoop; now you are rushing along the road, overtaking and passing a yellow truck, turning the knob to steer. At first you blunder into the dark trees on either side, and once the earth surges up over you in a chaos of writhing red shapes, but now you are learning, and you soar down past the crossroads, up the farther hill, and now, now you are on the big road, flying eastward, passing all the cars, rushing toward the great world where you long to be.

It took Smith six weeks to increase the efficiency of the image intensifier enough to bring up the ghost pictures clearly. When he succeeded, the image on the screen was instantly recognizable. It was a view of Jack McCranie's office; the picture was still dim, but sharp enough that Smith could see the expression on Jack's face. He was leaning back in his chair, hands behind his head. Beside him stood Peg Spatola in a purple dress, with her hand on an open folder. She was talking, and McCranie was listening. That was wrong, because Peg was not supposed to be back from Cleveland until next week.

Smith reached for the phone and punched McCranie's number.

"Yes, Tom?"

"Jack, is Peg in there?"

"Why, no—she's in Cleveland, Tom."

"Oh, yes."

McCranie sounded puzzled. "Is anything the matter?" In the screen, he had swiveled his chair and was talking to Peg, gesturing with short, choppy motions of his arm.

"No, nothing," said Smith. "That's all right, Jack, thank you." He broke the connection. After a moment he turned to the breadboard controls of the device and changed one setting slightly. In the screen, Peg turned and walked backward out of the office. When he turned the knob the other way, she repeated these actions in reverse. Smith tinkered with the other controls until he got a view of the calendar on Jack's desk. It was Friday, June 15—last week.

Smith locked up the device and all his notes, went home and spent the rest of the day thinking.

By the end of July he had refined and miniaturized the device and had extended its sensitivity range into the infrared. He spent most of August, when he should have been on vacation, trying various methods of detecting sound through the device. By focusing on the interior of a speaker's larynx and using infrared, he was able to convert the visible vibrations of the vocal cords into sound of fair quality, but that did not satisfy him. He worked for a while on vibrations picked up from panes of glass in windows and on framed pictures, and he experimented briefly with the diaphragms in speaker systems, intercoms and telephones. He kept on into October without stopping and finally achieved a system that would give tinny but recognizable sound from any vibrating surface—a wall, a floor, even the speaker's own cheek or forehead.

He redesigned the whole device, built a prototype and tested it, tore it down, redesigned, built another. It was Christmas before he was done. Once more he locked up the device and all his plans, drawings and notes.

At home he spent the holidays experimenting with commercial adhesives in various strengths. He applied these to coated paper, let them dry, and cut the paper into rectangles. He numbered these rectangles, pasted them onto letter envelopes, some of which he stacked loose; others he bundled together and secured with rubber bands. He opened the stacks and bundles and examined them at regular intervals. Some of the labels curled up and detached themselves after twenty-six hours without leaving any conspicuous trace. He made up another batch of these, typed his home address on six of them. On each of six envelopes he typed his office address, then covered it with one of the labels. He stamped the envelopes and dropped them into a mailbox. All six, minus their labels, were delivered to the office three days later.

Just after New Year's, he told his partner that he wanted to sell out and retire. They discussed it in general terms.

Using an assumed name and a post office box number which was not his, Smith wrote to a commission agent in Boston with whom he had never had any previous dealings. He mailed the letter, with the agent's address covered by one of his labels on which he had typed a fictitious address. The label detached itself in transit; the letter was delivered. When the agent replied, Smith was watching and read the letter as a secretary typed it. The agent followed his instruction to mail his reply in an envelope without return address. The owner of the post office box turned it in marked "not here"; it went to the dead-letter office and was returned in due time, but meanwhile Smith had acknowledged the letter and had mailed, in the same way, a large amount of cash. In subsequent letters he instructed the agent to take bids for components, plans for which he enclosed, from electronics manufacturers, for plastic casings from another, and for assembly and shipping from still another company. Through a second commission agent in New York, to whom he wrote in the same way, he contracted for ten thousand copies of an instruction booklet in four colors.

Late in February he bought a house and an electronics dealership in a small town in the Adirondacks. In March he signed over his interest in the company to his partner, cleaned out his lab and left. He sold his co-op apartment in Manhattan and his summer house in Connecticut, moved to his new home and became anonymous.

You are thirteen, chasing a fox with the big kids for the first time. They have put you in the north field, the worst place, but you know better than to leave it.

"He's in the glen."

"I see him; he's in the brook, going upstream."

You turn the viewer, racing forward through dappled shade, a brilliance of leaves: there is the glen, and now you see the fox, trotting through the shallows, blossoms of bright water at its feet.

"Ken and Nell, you come down ahead of him by the springhouse.

Wanda, you and Tim and Jean stay where you are. Everybody else come upstream, but stay back till I tell you."

That's Leigh, the oldest. You turn the viewer, catch a glimpse of Bobby running downhill though the woods, his long hair flying. Then back to the glen: the fox is gone.

"He's heading up past the corncrib!"

"Okay, keep spread out on both sides, everybody. Jim, can you and Edie head him off before he gets to the woods?"

"We'll try. There he is!"

And the chase is going away from you, as you knew it would, but soon you will be older, as old as Nell and Jim; then you will be in the middle of things, and your life will begin.

By trial and error, Smith has found the settings for Dallas, November 22, 1963: Dealey Plaza, 12:25 P.M. He sees the Presidential motorcade making the turn onto Elm Street. Kennedy slumps forward, raising his hands to his throat. Smith presses a button to hold the moment in time. He scans behind the motorcade, finds the sixth floor of the Book Depository Building, finds the window. There is no one behind the barricade of cartons; the room is empty. He scans the nearby rooms, finds nothing. He tries the floor below. At an open window a man kneels, holding a high-powered rifle. Smith photographs him. He returns to the motorcade, watches as the second shot strikes the President. He freezes time again, scans the surrounding buildings, finds a second marksman on a roof, photographs him. Back to the motorcade. A third and fourth shot, the last blowing off the side of the President's head. Smith freezes the action again, finds two gunmen on the grassy knoll, one aiming across the top of a station wagon, one kneeling in the shrubbery. He photographs them. He turns off the power, sits for a moment, then goes to the washroom, kneels beside the toilet and vomits.

The viewer is your babysitter, your television, your telephone (the telephone lines are still up, but they are used only as signaling devices; when you know that somebody wants to talk to you, you focus your viewer on him), your library, your school. Before puberty you watch other people having sex, but even then your curiosity is easily satisfied; after an older cousin initiates you at fourteen, you are much more interested in doing it yourself. The co-op teacher monitors your studies, sometimes makes suggestions, but more and more, as you grow older, leaves you to your own devices. You are intensely interested in African prehistory, in the European theater, and in the ant-civilization of Epsilon Eridani IV. Soon you will have to choose.

New York Harbor, November 4, 1872—a cold, blustery day. A two-masted ship rides at anchor; on her stern is lettered: *Mary Celeste*. Smith advances the time control. A flicker of darkness, light again, and the ship is gone. He turns back again until he finds it standing out under light canvas past Sandy Hook. Manipulating time and space controls at once, he follows it eastward through a flickering of storm and sun—loses it, finds it again, counting days as he goes. The farther eastward, the more he has to tilt the device downward, while the image of the ship tilts correspondingly away from him. Because of the angle, he can no longer keep the ship in view from a distance but must track it closely. November 21 and 22, violent storms: the ship is dashed upward by waves, falls again, visible only intermittently; it takes him five hours to pass through two days of real time. The 23rd is calmer, but on the 24th another storm blows up. Smith rubs his eyes, loses the ship, finds it again after a ten-minute search.

The gale blows itself out on the morning of the 26th. The sun is bright, the sea almost dead calm. Smith is able to catch glimpses of figures on deck, tilted above dark cross-sections of the hull. A sailor is splicing a rope in the stern, two others lowering a triangular sail between the foremast and the bowsprit, and a fourth is at the helm. A little group stands leaning on the starboard rail; one of them is a woman. The next glimpse is that of a running figure who advances into the screen and disappears. Now the men are lowering a boat over the side; the rail has been removed and lies on the deck. The men drop into the boat and row away. He hears them shouting to each other but cannot make out the words.

Smith turns to the ship again: the deck is empty. He dips below to look at the hold, filled with casks, then the cabin, then the forecastle. There is no sign of anything wrong—no explosion, no fire, no trace of violence. When he looks up again, he sees the sails flapping, then bellying out full. The sea is rising. He looks for the boat, but now too much time has passed and he cannot find it. He returns to the ship and now reverses the time control, tracks it backward until the men are again in their places on deck. He looks again at the group standing at the rail; now he sees that the woman has a child in her arms. The child struggles, drops over the rail. Smith hears the woman shriek. In a moment she too is over the rail and falling into the sea.

He watches the men running, sees them launch the boat. As they pull away, he is able to keep the focus near enough to see and hear them. One calls, "My God, who's at the helm?" Another, a bearded man with a face gone tallow-pale, replies, "Never mind—row!" They are staring down into the sea. After a moment one looks up, then another. The *Mary Celeste*, with three of the four sails on her foremast set, is gliding away, slowly, now faster; now she is gone.

Smith does not run through the scene again to watch the child and her mother drown, but others do.

The production model was ready for shipping in September. It was a simplified version of the prototype, with only two controls, one for space, one for time. The range of the device was limited to one thousand miles. Nowhere on the casing of the device or in the instruction booklet was a patent number or a pending patent mentioned. Smith had called the device Ozo, perhaps because he thought it sounded vaguely Japanese. The booklet described the device as a distant viewer and gave clear, simple instructions for its use. One sentence read cryptically: "Keep Time Control set at zero." It was like "Wet Paint—Do Not Touch."

During the week of September 23, seven thousand Ozos were shipped to domestic and Canadian addresses supplied by Smith: five hundred to electronics manufacturers and suppliers, six thousand, thirty to a carton, marked "On Consignment," to TV outlets in major cities, and the rest to private citizens chosen at random. The instruction booklets were in sealed envelopes packed with each device. Three thousand more went to Europe, South and Central America, and the Middle East.

A few of the outlets which received the cartons opened them the same day, tried the devices out, and put them on sale at prices ranging from $49.95 to $125. By the following day the word was beginning to spread, and by the close of business on the third day every store was sold out. Most people who got them, either through the mail or by purchase, used them to spy on their neighbors and on people in hotels.

In a house in Cleveland, a man watches his brother-in-law in the next room, who is watching his wife getting out of a taxi. She goes into the lobby of an apartment building. The husband watches as she gets into the elevator, rides to the fourth floor. She rings the bell beside the door marked 410. The door opens; a dark-haired man takes her in his arms; they kiss.

The brother-in-law meets him in the hall. "Don't do it, Charlie."

"Get out of my way."

"I'm not going to get out of your way, and I tell you, don't do it. Not now and not later."

"Why the hell shouldn't I?"

"Because if you do I'll kill you. If you want a divorce, OK, get a divorce. But don't lay a hand on her or I'll find you the farthest place you can go."

Smith got his consignment of Ozos early in the week, took one home and left it to his store manager to put a price on the rest. He did not bother to use the production model but began at once to build another prototype. It had controls calibrated to one-hundredth of a second and one millimeter, and a timer that would allow him to stop a scene, or advance or regress it at any desired rate. He ordered some clockwork from an astronomical supply house.

A high-ranking officer in Army Intelligence, watching the first demonstration of the Ozo in the Pentagon, exclaimed, "My God, with this we could dismantle half the establishment—all we've got to do is launch interceptors when we see them push the button."

"It's a good thing Senator Burkhart can't hear you say that," said another officer. But by the next afternoon everybody had heard it.

A Baptist minister in Louisville led the first mob against an Ozo assembly plant. A month later, while civil and criminal suits against all the rioters were still pending, tapes showing each one of them in compromising or ludicrous activities were widely distributed in the area.

The commission agents who had handled the orders for the first Ozos were found out and had to leave town. Factories were fire-bombed, but others took their place.

The first Ozo was smuggled into the Soviet Union from West Germany by Katerina Belov, a member of a dissident group in Moscow, who used it to document illegal government actions. The device was seized on December 13 by the KGB; Belov and two other members of the group were arrested, imprisoned and tortured. By that time over forty other Ozos were in the hands of dissidents.

You are watching an old movie, *Bob and Ted and Carol and Alice.* The humor seems infantile and unimaginative to you; you are not interested in the actresses' occasional seminudity. What strikes you as hilarious is the coyness, the sidelong glances, smiles, grimaces hinting at things that will never be shown on the screen. You realize that these people have never seen anyone but their most intimate friends without clothing, have never seen any adult shit or piss, and would be embarrassed or disgusted if they did. Why did children say "pee-pee" and "poo-poo," and then giggle? You have read scholarly books about taboos on "bodily functions," but why was shitting worse than sneezing?

Cora Zickwolfe, who lived in a remote rural area of Arizona and whose husband commuted to Tucson, arranged with her nearest neighbor, Phyllis Mell, for each of them to keep an Ozo focused on the bulletin board in the other's kitchen. On the bulletin board was a note that said "OK." If there was any trouble and she couldn't get to the phone, she would take down the note, or if she had time, write another.

In April 1992, about the time her husband usually got home, an intruder broke into the house and seized Mrs. Zickwolfe before she had time to get to the bulletin board. He dragged her into the bedroom and forced her to disrobe. The state troopers got there in fifteen minutes, and Cora never spoke to her friend Phyllis again.

•   •   •

Between 1992 and 2002 more than six hundred improvements and supplements to the Ozo were recorded. The most important of these was the power system created by focusing the Ozo at a narrow aperture on the interior of the Sun. Others included the system of satellite slave units in stationary orbits and a computerized tracer device which would keep the Ozo focused on any subject.

Using the tracer, an entomologist in Mexico City is following the ancestral line of a honey bee. The images bloom and expire, ten every second: the tracer is following each queen back to the egg, then the egg to the queen that laid it, then that queen to the egg. Tens of thousands of generations have passed; in two thousand hours, beginning with a Paleocene bee, he has traveled back into the Cretaceous. He stops at intervals to follow the bee in real time, then accelerates again. The hive is growing smaller, more primitive. Now it is only a cluster of round cells, and the bee is different, more like a wasp. His year's labor is coming to fruition. He watches, forgetting to eat, almost to breathe.

In your mother's study after she dies, you find an elaborate chart of her ancestors and your father's. You retrieve the program for it, punch it in, and idly watch a random sampling, back into time, first the female line, then the male . . . a teacher of biology in Boston, a suffragette, a corn merchant, a singer, a Dutch farmer in New York, a British sailor, a German musician. Their faces glow in the screen, bright-eyed, cheeks flushed with life. Someday you too will be only a series of images in a screen.

Smith is watching the planet Mars. The clockwork which turns the Ozo to follow the planet, even when it is below the horizon, makes it possible for him to focus instantly on the surface, but he never does this. He takes up his position hundreds of thousands of miles away, then slowly approaches, in order to see the red spark grow to a disk, then to a yellow sunlit ball hanging in darkness. Now he can make out the surface features: Syrtis Major and Thoth-Nepenthes leading in a long gooseneck to Utopia and the frostcap.

The image as it swells hypnotically toward him is clear and sharp, without tremor or atmospheric distortion. It is summer in the northern hemisphere: Utopia is wide and dark. The planet fills the screen, and now he turns northward, over the cratered desert still hundreds of miles distant. A dust storm, like a yellow veil, obscures the curved neck of Thoth-Nepenthes; then he is beyond it, drifting down to the edge of the frostcap. The limb of the planet reappears; he floats like a glider over the dark surface tinted with rose and violet-gray; now he can see its nubbly texture; now he can make out individual plants. He is drifting among their gnarled gray stems, their leaves of violet horn; he sees the curious misshapen growths that may be air bladders or some grotesque analogue of blossoms. Now, at the edge of the screen, something black and spindling leaps. He follows it instantly, finds it, brings it hugely magnified into the center of the screen: a thing like a hairy beetle, its body covered with thick black hairs or spines; it stands on six jointed legs, waving its antennae, its mouth parts busy. And its four bright eyes stare into his, across forty million miles.

Smith's hair got whiter and thinner. Before the 1992 Crash, he made heavy contributions to the International Red Cross and to volunteer organizations in Europe, Asia and Africa. He got drunk periodically, but always alone. From 1993 to 1996 he stopped reading the newspapers.

He wrote down the coordinates for the plane crash in which his daughter and her husband had died, but never used them.

At intervals while dressing or looking into the bathroom mirror, he stared as if into an invisible camera and raised one finger. In his last years he wrote some poems.

We know his name. Patient researchers, using advanced scanning techniques, followed his letters back through the postal system and found him, but by that time he was safely dead.

The whole world has been at peace for more than a generation. Crime is almost unheard of. Free energy has made the world rich, but the population is stable, even though early detection has wiped out most diseases. Everyone can do whatever he likes, providing his neighbors would not disapprove, and after all, their views are the same as his own.

You are forty, a respected scholar, taking a few days out to review your life, as many people do at your age. You have watched your mother and father coupling on the night they conceived you, watched yourself growing in her womb, first a red tadpole, then a thing like an embryo chicken, then a big-headed baby kicking and squirming. You have seen yourself delivered, seen the first moment when your bloody head broke into the light. You have seen yourself staggering about the nursery in rompers, clutching a yellow plastic duck. Now you are watching yourself hiding behind the fallen tree on the hill, and you realize that there are no secret places. And beyond you in the ghostly future you know that someone is watching you as you watch; and beyond that watcher another, and beyond that another. . . . Forever.

MASKS

The eight pens danced against the moving strip of paper, like the nervous claws of some mechanical lobster. Roberts, the technician, frowned over the tracings while the other two watched.

"Here's the wake-up impulse," he said, pointing with a skinny finger. "Then here, look, seventeen seconds more, still dreaming."

"Delayed response," said Babcock, the project director. His heavy face was flushed and he was sweating. "Nothing to worry about."

"Okay, delayed response, but look at the difference in the tracings. Still dreaming, after the wake-up impulse, but the peaks are closer together. Not the same dream. More anxiety, more motor pulses."

"Why does he have to sleep at all?" asked Sinescu, the man from Washington. He was dark, narrow-faced. "You flush the fatigue poisons out, don't you? So what is it, something psychological?"

"He needs to dream," said Babcock. "It's true he has no physiological need for sleep, but he's got to dream. If he didn't, he'd start to hallucinate, maybe go psychotic."

"Psychotic," said Sinescu. "Well—that's the question, isn't it? How long has he been doing this?"

"About six months."

"In other words, about the time he got his new body—and started wearing a mask?"

"About that. Look, let me tell you something, he's rational. Every test—"

"Yes, okay, I know about tests. Well—so he's awake now?"

The technician glanced at the monitor board. "He's up. Sam and Irma are with him." He hunched his shoulders, staring at the EEG tracings again. "I don't know why it should bother me. It stands to reason, if he has dream needs of his own that we're not satisfying with the programmed stuff, this is where he gets them in." His face hardened. "I don't know. Something about those peaks I don't like."

Sinescu raised his eyebrows. "You program his dreams?"

"Not program," said Babcock impatiently. "A routine suggestion to dream the sort of thing we tell him to. Somatic stuff, sex, exercise, sport."

"And whose idea was that?"

"Psych section. He was doing fine neurologically, every other way, but he was withdrawing. Psych decided he needed that somatic input in some form, we had to keep him in touch. He's alive, he's functioning, everything works. But don't forget, he spent forty-three years in a normal human body."

In the hush of the elevator, Sinescu said, ". . . Washington."

Swaying, Babcock said, "I'm sorry, what?"

"You look a little rocky. Getting any sleep?"

"Not lately. What did you say before?"

"I said they're not happy with your reports in Washington."

"Goddamn it, I know that." The elevator door silently opened. A tiny foyer, green carpet, gray walls. There were three doors, one metal, two heavy glass. Cool, stale air. "This way."

Sinescu paused at the glass door, glanced through: a gray-carpeted living room, empty. "I don't see him."

"Around the ell. Getting his morning checkup."

The door opened against slight pressure; a battery of ceiling lights went on as they entered. "Don't look up," said Babcock. "Ultraviolet." A faint hissing sound stopped when the door closed.

"And positive pressure in here? To keep out germs? Whose idea was that?"

"His." Babcock opened a chrome box on the wall and took out two surgical masks. "Here, put this on."

Voices came muffled from around the bend of the room. Sinescu looked with distaste at the white mask, then slowly put it over his head.

They stared at each other. "Germs," said Sinescu through the mask. "Is that rational?"

"All right, he can't catch a cold or what have you, but think about it a minute. There are just two things now that could kill him. One is a prosthetic failure, and we guard against that; we've got five hundred people here, we check him out like an airplane. That leaves a cerebrospinal infection. Don't go in there with a closed mind."

The room was large, part living room, part library, part workshop. Here was a cluster of Swedish-modern chairs, a sofa, coffee table; here a workbench with a metal lathe, electric crucible, drill press, parts bins, tools on wallboards; here a drafting table; here a free-standing wall of bookshelves that Sinescu fingered curiously as they passed. Bound volumes of project reports, technical journals, reference books; no fiction except for *Fire* and *Storm* by George Stewart and *The Wizard of Oz* in a worn blue binding. Behind the bookshelves, set into a little alcove, was a glass door through which they glimpsed another living room, differently furnished: upholstered chairs, a tall philodendron in a ceramic pot. "There's Sam," Babcock said.

A man had appeared in the other room. He saw them, turned to call to someone they could not see, then came forward, smiling. He was bald and stocky, deeply tanned. Behind him, a small, pretty woman hurried up. She crowded through after her husband, leaving the door open. Neither of them wore a mask.

"Sam and Irma have the next suite," Babcock said. "Company for him; he's got to have somebody around. Sam is an old air-force buddy of his, and besides, he's got a tin arm."

The stocky man shook hands, grinning. His grip was firm and warm. "Want to guess which one?" He wore a flowered sport shirt. Both arms were brown, muscular and hairy, but when Sinescu looked more closely, he saw that the right one was a slightly different color, not quite authentic.

Embarrassed, he said, "The left, I guess."

"Nope." Grinning wider, the stocky man pulled back his right sleeve to show the straps.

"One of the spin-offs from the project," said Babcock. "Myoelectric, servo-controlled, weighs the same as the other one. Sam, they about through in there?"

"Maybe so. Let's take a peek. Honey, you think you could rustle up some coffee for the gentlemen?"

"Oh, why, sure." The little woman turned and darted back through the open doorway.

The far wall was glass, covered by a translucent white curtain. They turned the corner. The next bay was full of medical and electronic equipment, some built into the walls, some in tall black cabinets on wheels. Four men in white coats were gathered around what looked like an astronaut's couch. Sinescu could see someone lying on it: feet in Mexican woven-leather shoes, dark socks, gray slacks. A mutter of voices.

"Not through yet," Babcock said. "Must have found something else they didn't like. Let's go out onto the patio a minute."

"Thought they checked him at night—when they exchange his blood, and so on . . . ?"

"They do," Babcock said. "And in the morning, too." He turned and pushed open the heavy glass door. Outside, the roof was paved with cut stone, enclosed by a green plastic canopy and tinted-glass walls. Here and there were concrete basins, empty. "Idea was to have a roof garden out here, something green, but he didn't want it. We had to take all the plants out, glass the whole thing in."

Sam pulled out metal chairs around a white table and they all sat down. "How is he, Sam?" asked Babcock.

He grinned and ducked his head. "Mean in the mornings."

"Talk to you much? Play any chess?"

"Not too much. Works, mostly. Reads some, watches the box a little." His smile was forced; his heavy fingers were clasped together and Sinescu saw now that the fingertips of one hand had turned darker, the others not. He looked away.

"You're from Washington, that right?" Sam asked politely. "First time here? Hold on." He was out of his chair. Vague upright shapes were passing behind the curtained glass door. "Looks like they're through. If you gentlemen would just wait here a minute, till I see." He strode across the roof. The two men sat in silence. Babcock had pulled down his surgical mask; Sinescu noticed and did the same.

"Sam's wife is a problem," Babcock said, leaning nearer. "It seemed like a good idea at the time, but she's lonely here, doesn't like it—no kids—"

The door opened again and Sam appeared. He had a mask on, but it was hanging under his chin. "If you gentlemen would come in now."

In the living area, the little woman, also with a mask hanging around her neck, was pouring coffee from a flowered ceramic jug. She was smiling brightly but looked unhappy. Opposite her sat some-one tall, in gray shirt and slacks, leaning back, legs out, arms on the arms of his chair, motionless. Something was wrong with his face.

"Well, now," said Sam heartily. His wife looked up at him with an agonized smile.

The tall figure turned its head and Sinescu saw with an icy shock that its face was silver, a mask of metal with oblong slits for eyes, no nose or mouth, only curves that were faired into each other. ". . . project," said an inhuman voice.

Sinescu found himself half bent over a chair. He sat down. They were all looking at him. The voice resumed, "I said, are you here to pull the plug on the project." It was unaccented, indifferent.

"Have some coffee." The woman pushed a cup toward him.

Sinescu reached for it, but his hand was trembling and he drew it back. "Just a fact-finding expedition," he said.

"Bull. Who sent you—Senator Hinkel."

"That's right."

"Bull. He's been here himself; why send you? If you are going to pull the plug, might as well tell me." The face behind the mask did not move when he spoke; the voice did not seem to come from it.

"He's just looking around, Jim," said Babcock.

"Two hundred million a year," said the voice, "to keep one man alive. Doesn't make much sense, does it. Go on, drink your coffee."

Sinescu realized that Sam and his wife had already finished theirs and that they had pulled up their masks. He reached for his cup hastily.

"Hundred percent disability in my grade is thirty thousand a year. I could get along on that easy. For almost an hour and a half."

"There's no intention of terminating the project," Sinescu said.

"Phasing it out, though. Would you say phasing it out."

"Manners, Jim," said Babcock.

"Okay. My worst fault. What do you want to know."

Sinescu sipped his coffee. His hands were still trembling. "That mask you're wearing," he started.

"Not for discussion. No comment, no comment. Sorry about that, don't mean to be rude; a personal matter. Ask me something—" Without warning, he stood up, blaring, "Get that damn thing out of here!" Sam's wife's cup smashed, coffee brown across the table. A fawn-colored puppy was sitting in the middle of the carpet, cocking its head, bright-eyed, tongue out.

The table tipped, Sam's wife struggled up behind it. Her face was pink, dripping with tears. She scooped up the puppy without pausing and ran out. "I better go with her," Sam said, getting up.

"Go on; and, Sam, take a holiday. Drive her into Winnemucca, see a movie."

"Yeah, guess I will." He disappeared behind the bookshelf wall.

The tall figure sat down again, moving like a man; it leaned back in the same posture, arms on the arms of the chair. It was still. The hands gripping the wood were shapely and perfect but unreal: there was something wrong about the fingernails. The brown, well-combed hair above the mask was a wig; the ears were wax. Sinescu nervously fumbled his surgical mask up over his mouth and nose. "Might as well get along," he said, and stood up.

"That's right, I want to take you over to Engineering and R and D," said Babcock. "Jim, I'll be back in a little while. Want to talk to you."

"Sure," said the motionless figure.

Babcock had had a shower, but sweat was soaking through the armpits of his shirt again. The silent elevator, the green carpet, a little blurred. The air cool, stale. Seven years, blood and money, five hundred good men. Psych section, Cosmetic, Engineering, R and D, Medical, Immunology, Supply, Serology, Administration. The glass doors. Sam's apartment empty, gone to Winnemucca with Irma. Psych. Good men, but were they the best? Three of the best had turned it down. Buried the files. *Not like an ordinary amputation, this man has had everything cut off.*

The tall figure had not moved. Babcock sat down. The silver mask looked back at him.

"Jim, let's level with each other."

"Bad, huh."

"Sure it's bad. I left him in his room with a bottle. I'll see him again before he leaves, but God knows what he'll say in Washington. Listen, do me a favor, take that thing off."

"Sure." The hand rose, plucked at the edge of the silver mask, lifted it away. Under it, the tan-pink face, sculptured nose and lips, eyebrows, eyelashes, not handsome but good-looking, normal-looking. Only the eyes wrong; pupils too big. And the lips that did not open or move when it spoke. "I can take anything off. What does that prove."

"Jim. Cosmetic spent eight and a half months on that model and the first thing you do is slap a mask over it. We've asked you what's wrong, offered to make any changes you want."

"No comment."

"You talked about phasing out the project. Did you think you were kidding?"

A pause. "Not kidding."

"All right, then open up, Jim, tell me; I have to know. They won't shut the project down; they'll keep you alive but that's all. There are seven hundred on the volunteer list, including two U.S. senators. Suppose one of them gets pulled out of an auto wreck tomorrow. We can't wait till then to decide; we've got to know now. Whether to let the next one die or put him into a TP body like yours. So talk to me."

"Suppose I tell you something but it isn't the truth."

"Why would you lie?"

"Why do you lie to a cancer patient."

"I don't get it. Come on, Jim."

"Okay, try this. Do I look like a man to you."

"Sure."

"Bull. Look at this face." Calm and perfect. Beyond the fake irises, a wink of metal. "Suppose we had all the other problems solved and I could go into Winnemucca tomorrow; can you see me walking down the street, going into a bar, taking a taxi."

"Is that all it is?" Babcock drew a deep breath. "Jim, sure there's a difference, but for Christ's sake, it's like any other prosthesis—people get used to it. Like that arm of Sam's. You see it, but after a while you forget it, you don't notice."

"Bull. You pretend not to notice. Because it would embarrass the cripple."

Babcock looked down at his clasped hands. "Sorry for yourself?"

"Don't give me that," the voice blared. The tall figure was standing. The hands slowly came up, the fists clenched. "I'm in this thing, I've been in it for two years. I'm in it when I go to sleep, and when I wake up, I'm still in it."

Babcock looked up at him. "What do you want, facial mobility? Give us twenty years, maybe ten, we'll lick it."

"No. No."

"Then what?"

"I want you to close down Cosmetic."

"But that's—"

"Just listen. The first model looked like a tailor's dummy, so you spent eight months and came up with this one, and it looks like a corpse. The whole idea was to make me look like a man, the first model pretty good, the second model better, until you've got something that can smoke cigars and joke with women and go bowling and nobody will know the difference. You can't do it, and if you could, what for?"

"I don't—Let me think about this. What do you mean, a metal—"

"Metal, sure, but what difference does that make. I'm talking about shape. Function. Wait a minute." The tall figure strode across the room, unlocked a cabinet, came back with rolled sheets of paper. "Look at this."

The drawing showed an oblong metal box on four jointed legs. From one end protruded a tiny mushroom-shaped head on a jointed stem and a cluster of arms ending in probes, drills, grapples. "For moon prospecting."

"Too many limbs," said Babcock after a moment. "How would you—"

"With the facial nerves. Plenty of them left over. Or here." Another drawing. "A module plugged into the control system of a spaceship. That's where I belong, in space. Sterile environment, low grav, I can go where a man can't go and do what a man can't do. I can be an asset, not a goddamn billion-dollar liability."

Babcock rubbed his eyes. "Why didn't you say anything before?"

"You were all hipped on prosthetics. You would have told me to tend my knitting."

Babcock's hands were shaking as he rolled up the drawings. "Well, by God, this just may do it. It just might." He stood up and turned toward the door. "Keep your—" He cleared his throat. "I mean, hang tight, Jim."

"I'll do that."

•   •   •

When he was alone, he put on his mask again and stood motionless a moment, eye shutters closed. Inside, he was running clean and cool; he could feel the faint reassuring hum of pumps, click of valves and relays. They had given him that: cleaned out all the offal, replaced it with machinery that did not bleed, ooze or suppurate. He thought of the lie he had told Babcock. *Why do you lie to a cancer patient?* But they would never get it, never understand.

He sat down at the drafting table, clipped a sheet of paper to it and with a pencil began to sketch a rendering of the moon-prospector design. When he had blocked in the prospector itself, he began to draw the background of craters. His pencil moved more slowly and stopped; he put it down with a click.

No more adrenal glands to pump adrenaline into his blood, so he could not feel fright or rage. They had released him from all that—love, hate, the whole sloppy mess—but they had forgotten there was still one emotion he could feel.

Sinescu, with the black bristles of his beard sprouting through his oily skin. A whitehead ripe in the crease beside his nostril.

Moon landscape, clean and cold. He picked up the pencil again.

Babcock, with his broad pink nose shining with grease, crusts of white matter in the corners of his eyes. Food mortar between his teeth.

Sam's wife, with raspberry-colored paste on her mouth. Face smeared with tears, a bright bubble in one nostril. And the damn dog, shiny nose, wet eyes . . .

He turned. The dog was there, sitting on the carpet, wet red tongue out—*left the door open again*—dripping, wagged its tail twice, then started to get up. He reached for the metal T square, leaned back, swinging it like an ax, and the dog yelped once as metal sheared bone, one eye spouting red, writhing on its back, dark stain of piss across the carpet, and he hit it again, hit it again.

The body lay twisted on the carpet, fouled with blood, ragged black lips drawn back from teeth. He wiped off the T square with a paper towel, then scrubbed it in the sink with soap and steel wool, dried it and hung it up. He got a sheet of drafting paper, laid it on the floor, rolled up the body over onto it without spilling any blood on the carpet. He lifted the body in the paper, carried it out onto the patio, then onto the unroofed section, opening the doors with his shoulder. He looked over the wall. Two stories down, concrete roof, vents ticking out of it, nobody watching. He held the dog out, let it slide off the paper, twisting as it fell. It struck one of the vents, bounced, a red smear. He carried the paper back inside, poured the blood down the drain, then put the paper into the incinerator chute.

Splashes of blood were on the carpet, the feet of the drafting table, the cabinet, his trouser legs. He sponged them all up with paper towels and warm water. He took off his clothing, examined it minutely, scrubbed it in the sink, then put it in the washer. He washed the sink, rubbed himself down with disinfectant and dressed again. He walked through into Sam's silent apartment, closing the glass door behind him. Past the potted philodendron, overstuffed furniture, red-and-yellow painting on the wall, out onto the roof, leaving the door ajar. Then back through the patio, closing the doors.

Too bad. How about some goldfish.

He sat down at the drafting table. He was running clean and cool. The dream this morning came back to his mind, the last one, as he was struggling up out of sleep: *slithery kidneys burst gray lungs blood and hair ropes of guts covered with yellow fat oozing and sliding and oh god the stink like the breath of an outhouse no sound nowhere he was putting a yellow stream down the slide of the dunghole and*

He began to ink in the drawing, first with a fine steel pen, then with a nylon brush. *his heel slid and he was falling could not stop himself falling into slimy bulging softness higher than his chin, higher and he could not move paralyzed and he tried to scream tried to scream tried to scream*

The prospector was climbing a crater slope with its handling members retracted and its head tilted up. Behind it in the distant ringwall and the horizon, the black sky, the pin-point stars. And he was there, and it was not far enough, not yet, for the earth hung overhead like a rotten fruit, blue with mold, crawling, wrinkling, purulent and alive.

A. E. VAN VOGT

1912–2000

A. E. van Vogt was born in Canada and lived there until, at the age of 32, he pulled up stakes and moved to Southern California. While still in his twenties he had done some writing in other fields, without attracting much attention, but when, in 1939, he turned his attention to science fiction the results were amazing. Well, *Astounding*, that is, because it was to John Campbell's magazine that he sent his first story, "Black Destroyer."

It is possible to trace the shaping of modern science fiction in terms of a few specific paradigm-shifting stories written by a handful of individuals. H. G. Wells contributed the themes of time travel and Martian invaders; Doc Smith gave us the high galactic adventure of space opera; in "A Martian Odyssey" Stanley G. Weinbaum showed that an alien from space could be written about as a person, possessed of as many individual personality traits as any human, rather than as a generic menace ruthlessly attempting to steal Earth's water or women. Those particular writers may not have been the first to touch on such themes, but they were the ones who succeeded in using them to tell stories that had not been told before . . . and that inspired the same sorts of stories from all the writers who followed.

Thus van Vogt in "The Black Destroyer." The story is about conflict between the human crew of a spaceship and an intelligent, highly involved alien aboard. What makes it revolutionary is that van Vogt told the story from the point of view of the alien, letting us feel the creature's nonhuman needs, goals, and constraints. Scores of writers have used that same device since then. But not before.

"The Black Destroyer" was not a flash in the pan. Over the next decade van Vogt became one of Campbell's principal contributors, and—with Heinlein, Theodore Sturgeon, and a handful of others— the exemplar of *Astounding*'s Golden Age. He published more than thirty stories in the magazine in that period, shorts, novelettes, novellas, full-length novels. His novel, *Slan*, concerned a mutant boy, superior to ordinary humans but trying to survive in a society that feared his kind and wanted them all dead. That was an engaging notion for a lot of science fiction fans, who had suspicions of their own superiority and persecution. When one group of Midwest fans established a communal home they called it "the Slan Shack."

A lot of van Vogt's intellectual autobiography shows up in his stories of that period. He was a seeker. He hoped to find some line of thought that would explain the world and the human condition, and make them both better. Alfred Korzybski's general semantics looked as though it might be a winner, and van Vogt's interest in it shows up in novels like *The World of Ā*. He was attracted for a time to the then voguish Bates method of eye care, which shows up in the Weapon Shops stories. Then, around 1950, he discovered L. Ron Hubbard's new "science of mental health," Dianetics, then being heavily promoted by Campbell. That didn't have the same effect as the others, however. Other writers did quickly begin to produce a spate of Dianetics-related stories for Campbell's magazine. Van Vogt did not, however. Quite to the contrary, he stopped writing science fiction entirely. For fourteen years.

In the 1960s I was editor of two science fiction magazines, *Galaxy* and *If*. I had admired the editorial skills of some of my predecessors, particularly Horace Gold and John Campbell, and did my best to emulate them. Both editors had spent a lot of effort in trying to cajole the writers they most wanted to publish into writing for them. So did I; and one of the writers I worked hardest on was A. E. van Vogt. It took a couple of years of letters and (when I happened to be in Los Angeles) lunches, but by 1964 I had the first of van Vogt's "Silkie" stories, followed by a number of others. And when I left the magazines in 1969 Van kept on writing.

Although A. E. van Vogt was unquestionably a major figure among American science fiction writers of the twentieth century, it is a curious fact that his greatest fame lay in another country. My French editors, one and all, assured me that no other SF writer matched van Vogt in fame and devotion in that country; also-rans like Heinlein, Clarke, Bradbury, and Asimov were certainly popular enough, in their way, but in France van Vogt's work (perhaps helped by a splendid translator) outshone them all. So it is not merely parochial Americans but an international audience which makes A. E. van Vogt a true Grand Master.

Recommended Reading
by A. E. van Vogt

Slan
The World of Ā
The Weapon Shops of Isher
The Voyage of the Space Beagle
The War Against the Rull

BLACK DESTROYER

On and on Coeurl prowled! The black, moonless, almost starless night yielded reluctantly before a grim reddish dawn that crept up from his left. A vague, dull light it was, that gave no sense of approaching warmth, no comfort, nothing but a cold, diffuse lightness, slowly revealing a nightmare landscape.

Black, jagged rock and black, unliving plain took form around him, as a pale-red sun peered at last above the grotesque horizon. It was then Coeurl recognized suddenly that he was on familiar ground.

He stopped short. Tenseness flamed along his nerves. His muscles pressed with sudden, unrelenting strength against his bones. His great forelegs—twice as long as his hindlegs—twitched with a shuddering movement that arched every razor-sharp claw. The thick tentacles that sprouted from his shoulders ceased their weaving undulation, and grew taut with anxious alertness.

Utterly appalled, he twisted his great cat head from side to side, while the little hairlike tendrils that formed each ear vibrated frantically, testing every vagrant breeze, every throb in the ether.

But there was no response, no swift tingling along his intricate nervous system, not the faintest suggestion anywhere of the presence of the all-necessary id. Hopelessly, Coeurl crouched, an enormous catlike figure silhouetted against the dim reddish skyline, like a distorted etching of a black tiger resting on a black rock in a shadow world.

He had known this day would come. Through all the centuries of restless search, this day had loomed ever nearer, blacker, more frightening—this inevitable hour when he must return to the point where he began his systematic hunt in a world almost depleted of id-creatures.

The truth struck in waves like an endless, rhythmic ache at the seat of his ego. When he had started, there had been a few id-creatures in every hundred square miles, to be mercilessly rooted out. Only too well Coeurl knew in this ultimate hour that he had missed none. There were no id-creatures left to eat. In all the hundreds of thousands of square miles that he had made his own by right of ruthless conquest—until no neighboring coeurl dared to question his sovereignty—there was no id to feed the otherwise immortal engine that was his body.

Square foot by square foot he had gone over it. And now—he recognized the knoll of rock just ahead, and the black rock bridge that formed a queer, curling tunnel to his right. It was in that tunnel he had lain for days, waiting for the simple-minded, snakelike id-creature to come forth from its hole in the rock to bask in the sun—his first kill after he had realized the absolute necessity of organized extermination.

He licked his lips in brief gloating memory of the moment his slavering jaws tore the victim into precious toothsome bits. But the dark fear of an idless universe swept the sweet remembrance from his consciousness, leaving only certainty of death.

He snarled audibly, a defiant, devilish sound that quavered on the air, echoed and re-echoed among the rocks, and shuddered back along his nerves—instinctive and hellish expression of his will to live.

And then—abruptly—it came.

He saw it emerge out of the distance on a long downward slant, a tiny glowing spot that grew enormously into a metal ball. The great shining globe hissed by above Coeurl, slowing visibly in quick deceleration. It sped over a black line of hills to the right, hovered almost motionless for a second, then sank down out of sight.

Coeurl exploded from his startled immobility. With tiger speed, he flowed down among the rocks. His round, black eyes burned with the horrible desire that was an agony within him. His ear tendrils vibrated a message of id in such tremendous quantities that his body felt sick with the pangs of his abnormal hunger.

The little red sun was a crimson ball in the purple-black heavens when he crept up from behind a mass of rock and gazed from its shadows at the crumbling, gigantic ruins of the city that sprawled below him. The silvery globe, in spite of its great size, looked strangely inconspicuous against that vast, fairylike reach of ruins. Yet about it was a leashed aliveness, a dynamic quiescence that, after a moment, made it stand out, dominating the foreground. A massive, rock-crushing thing of metal, it rested on a cradle made by its own weight in the harsh, resisting plain which began abruptly at the outskirts of the dead metropolis.

Coeurl gazed at the strange, two-legged creatures who stood in little groups near the brilliantly lighted opening that yawned at the base of the ship. His throat thickened with the immediacy of his need; and his brain grew dark with the first wild impulse to burst forth in furious charge and smash these flimsy, helpless-looking creatures whose bodies emitted the id-vibrations.

Mists of memory stopped that mad rush when it was still only electricity surging through his muscles. Memory that brought fear in an acid stream of weakness, pouring along his nerves, poisoning the reservoirs of his strength. He had time to see that the creature wore things over their real bodies, shimmering transparent material that glittered in strange, burning flashes in the rays of the sun.

Other memories came suddenly. Of dim days when the city that spread below was the living, breathing heart of an age of glory that dissolved in a single century before flaming guns whose wielders knew only that for the survivors there would be an ever-narrowing supply of id.

It was the remembrance of those guns that held him there, cringing in a wave of terror that blurred his reason. He saw himself smashed by balls of metal and burned by searing flame.

Came cunning—understanding of the presence of these creatures. This, Coeurl reasoned for the first time, was a scientific expedition from another star. In the olden days, the coeurls had thought of space travel, but disaster came too swiftly for it ever to be more than a thought.

Scientists meant investigation, not destruction. Scientists in their way were fools. Bold with his knowledge, he emerged into the open. He saw the creatures become aware of him. They turned and stared. One, the smallest of the group, detached a shining metal rod from a sheath, and held it casually in one hand. Coeurl loped on, shaken to his core by the action; but it was too late to turn back.

Commander Hal Morton heard little Gregory Kent, the chemist, laugh with the embarrassed half gurgle with which he invariably announced inner uncertainty. He saw Kent fingering the spindly metalite weapon.

Kent said: "I'll take no chances with anything as big as that."

Commander Morton allowed his own deep chuckle to echo along the communicators. "That," he grunted finally, "is one of the reasons why you're on this expedition, Kent—because you never leave anything to chance."

His chuckle trailed off into silence. Instinctively, as he watched the monster approach them across the black rock plain, he moved forward until he stood a little in advance of the others, his huge form bulking the transparent metalite suit. The comments of the men pattered through the radio communicator into his ears:

"I'd hate to meet that baby on a dark night in an alley."

"Don't be silly. This is obviously an intelligent creature. Probably a member of the ruling race."

"It looks like nothing else than a big cat, if you forget those tentacles sticking out from its shoulders, and make allowances for those monster forelegs."

"Its physical development," said a voice, which Morton recognized as that of Siedel, the psychologist, "presupposes an animal-like adaptation to surroundings, not an intellectual one. On the other hand, its coming to us like this is not the act of an animal but of a creature possessing a mental awareness of our possible identity. You will notice that its movements are stiff, denoting caution, which suggests fear and consciousness of our weapons. I'd like to get a good look at the end of its tentacles. If they taper into handlike appendages that can really grip objects, then the conclusion would be inescapable that it is a descendant of the inhabitants of this city. It would be a great help if we could establish communication with it, even though appearances indicate that it has degenerated into a historyless primitive."

Coeurl stopped when he was still ten feet from the foremost creature. The sense of id was so overwhelming that his brain drifted to the ultimate verge of chaos. He felt as if his limbs were bathed in molten liquid; his very vision was not quite clear, as the sheer sensuality of his desire thundered through his being.

The men—all except the little one with the shining metal rod in his fingers—came closer. Coeurl saw that they were frankly and curiously examining him. Their lips were moving, and their voices beat in a monotonous, meaningless rhythm on his ear tendrils. At the same time he had the sense of waves of a much higher frequency—his own communication level—only it was a machinelike clicking that jarred his brain. With a distinct effort to appear friendly, he broadcast his name from his ear tendrils, at the same time pointing at himself with one curving tentacle.

Gourlay, chief of communications, drawled: "I got a sort of static in my radio when he wiggled those hairs, Morton. Do you think—"

"Looks very much like it," the leader answered the unfinished question. "That means a job for you, Gourlay. If it speaks by means of radio waves, it might not be altogether impossible that you can create some sort of television picture of its vibrations, or teach him the Morse code."

"Ah," said Siedel. "I was right. The tentacles each develop into seven strong fingers. Provided the nervous system is complicated enough, those fingers could, with training, operate any machine."

Morton said: "I think we'd better go in and have some lunch. Afterward, we've got to get busy. The material men can set up their machines and start gathering data on the planet's metal possibilities, and so on. The others can do a little careful exploring. I'd like some notes on architecture and on the scientific development of this race, and particularly what happened to wreck the civilization. On earth civilization after civilization crumbled, but always a new one sprang up in its dust. Why didn't that happen here? Any questions?"

"Yes. What about pussy? Look, he wants to come in with us."

Commander Morton frowned, an action that emphasized the deep-space pallor of his face. "I wish there was some way we could take it in with us, without forcibly capturing it. Kent, what do you think?"

"I think we should first decide whether it's an it or a him, and call it one or the other. I'm in favor of him. As for the taking him in with us—" The little chemist shook his head decisively. "Impossible. This atmosphere is twenty-eight per cent chlorine. Our oxygen would be pure dynamite to his lungs."

The commander chuckled. "He doesn't believe that, apparently." He watched the catlike monster follow the first two men through the great door. The men kept an anxious distance from him, then glanced at Morton questioningly. Morton waved his hand. "O. K. Open the second lock and let him get a whiff of the oxygen. That'll cure him."

A moment later, he cursed his amazement. "By Heaven, he doesn't even notice the difference! That means he hasn't any lungs, or else the chlorine is not what his lungs use. Let him in! You bet he can go in! Smith, here's a treasure house for a biologist—harmless enough if we're careful. We can always handle him. But what a metabolism!"

Smith, a tall, thin, bony chap with a long, mournful face, said in an oddly forceful voice: "In all our travels, we've found only two higher forms of life. Those dependent on chlorine, and those who need oxygen—the two elements that support combustion. I'm prepared to stake my reputation that no complicated organism could ever adapt itself to both gases in a natural way. At first thought I should say here is an extremely advanced form of life. This race long ago discovered truths of biology that we are just beginning to suspect. Morton, we mustn't let this creature get away if we can help it."

"If his anxiety to get inside is any criterion," Commander Morton laughed, "then our difficulty will be to get rid of him."

He moved into the lock with Coeurl and the two men. The automatic machinery hummed; and in a few minutes they were standing at the bottom of a series of elevators that led up to the living quarters.

"Does that go up?" One of the men flicked a thumb in the direction of the monster.

"Better send him up alone, if he'll go in."

Coeurl offered no objection, until he heard the door slam behind him; and the closed cage shot upward. He whirled with a savage snarl, his reason swirling into chaos. With one leap, he pounced at the door. The metal bent under his plunge, and the desperate pain maddened him. Now, he was all trapped animal. He smashed at the metal with his paws, bending it like so much tin. He tore great bars loose with his thick tentacles. The machinery screeched; there were horrible jerks as the limitless power pulled the cage along in spite of projecting pieces of metal that scraped the outside walls. And then the cage stopped, and he snatched off the rest of the door and hurtled into the corridor.

He waited there until Morton and the men came up with drawn weapons. "We're fools," Morton said. "We should have shown him how it works. He thought we'd double-crossed him."

He motioned to the monster, and saw the savage glow fade from the coal-black eyes as he opened and closed the door with elaborate gestures to show the operation.

Coeurl ended the lesson by trotting into the large room to his right. He lay down on the rugged floor, and fought down the electric tautness of his nerves and muscles. A very fury of rage against himself for his fright consumed him. It seemed to his burning brain that he had lost the advantage of appearing a mild and harmless creature. His strength must have startled and dismayed them.

It meant greater danger in the task which he now knew he must accomplish: To kill everything in the ship, and take the machine back to their world in search of unlimited id.

With unwinking eyes, Coeurl lay and watched the two men clearing away the loose rubble from the metal doorway of the huge old building. His whole body ached with the hunger of his cells for id. The craving tore through his palpitant muscles, and throbbed like a living thing in his brain. His every nerve quivered to be off after the men who had wandered into the city. One of them, he knew, had gone— alone.

The dragging minutes fled; and still he restrained himself, still he lay there watching, aware that the men knew he watched. They floated a metal machine from the ship to the rock mass that blocked the great half-open door, under the direction of a third man. No flicker of their fingers escaped his fierce stare, and slowly, as the simplicity of the machinery became apparent to him, contempt grew upon him.

He knew what to expect finally, when the flame flared in incandescent violence and ate ravenously at the hard rock beneath. But in spite of his preknowledge, he deliberately jumped and snarled as if in fear, at that white heat burst forth. His ear tendrils caught the laughter of the men, their curious pleasure at his simulated dismay.

The door was released, and Morton came over and went inside with the third man. The latter shook his head.

"It's a shambles. You can catch the drift of the stuff. Obviously, they used atomic energy, but . . . but it's in wheel form. That's a peculiar development. In our science, atomic energy brought in the nonwheel machine. It's possible that here they've progressed further to a new type of wheel mechanics. I hope their libraries are better preserved than this, or we'll never know. What could have happened to a civilization to make it vanish like this?"

A third voice broke through the communicators: "This is Siedel. I heard your question, Pennons. Psychologically and sociologically speaking, the only reason why a territory becomes uninhabited is lack of food."

"But they're so advanced scientifically, why didn't they develop space flying and go elsewhere for their food?"

"Ask Gunlie Lester," interjected Morton. "I heard him expounding some theory even before we landed."

The astronomer answered the first call. "I've still got to verify all my facts, but this desolate world is the only planet revolving around that miserable red sun. There's nothing else. No moon, not even a planetoid. And the nearest star system is *nine hundred light-years* away.

"So tremendous would have been the problem of the ruling race of this world, that in one jump they would not only have had to solve interplanetary but interstellar space traveling. When you consider how slow our own development was—first the moon, then Venus—each success leading to the next, and after centuries to the nearest stars; and last of all to the anti-accelerators that permitted galactic travel—considering all this, I maintain it would be impossible for any race to create such machines without practical experience. And, with the nearest star so far away, they had no incentive for the space adventuring that makes for experience."

Coeurl was trotting briskly over to another group. But now, in the driving appetite that consumed him, and in the frenzy of his high scorn, he paid no attention to what they were doing. Memories of past knowledge, jarred into activity by what he had seen, flowed into his consciousness in an ever developing and more vivid stream.

From group to group he sped, a nervous dynamo—jumpy, sick with his awful hunger. A little car rolled up, stopping in front of him, and a formidable camera whirred as it took a picture of him. Over on a mound of rock, a gigantic telescope was rearing up toward the sky. Nearby, a disintegrating machine drilled its searing fire into an ever-deepening hole, down and down, straight down.

Coeurl's mind became a blur of things he watched with half attention. And ever more imminent grew the moment when he knew he could no longer carry on the torture of acting. His brain strained with an irresistible impatience; his body burned with the fury of his eagerness to be off after the man who had gone alone into the city.

He could stand it no longer. A green foam misted his mouth, maddening him. He saw that, for the bare moment, nobody was looking.

Like a shot from a gun, he was off. He floated along in great, gliding leaps, a shadow among the shadows of the rocks. In a minute, the harsh terrain hid the spaceship and the two-legged beings.

Coeurl forgot the ship, forgot everything but his purpose, as if his brain had been wiped clear by a magic, memory-erasing brush. He circled widely, then raced into the city, along deserted streets, taking short cuts with the ease of familiarity, through gaping holes in time-weakened walls, through long corridors of moldering buildings. He slowed to a crouching lope as his ear tendrils caught the id vibrations.

Suddenly, he stopped and peered from a scatter of fallen rock. The man was standing at what must once have been a window, sending the glaring rays of his flashlight into the gloomy interior. The flashlight clicked off. The man, a heavy-set, powerful fellow, walked off with quick, alert steps. Coeurl didn't like that alertness. It presaged trouble; it meant lightning reaction to danger.

Coeurl waited till the human being had vanished around a corner, then he padded into the open. He was running now, tremendously faster than a man could walk, because his plan was clear in his brain. Like a wraith, he slipped down the next street, past a long block of buildings. He turned the first corner at top speed; and then, with dragging belly, crept into the half-darkness between the building and a huge chunk of débris. The street ahead was barred by a solid line of loose rubble that made it like a valley, ending in a narrow, bottlelike neck. The neck had its outlet just below Coeurl.

His ear tendrils caught the low-frequency waves whistling. The sound throbbed through his being; and suddenly terror caught with icy fingers at his brain. The man would have a gun. Suppose he leveled one burst of atomic energy—one burst—before his own muscles could whip out in murder fury.

A little shower of rocks streamed past. And then the man was beneath him. Coeurl reached out and struck a single crushing blow at the shimmering transparent headpiece of the spacesuit. There was a tearing sound of metal and a gushing of blood. The man doubled up as if part of him had been telescoped. For a moment, his bones and legs and muscles combined miraculously to keep him standing. Then he crumpled with a metallic clank of his space armor.

Fear completely evaporated, Coeurl leaped out of hiding. With ravenous speed, he smashed the metal and the body within it to bits. Great chunks of metal, torn piecemeal from the suit, sprayed the ground. Bones cracked. Flesh crunched.

It was simple to tune in on the vibrations of the id, and to create the violent chemical disorganization that freed it from the crushed bone. The id was, Coeurl discovered, mostly in the bone.

He felt revived, almost reborn. Here was more food than he had had in a whole past year.

Three minutes, and it was over, and Coeurl was off like a thing fleeing dire danger. Cautiously, he approached the glistening globe from the opposite side to that by which he had left. The men were all busy at their tasks. Gliding noiselessly, Coeurl slipped unnoticed up to a group of men.

Morton stared down at the horror of tattered flesh, metal and blood on the rock at his feet, and felt a tightening in his throat that prevented speech. He heard Kent say:

"He *would* go alone, damn him!" The little chemist's voice held a sob imprisoned; and Morton remembered that Kent and Jarvey had chummed together for years in the way only two men can.

"The worst part of it is," shuddered one of the men, "it looks like a senseless murder. His body is spread out like little lumps of flattened jelly, but it seems to be all there. I'd almost wager that if we weighed everything here, there'd still be one hundred and seventy-five pounds by earth gravity. That'd be about one hundred and seventy pounds here."

Smith broke in, his mournful face lined with gloom: "The killer attacked Jarvey, and then discovered his flesh was alien—uneatable. Just like our big cat. Wouldn't eat anything we set before him—" His words died out in sudden, queer silence. Then he said slowly: "Say, what about that creature? He's big enough and strong enough to have done this with his own little paws."

Morton frowned. "It's a thought. After all, he's the only living thing we've seen. We can't just execute him on suspicion, of course—"

"Besides," said one of the men, "he was never out of my sight."

Before Morton could speak, Siedel, the psychologist, snapped, "Positive about that?"

The man hesitated. "Maybe he was for a few minutes. He was wandering around so much, looking at everything."

"Exactly," said Siedel with satisfaction. He turned to Morton. "You see, commander, I, too, had the impression that he was always around; and yet, thinking back over it, I find gaps. There were moments—probably long minutes—when he was completely out of sight."

Morton's face was dark with thought, as Kent broke in fiercely: "I say, take no chances. Kill the brute on suspicion before he does any more damage."

Morton said slowly: "Korita, you've been wandering around with Cranessy and Van Horne. Do you think pussy is a descendant of the ruling class of this planet?"

The tall Japanese archeologist stared at the sky as if collecting his mind. "Commander Morton," he said finally, respectfully, "there is a mystery here. Take a look, all of you, at that majestic skyline. Notice the almost Gothic outline of the architecture. In spite of the megalopolis which they created, these people were close to the soil. The buildings are not simply ornamented. They are ornamental in themselves. Here is the equivalent of the Doric column, the Egyptian pyramid, the Gothic cathedral, growing out of the ground, earnest, big with destiny. If this lonely, desolate world can be regarded as a mother earth, then the land had a warm, a spiritual place in the hearts of the race.

"The effect is emphasized by the winding streets. Their machines prove they were mathematicians, but they were artists first; and so they did not create the geometrically designed cities of the ultrasophisticated world metropolis. There is a genuine artistic abandon, a deep joyous emotion written in the curving and unmathematical arrangements of houses, buildings and avenues; a sense of intensity, of divine belief in an inner certainty. This is not a decadent, hoary-with-age civilization, but a young and vigorous culture, confident, strong with purpose.

"There it ended. Abruptly, as if at this point culture had its Battle of Tours, and began to collapse like the ancient Mohammedan civilization. Or as if in one leap it spanned the centuries and entered the period of contending states. In the Chinese civilization that period occupied 480–230 B.C., at the end of which the State of Tsin saw the beginning of the Chinese Empire. This phase Egypt experienced between 1780–1580 B.C., of which the last century was the 'Hyksos'—unmentionable—time. The classical experienced it from Chaeronea—338—and, at the pitch of horror, from the Gracchi—133—to Actium—31 B.C. The West European Americans were devastated by it in the nineteenth and twentieth centuries, and modern historians agree that, nominally, we entered the same phase fifty years ago; though, of course, we have solved the problem.

"You may ask, Commander, what has all this to do with your question? My answer is: There is no record of a culture entering abruptly into the period of contending states. It is always a slow development; and the first step is a merciless questioning of all that was once held sacred. Inner certainties cease to exist, are dissolved before the ruthless probings of scientific and analytic minds. The skeptic becomes the highest type of being.

"I say that this culture ended abruptly in its most flourishing age. The sociological effects of such a catastrophe would be a sudden vanishing of morals, a reversion to almost bestial criminality, unleavened by any sense of ideal, a callous indifference to death. If this . . . this pussy is a descendant of such a race, then he will be a cunning creature, a thief in the night, a cold-blooded murderer, who would cut his own brother's throat for gain."

"That's enough!" It was Kent's clipped voice. "Commander, I'm willing to act the role of executioner."

Smith interrupted sharply: "Listen, Morton, you're not going to kill that cat yet, even if he is guilty. He's a biological treasure house."

Kent and Smith were glaring angrily at each other. Morton frowned at them thoughtfully, then said: "Korita, I'm inclined to accept your theory as a working basis. But one question: Pussy comes from a period earlier than our own? That is, we are entering the highly civilized era of our culture, while he became suddenly histo-ryless in the most vigorous period of his. *But* is it possible that his culture is a later one on this planet than ours is in the galactic-wide system we have civilized?"

"Exactly. His may be the middle of the tenth civilization of his world; while ours is the end of the eighth sprung from earth, each of the ten, of course, having been built on the ruins of the one before it."

"In that case, pussy would not know anything about the skep-ticism that made it possible for us to find him out so positively as a criminal and murderer?"

"No; it would be literally magic to him."

Morton was smiling grimly. "Then I think you'll get your wish, Smith. We'll let pussy live; and if there are any fatalities, now that we know him, it will be due to rank carelessness. There's just the chance, of course, that we're wrong. Like Siedel, I also have the impression that he was always around. But now—we can't leave poor Jarvey here like this. We'll put him in a coffin and bury him."

"No, we won't!" Kent barked. He flushed. "I beg your pardon, Commander. I didn't mean it that way. I maintain pussy wanted something from that body. It looks to be all there, but something must be missing. I'm going to find out what, and pin this murder on him so that you'll have to believe it beyond the shadow of a doubt."

It was late night when Morton looked up from a book and saw Kent emerge through the door that led from the laboratories below.

Kent carried a large, flat bowl in his hands; his tired eyes flashed across at Morton, and he said in a weary, yet harsh, voice: "Now watch!"

He started toward Coeurl, who lay sprawled on the great rug, pretending to be asleep.

Morton stopped him. "Wait a minute, Kent. Any other time, I wouldn't question your actions, but you look ill; you're overwrought. What have you got there?"

Kent turned, and Morton saw that his first impression had been but a flashing glimpse of the truth. There were dark pouches under the little chemist's gray eyes—eyes that gazed feverishly from sunken cheeks in an ascetic face.

"I've found the missing element," Kent said. "It's phosphorus. There wasn't so much as a square millimeter of phosphorus left in Jarvey's bones. Every bit of it had been drained out—by what super-chemistry I don't know. There are ways of getting phosphorus out of the human body. For instance, a quick way was what happened to the workman who helped build this ship. Remember, he fell into fifteen tons of molten metalite—at least, so his relatives claimed—but the company wouldn't pay compensation until the metalite, on analysis, was found to contain a high percentage of phosphorus—"

"What about the bowl of food?" somebody interrupted. Men were putting away magazines and books, looking up with interest.

"It's got organic phosphorus in it. He'll get the scent, or whatever it is that he uses instead of scent—"

"I think he gets the vibrations of things," Gourlay interjected lazily. "Sometimes, when he wiggles those tendrils, I get a distinct static on the radio. And then, again, there's no reaction, just as if he's moved higher or lower on the wave scale. He seems to control the vibrations at will."

Kent waited with obvious impatience until Gourlay's last word, then abruptly went on: "All right, then, when he gets the vibration of the phosphorus and reacts to it like an animal, then—well, we can decide what we've proved by his reaction. May I go ahead, Morton?"

"There are three things wrong with your plan," Morton said. "In the first place, you seem to assume that he is only animal; you seem to have forgotten he may not be hungry after Jarvey; you seem to think that he will not be suspicious. But set the bowl down. His reaction may tell us something."

Coeurl stared with unblinking black eyes as the man set the bowl before him. His ear tendrils instantly caught the id-vibrations from the contents of the bowl—and he gave it not even a second glance.

He recognized this two-legged being as the one who had held the weapon that morning. Danger! With a snarl, he floated to his feet. He caught the bowl with the fingerlike appendages at the end of one looping tentacle, and emptied its contents into the face of Kent, who shrank back with a yell.

Explosively, Coeurl flung the bowl aside and snapped a hawser-thick tentacle around the cursing man's waist. He didn't bother with the gun that hung from Kent's belt. It was only a vibration gun, he sensed—atomic powered, but not an atomic disintegrator. He tossed the kicking Kent onto the nearest couch—and realized with a hiss of dismay that he should have disarmed the man.

Not that the gun was dangerous—but, as the man furiously wiped the gruel from his face with one hand, he reached with the other for his weapon. Coeurl crouched back as the gun was raised slowly and a white beam of flame was discharged at his massive head.

His ear tendrils hummed as they canceled the efforts of the vibration gun. His round, black eyes narrowed as he caught the movement of men reaching for the metalite guns. Morton's voice lashed across the silence.

"Stop!"

Kent clicked off his weapon; and Coeurl crouched down, quivering with fury at this man who had forced him to reveal something of his power.

"Kent," said Morton coldly, "you're not the type to lose your head. You deliberately tried to kill pussy, knowing that the majority of us are in favor of keeping him alive. You know what our rule is: If anyone objects to my decisions, he must say so at the time. If the majority object, my decisions are overruled. In this case, no one but you objected, and, therefore, your action in taking the law into your own hands is most reprehensible, and automatically debars you from voting for a year."

Kent stared grimly at the circle of faces. "Korita was right when he said ours was a highly civilized age. It's decadent." Passion flamed harshly in his voice. "My God, isn't there a man here who can see the horror of the situation? Jarvey dead only a few hours, and this creature, whom we all know to be guilty, lying there unchained, planning his next murder; and the victim is right here in this room. What kind of men are we—fools, cynics, ghouls—or is it that our civilization is so steeped in reason that we can contemplate a murderer sympathetically?"

He fixed brooding eyes on Coeurl. "You were right, Morton, that's no animal. That's a devil from the deepest hell of this forgotten planet, whirling its solitary way around a dying sun."

"Don't go melodramatic on us," Morton said. "Your analysis is all wrong, so far as I am concerned. We're not ghouls or cynics; we're simply scientists, and pussy here is going to be studied. Now that we suspect him, we doubt his ability to trap any of us. One against a hundred hasn't a chance." He glanced around. "Do I speak for all of us?"

"Not for me, Commander!" It was Smith who spoke, and, as Morton stared in amazement, he continued: "In the excitement and momentary confusion, no one seems to have noticed that when Kent fired his vibration gun, the beam hit this creature squarely on his cat head—and didn't hurt him."

Morton's amazed glance went from Smith to Coeurl, and back to Smith again. "Are you certain it hit him? As you say, it all happened so swiftly—when pussy wasn't hurt I simply assumed that Kent had missed him."

"He hit him in the face," Smith said positively. "A vibration gun, of course, can't even kill a man right away—but it can injure him. There's no sign of injury on pussy, though, not even a singed hair."

"Perhaps his skin is a good insulation against heat of any kind."

"Perhaps. But in view of our uncertainty, I think we should lock him up in the cage."

While Morton frowned darkly in thought, Kent spoke up. "Now you're talking sense, Smith."

Morton asked: "Then you would be satisfied, Kent, if we put him in the cage?"

Kent considered, finally: "Yes. If four inches of micro-steel can't hold him, we'd better give him the ship."

Coeurl followed the men as they went out into the corridor. He trotted docilely along as Morton unmistakably motioned him through a door he had not hitherto seen. He found himself in a square, solid metal room. The door clanged metallically behind him; he felt the flow of power as the electric lock clicked home.

His lips parted in a grimace of hate, as he realized the trap, but he gave no other outward reaction. It occurred to him that he had progressed a long way from the sunk-into-primitiveness creature who, a few hours before, had gone incoherent with fear in an elevator cage. Now, a thousand memories of his powers were reawakened in his brain; ten thousand cunnings were, after ages of disuse, once again part of his very being.

He sat quite still for a moment on the short, heavy haunches into which his body tapered, his ear tendrils examining his surroundings. Finally, he lay down, his eyes glowing with contemptuous fire. The fools! The poor fools!

It was about an hour later when he heard the man—Smith—fumbling overhead. Vibrations poured upon him, and for just an instant he was startled. He leaped to his feet in pure terror—and then realized that the vibrations were vibrations, not atomic explosions. Somebody was taking pictures of the inside of his body.

He crouched down again, but his ear tendrils vibrated, and he thought contemptuously: the silly fool would be surprised when he tried to develop those pictures.

After a while the man went away, and for a long time there were noises of men doing things far away. That, too, died away slowly.

Coeurl lay waiting, as he felt the silence creep over the ship. In the long ago, before the dawn of immortality, the coeurls, too, had slept at night; and the memory of it had been revived the day before when he saw some of the men dozing. At last, the vibration of two pairs of feet, pacing, pacing endlessly, was the only human-made frequency that throbbed on his ear tendrils.

Tensely, he listened to the two watchmen. The first one walked slowly past the cage door. Then about thirty feet behind him came the second. Coeurl sensed the alertness of these men; knew that he could never surprise either while they walked separately. It meant—he must be doubly careful!

Fifteen minutes, and they came again. The moment they were past, he switched his senses from their vibrations to a vastly higher range. The pulsating violence of the atomic engines stammered its soft story to his brain. The electric dynamos hummed their muffled song of pure power. He felt the whisper of that flow through the wires in the walls of his cage, and through the electric lock of his door. He forced his quivering body into straining immobility, his senses seeking, searching, to tune in on that sibilant tempest of energy. Suddenly, his ear tendrils vibrated in harmony—he caught the surging change into shrillness of that rippling force wave.

There was a sharp click of metal on metal. With a gentle touch of one tentacle, Coeurl pushed open the door, and glided out into the dully gleaming corridor. For just a moment he felt contempt, a glow of superiority, as he thought of the stupid creatures who dared to match their wit against a coeurl. And in that moment, he suddenly thought of other coeurls. A queer, exultant sense of race pounded through his being; the driving hate of centuries of ruthless competition yielded reluctantly before pride of kinship with the future rulers of all space.

·   ·   ·

Suddenly, he felt weighed down by his limitations, his need for other coeurls, his aloneness—one against a hundred, with the stake all eternity; the starry universe itself beckoned his rapacious, vaulting ambition. If he failed, there would never be a second chance—no time to revive long-rotted machinery, and attempt to solve the secret of space travel.

He padded along on tensed paws—through the salon—into the next corridor—and came to the first bedroom door. It stood half open. One swift flow of synchronized muscles, one swiftly lashing tentacle that caught the unresisting throat of the sleeping man, crushing it; and the lifeless head rolled crazily, the body twitched once.

Seven bedrooms; seven dead men. It was the seventh taste of murder that brought a sudden return of lust, a pure, unbounded desire to kill, return of a millennium-old habit of destroying everything containing the precious id.

As the twelfth man slipped convulsively into death, Coeurl emerged abruptly from the sensuous joy of the kill to the sound of footsteps.

They were not near—that was what brought wave after wave of fright swirling into the chaos that suddenly became his brain.

The watchmen were coming slowly along the corridor toward the door of the cage where he had been imprisoned. In a moment, the first man would see the open door—and sound the alarm.

Coeurl caught at the vanishing remnants of his reason. With frantic speed, careless now of accidental sounds, he raced—along the corridor with its bedroom doors—through the salon. He emerged into the next corridor, cringing in awful anticipation of the atomic flame he expected would stab into his face.

The two men were together, standing side by side. For one single instant, Coeurl could scarcely believe his tremendous good luck. Like a fool the second had come running when he saw the other stop before the open door. They looked up, paralyzed, before the nightmare of claws and tentacles, the ferocious cat head and hate-filled eyes.

The first man went for his gun, but the second, physically frozen before the doom he saw, uttered a shriek, a shrill cry of horror that floated along the corridors—and ended in a curious gurgle, as Coeurl flung the two corpses with one irresistible motion the full length of the corridor. He didn't want the dead bodies found near the cage. That was his one hope.

Shaking in every nerve and muscle, conscious of the terrible error he had made, unable to think coherently, he plunged into the cage. The door clicked softly shut behind him. Power flowed once more through the electric lock.

He crouched tensely, simulating sleep, as he heard the rush of many feet, caught the vibration of excited voices. He knew when somebody actuated the cage audioscope and looked in. A few moments now, and the other bodies would be discovered.

"Siedel gone!" Morton said numbly. "What are we going to do without Siedel? And Breckenridge! And Coulter and—Horrible!"

He covered his face with his hands, but only for an instant. He looked up grimly, his heavy chin outthrust as he stared into the stern faces that surrounded him. "If anybody's got so much as a germ of an idea, bring it out."

"Space madness!"

"I've thought of that. But there hasn't been a case of a man going mad for fifty years. Dr. Eggert will test everybody, of course, and right now he's looking at the bodies with that possibility in mind."

As he finished, he saw the doctor coming through the door. Men crowded aside to make way for him.

"I heard you, Commander," Dr. Eggert said, "and I think I can say right now that the space-madness theory is out. The throats of these men have been squeezed to a jelly. No human being could have exerted such enormous strength without using a machine."

Morton saw that the doctor's eyes kept looking down the corridor, and he shook his head and groaned:

"It's no use suspecting pussy, Doctor. He's in his cage, pacing up and down. Obviously heard the racket and—Man alive! You can't suspect him. That cage was built to hold literally anything—four inches of micro-steel—and there's not a scratch on the door. Kent, even you won't say, 'Kill him on suspicion,' because there can't be any suspicion, unless there's a new science here, beyond anything we can imagine—"

"On the contrary," said Smith flatly, "we have all the evidence we need. I used the telefluor on him—you know the arrangement we have on top of the cage—and tried to take some pictures. They just blurred. Pussy jumped when the telefluor was turned on, as if he felt the vibrations.

"You all know what Gourlay said before? This beast can apparently receive and send vibrations of any lengths. The way he dominated the power of Kent's gun is final proof of his special ability to interfere with energy."

"What in the name of all the hells have we got here?" One of the men groaned. "Why, if he can control that power, and sent it out in any vibrations, there's nothing to stop him killing all of us."

"Which proves," snapped Morton, "that he isn't invincible, or he would have done it long ago."

Very deliberately, he walked over to the mechanism that controlled the prison cage.

"You're not going to open the door!" Kent gasped, reaching for his gun.

"No, but if I pull this switch, electricity will flow through the floor, and electrocute whatever's inside. We've never had to use this before, so you had probably forgotten about it."

He jerked the switch hard over. Blue fire flashed from the metal, and a bank of fuses above his head exploded with a single bang.

Morton frowned. "That's funny. Those fuses shouldn't have blown! Well, we can't even look in, now. That wrecked the audios, too."

Smith said: "If he could interfere with the electric lock, enough to open the door, then he probably probed every possible danger and was ready to interfere when you threw that switch."

"At least, it proves he's vulnerable to our energies!" Morton smiled grimly. "Because he rendered them harmless. The important thing is, we've got him behind four inches of the toughest of metal. At the worst we can open the door and ray him to death. But first, I think we'll try to use the telefluor power cable—"

A commotion from inside the cage interrupted his words. A heavy body crashed against a wall, followed by a dull thump.

"He knows what we were trying to do!" Smith grunted to Morton. "And I'll bet it's a very sick pussy in there. What a fool he was to go back into that cage and does he realize it!"

The tension was relaxing; men were smiling nervously, and there was even a ripple of humorless laughter at the picture Smith drew of the monster's discomfiture.

"What I'd like to know," said Pennons, the engineer, "is, why did the telefluor meter dial jump and waver at full power when pussy made that noise? It's right under my nose here, and the dial jumped like a house afire!"

There was silence both without and within the cage, then Morton said: "It may mean he's coming out. Back, everybody, and keep your guns ready. Pussy was a fool to think he could conquer a hundred men, but he's by far the most formidable creature in the galactic system. He may come out of that door, rather than die like a rat in a trap. And he's just tough enough to take some of us with him—if we're not careful."

The men backed slowly in a solid body; and somebody said: "That's funny. I thought I heard the elevator."

"Elevator!" Morton echoed. "Are you sure, man?"

"Just for a moment I was!" The man, a member of the crew, hesitated. "We were all shuffling our feet—"

"Take somebody with you, and go look. Bring whoever dared to run off back here—"

There was a jar, a horrible jerk, as the whole gigantic body of the ship careened under them. Morton was flung to the floor with a violence that stunned him. He fought back to consciousness, aware of the other men lying all around him. He shouted: "Who the devil started those engines!"

The agonizing acceleration continued; his feet dragged with awful exertion, as he fumbled with the nearest audioscope, and punched the engine-room number. The picture that flooded onto the screen brought a deep bellow to his lips:

"It's pussy! He's in the engine room—and we're heading straight out into space."

The screen went black even as he spoke, and he could see no more.

It was Morton who first staggered across the salon floor to the supply room where the spacesuits were kept. After fumbling almost blindly into his own suit, he cut the effects of the body-torturing acceleration, and brought suits to the semiconscious men on the floor. In a few moments, other men were assisting him; and then it was only a matter of minutes before everybody was clad in metalite, with anti-acceleration motors running at half power.

It was Morton then who, after first looking into the cage, opened the door and stood, silent as the others crowded about him, to stare at the gaping hole in the rear wall. The hole was a frightful thing of jagged edges and horribly bent metal, and it opened upon another corridor.

"I'll swear," whispered Pennons, "that it's impossible. The ten-ton hammer in the machine shops couldn't more than dent four inches of micro with one blow—and we only heard one. It would take at least a minute for an atomic disintegrator to do the job. Morton, this is a super-being."

Morton saw that Smith was examining the break in the wall. The biologist looked up. "If only Breckinridge weren't dead! We need a metallurgist to explain this. Look!"

He touched the broken edge of the metal. A piece crumbled in his finger and slithered away in a fine shower of dust to the floor. Morton noticed for the first time that there was a little pile of metallic debris and dust.

"You've hit it." Morton nodded. "No miracle of strength here. The monster merely used his special powers to interfere with the electronic tensions holding the metal together. That would account, too, for the drain on the telefluor power cable that Pennons noticed. The thing used the power with his body as a transforming medium, smashed through the wall, ran down the corridor to the elevator shaft, and so down to the engine room."

"In the meantime, Commander," Kent said quietly, "we are faced with a super-being in control of the ship, completely dominating the engine room and its almost unlimited power, and in possession of the best part of the machine shops."

Morton felt the silence, while the men pondered the chemist's words. Their anxiety was a tangible thing that lay heavily upon their faces; in every expression was the growing realization that here was the ultimate situation in their lives; their very existence was at stake and perhaps much more. Morton voiced the thought in everybody's mind:

"Suppose he wins. He's utterly ruthless, and he probably sees galactic power within his grasp."

"Kent is wrong," barked the chief navigator. "The thing doesn't dominate the engine room. We've still got the control room, and that gives us first control of all the machines. You fellows may not know the mechanical set-up we have; but, though he can eventually disconnect us, we can cut off all the switches in the engine room now. Commander, why didn't you just shut off the power instead of putting us into spacesuits? At the very least you could have adjusted the ship to the acceleration."

"For two reasons," Morton answered. "Individually, we're safer within the force fields of our spacesuits. And we can't afford to give up our advantages in panicky moves."

"Advantages! What other advantages have we got?"

"We know things about him," Morton replied. "And right now, we're going to make a test. Pennons, detail five men to each of the four approaches to the engine room. Take atomic disintegrators to blast through the big doors. They're all shut, I noticed. He's locked himself in.

"Selenski, you go up to the control room and shut off everything except the drive engines. Gear them to the master switch, and shut them off all at once. One thing, though—leave the acceleration on full blast. No anti-acceleration must be applied to the ship. Understand?"

"Aye, sir!" The pilot saluted.

"And report to me through the communicators if any of the machines start to run again." He faced the men. "I'm going to lead the main approach. Kent, you take No. 2; Smith, No. 3, and Pennons, No. 4. We're going to find out right now if we're dealing with unlimited science, or a creature limited like the rest of us. I'll bet on the second possibility."

Morton had an empty sense of walking endlessly, as he moved, a giant of a man in his transparent space armor, along the glistening metal tube that was the main corridor of the engine-room floor. Reason told him the creature had already shown feet of clay, yet the feeling that here was an invincible being persisted.

He spoke into the communicator: "It's no use trying to sneak up on him. He can probably hear a pin drop. So just wheel up your units. He hasn't been in that engine room long enough to do anything.

"As I've said, this is largely a test attack. In the first place, we could never forgive ourselves if we didn't try to conquer him now, before he's had time to prepare against us. But, aside from the possibility that we can destroy him immediately, I have a theory.

"The idea goes something like this: Those doors are built to withstand accidental atomic explosions, and it will take fifteen minutes for the atomic disintegrators to smash them. During that period the monster will have no power. True, the drive will be on, but that's straight atomic explosion. My theory is, he can't touch stuff like that; and in a few minutes you'll see what I mean—I hope."

His voice was suddenly crisp: "Ready, Selenski?"

"Aye, ready."

"Then cut the master switch."

The corridor—the whole ship, Morton knew—was abruptly plunged into darkness. Morton clicked on the dazzling light of his spacesuit; the other men did the same, their faces pale and drawn.

"Blast!" Morton barked into his communicator.

The mobile units throbbed; and then pure atomic flame ravened out and poured upon the hard metal of the door. The first molten droplet rolled reluctantly, not down, but up the door. The second was more normal. It followed a shaky downward course. The third rolled sideways—for this was pure force, not subject to gravitation. Other drops followed until a dozen streams trickled sedately yet unevenly in every direction—streams of hellish, sparkling fire, bright as fairy gems, alive with the coruscating fury of atoms suddenly tortured, and running blindly, crazy with pain.

The minutes ate at time like a slow acid. At last Morton asked huskily:

"Selenski?"

"Nothing yet, Commander."

Morton half whispered: "But he must be doing something. He can't be just waiting in there like a cornered rat. Selenski?"

"Nothing, Commander."

Seven minutes, eight minutes, then twelve.

"Commander!" It was Selenski's voice, taut. "He's got the electric dynamo running."

Morton drew a deep breath, and heard one of his men say:

"That's funny. We can't get any deeper. Boss, take a look at this."

Morton looked. The little scintillating streams had frozen rigid.

The ferocity of the disintegrators vented in vain against metal grown suddenly invulnerable.

Morton sighed. "Our test is over. Leave two men guarding every corridor. The others come up to the control room."

He seated himself a few minutes later before the massive control keyboard. "So far as I'm concerned the test was a success. We know that of all the machines in the engine room, the most important to the monster was the electric dynamo. He must have worked in a frenzy of terror while we were at the doors."

"Of course, it's easy to see what he did," Pennons said. "Once he had the power he increased the electronic tensions of the door to their ultimate."

"The main thing is this," Smith chimed in. "He works with vibrations only so far as his special powers are concerned, and the energy must come from outside himself. Atomic energy in its pure form, not being vibration, he can't handle any differently than we can."

Kent said glumly: "The main point in my opinion is that he stopped us cold. What's the good of knowing that his control over vibrations did it? If we can't break through those doors with our atomic disintegrators, we're finished."

Morton shook his head. "Not finished—but we'll have to do some planning. First, though, I'll start these engines. It'll be harder for him to get control of them when they're running."

He pulled the master switch back into place with a jerk. There was a hum, as scores of machines leaped into violent life in the engine room a hundred feet below. The noises sank to a steady vibration of throbbing power.

Three hours later, Morton paced up and down before the men gathered in the salon. His dark hair was uncombed; the space pallor of his strong face emphasized rather than detracted from the outthrust aggressiveness of his jaw. When he spoke, his deep voice was crisp to the point of sharpness:

"To make sure that our plans are fully co-ordinated, I'm going to ask each expert in turn to outline his part in the overpowering of this creature. Pennons first!"

Pennons stood up briskly. He was not a big man, Morton

thought, yet he looked big, perhaps because of his air of authority. This man knew engines, and the history of engines. Morton had heard him trace a machine through its evolution from a simple toy to the highly complicated modern instrument. He had studied machine development on a hundred planets; and there was literally nothing fundamental that he didn't know about mechanics. It was almost weird to hear Pennons, who could have spoken for a thousand hours and still only have touched upon his subject, say with absurd brevity:

"We've set up a relay in the control room to start and stop every engine rhythmically. The trip lever will work a hundred times a second, and the effect will be to create vibrations of every description. There is just a possibility that one or more of the machines will burst, on the principle of soldiers crossing a bridge in step—you've heard that old story, no doubt—but in my opinion there is no real danger of a break of that tough metal. The main purpose is simply to interfere with the interference of the creature, and smash through the doors."

"Gourlay next!" barked Morton.

Gourlay climbed lazily to his feet. He looked sleepy, as if he was somewhat bored by the whole proceedings, yet Morton knew he loved people to think him lazy, a good-for-nothing slouch, who spent his days in slumber and his nights catching forty winks. His title was chief communication engineer, but his knowledge extended to every vibration field; and he was probably, with the possible exception of Kent, the fastest thinker on the ship. His voice drawled out, and—Morton noted—the very deliberate assurance of it had a soothing effect on the men—anxious faces relaxed, bodies leaned back more restfully:

"Once inside," Gourlay said, "we've rigged up vibration screens of pure force that should stop nearly everything he's got on the ball. They work on the principle of reflection, so that everything he sends will be reflected back to him. In addition, we've got plenty of spare electric energy that we'll just feed him from mobile copper cups. There must be a limit to his capacity for handling power with those insulated nerves of his."

"Selenski!" called Morton.

The chief pilot was already standing, as if he had anticipated Morton's call. And that, Morton reflected, was the man. His nerves had that rocklike steadiness which is the first requirement of the master controller of a great ship's movements; yet that very steadiness seemed to rest on dynamite ready to explode at its owner's volition. He was not a man of great learning, but he "reacted" to stimuli so fast that he always seemed to be anticipating.

"The impression I've received of the plan is that it must be cumulative. Just when the creature thinks that he can't stand any more, another thing happens to add to his trouble and confusion. When the uproar's at its height, I'm supposed to cut in the anti-accelerators. The commander thinks with Gunlie Lester that these creatures will know nothing about anti-acceleration. It's a development, pure and simple, of the science of interstellar flight, and couldn't have been developed in any other way. We think when the creature feels the first effects of the anti-acceleration—you all remember the caved-in feeling you had the first month—it won't know what to think or do."

"Korita next."

"I can only offer you encouragement," said the archeologist, "on the basis of my theory that the monster has all the characteristics of a criminal of the early ages of any civilization, complicated by an apparent reversion to primitiveness. The suggestion has been made by Smith that his knowledge of science is puzzling, and could only mean that we are dealing with an actual inhabitant, not a descendant of the inhabitants of the dead city we visited. This would ascribe a virtual immortality to our enemy, a possibility which is borne out by his ability to breathe both oxygen and chlorine—or neither—but even that makes no difference. He comes from a certain age in his civilization; and he has sunk so low that his ideas are mostly memories of that age.

"In spite of all the powers of his body, he lost his head in the elevator the first morning, until he remembered. He placed himself in such a position that he was forced to reveal his special powers against vibrations. He bungled the mass murders a few hours ago. In fact, his whole record is one of the low cunning of the primitive, egotistical mind which has little or no conception of the vast organization with which it is confronted.

"He is like the ancient German soldier who felt superior to the elderly Roman scholar, yet the latter was part of a mighty civilization of which the Germans of that day stood in awe.

"You may suggest that the sack of Rome by the Germans in later years defeats my argument; however, modern historians agree that the 'sack' was an historical accident, and not history in the true sense of the word. The movement of the 'Sea-peoples' which set in against the Egyptian civilization from 1400 B.C. succeeded only as regards the Cretan island-realm—their mighty expeditions against the Libyan and Phoenician coasts, with the accompaniment of viking fleets, failed as those of the Huns failed against the Chinese Empire. Rome would have been abandoned in any event. Ancient, glorious Samarra was desolate by the tenth century; Pataliputra, Asoka's great capital, was an immense and completely uninhabited waste of houses when the Chinese traveler Hsinan-tang visited it about A.D. 635.

"We have, then, a primitive, and that primitive is now far out in space, completely outside of his natural habitat. I say, let's go in and win."

One of the men grumbled, as Korita finished: "You can talk about the sack of Rome being an accident, and about this fellow being a primitive, but the facts are facts. It looks to me as if Rome is about to fall again; and it won't be no primitive that did it, either. This guy's got plenty of what it takes."

Morton smiled grimly at the man, a member of the crew. "We'll see about that—right now!"

In the blazing brilliance of the gigantic machine shop, Coeurl slaved. The forty-foot, cigar-shaped spaceship was nearly finished. With a grunt of effort, he completed the laborious installation of the drive engines, and paused to survey his craft.

Its interior, visible through the one aperture in the outer wall, was pitifully small. There was literally room for nothing but the engines—and a narrow space for himself.

He plunged frantically back to work as he heard the approach of the men, and the sudden change in the tempest-like thunder of the engines—a rhythmical off-and-on hum, shriller in tone, sharper, more nerve-racking than the deep-throated, steady throb that had preceded it. Suddenly, there were the atomic disintegrators again at the massive outer doors.

He fought them off, but never wavered from his task. Every mighty muscle of his powerful body strained as he carried great loads of tools, machines and instruments, and dumped them into the bottom of his makeshift ship. There was no time to fit anything into place, no time for anything—no time—no time.

The thought pounded at his reason. He felt strangely weary for the first time in his long and vigorous existence. With a last, tortured heave, he jerked the gigantic sheet of metal into the gaping aperture of the ship—and stood there for a terrible minute, balancing it precariously.

He knew the doors were going down. Half a dozen disintegrators concentrating on one point were irresistibly, though slowly, eating away the remaining inches. With a gasp, he released his mind from the doors and concentrated every ounce of his mind on the yard-thick outer wall, toward which the blunt nose of his ship was pointing.

His body cringed from the surging power that flowed from the electric dynamo through his ear tendrils into that resisting wall. The whole inside of him felt on fire, and he knew that he was dangerously close to carrying his ultimate load.

And still he stood there, shuddering with the awful pain, holding the unfastened metal plate with hard-clenched tentacles. His massive head pointed as in dread fascination at that bitterly hard wall.

He heard one of the engine-room doors crash inward. Men shouted; disintegrators rolled forward, their raging power unchecked. Coeurl heard the floor of the engine room hiss in protest, as those beams of atomic energy tore everything in their path to bits. The machines rolled closer; cautious footsteps sounded behind them. In a minute they would be at the flimsy doors separating the engine room from the machine shop.

Suddenly, Coeurl was satisfied. With a snarl of hate, a vindictive glow of feral eyes, he ducked into his little craft, and pulled the metal plate down into place as if it was a hatchway.

His ear tendrils hummed, as he softened the edges of the surrounding metal. In an instant, the plate was more than welded—it was part of his ship, a seamless, rivetless part of a whole that was solid opaque metal except for two transparent areas, one in the front, one in the rear.

His tentacle embraced the power drive with almost sensuous tenderness. There was a forward surge of his fragile machine, straight at the great outer wall of the machine shops. The nose of the forty-foot craft touched—and the wall dissolved in a glittering shower of dust.

Coeurl felt the barest retarding movement; and then he kicked the nose of the machine out into the cold of space, twisted it about, and headed back in the direction from which the big ship had been coming all these hours.

Men in space armor stood in the jagged hole that yawned in the lower reaches of the gigantic globe. The men and the great ship grew smaller. Then the men were gone; and there was only the ship with its blaze of a thousand blurring portholes. The ball shrank incredibly, too small now for individual portholes to be visible.

Almost straight ahead, Coeurl saw a tiny, dim, reddish ball—his own sun, he realized. He headed toward it at full speed. There were caves where he could hide and with other coeurls build secretly a spaceship in which they could reach other planets safely—now that he knew how.

His body ached from the agony of acceleration, yet he dared not let up for a single instant. He glanced back, half in terror. The globe was still there, a tiny dot of light in the immense blackness of space. Suddenly it twinkled and was gone.

For a brief moment, he had the empty, frightened impression that just before it disappeared, it moved. But he could see nothing. He could not escape the belief that they had shut off all their lights, and were sneaking up on him in the darkness. Worried and uncertain, he looked through the forward transparent plate.

A tremor of dismay shot through him. The dim red sun toward which he was heading was not growing larger. *It was becoming smaller* by the instant, and it grew visibly tinier during the next five minutes, became a pale-red dot in the sky—and vanished like the ship.

Fear came then, a blinding surge of it, that swept through his being and left him chilled with the sense of the unknown. For minutes, he stared frantically into the space ahead, searching for some landmark. But only the remote stars glimmered there, unwinking points against a velvet background of unfathomable distance.

Wait! One of the points was growing larger. With every muscle and nerve tensed, Coeurl watched the point becoming a dot, a round ball of light—red light. Bigger, bigger, it grew. Suddenly, the red light shimmered and turned white—and there, before him, was the great globe of the spaceship, lights glaring from every porthole, the very ship which a few minutes before he had watched vanish behind him.

Something happened to Coeurl in that moment. His brain was

spinning like a flywheel, faster, faster, more incoherently. Suddenly, the wheel flew apart into a million aching fragments. His eyes almost started from their sockets as, like a maddened animal, he raged in his small quarters.

His tentacles clutched at precious instruments and flung them insensately; his paws smashed in fury at the very walls of his ship. Finally, in a brief flash of sanity, he knew that he couldn't face the inevitable fire of atomic disintegrators.

It was a simple thing to create the violent disorganization that freed every drop of id from his vital organs.

They found him lying dead in a little pool of phosphorus.

"Poor pussy," said Morton. "I wonder what he thought when he saw us appear ahead of him, after his own sun disappeared. Knowing nothing of anti-accelerators, he couldn't know that we could stop short in space, whereas it would take him more than three hours to decelerate; and in the meantime he'd be drawing farther and farther away from where he wanted to go. He couldn't know that by stopping, we flashed past him at millions of miles a second. Of course, he didn't have a chance once he left our ship. The whole world must have seemed topsy-turvy."

"Never mind the sympathy," he heard Kent say behind him. "We've got a job—to kill every cat in that miserable world."

Korita murmured softly: "That should be simple. They are but primitives; and we have merely to sit down, and they will come to us, cunningly expecting to delude us."

Smith snapped: "You fellows make me sick! Pussy was the toughest nut we ever had to crack. He had everything he needed to defeat us—"

Morton smiled as Korita interrupted blandly: "Exactly, my dear Smith, except that he reacted according to the biological impulses of his type. His defeat was already foreshadowed when we unerringly analyzed him as a criminal from a certain era of his civilization.

"It was history, honorable Mr. Smith, our knowledge of history that defeated him," said the Japanese archeologist, reverting to the ancient politeness of his race.

FAR CENTAURUS

I wakened with a start, and thought: How was Renfrew taking it?

I must have moved physically, for blackness edged with pain closed over me. How long I lay in that agonized faint, I have no means of knowing. My next awareness was of the thrusting of the engines that drove the spaceship.

Slowly this time, consciousness returned. I lay very quiet, feeling the weight of my years of sleep, determined to follow the routine prescribed so long ago by Pelham.

I didn't want to faint again.

I lay there, and I thought: It was silly to have worried about Jim Renfrew. He wasn't due to come out of his state of suspended animation for another fifty years.

I began to watch the illuminated face of the clock in the ceiling. It has registered 23:12, now it was 23:22. The ten minutes Pelham had suggested for a time lapse between passivity and initial action was up.

Slowly, I pushed my hand toward the edge of the bed. *Click!* My fingers pressed the button that was there. There was a faint hum. The automatic massager began to fumble gently over my naked form.

First, it rubbed my arms; then it moved to my legs, and so on over my body. As it progressed, I could feel the fine slick of oil that oozed from it working into my dry skin.

A dozen times I could have screamed from the pain of life returning. But in an hour I was able to sit up and turn on the lights.

The small, sparsely furnished, familiar room couldn't hold my attention for more than an instant. I stood up.

The movement must have been too abrupt. I swayed, caught on to the metal column of the bed, and retched discolored stomach juices.

The nausea passed. But it required an effort of will for me to walk to the door, open it, and head along the narrow corridor that led to the control room.

I wasn't supposed to so much as pause there, but a spasm of absolutely dreadful fascination seized me; and I couldn't help it. I leaned over the control chair, and glanced at the chronometer.

It said: 53 years, 7 months, 2 weeks, 0 days, 0 hours and 27 minutes.

Fifty-three years! A little blindly, almost blankly, I thought: Back on Earth, the people we had known, the young men we'd gone to college with, that girl who had kissed me at the party given us the night we left—they were all dead. Or dying of old age.

I remembered the girl very vividly. She was pretty, vivacious, a complete stranger. She had laughed as she offered her red lips, and she had said "A kiss for the ugly one, too."

She'd be a grandmother now, or in her grave.

Tears came to my eyes. I brushed them away, and began to heat the can of concentrated liquid that was to be my first food. Slowly, my mind calmed.

Fifty-three years and seven and one half months, I thought drably. Nearly four years over my allotted time. I'd have to do some figuring before I took another dose of Eternity drug. Twenty grains had been calculated to preserve my flesh and my life for exactly fifty years.

The stuff was evidently more potent than Pelham had been able to estimate from his short period advance tests.

I sat tense, narrow-eyed, thinking about that. Abruptly, I grew conscious of what I was doing. Laughter spat from my lips. The sound split the silence like a series of pistol shots, startling me.

But it also relieved me. Was I sitting here actually being critical?

A miss of only four years was bull's-eye across that span of years.

Why, I was alive and still young. Time and space had been conquered. The universe belonged to man.

I ate my "soup," sipping each spoonful deliberately. I made the bowl last every second of thirty minutes. Then, greatly refreshed, I made my way back to the control room.

This time I paused for a long look through the plates. It took only a few moments to locate Sol, a very brightly glowing star in the approximate center of the rearview plate.

Alpha Centauri required longer to locate. But it shone finally, a glow point in a light sprinkled darkness.

I wasted no time trying to estimate their distances. They *looked* right. In fifty-four years we had covered approximately one tenth of the four and one third light years to the famous nearest star system.

Satisfied, I threaded my way back to the living quarters. Take them in a row, I thought. Pelham first.

As I opened the air-tight door of Pelham's room, a sickening odor of decayed flesh tingled in my nostrils. With a gasp I slammed the door, stood there in the narrow hallway, shuddering.

After a minute, there was still nothing but the reality.

Pelham was dead.

I cannot clearly remember what I did then. I ran; I know that. I flung open Renfrew's door, then Blake's. The clean, sweet smell of their rooms, the sight of their silent bodies on their beds brought back a measure of my sanity.

A great sadness came to me. Poor, brave Pelham. Inventor of the Eternity drug that had made the great plunge into interstellar space possible, he lay dead now from his own invention.

What was it he had said: "The chances are greatly against any of us dying. But there is what I am calling a death factor of about ten percent, a by-product of the first dose. If our bodies survive the initial shock, they will survive additional doses."

The death factor must be greater than ten percent. That extra four years the drug had kept me asleep—

Gloomily, I went to the storeroom, and procured my personal spacesuit and a tarpaulin. But even with their help, it was a horrible business. The drug had preserved the body to some extent, but pieces kept falling off as I lifted it.

At last, I carried the tarpaulin and its contents to the air lock, and shoved it into space.

I felt pressed now for time. These waking periods were to be brief affairs, in which what we called the "current" oxygen was to be used up, but the main reserves were not to be touched. Chemicals in each room slowly refreshed the "current" air over the years, readying it for the next to awaken.

In some curious defensive fashion, we had neglected to allow for an emergency like the death of one of our members; even as I climbed out of the spacesuit, I could feel the difference in the air I was breathing.

I went first to the radio. It had been calculated that half a light year was the limit of radio reception, and we were approaching that limit now.

Hurriedly, though carefully, I wrote my report out, then read it into a transcription record, and started sending. I set the record to repeat a hundred times.

In a little more than five months hence, headlines would be flaring on Earth.

I clamped my written report into the ship log book, and added a note for Renfrew at the bottom. It was a brief tribute to Pelham. My praise was heartfelt, but there was another reason behind my note. They had been pals, Renfrew, the engineering genius who built the ship, and Pelham, the great chemist-doctor, whose Eternity drug had made it possible for men to take this fantastic journey into vastness.

It seemed to me that Renfrew, waking up into the great silence of the hurtling ship, would need my tribute to his friend and colleague. It was little enough for me to do, who loved them both.

The note written, I hastily examined the glowing engines, made notations of several instrument readings, and then counted out fifty-five grains of Eternity drug. That was as close as I could get to the amount I felt would be required for one hundred and fifty years.

For a long moment before sleep came, I thought of Renfrew and the terrible shock that was coming to him on top of all the natural reactions to his situations, that would strike deep into his peculiar, sensitive nature—

I stirred uneasily at the picture.

The worry was still in my mind when darkness came.

Almost instantly, I opened my eyes. I lay thinking: The drug! It hadn't worked.

The draggy feel of my body warned me of the truth. I lay very still watching the clock overhead. This time it was easier to follow the routine except that, once more, I could not refrain from examining the chronometer as I passed through the galley.

It read: 201 years, 1 month, 3 weeks, 5 days, 7 hours, 8 minutes.

I sipped my bowl of that super soup, then went eagerly to the big log book.

It is utterly impossible for me to describe the thrill that coursed through me, as I saw the familiar handwriting of Blake, and then, as I turned back the pages, of Renfrew.

My excitement drained slowly, as I read what Renfrew had written. It was a report; nothing more: gravitometric readings, a careful calculation of the distance covered, a detailed report on the performance of the engines, and, finally, an estimate of our speed variations, based on the seven consistent factors.

It was a splendid mathematical job, a first-rate scientific analysis. But that was all there was. No mention of Pelham, not a word of comment on what I had written or on what had happened.

Renfrew had wakened; and, if his report was any criterion, he might as well have been a robot.

I knew better than that.

So—I saw as I began to read Blake's report—did Blake.

Bill:

TEAR THIS SHEET OUT WHEN YOU'VE READ IT!

Well, the worst has happened. We couldn't have asked fate to give us an unkindlier kick in the pants. I hate to think of Pelham being dead. What a man he was, what a friend! But we all knew the risk we were taking, he more than any of us. So all we can say is, "Sleep well, good friend. We'll never forget you."

But Renfrew's case is now serious. After all, we were worried, wondering how he'd take his first awakening, let alone a bang between the eyes like Pelham's death. And I think that the first anxiety was justified.

As you and I have always known, Renfrew was one of Earth's fairhaired boys. Just imagine any one human being born with his combination of looks, money and intelligence. His great fault was that he never let the future trouble him. With that dazzling personality of his, and the crew of worshipping women and yes-men around him, he didn't have much time for anything but the present.

Realities always struck him like a thunderbolt. He could leave those three ex-wives of his—and they weren't so ex, if you ask me—without grasping that it was forever.

That good-by party was enough to put anyone into a sort of mental haze when it came to realities. To wake up a hundred years later, and realize that those he loved had withered, died and been eaten by worms—well-l-l!

(I deliberately put it as baldly as that, because the human mind thinks of awfully strange angles, no matter how it censures speech.)

I personally counted on Pelham acting as a sort of psychological support to Renfrew; and we both know that Pelham recognized the extent of his influence over Renfrew. That influence must be replaced. Try to think of something, Bill, while you're charging around doing the routine work. We've got to live with that guy after we all wake up at the end of five hundred years.

Tear out this sheet. What follows is routine.

Ned

I burned the letter in the incinerator, examined the two sleeping bodies—how deathly quiet they lay!—and then returned to the control room.

In the plate, the sun was a very bright star, a jewel set in black velvet, a gorgeous, shining brilliant.

Alpha Centauri was brighter. It was a radiant light in that panoply of black and glitter. It was still impossible to make out the separate suns of Alpha A, B, C, and Proxima, but their combined light brought a sense of awe and majesty.

Excitement blazed inside me; and consciousness came of the glory of this trip we were making, the first men to head for far Centaurus, the first men to dare aspire to the stars.

Even the thought of Earth failed to dim that surging tide of wonder; the thought that seven, possibly eight generations, had been born since our departure; the thought that the girl who had given me the sweet remembrance of her red lips, was now known to her descendants as their great-great-great-great-grandmother—if she were remembered at all.

The immense time involved, the whole idea, was too meaningless for emotion.

I did my work, took my third dose of the drug, and went to bed. The sleep found me still without a plan about Renfrew.

When I woke up, alarm bells were ringing.

I lay still. There was nothing else to do. If I had moved, consciousness would have slid from me. Though it was mental torture even to think it, I realized that, no matter what the danger, the quickest way was to follow my routine to the second and in every detail.

Somehow I did it. The bells clanged and *brrred*, but I lay there until it was time to get up. The clamor was hideous, as I passed through the control room. But I *passed* through and sat for half an hour sipping my soup.

The conviction came to me that if that sound continued much longer, Blake and Renfrew would surely waken from their sleep.

At last, I felt free to cope with the emergency. Breathing hard, I eased myself into the control chair, cut off the mind-wrecking alarms, and switched on the plates.

A fire glowed at me from the rear-view plate. It was a colossal *white* fire, longer than it was wide, and filling nearly a quarter of the whole sky. The hideous thought came to me that we must be within a few million miles of some monstrous sun that had recently roared into this part of space.

Frantically, I manipulated the distance estimators—and then for a moment stared in blank disbelief at the answers that clicked metallically onto the product plate.

Seven miles! *Only* seven miles! Curious is the human mind. A moment before, when I had thought of it as an abnormally shaped sun, it hadn't resembled anything but an incandescent mass. Abruptly, now, I saw that it had a solid outline, an unmistakable material shape.

Stunned, I leaped to my feet because—

It was a spaceship! An enormous, mile-long ship. Rather—I sank back into my seat, subdued by the catastrophe I was witnessing, and consciously adjusting my mind—the flaming hell of what had been a spaceship. Nothing that had been alive could possibly still be conscious in that horror of ravenous fire. The only possibility was that the crew had succeeded in launching lifeboats.

Like a madman, I searched the heavens for a light, a glint of metal that would show the presence of survivors.

There was nothing but the night and the stars and the hell of burning ship.

After a long time, I noticed that it was farther away, and seemed to be receding. Whatever drive forces had matched its velocity to ours must be yielding to the fury of the energies that were consuming the ship.

I began to take pictures, and I felt justified in turning on the oxygen reserves. As it withdrew into distance, the miniature nova that had been a torpedo-shaped space liner began to change color, to lose its white intensity. It became a red fire silhouetted against darkness. My last glimpse showed it as a long, dull glow that looked like nothing else than a cherry colored nebula seen edge on, like a blaze reflecting from the night beyond a far horizon.

I had already, in between observations, done everything else required of me; and now, I re-connected the alarm system and, very reluctantly, my mind seething with speculation, returned to bed.

As I lay waiting for my final dosage of the trip to take effect, I thought: the great star system of Alpha Centauri must have inhabited planets. If my calculations were correct, we were only one point six light years from the main Alpha group of suns, slightly nearer than that to red Proxima.

Here was proof that the universe had at least one other supremely intelligent race. Wonders beyond our wildest expectation were in store for us. Thrill on thrill of anticipation raced through me.

It was only at the last instant, as sleep was already grasping at my brain, that the realization struck that I had completely forgotten about the problem of Renfrew.

I felt no alarm. Surely, even Renfrew would come alive in that great fashion of his when confronted by a complex alien civilization.

Our troubles were over.

Excitement must have bridged that final one hundred fifty years of time. Because, when I wakened, I thought:

"We're here! It's over, the long night, the incredible journey. We'll all be waking, seeing each other, as well as the civilization out there. Seeing, too, the great Centauri suns."

The strange thing, it struck me as I lay there exulting, was that the time seemed long. And yet . . . yet I had been awake only three times, and only once for the equivalent of a full day.

In the truest sense of meaning, I had seen Blake and Renfrew— and Pelham—no more than a day and a half ago. I had had only thirty-six hours of consciousness since a pair of soft lips had set themselves against mine, and clung in the sweetest kiss of my life.

Then why this feeling that millenniums had ticked by, second on slow second? Why this eerie, empty awareness of a journey through fathomless, unending night?

Was the human mind so easily fooled?

It seemed to me, finally, that the answer was that *I* had been alive for those five hundred years, all my cells and my organs had existed, and it was not even impossible that some part of my brain had been horrendously aware throughout the entire unthinkable period.

And there was, of course, the additional psychological fact that I knew now that five hundred years had gone by, and that—

I saw with a mental start, that my ten minutes were up. Cautiously, I turned on the massager.

The gentle, padded hands had been working on me for about fifteen minutes when my door opened; the light clicked on, and there stood Blake.

The too-sharp movement of turning my head to look at him made me dizzy. I closed my eyes, and heard him walk across the room toward me.

After a minute, I was able to look at him again without seeing blurs. I saw then that he was carrying a bowl of the soup. He stood staring down at me with a strangely grim expression on his face.

At last, his long, thin countenance relaxed into a wan grin.

" 'Lo, Bill," he said. "*Ssshh!*" he hissed immediately. "Now, don't try to speak. I'm going to start feeding you this soup while you're still lying down. The sooner you're up, the better I'll like it."

He was grim again, as he finished almost as if it were an after-thought: "I've been up for two weeks."

He sat down on the edge of the bed, and ladled out a spoonful of soup. There was silence, then, except for the rustling sound of the massager. Slowly, the strength flowed through my body; and with each passing second, I became more aware of the grimness of Blake.

"What about Renfrew?" I managed finally, hoarsely. "He awake?"

Blake hesitated, then nodded. His expression darkened with frown; he said simply:

"He's mad, Bill; stark, staring mad. I had to tie him up. I've got him now in his room. He's quieter now, but at the beginning he was a gibbering maniac."

"Are you crazy?" I whispered at last. "Renfrew was never so sensitive as that. Depressed and sick, yes; but the mere passage of time, abrupt awareness that all his friends are dead, couldn't make him insane."

Blake was shaking his head. "It isn't only that. Bill—"

He paused, then: "Bill, I want you to prepare your mind for the greatest shock it's ever had."

I stared up at him with an empty feeling inside me. "What do you mean?"

He went on grimacing: "I know you'll be able to take it. So don't get scared. You and I, Bill, are just a couple of lugs. We're along because we went to U with Renfrew and Pelham. Basically, it wouldn't matter to insensitives like us whether we landed in 1,000,000 B.C. or A.D. We'd just look around and say: 'Fancy seeing you here, mug!' or 'Who was that pterodactyl I saw you with last night? That wasn't no pterodactyl; that was Unthahorsten's bulbous brained wife.'"

I whispered, "Get to the point. What's up?"

Blake rose to his feet. "Bill, after I'd read your reports about, and seen the photographs of, that burning ship, I got an idea. The Alpha suns were pretty close two weeks ago, only about six months away at our average speed of five hundred miles a second. I thought to myself: 'I'll see if I can tune in some of their radio stations.'

"Well," he smiled wryly, "I got hundreds in a few minutes. They came in all over the seven wave dials, with bell-like clarity."

He paused; he stared down at me, and his smile was a sickly thing. "Bill," he groaned, "we're the prize fools in creation. When I told Renfrew the truth, he folded up like ice melting into water."

Once more, he paused; the silence was too much for my straining nerves.

"For Heaven's sake, man—" I began. And stopped. And lay there, very still. Just like that the lightning of understanding flashed on me. My blood seemed to thunder through my veins. At last, weakly, I said: "You mean—"

Blake nodded. "Yeah," he said. "That's the way it is. And they've already spotted us with their spy rays and energy screens. A ship's coming out to meet us.

"I only hope," he finished gloomily, "they can do something for Jim."

I was sitting in the control chair an hour later when I saw the glint in the darkness. There was a flash of bright silver, that exploded into size. The next instant, an enormous spaceship had matched our velocity less than a mile away.

Blake and I looked at each other. "Did they say," I said shakily, "that that ship left its hangar ten minutes ago?"

Blake nodded. "They can make the trip from Earth to Centauri in three hours," he said.

I hadn't heard that before. Something happened inside my brain. "What!" I shouted. "Why, it's taken us five hund—"

I stopped; I sat there. "Three hours!" I whispered. "How *could* we have forgotten human progress?"

In the silence that fell then, we watched a dark hole open in the clifflike wall that faced us. Into this cavern, I directed our ship.

The rear-view plate showed that the cave entrance was closing. Ahead of us lights flashed on, and focused on a door. As I eased our craft to the metal floor, a face flickered onto our radio plate.

"Cassellahat!" Blake whispered in my ear. "The only chap who's talked direct to me so far."

It was a distinguished, a scholarly looking head and face that peered at us. Cassellahat smiled, and said:

"You may leave your ship, and go through the door you see."

I had a sense of empty spaces around us, as we climbed gingerly out into the vast receptor chamber. Interplanetary spaceship hangars were like that, I reminded myself. Only this one had an alien quality that—

"Nerves!" I thought sharply.

But I could see that Blake felt it, too. A silent duo, we filed through the doorway into a hallway, that opened into a very large, luxurious room.

It was such a room as a king or a movie actress on set might have walked into without blinking. It was all hung with gorgeous tapestries—that is, for a moment, I thought they were tapestries; then I saw they weren't. They were—I couldn't decide.

I had seen expensive furniture in some of the apartments Renfrew maintained. But these settees, chairs, and tables glittered at us, as if they were made of a matching design of differently colored fires. No, that was wrong; they didn't glitter at all. They—

Once more I couldn't decide.

I had no time for more detailed examination. For a man arrayed very much as we were, was rising from one of the chairs. I recognized Cassellahat.

He came forward, smiling. Then he slowed, his nose wrinkling. A moment later, he hastily shook our hands, then swiftly retreated to a chair ten feet away, and sat down rather primly.

It was an astoundingly ungracious performance. But I was glad that he had drawn back that way. Because, as he shook my hand so briefly, I had caught a faint whiff of perfume from him. It was a vaguely unpleasant odor; and, besides—a man using perfume in quantities!

I shuddered. What kind of foppish nonsense had the human race gone in for?

He was motioning us to sit down. I did so, wondering: Was this our reception? The erstwhile radio operator began:

"About your friend, I must caution you. He is a schizoid type, and our psychologists will be able to effect a temporary recovery only for the moment. A permanent cure will require a longer period, and your fullest co-operation. Fall in readily with all Mr. Renfrew's plans, unless, of course, he takes a dangerous turn.

"But now"—he squirted us a smile—"permit me to welcome you to the four planets of Centauri. It is a great moment for me, personally. From early childhood, I have been trained for the sole purpose of being your mentor and guide; and naturally I am overjoyed that the time has come when my exhaustive studies of the middle period American language and customs can be put to the practical use for which they were intended."

He didn't look overjoyed. He was wrinkling his nose in that funny way I had already noticed, and there was a generally pained expression on his face. But it was his words that shocked me.

"What do you mean," I asked, "studies in American? Don't people speak the universal language any more?"

"Of course"—he smiled—"but the language has developed to a point where—I might as well be frank—you would have difficulty understanding such a simple word as 'yeih.' "

"Yeih?" Blake echoed.

"Meaning 'yes.' "

"Oh!"

We sat silent. Blake chewing his lower lip. It was Blake who finally said:

"What kind of places are the Centauri planets? You said something on the radio about the population centers having reverted to the city structure again."

"I shall be happy," said Cassellahat, "to show you as many of our great cities as you care to see. You are our guests, and several million credits have been placed to your separate accounts for you to use as you see fit."

"Gee!" said Blake.

"I must, however," Cassellahat went on, "give you a warning. It is important that you do not disillusion our peoples about yourselves. Therefore, you must never wander around the streets, or mingle with the crowds in any way. Always, your contact should be via newsreels, radio, or from the *inside* of a closed machine. If you have any plan to marry, you must now finally give up the idea."

"I don't get it!" Blake said wonderingly; and he spoke for us both.

Cassellahat finished firmly: "It is important that no one becomes aware that you have an offensive physical odor. It might damage your financial prospects considerably.

"And now"—he stood up—"for the time being, I shall leave you. I hope you don't mind if I wear a mask in the future in your presence. I wish you well, gentlemen, and—"

He paused, glanced past us, said: "Ah, here is your friend."

I whirled, and I could see Blake twisting, staring—

"Hi, there, fellows," Renfrew said cheerfully from the door, then wryly: "Have we ever been a bunch of suckers?"

I felt choked. I raced up to him, caught his hand, hugged him. Blake was trying to do the same.

When we finally released Renfrew, and looked around, Cassellahat was gone.

Which was just as well. I had been wanting to punch him in the nose for his final remarks.

"Well, here goes!" Renfrew said.

He looked at Blake and me, grinned, rubbed his hands together gleefully, and added:

"For a week I've been watching, thinking up questions to ask this cluck and—"

He faced Cassellahat. "What," he began, "makes the speed of light constant?"

Cassellahat did not even blink. "Velocity equals the cube of the cube root of gd," he said, "d being the depth of the space time continuum, g the total toleration or gravity, as you would say, of all the matter in that continuum."

"How are planets formed?"

"A sun must balance itself in the space that it is in. It throws out matter as a sea vessel does anchors. That's a very rough description. I could give it to you in mathematical formula, but I'd have to write it down. After all, I'm not a scientist. These are merely facts that I've known from childhood, or so it seems."

"Just a minute," said Renfrew, puzzled. "A sun throws this matter out without any pressure other than its—desire—to balance itself?"

Cassellahat stared at him. "Of course not. The reason, the pressure involved, is very potent, I assure you. Without such a balance, the sun would fall out of this space. Only a few bachelor suns have learned how to maintain stability without planets."

"A few what?" echoed Renfrew.

I could see that he had been jarred into forgetting the questions he had been intending to ask one by swift one. Cassellahat's words cut across my thought; he said:

"A bachelor sun is a very old, cooled class M star. The hottest one known has a temperature of one hundred ninety degrees F., the coldest forty-eight. Literally, a bachelor is a rogue, crotchety with age. Its main feature is that it permits no matter, no planets, not even gases in its vicinity."

Renfrew sat silent, frowning, thoughtful. I seized the opportunity to carry on a train of idea.

"This business," I said, "of knowing all this stuff without being a scientist, interests me. For instance, back home every kid understood the atomic-rocket principle practically from the day he was born. Boys of eight and ten rode around in specially made toys, took them apart and put them together again. They *thought* rocket-atomic, and any new development in the field was just pie for them to absorb.

"Now, here's what I'd like to know: what is the parallel here to that particular angle?"

"The adeledicnander force," said Cassellahat. "I've already tried to explain it to Mr. Renfrew, but his mind seems to balk at some of the most simple aspects."

Renfrew roused himself, grimaced. "He's been trying to tell me that electrons think; and I won't swallow it."

Cassellahat shook his head. "Not think; they don't think. But they have a psychology."

"Electronic psychology!" I said.

"Simply adeledicnander," Cassellahat replied. "Any child—"

Renfrew groaned: "I know. Any child of six could tell me."

He turned to us. "That's why I lined up a lot of questions. I figured that if we got a good intermediate grounding, we might be able to slip into this adeledicnander stuff the way their kids do."

He faced Cassellahat. "Next question," he said. "What—"

Cassellahat had been looking at his watch. "I'm afraid, Mr. Renfrew," he interrupted, "that if you and I are going to be on the ferry to the Pelham planet, we'd better leave now. You can ask your questions on the way."

"What's all this?" I chimed in.

Renfrew explained: "He's taking me to the great engineering laboratories in the European mountains of Pelham. Want to come along?"

"Not me," I said.

Blake shrugged. "I don't fancy getting into one of those suits Cassellahat has provided for us, designed to keep our odor in, but not theirs out."

He finished: "Bill and I will stay here and play poker for some of that five million credits worth of dough we've got in the State bank."

Cassellahat turned at the door; there was a distinct frown on the flesh mask he wore. "You treat our government gift very lightly."

"Yeih!" said Blake.

"So we stink," said Blake.

It was nine days since Cassellahat had taken Renfrew to the planet Pelham; and our only contact had been a radio telephone call from Renfrew on the third day, telling us not to worry.

Blake was standing at the window of our penthouse apartment in the city of Newmerica; and I was on my back on a couch, in my mind a mixture of thoughts involving Renfrew's potential insanity and all the things I had heard and seen about the history of the past five hundred years.

I roused myself. "Quit it," I said. "We're faced with a change in the metabolism of the human body, probably due to the many different foods from remote stars that they eat. They must be able to smell better, too, because just being near us is agony to Cassellahat, whereas we only notice an unpleasantness from him. It's a case of three of us against billions of them. Frankly, I don't see an early victory over the problem, so let's just take it quietly."

There was no answer; so I returned to my reverie. My first radio message to Earth had been picked up; and so, when the interstellar drive was invented in 2320 A.D., less than one hundred forty years after our departure, it was realized what would eventually happen.

In our honor, the four habitable planets of the Alpha A and B suns were called Renfrew, Pelham, Blake, and Endicott. Since 2320, the populations of the four planets had become so dense that a total of nineteen billion people now dwelt on their narrowing land spaces. This in spite of migrations to the planets of more distant stars.

The space liner I had seen burning in 2511 A.D. was the only ship ever lost on the Earth-Centauri lane. Traveling at full speed, its screens must have reacted against our spaceship. All the automatics would instantly have flashed on; and, as those defenses were not able at that time to stop a ship that had gone Minus Infinity, every recoil engine aboard had probably blown up.

Such a thing could not happen again. So enormous had been the progress in the adeledicnander field of power, that the greatest liners could stop dead in the full fury of midflight.

We had been told not to feel any sense of blame for that one disaster, as many of the most important advances in adeledicnander electronic psychology had been made as the result of the theoretical analyses of that great catastrophe.

I grew aware that Blake had flung himself disgustedly into a nearby chair.

"Boy, oh, boy," he said, "this is going to be some life for us. We can all anticipate about fifty more years of being pariahs in a civilization where we can't even understand how the simplest machines work."

I stirred uneasily. I had had similar thoughts. But I said nothing. Blake went on:

"I must admit, after I first discovered the Centauri planets had been colonized, I had pictures of myself bowling over some dame, and marrying her."

Involuntarily my mind leaped to the memory of a pair of lips lifting up to mine. I shook myself. I said:

"I wonder how Renfrew is taking all this. He—"

A familiar voice from the door cut off my words. "Renfrew," it said, "is taking things beautifully now that the first shock has yielded to resignation, and resignation to purpose."

We had turned to face him by the time he finished. Renfrew

walked slowly toward us, grinning. Watching him, I felt uncertain as to just how to take his built-up sanity.

He was at his best. His dark, wavy hair was perfectly combed. His startlingly blue eyes made his whole face come alive. He was a natural physical wonder; and at his normal he had all the shine and swagger of an actor in a carefully tailored picture.

He wore that shine and swagger now, He said:

"I've bought a spaceship, fellows. Took all my money and part of yours, too. But I knew you'd back me up. Am I right?"

"Why, sure," Blake and I echoed.

Blake went on alone: "What's the idea."

"I get it," I chimed in. "We'll cruise all over the universe, live our life span exploring new worlds. Jim, you've got something there. Blake and I were just going to enter a suicide pact."

Renfrew was smiling. "We'll cruise for a while anyway."

Two days later, Cassellahat having offered no objection and no advice about Renfrew, we were in space.

It was a curious three months that followed. For a while I felt a sense of awe at the vastness of the cosmos. Silent planets swung into our viewing plates, and faded into remoteness behind us, leaving nostalgic memory of uninhabited, windlashed forests and plains, deserted, swollen seas, and nameless suns.

The sight and the remembrance brought loneliness like an ache, and the knowledge, the slow knowledge, that this journeying was not lifting the weight of strangeness that had settled upon us ever since our arrival at Alpha Centauri.

There was nothing here for our souls to feed on, nothing that would satisfactorily fill one year of our life, let alone fifty.

I watched the realization grow on Blake, and I waited for a sign from Renfrew that he felt it, too. The sign didn't come. That of itself worried me; then I grew aware of something else. Renfrew was watching us. Watching us with a hint in his manner of secret knowledge, a suggestion of secret purpose.

My alarm grew; and Renfrew's perpetual cheerfulness didn't help any. I was lying on my bunk at the end of the third month, thinking uneasily about the whole unsatisfactory situation, when my door opened and Renfrew came in.

He carried a paralyzer gun and a rope. He pointed the gun at me, and said:

"Sorry, Bill. Cassellahat told me to take no chances, so just lie quiet while I tie you up."

"Blake!" I bellowed.

Renfrew shook his head gently. "No use," he said. "I was in his room first."

The gun was steady in his fingers, his blue eyes were steely. All I could do was tense my muscles against the ropes as he tied me, and trust to the fact that I was twice as strong, at least, as he was.

I thought in dismay: Surely I could prevent him from tying me too tightly.

He stepped back finally, said again, "Sorry, Bill." He added "I hate to tell you this, but both of you went off the deep end mentally when we arrived at Centauri; and this is the cure prescribed by the psychologist whom Cassellahat consulted. You're supposed to get a shock as big as the one that knocked you for a loop."

The first time I'd paid no attention to his mention of Cassellahat's name. Now my mind flared with understanding.

Incredibly, Renfrew had been told that Blake and I were mad. All these months he had been held steady by a sense of responsibility toward us. It was a beautiful psychological scheme. The only thing, was: *what* shock was going to be administered?

Renfrew's voice cut off my thought. He said:

"It won't be long now. We're already entering the field of the bachelor sun."

"Bachelor sun!" I yelled.

He made no reply. The instant the door closed behind him, I began to work on my bonds; all the time I was thinking:

What was it Cassellahat had said? Bachelor suns maintained themselves in this space by a precarious balancing.

In *this* space! The sweat poured down my face, as I pictured ourselves being precipitated into another plane of the space-time continuum—I could feel the ship falling when I finally worked my hands free of the rope.

I hadn't been tied long enough for the cords to interfere with my circulation. I headed for Blake's room. In two minutes we were on our way to the control cabin.

Renfrew didn't see us till we had him. Blake grabbed his gun; I hauled him out of the control chair with one mighty heave, and dumped him onto the floor.

He lay there, unresisting, grinning up at us. "Too late," he taunted. "We're approaching the first point of intolerance, and there's nothing you can do except prepare for the shock."

I scarcely heard him. I plumped myself into the chair, and glared into the viewing plates. Nothing showed. That stumped me for a second. Then I saw the recorder instruments. They were trembling furiously, registering a body of INFINITE size.

For a long moment I stared crazily at those incredible figures. Then I plunged the decelerator far over. Before that pressure of full-driven adeledicnander, the machine grew rigid; I had a sudden fantastic picture of two irresistible forces in full collision. Gasping, I jerked the power out of gear.

We were still falling.

"An orbit," Blake was saying. "Get us into an orbit."

With shaking fingers, I pounded one out on the keyboard, basing my figures on a sun of Sol-ish size, gravity, and mass.

The bachelor wouldn't let us have it.

I tried another orbit, and a third, and more—finally one that would have given us an orbit around mighty Antares itself. But the deadly reality remained. The ship plunged on, down and down.

And there was nothing visible on the plates, not a real shadow of substance. It seemed to me once that I could make out a vague blur of greater darkness against the black reaches of space. But the stars were few in every direction and it was impossible to be sure.

Finally, in despair, I whirled out of the seat, and knelt beside Renfrew, who was still making no effort to get up.

"Listen, Jim," I pleaded, "what did you do this for? What's going to happen?"

He was smiling easily. "Think," he said, "of an old, crusty, human bachelor. He maintains a relationship with his fellows, but the association is as remote as that which exists between a bachelor sun and the stars in the galaxy of which it is a part."

He added: "Any second now we'll strike the first period of intolerance. It works in jumps like quantum, each period being four hundred ninety-eight years, seven months and eight days plus a few hours."

It sounded like gibberish. "But what's going to happen?" I urged. "For Heaven's sake, man!"

He gazed up at me blandly; and, looking up at him, I had the sudden, wondering realization that he was sane, the old, completely rational Jim Renfrew, made better somehow, stronger. He said quietly:

"Why, it'll just knock us out of its toleration area; and in doing so will put us back—"

JERK!

The lurch was immensely violent. With a bang, I struck the floor, skidded, and then a hand—Renfrew's—caught me. And it was all over.

I stood up, conscious that we were no longer falling. I looked at the instrument board. All the lights were dim, untroubled, the needles firmly at zero. I turned and stared at Renfrew, and at Blake, who was ruefully picking himself from the floor.

Renfrew said persuasively: "Let me at the control board, Bill. I want to set our course for Earth."

For a long minute, I gazed at him; and then, slowly, I stepped aside. I stood by as he set the controls and pulled the accelerator over. Renfrew looked up.

"We'll reach Earth in about eight hours," he said, "and it'll be about a year and a half after we left five hundred years ago."

Something began to tug at the roof of my cranium. It took several seconds before I decided that it was probably my brain jumping with the tremendous understanding that suddenly flowed in upon me.

The bachelor sun, I thought dazedly. In easing us out of its field of toleration, it had simply precipitated us into a period of time beyond its field. Renfrew had said . . . had said that it worked in jumps of . . . four hundred ninety-eight years and some seven months and—

But what about the ship? Wouldn't twenty-seventh-century adeledicnander brought to the twenty-second century, before it was invented, change the course of history? I mumbled the question.

Renfrew shook his head. "Do *we* understand it? Do we even dare monkey with the raw power inside those engines? I'll say not. As for the ship, we'll keep it for our own private use."

"B-but—" I began.

He cut me off. "Look, Bill," he said, "here's the situation: that girl who kissed you—don't think I didn't see you falling like a ton of bricks—is going to be sitting beside you fifty years from now, when *your* voice from space reports to Earth that you had wakened on your first lap of the first trip to Centaurus."

That's exactly what happened.

VAULT OF THE BEAST

The creature crept. It whimpered from fear and pain, a thin, slobbering sound horrible to hear. Shapeless, formless thing yet changing shape and form with every jerky movement.

It crept along the corridor of the space freighter, fighting the terrible urge of its elements to take the shape of its surroundings. A gray blob of disintegrating stuff, it crept, it cascaded, it rolled, flowed, dissolved, every movement an agony of struggle against the abnormal need to become a stable shape.

Any shape! The hard, chilled-blue metal wall of the Earth-bound freighter, the thick, rubbery floor. The floor was easy to fight. It wasn't like the metal that pulled and pulled. It would be easy to become metal for all eternity.

But something prevented it. An implanted purpose. A purpose that drummed from electron to electron, vibrated from atom to atom with an unvarying intensity that was like a special pain: *Find the greatest mathematical mind in the Solar System, and bring it to the vault of the Martian ultimate metal. The Great One must be freed! The prime number time lock must be opened!*

That was the purpose that hummed with unrelenting agony through its elements. That was the thought that had been seared into its fundamental consciousness by the great and evil minds that had created it.

There was movement at the far end of the corridor. A door opened. Footsteps sounded. A man whistling to himself. With a metallic hiss, almost a sigh, the creature dissolved, looking momentarily like diluted mercury. Then it turned brown like the floor. It became the floor, a slightly thicker stretch of dark-brown rubber spread out for yards.

It was ecstasy just to lie there, to be flat and to have shape; and to be so nearly dead that there was no pain. Death was so sweet, so utterly desirable. And life such an unbearable torment of agony, such a throbbing, piercing nightmare of anguished convulsion. If only the life that was approaching would pass swiftly. If the life stopped, it would pull it into shape. Life could do that. Life was stronger than metal, stronger than anything. The approaching life meant torture, struggle, pain.

The creature tensed its now flat, grotesque body—the body that could develop muscles of steel—and waited in terror for the death struggle.

Spacecraftsman Parelli whistled happily as he strode along the gleaming corridor that led from the engine room. He had just received a wireless from the hospital. His wife was doing well, and it was a boy. Eight pounds, the radiogram had said. He suppressed a desire to whoop and dance. A boy. Life sure was good.

Pain came to the thing on the floor. Primeval pain that sucked through its elements like acid burning, burning. The brown floor shuddered in every atom as Parelli strode over it. The aching urge to pull toward him, to take his shape. The thing fought its horrible desire, fought with anguish and shivering dread, more consciously now that it could think with Parelli's brain. A ripple of floor rolled after the man.

Fighting didn't help. The ripple grew into a blob that momentarily seemed to become a human head. Gray, hellish nightmare of demoniac shape. The creature hissed metallically in terror, then collapsed palpitating, slobbering with fear and pain and hate as Parelli strode on rapidly—too rapidly for its creeping pace.

The thin, horrible sound died; the thing dissolved into brown floor, and lay quiescent yet quivering in every atom from its unquenchable, uncontrollable urge to live—live in spite of pain, in spite of abysmal terror and primordial longing for stable shape. To live and fulfill the purpose of its lusting and malignant creators.

Thirty feet up the corridor, Parelli stopped. He jerked his mind from its thoughts of child and wife. He spun on his heels, and stared uncertainly along the passageway from the engine room.

"Now, what the devil was that?" he pondered aloud.

A sound—a queer, faint yet unmistakably horrid sound was echoing and re-echoing through his consciousness. A shiver ran the length of his spine. That sound—that devilish sound.

He stood there, a tall, magnificently muscled man, stripped to the waist, sweating from the heat generated by the rockets that were decelerating the craft after its meteoric flight from Mars. Shuddering, he clenched his fists, and walked slowly back the way he had come.

The creature throbbed with the pull of him, a gnawing, writhing, tormenting struggle that pierced into the deeps of every restless, agitated cell, stabbing agonizingly along the alien nervous system; and then became terrifyingly aware of the inevitable, the irresistible need to take the shape of the life.

Parelli stopped uncertainly. The floor moved under him, a visible wave that reared brown and horrible before his incredulous eyes and grew into a bulbous, slobbering, hissing mass. A venomous demon head reared on twisted, half-human shoulders. Gnarled hands on apelike, malformed arms clawed at his face with insensate rage—and changed even as they tore at him.

"Good God!" Parelli bellowed.

The hands, the arms that clutched him grew more normal, more human, brown, muscular. The face assumed familiar lines, sprouted a nose, eyes, a red gash of mouth. The body was suddenly his own, trousers and all, sweat and all.

"—God!" his image echoed; and pawed at him with letching fingers and an impossible strength.

Gasping, Parelli fought free, then launched one crushing blow straight into the distorted face. A drooling scream of agony came from the thing. It turned and ran, dissolving as it ran, fighting dissolution, uttering strange half-human cries.

And, struggling against horror, Parelli chased it, his knees weak and trembling from sheer funk and incredulity. His arm reached out, and plucked at the disintegrating trousers. A piece came away in his hand, a cold, slimy, writhing lump like wet clay.

The feel of it was too much. His gorge rising in disgust, he faltered in his stride. He heard the pilot shouting ahead:

"What's the matter?"

Parelli saw the open door of the storeroom. With a gasp, he dived in, came out a moment later, wild-eyed, an ato-gun in his fingers. He saw the pilot, standing with staring, horrified brown eyes, white face and rigid body, facing one of the great windows.

"There it is!" the man cried.

A gray blob was dissolving into the edge of the glass, becoming glass. Parelli rushed forward, ato-gun poised. A ripple went through the glass, darkening it; and then, briefly, he caught a glimpse of a blob emerging on the other side of the glass into the cold of space.

The officer stood gaping beside him; the two of them watched the gray, shapeless mass creep out of sight along the side of the rushing freight liner.

Parelli sprang to life. "I got a piece of it!" he gasped. "Flung it down on the floor of the storeroom."

It was Lieutenant Morton who found it. A tiny section of floor reared up, and then grew amazingly large as it tried to expand into human shape. Parelli with distorted, crazy eyes scooped it up in a shovel. It hissed; it nearly became a part of the metal shovel, but couldn't because Parelli was so close. Changing, fighting for shape, it slobbered and hissed as Parelli staggered with it behind his superior officer. He was laughing hysterically. "I touched it," he kept saying, "I touched it."

A large blister of metal on the outside of the space freighter stirred into sluggish life, as the ship tore into the Earth's atmosphere. The metal walls of the freighter grew red, then white-hot, but the creature, unaffected, continued its slow transformation into gray mass. Vague thought came to the thing, realization that it was time to act.

Suddenly, it was floating free of the ship, falling slowly, heavily, as if somehow the gravitation of Earth had no serious effect upon it. A minute distortion in its electrons started it falling faster, as in some alien way it suddenly became more allergic to gravity.

The Earth was green below; and in the dim distance a gorgeous and tremendous city of spires and massive buildings glittered in the sinking Sun. The thing slowed, and drifted like a falling leaf in a breeze toward the still-distant Earth. It landed in an arroyo beside a bridge at the outskirts of the city.

A man walked over the bridge with quick, nervous steps. He would have been amazed, if he had looked back, to see a replica of himself climb from the ditch to the road, and start walking briskly after him.

Find the—greatest mathematician!

It was an hour later; and the pain of that throbbing thought was a dull, continuous ache in the creature's brain, as it walked along the crowded street. There were other pains, too. The pain of fighting the pull of the pushing, hurrying mass of humanity that swarmed by with unseeing eyes. But it was easier to think, easier to hold form now that it had the brain and body of a man.

Find—mathematician!

"Why?" asked the man's brain of the thing; and the whole body shook with startled shock at such heretical questioning. The brown eyes darted in fright from side to side, as if expecting instant and terrible doom. The face dissolved a little in that brief moment of mental chaos, became successively the man with the hooked nose who swung by, the tanned face of the tall woman who was looking into the shop window, the—

With a second gasp, the creature pulled its mind back from fear, and fought to readjust its face to that of the smooth-shaven young man who sauntered idly in from a side street. The young man glanced at him, looked away, then glanced back again startled. The creature echoed the thought in the man's brain: "Who the devil is that? Where have I seen that fellow before?"

Half a dozen women in a group approached. The creature shrank aside as they passed, its face twisted with the agony of the urge to become woman. Its brown suit turned just the faintest shade of blue, the color of the nearest dress, as it momentarily lost control of its outer atoms. Its mind hummed with the chatter of clothes and "My dear, didn't she look dreadful in that awful hat?"

There was a solid cluster of giant buildings ahead. The thing shook its human head consciously. So many buildings meant metal; and the forces that held metal together would pull and pull at its human shape. The creature comprehended the reason for this with the understanding of the slight man in a dark suit who wandered by dully. The slight man was a clerk; the thing caught his thought. He was thinking enviously of his boss who was Jim Brender, of the financial firm of J. P. Brender & Co.

The overtones of that thought struck along the vibrating elements of the creature. It turned abruptly and followed Lawrence Pearson, bookkeeper. If people ever paid attention to other people on the street, they would have been amazed after a moment to see two Lawrence Pearsons proceeding down the street, one some fifty feet behind the other. The second Lawrence Pearson had learned from the mind of the first that Jim Brender was a Harvard graduate in mathematics, finance and political economy, the latest of a long line of financial geniuses, thirty years old, and the head of the tremendously wealthy J. P. Brender & Co. Jim Brender had just married the most beautiful girl in the world; and this was the reason for Lawrence Pearson's discontent with life.

"Here I'm thirty, too," his thoughts echoed in the creature's mind, "and I've got nothing. He's got everything—everything while all I've got to look forward to is the same old boardinghouse till the end of time."

It was getting dark as the two crossed the river. The creature quickened its pace, striding forward with aggressive alertness that Lawrence Pearson in the flesh could never have managed. Some glimmering of its terrible purpose communicated itself in that last instant to the victim. The slight man turned; and let out a faint squawk as those steel-muscled fingers jerked at his throat, a single, fearful snap.

The creature's brain went black with dizziness as the brain of Lawrence Pearson crashed into the night of death. Gasping, whimpering, fighting dissolution, it finally gained control of itself. With one sweeping movement, it caught the dead body and flung it over the cement railing. There was a splash below, then a sound of gurgling water.

The thing that was now Lawrence Pearson walked on hurriedly, then more slowly till it came to a large, rambling brick house. It looked anxiously at the number, suddenly uncertain if it had remembered rightly. Hesitantly, it opened the door.

A streamer of yellow light splashed out, and laughter vibrated in the thing's sensitive ears. There was the same hum of many thoughts and many brains, as there had been in the street. The creature fought against the inflow of thought that threatened to crowd out the mind of Lawrence Pearson. A little dazed by the struggle, it found itself in a large, bright hall, which looked through a door into a room where a dozen people were sitting around a dining table.

"Oh, it's you, Mr. Pearson," said the landlady from the head of the table. She was a sharp-nosed, thin-mouthed woman at whom the creature stared with brief intentness. From her mind, a thought had come. She had a son who was a mathematics teacher in a high school. The creature shrugged. In one penetrating glance, the truth throbbed along the intricate atomic structure of its body. This woman's son was as much of an intellectual lightweight as his mother.

"You're just in time," she said incuriously. "Sarah, bring Mr. Pearson's plate."

"Thank you, but I'm not feeling hungry," the creature replied; and its human brain vibrated to the first silent, ironic laughter that it had ever known. "I think I'll just lie down."

All night long it lay on the bed of Lawrence Pearson, bright-eyed, alert, becoming more and more aware of itself. It thought:

"I'm a machine, without a brain of my own. I use the brains of other people, but somehow my creators made it possible for me to be more than just an echo. I use people's brains to carry out my purpose."

It pondered about those creators, and felt a surge of panic sweeping along its alien system, darkening its human mind. There was a vague physiological memory of pain unutterable, and of tearing chemical action that was frightening.

The creature rose at dawn, and walked the streets till half past nine. At that hour, it approached the imposing marble entrance of J. P. Brender & Co. Inside, it sank down in the comfortable chair initialed L. P.; and began painstakingly to work at the books Lawrence Pearson had put away the night before.

At ten o'clock, a tall young man in a dark suit entered the arched hallway and walked briskly through the row after row of offices. He smiled with easy confidence to every side. The thing did not need the chorus of "Good morning, Mr. Brender" to know that its prey had arrived.

Terrible in its slow-won self-confidence, it rose with a lithe, graceful movement that would have been impossible to the real

Lawrence Pearson, and walked briskly to the washroom. A moment later, the very image of Jim Brender emerged from the door and walked with easy confidence to the door of the private office which Jim Brender had entered a few minutes before.

The thing knocked and walked in—and simultaneously became aware of three things: The first was that it had found the mind after which it had been sent. The second was that its image mind was incapable of imitating the finer subtleties of the razor-sharp brain of the young man who was staring up from dark-gray eyes that were a little startled. And the third was the large metal bas-relief that hung on the wall.

With a shock that almost brought chaos, it felt the overpowering tug of that metal. And in one flash it knew that this was ultimate metal, product of the fine craft of the ancient Martians, whose metal cities, loaded with treasures of furniture, art and machinery, were slowly being dug up by enterprising human beings from the sands under which they had been buried for thirty or fifty million years.

The ultimate metal! The metal that no heat would even warm, that no diamond or other cutting device, could scratch, never duplicated by human beings, as mysterious as the *ieis* force which the Martians made from apparent nothingness.

All these thoughts crowded the creature's brain, as it explored the memory cells of Jim Brender. With an effort that was a special pain, the thing wrenched its mind from the metal, and fastened its eyes on Jim Brender. It caught the full flood of the wonder in his mind, as he stood up.

"Good lord," said Jim Brender, "who are you?"

"My name's Jim Brender," said the thing, conscious of grim amusement, conscious, too, that it was progress for it to be able to feel such an emotion.

The real Jim Brender had recovered himself. "Sit down, sit down," he said heartily. "This is the most amazing coincidence I've ever seen."

He went over to the mirror that made one panel of the left wall. He stared, first at himself, then at the creature. "Amazing," he said. "Absolutely amazing."

"Mr. Brender," said the creature, "I saw your picture in the paper, and I thought our astounding resemblance would make you listen,

334   A. E. VAN VOGT

where otherwise you might pay no attention. I have recently returned from Mars, and I am here to persuade you to come back to Mars with me."

"That," said Jim Brender, "is impossible."

"Wait," the creature said, "until I have told you why. Have you ever heard of the Tower of the Beast?"

"The Tower of the Beast!" Jim Brender repeated slowly. He went around his desk and pushed a button.

A voice from an ornamental box said: "Yes, Mr. Brender?"

"Dave, get me all the data on the Tower of the Beast and the legendary city of Li in which it is supposed to exist."

"Don't need to look it up," came the crisp reply. "Most Martian histories refer to it as the beast that fell from the sky when Mars was young—some terrible warning connected with it—the beast was unconscious when found—said to be the result of its falling out of sub-space. Martians read its mind; and were so horrified by its subconscious intentions they tried to kill it, but couldn't. So they built a huge vault, about fifteen hundred feet in diameter and a mile high—and the beast, apparently of these dimensions, was locked in. Several attempts have been made to find the city of Li, but without success. Generally believed to be a myth. That's all, Jim."

"Thank you!" Jim Brender clicked off the connection, and turned to his visitor. "Well?"

"It is not a myth. I know where the Tower of the Beast is; and I also know that the beast is still alive."

"Now, see here," said Brender good-humoredly, "I'm intrigued by your resemblance to me; and as a matter of fact I'd like Pamela— my wife—to see you. How about coming over to dinner? But don't, for Heaven's sake, expect me to believe such a story. The beast, if there is such a thing, fell from the sky when Mars was young. There are some authorities who maintain that the Martian race died out a hundred million years ago, though twenty-five million is the conservative estimate. The only things remaining of their civilization are their constructions of ultimate metal. Fortunately, toward the end they build almost everything from that indestructible metal."

"Let me tell you about the Tower of the Beast," said the thing quietly. "It is a tower of gigantic size, but only a hundred feet or so projected above the sand when I saw it. The whole top is a door, and that door is geared to a time lock, which in turn has been integrated along a line of ieis to the ultimate prime number."

Jim Brender stared; and the thing caught his startled thought, the first uncertainty, and the beginning of belief.

"Ultimate prime number!" Brender ejaculated. "What do you mean?" He caught himself. "I know of course that a prime number is a number divisible only by itself and by one."

He snatched at a book from the little wall library beside his desk, and rippled through it. "The largest known prime is—ah, here it is— is 230584300921393951. Some others, according to this authority, are 77843839397, 182521213001, and 78875943472201."

He frowned. "That makes the whole thing ridiculous. The ultimate prime would be an indefinite number." He smiled at the thing. "If there is a beast, and it is locked up in a vault of ultimate metal, the door of which is geared to a time lock, integrated along a line of ieis to the ultimate prime number—then the beast is caught. Nothing in the world can free it."

"To the contrary," said the creature. "I have been assured by the beast that it is within the scope of human mathematics to solve the problem, but that what is required is a born mathematical mind, equipped with all the mathematical training that Earth science can afford. You are that man."

"You expect me to release this evil creature—even if I could perform this miracle of mathematics."

"Evil nothing!" snapped the thing. "That ridiculous fear of the unknown which made the Martians imprison it has resulted in a very grave wrong. The beast is a scientist from another space, accidentally caught in one of his experiments. I say 'his' when of course I do not know whether this race has a sexual differentiation."

"You actually talked with the beast?"

"It communicated with me by mental telepathy."

"It has been proven that thoughts cannot penetrate ultimate metal."

"What do humans know about telepathy? They cannot even communicate with each other except under special conditions." The creature spoke contemptuously.

"That's right. And if your story is true, then this is a matter for the Council."

"This is a matter for two men, you and I. Have you forgotten that the vault of the beast is the central tower of the great city of Li—billions of dollars' worth of treasure ·in furniture, art and machinery? The beast demands release from its prison before it will permit anyone to mine that treasure. You can release it. We can share the treasure."

"Let me ask you a question," said Jim Brender. "What is your real name?"

"P-Pierce Lawrence!" the creature stammered. For the moment, it could think of no greater variation of the name of its first victim than reversing the two words, with a slight change on "Pearson." Its thoughts darkened with confusion as the voice of Brender pounded:

"On what ship did you come from Mars?"

"O-on *F 4961*," the thing stammered chaotically, fury adding to the confused state of its mind. It fought for control, felt itself slipping, suddenly felt the pull of the ultimate metal that made up the bas-relief on the wall, and knew by that tug that it was dangerously near dissolution.

"That would be a freighter," said Jim Brender. He pressed a button. "Carltons, find out if the *F 4961* had a passenger or person aboard, named Pierce Lawrence. How long will it take?"

"About a minute, sir."

"You see," said Jim Brender, leaning back, "this is mere formality. If you were on that ship, then I shall be compelled to give serious attention to your statements. You can understand, of course, that I could not possibly go into a thing like this blindly. I—"

The buzzer rang. "Yes?" said Jim Brender.

"Only the crew of two was on the *F 4961* when it landed yesterday. No such person as Pierce Lawrence was aboard."

"Thank you." Jim Brender stood up. He said coldly, "Good-by, Mr. Lawrence. I cannot imagine what you hoped to gain by this ridiculous story. However, it has been most intriguing, and the problem you presented was very ingenious indeed—"

The buzzer was ringing. "What is it?"

"Mr. Gorson to see you, sir."

"Very well, send him right in."

The thing had greater control of its brain now, and it saw in Brender's mind that Gorson was a financial magnate, whose business ranked with the Brender firm. It saw other things, too; things that made it walk out of the private office, out of the building, and wait patiently until Mr. Gorson emerged from the imposing entrance. A few minutes later, there were two Mr. Gorsons walking down the street.

•   •   •

Mr. Gorson was a vigorous man in his early fifties. He had lived a clean, active life; and the hard memories of many climates and several planets were stored away in his brain. The thing caught the alertness of this man on its sensitive elements, and followed him warily, respectfully, not quite decided whether it would act.

It thought: "I've come a long way from the primitive life that couldn't hold its shape. My creators, in designing me, gave to me powers of learning, developing. It is easier to fight dissolution, easier to be human. In handling this man, I must remember that my strength is invincible when properly used."

With minute care, it explored in the mind of its intended victim the exact route of his walk to his office. There was the entrance to a large building clearly etched on his mind. Then a long, marble corridor, into an automatic elevator up to the eighth floor, along a short corridor with two doors. One door led to the private entrance of the man's private office. The other to a storeroom used by the janitor. Gorson had looked into the place on various occasions; and there was in his mind, among other things, the memory of a large chest—

The thing waited in the storeroom till the unsuspecting Gorson was past the door. The door creaked. Gorson turned, his eyes widening. He didn't have a chance. A fist of solid steel smashed his face to a pulp, knocking the bones back into his brain.

This time, the creature did not make the mistake of keeping its mind tuned to that of its victim. It caught him viciously as he fell, forcing its steel fist back to a semblance of human flesh. With furious speed, it stuffed the bulky and athletic form into the large chest, and clamped the lid down tight.

Alertly, it emerged from the storeroom, entered the private office of Mr. Gorson, and sat down before the gleaming desk of oak. The man who responded to the pressing of a button saw John Gorson sitting there, and heard John Gorson say:

"Crispins, I want you to start selling these stocks through the secret channels right away. Sell until I tell you to stop, even if you think it's crazy. I have information of something big on."

Crispins glanced down the row after row of stock names; and his eyes grew wider and wider. "Good lord, man!" he gasped finally, with that familiarity which is the right of a trusted adviser, "these are all the gilt-edged stocks. Your whole fortune can't swing a deal like this."

"I told you I'm not in this alone."

"But it's against the law to break the market," the man protested.

"Crispins, you heard what I said. I'm leaving the office. Don't try to get in touch with me. I'll call you."

The thing that was John Gorson stood up, paying no attention to the bewildered thoughts that flowed from Crispins. It went out of the door by which it had entered. As it emerged from the building, it was thinking: "All I've got to do is kill half a dozen financial giants, start their stocks selling, and then—"

By one o'clock it was over. The exchange didn't close till three, but at one o'clock, the news was flashed on the New York tickers. In London, where it was getting dark, the papers brought out an extra. In Hankow and Shanghai, a dazzling new day was breaking as the newsboys ran along the streets in the shadows of skyscrapers, and shouted that J. P. Brender & Co. had assigned; and that there was to be an investigation—

"We are facing," said the chairman of the investigation committee, in his opening address the following morning, "one of the most astounding coincidences in all history. An ancient and respected firm, with worldwide affiliations and branches, with investments in more than a thousand companies of every description, is struck bankrupt by an unexpected crash in every stock in which the firm was interested. It will require months to take evidence on the responsibility for the short-selling which brought about this disaster. In the meantime, I see no reason, regrettable as the action must be to all the old friends of the late J. P. Brender, and of his son, why the demands of the creditors should not be met, and the properties liquidated through auction sales and such other methods as may be deemed proper and legal—"

"Really, I don't blame her," said the first woman, as they wandered through the spacious rooms of the Brenders' Chinese palace. "I have no doubt she does love Jim Brender, but no one could seriously expect her to remain married to him *now*. She's a woman of the world, and it's utterly impossible to expect her to live with a man who's going to be a mere pilot or space hand or something on a Martian spaceship—"

•   •   •

Commander Hughes of Interplanetary Spaceways entered the office of his employer truculently. He was a small man, but extremely wiry; and the thing that was Louis Dyer gazed at him tensely, conscious of the force and power of this man.

Hughes began: "You have my report on this Brender case?"

The thing twirled the mustache of Louis Dyer nervously; then picked up a small folder, and read out loud:

"Dangerous for psychological reasons . . . to employ Brender. . . . So many blows in succession. Loss of wealth, position and wife. . . . No normal man could remain normal under . . . circumstances. Take him into office . . . befriend him . . . give him a sinecure, or position where his undoubted great ability . . . but not on a spaceship, where the utmost hardiness, both mental, moral, spiritual and physical is required—"

Hughes interrupted: "Those are exactly the points which I am stressing. I knew you would see what I meant, Louis."

"Of course, I see," said the creature, smiling in grim amusement, for it was feeling very superior these days. "Your thoughts, your ideas, your code and your methods are stamped irrevocably on your brain and"—it added hastily—"you have never left me in doubt as to where you stand. However, in this case I must insist. Jim Brender will not take an ordinary position offered by his friends. And it is ridiculous to ask him to subordinate himself to men to whom he is in every way superior. He has commanded his own space yacht; he knows more about the mathematical end of the work than our whole staff put together; and that is no reflection on our staff. He knows the hardships connected with space flying, and believes that it is exactly what he needs. I, therefore, command you, for the first time in our long association, Peter, to put him on space freighter F 4961 in the place of Spacecraftsman Parelli who collapsed into a nervous breakdown after that curious affair with the creature from space, as Lieutenant Morton described it—By the way, did you find the . . . er . . . sample of that creature yet?"

"No, sir, it vanished the day you came in to look at it. We've searched the place high and low—queerest stuff you ever saw. Goes through glass as easy as light; you'd think it was some form of light-stuff—scares me, too. A pure sympodial development—actually more adaptable to environment than anything hitherto discovered; and that's putting it mildly. I tell you, sir—But see here, you can't steer me off the Brender case like that."

"Peter, I don't understand your attitude. This is the first time I've interfered with your end of the work and—"

"I'll resign," groaned that sorely beset man.

The thing stifled a smile. "Peter, you've built up the staff of Spaceways. It's your child, your creation; you can't give it up, you know you can't—"

The words hissed softly into alarm; for into Hughes' brain had flashed the first real intention of resigning. Just hearing of his accomplishments and the story of his beloved job brought such a rush of memories, such a realization of how tremendous an outrage was this threatened interference. In one mental leap, the creature saw what this man's resignation would mean: The discontent of the men; the swift perception of the situation by Jim Brender; and his refusal to accept the job. There was only one way out—that Brender would get to the ship without finding out what had happened. Once on it, he must carry through with one trip to Mars; and that was all that was needed.

The thing pondered the possibility of imitating Hughes' body; then agonizingly realized that it was hopeless. Both Louis Dyer and Hughes must be around until the last minute.

"But, Peter, listen!" the creature began chaotically. Then it said, "Damn!" for it was very human in its mentality; and the realization that Hughes took its words as a sign of weakness was maddening. Uncertainty descended like a black cloud over its brain.

"I'll tell Brender when he arrives in five minutes how I feel about all this!" Hughes snapped; and the creature knew that the worst had happened. "If you forbid me to tell him then I resign. I—Good God, man, your face!"

Confusion and horror came to the creature simultaneously. It knew abruptly that its face had dissolved before the threatened ruin of its plans. It fought for control, leaped to its feet, seeing the incredible danger. The large office just beyond the frosted glass door— Hughes' first outcry would bring help—

With a half sob, it sought to force its arm into an imitation of a metal fist, but there was no metal in the room to pull it into shape. There was only the solid maple desk. With a harsh cry, the creature leaped completely over the desk, and sought to bury a pointed shaft of stick into Hughes' throat.

Hughes cursed in amazement, and caught at the stick with furious strength. There was sudden commotion in the outer office, raised voices, running feet—

It was quite accidental the way it happened. The surface cars swayed to a stop, drawing up side by side as the red light blinked on ahead. Jim Brender glanced at the next car.

A girl and a man sat in the rear of the long, shiny, streamlined affair, and the girl was desperately striving to crouch down out of his sight, striving with equal desperation not to be too obvious in her intention. Realizing that she was seen, she smiled brilliantly, and leaned out of the window.

"Hello, Jim, how's everything?"

"Hello, Pamela!" Jim Brender's fingers tightened on the steering wheel till the knuckles showed white, as he tried to keep his voice steady. He couldn't help adding: "When does the divorce become final?"

"I get my papers tomorrow," she said, "but I suppose you won't get yours till you return from your first trip. Leaving today, aren't you?"

"In about fifteen minutes." He hesitated. "When is the wedding?"

The rather plump, white-faced man who had not participated in the conversation so far, leaned forward.

"Next week," he said. He put his fingers possessively over Pamela's hand. "I wanted it tomorrow but Pamela wouldn't—er, good-by."

His last words were hastily spoken, as the traffic lights switched, and the cars rolled on, separating at the first corner.

The rest of the drive to the spaceport was a blur. He hadn't expected the wedding to take place so soon. Hadn't, when he came right down to it, expected it to take place at all. Like a fool, he had hoped blindly—

Not that it was Pamela's fault. Her training, her very life made this the only possible course of action for her. But—*one week!* The spaceship would be one fourth of the long trip to Mars—

He parked his car. As he paused beside the runway that led to the open door of F 4961—a huge globe of shining metal, three hundred feet in diameter—he saw a man running toward him. Then he recognized Hughes.

The thing that was Hughes approached, fighting for calmness. The whole world was a flame of cross-pulling forces. It shrank from the thoughts of the people milling about in the office it had just left. Everything had gone wrong. It had never intended to do what it now had to do. It had intended to spend most of the trip to Mars as a blister of metal on the outer shield of the ship. With an effort, it controlled its funk, its terror, its brain.

"We're leaving right away," it said.

Brender looked amazed. "But that means I'll have to figure out a new orbit under the most difficult—"

"Exactly," the creature interrupted. "I've been hearing a lot about your marvelous mathematical ability. It's time the words were proved by deeds."

Jim Brender shrugged. "I have no objection. But how is it that you're coming along?"

"I always go with a new man."

It sounded reasonable. Brender climbed the runway, closely followed by Hughes. The powerful pull of the metal was the first real pain the creature had known for days. For a long month, it would now have to fight the metal, fight to retain the shape of Hughes— and carry on a thousand duties at the same time.

The first stabbing pain tore along its elements, and smashed the confidence that days of being human had built up. And then, as it followed Brender through the door, it heard a shout behind it. It looked back hastily. People were streaming out of several doors, running toward the ship.

Brender was several yards along the corridor. With a hiss that was almost a sob, the creature leaped inside, and pulled the lever that clicked the great door shut.

There was an emergency lever that controlled the antigravity plates. With one jerk, the creature pulled the heavy lever hard over. There was a sensation of lightness and a sense of falling.

Through the great plate window, the creature caught a flashing glimpse of the field below, swarming with people. White faces turning upward, arms waving. Then the scene grew remote, as a thunder of rockets vibrated through the ship.

"I hope," said Brender, as Hughes entered the control room, "you wanted me to start the rockets."

"Yes," the thing replied, and felt brief panic at the chaos in its brain, the tendency of its tongue to blur. "I'm leaving the mathematical end entirely in your hands."

It didn't dare to stay so near the heavy metal engines, even with Brender's body there to help it keep its human shape. Hurriedly, it started up the corridor. The best place would be the insulated bedroom—

Abruptly, it stopped in its headlong walk, teetered for an instant on tiptoes. From the control room it had just left, a thought was trickling—a thought from Brender's brain. The creature almost dissolved in terror as it realized that Brender was sitting at the radio, answering an insistent call from Earth—

It burst into the control room, and braked to a halt, its eyes widening with humanlike dismay. Brender whirled from before the radio with a single twisting step. In his fingers, he held a revolver. In his mind, the creature read a dawning comprehension of the whole truth. Brender cried:

"You're the . . . thing that came to my office, and talked about prime numbers and the vault of the beast."

He took a step to one side to cover an open doorway that led down another corridor. The movement brought the telescreen into the vision of the creature. In the screen was the image of the real Hughes. Simultaneously, Hughes saw the thing.

"Brender," he bellowed, "it's the monster that Morton and Parelli saw on their trip from Mars. It doesn't react to heat or any chemicals, but we never tried bullets. Shoot, you fool!"

It was too much, there was too much metal, too much confusion. With a whimpering cry, the creature dissolved. The pull of the metal twisted it horribly into thick half metal; the struggle to be human left it a malignant structure of bulbous head, with one eye half gone, and two snakelike arms attached to the half metal of the body.

Instinctively, it fought closer to Brender, letting the pull of his body make it more human. The half metal became fleshlike stuff that sought to return to its human shape.

"Listen, Brender!" Hughes' voice came urgently. "The fuel vats in the engine room are made of ultimate metal. One of them is empty. We caught a part of this thing once before, and it couldn't get out of the small jar of ultimate metal. If you could drive it into the vat while it's lost control of itself, as it seems to do very easily—"

"I'll see what lead can do!" Brender rapped in a brittle voice.

Bang! The half-human creature screamed from its half-formed slit of mouth, and retreated, its legs dissolving into gray dough.

"It hurts, doesn't it?" Brender ground out. "Get over into the engine room, you damned thing, into the vat!"

"Go on, go on!" Hughes was screaming from the telescreen.

Brender fired again. The creature made a horrible slobbering sound, and retreated once more. But it was bigger again, more human; and in one caricature hand a caricature of Brender's revolver was growing.

It raised the unfinished, unformed gun. There was an explosion, and a shriek from the thing. The revolver fell, a shapeless, tattered blob, to the floor. The little gray mass of it scrambled frantically toward the parent body, and attached itself like some monstrous canker to the right foot.

And then, for the first time, the mighty and evil brains that had created the thing, sought to dominate their robot. Furious, yet conscious that the game must be carefully played, the Controller forced the terrified and utterly beaten thing to its will. Scream after agonized scream rent the air, as the change was forced upon the unstable elements. In an instant, the thing stood in the shape of Brender, but instead of a revolver, there grew from one browned, powerful hand a pencil of shining metal. Mirror bright, it glittered in every facet like some incredible gem.

The metal glowed ever so faintly, an unearthly radiance. And where the radio had been, and the screen with Hughes' face on it, there was a gaping hole Desperately, Brender pumped bullets into the body before him, but though the shape trembled, it stared at him now, unaffected. The shining weapon swung toward him.

"When you are quite finished," it said, "perhaps we can talk."

It spoke so mildly that Brender, tensing to meet death, lowered his gun in amazement. The thing went on:

"Do not be alarmed. This which you hear and see is a robot, designed by us to cope with your space and number world. Several of us are working here under the most difficult conditions to maintain this connection, so I must be brief.

"We exist in a time world immeasurably more slow than your own. By a system of synchronization, we have geared a number of these spaces in such fashion that, though one of our days is millions of your years, we can communicate. Our purpose is to free our colleague, Kalorn, from the Martian vault. Kalorn was caught accidentally in a time warp of his own making and precipitated onto the planet you know as Mars. The Martians, needlessly fearing his great size, constructed a most diabolical prison, and we need your knowledge of the mathematics peculiar to your space and number world—and to it alone—in order to free him."

The calm voice continued, earnest but not offensively so, insistent but friendly. He regretted that their robot had killed human beings. In greater detail, he explained that every space was constructed on a different numbers system, some all negative, some all positive, some a mixture of the two, the whole an infinite variety, and every mathematic interwoven into the very fabric of the space it ruled.

Ieis force was not really mysterious. It was simply a flow from one space to another, the result of a difference in potential. This flow, however, was one of the universal forces, which only one other force could affect, the one he had used a few minutes before. Ultimate metal was *actually* ultimate.

In their space they had a similar metal, built up from negative atoms. He could see from Brender's mind that the Martians had known nothing about minus numbers, so that they must have built it up from ordinary atoms. It could be done that way, too, though not so easily. He finished:

"The problem narrows down to this: Your mathematics must tell us how, with our universal force, we can short-circuit the ultimate prime number—that is, factor it—so that the door will open any time. You may ask how a prime can be factored when it is divisible only by itself and by one. That problem is, for your system, solvable only by your mathematics. Will you do it?"

Brender realized with a start that he was still holding his revolver. He tossed it aside. His nerves were calm as he said:

"Everything you have said sounds reasonable and honest. If you were desirous of making trouble, it would be the simplest thing in the world to send as many of your kind as you wished. Of course, the whole affair must be placed before the Council—"

"Then it is hopeless—the Council could not possibly accede—"

"And you expect me to do what you do not believe the highest governmental authority in the System would do?" Brender exclaimed.

"It is inherent in the nature of a democracy that it cannot gamble with the lives of its citizens. We have such a government here; and its members have already informed us that, in a similar condition, they would not consider releasing an unknown beast upon their people. Individuals, however, can gamble where governments must not. You have agreed that our argument is logical. What system do men follow if not that of logic?"

The Controller, through its robot, watched Brender's thoughts alertly. It saw doubt and uncertainty, opposed by a very human desire to help, based upon the logical conviction that it was safe. Probing his mind, it saw swiftly that it was unwise, in dealing with men, to trust too much to logic. It pressed on:

"To an individual we can offer—everything. In a minute, with your permission, we shall transfer this ship to Mars; not in thirty days, but in thirty seconds. The knowledge of how this is done will remain with you. Arrived at Mars, you will find yourself the only living person who knows the whereabouts of the ancient city of Li, of which the vault of the beast is the central tower. In this city will be found literally billions of dollars' worth of treasure made of ultimate metal; and according to the laws of Earth, fifty percent will be yours. Your fortune re-established, you will be able to return to Earth this very day, and reclaim your former wife, and your position. Poor silly child, she loves you still, but the iron conventions and training of her youth leave her no alternative. If she were older, she would have the character to defy those conventions. You must save her from herself. Will you do it?"

Brender was as white as a sheet, his hands clenching and unclenching. Malevolently, the thing watched the flaming thought sweeping through his brain—the memory of a pudgy white hand closing over Pamela's fingers, watched the reaction of Brender to its words, those words that expressed exactly what he had always thought. Brender looked up with tortured eyes.

"Yes," he said, "I'll do what I can."

A bleak range of mountains fell away into a valley of reddish gray sand. The thin winds of Mars blew a mist of sand against the building.

Such a building! At a distance, it had looked merely big. A bare hundred feet projected above the desert, a hundred feet of length and *fifteen hundred feet of diameter*. Literally thousands of feet must extend beneath the restless ocean of sand to make the perfect balance of form, the graceful flow, the fairylike beauty, which the long-dead Martians demanded of all their constructions, however massive. Brender felt suddenly small and insignificant as the rockets of his spacesuit pounded him along a few feet above the sand toward that incredible building.

At close range the ugliness of sheer size was miraculously lost in the wealth of the decorative. Columns and pilasters assembled in groups and clusters, broke up the façades, gathered and dispersed again restlessly. The flat surfaces of wall and roof melted into a wealth of ornaments and imitation stucco work, vanished and broke into a play of light and shade.

The creature floated beside Brender; and its Controller said: "I see that you have been giving considerable thought to the problem, but this robot seems incapable of following abstract thoughts, so I have no means of knowing the source of your speculations. I see however that you seem to be satisfied."

"I think I've got the answer," said Brender, "but first I wish to see the time lock. Let's climb."

They rose into the sky, dipping over the lip of the building. Brender saw a vast flat expanse; and in the center—He caught his breath!

The meager light from the distant sun of Mars shone down on a structure located at what seemed the exact center of the great door. The structure was about fifty feet high, and seemed nothing less than a series of quadrants coming together at the center, which was a metal arrow pointing straight up.

The arrow head was not solid metal. Rather it was as if the metal had divided in two parts, then curved together again. But not quite together. About a foot separated the two sections of metal. But that foot was bridged by a vague, thin, green flame of ieis force.

"The time lock!" Brender nodded. "I thought it would be something like that, though I expected it would be bigger, more substantial."

"Do not be deceived by its fragile appearance," answered the thing. "Theoretically, the strength of ultimate metal is infinite; and the ieis force can only be affected by the universal I have mentioned.

Exactly what the effect will be, it is impossible to say as it involves the temporary derangement of the whole number system upon which that particular area of space is built. But now tell us what to do."

"Very well." Brender eased himself onto a bank of sand, and cut off his antigravity plates. He lay on his back, and stared thoughtfully into the blue-black sky. For the time being all doubts, worries and fears were gone from him, forced out by sheer will power. He began to explain:

"The Martian mathematic, like that of Euclid and Pythagoras, was based on endless magnitude. Minus numbers were beyond their philosophy. On Earth, however, beginning with Descartes, an analytical mathematic was evolved. Magnitude and perceivable dimensions were replaced by that of variable relation-values between positions in space.

"For the Martians, there was only one number between 1 and 3. Actually, the totality of such numbers is an infinite aggregate. And with the introduction of the idea of the square root of minus one—or i—and the complex numbers, mathematics definitely ceased to be a simple thing of magnitude, perceivable in pictures. Only the intellectual step from the infinitely small quantity to the lower limit of every possible finite magnitude brought out the conception of a variable number which oscillated beneath any assignable number that was not zero.

"The prime number, being a conception of pure magnitude, had no reality in *real* mathematics, but in this case was rigidly bound up with the reality of the ieis force. The Martians knew ieis as a pale-green flow about a foot in length and developing say a thousand horsepower. (It was actually 12.171 inches and 1021.23 horsepower, but that was unimportant.) The power produced never varied, the length never varied, from year end to year end, for tens of thousands of years. The Martians took the length as their basis of measurement, and called it one 'el'; they took the power as their basis of power and called it one 'rb.' And because of the absolute invariability of the flow they knew it was eternal.

"They knew furthermore that nothing could be eternal without being prime; their whole mathematic was based on numbers which could be factored, that is, disintegrated, destroyed, rendered less than they had been; and numbers which could not be factored, disintegrated or divided into smaller groups.

"Any number which could be factored was incapable of being

infinite. Contrariwise, the infinite number must be prime.

"Therefore, they built a lock and integrated it along a line of ieis, to operate when the ieis ceased to flow—which would be at the end of Time, provided it was not interfered with. To prevent interference, they buried the motivating mechanism of the flow in ultimate metal, which could not be destroyed or corroded in any way. According to their mathematic, that settled it."

"But you have the answer," said the voice of the thing eagerly.

"Simply this: The Martians set a value on the flow of one 'rb.' If you interfere with that flow to no matter what small degree, you no longer have an 'rb.' You have something less. The flow, which is a universal, becomes automatically less than a universal, less than infinite. The prime number ceases to be prime. Let us suppose that you interfere with it to the extent of *infinity minus one*. You will then have a number divisible by two. As a matter of fact, the number, like most large numbers, will immediately break into thousands of pieces, i.e., it will be divisible by tens of thousands of smaller numbers. If the present time falls anywhere near one of those breaks, the door would open then. In other words, the door will open immediately if you can so interfere with the flow that one of the factors occurs in immediate time."

"That is very clear," said the Controller with satisfaction and the image of Brender was smiling triumphantly. "We shall now use this robot to manufacture a universal; and Kalorn shall be free very shortly." He laughed aloud. "The poor robot is protesting violently at the thought of being destroyed, but after all it is only a machine, and not a very good one at that. Besides, it is interfering with my proper reception of your thoughts. Listen to it scream, as I twist it into shape."

The cold-blooded words chilled Brender, pulled him from the heights of his abstract thought. Because of the prolonged intensity of his thinking, he saw with sharp clarity something that had escaped him before.

"Just a minute," he said. "How is it that the robot, introduced from your world, is living at the same time rate as I am, whereas Kalorn continues to live at your time rate?"

"A very good question." The face of the robot was twisted into a triumphant sneer, as the Controller continued. "Because, my dear

Brender, you have been duped. It is true that Kalorn is living in our time rate, but that was due to a shortcoming in our machine. The machine which Kalorn built, while large enough to transport him, was not large enough in its adaptive mechanism to adapt him to each new space as he entered it. With the result that he was transported but not adapted. It was possible of course for us, his helpers, to transport such a small thing as the robot, though we have no more idea of the machine's construction than you have.

"In short, we can use what there is of the machine, but the secret of its construction is locked in the insides of our own particular ultimate metal, and in the brain of Kalorn. Its invention by Kalorn was one of those accidents which, by the law of averages, will not be repeated in millions of our years. Now that you have provided us with the method of bringing Kalorn back, we shall be able to build innumerable interspace machines. Our purpose is to control all spaces, all worlds—particularly those which are inhabited. We intend to be absolute rulers of the entire Universe."

The ironic voice ended; and Brender lay in his prone position the prey of horror. The horror was twofold, partly due to the Controller's monstrous plan, and partly due to the thought that was pulsing in his brain. He groaned, as he realized that warning thought must be ticking away on the automatic receiving brain of the robot. "Wait," his thought was saying, "that adds a new factor. Time—"

There was a scream from the creature as it was forcibly dissolved. The scream choked to a sob, then silence. An intricate machine of shining metal lay there on that great gray-brown expanse of sand and ultimate metal.

The metal glowed; and then the machine was floating in the air. It rose to the top of the arrow, and settled over the green flame of ieis.

Brender jerked on his antigravity screen, and leaped to his feet. The violent action carried him some hundred feet into the air. His rockets sputtered into staccato fire, and he clamped his teeth against the pain of acceleration.

Below him, the great door began to turn, to unscrew, faster and faster, till it was like a flywheel. Sand flew in all directions in a miniature storm.

At top acceleration, Brender darted to one side.

Just in time. First, the robot machine was flung off that tremendous wheel by sheer centrifugal power. Then the door came off, and, spinning now at an incredible rate, hurtled straight into the air, and vanished into space.

A puff of black dust came floating up out of the blackness of the vault. Suppressing his horror, yet perspiring from awful relief, he rocketed to where the robot had fallen into the sand.

Instead of glistening metal, a time-dulled piece of junk lay there. The dull metal flowed sluggishly and assumed a quasi-human shape. The flesh remained gray and in little rolls as if it were ready to fall apart from old age. The thing tried to stand up on wrinkled, horrible legs, but finally lay still. Its lips moved, mumbled:

"I caught your warning thought, but I didn't let them know. Now, Kalorn is dead. They realized the truth as it was happening. End of Time came—"

It faltered into silence; and Brender went on: "Yes, end of Time came when the flow became momentarily less than eternal—came at the factor point which occurred a few minutes ago."

"I was . . . only partly . . . within its . . . influence, Kalorn all the way. . . . Even if they're lucky . . . will be years before . . . they invent another machine . . . and one of their years is billions . . . of yours. . . . I didn't tell them. . . . I caught your thought . . . and kept it . . . from them—"

"But why did you do it? Why?"

"Because they were hurting me. They were going to destroy me. Because . . . I liked . . . being human. I was . . . somebody!"

The flesh dissolved. It flowed slowly into a pool of lavalike gray. The lava crinkled, split into dry, brittle pieces. Brender touched one of the pieces. It crumbled into a fine powder of gray dust. He gazed out across that grim, deserted valley of sand, and said aloud, pityingly:

"Poor Frankenstein."

He turned toward the distant spaceship, toward the swift trip to Earth. As he climbed out of the ship a few minutes later, one of the first persons he saw was Pamela.

She flew into his arms. "Oh, Jim, Jim," she sobbed. "What a fool I've been. When I heard what had happened, and realized you were in danger, I—Oh, Jim!"

Later, he would tell her about their new fortune.

DEAR PEN PAL

Planet Aurigae II

Dear Pen Pal:

When I first received your letter from the interstellar correspondence club, my impulse was to ignore it. The mood of one who has spent the last seventy planetary periods—years I suppose you would call them—in an Aurigaen prison, does not make for a pleasant exchange of letters. However, life is very boring, and so I finally settled myself to the task of writing you.

Your description of Earth sounds exciting. I would like to live there for a while, and I have a suggestion in this connection, but I won't mention it till I have developed it further.

You will have noticed the material on which this letter is written. It is a highly sensitive metal, very thin, very flexible, and I have inclosed several sheets of it for your use. Tungsten dipped in any strong acid makes an excellent mark on it. It is important to me that you do write on it, as my fingers are too hot—literally—to hold your paper without damaging it.

I'll say no more just now. It is possible you will not care to correspond with a convicted criminal, and therefore I shall leave the next move up to you. Thank you for your letter. Though you did not know its destination, it brought a moment of cheer into my drab life.

Skander

Aurigae II

Dear Pen Pal:

Your prompt reply to my letter made me happy. I am sorry your doctor thought it excited you too much, and sorry, also, if I have described my predicament in such a way as to make you feel badly. I welcome your many questions, and I shall try to answer them all.

You say the international correspondence club has no record of having sent any letters to Aurigae. That, according to them, the temperature on the second planet of the Aurigae sun is more than 500 degrees Fahrenheit. And that life is not known to exist there. Your club is right about the temperature and the letters. We have what your people would call a hot climate, but then we are not a hydrocarbon form of life, and find 500 degrees very pleasant.

I must apologize for deceiving you about the way your first letter was sent to me. I didn't want to frighten you away by telling you too much at once. After all, I could not be expected to know that you would be enthusiastic to hear from me.

The truth is that I am a scientist, and, along with the other members of my race, I have known for some centuries that there were other inhabited systems in the galaxy. Since I am allowed to experiment in my spare hours, I amused myself in attempts at communication. I developed several simple systems for breaking in on galactic communication operations, but it was not until I developed a subspacewave control that I was able to draw your letter (along with several others, which I did not answer) into a cold chamber.

I use the cold chamber as both sending and receiving center, and since you were kind enough to use the material which I sent you, it was easy for me to locate your second letter among the mass of mail that accumulated at the nearest headquarters of the interstellar correspondence club.

How did I learn your language? After all, it is a simple one, particularly the written language seems easy. I had no difficulty with it. If you are still interested in writing me, I shall be happy to continue the correspondence.

Skander

Aurigae II

Dear Pen Pal:

Your enthusiasm is refreshing. You say that I failed to answer your question about how I expected to visit Earth. I confess I deliberately ignored the question, as my experiment had not yet proceeded far enough. I want you to bear with me a short time longer, and then I will be able to give you the details. You are right in saying that it would be difficult for a being who lives at a temperature of 500 degrees Fahrenheit to mingle freely with the people of Earth.

This was never my intention, so please relieve your mind. However, let us drop that subject for the time being.

I appreciate the delicate way in which you approach the subject of my imprisonment. But it is quite unnecessary. I performed forbidden experiments upon my body in a way that was deemed to be dangerous to the public welfare. For instance, among other things, I once lowered my surface temperature to 150 degrees Fahrenheit, and so shortened the radioactive cycle-time of my surroundings. This caused an unexpected break in the normal person to person energy flow in the city where I lived, and so charges were laid against me. I have thirty more years to serve. It would be pleasant to leave my body behind and tour the universe—but as I said I'll discuss that later.

I wouldn't say that we're a superior race. We have certain qualities which apparently your people do not have. We live longer, not because of any discoveries we've made about ourselves, but because our bodies are built of a more enduring element—I don't know your name for it, but the atomic weight is 52.9#.* Our scientific discoveries are of the kind that would normally be made by a race with our kind of physical structure. The fact that we can work with temperatures of as high as—I don't know just how to put that—has been very helpful in the development of the subspace energies which are extremely hot, and require delicate adjustments. In the later stages these adjustments can be made by machinery, but in the development the work must be done by "hand"—I put that word in quotes, because we have no hands in the same way that you have.

I am enclosing a photographic plate, properly cooled and chemicalized for your climate. I wonder if you would set it up and take a picture of yourself. All you have to do is arrange it properly on the basis of the laws of light—that is, light travels in straight lines, so stand in front of it—and when you are ready *think* "Ready!" The picture will be automatically taken.

Would you do this for me? If you are interested, I will also send you a picture of myself, though I must warn you. My appearance will probably shock you.

Sincerely,
Skander

*A radioactive isotope of chromium.—Author's note.

Planet Aurigae II

Dear Pen Pal:

Just a brief note in answer to your question. It is not necessary to put the plate into a camera. You describe this as a dark box. The plate will take the picture when you think, "Ready!" I assure you it will be flooded with light.

Skander

Aurigae II

Dear Pen Pal:

You say that while you were waiting for the answer to my last letter you showed the photographic plate to one of the doctors at the hospital—I cannot picture what you mean by doctor or hospital, but let that pass—and he took the problem up with government authorities. Problem? I don't understand. I thought we were having a pleasant correspondence, private and personal.

I shall certainly appreciate your sending that picture of yourself.

Skander

Aurigae II

Dear Pen Pal:

I assure you I am not annoyed at your action. It merely puzzled me, and I am sorry the plate has not been returned to you. Knowing what governments are, I can imagine that it will not be returned to you for some time, so I am taking the liberty of inclosing another plate.

I cannot imagine why you should have been warned against continuing this correspondence. What do they expect me to do?—eat you up at long distance? I'm sorry but I don't like hydrogen in my diet.

In any event, I would like your picture as a memento of our friendship, and I will send mine as soon as I have received yours. You may keep it or throw it away, or give it to your governmental authorities—but at least I will have the knowledge that I've given a fair exchange.

With all the best wishes
Skander

Aurigae II

Dear Pen Pal:

Your last letter was so slow in coming that I thought you had decided to break off the correspondence. I was sorry to notice that you failed to inclose the photograph, puzzled by your reference to having a relapse, and cheered by your statement that you would send it along as soon as you felt better—whatever that means. However, the important thing is that you did write, and I respect the philosophy of your club which asks its members not to write of pessimistic matters. We all have our own problems which we regard as overshadowing the problems of others. Here I am in prison, doomed to spend the next 30 years tucked away from the main stream of life. Even the thought is hard on my restless spirit, though I know I have a long life ahead of me after my release.

In spite of your friendly letter, I won't feel that you have completely re-established contact with me until you send the photograph.

Yours in expectation
Skander

Aurigae II

Dear Pen Pal:

The photograph arrived. As you suggest, your appearance startled me. From your description I thought I had mentally reconstructed your body. It just goes to show that words cannot really describe an object which has never been seen.

You'll notice that I've inclosed a photograph of myself, as I promised I would. Chunky, metallic looking chap, am I not, very different, I'll wager, than you expected? The various races with whom we have communicated become wary of us when they discover we are highly radioactive, and that literally we are a radioactive form of life, the only such (that we know of) in the universe. It's been very trying to be so isolated and, as you know, I have occasionally mentioned that I had hopes of escaping not only the deadly imprisonment to which I am being subjected but also the body which cannot escape.

Perhaps you'll be interested in hearing how far this idea has developed. The problem involved is one of exchange of personalities with someone else. Actually, it is not really an exchange in the accepted meaning of the word. It is necessary to get an impress of both individuals, of their mind and of their thoughts as well as their bodies. Since this phase is purely mechanical, it is simply a matter of taking complete photographs and of exchanging them. By complete I mean of course every vibration must be registered. The next step is to make sure the two photographs are exchanged, that is, that each party has somewhere near him a complete photograph of the other. (It is already too late, Pen Pal. I have set in motion the sub-space energy interflow between the two plates, so you might as well read on.) As I have said it is not exactly an exchange of personalities. The original personality in each individual is suppressed, literally pushed back out of the consciousness, and the image personality from the "photographic" plate replaces it.

You will take with you a complete memory of your life on Earth, and I will take along memory of my life on Aurigae. Simultaneously, the memory of the receiving body will be blurrily at our disposal. A part of us will always be pushing up, striving to regain consciousness, but always lacking the strength to succeed.

As soon as I grow tired of Earth, I will exchange bodies in the same way with a member of some other race. Thirty years hence, I will be happy to reclaim my body, and you can then have whatever body I last happened to occupy.

This should be a very happy arrangement for us both. You, with your short life expectancy, will have out-lived all your contemporaries and will have had an interesting experience. I admit I expect to have the better of the exchange—but now, enough of explanation. By the time you reach this part of the letter it will be me reading it, not you. But if any part of you is still aware, so long for now, Pen Pal. It's been nice having all those letters from you. I shall write you from time to time to let you know how things are going with my tour.

                                                        Skander

                                                        Aurigae II
Dear Pen Pal:
    Thanks a lot for forcing the issue. For a long time I hesitated about letting you play such a trick on yourself. You see, the government scientists analyzed the nature of that first photographic plate you sent me, and so the final decision was really up to me. I decided that anyone as eager as you were to put one over should be allowed to succeed.

    Now I know I didn't have to feel sorry for you. Your plan to conquer Earth wouldn't have gotten anywhere, but the fact that you had the idea ends the need for sympathy.

By this time you will have realized for yourself that a man who has been paralyzed since birth, and is subject to heart attacks, cannot expect a long life span. I am happy to tell you that your once lonely pen pal is enjoying himself, and I am happy to sign myself with a name to which I expect to become accustomed.

With best wishes
Skander

JACK VANCE

b. 1916

In World War II John Holbrook (best known as "Jack") Vance served in the Merchant Marine. When you're not being torpedoed (as Vance was, twice) shipboard life leaves occasional stretches of time with few distractions. Like many another mariner before him— Joseph Conrad, A. Bertram Chandler—Vance used the time to write. His first sale was "The World Thinker," published in *Thrilling Wonder Stories* in 1945. After the war he kept on writing, primarily adventure SF stories about his picaresque character, Magnus Ridolph, generally for *Thrilling Wonder* and its companion magazine, *Startling Stories*.

Pulp adventure was not Vance's strongest point, however. By 1950 he had written half a dozen stories of a different kind. These dealt, ironically and sometimes poetically, with the far future of the human race, when science has been lost and the world is governed by magic. These stories were not the sort preferred by the *Thrilling* magazines, but Vance bundled them up and succeeded in having them published in book form, as *The Dying Earth*.

Other major Vance works from that period include *Big Planet*— about, as the title suggests, a planet so large that it is populated with scores of completely different societies, though all are the remote descendants of ourselves—and *The Languages of Pao*, in which Vance takes up the complex relationship between language and understanding.

Science fiction was not Vance's only field. Beginning in the 1960s he wrote a number of fine mysteries—signing them with his first two real names, as "John Holbrook"—and is one of the few writers to have won both science fiction's Hugo and the Mystery Writers of America's Edgar award.

•   •   •

The story which, for me, epitomizes all that is most wonderful about Jack Vance's science fiction is his novella, "The Dragon Masters," about a marvelous planet, far in the future, in which the human race and a race of saurians contest for dominance, along with their multitudinous evolved subspecies. Unhappily it is far too long to include in this collection.

When Vance's agent sent me the manuscript of "The Dragon Masters" I knew at once that I wanted to publish it in my magazine, Galaxy. Fortunately—and unusually—I had a little extra time before deadline, so I called in that wonderful artist Jack Gaughan, and we conspired to dress it up. In his artwork for "The Dragon Masters" Gaughan did not limit himself to illustrating particular scenes. Instead he made a lovely map of the far-off planet on which the story is set, and individual drawings of each of the species described. When the next year's voting time for awards came around, not only did "The Dragon Masters" win a best story Hugo, but Gaughan's drawings won the Hugo for best art—the only time the award was given for the drawings for a single story.

Vance is one of the best-loved science fiction writers in America, but, as with that other Grand Master, A. E. van Vogt, he is even more popular in some other parts of the world. I discovered this for myself some years ago when Jack and I made a joint appearance at a bookstore autographing session in the Hague, in the Netherlands. It was a humbling experience. The proprietors set us up in a room within the store; behind glass doors several score people were lined up, waiting to be admitted. Then the doors opened. A handful of readers headed toward my table, but the hordes poured in to line up for Jack.

I had not previously known that Jack Vance was far and away the favorite science fiction writer of the Dutch, more popular than even such stars as Asimov and Clarke. I found it out then and there. When I began to sign the third or fourth book someone had put before me, I noticed that it wasn't mine. "I'm sorry," I said to the woman who owned it, "but this one's by Jack Vance."

She nodded. "Yes, I know," she said, "but his line is too long."

•   •   •

In his eighties, Vance lives in northern California, in a hillside house much of which he built himself. He hasn't stopped writing, but physically it is no longer easy for him. His eyesight began failing long ago, so that he can read, or write, only large letters. He can manage only a few words to a page before he runs out of room and has to turn to the next . . . but, as always, they are very good words, as befit a Grand Master of Science Fiction.

Recommended Reading
by Jack Vance

Big Planet
The Dragon Masters
The Languages of Pao
The Dying Earth
The Complete Magnus Ridolph

SAIL 25

I

Henry Belt came limping into the conference room, mounted the dais, settled himself at the desk. He looked once around the room: a swift bright glance which, focusing nowhere, treated the eight young men who faced him to an almost insulting disinterest. He reached in his pocket, brought forth a pencil and a flat red book, which he placed on the desk. The eight young men watched in absolute silence. They were much alike: healthy, clean, smart, their expressions identically alert and wary. Each had heard legends of Henry Belt, each had formed his private plans and private determinations.

Henry Belt seemed a man of a different species. His face was broad, flat, roped with cartilage and muscle, with skin the color and texture of bacon rind. Coarse white grizzle covered his scalp, his eyes were crafty slits, his nose a misshapen lump. His shoulders were massive, his legs short and gnarled.

"First of all," said Henry Belt, with a gap-toothed grin, "I'll make it clear that I don't expect you to like me. If you do I'll be surprised and displeased. It will mean that I haven't pushed you hard enough."

He leaned back in his chair, surveyed the silent group. "You've heard stories about me. Why haven't they kicked me out of the service? Incorrigible, arrogant, dangerous Henry Belt. Drunken

Henry Belt. (This last, of course, is slander. Henry Belt has never been drunk in his life.) Why do they tolerate me? For one simple reason: out of necessity. No one wants to take on this kind of job. Only a man like Henry Belt can stand up to it: year after year in space, with nothing to look at but a half-dozen round-faced young scrubs. He takes them out, he brings them back. Not all of them, and not all of those who come back are spacemen today. But they'll all cross the street when they see him coming. Henry Belt? you say. They'll turn pale or go red. None of them will smile. Some of them are high placed now. They could kick me loose if they chose. Ask them why they don't. Henry Belt is a terror, they'll tell you. He's wicked, he's a tyrant. Cruel as an ax, fickle as a woman. But a voyage with Henry Belt blows the foam off the beer. He's ruined many a man, he's killed a few, but those that come out of it are proud to say, I trained with Henry Belt!

"Another thing you may hear: Henry Belt has luck. But don't pay any heed. Luck runs out. You'll be my thirteenth class, and that's unlucky. I've taken out seventy-two young sprats, no different from yourselves; I've come back twelve times: which is partly Henry Belt and partly luck. The voyages average about two years long: how can a man stand it? There's only one who could: Henry Belt. I've got more spacetime than any man alive, and now I'll tell you a secret: this is my last time out. I'm starting to wake up at night to strange visions. After this class I'll quit. I hope you lads aren't superstitious. A white-eyed woman told me that I'd die in space. She told me other things and they've all come true. We'll get to know each other well. And you'll be wondering on what basis I make my recommendations. Am I objective and fair? Do I put aside personal animosity? Naturally there won't be any friendship. Well, here's my system. I keep a red book. Here it is. I'll put your names down right now. You, sir?"

"I'm Cadet Lewis Lynch, sir."

"You?"

"Edward Culpepper, sir."

"Marcus Verona, sir."

"Vidal Weske, sir."

"Marvin McGrath, sir."

"Barry Ostrander, sir."

"Clyde von Gluck, sir."

"Joseph Sutton, sir."

Henry Belt wrote the names in the red book. "This is the system. When you do something to annoy me, I mark you down demerits. At the end of the voyage I total these demerits, add a few here and there for luck, and am so guided. I'm sure nothing could be clearer than this. What annoys me? Ah, that's a question which is hard to answer. If you talk too much: demerits. If you're surly and taciturn: demerits. If you slouch and laze and dog the dirty work: demerits. If you're overzealous and forever scuttling about: demerits. Obsequiousness: demerits. Truculence: demerits. If you sing and whistle: demerits. If you're a stolid bloody bore: demerits. You can see that the line is hard to draw. Here's a hint which can save you many marks. I don't like gossip, especially when it concerns myself. I'm a sensitive man, and I open my red book fast when I think I'm being insulted." Henry Belt once more leaned back in his chair. "Any questions?"

No one spoke.

Henry Belt nodded. "Wise. Best not to flaunt your ignorance so early in the game. In response to the thought passing through each of your skulls, I do not think of myself as God. But you may do so, if you choose. And this"—he held up the red book—"you may regard as the Syncretic Compendium. Very well. Any questions?"

"Yes, sir," said Culpepper.

"Speak, sir."

"Any objection to alcoholic beverages aboard ship, sir?"

"For the cadets, yes indeed. I concede that the water must be carried in any event, that the organic compounds present may be reconstituted, but unluckily the bottles weigh far too much."

"I understand, sir."

Henry Belt rose to his feet. "One last word. Have I mentioned that I run a tight ship? When I say jump, I expect every one of you to jump. This is dangerous work, of course. I don't guarantee your safety. Far from it, especially since we are assigned to old Twenty-Five, which should have been broken up long ago. There are eight of you present. Only six cadets will make the voyage. Before the week is over I will make the appropriate notifications. Any more questions? . . . Very well, then. Cheerio." Limping on his thin legs as if his feet hurt, Henry Belt departed into the back passage.

For a moment or two there was silence. Then von Gluck said in a soft voice, "My gracious."

"He's a tyrannical lunatic," grumbled Weske. "I've never heard anything like it! Megalomania!"

"Easy," said Culpepper. "Remember, no gossiping."

"Bah!" muttered McGrath. "This is a free country. I'll damn well say what I like."

Weske rose to his feet. "A wonder somebody hasn't killed him."

"I wouldn't want to try it," said Culpepper. "He looks tough." He made a gesture, stood up, brow furrowed in thought. Then he went to look along the passageway into which Henry Belt had made his departure. There, pressed to the wall, stood Henry Belt. "Yes, sir," said Culpepper suavely. "I forgot to inquire when you wanted us to convene again."

Henry Belt returned to the rostrum. "Now is as good a time as any." He took his seat, opened his red book. "You, Mr. von Gluck, made the remark 'My gracious' in an offensive tone of voice. One demerit. You, Mr. Weske, employed the terms 'tyrannical lunatic' and 'megalomania,' in reference to myself. Three demerits. Mr. McGrath, you observed that freedom of speech is the official doctrine of this country. It is a theory which presently we have no time to explore, but I believe that the statement in its present context carries an overtone of insubordination. One demerit. Mr. Culpepper, your imperturbable complacence irritates me. I prefer that you display more uncertainty, or even uneasiness."

"Sorry, sir."

"However, you took occasion to remind your colleagues of my rule, and so I will not mark you down."

"Thank you, sir."

Henry Belt leaned back in the chair, stared at the ceiling. "Listen closely, as I do not care to repeat myself. Take notes if you wish. Topic: Solar Sails, Theory and Practice Thereof. Material with which you should already be familiar, but which I will repeat in order to avoid ambiguity.

"First, why bother with the sail when nuclear jet-ships are faster, more dependable, more direct, safer and easier to navigate? The answer is threefold. First, a sail is not a bad way to move heavy cargo slowly but cheaply through space. Secondly, the range of the sail is unlimited, since we employ the mechanical pressure of light for thrust, and therefore need carry neither propulsive machinery, material to be ejected, nor energy source. The solar sail is much lighter than its nuclear-powered counterpart, and may carry a larger complement of men in a larger hull. Thirdly, to train a man for space there is no better instrument than the handling of a sail. The computer naturally calculates sail cant and plots the course; in fact, without the computer we'd be dead ducks. Nevertheless the control of a sail provides working familiarity with the cosmic elementals: light, gravity, mass, space.

"There are two types of sail: pure and composite. The first relies on solar energy exclusively, the second carries a secondary power source. We have been assigned Number Twenty-Five, which is the first sort. It consists of a hull, a large parabolic reflector which serves as radar and radio antenna, as well as reflector for the power generator; and the sail itself. The pressure of radiation, of course, is extremely slight—on the order of an ounce per acre at this distance from the sun. Necessarily the sail must be extremely large and extremely light. We use a fluoro-siliconic film a tenth of a mil in gauge, fogged with lithium to the state of opacity. I believe the layer of lithium is about a thousand two hundred molecules thick. Such a foil weighs about four tons to the square mile. It is fitted to a hoop of thin-walled tubing, from which mono-crystalline iron cords lead to the hull.

"We try to achieve a weight factor of six tons to the square mile, which produces an acceleration of between g/one hundred and g/one thousand, depending on proximity to the sun, angle of cant, circumsolar orbital speed, reflectivity of surface. These accelerations seem minute, but calculation shows them to be cumulatively enormous. G/one hundred yields a velocity increment of eight hundred miles per hour every hour, eighteen thousand miles per hour each day, or five miles per second each day. At this rate interplanetary distances are readily negotiable—with proper manipulation of the sail, I need hardly say.

"The virtues of the sail I've mentioned. It is cheap to build and cheap to operate. It requires neither fuel, nor ejectant. As it travels through space, the great area captures various ions, which may be expelled in the plasma jet powered by the parabolic reflector, which adds another increment to the acceleration.

"The disadvantages of the sail are those of the glider or sailing ship, in that we must use natural forces with great precision and delicacy.

"There is no particular limit to the size of the sail. On Twenty-Five we use about four square miles of sail. For the present voyage we will install a new sail, as the old is well worn and eroded.

"That will be all for today."

Once more Henry Belt limped down from the dais and out the passage. On this occasion there were no comments.

2

The eight cadets shared a dormitory, attended classes together, ate at the same table in the mess hall. In various shops and laboratories they assembled, disassembled and reassembled computers, pumps, generators, gyro-platforms, star-trackers, communication gear. "It's not enough to be clever with your hands," said Henry Belt. "Dexterity is not enough. Resourcefulness, creativity, the ability to make successful improvisations—these are more important. We'll test you out." And presently each of the cadets was introduced into a room on the floor of which lay a great heap of mingled housings, wires, flexes, gears, components of a dozen varieties of mechanism. "This is a twenty-six-hour test," said Henry Belt. "Each of you has an identical set of components and supplies. There shall be no exchange of parts or information between you. Those whom I suspect of this fault will be dropped from the class, without recommendation. What I want you to build is, first, one standard Aminex Mark Nine Computer. Second, a servo-mechanism to orient a mass ten kilograms toward Mu Hercules. Why Mu Hercules?"

"Because, sir, the solar system moves in the direction of Mu Hercules, and we thereby avoid parallax error. Negligible though it may be, sir."

"The final comment smacks of frivolity, Mr. McGrath, which serves only to distract the attention of those who are trying to take careful note of my instructions. One demerit."

"Sorry, sir. I merely intended to express my awareness that for many practical purposes such a degree of accuracy is unnecessary."

"That idea, cadet, is sufficiently elemental that it need not be labored. I appreciate brevity and precision."

"Yes, sir."

"Thirdly, from these materials, assemble a communication system, operating on one hundred watts, which will permit two-way conversation between Tycho Base and Phobos, at whatever frequency you deem suitable."

The cadets started in identical fashion by sorting the material into various piles, then calibrating and checking the test instruments.

Achievement thereafter was disparate. Culpepper and von Gluck, diagnosing the test as partly one of mechanical ingenuity and partly ordeal by frustration, failed to become excited when several indispensable components proved either to be missing or inoperative, and carried each project as far as immediately feasible. McGrath and Weske, beginning with the computer, were reduced to rage and random action. Lynch and Sutton worked doggedly at the computer, Verona at the communication system.

Culpepper alone managed to complete one of the instruments, by the process of sawing, polishing and cementing together sections of two broken crystals into a crude, inefficient, but operative maser unit.

The day after this test McGrath and Weske disappeared from the dormitory, whether by their own volition or notification from Henry Belt, no one ever knew.

The test was followed by weekend leave. Cadet Lynch, attending a cocktail party, found himself in conversation with a Lieutenant-Colonel Trenchard, who shook his head pityingly to hear that Lynch was training with Henry Belt.

"I was up with Old Horrors myself. I tell you, it's a miracle we ever got back. Belt was drunk two-thirds of the voyage."

"How does he escape court-martial?" asked Lynch.

"Very simple. All the top men seem to have trained under Henry Belt. Naturally they hate his guts but they all take a perverse pride in the fact. And maybe they hope that someday a cadet will take him apart."

"Have any ever tried?"

"Oh yes. I took a swing at Henry once. I was lucky to escape with a broken collarbone and two sprained ankles. If you come back alive, you'll stand a good chance of reaching the top."

The next evening Henry Belt passed the word. "Next Tuesday morning we go up. We'll be gone several months."

On Tuesday morning the cadets took their places in the angelwagon. Henry Belt presently appeared. The pilot readied for takeoff.

"Hold your hats. On the count . . ." The projectile thrust against the earth, strained, rose, went streaking up into the sky. An hour later the pilot pointed. "There's your boat. Old Twenty-Five. And Thirty-Nine right beside it, just in from space."

Henry Belt stared aghast from the port. "What's been done to the ship? The decoration? The red, the white, the yellow, the checkerboard?"

"Thank some idiot of a landlubber," said the pilot. "The word came to pretty the old boats for a junket of congressmen."

Henry Belt turned to the cadets. "Observe this foolishness. It is the result of vanity and ignorance. We will be occupied several days removing the paint."

They drifted close below the two sails: No. 39 just down from space, spare and polished beside the bedizened structure of No. 25. In 39's exit port a group of men waited, their gear floating at the end of cords.

"Observe those men," said Henry Belt. "They are jaunty. They have been on a pleasant outing around the planet Mars. They are poorly trained. When you gentlemen return you will be haggard and desperate and well trained. Now, gentlemen, clamp your helmets, and we will proceed."

The helmets were secured. Henry Belt's voice came by radio. "Lynch, Ostrander, will remain here to discharge cargo. Verona, Culpepper, von Gluck, Sutton, leap with cords to the ship; ferry across the cargo, stow it in the proper hatches."

Henry Belt took charge of his personal cargo, which consisted of several large cases. He eased them out into space, clipped on lines, thrust them toward 25, leaped after. Pulling himself and the cases to the entrance port he disappeared within.

Discharge of cargo was effected. The crew from 39 transferred to the carrier, which thereupon swung down and away, thrust itself dwindling back toward Earth.

When the cargo had been stowed, the cadets gathered in the wardroom. Henry Belt appeared from the master's cubicle.

"Gentlemen, how do you like the surroundings? Eh, Mr. Culpepper?"

"The hull is commodious, sir. The view is superb."

Henry Belt nodded. "Mr. Lynch? Your impressions?"

"I'm afraid I haven't sorted them out yet, sir."

"I see. You, Mr. Sutton?"

"Space is larger than I imagined it, sir."

"True. Space is unimaginable. A good spaceman must either be larger than space, or he must ignore it. Both difficult. Well, gentlemen, I will make a few comments, then I will retire and enjoy the voyage. Since this is my last time out, I intend to do nothing whatever. The operation of the ship will be completely in your hands. I will merely appear from time to time to beam benevolently about, or alas! to make marks in my red book. Nominally I shall be in command, but you six will enjoy complete control over the ship. If you return us safely to Earth I will make an approving entry in my red book. If you wreck us or fling us into the sun, you will be more unhappy than I, since it is my destiny to die in space. Mr. von Gluck, do I perceive a smirk on your face?"

"No, sir, it is a thoughtful half-smile."

"What is humorous in the concept of my demise, may I ask?"

"It will be a great tragedy, sir. I merely was reflecting upon the contemporary persistence of, well, not exactly superstition, but, let us say, the conviction of a subjective cosmos."

Henry Belt made a notation in the red book. "Whatever is meant by this barbaric jargon I'm sure I don't know, Mr. von Gluck. It is clear that you fancy yourself a philosopher and dialectician. I will not fault this, so long as your remarks conceal no overtones of malice and insolence, to which I am extremely sensitive. Now, as to the persistence of superstition, only an impoverished mind considers itself the repository of absolute knowledge. Hamlet spoke on this subject to Horatio, as I recall, in the well-known work by William Shakespeare. I myself have seen strange and terrifying sights. Were they hallucinations? Were they the manipulation of the cosmos by my mind or the mind of someone—or something—other than myself? I do not know. I therefore counsel a flexible attitude toward matters where the truth is still unknown. For this reason: the impact of an inexplicable experience may well destroy a mind which is too brittle. Do I make myself clear?"

"Perfectly, sir."

"Very good. To return, then. We shall set a system of watches whereby each man works in turn with each of the other five. I thereby hope to discourage the formation of special friendships, or cliques.

"You have inspected the ship. The hull is a sandwich of lithium-beryllium, insulating foam, fiber and an interior skin. Very light, held rigid by air pressure rather than by any innate strength of the material. We can therefore afford enough space to stretch our legs and provide all of us with privacy.

"The master's cubicle is to the left; under no circumstances is anyone permitted in my quarters. If you wish to speak to me, knock on my door. If I appear, good. If I do not appear, go away. To the right are six cubicles which you may now distribute among yourselves by lot.

"Your schedule will be two hours study, four hours on watch, six hours off. I will require no specific rate of study progress, but I recommend that you make good use of your time.

"Our destination is Mars. We will presently construct a new sail, then while orbital velocity builds up, you will carefully test and check all equipment aboard. Each of you will compute sail cant and course and work out among yourselves any discrepancies which may appear. I shall take no hand in navigation. I prefer that you involve me in no disaster. If any such occur I shall severely mark down the persons responsible.

"Singing, whistling, humming, are forbidden. I disapprove of fear and hysteria, and mark accordingly. No one dies more than once; we are well aware of the risks of this, our chosen occupation. There will be no practical jokes. You may fight, so long as you do not disturb me or break any instruments; however, I counsel against it, as it leads to resentment, and I have known cadets to kill each other. I suggest coolness and detachment in your personal relations. Use of the microfilm projector is of course at your own option. You may not use the radio either to dispatch or receive messages. In fact, I have put the radio out of commission, as is my practice. I do this to emphasize the fact that, sink or swim, we must make do with our own resources. Are there any questions? . . . Very good. You will find that if you all behave with scrupulous correctness and accuracy, we shall in due course return safe and sound, with a minimum of demerits and no casualties. I am bound to say, however, that in twelve previous voyages this has failed to occur. Now you select your cubicles, stow your gear. The carrier will bring up the new sail tomorrow, and you will go to work."

3

The carrier discharged a great bundle of three-inch tubing: paper-thin lithium hardened with beryllium, reinforced with filaments of mono-crystalline iron—a total length of eight miles. The cadets fitted the tubes end to end, cementing the joints. When the tube extended a quarter-mile it was bent bow shaped by a cord stretched between two ends, and further sections added. As the process continued the free end curved far out and around, and presently began to veer back in toward the hull. When the last tube was in place the loose end was hauled down, socketed home, to form a great hoop two and a half miles in diameter.

Henry Belt came out occasionally in his spacesuit to look on, and occasionally spoke a few words of sardonic comment, to which the cadets paid little heed. Their mood had changed; this was exhilaration, to be weightlessly afloat above the bright cloud-marked globe, with continent and ocean wheeling massively below. Anything seemed possible, even the training voyage with Henry Belt! When he came out to inspect their work, they grinned at each other with indulgent amusement. Henry Belt suddenly seemed a rather pitiful creature, a poor vagabond suited only for drunken bluster. Fortunate indeed that they were less naïve than Henry Belt's previous classes! They had taken Belt seriously; he had cowed them, reduced them to nervous pulp. Not this crew, not by a long shot! They saw through Henry Belt! Just keep your nose clean, do your work, keep cheerful. The training voyage won't last but a few months, and then real life begins. Gut it out, ignore Henry Belt as much as possible. This is the sensible attitude; the best way to keep on top of the situation.

Already the group had made a composite assessment of its members, arriving at a set of convenient labels. Culpepper: smooth, suave, easy-going. Lynch: excitable, argumentative, hot-tempered. Von Gluck: the artistic temperament, delicate with hands and sensibilities. Ostrander: prissy, finicky, overtidy. Sutton: moody, suspicious, competitive. Verona: the plugger, rough at the edges, but persistent and reliable.

Around the hull swung the gleaming hoop, and now the carrier brought up the sail, a great roll of darkly shining stuff. When unfolded and unrolled, and unfolded many times more, it became a tough gleaming film, flimsy as gold leaf. Unfolded to its fullest extent it was a shimmering disk, already rippling and bulging to the light of the sun. The cadets fitted the film to the hoop, stretched it taut as a drumhead, cemented it in place. Now the sail must carefully be held edge on to the sun, or it would quickly move away, under a thrust of about a hundred pounds.

From the rim, braided-iron threads were led to a ring at the back of the parabolic reflector, dwarfing this as the reflector dwarfed the hull, and now the sail was ready to move.

The carrier brought up a final cargo: water, food, spare parts, a new magazine for the microfilm viewer, mail. Then Henry Belt said, "Make sail."

This was the process of turning the sail to catch the sunlight while the hull moved around Earth away from the sun, canting it parallel to the sun-rays when the ship moved on the sunward leg of its orbit: in short, building up an orbital velocity which in due course would stretch loose the bonds of Terrestrial gravity and send Sail 25 kiting out toward Mars.

During this period the cadets checked every item of equipment aboard the vessel. They grimaced with disgust and dismay at some of the instruments: 25 was an old ship, with antiquated gear. Henry Belt seemed to enjoy their grumbling. "This is a training voyage, not a pleasure cruise. If you wanted your noses wiped, you should have taken a post on the ground. And, I have no sympathy for faultfinders. If you wish a model by which to form your own conduct, observe me."

The moody introspective Sutton, usually the most diffident and laconic of individuals, ventured an ill-advised witticism. "If we modeled ourselves after you, sir, there'd be no room to move for the whiskey."

Out came the red book. "Extraordinary impudence, Mr. Sutton. How can you yield so easily to malice?"

Sutton flushed pink; his eyes glistened, he opened his mouth to speak, then closed it firmly. Henry Belt, waiting politely expectant, turned away. "You gentlemen will perceive that I rigorously obey my own rules of conduct. I am regular as a clock. There is no better, more genial shipmate than Henry Belt. There is not a fairer man alive. Mr. Culpepper, you have a remark to make?"

"Nothing of consequence, sir."

Henry Belt went to the port, glared out at the sail. He swung around instantly. "Who is on watch?"

"Sutton and Ostrander, sir."

"Gentlemen, have you noticed the sail? It has swung about and is canting to show its back to the sun. In another ten minutes we shall be tangled in a hundred miles of guy-wires."

Sutton and Ostrander sprang to repair the situation. Henry Belt shook his head disparagingly. "This is precisely what is meant by the words 'negligence' and 'inattentiveness.' You two have committed a serious error. This is poor spacemanship. The sail must always be in such a position as to hold the wires taut."

"There seems to be something wrong with the sensor, sir," Sutton blurted. "It should notify us when the sail swings behind us."

"I fear I must charge you an additional demerit for making excuses, Mr. Sutton. It is your duty to assure yourself that all the warning devices are functioning properly, at all times. Machinery must never be used as a substitute for vigilance."

Ostrander looked up from the control console. "Someone has turned off the switch, sir. I do not offer this as an excuse, but as an explanation."

"The line of distinction is often hard to define, Mr. Ostrander. Please bear in mind my remarks on the subject of vigilance."

"Yes, sir, but—who turned off the switch?"

"Both you and Mr. Sutton are theoretically hard at work watching for any accident or occurrence. Did you not observe it?"

"No, sir."

"I might almost accuse you of further inattention and neglect, in this case."

Ostrander gave Henry Belt a long, dubious side-glance. "The only person I recall going near the console is yourself, sir. I'm sure you wouldn't do such a thing."

Henry Belt shook his head sadly. "In space you must never rely on anyone for rational conduct. A few moments ago Mr. Sutton unfairly imputed to me an unusual thirst for whiskey. Suppose this were the case? Suppose, as an example of pure irony, that I had indeed been drinking whiskey, that I was in fact drunk?"

"I will agree, sir, that anything is possible."

Henry Belt shook his head again. "That is the type of remark, Mr. Ostrander, that I have come to associate with Mr. Culpepper. A better response would have been, 'In the future, I will try to be ready for any conceivable contingency.' Mr. Sutton, did you make a hissing sound between your teeth?"

"I was breathing, sir."

"Please breathe with less vehemence."

Henry Belt turned away and wandered back and forth about the wardroom, scrutinizing cases, frowning at smudges on polished metal. Ostrander muttered something to Sutton, and both watched Henry Belt closely as he moved here and there. Presently Henry Belt lurched toward them. "You show great interest in my movements, gentlemen."

"We were on the watch for another unlikely contingency, sir."

"Very good, Mr. Ostrander. Stick with it. In space nothing is impossible. I'll vouch for this personally."

4

Henry Belt sent all hands out to remove the paint from the surface of the parabolic reflector. When this had been accomplished, incident sunlight was now focused upon an expanse of photoelectric cells. The power so generated was used to operate plasma jets, expelling ions collected by the vast expanse of sail, further accelerating the ship, thrusting it ever out into an orbit of escape. And finally one day, at an exact instant dictated by the computer, the ship departed from Earth and floated tangentially out into space, off at an angle for the orbit of Mars. At an acceleration of g/100, velocity built up rapidly. Earth dwindled behind; the ship was isolated in space. The cadets' exhilaration vanished, to be replaced by an almost funereal solemnity. The vision of Earth dwindling and retreating is an awesome symbol, equivalent to eternal loss, to the act of dying itself. The more impressionable cadets—Sutton, von Gluck, Ostrander—could not look astern without finding their eyes swimming with tears. Even the suave Culpepper was awed by the magnificence of the spectacle, the sun an aching pit not to be tolerated, Earth a plump pearl rolling on black velvet among a myriad glittering diamonds. And away from Earth, away from the sun, opened an exalted magnificence of another order entirely. For the first time the cadets became dimly aware that Henry Belt had spoken truly of strange visions. Here was death, here was peace, solitude, star-blazing beauty which promised not oblivion in death, but eternity. . . . Streams and spatters of stars. . . . The familiar constellation, the stars with their prideful names presenting themselves like heroes: Achernar, Fomalhaut, Sadal, Suud, Canopus. . . .

Sutton could not bear to look into the sky. "It's not that I feel fear," he told von Gluck, "or yes, perhaps it is fear. It sucks at me, draws me out there. . . . I suppose in due course I'll become accustomed to it."

"I'm not sure," said von Gluck. "I wouldn't be surprised if space could become a psychological addiction, a need—so that whenever you walked on Earth you felt hot and breathless."

Life settled into a routine. Henry Belt no longer seemed a man, but a capricious aspect of nature, like storm or lightning; and like some natural cataclysm, Henry Belt showed no favoritism, nor forgave one jot or tittle of offense. Apart from the private cubicles no place on the ship escaped his attention. Always he reeked of whiskey, and it became a matter of covert speculation as to exactly how much whiskey he had brought aboard. But no matter how he reeked or how he swayed on his feet, his eyes remained clever and steady, and he spoke without slurring in his paradoxically clear sweet voice.

One day he seemed slightly drunker than usual, and ordered all hands into spacesuits and out to inspect the sail for meteoric puncture. The order seemed sufficiently odd that the cadets stared at him in disbelief. "Gentlemen, you hesitate, you fail to exert yourselves, you luxuriate in sloth. Do you fancy yourselves at the Riviera? Into the spacesuits, on the double, and everybody into space. Check hoop, sail, reflector, struts and sensor. You will be adrift for two hours. When you return I want a comprehensive report. Mr. Lynch, I believe you are in charge of this watch. You will present the report."

"Yes, sir."

"One more matter. You will notice that the sail is slightly bellied by the continual radiation pressure. It therefore acts as a focusing device, the focal point presumably occurring behind the cab. But this is not a matter to be taken for granted. I have seen a man burned to death in such a freak accident. Bear this in mind."

For two hours the cadets drifted through space, propelled by tanks of gas and thrust tubes. All enjoyed the experience except Sutton, who found himself appalled by the immensity of his emotions. Probably least affected was the practical Verona, who inspected the sail with a care exacting enough to satisfy even Henry Belt.

The next day the computer went wrong. Ostrander was in charge of the watch and knocked on Henry Belt's door to make the report.

Henry Belt appeared in the doorway. He apparently had been asleep. "What is the difficulty, Mr. Ostrander?"

"We're in trouble, sir. The computer has gone out."

Henry Belt rubbed his grizzled pate. "This is not an unusual circumstance. We prepare for this contingency by schooling all cadets thoroughly in computer design and repair. Have you identified the difficulty?"

"The bearings which suspend the data-separation disks have broken. The shaft has several millimeters play and as a result there is total confusion in the data presented to the analyzer."

"An interesting problem. Why do you present it to me?"

"I thought you should be notified, sir. I don't believe we carry spares for this particular bearing."

Henry Belt shook his head sadly. "Mr. Ostrander, do you recall my statement at the beginning of this voyage, that you six gentlemen are totally responsible for the navigation of the ship?"

"Yes, sir. But—"

"This is an applicable situation. You must either repair the computer, or perform the calculations yourself."

"Very well, sir. I will do my best."

5

Lynch, Verona, Ostrander and Sutton disassembled the mechanism, removed the worn bearing. "Confounded antique!" said Lynch. "Why can't they give us decent equipment? Or if they want to kill us, why not shoot us and save us all trouble."

"We're not dead yet," said Verona. "You've looked for a spare?"

"Naturally. There's nothing remotely like this."

Verona looked at the bearing dubiously. "I suppose we could cast a babbitt sleeve and machine it to fit. That's what we'll have to do— unless you fellows are awfully fast with your math."

Sutton glanced out the port, quickly turned his eyes away. "I wonder if we should cut sail."

"Why?" asked Ostrander.

"We don't want to build up too much velocity. We're already going thirty miles a second."

"Mars is a long way off."

"And if we miss, we go shooting past. Then where are we?"

"Sutton, you're a pessimist. A shame to find morbid tendencies in one so young." This from von Gluck.

"I'd rather be a live pessimist than a dead comedian."

The new sleeve was duly cast, machined and fitted. Anxiously the alignment of the data disks was checked. "Well," said Verona doubtfully, "there's wobble. How much that affects the functioning remains to be seen. We can take some of it out by shimming the mount. . . ."

Chims of tissue paper were inserted and the wobble seemed to be reduced. "Now—feed in the data," said Sutton. "Let's see how we stand."

Coordinates were fed into the system; the indicator swung. "Enlarge sail cant four degrees," said von Gluck; "we're making too much left concentric. Projected course. . . ." He tapped buttons, watched the bright line extend across the screen, swing around a dot representing the center of gravity of Mars. "I make it an elliptical pass, about twenty thousand miles out. That's at present acceleration, and it should toss us right back at Earth."

"Great. Simply great. Let's go, Twenty-Five!" This was Lynch. "I've heard of guys dropping flat on their faces and kissing Earth when they put down. Me, I'm going to live in a cave the rest of my life."

Sutton went to look at the data disks. The wobble was slight but perceptible. "Good Lord," he said huskily. "The other end of the shaft is loose too."

Lynch started to spit curses; Verona's shoulders slumped. "Let's get to work and fix it."

Another bearing was cast, machined, polished, mounted. The disks wobbled, scraped. Mars, an ocher disk, shouldered ever closer in from the side. With the computer unreliable the cadets calculated and plotted the course manually. The results were at slight but significant variance with those of the computer. The cadets looked dourly at each other. "Well," growled Ostrander, "there's error. Is it the instruments? The calculation? The plotting? Or the computer?"

Culpepper said in a subdued voice, "Well, we're not about to crash head-on at any rate."

Verona went back to study the computer. "I can't imagine why the bearings don't work better. . . . The mounting brackets—could they have shifted?" He removed the side housing, studied the frame, then went to the case for tools.

"What are you going to do?" demanded Sutton.

"Try to ease the mounting brackets around. I think that's our trouble."

"Leave me alone! You'll bugger the machine so it'll never work."

Verona paused, looked questioningly around the group. "Well? What's the verdict?"

"Maybe we'd better check with the old man," said Ostrander nervously.

"All well and good—but you know what he'll say."

"Let's deal cards. Ace of spades goes to ask him."

Culpepper received the ace. He knocked on Henry Belt's door. There was no response. He started to knock again, but restrained himself.

He returned to the group. "Wait till he shows himself. I'd rather crash into Mars than bring forth Henry Belt and his red book."

The ship crossed the orbit of Mars well ahead of the looming red planet. It came toppling at them with a peculiar clumsy grandeur, a mass obviously bulky and globular, but so fine and clear was the detail, so absent the perspective, that the distance and size might have been anything. Instead of swinging in a sharp elliptical curve back toward Earth, the ship swerved aside in a blunt hyperbola and proceeded outward, now at a velocity of close to fifty miles a second. Mars receded astern and to the side. A new part of space lay ahead. The sun was noticeably smaller. Earth could no longer be differentiated from the stars. Mars departed quickly and politely, and space seemed lonely and forlorn.

Henry Belt had not appeared for two days. At last Culpepper went to knock on the door—once, twice, three times: a strange face looked out. It was Henry Belt, face haggard, skin like pulled taffy. His eyes glared red, his hair seemed matted and more unkempt than hair a quarter-inch should be. But he spoke in his quiet clear voice.

"Mr. Culpepper, your merciless din has disturbed me. I am quite put out with you."

"Sorry, sir. We feared that you were ill."

Henry Belt made no response. He looked past Culpepper, around the circle of faces. "You gentlemen are unwontedly serious. Has this presumptive illness of mine caused you all distress?"

Sutton spoke in a rush. "The computer is out of order."

"Why then, you must repair it."

"It's a matter of altering the housing. If we do it incorrectly—"

"Mr. Sutton, please do not harass me with the hour-by-hour minutiae of running the ship."

"But, sir, the matter has become serious; we need your advice. We missed the Mars turn-around—"

"Well, I suppose there's always Jupiter. Must I explain the basic elements of astrogation to you?"

"But the computer's out of order—definitely."

"Then, if you wish to return to Earth, you must perform the calculations with pencil and paper. Why is it necessary to explain the obvious?"

"Jupiter is a long way out," said Sutton in a shrill voice. "Why can't we just turn around and go home?" This last was almost a whisper.

"I see I've been too easy on you cads," said Henry Belt. "You stand around idly; you chatter nonsense while the machinery goes to pieces and the ship flies at random. Everybody into spacesuits for sail inspection. Come now. Let's have some snap. What are you all? Walking corpses? You, Mr. Culpepper, why the delay?"

"It occurred to me, sir, that we are approaching the asteroid belt. As I am chief of the watch, I consider it my duty to cant sail to swing us around the area."

"You may do this; then join the rest in hull-and-sail inspection."

"Yes, sir."

The cadets donned spacesuits, Sutton with the utmost reluctance. Out into the dark void they went, and now here was loneliness indeed.

When they returned, Henry Belt had returned to his compartment.

"As Mr. Belt points out, we have no great choice," said Ostrander. "We missed Mars, so let's hit Jupiter. Luckily it's in good position—otherwise we'd have to swing out to Saturn or Uranus—"

"They're off behind the sun," said Lynch. "Jupiter's our last chance."

"Let's do it right then. I say, let's make one last attempt to set those confounded bearings. . . ."

But now it seemed as if the wobble and twist had been eliminated. The disks tracked perfectly, the accuracy monitor glowed green.

"Great!" yelled Lynch. "Feed it the dope. Let's get going! All sail for Jupiter. Good Lord, but we're having a trip!"

"Wait till it's over," said Sutton. Since his return from sail inspection he had stood to one side, cheeks pinched, eyes staring. "It's not over yet. And maybe it's not meant to be."

The other five pretended not to have heard him. The computer spat out figures and angles. There was a billion miles to travel. Acceleration was less, due to the diminution in the intensity of sunlight. At least a month must pass before Jupiter came close.

6

The ship, great sail spread to the fading sunlight, fled like a ghost—out, always out. Each of the cadets had quietly performed the same calculation, and arrived at the same result. If the swing around Jupiter were not performed with exactitude, if the ship were not slung back like a stone on a string, there was nothing beyond. Saturn, Uranus, Neptune, Pluto were far around the sun; the ship, speeding at a hundred miles a second, could not be halted by the waning gravity of the sun, nor yet sufficiently accelerated in a concentric direction by sail and jet into a true orbit. The very nature of the sail made it useless as a brake; always the thrust was outward. Within the hull seven men lived and thought, and the psychic relationship worked and stirred like yeast in a vat of decaying fruit. The fundamental similarity, the human identity of the seven men, was utterly canceled; apparent only were the disparities. Each cadet appeared to others only as a walking characteristic, and Henry Belt was an incomprehensible Thing, who appeared from his compartment at unpredictable times, to move quietly here and there with the blind blank grin of an archaic Attic hero.

Jupiter loomed and bulked. The ship, at last within reach of the

Jovian gravity, sidled over to meet it. The cadets gave ever more careful attention to the computer, checking and counter-checking the instructions. Verona was the most assiduous at this, Sutton the most harassed and ineffectual. Lynch growled and cursed and sweat; Ostrander complained in a thin peevish voice. Von Gluck worked with the calm of pessimistic fatalism; Culpepper seemed unconcerned, almost debonair, a blandness which bewildered Ostrander, infuriated Lynch, awoke a malignant hate in Sutton. Verona and von Gluck on the other hand seemed to derive strength and refreshment from Culpepper's placid acceptance of the situation. Henry Belt said nothing. Occasionally he emerged from his compartment, to survey the wardroom and the cadets with the detached interest of a visitor to an asylum.

It was Lynch who made the discovery. He signaled it with an odd growl of sheer dismay, which brought a resonant questioning sound from Sutton. "My God, my God," muttered Lynch.

Verona was at his side. "What's the trouble?"

"Look. This gear. When we replaced the disks we dephased the whole apparatus one notch. This white dot and this other white dot should synchronize. They're one sprocket apart. All the results would check and be consistent because they'd all be off by the same factor."

Verona sprang into action. Off came the housing, off came various components. Gently he lifted the gear, set it back into correct alignment. The other cadets leaned over him as he worked, except Culpepper, who was chief of the watch.

Henry Belt appeared. "You gentlemen are certainly diligent in your navigation," he said presently. "Perfectionists almost."

"We do our best," grated Lynch between set teeth. "It's a damn shame sending us out with a machine like this."

The red book appeared. "Mr. Lynch, I mark you down not for your private sentiments, which are of course yours to entertain, but for voicing them and thereby contributing to an unhealthy atmosphere of despairing and hysterical pessimism."

A tide of red crept from Lynch's neck. He bent over the computer, made no comment. But Sutton suddenly cried out, "What else do you expect from us? We came out here to learn, not to suffer, or to fly on forever!" He gave a ghastly laugh. Henry Belt listened patiently. "Think of it!" cried Sutton. "The seven of us. In this capsule, forever!"

"I am afraid that I must charge you two demerits for your outburst, Mr. Sutton. A good spaceman maintains his dignity at all costs."

Lynch looked up from the computer. "Well, now we've got a corrected reading. Do you know what it says?"

Henry Belt turned him a look of polite inquiry.

"We're going to miss," said Lynch. "We're going to pass by just as we passed Mars. Jupiter is pulling us around and sending us out toward Gemini."

The silence was thick in the room. Henry Belt turned to look at Culpepper, who was standing by the porthole, photographing Jupiter with his personal camera.

"Mr. Culpepper?"

"Yes, sir."

"You seem unconcerned by the prospect which Mr. Sutton has set forth."

"I hope it's not imminent."

"How do you propose to avoid it?"

"I imagine that we will radio for help, sir."

"You forget that I have destroyed the radio."

"I remember noting a crate marked 'Radio Parts' stored in the starboard jet-pod."

"I am sorry to disillusion you, Mr. Culpepper. That case is mislabeled."

Ostrander jumped to his feet, left the wardroom. There was the sound of moving crates. A moment of silence. Then he returned. He glared at Henry Belt. "Whiskey, bottles of whiskey."

Henry Belt nodded. "I told you as much."

"But now we have no radio," said Lynch in an ugly voice.

"We never have had a radio, Mr. Lynch. You were warned that you would have to depend on your own resources to bring us home. You have failed, and in the process doomed me as well as yourself. Incidentally, I must mark you all down ten demerits for a faulty cargo check."

"Demerits," said Ostrander in a bleak voice.

"Now, Mr. Culpepper," said Henry Belt. "What is your next proposal?"

"I don't know, sir."

Verona spoke in a placatory voice. "What would you do, sir, if you were in our position?"

Henry Belt shook his head. "I am an imaginative man, Mr. Verona, but there are certain leaps of the mind which are beyond my powers." He returned to his compartment.

Von Gluck looked curiously at Culpepper. "It is a fact. You're not at all concerned."

"Oh, I'm concerned. But I believe that Mr. Belt wants to get home too. He's too good a spaceman not to know exactly what he's doing."

The door from Henry Belt's compartment slid back. Henry Belt stood in the opening. "Mr. Culpepper, I chanced to overhear your remark, and I now note down ten demerits against you. This attitude expresses a complacence as dangerous as Mr. Sutton's utter funk." He looked about the room. "Pay no heed to Mr. Culpepper. He is wrong. Even if I could repair this disaster, I would not raise a hand. For I expect to die in space."

7

The sail was canted vectorless, edgewise to the sun. Jupiter was a smudge astern. There were five cadets in the wardroom. Culpepper, Verona, and von Gluck sat talking in low voices. Ostrander and Lynch lay crouched, arms to knees, faces to the wall. Sutton had gone two days before. Quietly donning his spacesuit he had stepped into the exit chamber and thrust himself headlong into space. A propulsion unit gave him added speed, and before any of the cadets could intervene he was gone.

Shortly thereafter Lynch and Ostrander succumbed to inanition, a kind of despondent helplessness: manic-depression in its most stupefying phase. Culpepper the suave, Verona the pragmatic and von Gluck the sensitive remained.

They spoke quietly to themselves, out of earshot of Henry Belt's room. "I still believe," said Culpepper, "that somehow there is a means to get ourselves out of this mess, and that Henry Belt knows it."

Verona said, "I wish I could think so. . . . We've been over it a hundred times. If we set sail for Saturn or Neptune or Uranus, the outward vector of thrust plus the outward vector of our momentum will take us far beyond Pluto before we're anywhere near a trajectory of control. The plasma jets could stop us if we had enough energy, but the shield can't supply it and we don't have another power source. . . ."

Von Gluck hit his fist into his hand. "Gentlemen," he said in a soft, delighted voice. "I believe we have sufficient energy at hand. We will use the sail. Remember? It is bellied. It can function as a mirror. It spreads five square miles of surface. Sunlight out here is thin—but so long as we collect enough of it—"

"I understand!" said Culpepper. "We back off the hull till the reactor is at the focus of the sail and turn on the jets!"

Verona said dubiously, "We'll still be receiving radiation pressure. And what's worse, the jets will impinge back on the sail. Effect—cancellation. We'll be nowhere."

"If we cut the center out of the sail—just enough to allow the plasma through—we'd beat that objection. As for the radiation pressure—we'll surely do better with the plasma drive."

"What do we use to make plasma? We don't have the stock."

"Anything that can be ionized. The radio, the computer, your shoes, my shirt, Culpepper's camera, Henry Belt's whiskey. . . ."

<h1 style="text-align:center">8</h1>

The angel-wagon came up to meet Sail 25, in orbit beside Sail 40, which was just making ready to take out a new crew.

The cargo carrier drifted near, eased into position. Three men sprang across space to Sail 40, a few hundred yards behind 25, tossed lines back to the carrier, pulled bales of cargo and equipment across the gap.

The five cadets and Henry Belt, clad in spacesuits, stepped out into the sunlight. Earth spread below, green and blue, white and brown, the contours so precious and dear to bring tears to the eyes. The cadets transferring cargo to Sail 40 gazed at them curiously as they worked. At last they were finished, and the six men of Sail 25 boarded the carrier.

"Back safe and sound, eh Henry?" said the pilot. "Well, I'm always surprised."

Henry Belt made no answer. The cadets stowed their cargo, and standing by the port, took a final look at Sail 25. The carrier retro-jetted; the two sails seemed to rise above them.

The lighter nosed in and out of the atmosphere, braked, extended its wings, glided to an easy landing on the Mojave Desert.

The cadets, their legs suddenly loose and weak to the unaccustomed gravity, limped after Henry Belt to the carry-all, seated themselves and were conveyed to the administration complex. They alighted from the carry-all, and now Henry Belt motioned the five to the side.

"Here, gentlemen, is where I leave you. Tonight I will check my red book and prepare my official report. But I believe I can present you an unofficial résumé of my impressions. Mr. Lynch and Mr. Ostrander, I feel that you are ill suited either for command or for any situation which might inflict prolonged emotional pressure upon you. I cannot recommend you for space-duty.

"Mr. von Gluck, Mr. Culpepper and Mr. Verona, all of you meet my minimum requirements for a recommendation, although I shall write the words 'Especially Recommended' only beside the names Clyde von Gluck and Marcus Verona. You brought the sail back to Earth by essentially faultless navigation.

"So now our association ends. I trust you have profited by it." Henry Belt nodded briefly to each of the five and limped off around the building.

The cadets looked after him. Culpepper reached in his pocket and brought forth a pair of small metal objects which he displayed in his palm. "Recognize these?"

"Hmf," said Lynch in a flat voice. "Bearings for the computer disks. The original ones."

"I found them in the little spare parts tray. They weren't there before."

Von Gluck nodded. "The machinery always seemed to fail immediately after sail check, as I recall."

Lynch drew in his breath with a sharp hiss. He turned, strode away. Ostrander followed him. Culpepper shrugged. To Verona he gave one of the bearings, to von Gluck the other. "For souvenirs— or medals. You fellows deserve them."

"Thanks, Ed," said von Gluck.

"Thanks," muttered Verona. "I'll make a stickpin of this thing."

The three, not able to look at each other, glanced up into the sky where the first stars of twilight were appearing, then continued on into the building where family and friends and sweethearts awaited them.

ULLWARD'S RETREAT

Bruham Ullward had invited three friends to lunch at his ranch: Ted and Ravelin Seehoe, and their adolescent daughter Iugenae. After an eye-bulging feast, Ullward offered around a tray of the digestive pastilles which had won him his wealth.

"A wonderful meal," said Ted Seehoe reverently. "Too much, really. I'll need one of these. The algae was absolutely marvelous."

Ullward made a smiling easy gesture. "It's the genuine stuff."

Ravelin Seehoe, a fresh-faced, rather positive young woman of eighty or ninety, reached for a pastille. "A shame there's not more of it. The synthetic we get is hardly recognizable as algae."

"It's a problem," Ullward admitted. "I clubbed up with some friends; we bought a little mat in the Ross Sea and grow all our own."

"Think of that!" exclaimed Ravelin. "Isn't it frightfully expensive?"

Ullward pursed his lips whimsically. "The good things in life come high. Luckily, I'm able to afford a bit extra."

"What I keep telling Ted—" began Ravelin, then stopped as Ted turned her a keen warning glance.

Ullward bridged the rift. "Money isn't everything. I have a flat of algae, my ranch; you have your daughter—and I'm sure you wouldn't trade."

Ravelin regarded Iugenae critically. "I'm not so sure."

Ted patted Iugenae's hand. "When do you have your own child, Lamster Ullward?" (*Lamster: contraction of Landmaster—the polite form of address in current use.*)

"Still some time yet. I'm thirty-seven billion down the list."

"A pity," said Ravelin Seehoe brightly, "when you could give a child so many advantages."

"Someday, someday, before I'm too old."

"A shame," said Ravelin, "but it has to be. Another fifty billion people and we'd have no privacy whatever!" She looked admiringly around the room, which was used for the sole purpose of preparing food and dining.

Ullward put his hands on the arms of his chair, hitched forward a little. "Perhaps you'd like to look around the ranch?" He spoke in a casual voice, glancing from one to the other.

Iugenae clapped her hands; Ravelin beamed. "If it wouldn't be too much trouble!" "Oh, we'd love to, Lamster Ullward!" cried Iugenae. "I've always wanted to see your ranch," said Ted. "I've heard so much about it."

"It's an opportunity for Iugenae I wouldn't want her to miss," said Ravelin. She shook her finger at Iugenae. "Remember, Miss Puss, notice everything very carefully—and don't *touch*!"

"May I take pictures, Mother?"

"You'll have to ask Lamster Ullward."

"Of course, of course," said Ullward. "Why in the world not?" He rose to his feet—a man of more than middle stature, more than middle pudginess, with straight sandy hair, round blue eyes, a prominent beak of a nose. Almost three hundred years old, he guarded his health with great zeal, and looked little more than two hundred.

He stepped to the door, checked the time, touched a dial on the wall. "Are you ready?"

"Yes, we're quite ready," said Ravelin.

Ullward snapped back the wall, to reveal a view over a sylvan glade. A fine oak tree shaded a pond growing with rushes. A path led through a field toward a wooded valley a mile in the distance.

"Magnificent," said Ted. "Simply magnificent!"

They stepped outdoors into the sunlight. Iugenae flung her arms out, twirled, danced in a circle. "Look! I'm all alone! I'm out here all by myself!"

"Iugenae!" called Ravelin sharply. "Be careful! Stay on the path! That's real grass and you mustn't damage it."

Iugenae ran ahead to the pond. "Mother!" she called back. "Look at these funny little jumpy things! And look at the flowers!"

"The animals are frogs," said Ullward. "They have a very interesting life-history. You see the little fishlike things in the water?"

"Aren't they funny! Mother, do come here!"

"Those are called tadpoles and they will presently become frogs, indistinguishable from the ones you see."

Ravelin and Ted advanced with more dignity, but were as interested as Iugenae in the frogs.

"Smell the fresh air," Ted told Ravelin. "You'd think you were back in the early times."

"It's absolutely exquisite," said Ravelin. She looked around her. "One has the feeling of being able to wander on and on and on."

"Come around over here," called Ullward from beyond the pool. "This is the rock garden."

In awe, the guests stared at the ledge of rock, stained with red and yellow lichen, tufted with green moss. Ferns grew from a crevice; there were several fragile clusters of white flowers.

"Smell the flowers, if you wish," Ullward told Iugenae. "But please don't touch them; they stain rather easily."

Iugenae sniffed. "Mmmm!"

"Are they real?" asked Ted.

"The moss, yes. That clump of ferns and these little succulents are real. The flowers were designed for me by a horticulturist and are exact replicas of certain ancient species. We've actually improved on the odor."

"Wonderful, wonderful," said Ted.

"Now come this way—no, don't look back; I want you to get the total effect. . . ." An expression of vexation crossed his face.

"What's the trouble?" asked Ted.

"It's a damned nuisance," said Ullward. "Hear that sound?"

Ted became aware of a faint rolling rumble, deep and almost unheard. "Yes. Sounds like some sort of factory."

"It is. On the floor below. A rug-works. One of the looms creates this terrible row. I've complained, but they pay no attention. . . . Oh, well, ignore it. Now stand over here—look around!"

His friends gasped in rapture. The view from this angle was a rustic bungalow in an Alpine valley, the door being the opening into Ullward's dining room.

"What an illusion of distance!" exclaimed Ravelin. "A person would almost think he was alone."

"A beautiful piece of work," said Ted. "I'd swear I was looking into ten miles—at least five miles—of distance."

"I've got a lot of space here," said Ullward proudly. "Almost three-quarters of an acre. Would you like to see it by moonlight?"

"Oh, could we?"

Ullward went to a concealed switch-panel; the sun seemed to race across the sky. A fervent glow of sunset lighted the valley; the sky burned peacock blue, gold, green, then came twilight—and the rising full moon came up behind the hill.

"This is absolutely marvelous," said Ravelin softly. "How can you bring yourself to leave it?"

"It's hard," admitted Ullward. "But I've got to look after business too. More money, more space."

He turned a knob; the moon floated across the sky, sank. Stars appeared, forming the age-old patterns. Ullward pointed out the constellations and the first-magnitude stars by name, using a pencil-torch for a pointer. Then the sky flushed with lavender and lemon-yellow and the sun appeared once more. Unseen ducts sent a current of cool air through the glade.

"Right now I'm negotiating for an area behind this wall here." He tapped at the depicted mountainside, an illusion given reality and three-dimensionality by laminations inside the pane. "It's quite a large area—over a hundred square feet. The owner wants a fortune, naturally."

"I'm surprised he wants to sell," said Ted. "A hundred square feet means real privacy."

"There's been a death in the family," explained Ullward. "The owner's four-great-grandfather passed on and the space is temporarily surplus."

Ted nodded. "I hope you're able to get it."

"I hope so too. I've got rather flamboyant ambitions—eventually I hope to own the entire quarterblock—but it takes time. People don't like to sell their space and everyone is anxious to buy."

"Not we," said Ravelin cheerfully. "We have our little home. We're snug and cozy and we're putting money aside for investment."

"Wise," agreed Ullward. "A great many people are space-poor. Then when a chance to make real money comes up, they're undercapitalized. Until I scored with the digestive pastilles, I lived in a single rented locker. I was cramped—but I don't regret it today."

They returned through the glade toward Ullward's house, stopping at the oak tree. "This is my special pride," said Ullward. "A genuine oak tree!"

"Genuine?" asked Ted in astonishment. "I assumed it was simulated."

"So many people do," said Ullward. "No, it's genuine."

"Take a picture of the tree, Iugenae, please. But don't touch it. You might damage the bark."

"Perfectly all right to touch the bark," assured Ullward. He looked up into the branches, then scanned the ground. He stooped, picked up a fallen leaf. "This grew on the tree," he said. "Now, Iugenae, I want you to come with me." He went to the rock garden, pulled a simulated rock aside, to reveal a cabinet with washbasin. "Watch carefully." He showed her the leaf. "Notice? It's dry and brittle and brown."

"Yes, Lamster Ullward." Iugenae craned her neck.

"First I dip it in this solution." He took a beaker full of dark liquid from a shelf. "So. That restores the green color. We wash off the excess, then dry it. Now we rub this next fluid carefully into the surface. Notice, it's flexible and strong now. One more solution—a plastic coating—and there we are, a true oak leaf, perfectly genuine. It's yours."

"Oh, Lamster Ullward! Thank you ever so much!" She ran off to show her father and mother, who were standing by the pool, luxuriating in the feeling of space, watching the frogs. "See what Lamster Ullward gave me!"

"You be very careful with it," said Ravelin. "When we get home, we'll find a nice little frame and you can hang it in your locker."

The simulated sun hung in the western sky. Ullward led the group to a sundial. "An antique, countless years old. Pure marble, carved by hand. It works too—entirely functional. Notice. Three-fifteen by the shadow on the dial. . . ." He peered at his beltwatch, squinted at the sun. "Excuse me one moment." He ran to the control board, made an adjustment. The sun lurched ten degrees across the sky. Ullward returned, checked the sundial. "That's better. Notice. Three-fifty by the sundial, three-fifty by my watch. Isn't that something now?"

"It's wonderful," said Ravelin earnestly.

"It's the loveliest thing I've ever seen," chirped Iugenae.

Ravelin looked around the ranch, sighed wistfully. "We hate to leave, but I think we must be returning home."

"It's been a wonderful day, Lamster Ullward," said Ted. "A wonderful lunch, and we enjoyed seeing your ranch."

"You'll have to come out again," invited Ullward. "I always enjoy company."

He led them into the dining room, through the living room-bedroom to the door. The Seehoe family took a last look across the spacious interior, pulled on their mantles, stepped into their runshoes, made their farewells. Ullward slid back the door. The Seehoes looked out, waited till a gap appeared in the traffic. They waved good-bye, pulled the hoods over their heads, stepped out into the corridor.

The runshoes spun them toward their home, selecting the appropriate turnings, sliding automatically into the correct lift- and drop-pits. Deflection fields twisted them through the throngs. Like the Seehoes, everyone wore mantle and hood of filmy reflective stuff to safeguard privacy. The illusion-pane along the ceiling of the corridor presented a view of towers dwindling up into a cheerful blue sky, as if the pedestrian were moving along one of the windy upper passages.

The Seehoes approached their home. Two hundred yards away, they angled over to the wall. If the flow of traffic carried them past, they would be forced to circle the block and make another attempt to enter. Their door slid open as they spun near; they ducked into the opening, swinging around on a metal grab-bar.

They removed their mantles and runshoes, sliding skillfully past each other. Iugenae pivoted into the bathroom and there was room for both Ted and Ravelin to sit down. The house was rather small for the three of them; they could well have used another twelve square feet, but rather than pay exorbitant rent, they preferred to save the money with an eye toward Iugenae's future.

Ted sighed in satisfaction, stretching his legs luxuriously under Ravelin's chair. "Ullward's ranch notwithstanding, it's nice to be home."

Iugenae backed out of the bathroom.

Ravelin looked up. "It's time for your pill, dear."

Iugenae screwed up her face. "Oh, Mama! Why do I have to take pills? I feel perfectly well."

"They're good for you, dear."

Iugenae sullenly took a pill from the dispenser. "Runy says you make us take pills to keep us from growing up."

Ted and Ravelin exchanged glances.

"Just take your pill," said Ravelin, "and never mind what Runy says."

"But how is it that I'm thirty-eight and Ermara Burk's only thirty-two; and she's got a figure and I'm like a slat?"

"No arguments, dear. Take your pill."

Ted jumped to his feet. "Here, Babykin, sit down."

Iugenae protested, but Ted held up his hand. "I'll sit in the niche. I've got a few calls that I have to make."

He sidled past Ravelin, seated himself in the niche in front of the communication screen. The illusion-pane behind him was custom-built—Ravelin, in fact, had designed it herself. It simulated a merry little bandit's den, the walls draped in red and yellow silk, a bowl of fruit on the rustic table, a guitar on the bench, a copper teakettle simmering on the countertop stove. The pane had been rather expensive, but when anyone communicated with the Seehoes, it was the first thing they saw, and here the house-proud Ravelin had refused to stint.

Before Ted could make his call, the signal light flashed. He answered; the screen opened to display his friend Loren Aigle, apparently sitting in an airy arched rotunda, against a background of fleecy clouds—an illusion which Ravelin had instantly recognized as an inexpensive stock effect.

Loren and Elme, his wife, were anxious to hear of the Seehoe's visit to the Ullward ranch. Ted described the afternoon in detail.

"Space, space and more space! Isolation pure and simple! Absolute privacy! You can hardly imagine it! A fortune in illusion-panes."

"Nice," said Loren Aigle. "I'll tell you one you'll find hard to believe. Today I registered a whole planet to a man." Loren worked in the Certification Bureau of the Extraterrestrial Properties Agency.

Ted was puzzled and uncomprehending. "A whole planet? How so?"

Loren explained. "He's a free-lance spaceman. Still a few left."

"But what's he planning to do with an entire planet?"

"Live there, he claims."

"Alone?"

Loren nodded. "I had quite a chat with him. Earth is all very well, he says, but he prefers the privacy of his own planet. Can you imagine that?"

"Frankly, no! I can't imagine the fourth dimension either. What a marvel, though!"

The conversation ended and the screen faded. Ted swung around to his wife. "Did you hear that?"

Ravelin nodded; she had heard but not heeded. She was reading the menu supplied by the catering firm to which they subscribed. "We won't want anything heavy after that lunch. They've got simulated synthetic algae again."

Ted grunted. "It's never as good as the genuine synthetic."

"But it's cheaper and we've all had an enormous lunch."

"Don't worry about me, Mom!" sang Iugenae. "I'm going out with Runy."

"Oh, you are, are you? And where are you going, may I ask?"

"A ride around the world. We're catching the seven o'clock shuttle, so I've got to hurry."

"Come right home afterward," said Ravelin severely. "Don't go anywhere else."

"For heaven's sake, Mother, you'd think I was going to elope or something."

"Mind what I say, Miss Puss. I was a girl once myself. Have you taken your medicine?"

"Yes, I've taken my medicine."

Iugenae departed; Ted slipped back into the niche. "Who are you calling now?" asked Ravelin.

"Lamster Ullward. I want to thank him for going to so much trouble for us."

Ravelin agreed that an algae-and-margarine call was no more than polite.

Ted called, expressed his thanks, then—almost as an afterthought—chanced to mention the man who owned a planet.

"An entire planet?" inquired Ullward. "It must be inhabited."

"No, I understand not, Lamster Ullward. Think of it! Think of the privacy!"

"Privacy!" exclaimed Ullward bluffly. "My dear fellow, what do you call this?"

"Oh, naturally, Lamster Ullward—you have a real showplace."

"The planet must be very primitive," Ullward reflected. "An engaging idea, of course—if you like that kind of thing. Who is this man?"

"I don't know, Lamster Ullward. I could find out, if you like."

"No, no, don't bother. I'm not particularly interested. Just an idle thought." Ullward laughed his hearty laugh. "Poor man. Probably lives in a dome."

"That's possible, of course, Lamster Ullward. Well, thanks again, and good night."

The spaceman's name was Kennes Mail. He was short and thin, tough as synthetic herring, brown as toasted yeast. He had a close-cropped pad of gray hair, a keen, if ingenuous, blue gaze. He showed a courteous interest in Ullward's ranch, but Ullward thought his recurrent use of the word "clever" rather tactless.

As they returned to the house, Ullward paused to admire his oak tree.

"It's absolutely genuine, Lamster Mail! A living tree, survival of past ages! Do you have trees as fine as that on your planet?"

Kennes Mail smiled. "Lamster Ullward, that's just a shrub. Let's sit somewhere and I'll show you photographs."

Ullward had already mentioned his interest in acquiring extra-terrestrial property; Mail, admitting that he needed money, had given him to understand that some sort of deal might be arranged. They sat at a table; Mail opened his case. Ullward switched on the wall-screen.

"First I'll show you a map," said Mail. He selected a rod, dropped it into the table socket. On the wall appeared a world projection: oceans, an enormous equatorial landmass named Gaea; the smaller subcontinents Atalanta, Persephone, Alcyone. A box of descriptive information read:

MAIL'S PLANET
Claim registered and endorsed at Extraterrestrial Properties Agency

Surface area:	.87 Earth normal
Gravity:	.93 Earth normal
Diurnal rotation:	22.15 Earth hours
Annual revolution:	2.97 Earth years
Atmosphere:	Invigorating
Climate:	Salubrious
Noxious conditions and influences:	None
Population:	1

Mail pointed to a spot on the eastern shore of Gaea. "I live here. Just got a rough camp at present. I need money to do a bit better for myself. I'm willing to lease off one of the smaller continents, or, if you prefer, a section of Gaea, say from Murky Mountains west to the ocean."

Ullward, with a cheerful smile, shook his head. "No sections for me, Lamster Mail. I want to buy the world outright. You set your price; if it's within reason, I'll write a check."

Mail glanced at him sidewise. "You haven't even seen the photographs."

"True." In a businesslike voice, Ullward said, "By all means, the photographs."

Mail touched the projection button. Landscapes of an unfamiliar wild beauty appeared on the screen. There were mountain crags and roaring rivers, snow-powdered forests, ocean dawns and prairie sunsets, green hillsides, meadows spattered with blossoms, beaches white as milk.

"Very pleasant," said Ullward. "Quite nice." He pulled out his checkbook. "What's your price?"

Mail chuckled and shook his head. "I won't sell. I'm willing to lease off a section—providing my price is met and my rules are agreed to."

Ullward sat with compressed lips. He gave his head a quick little jerk. Mail started to rise to his feet.

"No, no," said Ullward hastily. "I was merely thinking. . . . Let's look at the map again."

Mail returned the map to the screen. Ullward made careful inspection of the various continents, inquired as to physiography, climate, flora and fauna.

Finally he made his decision. "I'll lease Gaea."

"No, Lamster Ullward!" declared Mail. "I'm reserving this entire area—from Murky Mountains and the Calliope River east. This western section is open. It's maybe a little smaller than Atalanta or Persephone, but the climate is warmer."

"There aren't any mountains on the western section," Ullward protested. "Only these insignificant Rock Castle Crags."

"They're not so insignificant," said Mail. "You've also got the Purple Bird Hills, and down here in the south is Mount Cairasco—a live volcano. What more do you need?"

Ullward glanced across his ranch. "I'm in the habit of thinking big."

"West Gaea is a pretty big chunk of property."

"Very well," said Ullward. "What are your terms?"

"So far as money goes, I'm not greedy," Mail said. "For a twenty-year lease: two hundred thousand a year, the first five years in advance."

Ullward made a startled protest. "Great guns, Lamster Mail! That's almost half my income!"

Mail shrugged. "I'm not trying to get rich. I want to build a lodge for myself. It costs money. If you can't afford it, I'll have to speak to someone who can."

Ullward said in a nettled voice, "I can afford it, certainly—but my entire ranch here cost less than a million."

"Well, either you want it or you don't," said Mail. "I'll tell you my rules, then you can make up your mind."

"What rules?" demanded Ullward, his face growing red.

"They're simple and their only purpose is to maintain privacy for both of us. First, you have to stay on your own property. No excursions hither and yon on my property. Second, no subleasing. Third, no residents except yourself, your family and your servants. I don't want any artists' colony springing up, nor any wild, noisy resort atmosphere. Naturally you're entitled to bring out your guests, but they've got to keep your property just like yourself."

He looked sidewise at Ullward's glum face. "I'm not trying to be tough, Lamster Ullward. Good fences make good neighbors, and it's better that we have the understanding now than hard words and beam-gun evictions later."

"Let me see the photographs again," said Ullward. "Show me West Gaea."

He looked, heaved a deep sigh. "Very well, I agree."

The construction crew had departed. Ullward was alone on West Gaea. He walked around the new lodge, taking deep breaths of pure quiet air, thrilling to the absolute solitude and privacy. The lodge had cost a fortune, but how many other people of Earth owned—leased, rather—anything to compare with this?

He walked out on the front terrace, gazed proudly across miles—genuine unsimulated miles—of landscape. For his home site, he had selected a shelf in the foothills of the Ullward Range (as he had renamed the Purple Bird Hills). In front spread a great golden savannah dotted with blue-green trees; behind rose a tall gray cliff.

A stream rushed down a cleft in the rock, leaping, splashing, cooling the air, finally flowing into a beautiful clear pool, beside which Ullward had erected a cabana of red, green and brown plastic. At the base of the cliff and in crevices grew clumps of spiky blue cactus, lush green bushes covered with red trumpet-flowers, a thick-leafed white plant holding up a stalk clustered with white bubbles.

Solitude! The real thing! No thumping of factories, no roar of traffic two feet from one's bed. One arm outstretched, the other pressed to his chest, Ullward performed a stately little jig of triumph on the terrace. Had he been able, he might have turned a cartwheel. When a person has complete privacy, absolutely nothing is forbidden!

Ullward took a final turn up and down the terrace, made a last appreciative survey of the horizon. The sun was sinking through banks of fire-fringed clouds. Marvelous depth of color, a tonal brilliance to be matched only in the very best illusion-panes!

He entered the lodge, made a selection from the nutrition locker. After a leisurely meal, he returned to the lounge. He stood thinking for a moment, then went out upon the terrace, strolled up and down. Wonderful! The night was full of stars, hanging like blurred white lamps, almost as he had always imagined them.

After ten minutes of admiring the stars, he returned into the lodge. Now what? The wallscreen, with its assortment of recorded programs. Snug and comfortable, Ullward watched the performance of a recent musical comedy.

Real luxury, he told himself. Pity he couldn't invite his friends out to spend the evening. Unfortunately impossible, considering the inconvenient duration of the trip between Mail's Planet and Earth. However—only three days until the arrival of his first guest. She was Elf Intry, a young woman who had been more than friendly with Ullward on Earth. When Elf arrived, Ullward would broach a subject which he had been mulling over for several months—indeed, ever since he had first learned of Mail's Planet.

Elf Intry arrived early in the afternoon, coming down to Mail's Planet in a capsule discharged from the weekly Outer Ring Express packet.

A woman of normally good disposition, she greeted Ullward in a seethe of indignation. "Just who is that brute around the other side of the planet? I thought you had absolute privacy here!"

"That's just old Mail," said Ullward evasively. "What's wrong?"

"The fool on the packet set me the wrong coordinates and the capsule came down on a beach. I noticed a house and then I saw a naked man jumping rope behind some bushes. I thought it was you, of course. I went over and said 'Boo!' You should have heard the language he used!" She shook her head. "I don't see why you allow such a boor on your planet."

The buzzer on the communication screen sounded. "That's Mail now," said Ullward. "You wait here. I'll tell him how to speak to my guests!"

He presently returned to the terrace. Elf came over to him, kissed his nose. "Ully, you're pale with rage! I hope you didn't lose your temper."

"No," said Ullward. "We merely—well, we had an understanding. Come along, look over the property."

He took Elf around to the back, pointing out the swimming pool, the waterfall, the mass of rock above. "You won't see that effect on any illusion-pane! That's genuine rock!"

"Lovely, Ully. Very nice. The color might be just a trifle darker, though. Rock doesn't look like that."

"No?" Ullward inspected the cliff more critically. "Well, I can't do anything about it. How about the privacy?"

"Wonderful! It's so quiet, it's almost eerie!"

"Eerie?" Ullward looked around the landscape. "It hadn't occurred to me."

"You're not sensitive to these things, Ully. Still, it's very nice, if you can tolerate that unpleasant creature Mail so close."

"Close?" protested Ullward. "He's on the other side of the continent!"

"True," said Elf. "It's all relative, I suppose. How long do you expect to stay out here?"

"That depends. Come along inside. I want to talk with you."

He seated her in a comfortable chair, brought her a globe of Gluco-Fructoid Nectar. For himself, he mixed ethyl alcohol, water, a few drops of Haig's Oldtime Esters.

"Elf, where do you stand in the reproduction list?"

She raised her fine eyebrows, shook her head. "So far down, I've lost count. Fifty or sixty billion."

"I'm down thirty-seven billion. It's one reason I bought this place. Waiting list, piffle! Nobody stops Bruham Ullward's breeding on his own planet!"

Elf pursed her lips, shook her head sadly. "It won't work, Ully."

"And why not?"

"You can't take the children back to Earth. The list would keep them out."

"True, but think of living here, surrounded by children. All the children you wanted! And utter privacy to boot! What more could you ask for?"

Elf sighed. "You fabricate a beautiful illusion-pane, Ully. But I think not. I love the privacy and solitude—but I thought there'd be more people to be private from."

The Outer Ring Express packet came past four days later. Elf kissed Ullward good-bye. "It's simply exquisite here, Ully. The solitude is so magnificent, it gives me gooseflesh. I've had a wonderful visit." She climbed into the capsule. "See you on Earth."

"Just a minute," said Ullward suddenly. "I want you to post a letter or two for me."

"Hurry. I've only got twenty minutes."

Ullward was back in ten minutes. "Invitations," he told her breathlessly. "Friends."

"Right." She kissed his nose. "Good-bye, Ully." She slammed the port; the capsule rushed away, whirling up to meet the packet.

The new guests arrived three weeks later; Frobisher Worbeck, Liornetta Stobart, Harris and Hyla Cabe, Ted and Ravelin and Iugenae Seehoe, Juvenal Aquister and his son Runy.

Ullward, brown from long days of lazing in the sun, greeted them with great enthusiasm. "Welcome to my little retreat! Wonderful to see you all! Frobisher, you pink-cheeked rascal! And Iugenae! Prettier than ever! Be careful, Ravelin—I've got my eye on your daughter! But Runy's here, guess I'm out of the picture! Liornetta, damned glad you could make it! And Ted! Great to see you, old chap! This is all your doing, you know! Harris, Hyla, Juvenal—come on up! We'll have a drink, a drink, a drink!"

Running from one to the other, patting arms, herding the slow-moving Frobisher Worbeck, he conducted his guests up the slope to the terrace. Here they turned to survey the panorama. Ullward listened to their remarks, mouth pursed against a grin of gratification.

"Magnificent!"

"Grand!"

"Absolutely genuine!"

"The sky is so far away, it frightens me!"

"The sunlight's so pure!"

"The genuine thing's always best, isn't it?"

Runy said a trifle wistfully, "I thought you were on a beach, Lamster Ullward."

"Beach? This is mountain country, Runy. Land of the wide open spaces! Look out over that plain!"

Liornetta Stobart patted Runy's shoulder. "Not every planet has beaches, Runy. The secret of happiness is to be content with what one has."

Ullward laughed gaily. "Oh, I've got beaches, never fear for that! There's a fine beach—ha, ha—five hundred miles due west. Every step Ullward domain!"

"Can we go?" said Iugenae excitedly. "Can we go, Lamster Ullward?"

"We certainly can! That shed down the slope is headquarters for the Ullward Airlines. We'll fly to the beach, swim in Ullward Ocean! But now refreshment! After that crowded capsule, your throats must be like paper!"

"It wasn't too crowded," said Ravelin Seehoe. "There were only nine of us." She looked critically up at the cliff. "If that were an illusion-pane, I'd consider it grotesque."

"My dear Ravelin!" cried Ullward. "It's impressive! Magnificent!"

"All of that," agreed Frobisher Worbeck, a tall sturdy man, white haired, red jowled, with a blue benevolent gaze. "And now, Bruham, what about those drinks?"

"Of course. Ted, I know you of old. Will you tend bar? Here's the alcohol, here's the water, here are the esters. Now, you two," Ullward called to Runy and Iugenae. "How about some nice cold soda pop?"

"What kind is there?" asked Runy.

"All kinds, all flavors. This is Ullward's Retreat! We've got

ULLWARD'S RETREAT   403

methylamyl glutamine, cycloprodacterol phosphate, metathiobromine-four-glycocitrose. . . ."

Runy and Iugenae expressed their preferences; Ullward brought the globes, then hurried to arrange tables and chairs for the adults. Presently everyone was comfortable and relaxed.

Iugenae whispered to Ravelin, who smiled and nodded indulgently. "Lamster Ullward, you remember the beautiful oak leaf you gave Iugenae?"

"Of course I do."

"It's still as fresh a green as ever. I wonder *if* Iugenae might have a leaf or two from some of these other trees?"

"My dear Ravelin!" Ullward roared with laughter. "She can have an entire tree!"

"Oh, Mother! Can—"

"Iugenae, don't be ridiculous!" snapped Ted. "How could we get it home? Where would we plant the thing? In the bathroom?"

Ravelin said, "You and Runy find some nice leaves, but don't wander too far."

"No, Mother." She beckoned to Runy. "Come along, dope. Bring a basket."

The others of the party gazed out over the plain. "A beautiful view, Ullward," said Frobisher Worbeck. "How far does your property extend?"

"Five hundred miles west to the ocean, six hundred miles east to the mountains, eleven hundred miles north and two hundred miles south."

Worbeck shook his head solemnly. "Nice. A pity you couldn't get the whole planet. Then you'd have real privacy!"

"I tried, of course," said Ullward. "The owner refused to consider the idea."

"A pity."

Ullward brought out a map. "However, as you see, I have a fine volcano, a number of excellent rivers, a mountain range, and down here on the delta of Cinnamon River an absolutely miasmic swamp."

Ravelin pointed to the ocean. "Why, it's Lonesome Ocean! I thought the name was Ullward Ocean."

Ullward laughed uncomfortably. "Just a figure of speech—so to speak. My rights extend ten miles. More than enough for swimming purposes."

"No freedom of the seas here, eh, Lamster Ullward?" laughed Harris Cabe.

"Not exactly," confessed Ullward.

"A pity," said Frobisher Worbeck.

Hyla Cabe pointed to the map. "Look at these wonderful mountain ranges! The Magnificent Mountains! And over here—the Elysian Gardens! I'd love to see them, Lamster Ullward."

Ullward shook his head in embarrassment. "Impossible, I'm afraid. They're not on my property. I haven't seen them myself."

His guests stared at him in astonishment. "But surely—"

"It's an atom-welded contract with Lamster Mail," Ullward explained. "He stays on his property, I stay on mine. In this way, our privacy is secure."

"Look," Hyla Cabe said aside to Ravelin. "The Unimaginable Caverns! Doesn't it make you simply wild not to be able to see them?"

Aquister said hurriedly, "It's a pleasure to sit here and just breathe this wonderful fresh air. No noise, no crowds, no bustle or hurry."

The party drank and chatted and basked in the sunshine until late afternoon. Enlisting the aid of Ravelin Seehoe and Hyla Cabe, Ullward set out a simple meal of yeast pellets, processed protein, thick pieces of algae crunch.

"No animal flesh, cooked vegetation?" questioned Worbeck curiously.

"Tried them the first day," said Ullward. "Revolting. Sick for a week."

After dinner, the guests watched a comic melodrama on the wallscreen. Then Ullward showed them to their various cubicles, and after a few minutes of badinage and calling back and forth, the lodge became quiet.

Next day, Ullward ordered his guests into their bathing suits. "We're off to the beach, we'll gambol on the sand, we'll frolic in the surf of Lonesome Ullward Ocean!"

The guests piled happily into the air-car. Ullward counted heads. "All aboard! We're off!"

They rose and flew west, first low over the plain, then high into the air, to obtain a panoramic view of the Rock Castle Crags.

"The tallest peak—there to the north—is almost ten thousand feet high. Notice how it juts up, just imagine the mass! Solid rock! How'd you like that dropped on your toe, Runy? Not so good, eh? In a moment, we'll see a precipice over a thousand feet straight up and down. There—now! Isn't that remarkable?"

"Certainly impressive," agreed Ted.

"What those Magnificent Mountains must be like!" said Harris Cabe with a wry laugh.

"How tall are they, Lamster Ullward?" inquired Liornetta Stobart.

"What? Which?"

"The Magnificent Mountains."

"I don't know for sure. Thirty or forty thousand feet, I suppose."

"What a marvelous sight they must be!" said Frobisher Worbeck. "Probably make these look like foothills."

"These are beautiful too," Hyla Cabe put in hastily.

"Oh, naturally," said Frobisher Worbeck. "A damned fine sight! You're a lucky man, Bruham!"

Ullward laughed shortly, turned the air-car west. They flew across a rolling forested plain and presently Lonesome Ocean gleamed in the distance. Ullward slanted down, landed the air-car on the beach, and the party alighted.

The day was warm, the sun hot. A fresh wind blew in from the ocean. The surf broke upon the sand in massive roaring billows.

The party stood appraising the scene. Ullward swung his arms. "Well, who's for it? Don't wait to be invited! We've got the whole ocean to ourselves!"

Ravelin said, "It's so rough! Look how that water crashes down!"

Liornetta Stobart turned away with a shake of her head. "Illusion-pane surf is always so gentle. This could lift you right up and give you a good shaking!"

"I expected nothing quite so vehement," Harris Cabe admitted.

Ravelin beckoned to Iugenae. "You keep well away, Miss Puss. I don't want you swept out to sea. You'd find it Lonesome Ocean indeed!"

Runy approached the water, waded gingerly into a sheet of retreating foam. A comber thrashed down at him and he danced quickly back up the shore.

"The water's cold," he reported.

Ullward poised himself. "Well, here goes! I'll show you how it's done!" He trotted forward, stopped short, then flung himself into the face of a great white comber.

The party on the beach watched.

"Where is he?" asked Hyla Cabe.

Iugenae pointed. "I saw part of him out there. A leg, or an arm."

"There he is!" cried Ted. "Woof! Another one's caught him. I suppose some people might consider it sport. . . ."

Ullward staggered to his feet, lurched through the retreating wash to shore. "Hah! Great! Invigorating! Ted! Harris! Juvenal! Take a go at it!"

Harris shook his head. "I don't think I'll try it today, Bruham."

"The next time for me too," said Juvenal Aquister. "Perhaps it won't be so rough."

"But don't let us stop you!" urged Ted. "You swim as long as you like. We'll wait here for you."

"Oh, I've had enough for now," said Ullward. "Excuse me while I change."

When Ullward returned, he found his guests seated in the air-car. "Hello! Everyone ready to go?"

"It's hot in the sun," explained Liornetta, "and we thought we'd enjoy the view better from inside."

"When you look through the glass, it's almost like an illusion-pane," said Iugenae.

"Oh, I see. Well, perhaps you're ready to visit other parts of the Ullward domain?"

The proposal met with approval; Ullward took the air-car into the air. "We can fly north over the pine woods, south over Mount Cairasco, which unfortunately isn't erupting just now."

"Anywhere you like, Lamster Ullward," said Frobisher Worbeck. "No doubt it's all beautiful."

Ullward considered the varied attractions of his leasehold. "Well, first to the Cinnamon Swamp."

For two hours they flew, over the swamp, across the smoking crater of Mount Cairasco, east to the edge of Murky Mountains, along Calliope River to its source in Goldenleaf Lake. Ullward pointed out noteworthy views, interesting aspects. Behind him, the murmurs of admiration dwindled and finally died.

"Had enough?" Ullward called back gaily. "Can't see half a continent in one day! Shall we save some for tomorrow?"

There was a moment's stillness. Then Liornetta Stobart said, "Lamster Ullward, we're simply dying for a peek at the Magnificent Mountains. I wonder—do you think we could slip over for a quick look? I'm sure Lamster Mail wouldn't really mind."

Ullward shook his head with a rather stiff smile. "He's made me agree to a very definite set of rules. I've already had one brush with him."

"How could he possibly find out?" asked Juvenal Aquister.

"He probably wouldn't find out," said Ullward, "but—"

"It's a damned shame for him to lock you off into this drab little peninsula!" Frobisher Worbeck said indignantly.

"Please, Lamster Ullward," Iugenae wheedled.

"Oh, very well," Ullward said recklessly.

He turned the air-car east. The Murky Mountains passed below. The party peered from the windows, exclaiming at the marvels of the forbidden landscape.

"How far are the Magnificent Mountains?" asked Ted.

"Not far. Another thousand miles."

"Why are you hugging the ground?" asked Frobisher Worbeck. "Up in the air, man! Let's see the countryside!"

Ullward hesitated. Mail was probably asleep. And, in the last analysis, he really had no right to forbid an innocent little—

"Lamster Ullward," called Runy, "there's an air-car right behind us."

The air-car drew up level. Kennes Mail's blue eyes met Ullward's across the gap. He motioned Ullward down.

Ullward compressed his mouth, swung the air-car down. From behind him came murmurs of sympathy and outrage.

Below was a dark pine forest; Ullward set down in a pretty little glade. Mail landed nearby, jumped to the ground, signaled to Ullward. The two men walked to the side. The guests murmured together and shook their heads.

Ullward presently returned to the air-car. "Everybody please get in," he said crisply.

They rose into the air and flew west. "What did the chap have to say for himself?" queried Worbeck.

Ullward chewed at his lips. "Not too much. Wanted to know if I'd lost the way. I told him one or two things. Reached an understanding. . . ." His voice dwindled, then rose in a burst of cheerfulness. "We'll have a party back at the lodge. What do we care for Mail and his confounded mountains?"

"That's the spirit, Bruham!" cried Frobisher Worbeck.

Both Ted and Ullward tended bar during the evening. Either one or the other mingled rather more alcohol to rather less esters into the drinks than standard practice recommended. As a result, the party became quite loud and gay. Ullward damned Mail's interfering habits; Worbeck explored six thousand years of common law in an effort to prove Mail a domineering tyrant; the women giggled; Iugenae and Runy watched cynically then presently went off to attend to their own affairs.

In the morning, the group slept late. Ullward finally tottered out on the terrace, to be joined one at a time by the others. Runy and Iugenae were missing.

"Young rascals," groaned Worbeck. "If they're lost, they'll have to find their own way back. No search parties for me."

At noon, Runy and Iugenae returned in Ullward's air-car.

"Good heavens," shrieked Ravelin. "Iugenae, come here this instant! Where have you been?"

Juvenal Aquister surveyed Runy sternly. "Have you lost your mind, taking Lamster Ullward's air-car without his permission?"

"I asked him last night," Runy declared indignantly. "He said yes, take anything except the volcano because that's where he slept when his feet got cold, and the swamp because that's where he dropped his empty containers."

"Regardless," said Juvenal in disgust, "you should have had better sense. Where have you been?"

Runy fidgeted. Iugenae said, "Well, we went south for a while, then turned and went east—I think it was east. We thought if we flew low, Lamster Mail wouldn't see us. So we flew low, through the mountains, and pretty soon we came to an ocean. We went along the beach and came to a house. We landed to see who lived there, but nobody was home."

Ullward stifled a groan.

"What would anyone want with a pen of birds?" asked Runy.

"Birds? What birds? Where?"

"At the house. There was a pen with a lot of big birds, but they kind of got loose while we were looking at them and all flew away."

"Anyway," Iugenae continued briskly, "we decided it was Lamster Mail's house, so we wrote a note, telling what everybody thinks of him and pinned it to his door."

Ullward rubbed his forehead. "Is that all?"

"Well, practically all." Iugenae became diffident. She looked at Runy and the two of them giggled nervously.

"There's more?" yelled Ullward. "What, in heaven's name?"

"Nothing very much," said Iugenae, following a crack in the terrace with her toe. "We put a booby-trap over the door—just a bucket of water. Then we came home."

The screen buzzer sounded from inside the lodge. Everybody looked at Ullward. Ullward heaved a deep sigh, rose to his feet, went inside.

That very afternoon, the Outer Ring Express packet was due to pass the junction point. Frobisher Worbeck felt sudden and acute qualms of conscience for the neglect his business suffered while he dawdled away hours in idle enjoyment.

"But my dear old chap!" exclaimed Ullward. "Relaxation is good for you!"

True, agreed Frobisher Worbeck, if one could make himself oblivious to the possibility of fiasco through the carelessness of underlings. Much as he deplored the necessity, in spite of his inclination to loiter for weeks, he felt impelled to leave—and not a minute later than that very afternoon.

Others of the group likewise remembered important business which they had to see to, and those remaining felt it would be a shame and an imposition to send up the capsule half empty and likewise decided to return.

Ullward's arguments met unyielding walls of obstinacy. Rather glumly, he went down to the capsule to bid his guests farewell. As they climbed through the port, they expressed their parting thanks:

"Bruham, it's been absolutely marvelous!"

"You'll never know how we've enjoyed this outing, Lamster Ullward!"

"The air, the space, the privacy—I'll never forget!"

"It was the most, to say the least."

The port thumped into its socket. Ullward stood back, waving rather uncertainly.

Ted Seehoe reached to press the *Active* button. Ullward sprang forward, pounded on the port.

"Wait!" he bellowed. "A few things I've got to attend to! I'm coming with you!"

"Come in, come in," said Ullward heartily, opening the door to three of his friends; Coble and his wife Heulia Sansom, and Coble's young, pretty cousin Landine. "Glad to see you!"

"And we're glad to come! We've heard so much of your wonderful ranch, we've been on pins and needles all day!"

"Oh, come now! It's not so marvelous as all that!"

"Not to you, perhaps—you live here!"

Ullward smiled. "Well, I must say I live here and still like it. Would you like to have lunch, or perhaps you'd prefer to walk around for a few minutes? I've just finished making a few changes, but I'm happy to say everything is in order."

"Can we just take a look?"

"Of course. Come over here. Stand just so. Now—are you ready?"

"Ready."

Ullward snapped the wall back.

"Ooh!" breathed Landine. "Isn't it beautiful!"

"The space, the open feeling!"

"Look, a tree! What a wonderful simulation!"

"That's no simulation," said Ullward. "That's a genuine tree!"

"Lamster Ullward, are you telling the truth?"

"I certainly am. I never tell lies to a lovely young lady. Come along, over this way."

"Lamster Ullward, that cliff is so convincing, it frightens me."

Ullward grinned. "It's a good job." He signaled a halt. "Now—turn around."

The group turned. They looked out across a great golden savannah, dotted with groves of blue-green trees. A rustic lodge commanded the view, the door being the opening into Ullward's living room.

The group stood in silent admiration. Then Heulia sighed. "Space. Pure space."

"I'd swear I was looking miles," said Coble.

Ullward smiled, a trifle wistfully. "Glad you like my little retreat. Now what about lunch? Genuine algae!"

THE MIRACLE WORKERS

I

The war party from Faide Keep moved eastward across the downs: a column of a hundred armored knights, five hundred foot soldiers, a train of wagons. In the lead rode Lord Faide, a tall man in his early maturity, spare and catlike, with a sallow dyspeptic face. He sat in the ancestral car of the Faides, a boat-shaped vehicle floating two feet above the moss, and carried, in addition to his sword and dagger, his ancestral side weapons.

An hour before sunset a pair of scouts came racing back to the column, their club-headed horses loping like dogs. Lord Faide braked the motion of his car. Behind him the Faide kinsmen, the lesser knights, and the leather-capped foot soldiers halted; to the rear the baggage train and the high-wheeled wagons of the jinxmen creaked to a stop.

The scouts approached at breakneck speed, at the last instant flinging their horses sidewise. Long shaggy legs kicked out, padlike hooves plowed through the moss. The scouts jumped to the ground, ran forward. "The way to Ballant Keep is blocked!"

Lord Faide rose in his seat, stood staring eastward over the gray-green downs. "How many knights? How many men?"

"No knights, no men, Lord Faide. The First Folk have planted a forest between North and South Wildwood."

Lord Faide stood a moment in reflection, then seated himself and pushed the control knob. The car wheezed, jerked, moved forward. The knights touched up their horses; the foot soldiers resumed their slouching gait. At the rear the baggage train creaked into motion, together with the six wagons of the jinxmen.

The sun, large, pale, and faintly pink, sank in the west. North Wildwood loomed down from the left, separated from South Wildwood by an area of stony ground, only sparsely patched with moss. As the sun passed behind the horizon, the new planting became visible: a frail new growth connecting the tracts of woodland like a canal between two seas.

Lord Faide halted his car, stepped down to the moss. He appraised the landscape, then gave the signal to make camp. The wagons were ranged in a circle, the gear unloaded. Lord Faide watched the activity for a moment, eyes sharp and critical, then turned and walked out across the downs through the lavender and green twilight. Fifteen miles to the east his last enemy awaited him: Lord Ballant of Ballant Keep. Contemplating the next day's battle, Lord Faide felt reasonably confident of the outcome. His troops had been tempered by a dozen campaigns; his kinsmen were loyal and singlehearted. Head Jinxman to Faide Keep was Hein Huss, and associated with him were three of the most powerful jinxmen of Pangborn: Isak Comandore, Adam McAdam, and the remarkable Enterlin, together with their separate troupes of cabalmen, spellbinders, and apprentices. Altogether, an impressive assemblage. Certainly there were obstacles to be overcome: Ballant Keep was strong; Lord Ballant would fight obstinately; Anderson Grimes, the Ballant Head Jinxman, was efficient and highly respected. There was also this nuisance of the First Folk and the new planting which closed the gap between North and South Wildwood. The First Folk were a pale and feeble race, no match for human beings in single combat, but they guarded their forests with traps and deadfalls. Lord Faide cursed softly under his breath. To circle either North or South Wildwood meant a delay of three days, which could not be tolerated.

Lord Faide returned to the camp. Fires were alight, pots bubbled, orderly rows of sleep holes had been dug into the moss. The knights groomed their horses within the corral of wagons; Lord Faide's own tent had been erected on a hummock, beside the ancient car.

Lord Faide made a quick round of inspection, noting every detail, speaking no word. The jinxmen were encamped a little distance apart from the troops. The apprentices and lesser spellbinders prepared food, while the jinxmen and cabalmen worked inside their tents, arranging cabinets and cases, correcting whatever disorder had been caused by the jolting of the wagons.

Lord Faide entered the tent of his Head Jinxman. Hein Huss

was an enormous man, with arms and legs heavy as tree trunks, a torso like a barrel. His face was pink and placid, his eyes were water-clear; a stiff gray brush rose from his head, which was innocent of the cap jinxmen customarily wore against the loss of hair. Hein Huss disdained such precautions; it was his habit, showing his teeth in a face-splitting grin, to rumble, "Why should any hoodoo me, old Hein Huss? I am so inoffensive. Whoever tried would surely die, of shame and remorse."

Lord Faide found Huss busy at his cabinet. The doors stood wide, revealing hundreds of manikins, each tied with a lock of hair, a bit of cloth, a fingernail clipping, daubed with grease, sputum, excrement, blood. Lord Faide knew well that one of these manikins represented himself. He also knew that should he request it Hein Huss would deliver it without hesitation. Part of Huss's *mana* derived from his enormous confidence, the effortless ease of his power. He glanced at Lord Faide and read the question in his mind. "Lord Ballant did not know of the new planting. Anderson Grimes has now informed him, and Lord Ballant expects that you will be delayed. Grimes has communicated with Gisborne Keep and Castle Cloud. Three hundred men march tonight to reinforce Ballant Keep. They will arrive in two days. Lord Ballant is much elated."

Lord Faide paced back and forth across the tent. "Can we cross this planting?"

Hein Huss made a heavy sound of disapproval. "There are many futures. In certain of these futures you pass. In others you do not pass. I cannot ordain these futures."

Lord Faide had long learned to control his impatience at what sometimes seemed to be pedantic obfuscation. He grumbled, "They are either very stupid or very bold planting across the downs in this fashion. I cannot imagine what they intend."

Hein Huss considered, then grudgingly volunteered an idea. "What if they plant west from North Wildwood to Sarrow Copse? What if they plant west from South Wildwood to Old Forest?"

"Then Faide Keep is almost ringed by forest."

"And what if they join Sarrow Copse to Old Forest?"

Lord Faide stood stock-still, his eyes narrow and thoughtful. "Faide Keep would be surrounded by forest. We would be imprisoned. . . . These plantings, do they proceed?"

"They proceed, so I have been told."

"What do they hope to gain?"

"I do not know. Perhaps they hope to isolate the keeps, to rid the planet of men. Perhaps they merely want secure avenues between the forests."

Lord Faide considered. Huss's final suggestion was reasonable enough. During the first centuries of human settlement, sportive young men had hunted the First Folk with clubs and lances, eventually had driven them from their native downs into the forests. "Evidently they are more clever than we realize. Adam McAdam asserts that they do not think, but it seems that he is mistaken."

Hein Huss shrugged. "Adam McAdam equates thought to the human cerebral process. He cannot telepathize with the First Folk, hence he deduces that they do not 'think.' But I have watched them at Forest Market, and they trade intelligently enough." He raised his head, appeared to listen, then reached into his cabinet and delicately tightened a noose around the neck of one of the manikins. From outside the tent came a sudden cough and a whooping gasp for air. Huss grinned, twitched open the noose. "That is Isak Comandore's apprentice. He hopes to complete a Hein Huss manikin. I must say he works diligently, going so far as to touch its feet into my footprints whenever possible."

Lord Faide went to the flap of the tent. "We break camp early. Be alert, I may require your help." He departed the tent.

Hein Huss continued the ordering of his cabinet. Presently he sensed the approach of his rival, Jinxman Isak Comandore, who coveted the office of Head Jinxman with all-consuming passion. Huss closed the cabinet and hoisted himself to his feet.

Comandore entered the tent, a man tall, crooked, and spindly. His wedge-shaped head was covered with coarse russet ringlets; hot red-brown eyes peered from under his red eyebrows. "I offer my complete rights to Keyril, and will include the masks, the headdress, the amulets. Of all the demons ever contrived he has won the widest public acceptance. To utter the name Keyril is to complete half the work of a possession. Keyril is a valuable property. I can give no more."

But Huss shook his head. Comandore's desire was the full simulacrum of Tharon Faide, Lord Faide's oldest son, complete with clothes, hair, skin, eyelashes, tears, excrement, sweat and sputum—the only one in existence, for Lord Faide guarded his son much more jealously than he did himself. "You offer convincingly," said Huss, "but my own demons suffice. The name Dant conveys fully as much terror as Keyril."

"I will add five hairs from the head of Jinxman Clarence Sears; they are the last, for he is now stark bald."

"Let us drop the matter; I will keep the simulacrum."

"As you please," said Comandore with asperity. He glanced out the flap of the tent. "That blundering apprentice. He puts the feet of the manikin backwards into your prints."

Huss opened his cabinet, thumped a manikin with his finger. From outside the tent came a grunt of surprise. Huss grinned. "He is young and earnest, and perhaps he is clever, who knows?" He went to the flap of the tent, called outside. "Hey, Sam Salazar, what do you do? Come inside."

Apprentice Sam Salazar came blinking into the tent, a thickset youth with a round florid face, overhung with a rather untidy mass of straw-colored hair. In one hand he carried a crude pot-bellied manikin, evidently intended to represent Hein Huss.

"You puzzle both your master and myself," said Huss. "There must be method in your folly, but we fail to perceive it. For instance, this moment you place my simulacrum backwards into my track. I feel a tug on my foot, and you pay for your clumsiness."

Sam Salazar showed small evidence of abashment. "Jinxman Comandore has warned that we must expect to suffer for our ambitions."

"If your ambition is jinxmanship," Comandore declared sharply, "you had best mend your ways."

"The lad is craftier than you know," said Hein Huss. "Look now." He took the manikin from the youth, spit into its mouth, plucked a hair from his head, thrust it into a convenient crevice. "He has a Hein Huss manikin, achieved at very small cost. Now, Apprentice Salazar, how will you hoodoo me?"

"Naturally, I would never dare. I merely want to fill the bare spaces in my cabinet."

Hein Huss nodded his approval. "As good a reason as any. Of course you own a simulacrum of Isak Comandore?"

Sam Salazar glanced uneasily at Isak Comandore. "He leaves none of his traces. If there is so much as an open bottle in the room, he breathes behind his hand."

"Ridiculous!" exclaimed Hein Huss. "Comandore, what do you fear?"

"I am conservative," said Comandore, dryly. "You make a fine gesture, but some day an enemy may own that simulacrum; then you will regret your bravado."

"Bah. My enemies are all dead, save one or two who dare not reveal themselves." He clapped Sam Salazar a great buffet on the shoulder. "Tomorrow, Apprentice Salazar, great things are in store for you."

"What manner of great things?"

"Honor, noble self-sacrifice. Lord Faide must beg permission from the First Folk to pass Wildwood, which galls him. But beg he must. Tomorrow, Sam Salazar, I will elect you to lead the way to the parley, to deflect deadfalls, scythes, and nettletraps from the more important person who follows."

Sam Salazar shook his head and drew back. "There must be others more worthy; I prefer to ride in the rear with the wagons."

Comandore waved him from the tent. "You will do as ordered. Leave us; we have had enough apprentice talk."

Sam Salazar departed. Comandore turned back to Hein Huss. "In connection with tomorrow's battle, Anderson Grimes is especially adept with demons. As I recall, he has developed and successfully publicized Pont, who spreads sleep; Everid, a being of wrath; Deigne, a force of fear. We must take care that in countering these effects we do not neutralize each other."

"True," rumbled Huss. "I have long maintained to Lord Faide that a single jinxman—the Head Jinxman in fact—is more effective than a group of cross-purposes. But he is consumed by ambition and does not listen."

"Perhaps he wants to be sure that should advancing years overtake the Head Jinxman other equally effective jinxmen are at hand."

"The future has many paths," agreed Hein Huss. "Lord Faide is well advised to seek early for my successor, so that I may train him over the years. I plan to access all the subsidiary jinxmen, and select the most promising. Tomorrow I relegate to you the demons of Anderson Grimes."

Isak Comandore nodded politely. "You are wise to give over responsibility. When I feel the weight of my years I hope I may act with similar forethought. Good night, Hein Huss. I go to arrange my demonmasks. Tomorrow Keyril must walk like a giant."

"Good night, Isak Comandore."

•   •   •

Comandore swept from the tent, and Huss settled himself on his stool. Sam Salazar scratched at the flap. "Well, lad?" growled Huss. "Why do you loiter?"

Sam Salazar placed the Hein Huss manikin on the table. "I have no wish to keep this doll."

"Throw it in a ditch, then." Hein Huss spoke gruffly. "You must stop annoying me with stupid tricks. You efficiently obtrude yourself upon my attention, but you cannot transfer from Comandore's troupe without his express consent."

"If I gain his consent?"

"You will incur his enmity; he will open his cabinet against you. Unlike myself, you are vulnerable to a hoodoo. I advise you to be content. Isak Comandore is highly skilled and can teach you much."

Sam Salazar still hesitated. "Jinxman Comandore, though skilled, is intolerant of new thoughts."

Hein Huss shifted ponderously on his stool, examined Sam Salazar with his water-clear eyes. "What new thoughts are these? Your own?"

"The thoughts are new to me, and for all I know new to Isak Comandore. But he will say neither yes nor no."

Hein Huss sighed, settled his monumental bulk more comfortably. "Speak then, describe these thoughts, and I will assess their novelty."

"First, I have wondered about trees. They are sensitive to light, to moisture, to wind, to pressure. Sensitivity implies sensation. Might a man feel into the soul of a tree for these sensations? If a tree were capable of awareness, this faculty might prove useful. A man might select trees as sentinels in strategic sites, and enter into them as he chose."

Hein Huss was skeptical. "An amusing notion, but practically not feasible. The reading of minds, the act of possession, televoyance, all similar interplay, require psychic congruence as a basic condition. The minds must be able to become identities at some particular stratum. Unless there is sympathy, there is no linkage. A tree is at opposite poles from a man; the images of tree and man are incommensurable. Hence, anything more than the most trifling flicker of comprehension must be a true miracle of jinxmanship."

Sam Salazar nodded mournfully. "I realized this, and at one time hoped to equip myself with the necessary identification."

"To do this you must become a vegetable. Certainly the tree will never become a man."

"So I reasoned," said Sam Salazar. "I went alone into a grove of trees, where I chose a tall conifer. I buried my feet in the mold, I stood silent and naked—in the sunlight, in the rain; at dawn, noon, dusk, midnight. I closed my mind to manthoughts, I closed my eyes to vision, my ears to sound. I took no nourishment except from rain and sun. I sent roots forth from my feet and branches from my torso. Thirty hours I stood, and two days later another thirty hours, and after two days another thirty hours. I made myself a tree, as nearly as possible to one of flesh and blood."

Hein Huss gave the great inward gurgle that signalized his amusement. "And you achieved sympathy?"

"Nothing useful," Sam Salazar admitted. "I felt something of the tree's sensations—the activity of light, the peace of dark, the coolness of rain. But visual and auditory experience—nothing. However, I do not regret the trial. It was a useful discipline."

"An interesting effort, even if inconclusive. The idea is by no means of startling originality, but the empiricism—to use an archaic word—of your method is bold, and no doubt antagonized Isak Comandore, who has no patience with the superstitions of our ancestors. I suspect that he harangued you against frivolity, metaphysics, and inspirationalism."

"True," said Sam Salazar. "He spoke at length."

"You should take the lesson to heart. Isak Comandore is sometimes unable to make the most obvious truth seem credible. However, I cite you the example of Lord Faide who considers himself an enlightened man, free from superstition. Still, he rides in his feeble car, he carries a pistol sixteen hundred years old, he relies on Hellmouth to protect Faide Keep."

"Perhaps—unconsciously—he longs for the old magical times," suggested Sam Salazar thoughtfully.

"Perhaps," agreed Hein Huss. "And you do likewise?"

Sam Salazar hesitated. "There is an aura of romance, a kind of wild grandeur to the old days—but of course," he added quickly, "mysticism is no substitute for orthodox logic."

"Naturally not," agreed Hein Huss. "Now go; I must consider the events of tomorrow."

Sam Salazar departed, and Hein Huss, rumbling and groaning, hoisted himself to his feet. He went to the flap of his tent, surveyed the camp. All now was quiet. The fires were embers, the warriors lay in the pits they had cut into the moss. To the north and south spread the woodlands. Among the trees and out on the downs were faint flickering luminosities, where the First Folk gathered spore-pods from the moss.

Hein Huss became aware of a nearby personality. He turned his head and saw approaching the shrouded form of Jinxman Enterlin, who concealed his face, who spoke only in whispers, who disguised his natural gait with a stiff stiltlike motion. By this means he hoped to reduce his vulnerability to hostile jinxmanship. The admission carelessly let fall of failing eyesight, of stiff joints, forgetfulness, melancholy, nausea might be of critical significance in controversy by hoodoo. Jinxmen therefore maintained the pose of absolute health and virility, even though they must grope blindly or limp doubled up from cramps.

Hein Huss called out to Enterlin, lifted back the flap to the tent. Enterlin entered; Huss went to the cabinet, brought forth a flask, poured liquor into a pair of stone cups. "A cordial only, free of overt significance."

"Good," whispered Enterlin, selecting the cup farthest from him. "After all, we jinxmen must relax into the guise of men from time to time." Turning his back on Huss, he introduced the cup through the folds of his hood, drank. "Refreshing," he whispered. "We need refreshment; tomorrow we must work."

Huss issued his reverberating chuckle. "Tomorrow Isak Comandore matches demons with Anderson Grimes. We others perform only subsidiary duties."

Enterlin seemed to make a quizzical inspection of Hein Huss through the black gauze before his eyes. "Comandore will relish this opportunity. His vehemence oppresses me, and his is a power which feeds on success. He is a man of fire, you are a man of ice."

"Ice quenches fire."

"Fire sometimes melts ice."

Hein Huss shrugged. "No matter. I grow weary. Time has passed all of us by. Only a moment ago a young apprentice showed me to myself."

"As a powerful jinxman, as Head Jinxman to the Faides, you have cause for pride."

Hein Huss drained the stone cup, set it aside. "No. I see myself at the top of my profession, with nowhere else to go. Only Sam Salazar the apprentice thinks to search for more universal lore; he comes to me for counsel, and I do not know what to tell him."

"Strange talk, strange talk!" whispered Enterlin. He moved to the flap of the tent. "I go now," he whispered. "I go to walk on the downs. Perhaps I will see the future."

"There are many futures."

Enterlin rustled away and was lost in the dark. Hein Huss groaned and grumbled, then took himself to his couch, where he instantly fell asleep.

II

The night passed. The sun, flickering with films of pink and green, lifted over the horizon. The new planting of the First Folk was silhouetted, a sparse stubble of saplings, against the green and lavender sky. The troops broke camp with practiced efficiency. Lord Faide marched to his car, leaped within; the machine sagged under his weight. He pushed a button, the car drifted forward, heavy as a waterlogged timber.

A mile from the new planting he halted, sent a messenger back to the wagons of the jinxmen. Hein Huss walked ponderously forward, followed by Isak Comandore, Adam McAdam, and Enterlin. Lord Faide spoke to Hein Huss. "Send someone to speak to the First Folk. Inform them we wish to pass, offering them no harm, but that we will react savagely to any hostility."

"I will go myself," said Hein Huss. He turned to Comandore, "Lend me, if you will, your brash young apprentice. I can put him to good use."

"If he unmasks a nettle trap by blundering into it, his first useful deed will be done," said Comandore. He signaled to Sam Salazar, who came reluctantly forward. "Walk in front of Head Jinxman Hein Huss that he may encounter no traps or scythes. Take a staff to probe the moss."

Without enthusiasm Sam Salazar borrowed a lance from one of the foot soldiers. He and Huss set forth, along the low rise that previously had separated North from South Wildwood. Occasionally outcroppings of stone penetrated the cover of moss; here and there grew bayberry trees, clumps of tarplant, ginger-tea, and rosewort.

A half mile from the planting Huss halted. "Now take care, for here the traps will begin. Walk clear of hummocks, these often conceal swing-scythes; avoid moss which shows a pale blue; it is dying or sickly and may cover a deadfall or a nettle trap."

"Why cannot you locate the traps by clairvoyance?" asked Sam Salazar in a rather sullen voice. "It appears an excellent occasion for the use of these faculties."

"The question is natural," said Hein Huss with composure. "However you must know that when a jinxman's own profit or security is at stake his emotions play tricks on him. I would see traps everywhere and would never know whether clairvoyance or fear prompted me. In this case, that lance is a more reliable instrument than my mind."

Sam Salazar made a salute of understanding and set forth, with Hein Huss stumping behind him. At first he prodded with care, uncovering two traps, then advanced more jauntily; so swiftly indeed that Huss called out in exasperation, "Caution, unless you court death!"

Sam Salazar obligingly slowed his pace. "There are traps all around us, but I detect the pattern, or so I believe."

"Ah, ha, you do? Reveal it to me, if you will. I am only Head Jinxman, and ignorant."

"Notice. If we walk where the spore-pods have recently been harvested, then we are secure."

Hein Huss grunted. "Forward then. Why do you dally? We must do battle at Ballant Keep today."

Two hundred yards farther, Sam Salazar stopped short. "Go on, boy, go on!" grumbled Hein Huss.

"The savages threaten us. You can see them just inside the planting. They hold tubes which they point toward us."

Hein Huss peered, then raised his head and called out in the sibilant language of the First Folk.

A moment or two passed, then one of the creatures came forth, a naked humanoid figure, ugly as a demonmask. Foam-sacs bulged under its arms, orange-lipped foam-vents pointed forward. Its back was wrinkled and loose, the skin serving as a bellows to blow air through the foam-sacs. The fingers of the enormous hands ended in chisel-shaped blades, the head was sheathed in chitin. Billion-faceted eyes swelled from either side of the head, glowing like black opals, merging without definite limit into the chitin. This was a representative of the original inhabitants of the planet, who until the coming of man had inhabited the downs, burrowing in the moss, protecting themselves behind masses of foam exuded from the underarm sacs.

The creature wandered close, halted. "I speak for Lord Faide of Faide Keep," said Huss. "Your planting bars his way. He wishes that you guide him through, so that his men do not damage the trees, or spring the traps you have set against your enemies."

"Men are our enemies," responded the autochthon. "You may spring as many traps as you care to; that is their purpose." It backed away.

"One moment," said Hein Huss sternly. "Lord Faide must pass. He goes to battle Lord Ballant. He does not wish to battle the First Folk. Therefore it is wise to guide him across the planting without hindrance."

The creature considered a second or two. "I will guide him." He stalked across the moss toward the war party.

Behind followed Hein Huss and Sam Salazar. The autochthon, legs articulated more flexibly than a man's, seemed to weave and wander, occasionally pausing to study the ground ahead.

"I am puzzled," Sam Salazar told Hein Huss. "I cannot understand the creature's actions."

"Small wonder," grunted Hein Huss. "He is one of the First Folk, you are human. There is no basis for understanding."

"I disagree," said Sam Salazar seriously.

"Eh?" Hein Huss inspected the apprentice with vast disapproval. "You engage in contention with me, Head Jinxman Hein Huss?"

"Only in a limited sense," said Sam Salazar. "I see a basis for understanding with the First Folk in our common ambition to survive."

"A truism," grumbled Hein Huss. "Granting this community of interests with the First Folk, what is your perplexity?"

"The fact that it first refused, then agreed to conduct us across the planting."

Hein Huss nodded. "Evidently the information which intervened, that we go to fight at Ballant Keep, occasioned the change."

"This is clear," said Sam Salazar. "But think—"

"You exhort me to think?" roared Hein Huss.

"—here is one of the First Folk, apparently without distinction, who makes an important decision instantly. Is he one of their leaders? Do they live in anarchy?"

"It is easy to put questions," Hein Huss said gruffly. "It is not as easy to answer them."

"In short—"

"In short, I do not know. In any event, they are pleased to see us killing one another."

III

The passage through the planting was made without incident. A mile to the east the autochthon stepped aside and without formality returned to the forest. The war party, which had been marching in single file, regrouped into its usual formation. Lord Faide called Hein Huss and made the unusual gesture of inviting him up into the seat beside him. The ancient car dipped and sagged; the power-mechanism whined and chattered. Lord Faide, in high good spirits, ignored the noise. "I feared that we might be forced into a time-consuming wrangle. What of Lord Ballant? Can you read his thoughts?"

Hein Huss cast his mind forth. "Not clearly. He knows of our passage. He is disturbed."

Lord Faide laughed sardonically. "For excellent reason! Listen now, I will explain the plan of battle so that all may coordinate their efforts."

"Very well."

"We approach in a wide line. Ballant's great weapon is of course Volcano. A decoy must wear my armor and ride in the lead. The yellow-haired apprentice is perhaps the most expendable member of the party. In this way we will learn the potentialities of Volcano. Like our own Hellmouth, it was built to repel vessels from space and cannot command the ground immediately under the keep. Therefore we will advance in dispersed formation, to regroup two hundred yards from the keep. At this point the jinxmen will impel Lord Ballant forth from the keep. You no doubt have made plans to this end."

Hein Huss gruffly admitted that such was the case. Like other jinxmen, he enjoyed the pose that his power sufficed for extemporaneous control of any situation.

Lord Faide was in no mood for niceties and pressed for further information. Grudging each word, Hein Huss disclosed his arrangements. "I have prepared certain influences to discomfit the Ballant defenders and drive them forth. Jinxman Enterlin will sit at his cabinet, ready to retaliate if Lord Ballant orders a spell against you. Anderson Grimes undoubtedly will cast a demon—probably Everid— into the Ballant warriors; in return, Jinxman Comandore will possess an equal or a greater number of Faide warriors with the demon Keyril, who is even more ghastly and horrifying."

"Good. What more?"

"There is need for no more, if your men fight well."

"Can you see the future? How does today end?"

"There are many futures. Certain jinxmen—Enterlin for instance—profess to see the thread which leads through the maze; they are seldom correct."

"Call Enterlin here."

Hein Huss rumbled his disapproval. "Unwise, if you desire victory over Ballant Keep."

Lord Faide inspected the massive jinxman from under his black saturnine brows. "Why do you say this?"

"If Enterlin foretells defeat, you will be dispirited and fight poorly. If he predicts victory, you become overconfident and likewise fight poorly."

Lord Faide made a petulant gesture. "The jinxmen are loud in their boasts until the test is made. Then they always find reasons to retract, to qualify."

"Ha, ha!" barked Hein Huss. "You expect miracles, not honest jinxmanship. I spit—" he spat. "I predict that the spittle will strike the moss. The probabilities are high. But an insect might fly in the way. One of the First Folk might raise through the moss. The chances are slight. In the next instant there is only one future. A minute hence there are four futures. Five minutes hence, twenty futures. A billion futures could not express all the possibilities of tomorrow. Of these billion, certain are more probable than others. It is true that these probable futures sometimes send a delicate influence into the jinxman's brain. But unless he is completely impersonal and disinterested, his own desires overwhelm this influence. Enterlin is a strange man. He hides himself, he has no appetites. Occasionally his auguries are exact. Nevertheless, I advise against consulting him. You do better to rely on the practical and real uses of jinxmanship."

Lord Faide said nothing. The column had been marching along the bottom of a low swale; the car had been sliding easily downslope. Now they came to a rise, and the power-mechanism complained so vigorously that Lord Faide was compelled to stop the car. He considered. "Once over the crest we will be in view of Ballant Keep. Now we must disperse. Send the least valuable man in your troupe forward—the apprentice who tested out the moss. He must wear my helmet and corselet and ride in the car."

Hein Huss alighted, returned to the wagons, and presently Sam Salazar came forward. Lord Faide eyed the round, florid face with distaste. "Come close," he said crisply. Sam Salazar obeyed. "You will now ride in my place," said Lord Faide. "Notice carefully. This rod impels a forward motion. This arm steers—to right, to left. To stop, return the rod to its first position."

Sam Salazar pointed to some of the other arms, toggles, switches, and buttons. "What of these?"

"They are never used."

"And these dials, what is their meaning?"

Lord Faide curled his lip, on the brink of one of his quick furies. "Since their use is unimportant to me, it is twenty times unimportant to you. Now. Put this cap on your head, and this helmet. See to it that you do not sweat."

Sam Salazar gingerly settled the magnificent black and green crest of Faide on his head, with a cloth cap underneath.

"Now this corselet."

The corselet was constructed of green and black metal sequins, with a pair of scarlet dragon-heads at either side of the breast.

"Now the cloak." Lord Faide flung the black cloak over Sam Salazar's shoulders. "Do not venture too close to Ballant Keep. Your purpose is to attract the fire of Volcano. Maintain a lateral motion around the keep, outside of dart range. If you are killed by a dart, the whole purpose of the deception is thwarted."

"You prefer me to be killed by Volcano?" inquired Sam Salazar.

"No. I wish to preserve the car and the crest. These are relics of great value. Evade destruction by all means possible. The ruse probably will deceive no one; but if it does, and if it draws the fire of Volcano, I must sacrifice the Faide car. Now—sit in my place."

Sam Salazar climbed into the car, settled himself on the seat.

"Sit straight," roared Lord Faide. "Hold your head up! You are simulating Lord Faide! You must not appear to slink!"

Sam Salazar heaved himself erect in the seat. "To simulate Lord Faide most effectively, I should walk among the warriors, with some-one else riding in the car."

Lord Faide glared, then grinned sourly. "No matter. Do as I have commanded."

IV

Sixteen hundred years before, with war raging through space, a group of space captains, their home bases destroyed, had taken refuge on Pangborn. To protect themselves against vengeful enemies, they built great forts armed with weapons from the dismantled spaceships.

The wars receded, Pangborn was forgotten. The newcomers drove the First Folk into the forests, planted and harvested the river valleys. Ballant Keep, like Faide Keep, Castle Cloud, Boghoten, and the rest, overlooked one of these valleys. Four squat towers of a dense black substance supported an enormous parasol roof, and were joined by walls two-thirds as high as the towers. At the peak of the roof a cupola housed Volcano, the weapon corresponding to Faide's Hell-mouth.

The Faide war party advancing over the rise found the great gates already secure, the parapets between the towers thronged with bow-men. According to Lord Faide's strategy, the war party advanced on a broad front. At the center rode Sam Salazar, resplendent in Lord Faide's armor. He made, however, small effort to simulate Lord Faide. Rather than sitting proudly erect, he crouched at the side of the seat, the crest canted at an angle. Lord Faide watched with disgust. Ap-prentice Salazar's reluctance to be demolished was understandable; if his impersonation failed to convince Lord Ballant, at least the Faide ancestral car might be spared. For a certainty Volcano was being manned; the Ballant weapon-tender could be seen in the cupola, and the snout protruded at a menacing angle.

Apparently the tactic of dispersal, offering no single tempting target, was effective. The Faide war party advanced quickly to a point two hundred yards from the keep, below Volcano's effective field, without drawing fire; first the knights, then the foot soldiers, then the rumbling wagons of the magicians. The slow-moving Faide car was far outdistanced; any doubt as to the nature of the ruse must now be extinguished.

Apprentice Salazar, disliking the isolation, and hoping to increase the speed of the car, twisted one of the other switches, then another. From under the floor came a thin screeching sound; the car quivered and began to rise. Sam Salazar peered over the side, threw out a leg to jump. Lord Faide ran forward, gesturing and shouting. Sam Salazar hastily drew back his leg, returned the switches to their previous condition. The car dropped like a rock. He snapped the switches up again, cushioning the fall.

"Get out of that car!" roared Lord Faide. He snatched away the helmet, dealt Sam Salazar a buffet which toppled him head over heels. "Out of the armor; back to your duties!"

Sam Salazar hurried to the jinxmen's wagons where he helped erect Isak Comandore's black tent. Inside the tent a black carpet with red and yellow patterns was laid; Comandore's cabinet, his chair, and his chest were carried in, and incense set burning in a censer. Directly in front of the main gate Hein Huss superintended the assembly of a rolling stage, forty feet tall and sixty feet long, the surface concealed from Ballant Keep by a tarpaulin.

Meanwhile, Lord Faide had dispatched an emissary, enjoining Lord Ballant to surrender. Lord Ballant delayed his response, hoping to delay the attack as long as possible. If he could maintain himself a day and a half, reinforcements from Gisborne Keep and Castle Cloud might force Lord Faide to retreat.

Lord Faide waited only until the jinxmen had completed their preparations, then sent another messenger, offering two more minutes in which to surrender.

One minute passed, two minutes. The envoys turned on their heels, marched back to the camp.

Lord Faide spoke to Hein Huss. "You are prepared?"

"I am prepared," rumbled Hein Huss.

"Drive them forth."

Huss raised his arm; the tarpaulin dropped from the face of his great display, to reveal a painted representation of Ballant Keep.

Huss retired to his tent, and pulled the flaps together. Braziers burnt fiercely, illuminating the faces of Adam McAdam, eight cabalmen, and six of the most advanced spellbinders. Each worked at a bench supporting several dozen dolls and a small glowing brazier. The cabalmen and spellbinders worked with dolls representing Ballant men-at-arms; Huss and Adam McAdam employed simulacra of the Ballant knights. Lord Ballant would not be hoodooed unless he ordered a jinx against Lord Faide—a courtesy the keep-lords extended each other.

Huss called out: "Sebastian!"

Sebastian, one of Huss's spellbinders, waiting at the flap to the tent, replied, "Ready, sir."

"Begin the display."

Sebastian ran to the stage, struck fire to a fuse. Watchers inside Ballant Keep saw the depicted keep take fire. Flame erupted from the windows, the roof glowed and crumbled. Inside the tent the two jinxmen, the cabalmen, and the spellbinders methodically took dolls, dipped them into the heat of the braziers, concentrating, reaching out for the mind of the man whose doll they burnt. Within the keep men became uneasy. Many began to imagine burning sensations, which became more severe as their minds grew more sensitive to the idea of fire. Lord Ballant noted the uneasiness. He signaled to his chief jinxman Anderson Grimes. "Begin the counterspell."

Down the front of the keep unrolled a display even larger than Hein Huss's, depicting a hideous beast. It stood on four legs and was shown picking up two men in a pair of hands, biting off their heads. Grimes's cabalmen meanwhile took up dolls representing the Faide warriors, inserted them into models of the depicted beast, and closed the hinged jaws, all the while projecting ideas of fear and disgust. And the Faide warriors, staring at the depicted monster, felt a sense of horror and weakness.

Inside Huss's tent the braziers reeked and dolls smoked. Eyes stared, brows glistened. From time to time one of the workers gasped—signaling the entry of his projection into an enemy mind. Within the keep warriors began to mutter, to slap at burning skin, to eye each other fearfully, noting each other's symptoms. Finally one cried out, and tore at his armor. "I burn! The cursed witches burn me!" His pain aggravated the discomfort of the others; there was a growing sound throughout the keep.

Lord Ballant's oldest son, his mind penetrated by Hein Huss himself, struck his shield with his mailed fist. "They burn me! They burn us all! Better to fight than burn!"

"Fight! Fight!" came the voices of the tormented men.

Lord Ballant looked around at the twisted faces, some displaying blisters, scaldmarks. "Our own spell terrifies them; wait yet a moment!" he pleaded.

His brother called hoarsely, "It is not your belly that Hein Huss toasts in the flames, it is mine! We cannot win a battle of hoodoos; we must win a battle of arms!"

Lord Ballant cried desperately, "Wait, our own effects are working! They will flee in terror; wait, wait!"

His cousin tore off his corselet. "It's Hein Huss! I feel him! My leg's in the fire, the devil laughs at me. Next my head, he says. Fight, or I go forth to fight alone!"

"Very well," said Lord Ballant in a fateful voice. "We go forth to fight. First—the beast goes forth. Then we follow and smite them in their terror."

The gates to the keep swung suddenly wide. Out sprang what appeared to be the depicted monster: legs moving, arms waving, eyes rolling, issuing evil sounds. Normally the Faide warriors would have seen the monster for what it was: a model carried on the backs of three horses. But their minds had been influenced; they had been infected with horror; they drew back with arms hanging flaccid. From behind the monster the Ballant knights galloped, followed by the Ballant foot soldiers. The charge gathered momentum, tore into the Faide center. Lord Faide bellowed orders; discipline asserted itself. The Faide knights disengaged, divided into three platoons, and engulfed the Ballant charge, while the foot soldiers poured darts into the advancing ranks.

There was the clatter and surge of battle; Lord Ballant, seeing that his sally had failed to overwhelm the Faide forces, and thinking to conserve his own forces, ordered a retreat. In good order the Ballant warriors began to back up toward the keep. The Faide knights held close contact, hoping to win to the courtyard. Close behind came a heavily loaded wagon pushed by armored horses, to be wedged against the gate.

Lord Faide called an order; a reserve platoon of ten knights charged from the side, thrust behind the main body of Ballant horsemen, rode through the footsoldiers, fought into the keep, cut down the gate-tenders.

Lord Ballant bellowed to Anderson Grimes, "They have won inside; quick with your cursed demon! If he can help us, let him do so now!"

"Demon-possession is not a matter of an instant," muttered the jinxman. "I need time."

"You have no time! Ten minutes and we're all dead!"

"I will do my best. Everid, Everid, come swift!"

He hastened into his workroom, donned his demonmask, tossed handful after handful of incense into the brazier. Against one wall stood a great form: black, slit-eyed, noseless. Great white fangs hung from its upper palate; it stood on heavy bent legs, arms reached forward to grasp. Anderson Grimes swallowed a cup of syrup, paced slowly back and forth. A moment passed.

"Grimes!" came Ballant's call from outside. "Grimes!"

A voice spoke. "Enter without fear."

Lord Ballant, carrying his ancestral side arm, entered. He drew back with an involuntary sound. "Grimes!" he whispered.

"Grimes is not here," said the voice. "I am here. Enter."

Lord Ballant came forward stiff-legged. The room was dark except for the feeble glimmer of the brazier. Anderson Grimes crouched in a corner, head bowed under his demonmask. The shadows twisted and pulsed with shapes and faces, forms struggling to become solid. The black image seemed to vibrate with life.

"Bring in your warriors," said the voice. "Bring them in five at a time, bid them look only at the floor until commanded to raise their eyes."

Lord Ballant retreated; there was no sound in the room.

A moment passed; then five limp and exhausted warriors filed into the room, eyes low.

"Look slowly up," said the voice. "Look at the orange fire. Breathe deeply. Then look at me. I am Everid, Demon of Hate. Look at me. Who am I?"

"You are Everid, Demon of Hate," quavered the warriors.

"I stand all around you, in a dozen forms. . . . I come closer. Where am I?"

"You are close."

"Now I am you. We are together."

There was a sudden quiver of motion. The warriors stood straighter, their faces distorted.

"Go forth," said the voice. "Go quietly into the court. In a few minutes we march forth to slay."

The five stalked forth. Five more entered.

Outside the wall the Ballant knights had retreated as far as the gate; within, seven Faide knights still survived, and with their backs to the wall held the Ballant warriors away from the gate mechanism.

In the Faide camp Huss called to Comandore, "Everid is walking. Bring forth Keyril."

"Send the men," came Comandore's voice, low and harsh. "Send the men to me. I am Keyril."

Within the keep twenty warriors came marching into the courtyard. Their steps were cautious, tentative, slow. Their faces had lost individuality, they were twisted and distorted, curiously alike.

"Bewitched!" whispered the Ballant soldiers, drawing back. The seven Faide knights watched with sudden fright. But the twenty warriors, paying them no heed, marched out the gate. The Ballant knights parted; for an instant there was a lull in the fighting. The twenty sprang like tigers. Their swords glistened, twinkling in water-bright arcs. They crouched, jerked, jumped; Faide arms, legs, heads were hewed off. The twenty were cut and battered, but the blows seemed to have no effect.

The Faide attack faltered, collapsed. The knights, whose armor was no protection against the demoniac swords, retreated. The twenty possessed warriors raced out into the open toward the foot soldiers, running with great strides, slashing and rending. The Faide foot soldiers fought for a moment, then they too gave way and turned to flee.

From behind Comandore's tent appeared thirty Faide warriors, marching stiffly, slowly. Like the Ballant twenty their faces were alike—but between the Everid-possessed and the Keyril-possessed was the difference between the face of Everid and the face of Keyril.

Keyril and Everid fought, using the men as weapons, without fear, retreat, or mercy. Hack, chop, cut. Arms, legs, sundered torsos. Bodies fought headless for moments before collapsing. Only when a body was minced, hacked to bits, did the demoniac vitality depart. Presently there were no more men of Everid, and only fifteen men of Keyril. These hopped and limped and tumbled toward the keep where Faide knights still held the gate. The Ballant knights met them in despair, knowing that now was the decisive moment. Leaping, leering from chopped faces, slashing from tireless arms, the warriors cut a hole into the iron. The Faide knights, roaring victory cries, plunged after. Into the courtyard surged the battle, and now there was no longer doubt of the outcome. Ballant Keep was taken.

Back in his tent Isak Comandore took a deep breath, shuddered, flung down his demonmask. In the courtyard the twelve remaining warriors dropped in their tracks, twitched, gasped, gushed blood and died.

Lord Ballant, in the last gallant act of a gallant life, marched forth brandishing his ancestral side arm. He aimed across the bloody field at Lord Faide, pulled the trigger. The weapon spewed a brief gout of light; Lord Faide's skin prickled and hair rose from his head. The weapon crackled, turned cherry-red, and melted. Lord Ballant threw down the weapon, drew his sword, marched forth to challenge Lord Faide.

Lord Faide, disinclined to unnecessary combat, signaled to his soldiers. A flight of darts ended Lord Ballant's life, saving him the discomfort of formal execution.

There was no further resistance. The Ballant defenders threw down their arms and marched grimly out to kneel before Lord Faide, while inside the keep the Ballant women gave themselves to mourning and grief.

V

Lord Faide had no wish to linger at Ballant Keep, for he took no relish in his victories. Inevitably, a thousand decisions had to be made. Six of the closest Ballant kinsmen were summarily stabbed and the title declared defunct. Others of the clan were offered a choice: an oath of lifelong fealty together with a moderate ransom, or death. Only two, eyes blazing hate, chose death and were instantly stabbed.

Lord Faide had now achieved his ambition. For over a thousand years the keep-lords had struggled for power; now one, now another gaining ascendancy. None before had ever extended his authority across the entire continent—which meant control of the planet, since all other land was either sun-parched rock or eternal ice. Ballant Keep had long thwarted Lord Faide's drive to power; now—success, total and absolute. It still remained to chastise the lords of Castle Cloud and Gisborne, both of whom, seeing opportunity to overwhelm Lord Faide, had ranged themselves behind Lord Ballant. But these were matters that might well be assigned to Hein Huss.

Lord Faide, for the first time in his life, felt a trace of uncertainty. Now what? No real adversaries remained. The First Folk must be whipped back, but here was no great problem; they were numerous, but no more than savages. He knew that dissatisfaction and controversy would ultimately arise among his kinsmen and allies. Inaction and boredom would breed irritability; idle minds would calculate the pros and cons of mischief. Even the most loyal would remember the campaigns with nostalgia and long for the excitement, the release, the license, of warfare. Somehow he must find means to absorb the energy of so many active and keyed-up men. How and where, this was the problem. The construction of roads? New farmland claimed from the downs? Yearly tournaments-at-arms? Lord Faide frowned at the inadequacy of his solutions, but his imagination was impoverished by the lack of tradition. The original settlers of Pangborn had been warriors, and had brought with them a certain amount of practical rule-of-thumb knowledge, but little else. The tales they passed down the generations described the great spaceships which moved with magic speed and certainty, the miraculous weapons, the wars in the void, but told nothing of human history or civilized achievement. And so Lord Faide, full of power and success, but with no goal toward which to turn his strength, felt more morose and saturnine than ever.

He gloomily inspected the spoils from Ballant Keep. They were of no great interest to him. Ballant's ancestral car was no longer used, but displayed behind a glass case. He inspected the weapon Volcano, but this could not be moved. In any event it was useless, its magic lost forever. Lord Faide now knew that Lord Ballant had ordered it turned against the Faide car, but that it had refused to spew its vaunted fire. Lord Faide saw with disdainful amusement that Volcano had been sadly neglected. Corrosion had pitted the metal, careless cleaning had twisted the exterior tubing, undoubtedly diminishing the potency of the magic. No such neglect at Faide Keep! Jambart the weapon-tender cherished Hellmouth with absolute devotion. Elsewhere were other ancient devices, interesting but useless—the same sort of curios that cluttered shelves and cases at Faide Keep. (Peculiar, these ancient men! thought Lord Faide: at once so clever, yet so primitive and impractical. Conditions had changed; there had been enormous advances since the dark ages sixteen hundred years ago. For instance, the ancients had used intricate fetishes of metal and glass to communicate with each other. Lord Faide need merely voice his needs; Hein Huss could project his mind a hundred miles to see, to hear, to relay Lord Faide's words.) The ancients had contrived dozens of such objects, but the old magic had worn away and they never seemed to function. Lord Ballant's side arm had melted, after merely stinging Lord Faide. Imagine a troop armed thus trying to cope with a platoon of demon-possessed warriors! Slaughter of the innocents!

Among the Ballant trove Lord Faide noted a dozen old books and several reels of microfilm. The books were worthless, page after page of incomprehensible jargon; the microfilm was equally undecipherable. Again Lord Faide wondered skeptically about the ancients. Clever of course, but to look at the hard facts, they were little more advanced than the First Folk: neither had facility with telepathy or voyance or demon-command. And the magic of the ancients: might there not be a great deal of exaggeration in the legends? Volcano, for instance. A joke. Lord Faide wondered about his own Hellmouth. But no—surely Hellmouth was more trustworthy; Jambart cleaned and polished the weapon daily and washed the entire cupola with vintage wine every month. If human care could induce faithfulness, then Hellmouth was ready to defend Faide Keep!

Now there was no longer need for defense. Faide was supreme. Considering the future, Lord Faide made a decision. There should no longer be keep-lords on Pangborn; he would abolish the appellation. Habitancy of the keeps would gradually be transferred to trusted bailiffs on a yearly basis. The former lords would be moved to comfortable but indefensible manor houses, with the maintenance of private troops forbidden. Naturally they must be allowed jinxmen, but these would be made accountable to himself—perhaps through some sort of licensing provision. He must discuss the matter with Hein Huss. A matter for the future, however. Now he merely wished to settle affairs and return to Faide Keep.

There was little more to be done. The surviving Ballant kinsmen he sent to their homes after Hein Huss had impregnated fresh dolls with their essences. Should they default on their ransoms, a twinge of fire, a few stomach cramps would more than set them right. Ballant Keep itself Lord Faide would have liked to burn—but the material of the ancients was proof to fire. But in order to discourage any new pretenders to the Ballant heritage Lord Faide ordered all the heirlooms and relics brought forth into the courtyard, and then, one at a time, in order of rank, he bade his men choose. Thus the Ballant wealth was distributed. Even the jinxmen were invited to choose, but they despised the ancient trinkets as works of witless superstition. The lesser spellbinders and apprentices rummaged through the leavings, occasionally finding an overlooked bauble or some anomalous implement. Isak Comandore was irritated to find Sam Salazar staggering under a load of the ancient books. "And what is your purpose with these?" he barked. "Why do you burden yourself with rubbish?"

Sam Salazar hung his head. "I have no definite purpose. Undoubtedly there was wisdom—or at least knowledge—among the ancients; perhaps I can use these symbols of knowledge to sharpen my own understanding."

Comandore threw up his hands in disgust. He turned to Hein Huss who stood nearby. "First he fancies himself a tree and stands in the mud; now he thinks to learn jinxmanship through a study of ancient symbols."

Huss shrugged. "They were men like ourselves, and, though limited, they were not entirely obtuse. A certain simian cleverness is required to fabricate these objects."

"Simian cleverness is no substitute for sound jinxmanship," retorted Isak Comandore. "This is a point hard to overemphasize; I have drummed it into Salazar's head a hundred times. And now, look at him."

Huss grunted noncommittally. "I fail to understand what he hopes to achieve."

Sam Salazar tried to explain, fumbling for words to express an idea that did not exist. "I thought perhaps to decipher the writing, if only to understand what the ancients thought, and perhaps to learn how to perform one or two of their tricks."

Comandore rolled up his eyes. "What enemy bewitched me when I consented to take you as apprentice? I can cast twenty hoodoos in an hour, more than any of the ancients could achieve in a lifetime."

"Nevertheless," said Sam Salazar, "I notice that Lord Faide rides in his ancestral car, and that Lord Ballant sought to kill us all with Volcano."

"I notice," said Comandore with feral softness, "that my demon Keyril conquered Lord Ballant's Volcano, and that riding on my wagon I can outdistance Lord Faide in his car."

Sam Salazar thought better of arguing further. "True, Jinxman Comandore, very true. I stand corrected."

"Then discard that rubbish and make yourself useful. We return to Faide Keep in the morning."

"As you wish, Jinxman Comandore." Sam Salazar threw the books back into the trash.

VI

The Ballant clan had been dispersed, Ballant Keep was despoiled. Lord Faide and his men banqueted somberly in the great hall, tended by silent Ballant servitors.

Ballant Keep had been built on the same splendid scale as Faide Keep. The great hall was a hundred feet long, fifty feet wide, fifty feet high, paneled in planks sawn from pale native hardwood, rubbed and waxed to a rich honey color. Enormous black beams supported the ceiling; from these hung candelabra, intricate contrivances of green, purple, and blue glass, knotted with ancient but still bright light-motes. On the far wall hung portraits of all the lords of Ballant Keep—105 grave faces in a variety of costumes. Below, a genealogical chart ten feet high detailed the descent of the Ballants and their connections with the other noble clans. Now there was a desolate air to the hall, and the 105 dead faces were meaningless and empty.

Lord Faide dined without joy, and cast dour side glances at those of his kinsmen who reveled too gladly. Lord Ballant, he thought, had conducted himself only as he himself might have done under the same circumstances; coarse exultation seemed in poor taste, almost as if it were disrespect for Lord Faide himself. His followers were quick to catch his mood, and the banquet proceeded with greater decorum.

The jinxmen sat apart in a smaller room to the side. Anderson Grimes, erstwhile Ballant Head Jinxman, sat beside Hein Huss, trying to put a good face on his defeat. After all, he had performed creditably against four powerful adversaries, and there was no cause to feel a diminution of *mana*. The five jinxmen discussed the battle, while the cabalmen and spellbinders listened respectfully. The conduct of the demon-possessed troops occasioned the most discussion. Anderson Grimes readily admitted that his conception of Everid was a force absolutely brutal and blunt, terrifying in its indomitable vigor. The other jinxmen agreed that he undoubtedly succeeded in projecting these qualities; Hein Huss however pointed out that Isak Commandore's Keyril, as cruel and vigorous as Everid, also combined a measure of crafty malice, which tended to make the possessed soldier a more effective weapon.

Anderson Grimes allowed that this might well be the case, and that in fact he had been considering such an augmentation of Everid's characteristics.

"To my mind," said Huss, "the most effective demon should be swift enough to avoid the strokes of the brute demons, such as Keyril and Everid. I cite my own Dant as example. A Dant-possessed warrior can easily destroy a Keyril or an Everid, simply through his agility. In an encounter of this sort the Keyrils and Everids presently lose their capacity to terrify, and thus half the effect is lost."

Isak Comandore pierced Huss with a hot russet glance. "You state a presumption as if it were fact. I have formulated Keyril with sufficient craft to counter any such displays of speed. I firmly believe Keyril to be the most fearsome of all demons."

"It may well be," rumbled Hein Huss thoughtfully. He beckoned to a steward, gave instructions. The steward reduced the light a trifle. "Behold," said Hein Huss. "There is Dant. He comes to join the banquet." To the side of the room loomed the tiger-striped Dant, a creature constructed of resilient metal, with four terrible arms, and a squat black head which seemed all gaping jaw.

"Look," came the husky voice of Isak Comandore. "There is Keyril." Keyril was rather more humanoid and armed with a cutlass. Dant spied Keyril. The jaws gaped wider, it sprang to the attack.

The battle was a thing of horror; the two demons rolled, twisted, bit, frothed, uttered soundless shrieks, tore each other apart. Suddenly Dant sprang away, circled Keyril with dizzying speed, faster, faster; became a blur, a wild coruscation of colors that seemed to give off a high-pitched wailing sound, rising higher and higher in pitch. Keyril hacked brutally with his cutlass, then seemed to grow feeble and wan. The light that once had been Dant blazed white, exploded in a mental shriek; Keyril was gone and Isak Comandore lay moaning.

Hein Huss drew a deep breath, wiped his face, looked about him with a complacent grin. The entire company sat rigid as stones, staring, all except the apprentice Sam Salazar, who met Hein Huss's glance with a cheerful smile.

"So," growled Huss, panting from his exertion, "you consider yourself superior to the illusion; you sit and smirk at one of Hein Huss's best efforts."

"No, no," cried Sam Salazar, "I mean no disrespect! I want to learn, so I watched you rather than the demons. What could they teach me? Nothing!"

"Ah," said Huss, mollified. "And what did you learn?"

"Likewise, nothing," said Sam Salazar, "but at least I do not sit like a fish."

Comandore's voice came soft but crackling with wrath. "You see in me the resemblance to a fish?"

"I except you, Jinxman Comandore, naturally," Sam Salazar explained.

"Please go to my cabinet, Apprentice Salazar, and fetch me the doll that is your likeness. The steward will bring a basin of water, and we shall have some sport. With your knowledge of fish you perhaps can breathe under water. If not—you may suffocate."

"I prefer not, Jinxman Comandore," said Sam Salazar. "In fact, with your permission, I now resign your service."

Comandore motioned to one of his cabalmen. "Fetch me the Salazar doll. Since he is no longer my apprentice, it is likely indeed that he will suffocate."

"Come now, Comandore," said Hein Huss gruffly. "Do not torment the lad. He is innocent and a trifle addled. Let this be an occasion of placidity and ease."

"Certainly, Hein Huss," said Comandore. "Why not? There is ample time in which to discipline this upstart."

"Jinxman Huss," said Sam Salazar, "since I am now relieved of my duties to Jinxman Comandore, perhaps you will accept me into your service."

Hein Huss made a noise of vast distaste. "You are not my responsibility."

"There are many futures, Hein Huss," said Sam Salazar. "You have said as much yourself."

Hein Huss looked at Sam Salazar with his water-clear eyes. "Yes, there are many futures. And I think that tonight sees the full amplitude of jinxmanship. . . . I think that never again will such power and skill gather at the same table. We shall die one by one and there shall be none to fill our shoes. . . . Yes, Sam Salazar. I will take you as apprentice. Isak Comandore, do you hear? This youth is now of my company."

"I must be compensated," growled Comandore.

"You have coveted my doll of Tharon Faide, the only one in existence. It is yours."

"Ah, ha!" cried Isak Comandore leaping to his feet. "Hein Huss, I salute you! You are generous indeed! I thank you and accept!"

Hein Huss motioned to Sam Salazar. "Move your effects to my wagon. Do not show your face again tonight."

Sam Salazar bowed with dignity and departed the hall.

The banquet continued, but now something of melancholy filled the room. Presently a messenger from Lord Faide came to warn all to bed, for the party returned to Faide Keep at dawn.

VII

The victorious Faide troops gathered on the heath before Ballant Keep. As a parting gesture Lord Faide ordered the great gate torn off the hinges, so that ingress could never again be denied him. But even after sixteen hundred years the hinges were proof to all the force the horses could muster, and the gates remained in place.

Lord Faide accepted the fact with good grace and bade farewell to his cousin Renfroy, whom he had appointed bailiff. He climbed into his car, settled himself, snapped the switch. The car groaned and moved forward. Behind came the knights and the foot soldiers, then the baggage train, laden with booty, and finally the wagons of the jinxmen.

Three hours the column marched across the mossy downs. Ballant Keep dwindled behind; ahead appeared North and South Wildwood, darkening all the sweep of the western horizon. Where once the break had existed, the First Folk's new planting showed a smudge lower and less intense than the old woodlands.

Two miles from the woodlands Lord Faide called a halt and signaled up his knights. Hein Huss laboriously dismounted from his wagon, came forward.

"In the event of resistance," Lord Faide told the knights, "do not be tempted into the forest. Stay with the column and at all times be on your guard against traps."

Hein Huss spoke. "You wish me to parley with the First Folk once more?"

"No," said Lord Faide. "It is ridiculous that I must ask permission of savages to ride over my own land. We return as we came; if they interfere, so much the worse for them."

"You are rash," said Huss with simple candor.

Lord Faide glanced down at him with black eyebrows raised. "What damage can they do if we avoid their traps? Blow foam at us?"

"It is not my place to advise or to warn," said Hein Huss. "However, I point out that they exhibit a confidence which does not come from conscious weakness; also, that they carried tubes, apparently hollow grasswood shoots, which imply missiles."

Lord Faide nodded. "No doubt. However, the knights wear armor, the soldiers carry bucklers. It is not fit that I, Lord Faide of Faide Keep, choose my path to suit the whims of the First Folk. This must be made clear, even if the exercise involves a dozen or so First Folk corpses."

"Since I am not a fighting man," remarked Hein Huss, "I will keep well to the rear, and pass only when the way is secure."

"As you wish." Lord Faide pulled down the visor of his helmet. "Forward."

The column moved toward the forest, along the previous track, which showed plain across the moss. Lord Faide rode in the lead, flanked by his brother, Gethwin Faide, and his cousin, Mauve Dermont-Faide.

A half mile passed, and another. The forest was only a mile distant. Overhead the great sun rode at zenith; brightness and heat poured down; the air carried the oily scent of thorn and tarbush. The column moved on, more slowly; the only sound the clanking of armor, the muffled thud of hooves in the moss, the squeal of wagon wheels.

Lord Faide rose up in his car, watching for any sign of hostile preparation. A half mile from the planting the forms of the First Folk, waiting in the shade along the forest's verge, became visible. Lord Faide ignored them, held a steady pace along the track they had traveled before.

The half-mile became a quarter-mile. Lord Faide turned to order the troops into single file and was just in time to see a hole suddenly open into the moss and his brother, Gethwin Faide, drop from sight. There was a rattle, a thud, the howling of the impaled horse; Gethwin's wild calls as the horse kicked and crushed him into the stakes. Mauve Dermont-Faide, riding beside Gethwin, could not control his own horse, which leaped aside from the pit and blundered upon a trigger. Up from the moss burst a tree trunk studded with foot-long thorns. It snapped, quick as a scorpion's tail; the thorns punctured Mauve Dermont-Faide's armor, his chest, and whisked him from his horse to carry him suspended, writhing and screaming. The tip of the scythe pounded into Lord Faide's car, splintered against the hull. The car swung groaning through the air. Lord Faide clutched at the windscreen to prevent himself from falling.

The column halted; several men ran to the pit, but Gethwin Faide lay twenty feet below, crushed under his horse. Others took Mauve Dermont-Faide down from the swaying scythe, but he, too, was dead.

Lord Faide's skin tingled with a gooseflesh of hate and rage. He looked toward the forest. The First Folk stood motionless. He beckoned to Bernard, sergeant of the foot soldiers. "Two men with lances to try out the ground ahead. All others ready with darts. At my signal spit the devils."

Two men came forward, and marching before Lord Faide's car, probed at the ground. Lord Faide settled in his seat. "Forward."

The column moved slowly toward the forest, every man tense and ready. The lances of the two men in the vanguard presently broke through the moss, to disclose a nettle trap—a pit lined with nettles, each frond ripe with globes of acid. Carefully they probed out a path to the side, and the column filed around, each man walking in the other's tracks.

At Lord Faide's side now rode his two nephews, Scolford and Edwin. "Notice," said Lord Faide in a voice harsh and tight. "These traps were laid since our last passage; an act of malice."

"But why did they guide us through before?"

Lord Faide smiled bitterly. "They were willing that we should die at Ballant Keep. But we have disappointed them."

"Notice, they carry tubes," said Scolford.

"Blowguns possibly," suggested Edwin.

Scolford disagreed. "They cannot blow through their foamvents."

"No doubt we shall soon learn," said Lord Faide. He rose in his seat, called to the rear. "Ready with the darts!"

The soldiers raised their crossbows. The column advanced slowly, now only a hundred yards from the planting. The white shapes of the First Folk moved uneasily at the forest's edges. Several of them raised their tubes, seemed to sight along the length. They twitched their great hands.

One of the tubes was pointed toward Lord Faide. He saw a small black object leave the opening, flit forward, gathering speed. He heard a hum, waxing to a rasping, clicking flutter. He ducked behind the windscreen; the projectile swooped in pursuit, struck the windscreen like a thrown stone. It fell crippled upon the forward deck of the car—a heavy black insect like a wasp, its broken proboscis oozing ocher liquid, horny wings beating feebly, eyes like dumbbells fixed on Lord Faide. With his mailed fist, he crushed the creature.

Behind him other wasps struck knights and men; Corex Faide-Battaro took the prong through his visor into the eye, but the armor of the other knights defeated the wasps. The foot soldiers, however, lacked protection; the wasps half buried themselves in flesh. The soldiers called out in pain, clawed away the wasps, squeezed the wounds. Corex Faide-Battaro toppled from his horse, ran blindly out over the heath, and after fifty feet fell into a trap. The stricken soldiers began to twitch, then fell on the moss, thrashed, leaped up to run with flapping arms, threw themselves in wild somersaults, forward, backward, foaming and thrashing.

In the forest, the First Folk raised their tubes again. Lord Faide bellowed, "Spit the creatures! Bowmen, launch your darts!"

There came the twang of crossbows, darts snapped at the quiet white shapes. A few staggered and wandered aimlessly away; most, however, plucked out the darts or ignored them. They took capsules from small sacks, put them to the end of their tubes.

"Beware the wasps!" cried Lord Faide. "Strike with your bucklers! Kill the cursed things in flight!"

The rasp of horny wings came again; certain of the soldiers found courage enough to follow Lord Faide's orders, and battered down the wasps. Others struck home as before; behind came another flight. The column became a tangle of struggling, crouching men.

"Footmen, retreat!" called Lord Faide furiously. "Footmen back! Knights to me!"

The soldiers fled back along the track, taking refuge behind the baggage wagons. Thirty of their number lay dying, or dead, on the moss.

Lord Faide cried out to his knights in a voice like a bugle. "Dismount, follow slow after me! Turn your helmets, keep the wasps from your eyes! One step at a time, behind the car! Edwin, into the car beside me, test the footing with your lance. Once in the forest there are no traps! Then attack!"

The knights formed themselves into a line behind the car. Lord Faide drove slowly forward, his kinsman Edwin prodding the ground ahead. The First Folk sent out a dozen more wasps, which dashed themselves vainly against the armor. Then there was silence . . . cessation of sound, activity. The First Folk watched impassively as the knights approached, step by step.

Edwin's lance found a trap, the column moved to the side. Another trap—and the column was diverted from the planting toward the forest. Step by step, yard by yard—another trap, another detour, and now the column was only a hundred feet from the forest. A trap to the left, a trap to the right: the safe path led directly toward an enormous heavy-branched tree. Seventy feet, fifty feet, then Lord Faide drew his sword.

"Prepare to charge, kill till your arms tire!"

From the forest came a crackling sound. The branches of the great tree trembled and swayed. The knights stared, for a moment frozen into place. The tree toppled forward, the knights madly tried to flee—to the rear, to the sides. Traps opened; the knights dropped upon sharp stakes. The tree fell; boughs cracked armored bodies like nuts; there was the hoarse yelling of pinned men, screams from the traps, the crackling subsidence of breaking branches. Lord Faide had been battered down into the car, and the car had been pressed groaning into the moss. His first instinctive act was to press the switch to rest position; then he staggered erect, clambered up through the boughs. A pale unhuman face peered at him; he swung his fist, crushed the faceted eye-bulge, and roaring with rage scrambled through the branches. Others of his knights were working themselves free, although almost a third were either crushed or impaled.

The First Folk came scrambling forward, armed with enormous thorns, long as swords. But now Lord Faide could reach them at close quarters. Hissing with vindictive joy he sprang into their midst, swinging his sword with both hands, as if demon-possessed. The sur-

viving knights joined him and the ground became littered with dis-
membered First Folk. They drew back slowly, without excitement.
Lord Faide reluctantly called back his knights. "We must succor those
still pinned, as many as still are alive."

As well as possible branches were cut away, injured knights
drawn forth. In some cases the soft moss had cushioned the impact
of the tree. Six knights were dead, another four crushed beyond hope
of recovery. To these Lord Faide himself gave the *coup de grâce*. Ten
minutes further hacking and chopping freed Lord Faide's car, while
the First Folk watched incuriously from the forest. The knights
wished to charge once more, but Lord Faide ordered retreat. Without
interference they returned the way they had come, back to the baggage train.

Lord Faide ordered a muster. Of the original war party, less than two-
thirds remained. Lord Faide shook his head bitterly. Galling to think
how easily he had been led into a trap! He swung on his heel, strode
to the rear of the column, to the wagons of the magicians. The
jinxmen sat around a small fire, drinking tea. "Which of you will
hoodoo these white forest vermin? I want them dead—stricken with
sickness, cramps, blindness, the most painful afflictions you can con-
trive!"

There was general silence. The jinxmen sipped their tea.

"Well?" demanded Lord Faide. "Have you no answer? Do I not
make myself plain?"

Hein Huss cleared his throat, spat into the blaze. "Your wishes
are plain. Unfortunately we cannot hoodoo the First Folk."

"And why?"

"There are technical reasons."

Lord Faide knew the futility of argument. "Must we slink home
around the forest? If you cannot hoodoo the First Folk, then bring
out your demons! I will march on the forest and chop out a path
with my sword!"

"It is not for me to suggest tactics," grumbled Hein Huss.

"Go on, speak! I will listen."

"A suggestion has been put to me, which I will pass to you.
Neither I nor the other jinxmen associate ourselves with it, since it
recommends the crudest of physical principles."

"I await the suggestion," said Lord Faide.

"It is merely this. One of my apprentices tampered with your car, as you may remember."

"Yes, and I will see he gets the hiding he deserves."

"By some freak he caused the car to rise high into the air. The suggestion is this: that we load the car with as much oil as the baggage train affords, that we send the car aloft and let it drift over the planting. At a suitable moment, the occupant of the car will pour the oil over the trees, then hurl down a torch. The forest will burn. The First Folk will be at least discomfited; at best a large number will be destroyed."

Lord Faide slapped his hands together. "Excellent! Quickly, to work!" He called a dozen soldiers, gave them orders; four kegs of cooking oil, three buckets of pitch, six demijohns of spirit were brought and lifted into the car. The engines grated and protested, and the car sagged almost to the moss.

Lord Faide shook his head sadly. "A rude use of the relic, but all in good purpose. Now, where is that apprentice? He must indicate which switches and which buttons he turned."

"I suggest," said Hein Huss, "that Sam Salazar be sent up with the car."

Lord Faide looked sidewise at Sam Salazar's round, bland countenance. "An efficient hand is needed, a seasoned judgment. I wonder if he can be trusted?"

"I would think so," said Hein Huss, "inasmuch as it was Sam Salazar who evolved the scheme in the first place."

"Very well. In with you, Apprentice! Treat my car with reverence! The wind blows away from us; fire this edge of the forest, in as long a strip as you can manage. The torch, where is the torch?"

The torch was brought and secured to the side of the car.

"One more matter," said Sam Salazar. "I would like to borrow the armor of some obliging knight, to protect myself from the wasps. Otherwise—"

"Armor!" bawled Lord Faide. "Bring armor!"

At last, fully accoutered and with visor down, Sam Salazar climbed into the car. He seated himself, peered intently at the buttons and switches. In truth he was not precisely certain as to which he had manipulated before. . . . He considered, reached forward, pushed, turned. The motors roared and screamed; the car shuddered, sluggishly rose into the air. Higher, higher, twenty feet, forty feet, sixty feet—a hundred, two hundred. The wind eased the car toward the forest; in the shade the First Folk watched. Several of them raised tubes, opened the shutters. The onlookers saw the wasps dart through the air to dash against Sam Salazar's armor.

The car drifted over the trees; Sam Salazar began ladling out the oil. Below, the First Folk stirred uneasily. The wind carried the car too far over the forest; Sam Salazar worked the controls, succeeded in guiding himself back. One keg was empty, and another; he tossed them out, presently emptied the remaining two, and the buckets of pitch. He soaked a rag in spirit, ignited it, threw it over the side, poured the spirit after.

The flaming rag fell into leaves. A crackle, fire blazed and sprang. The car now floated at a height of five hundred feet. Salazar poured over the remaining spirits, dropped the demijohns, guided the car back over the heath, and fumbling nervously with the controls dropped the car in a series of swoops back to the moss.

Lord Faide sprang forward, clapped him on the shoulder. "Excellently done! The forest blazes like tinder!"

The men of Faide Keep stood back, rejoicing to see the flames soar and lick. The First Folk scurried back from the heat, waving their arms; foam of a peculiar purple color issued from their vents as they ran, small useless puffs discharged as if by accident or through excitement. The flames ate through first the forest, then spread into the new planting, leaping through the leaves.

"Prepare to march!" called Lord Faide. "We pass directly behind the flames, before the First Folk return."

Off in the forest the First Folk perched in the trees, blowing out foam in great puffs and billows, building a wall of insulation. The flames had eaten half across the new planting, leaving behind smoldering saplings.

"Forward! Briskly!"

The column moved ahead. Coughing in the smoke, eyes smarting, they passed under still blazing trees and came out on the western downs.

Slowly the column moved forward, led by a pair of soldiers prodding the moss with lances. Behind followed Lord Faide with the knights, then came the foot soldiers, then the rumbling baggage train, and finally the six wagons of the jinxmen.

A thump, a creak, a snap. A scythe had broken up from the

moss; the soldiers in the lead dropped flat; the scythe whipped past, a foot from Lord Faide's face. At the same time a plaintive cry came from the rear guard. "They pursue! The First Folk come!"

Lord Faide turned to inspect the new threat. A clot of First Folk, two hundred or more, came across the moss, moving without haste of urgency. Some carried wasp tubes, others thorn-rapiers.

Lord Faid looked ahead. Another hundred yards should bring the army out upon safe ground; then he could deploy and maneuver. "Forward!"

The column proceeded, the baggage train and the jinxmen's wagons pressing close up against the soldiers. Behind and to the side came the First Folk, moving casually and easily.

At last Lord Faide judged they had reached secure ground. "Forward, now! Bring the wagons out, hurry now!"

The troops needed no urging; they trotted out over the heath, the wagons trundling after. Lord Faide ordered the wagons into a close double line, stationed the soldiers between, with the horses behind and protected from the wasps. The knights, now dismounted, waited in front.

The First Folk came listlessly, formlessly forward. Blank white faces stared; huge hands grasped tubes and thorns; traces of the purplish foam showed at the lips of their underarm orifices.

Lord Faide walked along the line of knights. "Swords ready. Allow them as close as they care to come. Then a quick charge." He motioned to the foot soldiers. "Choose a target . . . !" A volley of darts whistled overhead, to plunge into white bodies. With chisel-bladed fingers the First Folk plucked them out, discarded them with no evidence of vexation. One or two staggered, wandered confusedly across the line of approach. Others raised their tubes, withdrew the shutter. Out flew the insects, horny wings rasping, prongs thrust forward. Across the moss they flickered, to crush themselves against the armor of the knights, to drop to the ground, to be stamped upon. The soldiers cranked their crossbows back into tension, discharged another flight of darts, caused several more First Folk casualties.

The First Folk spread into a long line, surrounding the Faide troops. Lord Faide shifted half his knights to the other side of the wagons.

The First Folk wandered closer. Lord Faide called for a charge. The knights stepped smartly forward, swords swinging. The First Folk advanced a few more steps, then stopped short. The flaps of skin at their backs swelled, pulsed; white foam gushed through their vents; clouds and billows rose up around them. The knights halted uncertainly, prodding and slashing into the foam but finding nothing. The foam piled higher, rolling in and forward, pushing the knights back toward the wagons. They looked questioningly toward Lord Faide.

Lord Faide waved his sword. "Cut through to the other side! Forward!" Slashing two-handed with his sword, he sprang into the foam. He struck something solid, hacked blindly at it, pushed forward. Then his legs were seized; he was upended and fell with a spine-rattling jar. Now he felt the grate of a thorn searching his armor. It found a crevice under his corselet and pierced him. Cursing he raised on his hands and knees, and plunged blindly forward. Enormous hard hands grasped him, heavy forms fell on his shoulders. He tried to breathe, but the foam clogged his visor; he began to smother. Staggering to his feet he half ran, half fell out into the open air, carrying two of the First Folk with him. He had lost his sword, but managed to draw his dagger. The First Folk released him and stepped back into the foam. Lord Faide sprang to his feet. Inside the foam came the sounds of combat; some of his knights burst into the open; others called for help. Lord Faide motioned to the knights. "Back within; the devils slaughter our kinsmen! In and on to the center!"

He took a deep breath. Seizing his dagger he thrust himself back into the foam. A flurry of shapes came at him: he pounded with his fists, cut with his dagger, stumbled over a mass of living tissue. He kicked the softness, and stepped on metal. Bending, he grasped a leg but found it limp and dead. First Folk were on his back, another thorn found its mark; he groaned and thrust himself forward, and once again fell out into the open air.

A scant fifty of his knights had won back into the central clearing. Lord Faide cried out, "To the center; mount your horses!" Abandoning his car, he himself vaulted into a saddle. The foam boiled and billowed closer. Lord Faide waved his arm. "Forward, all; at a gallop! After us the wagons—out into the open!"

They charged, thrusting the frightened horses into the foam. There was white blindness, the feel of forms underneath, then the open air once again. Behind came the wagons, and the foot soldiers, running along the channel cut by the wagons. All won free—all but the knights who had fallen under the foam.

Two hundred yards from the great white clot of foam, Lord Faide halted, turned, looked back. He raised his fist, shook it in a passion. "My knights, my car, my honor! I'll burn your forests, I'll drive you into the sea, there'll be no peace till all are dead!" He swung around. "Come," he called bitterly to the remnants of his war party. "We have been defeated. We retreat to Faide Keep."

VIII

Faide Keep, like Ballant Keep, was constructed of a black, glossy substance, half metal, half stone, impervious to heat, force, and radiation. A parasol roof, designed to ward off hostile energy, rested on five squat outer towers, connected by walls almost as high as the lip of the overhanging roof.

The homecoming banquet was quiet and morose. The soldiers and knights ate lightly and drank much, but instead of becoming merry, lapsed into gloom. Lord Faide, overcome by emotion, jumped to his feet. "Everyone sits silent, aching with rage. I feel no differently. We shall take revenge. We shall put the forests to the torch. The cursed white savages will smother and burn. Drink now with good cheer; not a moment will be wasted. But we must be ready. It is no more than idiocy to attack as before. Tonight I take council with the jinxmen, and we will start a program of affliction."

The soldiers and knights rose to their feet, raised their cups and drank a somber toast. Lord Faide bowed and left the hall.

He went to his private trophy room. On the walls hung escutcheons, memorials, deathmasks, clusters of swords like many-petaled flowers; a rack of side arms, energy pistols, electric stilettos; a portrait of the original Faide, in ancient spacefarer's uniform, and a treasured, almost unique, photograph of the great ship that had brought the first Faide to Pangborn.

Lord Faide studied the ancient face for several moments, then summoned a servant. "Ask the Head Jinxman to attend me."

Hein Huss presently stumped into the room. Lord Faide turned away from the portrait, seated himself, motioned to Hein Huss to do likewise. "What of the keep-lords?" he asked. "How do they regard the setback at the hands of the First Folk?"

"There are various reactions," said Hein Huss. "At Boghoten, Candelwade, and Havve there is distress and anger."

Lord Faide nodded. "These are my kinsmen."

"At Gisborne, Graymar, Castle Cloud, and Alder there is satis-faction, veiled calculation."

"To be expected," muttered Lord Faide. "These lords must be humbled; in spite of oaths and undertakings, they still think rebel-lion."

"At Star Home, Julian-Douray, and Oak Hall I read surprise at the abilities of the First Folk, but in the main disinterest."

Lord Faide nodded sourly. "Well enough. There is no actual rebellion in prospect; we are free to concentrate on the First Folk. I will tell you what is in my mind. You report that new plantings are in progress between Wildwood, Old Forest, Sarrow Copse, and else-where—possibly with the intent of surrounding Faide Keep." He looked inquiringly at Hein Huss, but no comment was forthcoming. Lord Faide continued. "Possibly we have underestimated the cunning of the savages. They seem capable of forming plans and acting with almost human persistence. Or, I should say, more than human per-sistence, for it appears that after sixteen hundred years they still consider us invaders and hope to exterminate us."

"That is my own conclusion," said Hein Huss.

"We must take steps to strike first. I consider this a matter for the jinxmen. We gain no honor dodging wasps, falling into traps, or groping through foam. It is a needless waste of lives. Therefore, I want you to assemble your jinxmen, cabalmen, and spellbinders; I want you to formulate your most potent hoodoos—"

"Impossible."

Lord Faide's black eyebrows rose high. " 'Impossible'?"

Hein Huss seemed vaguely uncomfortable. "I read the wonder in your mind. You suspect me of disinterest, irresponsibility. Not true. If the First Folk defeat you, we suffer likewise."

"Exactly," said Lord Faide dryly. "You will starve."

"Nevertheless, the jinxmen cannot help you." He hoisted himself to his feet, started for the door.

"Sit," said Lord Faide. "It is necessary to pursue this matter."

Hein Huss looked around with his bland, water-clear eyes. Lord Faide met his gaze. Hein Huss sighed deeply. "I see I must ignore the precepts of my trade, break the habits of a lifetime. I must explain." He took his bulk to the wall, fingered the side arms in the rack, studied the portrait of the ancestral Faide. "These miracle workers of the old times—unfortunately we cannot use their magic! Notice the bulk of the spaceship! As heavy as Faide Keep." He turned his gaze on the table, teleported a candelabra two or three inches. "With considerably less effort they gave that spaceship enormous velocity, using ideas and forces they knew to be imaginary and irrational. We have advanced since then, of course. We no longer employ mysteries, arcane constructions, wild nonhuman forces. We are rational and practical—but we cannot achieve the effects of the ancient magicians."

Lord Faide watched Hein Huss with saturnine eyes. Hein Huss gave his deep rumbling laugh. "You think that I wish to distract you with talk? No, this is not the case. I am preparing to enlighten you." He returned to his seat, lowered his bulk with a groan. "Now I must talk at length, to which I am not accustomed. But you must be given to understand what we jinxmen can do and what we cannot do.

"First, unlike the ancient magicians, we are practical men. Naturally there is difference in our abilities. The best jinxman combines great telepathic facility, implacable personal force, and intimate knowledge of his fellow humans. He knows their acts, motives, desires, and fears; he understands the symbols that most vigorously represent these qualities. Jinxmanship in the main is drudgery—dangerous, difficult, and unromantic—with no mystery except that which we employ to confuse our enemies." Hein Huss glanced at Lord Faide to encounter the same saturnine gaze. "Ha! I still have told you nothing; I still have spent many words talking around my inability to confound the First Folk. Patience."

"Speak on," said Lord Faide.

"Listen then. What happens when I hoodoo a man? First I must enter into his mind telepathically. There are three operational levels: the conscious, the unconscious, the cellular. The most effective jinxing is done if all three levels are influenced. I feel into my victim, I learn as much as possible, supplementing my previous knowledge of him, which is part of my stock in trade. I take up his doll, which carries his traces. The doll is highly useful but not indispensable. It serves as a focus for my attention; it acts as a pattern, or a guide, as I fix upon the mind of the victim, and he is bound by his own telepathic capacity to the doll which bears his traces.

"So! Now! Man and doll are identified in my mind, and at one or more levels in the victim's mind. Whatever happens to the doll the victim feels to be happening to himself. There is no more to simple hoodooing than that, from the standpoint of the jinxman.

But naturally the victims differ greatly. Susceptibility is the key idea here. Some men are more susceptible than others. Fear and conviction breed susceptibility. As a jinxman succeeds he becomes ever more feared, and consequently the more efficacious he becomes. The process is self-generative.

"Demon-possession is a similar technique. Susceptibility is again essential; again conviction creates susceptibility. It is easiest and most dramatic when the characteristics of the demon are well known, as in the case of Comandore's Keyril. For this reason, demons can be exchanged or traded among jinxmen. The commodity actually traded is public acceptance and familiarity with the demon."

"Demons then do not actually exist?" inquired Lord Faide half-incredulously.

Hein Huss grinned vastly, showing enormous yellow teeth. "Telepathy works through a superstratum. Who knows what is created in this superstratum? Maybe the demons live on after they have been conceived; maybe they now are real. This of course is speculation, which we jinxmen shun.

"So much for demons, so much for the lesser techniques of jinxmanship. I have explained sufficient to serve as background to the present situation."

"Excellent," said Lord Faide. "Continue."

"The question, then, is: How does one cast a hoodoo into a creature of an alien race?" He looked inquiringly at Lord Faide. "Can you tell me?"

"I?" asked Lord Faide surprised. "No."

"The method is basically the same as in the hoodooing of men. It is necessary to make the creature believe, in every cell of his being, that he suffers or dies. This is where the problems begin to arise. Does the creature think—that is to say, does he arrange the processes of his life in the same manner as men? This is a very important distinction. Certain creatures of the universe use methods other than the human nerve-node system to control their environments. We call the human system 'intelligence'—a word which properly should be restricted to human activity. Other creatures use different agencies, different systems, arriving sometimes at similar ends. To bring home these generalities, I cannot hope to merge my mind with the corresponding capacity in the First Folk. The key will not fit the lock. At least, not altogether. Once or twice when I watched the First Folk trading with men at Forest Market, I felt occasional weak significances. This implies that the First Folk mentality creates something similar to human telepathic impulses. Nevertheless, there is no real sympathy between the two races.

"This is the first and the least difficulty. If I were able to make complete telepathic contact—what then? The creatures are different from us. They have no words for 'fear,' 'hate,' 'rage,' 'pain,' 'bravery,' 'cowardice.' One may deduce that they do not feel these emotions. Undoubtedly they know other sensations, possibly as meaningful. Whatever these may be, they are unknown to me, and therefore I cannot either form or project symbols for these sensations."

Lord Faide stirred impatiently. "In short, you tell me that you cannot efficiently enter these creatures' minds; and that if you could, you do not know what influences you could plant there to do them harm."

"Succinct," agreed Hein Huss. "Substantially accurate."

Lord Faide rose to his feet. "In that case you must repair these deficiencies. You must learn to telepathize with the First Folk; you must find what influences will harm them. As quickly as possible."

Hein Huss stared reproachfully at Lord Faide. "But I have gone to great lengths to explain the difficulties involved! To hoodoo the First Folk is a monumental task! It would be necessary to enter Wildwood, to live with the First Folk, to become one of them, as my apprentice thought to become a tree. Even then an effective hoodoo is improbable! The First Folk must be susceptible to conviction! Otherwise there would be no bite to the hoodoo! I could guarantee no success. I would predict failure. No other jinxman would dare tell you this, no other would risk his *mana*. I dare because I am Hein Huss, with life behind me."

"Nevertheless we must attempt every weapon at hand," said Lord Faide in a dry voice. "I cannot risk my knights, my kinsmen, my soldiers against these pallid half-creatures. What a waste of good flesh and blood to be stuck by a poison insect! You must go to Wildwood; you must learn how to hoodoo the First Folk."

Hein Huss heaved himself erect. His great round face was stony; his eyes were like bits of water-worn glass. "It is likewise a waste to go on a fool's errand. I am no fool, and I will not undertake a hoodoo which is futile from the beginning."

"In that case," said Lord Faide, "I will find someone else." He went to the door, summoned a servant. "Bring Isak Comandore here."

Hein Huss lowered his bulk into the chair. "I will remain during the interview, with your permission."

"As you wish."

Isak Comandore appeared in the doorway, tall, loosely articulated, head hanging forward. He darted a glance of swift appraisal at Lord Faide, at Hein Huss, then stepped into the room.

Lord Faide crisply explained his desires. "Hein Huss refuses to undertake the mission. Therefore I call on you."

Isak Comandore calculated. The pattern of his thinking was clear: he possibly could gain much *mana*; there was small risk of diminution, for had not Hein Huss already dodged away from the project? Comandore nodded. "Hein Huss has made clear the difficulties; only a very clever and very lucky jinxman can hope to succeed. But I accept the challenge, I will go."

"Good," said Hein Huss. "I will go, too." Isak Comandore darted him a sudden hot glance. "I wish only to observe. To Isak Comandore goes the responsibility and whatever credit may ensue."

"Very well," said Comandore presently. "I welcome your company. Tomorrow morning we leave. I go to order our wagon."

Late in the evening Apprentice Sam Salazar came to Hein Huss where he sat brooding in his workroom. "What do you wish?" growled Huss.

"I have a request to make of you, Head Jinxman Huss."

"Head Jinxman in name only," grumbled Hein Huss. "Isak Comandore is about to assume my position."

Sam Salazar blinked, laughed uncertainly. Hein Huss fixed wintry-pale eyes on him. "What do you wish?"

"I have heard that you go on an expedition to Wildwood, to study the First Folk."

"True, true. What then?"

"Surely they will now attack all men?"

Hein Huss shrugged. "At Forest Market they trade with men. At Forest Market men have always entered the forest. Perhaps there will be change, perhaps not."

"I would go with you, if I may," said Sam Salazar.

"This is no mission for apprentices."

"An apprentice must take every opportunity to learn," said Sam Salazar. "Also you will need extra hands to set up tents, to load and unload cabinets, to cook, to fetch water, and other such matters."

"Your argument is convincing," said Hein Huss. "We depart at dawn; be on hand."

IX

As the sun lifted over the heath the jinxmen departed Faide Keep. The high-wheeled wagon creaked north over the moss, Hein Huss and Isak Comandore riding the front seat, Sam Salazar with his legs hanging over the tail. The wagon rose and fell with the dips and mounds of the moss, wheels wobbling, and presently passed out of sight behind Skywatcher's Hill.

Five days later, an hour before sunset, the wagon reappeared. As before, Hein Huss and Isak Comandore rode the front seat, with Sam Salazar perched behind. They approached the keep, and without giving so much as a sign or a nod, drove through the gate into the courtyard.

Isak Comandore unfolded his long legs, stepped to the ground like a spider; Hein Huss lowered himself with a grunt. Both went to their quarters, while Sam Salazar led the wagon to the jinxmen's warehouse.

Somewhat later Isak Comandore presented himself to Lord Faide, who had been waiting in his trophy room, forced to a show of indifference through considerations of position, dignity, and protocol. Isak Comandore stood in the doorway, grinning like a fox. Lord Faide eyed him with sour dislike, waiting for Comandore to speak. Hein Huss might have stationed himself an entire day, eyes placidly fixed on Lord Faide, awaiting the first word; Isak Comandore lacked the absolute serenity. He came a step forward. "I have returned from Wildwood."

"With what results?"

"I believe that it is possible to hoodoo the First Folk."

Hein Huss spoke from behind Comandore. "I believe that such an undertaking, if feasible, would be useless, irresponsible, and possibly dangerous." He lumbered forward.

Isak Comandore's eyes glowed hot red-brown; he turned back to Lord Faide. "You ordered me forth on a mission; I will render a report."

"Seat yourselves. I will listen."

Isak Comandore, nominal head of the expedition, spoke. "We rode along the river bank to Forest Market. Here was no sign of disorder or of hostility. A hundred First Folk traded timber, planks, posts, and poles for knife blades, iron wire, and copper pots. When they returned to their barge we followed them aboard, wagon, horses, and all. They showed no surprise—"

"Surprise," said Hein Huss heavily, "is an emotion of which they have no knowledge."

Isak Comandore glared briefly. "We spoke to the barge-tenders, explaining that we wished to visit the interior of Wildwood. We asked if the First Folk would try to kill us to prevent us from entering the forest. They professed indifference as to either our well-being or our destruction. This was by no means a guarantee of safe conduct; however, we accepted it as such, and remained aboard the barge." He spoke on with occasional emendations from Hein Huss.

They had proceeded up the river, into the forest, the First Folk poling against the slow current. Presently they put away the poles; nevertheless the barge moved as before. The mystified jinxmen discussed the possibility of teleportation, or symboligical force, and wondered if the First Folk had developed jinxing techniques unknown to men. Sam Salazar, however, noticed that four enormous water beetles, each twelve feet long with oil-black carapaces and blunt heads, had risen from the river bed and pushed the barge from behind—apparently without direction or command. The First Folk stood at the bow, turning the nose of the barge this way or that to follow the winding of the river. They ignored the jinxmen and Sam Salazar as if they did not exist.

The beetles swam tirelessly; the barge moved for four hours as fast as a man could walk. Occasionally, First Folk peered from the forest shadows, but none showed interest or concern in the barge's unusual cargo. By midafternoon the river widened, broke into many channels and became a marsh; a few minutes later the barge floated out into the open water of a small lake. Along the shore, behind the first line of trees appeared a large settlement. The jinxmen were interested and surprised. It had always been assumed that the First Folk wandered at random through the forest, as they had originally lived in the moss of the downs.

The barge grounded; the First Folk walked ashore, the men followed with the horses and wagon. Their immediate impressions were of swarming numbers, of slow but incessant activity, and they were attacked by an overpoweringly evil smell.

Ignoring the stench, the men brought the wagon in from the shore, paused to take stock of what they saw. The settlement appeared to be a center of many diverse activities. The trees had been stripped of lower branches, and supported blocks of hardened foam three hundred feet long, fifty feet high, twenty feet thick, with a space of a man's height intervening between the underside of the foam and the ground. There were a dozen of these blocks, apparently of cellular construction. Certain of the cells had broken open and seethed with small white fishlike creatures—the First Folk young.

Below the blocks masses of First Folk engaged in various occupations, in the main unfamiliar to the jinxmen. Leaving the wagon in the care of Sam Salazar, Hein Huss and Isak Comandore moved forward among the First Folk, repelled by the stench and the pressure of alien flesh, but drawn by curiosity. They were neither heeded nor halted; they wandered everywhere about the settlement. One area seemed to be an enormous zoo, divided into a number of sections. The purpose of one of these sections—a kind of range two hundred feet long—was all too clear. At one end a human corpse hung on a rope—a Faide casualty from the battle at the new planting. Certain of the wasps flew straight at the corpse; just before contact they were netted and removed. Others flew up and away or veered toward the First Folk who stood along the side of the range. These latter also were netted and killed at once.

The purpose of the business was clear enough. Examining some of the other activity in this new light, the jinxmen were able to interpret much that had hitherto puzzled them.

They saw beetles tall as dogs with heavy saw-toothed pincers attacking objects resembling horses; pens of insects even larger, long narrow, segmented, with dozens of heavy legs and nightmare heads. All these creatures—wasps, beetles, centipedes—in smaller and less formidable form were indigenous to the forest; it was plain that the First Folk had been practicing selective breeding for many years, perhaps centuries.

Not all the activity was warlike. Moths were trained to gather nuts, worms to gnaw straight holes through timber; in another section caterpillars chewed a yellow mash, molded it into identical spheres. Much of the evil odor emanated from the zoo; the jinxmen departed without reluctance, and returned to the wagon. Sam Salazar pitched the tent and built a fire, while Hein Huss and Isak Comandore discussed the settlement.

Night came; the blocks of foam glowed with imprisoned light; the activity underneath proceeded without cessation. The jinxmen retired to the tent and slept, while Sam Salazar stood guard.

The following day Hein Huss was able to engage one of the First Folk in conversation; it was the first attention of any sort given to them.

The conversation was long; Hein Huss reported only the gist of it to Lord Faide. (Isak Comandore turned away, ostentatiously disassociating himself from the matter.)

Hein Huss first of all had inquired as to the purpose of the sinister preparations: the wasps, beetles, centipedes, and the like.

"We intend to kill men," the creature had reported ingenuously. "We intend to return to the moss. This has been our purpose ever since men appeared on the planet."

Huss had stated that such an ambition was shortsighted, that there was ample room for both men and First Folk on Pangborn. "The First Folk," said Hein Huss, "should remove their traps and cease their efforts to surround the keeps with forest."

"No," came the response, "men are intruders. They mar the beautiful moss. All will be killed."

Isak Comandore returned to the conversation. "I noticed here a significant fact. All the First Folk within sight had ceased their work; all looked toward us, as if they, too, participated in the discussion. I reached the highly important conclusion that the First Folk are not complete individuals but components of a larger unity, joined to a greater or less extent by a telepathic phase not unlike our own."

Hein Huss continued placidly, "I remarked that if we were attacked, many of the First Folk would perish. The creature showed no concern, and in fact implied much of what Jinxman Comandore had already induced: "There are always more in the cells to replace the elements which die. But if the community becomes sick, all suffer. We have been forced into the forests, into a strange existence. We must arm ourselves and drive away the men, and to this end we have developed the methods of men to our own purposes!' "

Isak Comandore spoke. "Needless to say, the creature referred to the ancient men, not ourselves."

"In any event," said Lord Faide, "they leave no doubt as to their intentions. We should be fools not to attack them at once, with every weapon at our disposal."

Hein Huss continued imperturbably. "The creature went on at some length. 'We have learned the value of irrationality.' 'Irrationality' of course was not his word or even his meaning. He said something like 'a series of vaguely motivated trials'—as close as I can translate. He said, 'We have learned to change our environment. We use insects and trees and plants and waterslugs. It is an enormous effort for us who would prefer a placid life in the moss. But you men have forced this life on us, and now you must suffer the consequences.' I pointed out once more that men were not helpless, that many First Folk would die. The creature seemed unworried. 'The community persists.' I asked a delicate question, 'If your purpose is to kill men, why do you allow us here?' He said, 'The entire community of men will be destroyed.' Apparently they believe the human society to be similar to their own, and therefore regard the killing of three wayfaring individuals as pointless effort."

Lord Faide laughed grimly. "To destroy us they must first win past Hellmouth, then penetrate Faide Keep. This they are unable to do."

Isak Comandore resumed his report. "At this time I was already convinced that the problem was one of hoodooing not an individual but an entire race. In theory this should be no more difficult than hoodooing one. It requires no more effort to speak to twenty than to one. With this end in view I ordered the apprentice to collect substances associated with the creatures. Skinflakes, foam, droppings, all other exudations obtainable. While he did so, I tried to put myself in rapport with the creatures. It is difficult, for their telepathy works across a different stratum from ours. Nevertheless, to a certain extent I have succeeded."

"Then you can hoodoo the First Folk?" asked Lord Faide.

"I vouchsafe nothing until I try. Certain preparations must be made."

"Go then; make your preparations."

Comandore rose to his feet and with a sly side glance for Hein Huss left the room. Huss waited, pinching his chin with heavy fingers. Lord Faide looked at him coldly. "You have something to add?"

Huss grunted, hoisted himself to his feet. "I wish that I did. But my thoughts are confused. Of the many futures, all seem troubled and angry. Perhaps our best is not good enough."

Lord Faide looked at Hein Huss with surprise; the massive Head Jinxman had never before spoken in terms so pessimistic and melancholy. "Speak then; I will listen."

Hein Huss said gruffly, "If I knew any certainties I would speak gladly. But I am merely beset by doubts. I fear that we can no longer depend on logic and careful jinxmanship. Our ancestors were miracle workers, magicians. They drove the First Folk into the forest. To put us to flight in our turn the First Folk have adopted the ancient methods: random trial and purposeless empiricism. I am dubious. Perhaps we must turn our backs on sanity and likewise return to the mysticism of our ancestors."

Lord Faide shrugged. "If Isak Comandore can hoodoo the First Folk, such a retreat may be unnecessary."

"The world changes," said Hein Huss. "Of so much I feel sure: the old days of craft and careful knowledge are gone. The future is for men of cleverness, of imagination untroubled by discipline; the unorthodox Sam Salazar may become more effective than I. The world changes."

Lord Faide smiled his sour dyspeptic smile. "When that day comes I will appoint Sam Salazar Head Jinxman and also name him Lord Faide, and you and I will retire together to a hut on the downs."

Hein Huss made a heavy fateful gesture and departed.

X

Two days later Lord Faide, coming upon Isak Comandore, inquired as to his progress. Comandore took refuge in generalities. After another two days Lord Faide inquired again and this time insisted on particulars. Comandore grudgingly led the way to his workroom, where a dozen cabalmen, spellbinders, and apprentices worked around a large table, building a model of the First Folk settlement in Wildwood.

"Along the lakeshore," said Comandore, "I will range a great number of dolls, daubed with First Folk essences. When this is complete I will work up a hoodoo and blight the creatures."

"Good. Perform well." Lord Faide departed the workroom, mounted to the topmost pinnacle of the keep, to the cupola where the ancestral weapon Hellmouth was housed. "Jambart! Where are you?"

Weapon-tender Jambart, short, blue-jowled, red-nosed and big-bellied, appeared. "My lord?"

"I come to inspect Hellmouth. Is it prepared for instant use?"

"Prepared, my lord, and ready. Oiled, greased, polished, scraped, burnished, tended—every part smooth as an egg."

Lord Faide made a scowling examination of Hellmouth—a heavy cylinder six feet in diameter, twelve feet long, studded with half-domes interconnected with tubes of polished copper. Jambart undoubtedly had been diligent. No trace of dirt or rust or corrosion showed; all was gleaming metal. The snout was covered with a heavy plate of metal and tarred canvas; the ring upon which the weapon swiveled was well greased.

Lord Faide surveyed the four horizons. To the south was fertile Faide Valley; to the west open downs; to north and east the menacing loom of Wildwood.

He turned back to Hellmouth and pretended to find a smear of grease. Jambart boiled with expostulations and protestations; Lord Faide uttered a grim warning, enjoining less laxity, then descended to the workroom of Hein Huss. He found the Head Jinxman reclining on a couch, staring at the ceiling. At a bench stood Sam Salazar surrounded by bottles, flasks, and dishes.

Lord Faide stared balefully at the confusion. "What are you doing?" he asked the apprentice.

Sam Salazar looked up guiltily. "Nothing in particular, my lord."

"If you are idle, go then and assist Isak Comandore."

"I am not idle, Lord Faide."

"Then what do you do?"

Sam Salazar gazed sulkily at the bench. "I don't know."

"Then you are idle!"

"No, I am occupied. I pour various liquids on this foam. It is First Folk foam. I wonder what will happen. Water does not dissolve it, nor spirits. Heat chars and slowly burns it, emitting a foul smoke."

Lord Faide turned away with a sneer. "You amuse yourself as a child might. Go to Isak Comandore; he can find use for you. How do you expect to become a jinxman, dabbling and prattling like a baby among pretty rocks?"

Hein Huss gave a deep sound: a mingling of sigh, snort, grunt, and clearing of the throat. "He does no harm, and Isak Comandore has hands enough. Salazar will never become a jinxman; that has been clear a long time."

Lord Faide shrugged. "He is your apprentice, and your responsibility. Well, then. What news from the keeps?"

Hein Huss, groaning and wheezing, swung his legs over the edge of the couch. "The lords share your concern, to greater or less extent. Your close allies will readily place troops at your disposal; the others likewise if pressure is brought to bear."

Lord Faide nodded in dour satisfaction. "For the moment there is no urgency. The First Folk hold to their forests. Faide Keep of course is impregnable, although they might ravage the valley. . . ." he paused thoughtfully. "Let Isak Comandore cast his hoodoo. Then we will see."

From the direction of the bench came a hiss, a small explosion, a whiff of acrid gas. Sam Salazar turned guiltily to look at them, his eyebrows singed. Lord Faide gave a snort of disgust and strode from the room.

"What did you do?" Hein Huss inquired in a colorless voice.

"I don't know."

Now Hein Huss likewise snorted in disgust. "Ridiculous. If you wish to work miracles, you must remember your procedures. Miracle working is not jinxmanship, with established rules and guides. In matters so complex it is well that you take notes, so that the miracles may be repeated."

Sam Salazar nodded in agreement and turned back to the bench.

XI

Late during the day, news of new First Folk truculence reached Faide Keep. On Honeymoss Hill, not far west of Forest Market, a camp of shepherds had been visited by a wandering group of First Folk, who began to kill the sheep with thorn-swords. When the shepherds protested they, too, were attacked, and many were killed. The remainder of the sheep were massacred.

The following day came other news: four children swimming in Brastock River at Gilbert Ferry had been seized by enormous water-beetles and cut into pieces. On the other side of Wildwood, in the foothills immediately below Castle Cloud, peasants had cleared several hillsides and planted them to vines. Early in the morning they had discovered a horde of black disklike flukes devouring the vines— leaves, branches, trunks, and roots. They set about killing the flukes with spades and at once were stung to death by wasps.

Adam McAdam reported the incidents to Lord Faide, who went to Isak Comandore in a fury. "How soon before you are prepared?"

"I am prepared now. But I must rest and fortify myself. Tomorrow morning I work the hoodoo."

"The sooner the better! The creatures have left their forest; they are out killing men!"

Isak Comandore pulled his long chin. "That was to be expected; they told us as much."

Lord Faide ignored the remark. "Show me your tableau."

Isak Comandore took him into his workroom. The model was now complete, with the masses of simulated First Folk properly daubed and sensitized, each tied with a small wad of foam. Isak Comandore pointed to a pot of dark liquid. "I will explain the basis of the hoodoo. When I visited the camp I watched everywhere for powerful symbols. Undoubtedly there were many at hand, but I could not discern them. However, I remembered a circumstance from the battle at the planting: when the creatures were attacked, threatened with fire and about to die, they spewed foam of dull purple color. Evidently this purple foam is associated with death. My hoodoo will be based upon this symbol."

"Rest well, then, so that you may hoodoo to your best capacity."

The following morning Isak Comandore dressed in long robes of black, and set a mask of the demon Nard on his head to fortify himself. He entered his workroom, closed the door.

An hour passed, two hours. Lord Faide sat at breakfast with his kin, stubbornly maintaining a pose of cynical unconcern. At last he could contain himself no longer and went out into the courtyard where Comandore's underlings stood fidgeting and uneasy. "Where is Hein Huss?" demanded Lord Faide. "Summon him here."

Hein Huss came stumping out of his quarters. Lord Faide motioned to Comandore's workshop. "What is happening? Is he succeeding?"

Hein Huss looked toward the workshop. "He is casting a powerful hoodoo. I feel confusion, anger—"

"In Comandore, or in the First Folk?"

"I am not in rapport. I think he has conveyed a message to their minds. A very difficult task, as I explained to you. In this preliminary aspect he has succeeded."

" 'Preliminary'? What else remains?"

"The two most important elements of the hoodoo: the susceptibility of the victim and the appropriateness of the symbol."

Lord Faide frowned. "You do not seem optimistic."

"I am uncertain. Isak Comandore may be right in his assumption. If so, and if the First Folk are highly susceptible, today marks a great victory, and Comandore will achieve tremendous *mana*!"

Lord Faide stared at the door to the workshop. "What now?"

Hein Huss's eyes went blank with concentration. "Isak Comandore is near death. He can hoodoo no more today."

Lord Faide turned, waved his arm to the cabalmen. "Enter the workroom! Assist your master!"

The cabalmen raced to the door, flung it open. Presently they emerged supporting the limp form of Isak Comandore, his black robe spattered with purple foam. Lord Faide pressed close. "What did you achieve? Speak!"

Isak Comandore's eyes were half closed, his mouth hung loose and wet. "I spoke to the First Folk, to the whole race. I sent the symbol into their minds—" His head fell limply sidewise.

Lord Faide moved back. "Take him to his quarters. Put him on his couch." He turned away, stood indecisively, chewing at his drooping lower lip. "Still we do not know the measure of his success."

"Ah," said Hein Huss, "but we do!"

Lord Faide jerked around. "What is this? What do you say?"

"I saw into Comandore's mind. He used the symbol of purple foam; with tremendous effort he drove it into their minds. Then he learned that purple foam means not death—purple foam means fear for the safety of the community, purple foam means desperate rage."

"In any event," said Lord Faide after a moment, "there is no harm done. The First Folk can hardly become more hostile."

Three hours later a scout rode furiously into the courtyard, threw himself off his horse, ran to Lord Faide. "The First Folk have left the forest! A tremendous number! Thousands! They are advancing on Faide Keep!"

"Let them advance!" said Lord Faide. "The more the better! Jambart, where are you?"

"Here, sir."

"Prepare Hellmouth! Hold all in readiness!"

"Hellmouth is always ready, sir!"

Lord Faide struck him across the shoulders. "Off with you! Bernard!"

The sergeant of the Faide troops came forward. "Ready, Lord Faide."

"The First Folk attack. Armor your men against wasps, feed them well. We will need all our strength."

Lord Faide turned to Hein Huss. "Send to the keeps, to the manor houses, order our kinsmen to join us, with all their troops and all their armor. Send to Bellgard Hall, to Boghoten, Camber, and Candelwade. Haste, haste, it is only hours from Wildwood."

Huss held up his hand. "I have already done so. The keeps are warned. They know your need."

"And the First Folk—can you feel their minds?"

"No."

Lord Faide walked away. Hein Huss lumbered out the main gate, walked around the keep, casting appraising glances up the black walls of the squat towers, windowless and proof even against the ancient miracle-weapons. High on top the great parasol roof Jambart the weapon-tender worked in the cupola, polishing that which already glistened, greasing surfaces already heavy with grease.

Hein Huss returned within. Lord Faide approached him, mouth hard, eyes bright. "What have you seen?"

"Only the keep, the walls, the towers, the roof, and Hellmouth."

"And what do you think?"

"I think many things."

"You are noncommittal; you know more than you say. It is best that you speak, because if Faide Keep falls to the savages you die with the rest of us."

Hein Huss's water-clear eyes met the brilliant black gaze of Lord Faide. "I know only what you know. The First Folk attack. They have proved they are not stupid. They intend to kill us. They are not jinxmen; they cannot afflict us or force us out. They cannot break in the walls. To burrow under, they must dig through solid rock. What are their plans? I do not know. Will they succeed? Again, I do not know. But the day of the jinxman and his orderly array of knowledge is past. I think that we must grope for miracles, blindly and foolishly, like Salazar pouring liquids on foam."

A troop of armored horsemen rode in through the gates: warriors from nearby Bellgard Hall. And as the hours passed contingents from other keeps came to Faide Keep, until the courtyard was dense with troops and horses.

Two hours before sunset the First Folk were sighted across the downs. They seemed a very large company, moving in an undisciplined clot with a number of stragglers, forerunners and wanderers out on the flanks.

The hotbloods from outside keeps came clamoring to Lord Faide, urging a charge to cut down the First Folk; they found no seconding voices among the veterans of the battle at the planting. Lord Faide, however, was pleased to see the dense mass of First Folk. "Let them approach only a mile more—and Hellmouth will take them! Jambart!"

"At your call, Lord Faide."

"Come, Hellmouth speaks!" He strode away with Jambart after. Up to the cupola they climbed.

"Roll forth Hellmouth, direct it against the savages!"

Jambart leaped to the glistening array of wheels and levers. He hesitated in perplexity, then tentatively twisted a wheel. Hellmouth responded by twisting slowly around on its radial track, to the groan and chatter of long-frozen bearings. Lord Faide's brows lowered into a menacing line. "I hear evidence of neglect."

"Neglect, my lord, never! Find one spot of rust, a shadow of grime, you may have me whipped!"

"What of the sound?"

"That is internal and invisible—none of my responsibility."

Lord Faide said nothing. Hellmouth now pointed toward the great pale tide from Wildwood. Jambart twisted a second wheel and Hellmouth thrust forth its heavy snout. Lord Faide, in a voice harsh with anger, cried, "The cover, fool!"

"An oversight, my lord, easily repaired." Jambart crawled out along the top of Hellmouth, clinging to the protuberances for dear life, with below only the long smooth sweep of roof. With considerable difficulty he tore the covering loose, then grunting and cursing, inched himself back, jerking with his knees, rearing his buttocks.

The First Folk had slowed their pace a trifle, the main body only a half-mile distant.

"Now," said Lord Faide in high excitement, "before they disperse, we exterminate them!" He sighted through a telescopic tube, squinting through the dimness of internal films and incrustations, signaled to Jambart for the final adjustments. "Now! Fire!"

Jambart pulled the firing lever. Within the great metal barrel came a sputter of clicking sounds. Hellmouth whined, roared. Its snout glowed red, orange, white, and out poured a sudden gout of blazing purple radiation—which almost instantly died. Hellmouth's barrel quivered with heat, fumed, seethed, hissed. From within came a faint pop. Then there was silence.

A hundred yards in front of the First Folk a patch of moss burnt black where the bolt had struck. The aiming device was inaccurate. Hellmouth's bolt had killed perhaps twenty of the First Folk vanguard.

Lord Faide made feverish signals. "Quick! Raise the barrel. Now! Fire again!"

Jambart pulled the firing arm, to no avail. He tried again, with the same lack of success. "Hellmouth evidently is tired."

"Hellmouth is dead," cried Lord Faide. "You have failed me. Hellmouth is extinct."

"No, no," protested Jambart. "Hellmouth rests! I nurse it as my own child! It is polished like glass! Whenever a section wears off or breaks loose, I neatly remove the fracture, and every trace of cracked glass."

Lord Faide threw up his arms, shouted in vast, inarticulate grief, ran below. "Huss! Hein Huss!"

Hein Huss presented himself. "What is your will?"

"Hellmouth has given up its fire. Conjure me more fire for Hellmouth, and quickly!"

"Impossible."

"Impossible!" cried Lord Faide. "That is all I hear from you! Impossible, useless, impractical! You have lost your ability. I will consult Isak Comandore."

"Isak Comandore can put no more fire into Hellmouth than can I."

"What sophistry is this? He puts demons into men, surely he can put fire into Hellmouth!"

"Come, Lord Faide, you are overwrought. You know the difference between jinxmanship and miracle working."

Lord Faide motioned to a servant. "Bring Isak Comandore here to me!"

Isak Comandore, face haggard, skin waxy, limped into the court-yard. Lord Faide waved preemptorily. "I need your skill. You must restore fire to Hellmouth."

Comandore darted a quick glance at Hein Huss, who stood solid and cold. Comandore decided against dramatic promises that could not be fulfilled. "I cannot do this, my lord."

"What! You tell me this, too?"

"Remark the difference, Lord Faide, between man and metal. A man's normal state is something near madness; he is at all times balanced on a knife-edge between hysteria and apathy. His senses tell him far less of the world than he thinks they do. It is a simple trick to deceive a man, to possess him with a demon, to drive him out of his mind, to kill him. But metal is insensible; metal reacts only as its shape and condition dictates, or by the working of mira-cles."

"Then you must work miracles!"

"Impossible."

Lord Faide drew a deep breath, collected himself. He walked swiftly across the court. "My armor, my horse. We attack."

The column formed, Lord Faide at the head. He led the knights through the portals, with armored footmen behind.

"Beware the foam!" called Lord Faide. "Attack, strike, cut, draw back. Keep your visors drawn against the wasps! Each man must kill a hundred! Attack!"

The troop rode forth against the horde of First Folk, knights in the lead. The hooves of the horses pounded softly over the thick moss; in the west the large pale sun hung close to the horizon.

Two hundred yards from the First Folk the knights touched the club-headed horses into a lope. They raised their swords, and shout-ing, plunged forward, each man seeking to be first. The clotted mass of First Folk separated: black beetles darted forth and after them long segmented centipede creatures. They dashed among the horses, man-dibles clicking, snouts slashing. Horses screamed, reared, fell over backwards; beetles cut open armored knights as a dog cracks a bone. Lord Faide's horse threw him and ran away; he picked himself up, hacked at a nearby beetle, lopped off its front leg. It darted forward, he lopped off the leg opposite; the heavy head dipped, tore up the moss. Lord Faide cut off the remaining legs, and it lay helpless.

"Retreat," he bellowed. "Retreat!"

The knights moved back, slashing and hacking at beetles and centipedes, killing or disabling all which attacked.

"Form into a double line, knights and men. Advance slowly, supporting each other!"

The men advanced. The First Folk dispersed to meet them, armed with their thorn-swords and carrying pouches. Ten yards from the men they reached into the pouches, brought dark balls which they threw at the men. The balls broke and spattered on the armor.

"Charge!" bawled Lord Faide. The men sprang forward into the mass of First Folk, cutting, slashing, killing. "Kill!" called Lord Faide in exultation. "Leave not one alive!"

A pang struck him, a sting inside his armor, followed by another and another. Small things crawled inside the metal, stinging, biting, crawling. He looked about: on all sides were harassed expressions, faces working in anguish. Sword arms fell limp as hands beat on the metal, futilely trying to scratch, rub. Two men suddenly began to tear off their armor.

"Retreat," cried Lord Faide. "Back to the keep!"

The retreat was a rout, the soldiers shedding articles of armor as they ran. After them came a flight of wasps—a dozen or more, and half as many men cried out as the poison prongs struck into their backs.

Inside the keep stormed the disorganized company, casting aside the last of their armor, slapping their skin, scratching, rubbing, crushing the ferocious red mites that infested them.

"Close the gates," roared Lord Faide.

The gates slid shut. Faide Keep was besieged.

XII

During the night the First Folk surrounded the keep, forming a ring fifty yards from the walls. All night there was motion, ghostly shapes coming and going in the starlight.

Lord Faide watched from a parapet until midnight, with Hein Huss at his side. Repeatedly, he asked, "What of the other keeps? Do they send further reinforcements?" to which Hein Huss each time gave the same reply: "There is confusion and doubt. The keep-lords are anxious to help but do not care to throw themselves away. At this moment they consider and take stock of the situation."

Lord Faide at last left the parapet, signaling Hein Huss to follow. He went to his trophy room, threw himself into a chair, motioned Hein Huss to be seated. For a moment he fixed the jinxman with a cool, calculating stare. Hein Huss bore the appraisal without discomfort.

"You are Head Jinxman," said Lord Faide finally. "For twenty years you have worked spells, cast hoodoos, performed auguries— more effectively than any other jinxman of Pangborn. But now I find you inept and listless. Why is this?"

"I am neither inept nor listless. I am unable to achieve beyond my abilities. I do not know how to work miracles. For this you must consult my apprentice Sam Salazar, who does not know either, but who earnestly tries every possibility and many impossibilities."

"You believe in this nonsense yourself! Before my very eyes you become a mystic!"

Hein Huss shrugged. "There are limitations to my knowledge. Miracles occur—that we know. The relics of our ancestors lie everywhere. Their methods were supernatural, repellent to our own mental processes—but think! Using these same methods the First Folk threaten to destroy us. In the place of metal they use living flesh— but the result is similar. The men of Pangborn, if they assemble and accept casualties, can drive the First Folk back to Wildwood—but for how long? A year? Ten years? The First Folk plant new trees, dig more traps—and presently come forth again, with more terrible weapons: flying beetles, large as a horse; wasps strong enough to pierce armor, lizards to scale the walls of Faide Keep."

Lord Faide pulled at his chin. "And the jinxmen are helpless?"

"You saw for yourself. Isak Comandore intruded enough into their consciousness to anger them, no more."

"So then—what must we do?"

Hein Huss held out his hands. "I do not know. I am Hein Huss, jinxman. I watch Sam Salazar with fascination. He learns nothing, but he is either too stupid or too intelligent to be discouraged. If this is the way to work miracles, he will work them."

Lord Faide rose to his feet. "I am deathly tired. I cannot think, I must sleep. Tomorrow we will know more."

Hein Huss left the trophy room, returned to the parapet. The ring of First Folk seemed closer to the walls, almost within dart-range. Behind them and across the moors stretched a long pale column of marching First Folk. A little back from the keep a pile of white material began to grow, larger and larger as the night proceeded.

Hours passed, the sky lightened; the sun rose in the east. The First Folk tramped the downs like ants, bringing long bars of hardened foam down from the north, dropping them into piles around the keep, returning into the north once more.

Lord Faide came up on the parapet, haggard and unshaven. "What is this? What do they do?"

Bernard the sergeant responded. "They puzzle us all, my lord."

"Hein Huss! What of the other keeps?"

"They have armed and mounted; they approach cautiously."

"Can you communicate our urgency?"

"I can, and I have done so. I have only accentuated their caution."

"Bah!" cried Lord Faide in disgust. "Warriors they call themselves! Loyal and faithful allies!"

"They know of your bitter experience," said Hein Huss. "They ask themselves, reasonably enough, what they can accomplish which you who are already here cannot do first."

Lord Faide laughed sourly. "I have no answer for them. In the meantime we must protect ourselves against the wasps. Armor is useless; they drive us mad with mites. . . . Bernard!"

"Yes, Lord Faide."

"Have each of your men construct a frame two-feet square, fixed with a short handle. To these frames should be sewed a net of heavy mesh. When these frames are built we will sally forth, two soldiers to guard one half-armored knight on foot."

"In the meantime," said Hein Huss, "the First Folk proceed with their plans."

Lord Faide turned to watch. The First Folk came close up under the walls carrying rods of hardened foam. "Bernard! Put your archers to work! Aim for the heads!"

Along the walls bowmen cocked their weapons. Darts spun down into the First Folk. A few were affected, turned and staggered away; others plucked away the bolts without concern. Another flight of bolts, a few more First Folk were disabled. The others planted the rods in the moss, exuded foam in great gushes, their back-flaps vigorously pumping air. Other First Folk brought more rods, pushed them into the foam. Entirely around the keep, close under the walls, extended the mound of foam. The ring of First Folk now came close and all gushed foam; it bulked up swiftly. More rods were brought, thrust into the foam, reinforcing and stiffening the mass.

"More darts!" barked Lord Faide. "Aim for the heads! Bernard— your men, have they prepared the wasp nets?"

"Not yet, Lord Faide. The project requires some little time."

Lord Faide became silent. The foam, now ten feet high, rapidly piled higher. Lord Faide turned to Hein Huss. "What do they hope to achieve?"

Hein Huss shook his head. "For the moment I am uncertain."

The first layer of foam had hardened; on top of this the First Folk spewed another layer, reinforcing again with the rods, criss-crossing, horizontal and vertical. Fifteen minutes later, when the second layer was hard the First Folk emplaced and mounted rude ladders to raise a third layer. Surrounding the keep now was a ring of foam thirty feet high and forty feet thick at the base.

"Look," said Hein Huss. He pointed up. The parasol roof overhanging the walls ended only thirty feet above the foam. "A few more layers and they will reach the roof."

"So then?" asked Lord Faide. "The roof is as strong as the walls."

"And we will be sealed within."

Lord Faide studied the foam in the light of this new thought. Already the First Folk, climbing laboriously up ladders along the outside face of their wall of foam, were preparing to lay on a fourth layer. First—rods, stiff and dry, then great gushes of white. Only twenty feet remained between roof and foam.

Lord Faide turned to the sergeant. "Prepare the men to sally forth."

"What of the wasp nets, sir?"

"Are they almost finished?"

"Another ten minutes, sir."

"Another ten minutes will see us smothering. We must force a passage through the foam."

Ten minutes passed, and fifteen. The First Folk created ramps behind their wall: first, dozens of the rods, then foam, and on top, to distribute the weight, reed mats.

Bernard the sergeant reported to Lord Faide. "We are ready."

"Good." Lord Faide descended into the courtyard. He faced the men, gave them their orders. "Move quickly, but stay together; we must not lose ourselves in the foam. As we proceed, slash ahead and to the sides. The First Folk see through the foam; they have the advantage of us. When we break through, we use the wasp nets. Two foot soldiers must guard each knight. Remember, quickly through the foam, that we do not smother. Open the gates."

The gates slid back, the troops marched forth. They faced an unbroken blank wall of foam. No enemy could be seen.

Lord Faide waved his sword. "Into the foam." He strode forward, pushed into the white mass, now crisp and brittle and harder than he had bargained for. It resisted him; he cut and hacked. His troops joined him, carving a way into the foam. First Folk appeared above them, crawling carefully on the mats. Their back flaps puffed, pumped; foam issued from their vents, falling in a cascade over the troops.

Hein Huss sighed. He spoke to Apprentice Sam Salazar. "Now they must retreat, otherwise they smother. If they fail to win through, we all smother."

Even as he spoke the foam, piling up swiftly, in places reached the roof. Below, bellowing and cursing, Lord Faide backed out from under, wiped his face clear. Once again, in desperation, he charged forward, trying at a new spot.

The foam was friable and cut easily, but the chunks detached still blocked the opening. And again down tumbled a cascade of foam, covering the soldiers.

Lord Faide retreated, waved his men back into the keep. At the same moment First Folk crawling on mats on the same level as the parapet over the gate laid rods up from the foam to rest against the projecting edge of the roof. They gushed foam; the view of the sky was slowly blocked from the view of Hein Huss and Sam Salazar.

"In an hour, perhaps two, we will die," said Hein Huss. "They have now sealed us in. There are many men here in the keep, and all will now breathe deeply."

Sam Salazar said nervously, "There is a possibility we might be able to survive—or at least not smother."

"Ah?" inquired Hein Huss with heavy sarcasm. "You plan to work a miracle?"

"If a miracle, the most trivial sort. I observed that water has no effect on the foam, nor a number of other liquids: milk, spirits, wine, or caustic. Vinegar, however, instantly dissolves the foam."

"Aha," said Hein Huss. "We must inform Lord Faide."

"Better that you do so," said Sam Salazar. "He will pay me no heed."

XIII

Half an hour passed. Light filtered into Faide Keep only as a dim gray gloom. Air tasted flat, damp, and heavy. Out from the gates sallied the troops. Each carried a crock, a jug, a skin, or a pan containing strong vinegar.

"Quickly now," called Lord Faide, "but careful! Spare the vinegar, don't throw it wildly. In close formation now—forward."

The soldiers approached the wall, threw ladles of vinegar ahead. The foam crackled, melted.

"Waste no vinegar," shouted Lord Faide. "Forward, quickly now; bring forward the vinegar!"

Minutes later they burst out upon the downs. The First Folk stared at them, blinking.

"Charge," croaked Lord Faide, his throat thick with fumes. "Mind now, wasp nets! Two soldiers to each knight! Charge, double-quick. Kill the white beasts."

The men dashed ahead. Wasp tubes were leveled. "Halt!" yelled Lord Faide. "Wasps!"

The wasps came, wings rasping. Nets rose up; wasps struck with a thud. Down went the nets; hard feet crushed the insects. The beetles and the lizard-centipedes appeared, not so many as of the last evening, for a great number had been killed. They darted forward, and a score of men died, but the insects were soon hacked into chunks of reeking brown flesh. Wasps flew, and some struck home; the agonies of the dying men were unnerving. Presently the wasps likewise decreased in number, and soon there were no more.

The men faced the First Folk, armed only with thorn-swords and their foam, which now came purple with rage.

Lord Faide waved his sword; the men advanced and began to kill the First Folk, by dozens, by hundreds.

Hein Huss came forth and approached Lord Faide. "Call a halt."

"A halt? Why? Now we kill these bestial things."

"Far better not. Neither need kill the other. Now is the time to show great wisdom."

"They have besieged us, caught us in their traps, stung us with their wasps! And you say halt?"

"They nourish a grudge sixteen hundred years old. Best not to add another one."

Lord Faide stared at Hein Huss. "What do you propose?"

"Peace between the two races, peace and cooperation."

"Very well. No more traps, no more plantings, no more breeding of deadly insects."

"Call back your men. I will try."

Lord Faide cried out, "Men, fall back, Disengage."

Reluctantly the troops drew back. Hein Huss approached the huddled mass of purple-foaming First Folk. He waited a moment. They watched him intently. He spoke in their language.

"You have attacked Faide Keep; you have been defeated. You planned well, but we have proved stronger. At this moment we can kill you. Then we can go on to fire the forest, starting a hundred blazes. Some of the fires you can control. Others not. We can destroy Wildwood. Some First Folk may survive, to hide in the thickets and breed new plans to kill men. This we do not want. Lord Faide has agreed to peace, if you likewise agree. This means no more death traps. Men will freely approach and pass through the forests. In your turn you may freely come out on the moss. Neither race shall molest the other. Which do you choose? Extinction—or peace?"

The purple foam no longer dribbled from the vents of the First Folk. "We choose peace."

"There must be no more wasps, beetles. The death traps must be disarmed and never replaced."

"We agree. In our turn we must be allowed freedom of the moss."

"Agreed. Remove your dead and wounded, haul away the foam rods."

Hein Huss returned to Lord Faide. "They have chosen peace."

Lord Faide nodded. "Very well. It is for the best." He called to his men. "Sheathe your weapons. We have won a great victory." He ruefully surveyed Faide Keep, swathed in foam and invisible except for the parasol roof. "A hundred barrels of vinegar will not be enough."

Hein Huss looked off into the sky. "Your allies approach quickly. Their jinxmen have told them of your victory."

Lord Faide laughed his sour laugh. "To my allies will fall the task of removing the foam from Faide Keep."

XIV

In the hall of Faide Keep, during the victory banquet, Lord Faide called jovially across to Hein Huss. "Now, Head Jinxman, we must deal with your apprentice, the idler and the waster Sam Salazar."

"He is here, Lord Faide. Rise, Sam Salazar, take cognizance of the honor being done you."

Sam Salazar rose to his feet, bowed.

Lord Faide proffered him a cup. "Drink, Sam Salazar, enjoy yourself. I freely admit that your idiotic tinkerings saved the lives of us all. Sam Salazar, we salute you, and thank you. Now, I trust that you will put frivolity aside, apply yourself to your work, and learn honest jinxmanship. When the time comes, I promise that you shall find a lifetime of employment at Faide Keep."

"Thank you," said Sam Salazar modestly. "However, I doubt if I will become a jinxman."

"No? You have other plans?"

Sam Salazar stuttered, grew faintly pink in the face, then straightened himself, and spoke as clearly and distinctly as he could. "I prefer to continue what you call my frivolity. I hope I can persuade others to join me."

"Frivolity is always attractive," said Lord Faide. "No doubt you can find other idlers and wasters, runaway farm boys, and the like."

Sam Salazar said staunchly, "This frivolity might become serious. Undoubtedly the ancients were barbarians. They used symbols to control entities they were unable to understand. We are methodical and rational; why can't we systematize and comprehend the ancient miracles?"

"Well, why can't we?" asked Lord Faide. "Does anyone have an answer?"

No one responded, although Isak Comandore hissed between his teeth and shook his head.

"I personally may never be able to work miracles; I suspect it is more complicated than it seems," said Sam Salazar. "However, I hope that you will arrange for a workshop where I and others who might share my views can make a beginning. In this matter I have the encouragement and the support of Head Jinxman Hein Huss."

Lord Faide lifted his goblet. "Very well, Apprentice Sam Salazar. Tonight I can refuse you nothing. You shall have exactly what you wish, and good luck to you. Perhaps you will produce a miracle during my lifetime."

Isak Comandore said huskily to Hein Huss, "This is a sad event! It signalizes intellectual anarchy, the degradation of jinxmanship, the prostitution of logic. Novelty has a way of attracting youth; already I see apprentices and spellbinders whispering in excitement. The jinxmen of the future will be sorry affairs. How will they go about demon-possession? With a cog, a gear, and a push-button. How will they cast a hoodoo? They will find it easier to strike their victim with an axe."

"Times change," said Hein Huss. "There is now the one rule of Faide on Pangborn, and the keeps no longer need to employ us. Perhaps I will join Sam Salazar in his workshop."

"You depict a depressing future," said Isak Comandore with a sniff of disgust.

"There are many futures, some of which are undoubtedly depressing."

Lord Faide raised his glass. "To the best of your many futures, Hein Huss. Who knows? Sam Salazar may conjure a spaceship to lead us back to home-planet."

"Who knows?" said Hein Huss. He raised his goblet. "To the best of the futures!"